SHURI
WAKANDA FOREVER

WRITERS

NNEDI OKORAFOR (#1-7)
& **VITA AYALA** (#8-10)

ARTISTS

LEONARDO ROMERO (#1-5),
PAUL DAVIDSON (#6-7) & **RACHAEL STOTT** (#8-10)

COLORISTS

JORDIE BELLAIRE (#1-5),
TRÍONA FARRELL (#6-7) & **CARLOS LOPEZ** (#8-10)

LETTERER

VC'S JOE SABINO

COVER ART

SAM SPRATT (#1-5) & **CHRISTINA STRAIN** (#6-10)

ASSOCIATE EDITOR

SARAH BRUNSTAD

EDITOR

Howell Carnegie District Library
314 W. Grand River Ave.
Howell, MI 48843

MAR 2 2 2021

collection editor JENNIFER GRÜNWALD
assistant managing editor MAIA LOY
assistant managing editor LISA MONTALBANO
editor, special projects MARK D. BEAZLEY

vp production & special projects JEFF YOUNGQUIST
svp print, sales & marketing DAVID GABRIEL
director, licensed publishing SVEN LARSEN
editor in chief C.B. CEBULSKI

3 2140 00517 6603

SHURI: WAKANDA FOREVER. Contains material originally published in magazine form as SHURI (2018) #1-10. First printing 2020. ISBN 978-1-302-92369-3. Published by MARVEL WORLDWIDE, INC., a subsidiary of MARVEL ENTERTAINMENT, LLC. OFFICE OF PUBLICATION: 1290 Avenue of the Americas, New York, NY 10104. © 2020 MARVEL No similarity between any of the names, characters, persons, and/or institutions in this magazine with those of any living or dead person or institution is intended, and any such similarity which may exist is purely coincidental. **Printed in Canada.** KEVIN FEIGE, Chief Creative Officer; DAN BUCKLEY, President, Marvel Entertainment; JOHN NEE, Publisher; JOE QUESADA, EVP & Creative Director; TOM BREVOORT, SVP of Publishing; DAVID BOGART, Associate Publisher & SVP of Talent Affairs; Publishing & Partnership; DAVID GABRIEL, VP of Print & Digital Publishing; JEFF YOUNGQUIST, VP of Production & Special Projects; DAN CARR, Executive Director of Publishing Technology; ALEX MORALES, Director of Publishing Operations; DAN EDINGTON, Managing Editor; RICKEY PURDIN, Director of Talent Relations; SUSAN CRESPI, Production Manager; STAN LEE, Chairman Emeritus. For information regarding advertising in Marvel Comics or on Marvel.com, please contact Vit DeBellis, Custom Solutions & Integrated Advertising Manager, at vdebellis@marvel.com. For Marvel subscription inquiries, please call 888-511-5480. **Manufactured between 9/25/2020 and 10/27/2020 by SOLISCO PRINTERS, SCOTT, QC, CANADA.**

10 9 8 7 6 5 4 3 2 1

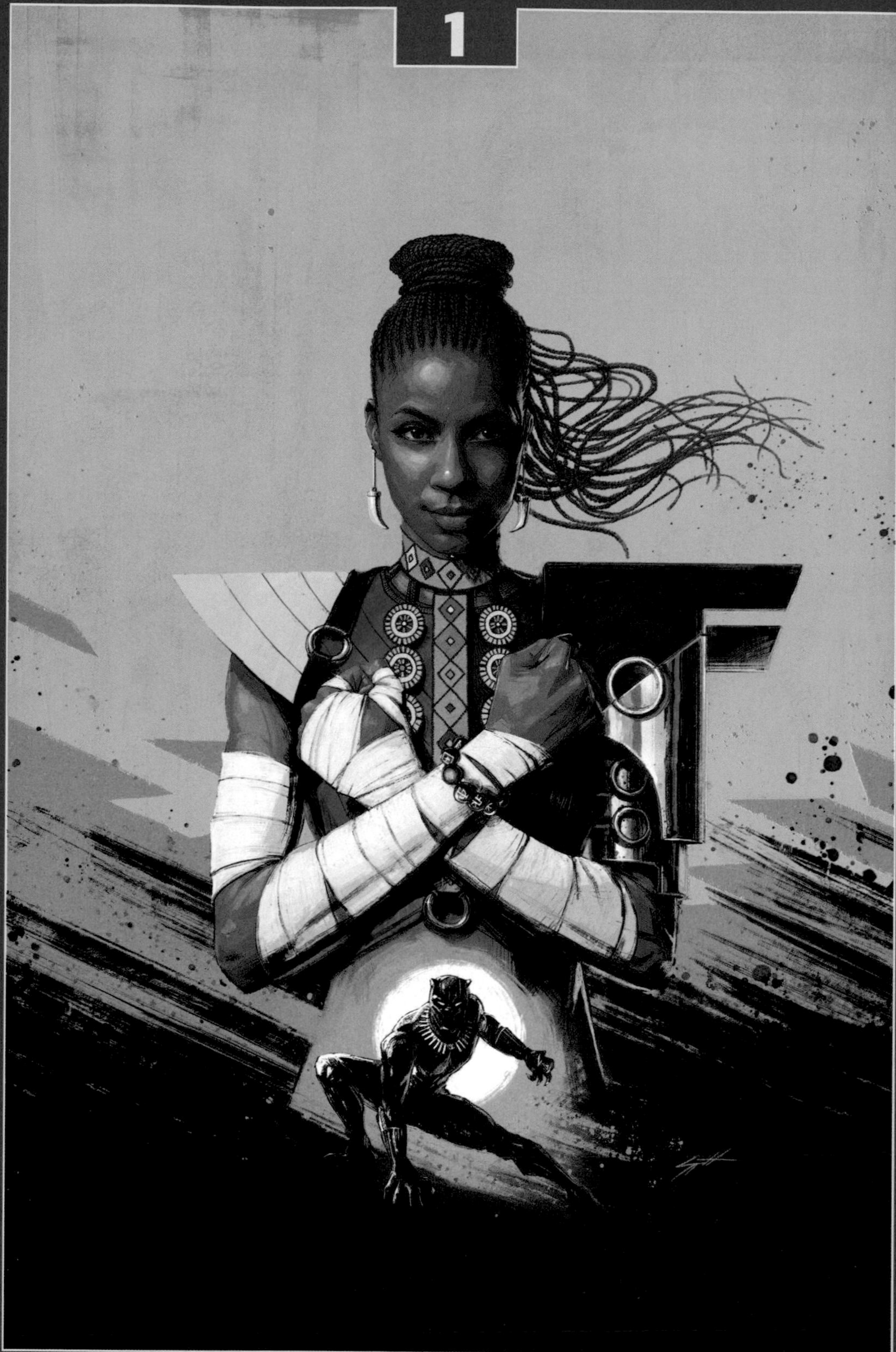
1

"GONE"

SHURI
WAKANDA FOREVER

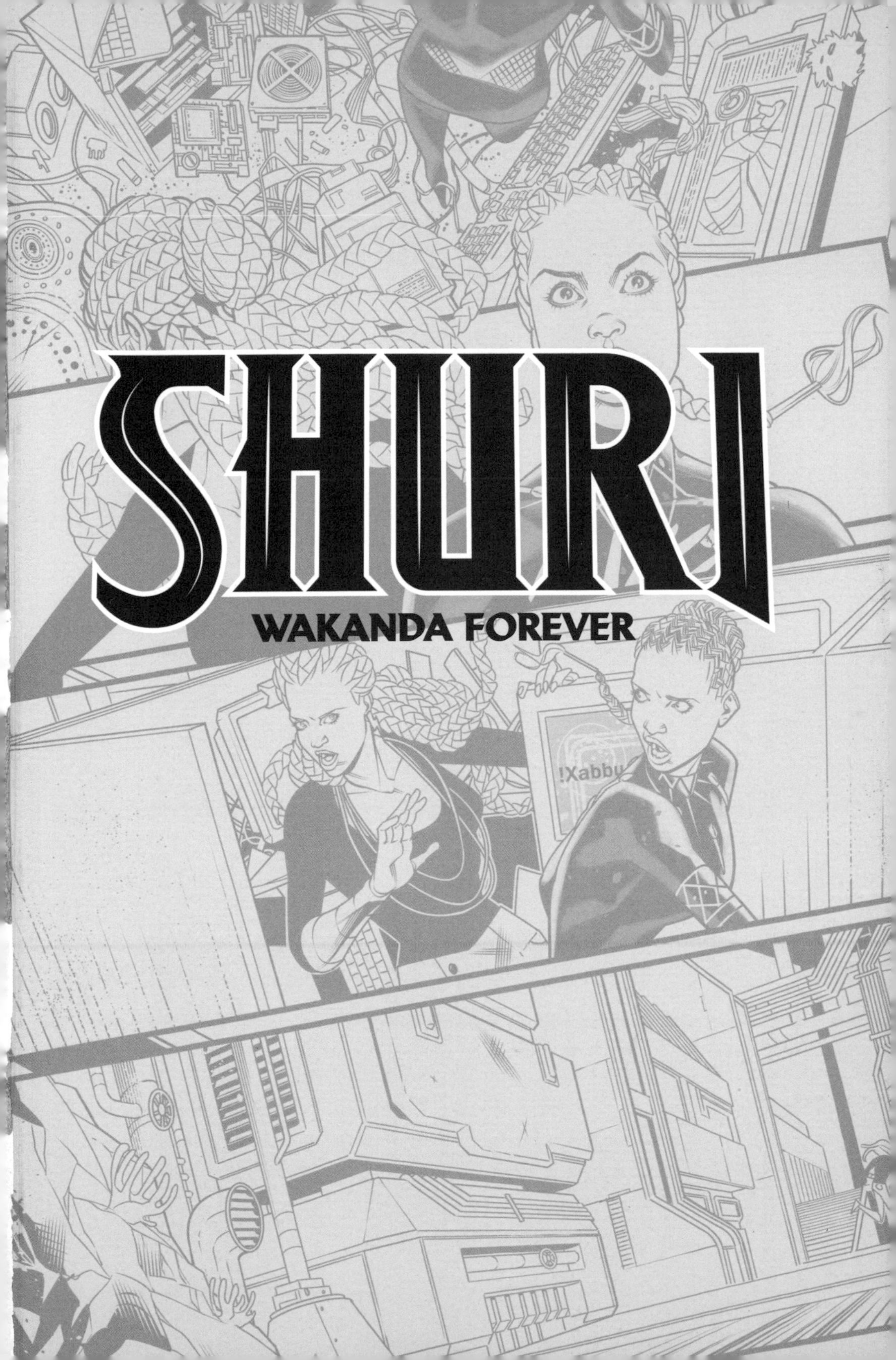
!Xabbu

CONTENTS

Issue #1 4
Issue #2 26
Issue #3 47
Issue #4 68
Issue #5 89
Issue #6 110
Issue #7 131
Issue #8 152
Issue #9 173
Issue #10 194

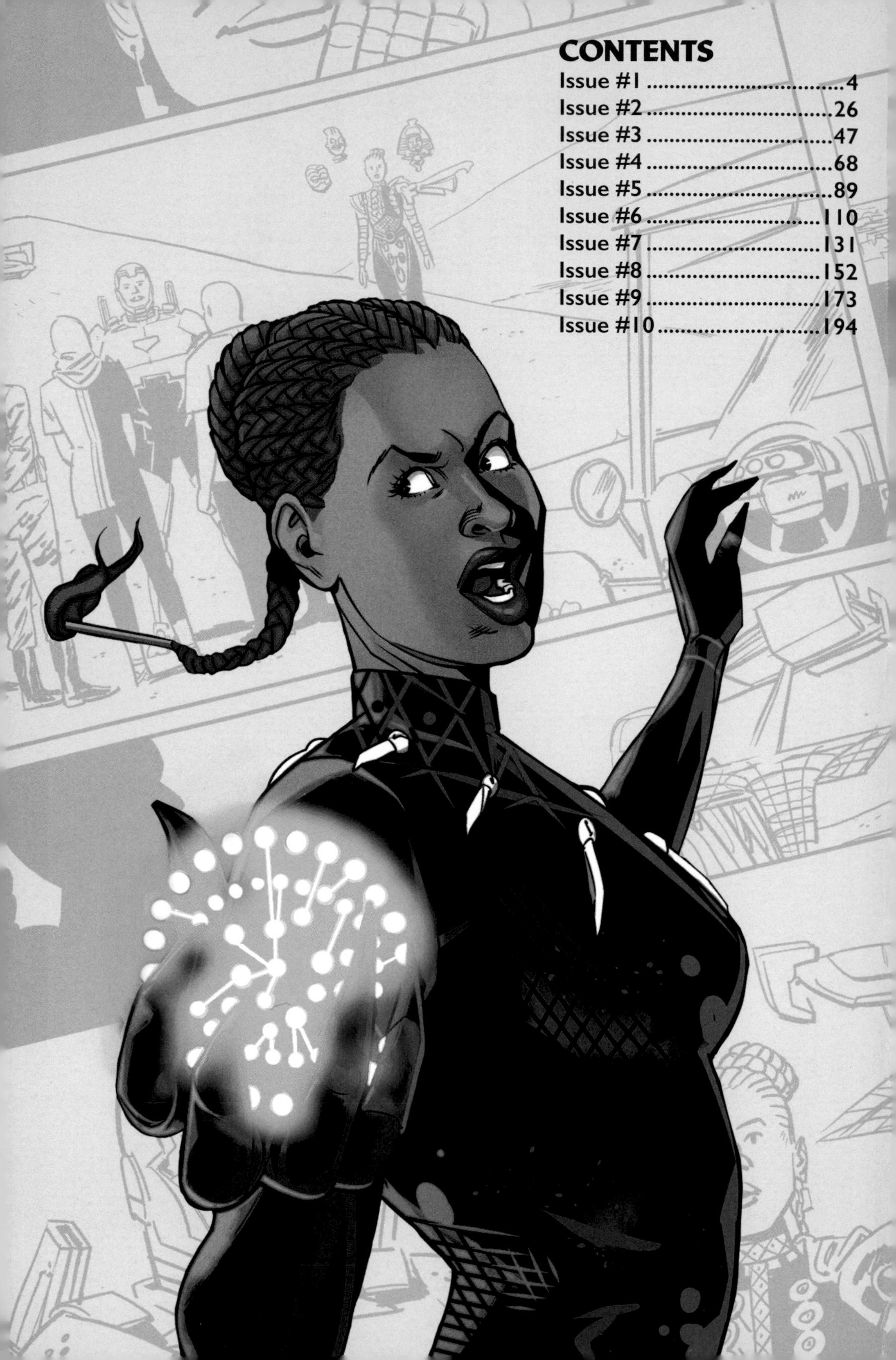

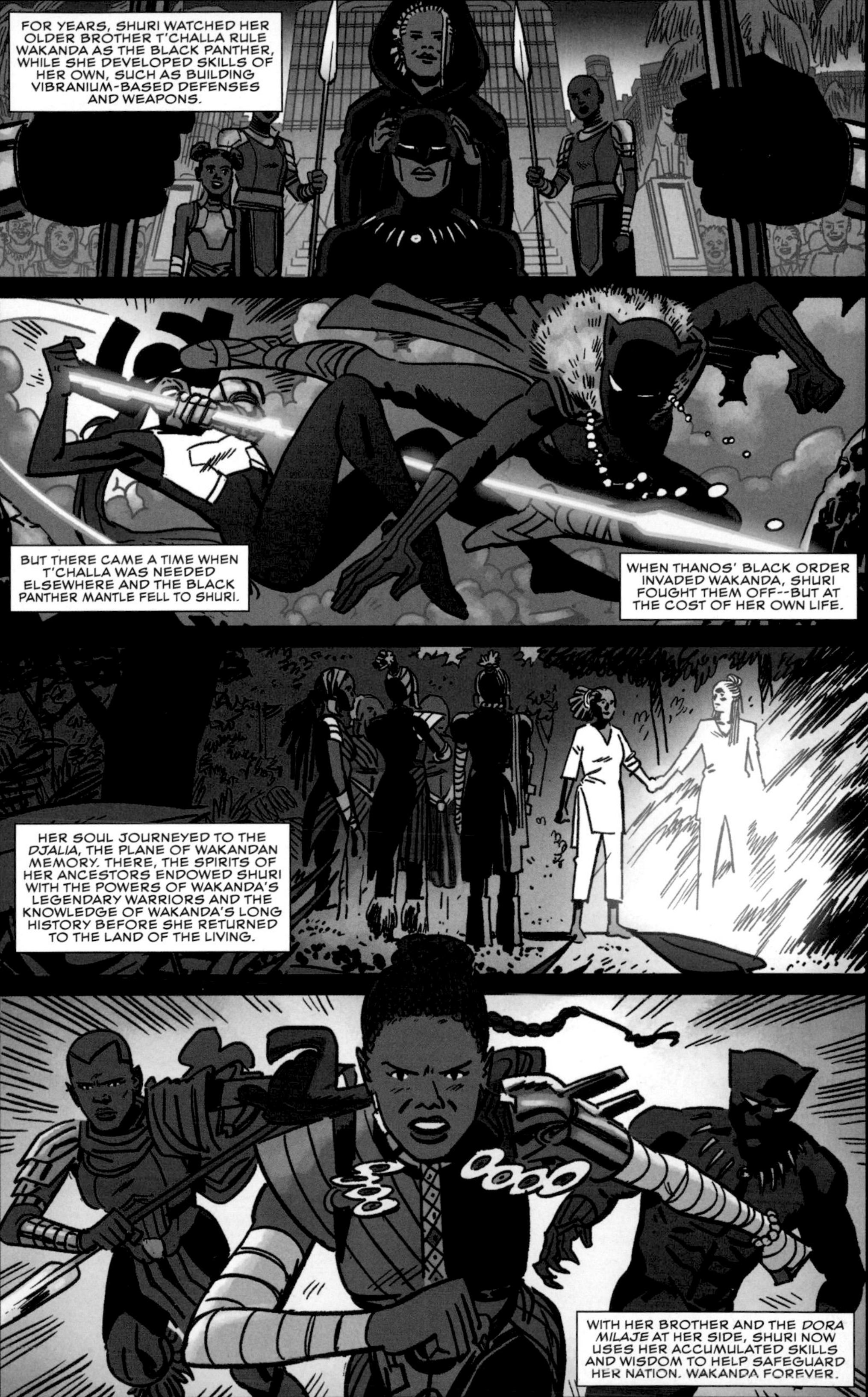
FOR YEARS, SHURI WATCHED HER OLDER BROTHER T'CHALLA RULE WAKANDA AS THE BLACK PANTHER, WHILE SHE DEVELOPED SKILLS OF HER OWN, SUCH AS BUILDING VIBRANIUM-BASED DEFENSES AND WEAPONS.
BUT THERE CAME A TIME WHEN T'CHALLA WAS NEEDED ELSEWHERE AND THE BLACK PANTHER MANTLE FELL TO SHURI.
WHEN THANOS' BLACK ORDER INVADED WAKANDA, SHURI FOUGHT THEM OFF--BUT AT THE COST OF HER OWN LIFE.
HER SOUL JOURNEYED TO THE *DJALIA*, THE PLANE OF WAKANDAN MEMORY. THERE, THE SPIRITS OF HER ANCESTORS ENDOWED SHURI WITH THE POWERS OF WAKANDA'S LEGENDARY WARRIORS AND THE KNOWLEDGE OF WAKANDA'S LONG HISTORY BEFORE SHE RETURNED TO THE LAND OF THE LIVING.
WITH HER BROTHER AND THE *DORA MILAJE* AT HER SIDE, SHURI NOW USES HER ACCUMULATED SKILLS AND WISDOM TO HELP SAFEGUARD HER NATION. WAKANDA FOREVER.

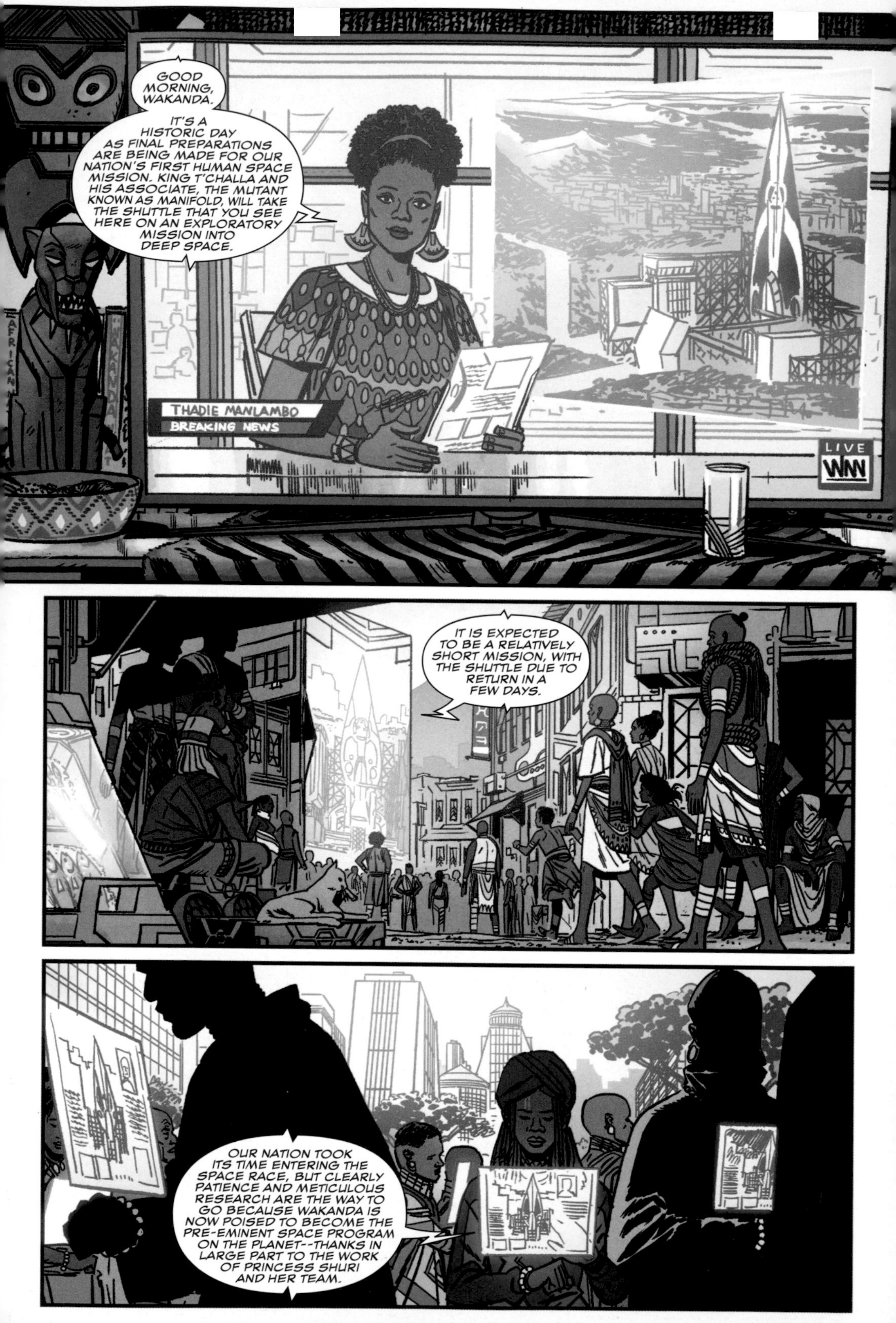
GOOD MORNING, WAKANDA.
IT'S A HISTORIC DAY AS FINAL PREPARATIONS ARE BEING MADE FOR OUR NATION'S FIRST HUMAN SPACE MISSION. KING T'CHALLA AND HIS ASSOCIATE, THE MUTANT KNOWN AS MANIFOLD, WILL TAKE THE SHUTTLE THAT YOU SEE HERE ON AN EXPLORATORY MISSION INTO DEEP SPACE.
THADIE MANLAMBO
BREAKING NEWS
LIVE
WNN
IT IS EXPECTED TO BE A RELATIVELY SHORT MISSION, WITH THE SHUTTLE DUE TO RETURN IN A FEW DAYS.
OUR NATION TOOK ITS TIME ENTERING THE SPACE RACE, BUT CLEARLY PATIENCE AND METICULOUS RESEARCH ARE THE WAY TO GO BECAUSE WAKANDA IS NOW POISED TO BECOME THE PRE-EMINENT SPACE PROGRAM ON THE PLANET--THANKS IN LARGE PART TO THE WORK OF PRINCESS SHURI AND HER TEAM.

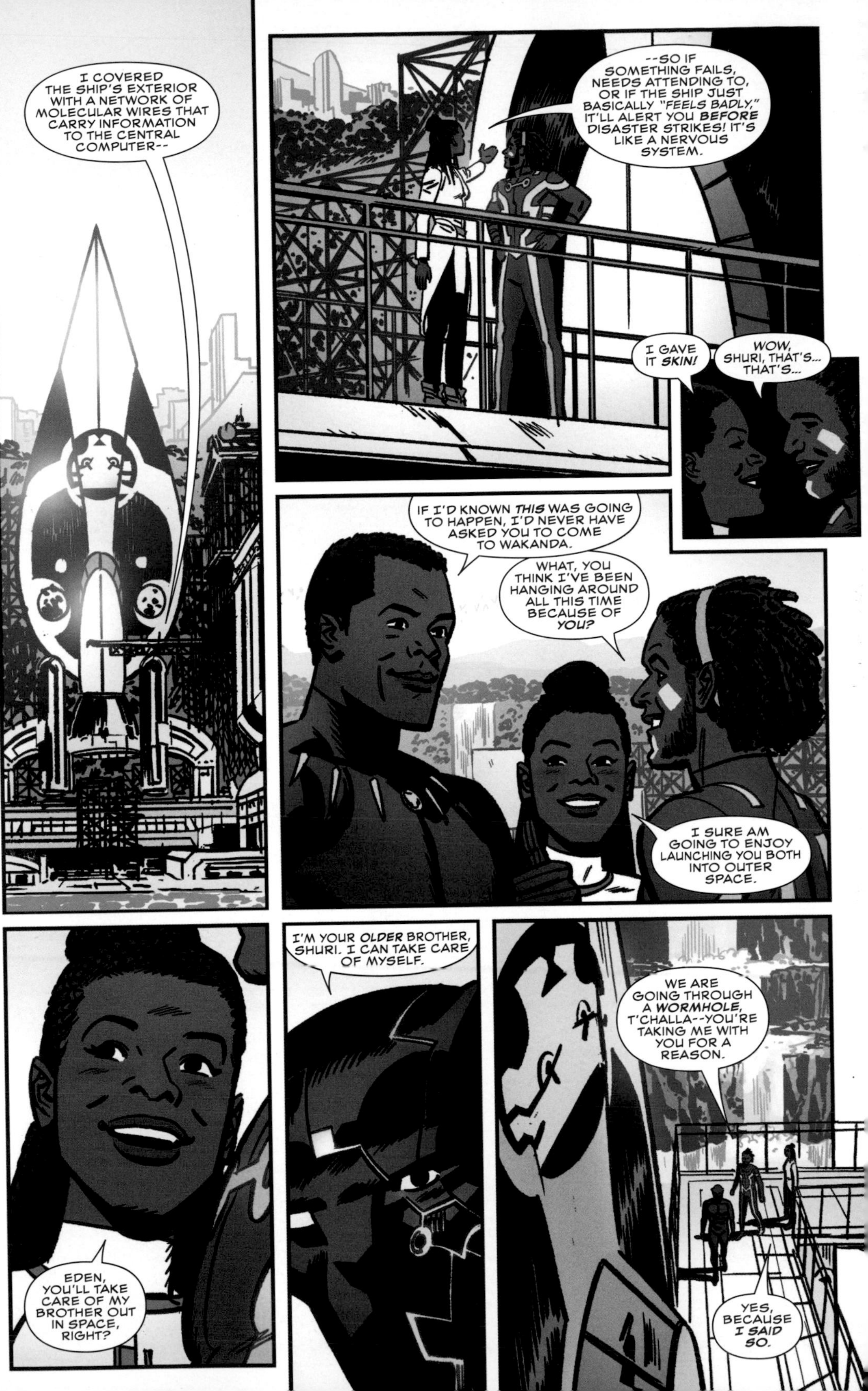
I COVERED THE SHIP'S EXTERIOR WITH A NETWORK OF MOLECULAR WIRES THAT CARRY INFORMATION TO THE CENTRAL COMPUTER--
--SO IF SOMETHING FAILS, NEEDS ATTENDING TO, OR IF THE SHIP JUST BASICALLY "FEELS BADLY," IT'LL ALERT YOU BEFORE DISASTER STRIKES! IT'S LIKE A NERVOUS SYSTEM.
I GAVE IT SKIN!
WOW, SHURI, THAT'S... THAT'S...
IF I'D KNOWN THIS WAS GOING TO HAPPEN, I'D NEVER HAVE ASKED YOU TO COME TO WAKANDA.
WHAT, YOU THINK I'VE BEEN HANGING AROUND ALL THIS TIME BECAUSE OF YOU?
I SURE AM GOING TO ENJOY LAUNCHING YOU BOTH INTO OUTER SPACE.
EDEN, YOU'LL TAKE CARE OF MY BROTHER OUT IN SPACE, RIGHT?
I'M YOUR OLDER BROTHER, SHURI. I CAN TAKE CARE OF MYSELF.
WE ARE GOING THROUGH A WORMHOLE, T'CHALLA--YOU'RE TAKING ME WITH YOU FOR A REASON.
YES, BECAUSE I SAID SO.

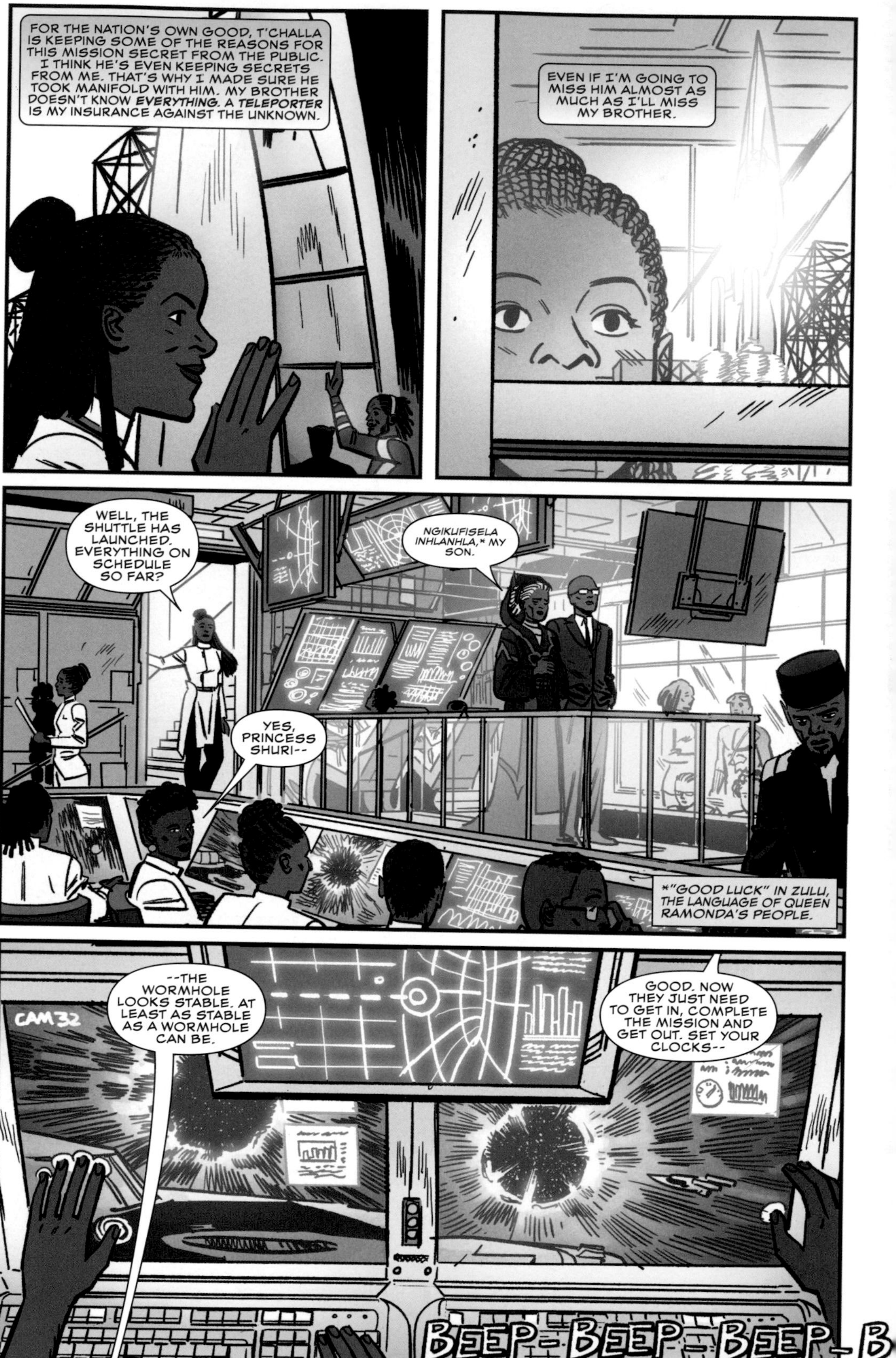
FOR THE NATION'S OWN GOOD, T'CHALLA IS KEEPING SOME OF THE REASONS FOR THIS MISSION SECRET FROM THE PUBLIC. I THINK HE'S EVEN KEEPING SECRETS FROM ME. THAT'S WHY I MADE SURE HE TOOK MANIFOLD WITH HIM. MY BROTHER DOESN'T KNOW *EVERYTHING*. A *TELEPORTER* IS MY INSURANCE AGAINST THE UNKNOWN.
EVEN IF I'M GOING TO MISS HIM ALMOST AS MUCH AS I'LL MISS MY BROTHER.
WELL, THE SHUTTLE HAS LAUNCHED. EVERYTHING ON SCHEDULE SO FAR?
NGIKUFISELA INHLANHLA,* MY SON.
YES, PRINCESS SHURI--
*"GOOD LUCK" IN ZULU, THE LANGUAGE OF QUEEN RAMONDA'S PEOPLE.
CAM 32
--THE WORMHOLE LOOKS STABLE. AT LEAST AS STABLE AS A WORMHOLE CAN BE.
GOOD. NOW THEY JUST NEED TO GET IN, COMPLETE THE MISSION AND GET OUT. SET YOUR CLOCKS--
BEEP-BEEP-BEEP-B

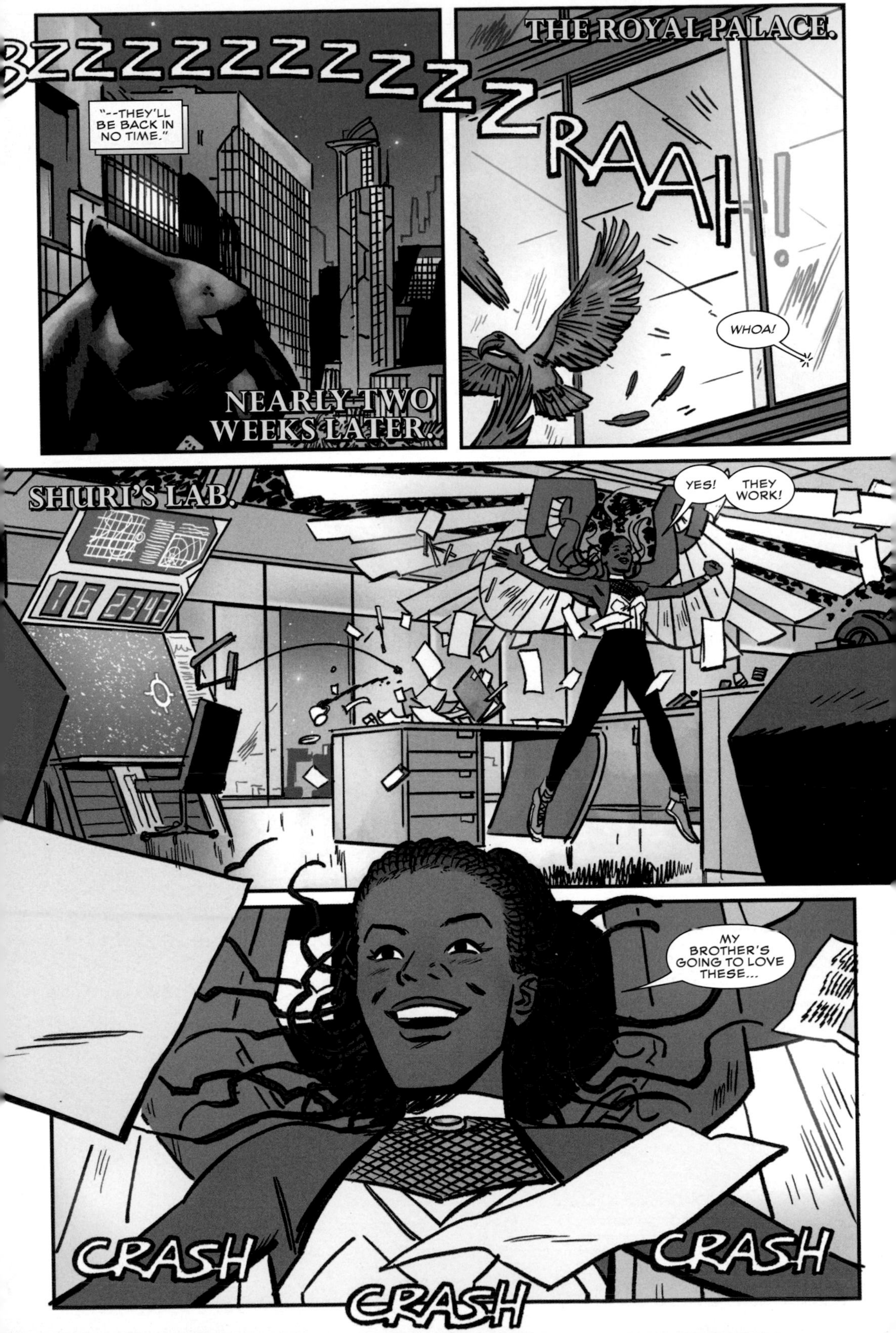
BZZZZZZZZZZZZ
"--THEY'LL BE BACK IN NO TIME."
NEARLY TWO WEEKS LATER.
THE ROYAL PALACE.
ZRAAH!
WHOA!
SHURI'S LAB.
YES!
THEY WORK!
MY BROTHER'S GOING TO LOVE THESE...
CRASH
CRASH
CRASH

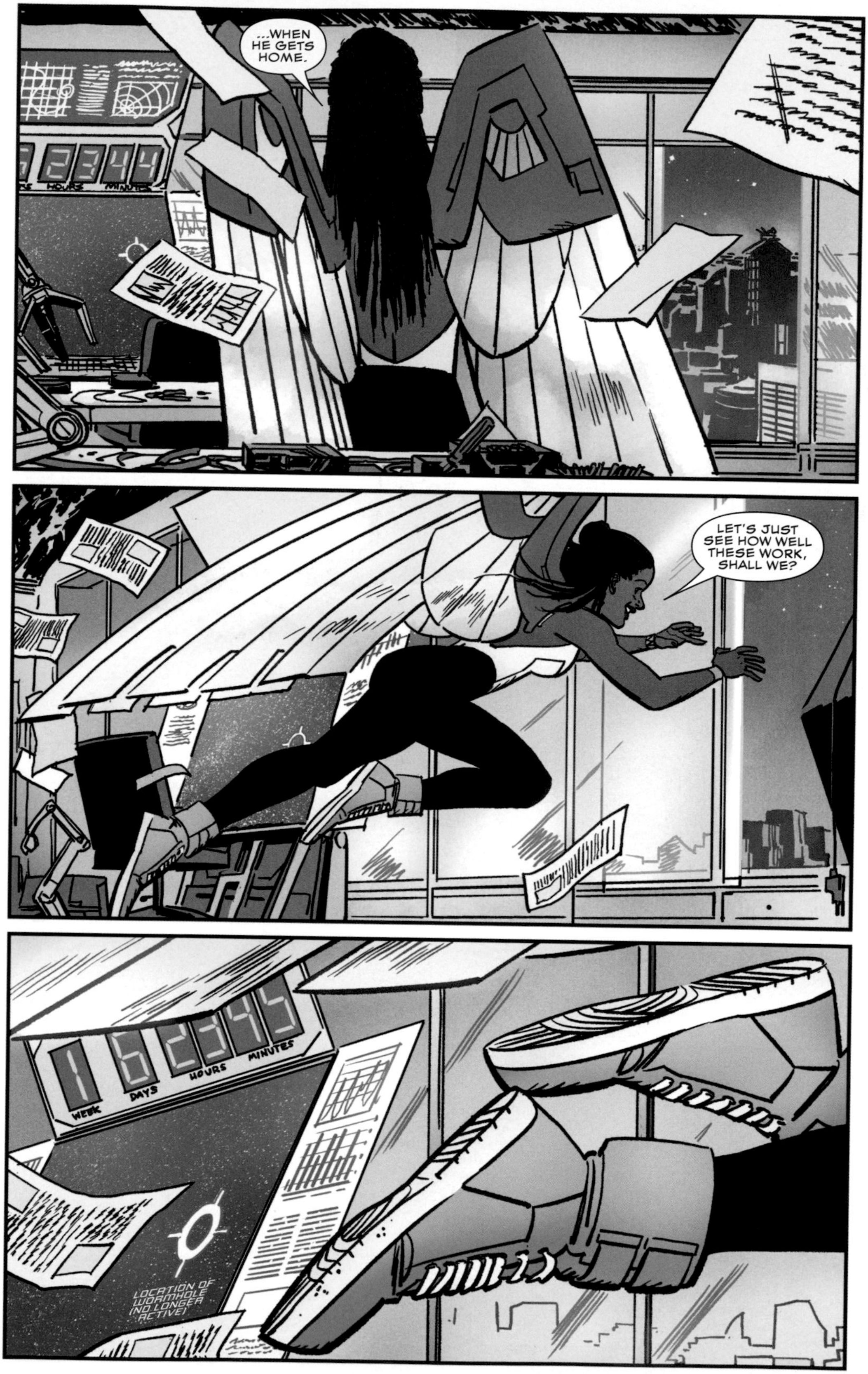
...WHEN HE GETS HOME.
LET'S JUST SEE HOW WELL THESE WORK, SHALL WE?
WEEK DAYS HOURS MINUTES
LOCATION OF WORMHOLE (NO LONGER ACTIVE)

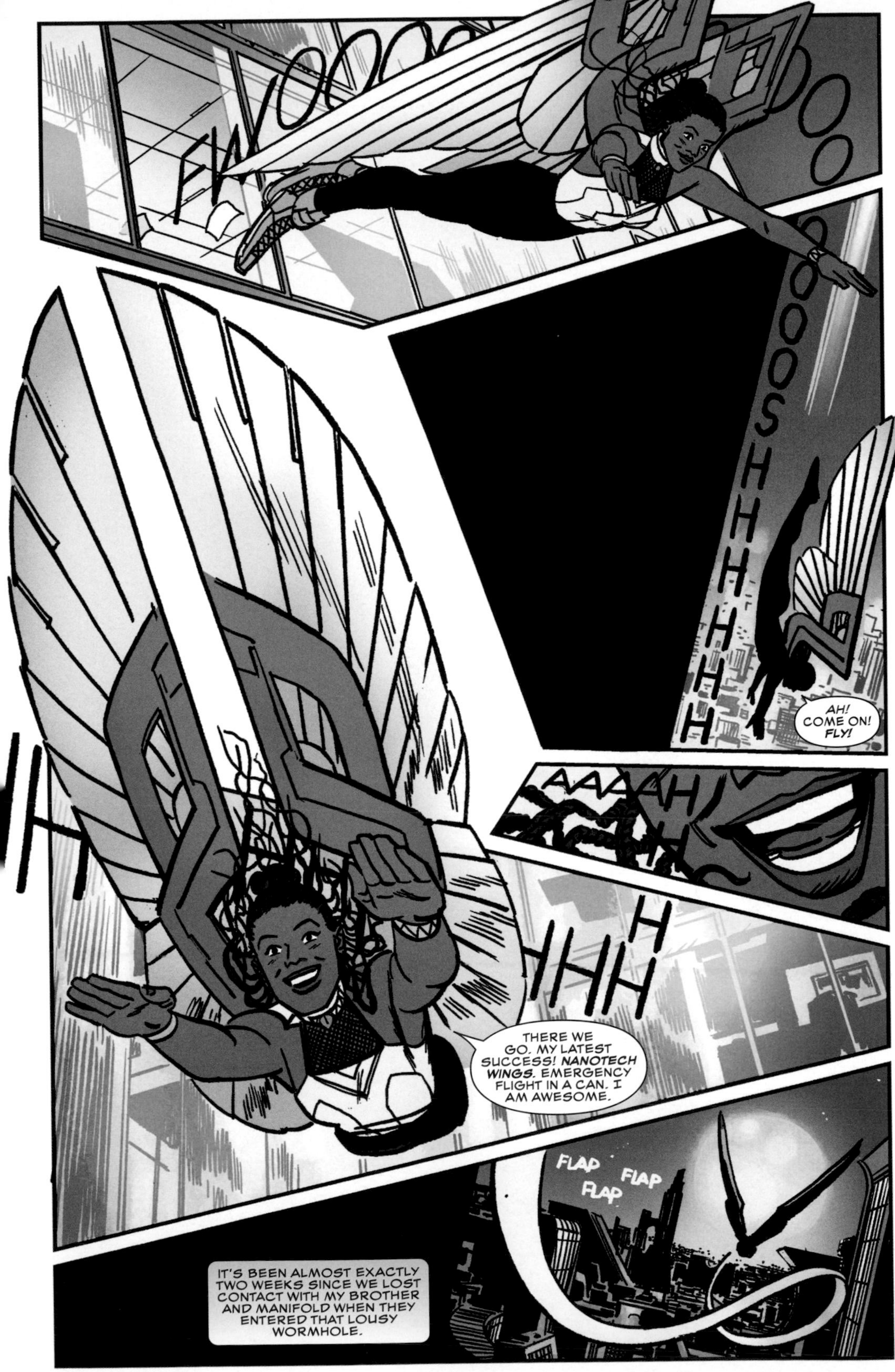
FWOOOOOOOOOOOOOOSHHHHHHHHH
AH! COME ON! FLY!
AAAAAHHHHHH
THERE WE GO. MY LATEST SUCCESS! NANOTECH WINGS. EMERGENCY FLIGHT IN A CAN. I AM AWESOME.
FLAP FLAP FLAP
IT'S BEEN ALMOST EXACTLY TWO WEEKS SINCE WE LOST CONTACT WITH MY BROTHER AND MANIFOLD WHEN THEY ENTERED THAT LOUSY WORMHOLE.

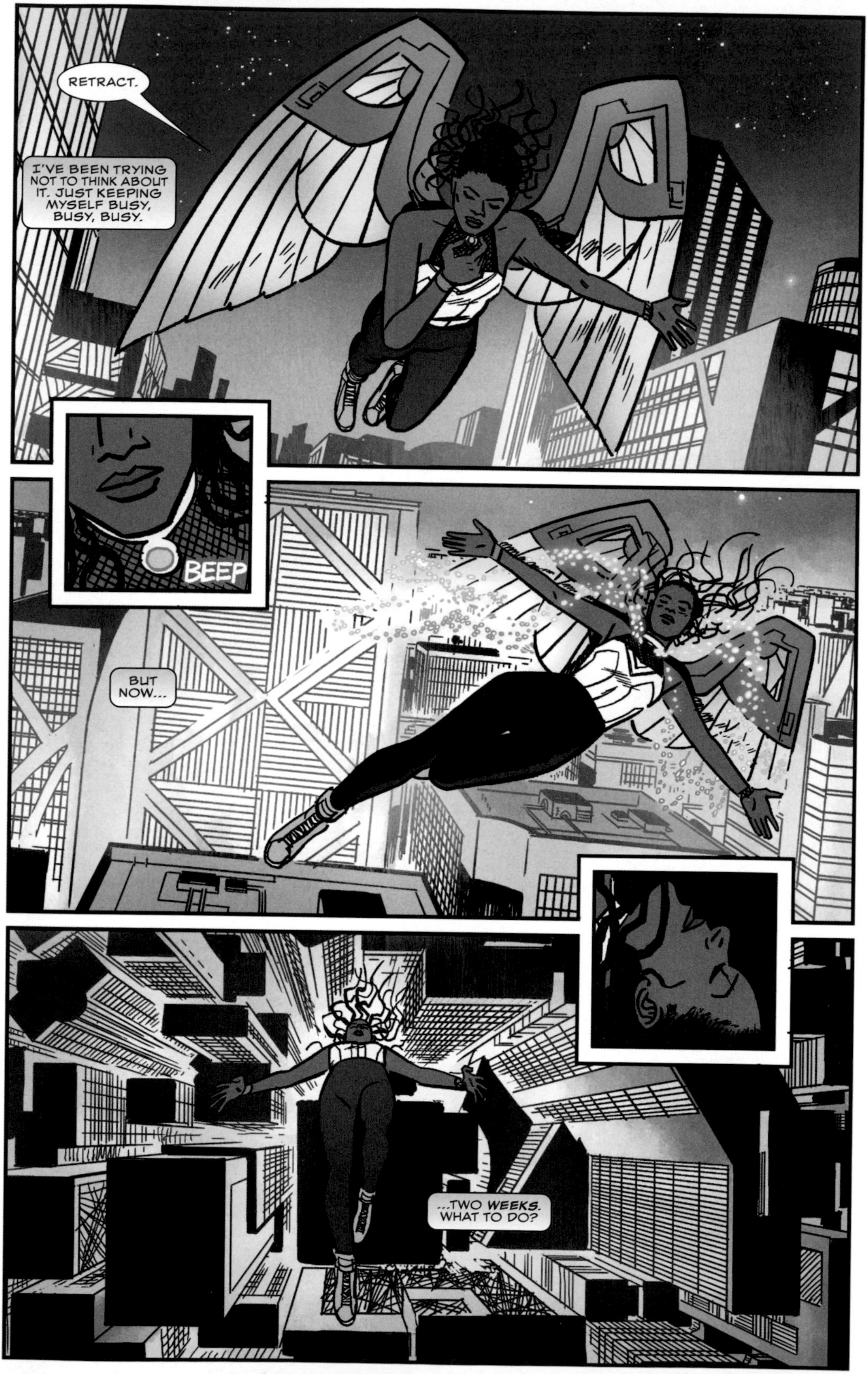

RETRACT.
I'VE BEEN TRYING NOT TO THINK ABOUT IT. JUST KEEPING MYSELF BUSY, BUSY, BUSY.
BEEP
BUT NOW...
...TWO WEEKS. WHAT TO DO?

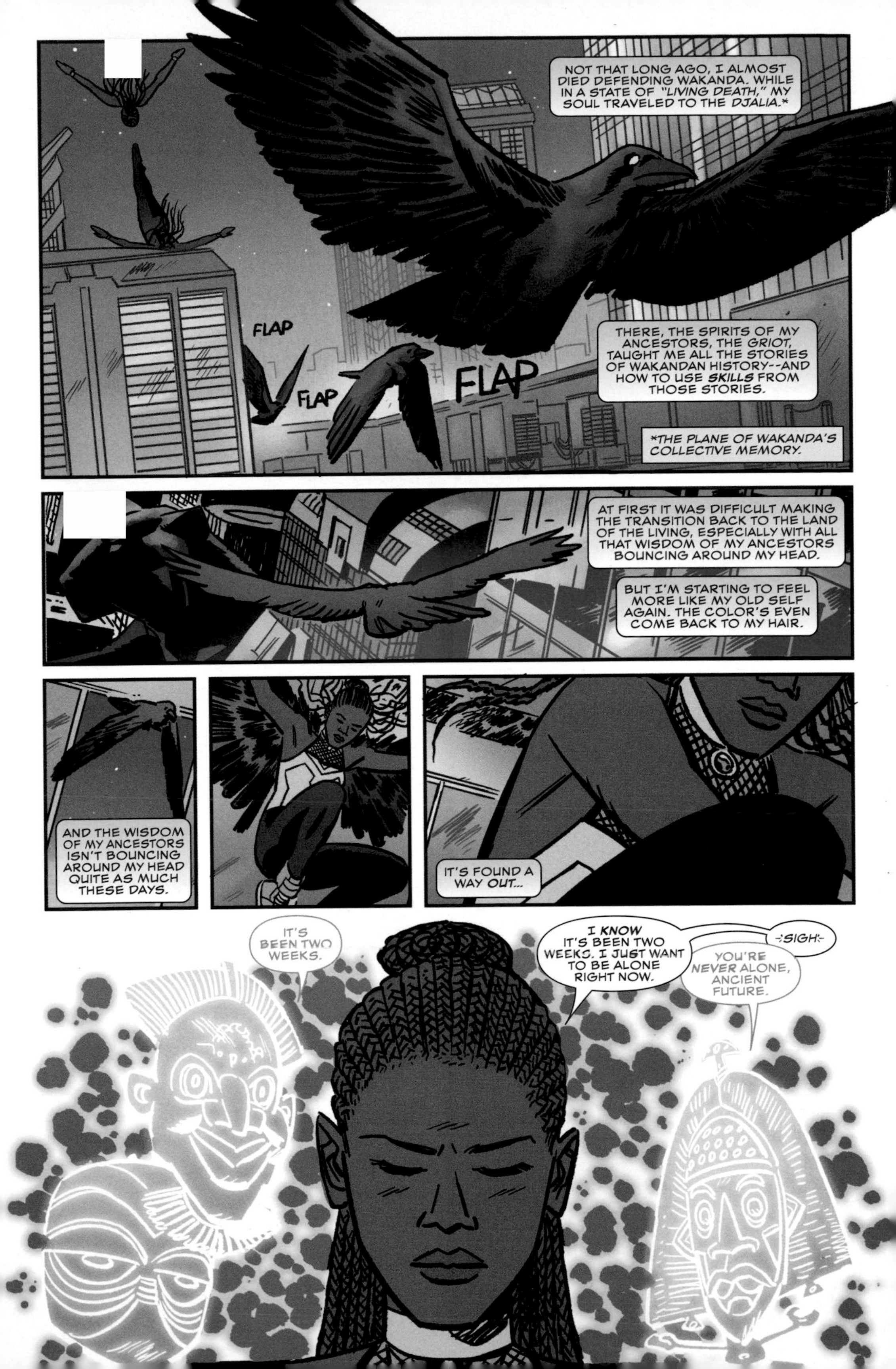

NOT THAT LONG AGO, I ALMOST DIED DEFENDING WAKANDA. WHILE IN A STATE OF "LIVING DEATH," MY SOUL TRAVELED TO THE DJALIA.*
FLAP
FLAP
FLAP
THERE, THE SPIRITS OF MY ANCESTORS, THE GRIOT, TAUGHT ME ALL THE STORIES OF WAKANDAN HISTORY--AND HOW TO USE SKILLS FROM THOSE STORIES.
*THE PLANE OF WAKANDA'S COLLECTIVE MEMORY.
AT FIRST IT WAS DIFFICULT MAKING THE TRANSITION BACK TO THE LAND OF THE LIVING, ESPECIALLY WITH ALL THAT WISDOM OF MY ANCESTORS BOUNCING AROUND MY HEAD.
BUT I'M STARTING TO FEEL MORE LIKE MY OLD SELF AGAIN. THE COLOR'S EVEN COME BACK TO MY HAIR.
AND THE WISDOM OF MY ANCESTORS ISN'T BOUNCING AROUND MY HEAD QUITE AS MUCH THESE DAYS.
IT'S FOUND A WAY OUT...
IT'S BEEN TWO WEEKS.
I KNOW IT'S BEEN TWO WEEKS. I JUST WANT TO BE ALONE RIGHT NOW.
SIGH
YOU'RE NEVER ALONE, ANCIENT FUTURE.

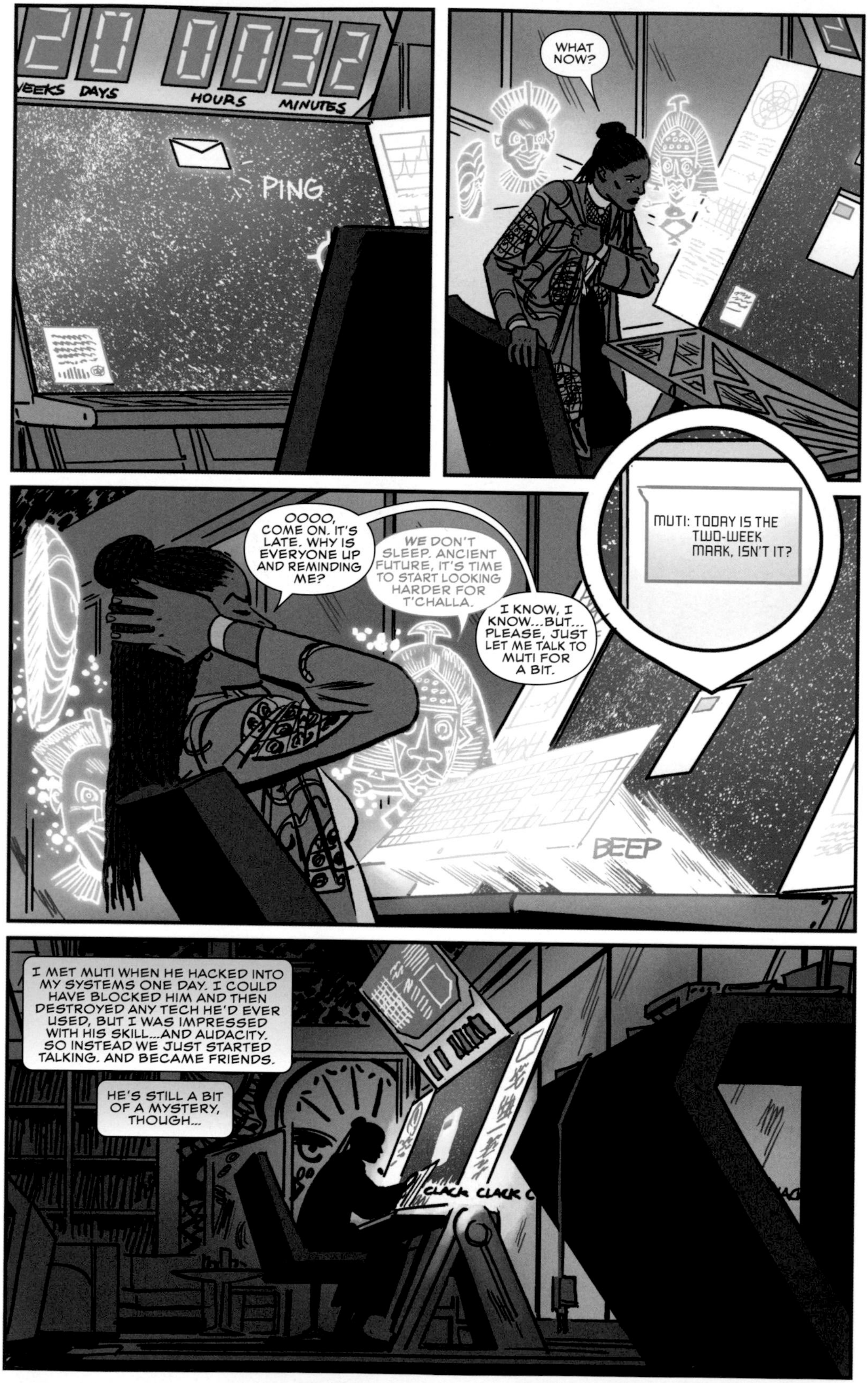
20 00 32
WEEKS DAYS HOURS MINUTES
PING
WHAT NOW?
MUTI: TODAY IS THE TWO-WEEK MARK, ISN'T IT?
OOOO, COME ON. IT'S LATE. WHY IS EVERYONE UP AND REMINDING ME?
WE DON'T SLEEP. ANCIENT FUTURE, IT'S TIME TO START LOOKING HARDER FOR T'CHALLA.
I KNOW, I KNOW...BUT... PLEASE, JUST LET ME TALK TO MUTI FOR A BIT.
BEEP
I MET MUTI WHEN HE HACKED INTO MY SYSTEMS ONE DAY. I COULD HAVE BLOCKED HIM AND THEN DESTROYED ANY TECH HE'D EVER USED, BUT I WAS IMPRESSED WITH HIS SKILL...AND AUDACITY. SO INSTEAD WE JUST STARTED TALKING. AND BECAME FRIENDS.
HE'S STILL A BIT OF A MYSTERY, THOUGH...
CLACK CLACK

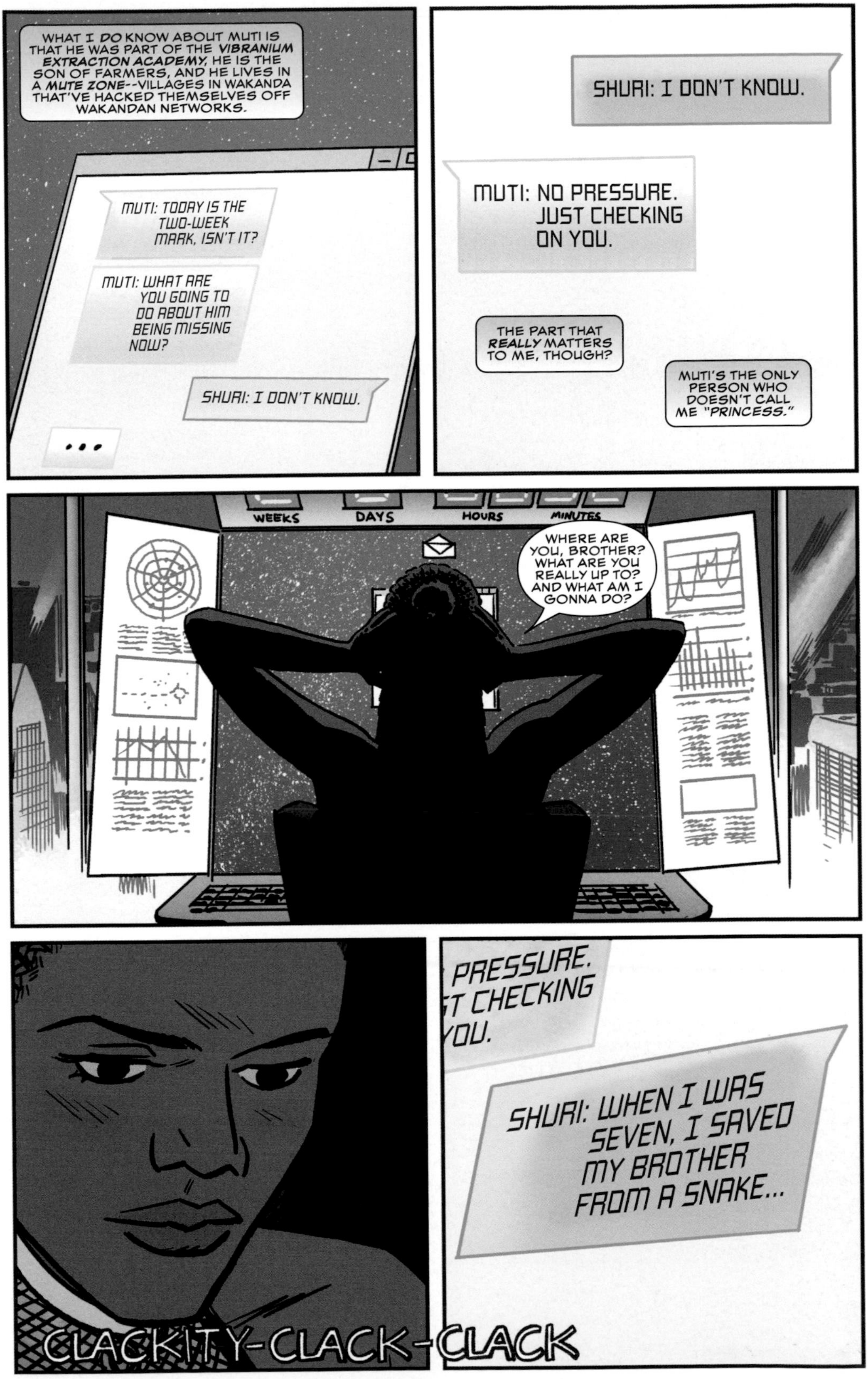
WHAT I DO KNOW ABOUT MUTI IS THAT HE WAS PART OF THE VIBRANIUM EXTRACTION ACADEMY, HE IS THE SON OF FARMERS, AND HE LIVES IN A MUTE ZONE--VILLAGES IN WAKANDA THAT'VE HACKED THEMSELVES OFF WAKANDAN NETWORKS.
MUTI: TODAY IS THE TWO-WEEK MARK, ISN'T IT?
MUTI: WHAT ARE YOU GOING TO DO ABOUT HIM BEING MISSING NOW?
SHURI: I DON'T KNOW.
...
SHURI: I DON'T KNOW.
MUTI: NO PRESSURE. JUST CHECKING ON YOU.
THE PART THAT REALLY MATTERS TO ME, THOUGH?
MUTI'S THE ONLY PERSON WHO DOESN'T CALL ME "PRINCESS."
WEEKS
DAYS
HOURS
MINUTES
WHERE ARE YOU, BROTHER? WHAT ARE YOU REALLY UP TO? AND WHAT AM I GONNA DO?
PRESSURE. T CHECKING YOU.
SHURI: WHEN I WAS SEVEN, I SAVED MY BROTHER FROM A SNAKE...
CLACKITY-CLACK-CLACK

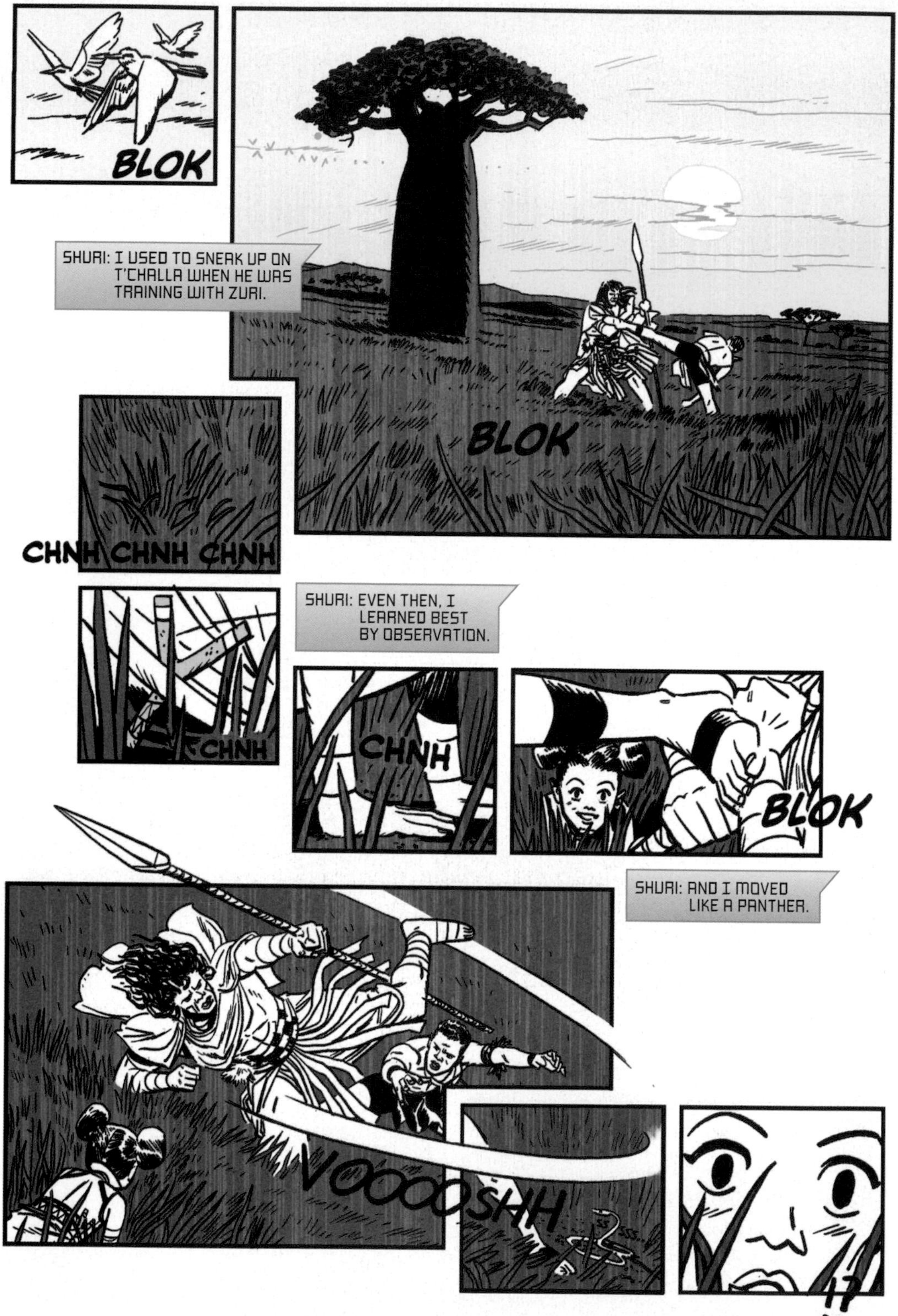
BLOK
SHURI: I USED TO SNEAK UP ON T'CHALLA WHEN HE WAS TRAINING WITH ZURI.
BLOK
CHNH CHNH CHNH
SHURI: EVEN THEN, I LEARNED BEST BY OBSERVATION.
CHNH
CHNH
BLOK
SHURI: AND I MOVED LIKE A PANTHER.
VOOOOOSHH
!?

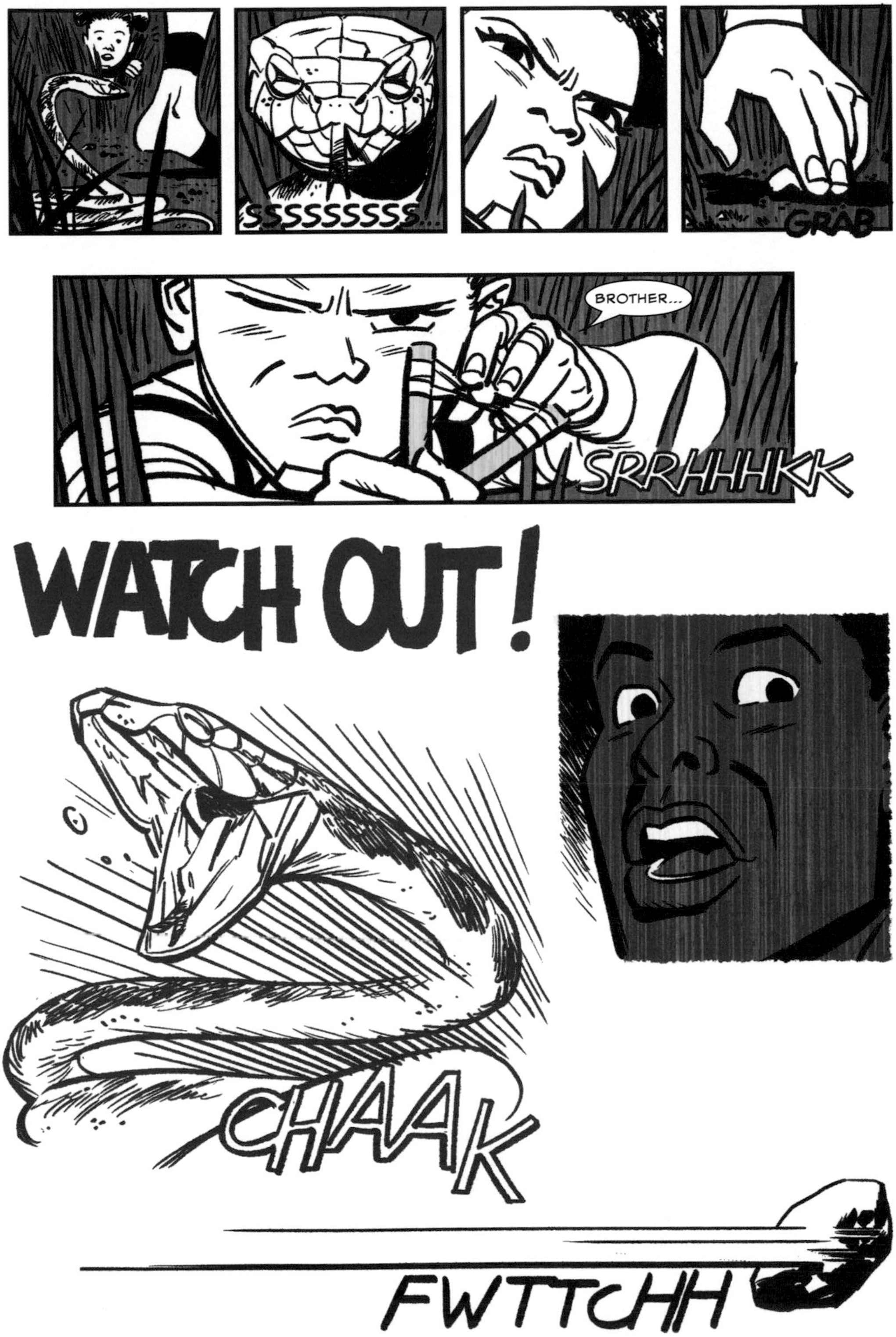
SSSSSSSSSS...
GRAB
BROTHER...
SRRHHHKK
WATCH OUT!
CHAAK
FWTTCHH

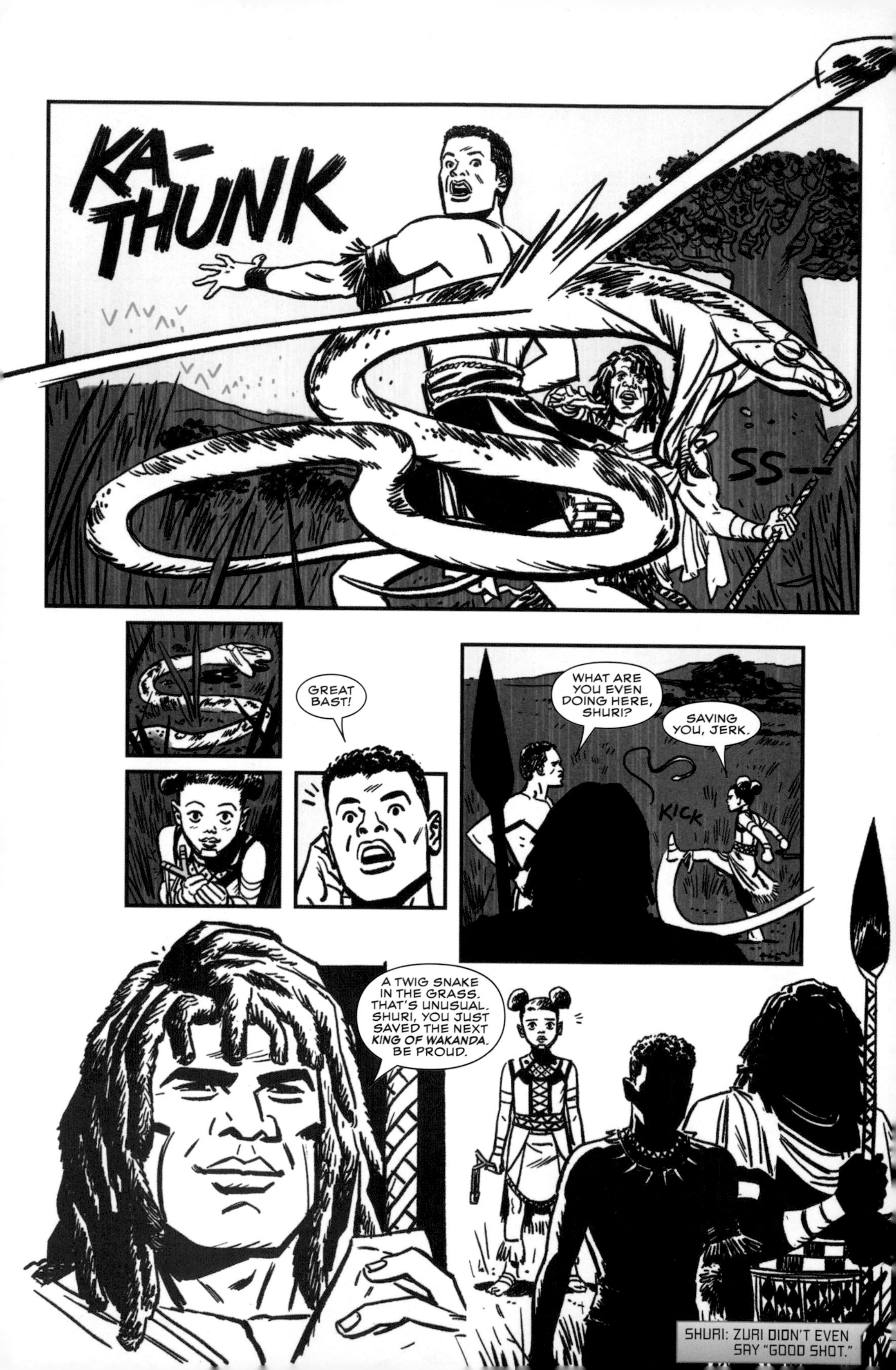
KA-THUNK
SS--
GREAT BAST!
WHAT ARE YOU EVEN DOING HERE, SHURI?
SAVING YOU, JERK.
KICK
A TWIG SNAKE IN THE GRASS. THAT'S UNUSUAL. SHURI, YOU JUST SAVED THE NEXT *KING OF WAKANDA*. BE PROUD.
SHURI: ZURI DIDN'T EVEN SAY "GOOD SHOT."

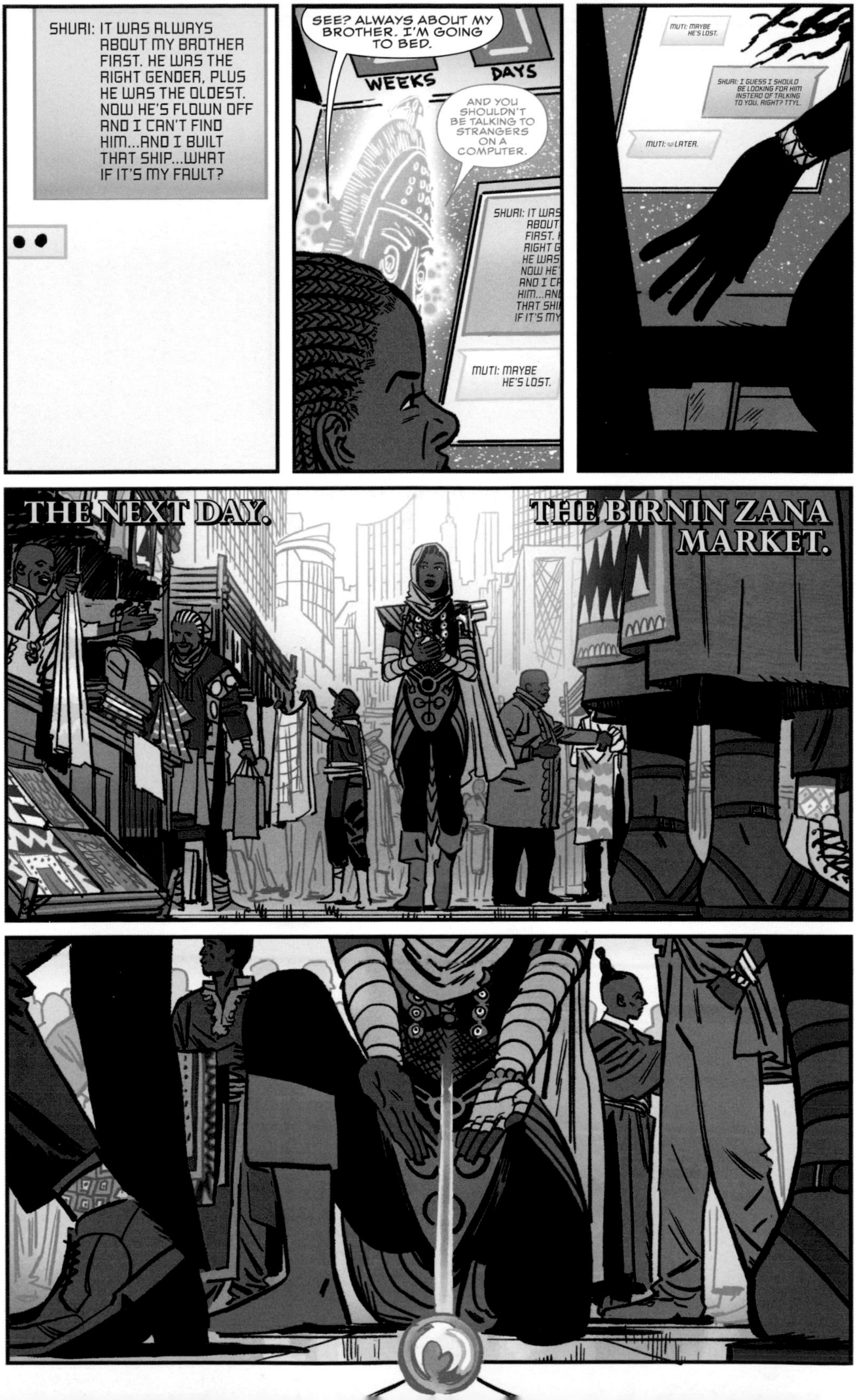

SHURI: IT WAS ALWAYS ABOUT MY BROTHER FIRST. HE WAS THE RIGHT GENDER, PLUS HE WAS THE OLDEST. NOW HE'S FLOWN OFF AND I CAN'T FIND HIM...AND I BUILT THAT SHIP...WHAT IF IT'S MY FAULT?
SEE? ALWAYS ABOUT MY BROTHER. I'M GOING TO BED.
WEEKS
DAYS
AND YOU SHOULDN'T BE TALKING TO STRANGERS ON A COMPUTER.
MUTI: MAYBE HE'S LOST.
MUTI: MAYBE HE'S LOST.
SHURI: I GUESS I SHOULD BE LOOKING FOR HIM INSTEAD OF TALKING TO YOU, RIGHT? TTYL.
MUTI: LATER.
THE NEXT DAY.
THE BIRNIN ZANA MARKET.

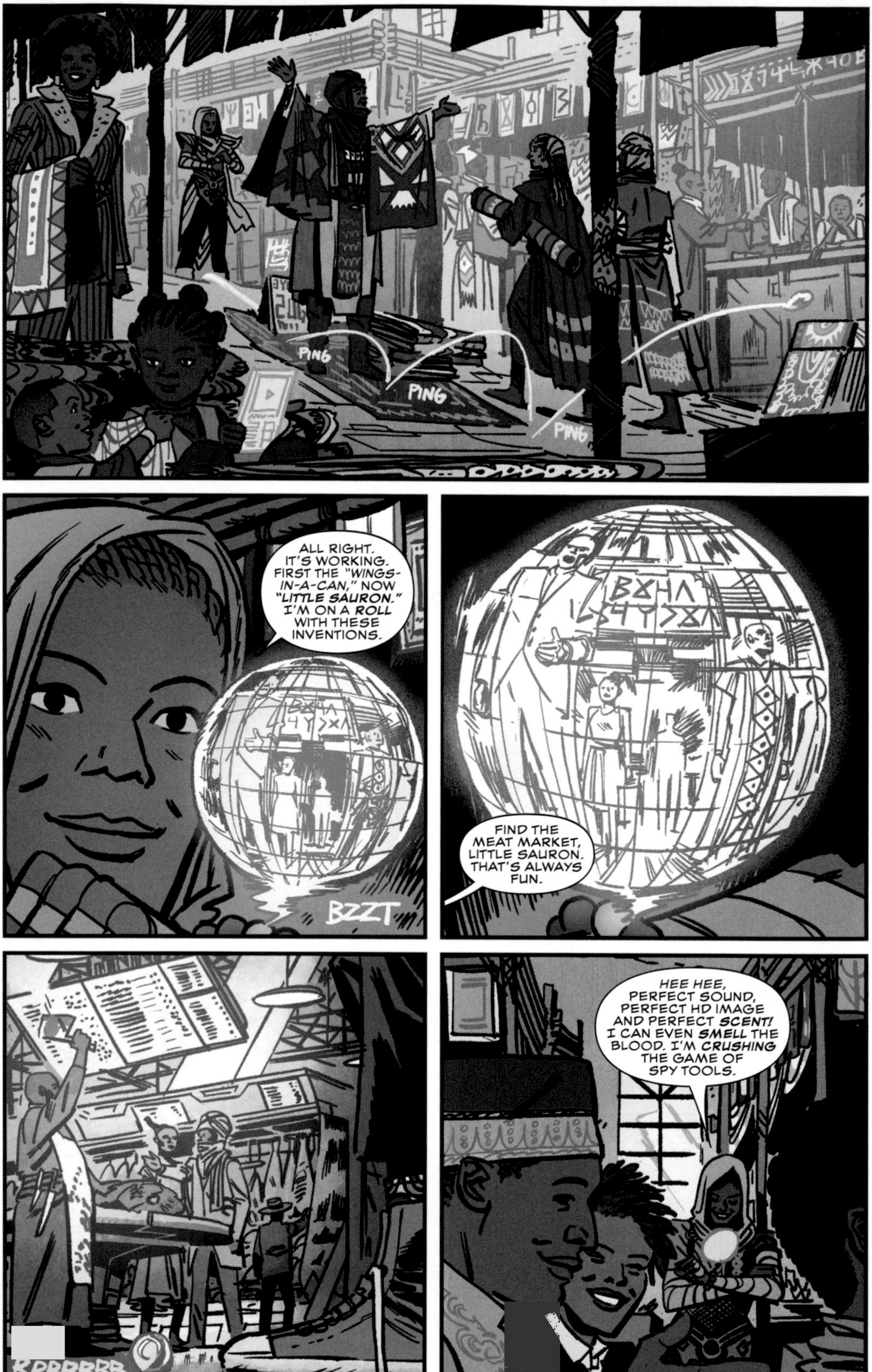
PING
PING
PING
ALL RIGHT. IT'S WORKING. FIRST THE "WINGS-IN-A-CAN," NOW "LITTLE SAURON." I'M ON A ROLL WITH THESE INVENTIONS.
BZZT
FIND THE MEAT MARKET, LITTLE SAURON. THAT'S ALWAYS FUN.
KRRRRRR
HEE HEE, PERFECT SOUND, PERFECT HD IMAGE AND PERFECT SCENT! I CAN EVEN SMELL THE BLOOD. I'M CRUSHING THE GAME OF SPY TOOLS.

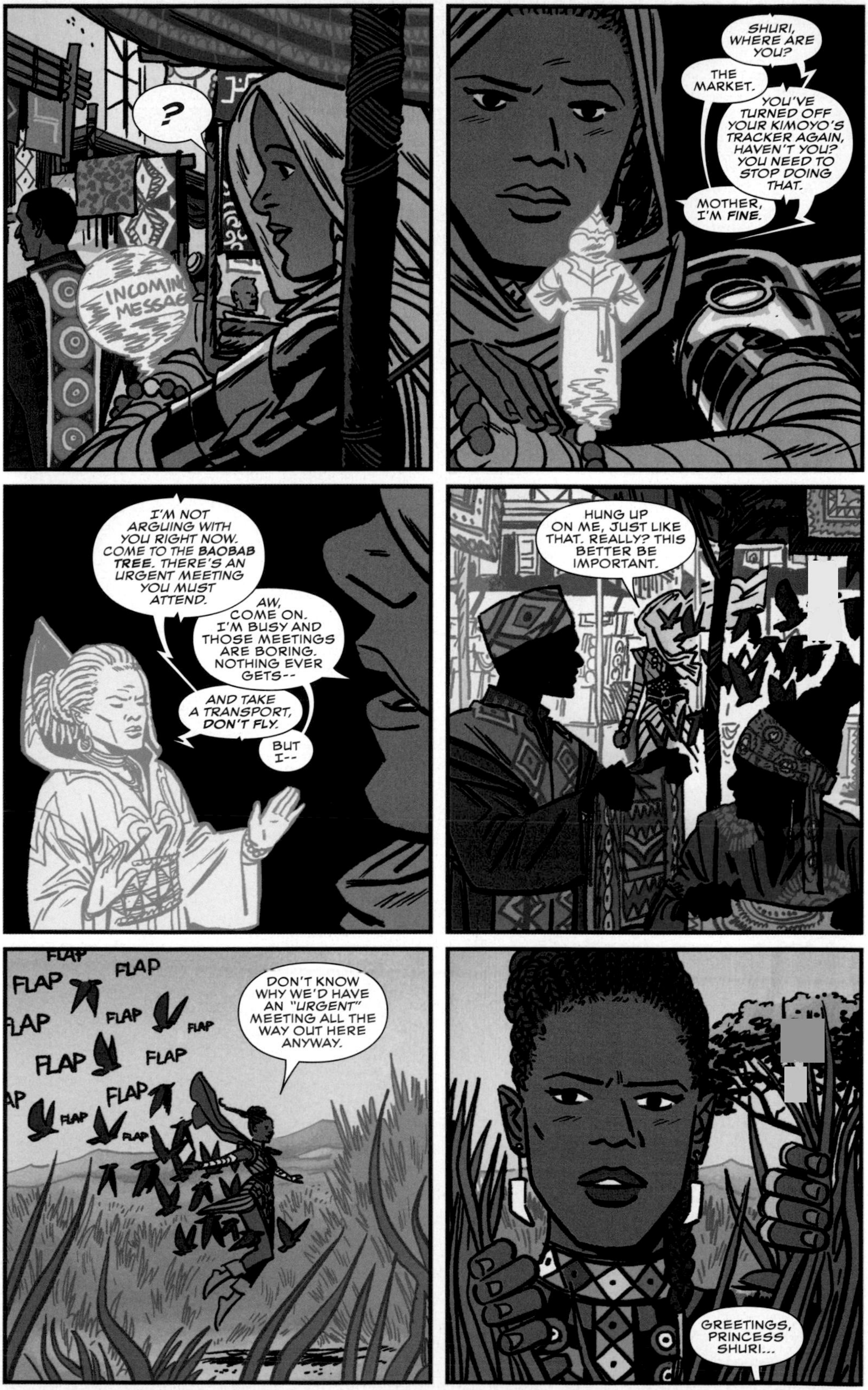
?
INCOMING MESSAGE
SHURI, WHERE ARE YOU?
THE MARKET.
YOU'VE TURNED OFF YOUR KIMOYO'S TRACKER AGAIN, HAVEN'T YOU? YOU NEED TO STOP DOING THAT.
MOTHER, I'M *FINE*.
I'M NOT ARGUING WITH YOU RIGHT NOW. COME TO THE **BAOBAB TREE**. THERE'S AN URGENT MEETING YOU MUST ATTEND.
AW, COME ON. I'M BUSY AND THOSE MEETINGS ARE BORING. NOTHING EVER GETS--
AND TAKE A TRANSPORT, *DON'T FLY*.
BUT I--
HUNG UP ON ME, JUST LIKE THAT. REALLY? THIS BETTER BE IMPORTANT.
FLAP FLAP FLAP FLAP FLAP FLAP FLAP FLAP FLAP FLAP FLAP FLAP
DON'T KNOW WHY WE'D HAVE AN *"URGENT"* MEETING ALL THE WAY OUT HERE ANYWAY.
GREETINGS, PRINCESS SHURI...

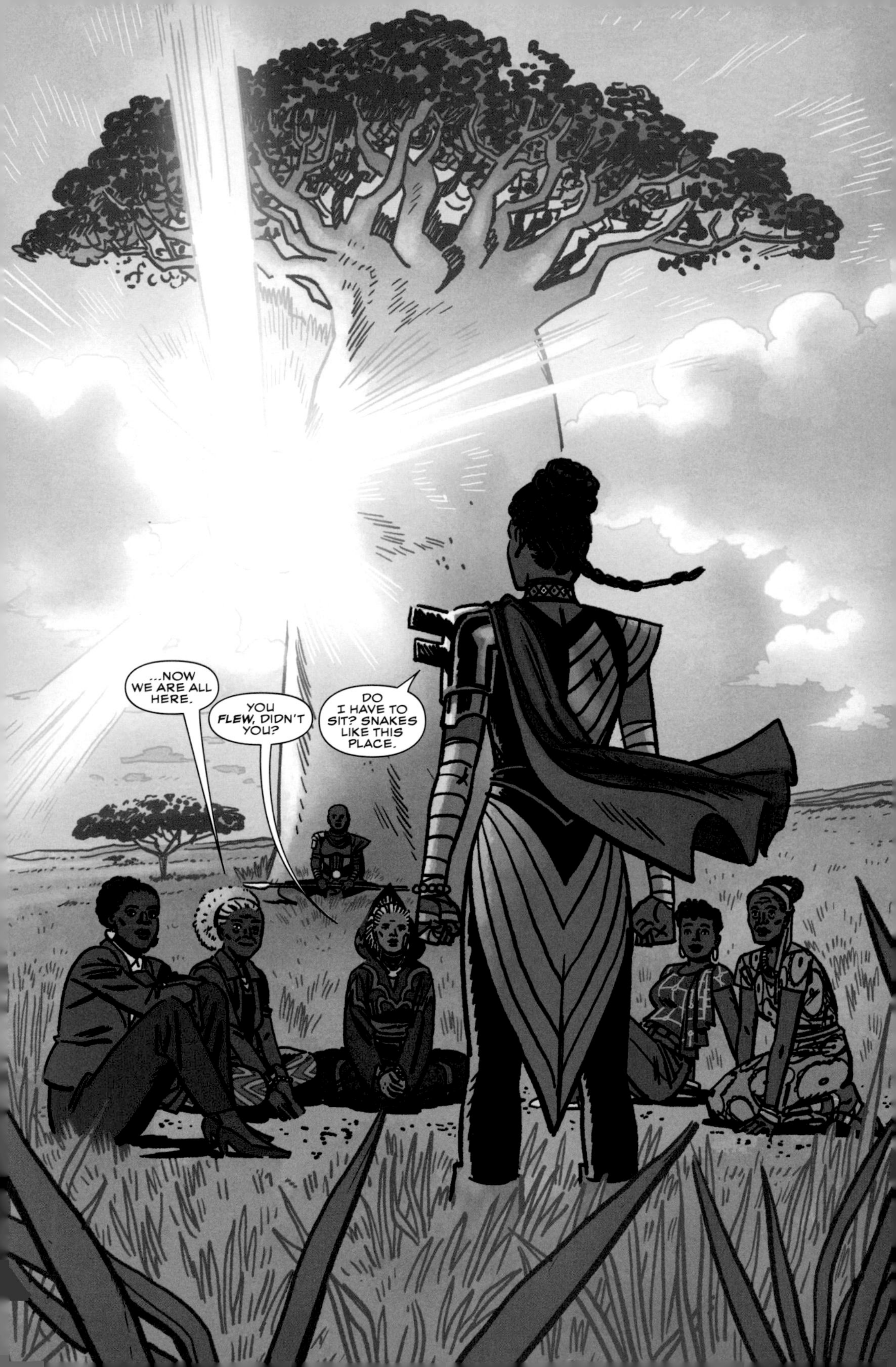
...NOW WE ARE ALL HERE.
YOU *FLEW*, DIDN'T YOU?
DO I HAVE TO SIT? SNAKES LIKE THIS PLACE.

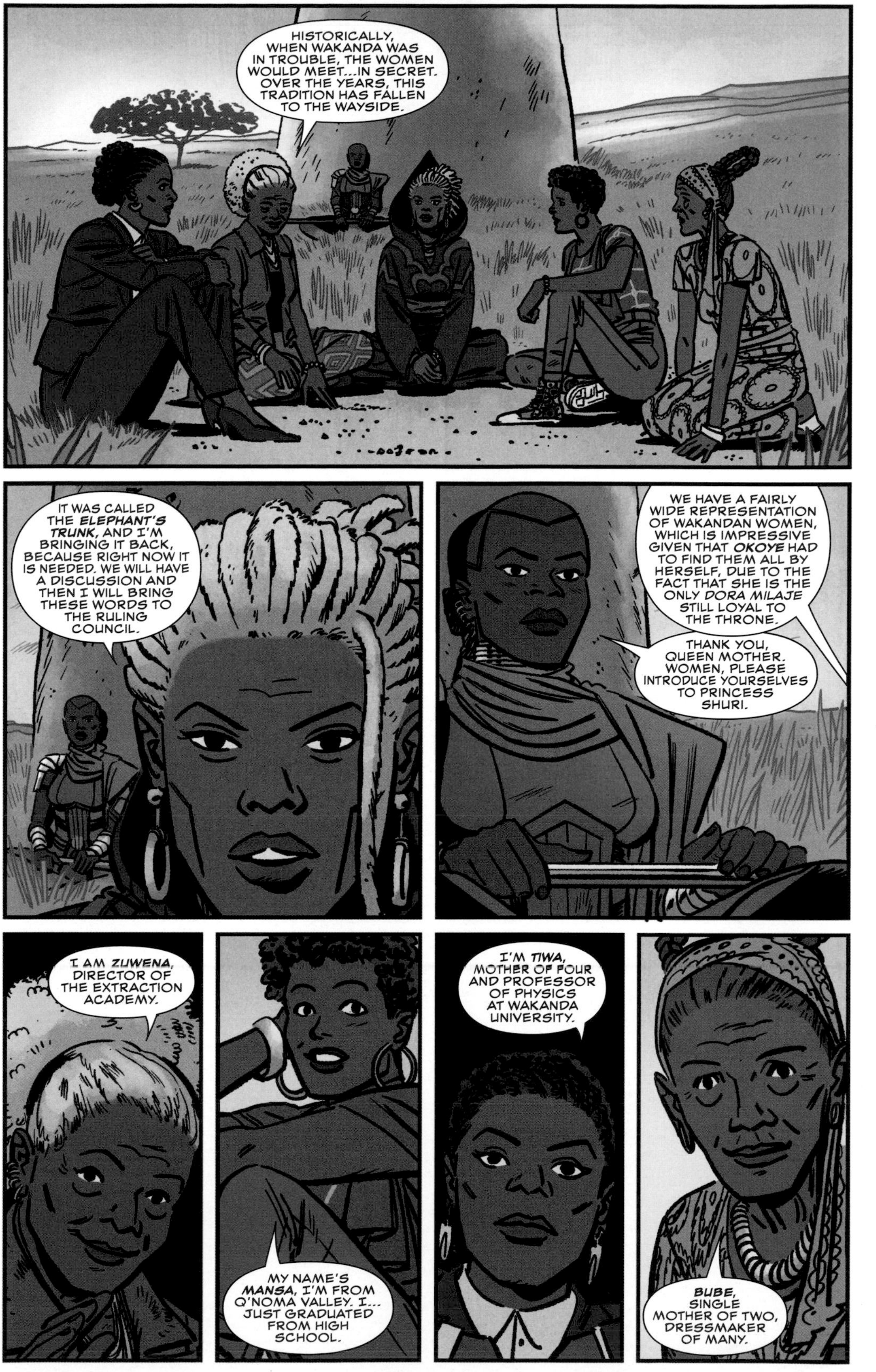
HISTORICALLY, WHEN WAKANDA WAS IN TROUBLE, THE WOMEN WOULD MEET...IN SECRET. OVER THE YEARS, THIS TRADITION HAS FALLEN TO THE WAYSIDE.
IT WAS CALLED THE ELEPHANT'S TRUNK, AND I'M BRINGING IT BACK, BECAUSE RIGHT NOW IT IS NEEDED. WE WILL HAVE A DISCUSSION AND THEN I WILL BRING THESE WORDS TO THE RULING COUNCIL.
WE HAVE A FAIRLY WIDE REPRESENTATION OF WAKANDAN WOMEN, WHICH IS IMPRESSIVE GIVEN THAT OKOYE HAD TO FIND THEM ALL BY HERSELF, DUE TO THE FACT THAT SHE IS THE ONLY DORA MILAJE STILL LOYAL TO THE THRONE.
THANK YOU, QUEEN MOTHER. WOMEN, PLEASE INTRODUCE YOURSELVES TO PRINCESS SHURI.
I AM ZUWENA, DIRECTOR OF THE EXTRACTION ACADEMY.
MY NAME'S MANSA, I'M FROM Q'NOMA VALLEY. I... JUST GRADUATED FROM HIGH SCHOOL.
I'M TIWA, MOTHER OF FOUR AND PROFESSOR OF PHYSICS AT WAKANDA UNIVERSITY.
BUBE, SINGLE MOTHER OF TWO, DRESSMAKER OF MANY.

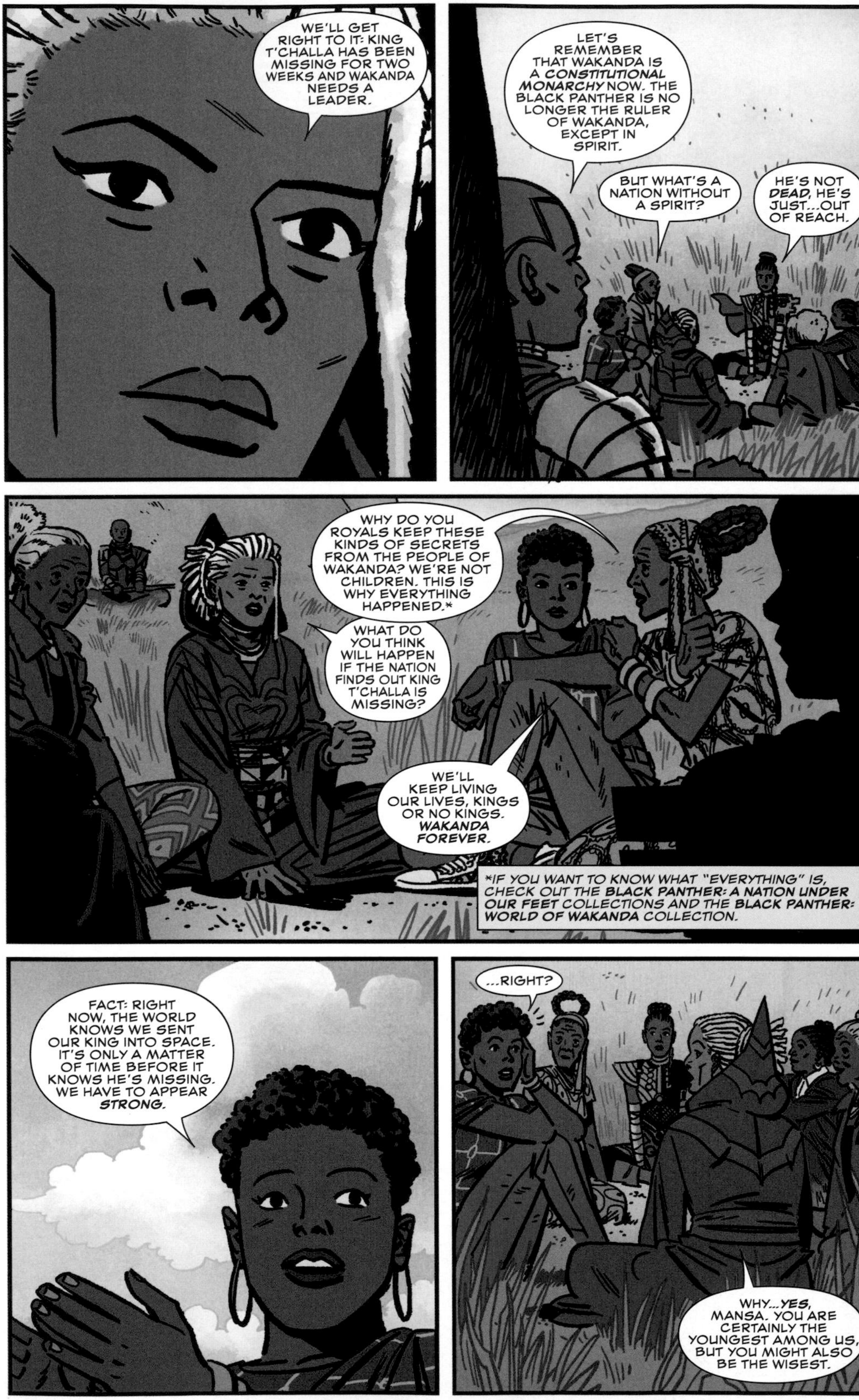
WE'LL GET RIGHT TO IT: KING T'CHALLA HAS BEEN MISSING FOR TWO WEEKS AND WAKANDA NEEDS A LEADER.
LET'S REMEMBER THAT WAKANDA IS A CONSTITUTIONAL MONARCHY NOW. THE BLACK PANTHER IS NO LONGER THE RULER OF WAKANDA, EXCEPT IN SPIRIT.
BUT WHAT'S A NATION WITHOUT A SPIRIT?
HE'S NOT DEAD, HE'S JUST...OUT OF REACH.
WHY DO YOU ROYALS KEEP THESE KINDS OF SECRETS FROM THE PEOPLE OF WAKANDA? WE'RE NOT CHILDREN. THIS IS WHY EVERYTHING HAPPENED.*
WHAT DO YOU THINK WILL HAPPEN IF THE NATION FINDS OUT KING T'CHALLA IS MISSING?
WE'LL KEEP LIVING OUR LIVES, KINGS OR NO KINGS. WAKANDA FOREVER.
*IF YOU WANT TO KNOW WHAT "EVERYTHING" IS, CHECK OUT THE BLACK PANTHER: A NATION UNDER OUR FEET COLLECTIONS AND THE BLACK PANTHER: WORLD OF WAKANDA COLLECTION.
FACT: RIGHT NOW, THE WORLD KNOWS WE SENT OUR KING INTO SPACE. IT'S ONLY A MATTER OF TIME BEFORE IT KNOWS HE'S MISSING. WE HAVE TO APPEAR STRONG.
...RIGHT?
WHY...YES, MANSA. YOU ARE CERTAINLY THE YOUNGEST AMONG US, BUT YOU MIGHT ALSO BE THE WISEST.

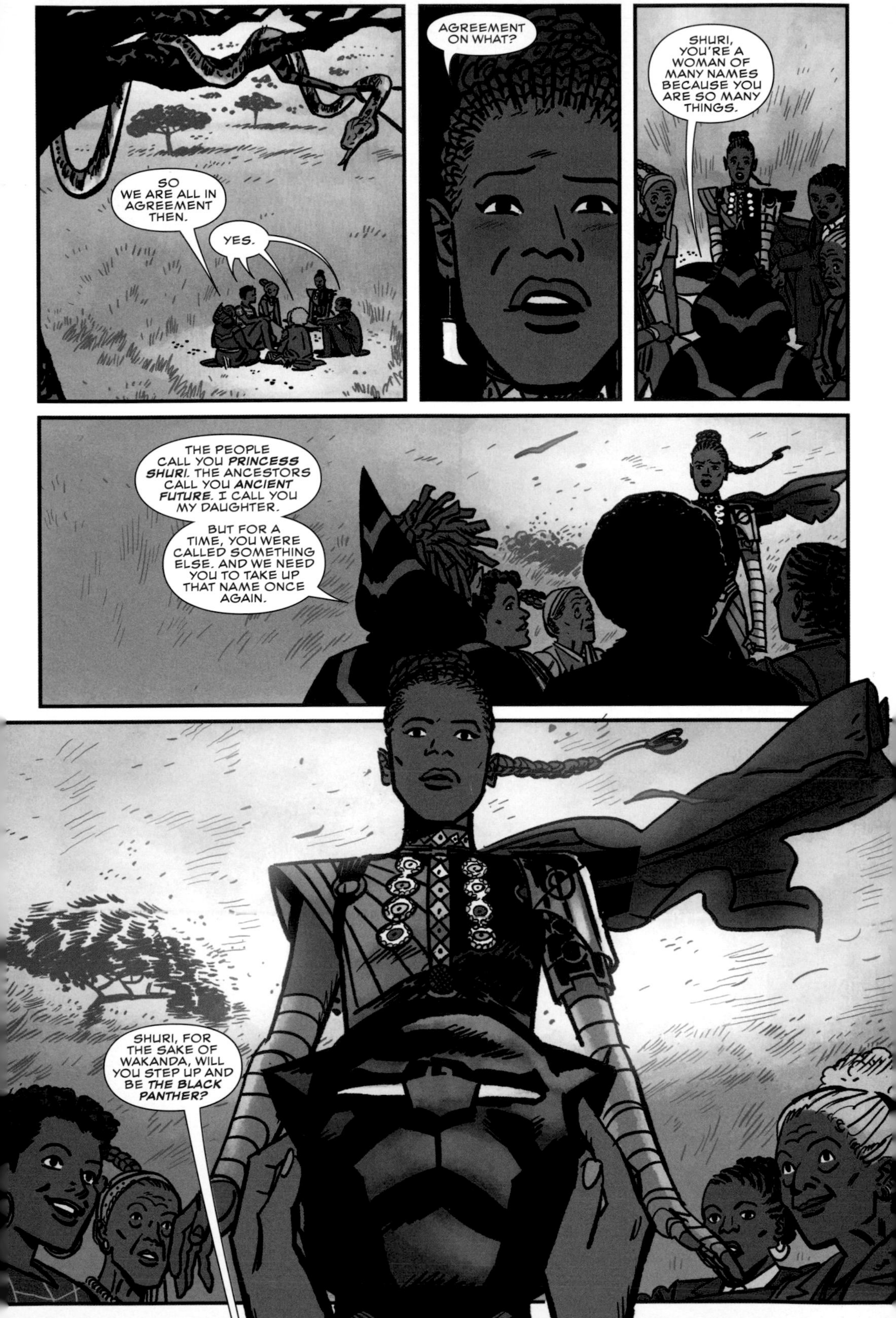
SO WE ARE ALL IN AGREEMENT THEN.
YES.
AGREEMENT ON WHAT?
SHURI, YOU'RE A WOMAN OF MANY NAMES BECAUSE YOU ARE SO MANY THINGS.
THE PEOPLE CALL YOU PRINCESS SHURI. THE ANCESTORS CALL YOU ANCIENT FUTURE. I CALL YOU MY DAUGHTER.
BUT FOR A TIME, YOU WERE CALLED SOMETHING ELSE. AND WE NEED YOU TO TAKE UP THAT NAME ONCE AGAIN.
SHURI, FOR THE SAKE OF WAKANDA, WILL YOU STEP UP AND BE THE BLACK PANTHER?

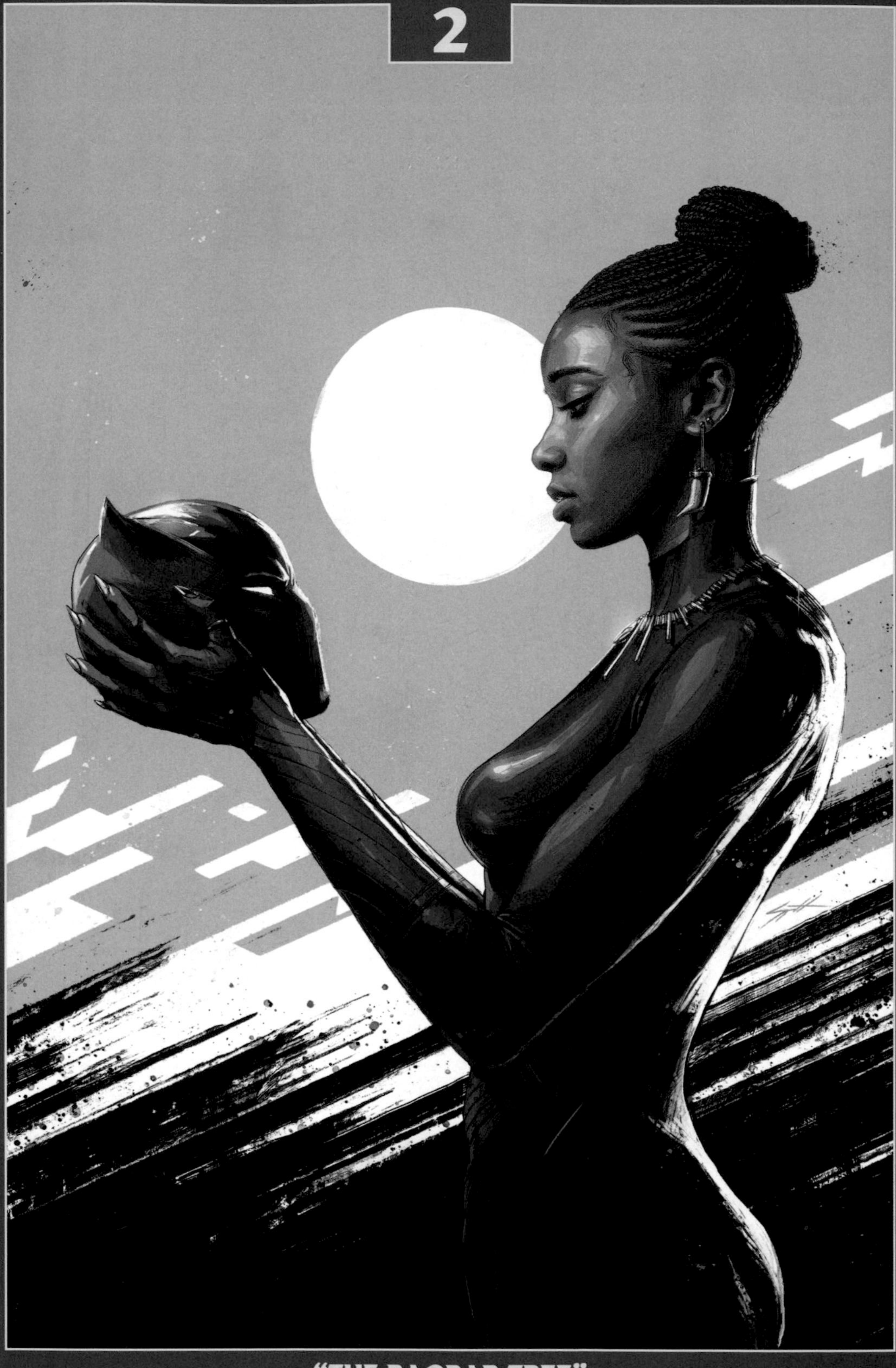
2

"THE BAOBAB TREE"

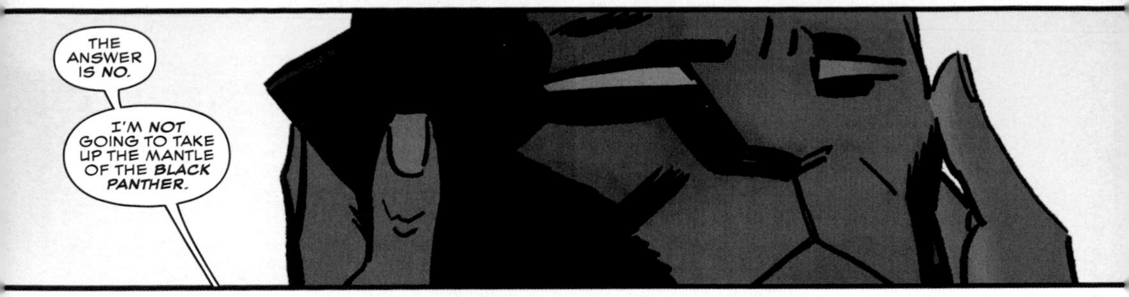
THE ANSWER IS NO.
I'M NOT GOING TO TAKE UP THE MANTLE OF THE BLACK PANTHER.

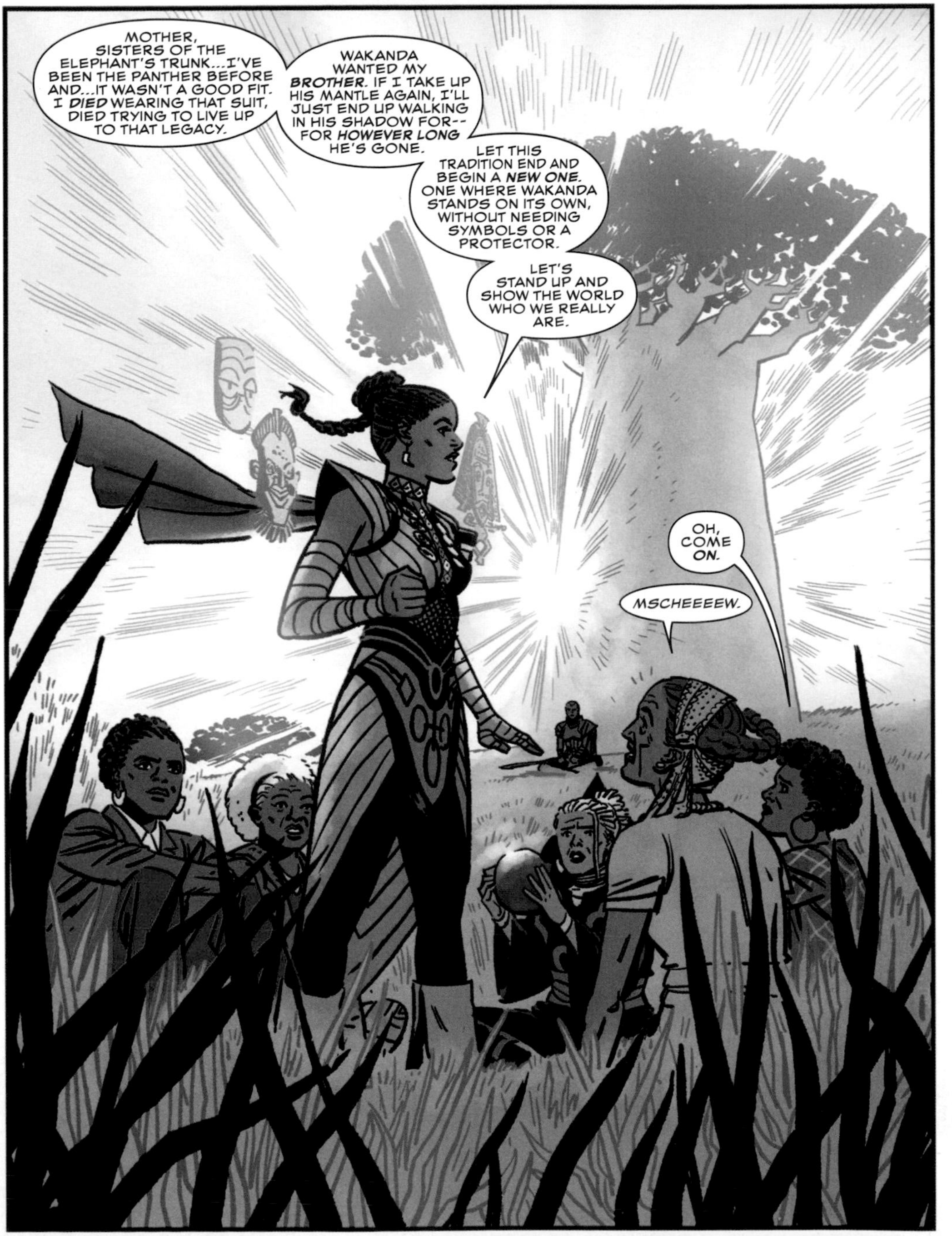
MOTHER, SISTERS OF THE ELEPHANT'S TRUNK...I'VE BEEN THE PANTHER BEFORE AND...IT WASN'T A GOOD FIT. I DIED WEARING THAT SUIT, DIED TRYING TO LIVE UP TO THAT LEGACY.
WAKANDA WANTED MY BROTHER. IF I TAKE UP HIS MANTLE AGAIN, I'LL JUST END UP WALKING IN HIS SHADOW FOR-- FOR HOWEVER LONG HE'S GONE.
LET THIS TRADITION END AND BEGIN A NEW ONE. ONE WHERE WAKANDA STANDS ON ITS OWN, WITHOUT NEEDING SYMBOLS OR A PROTECTOR.
LET'S STAND UP AND SHOW THE WORLD WHO WE REALLY ARE.
OH, COME ON.
MSCHEEEEW.

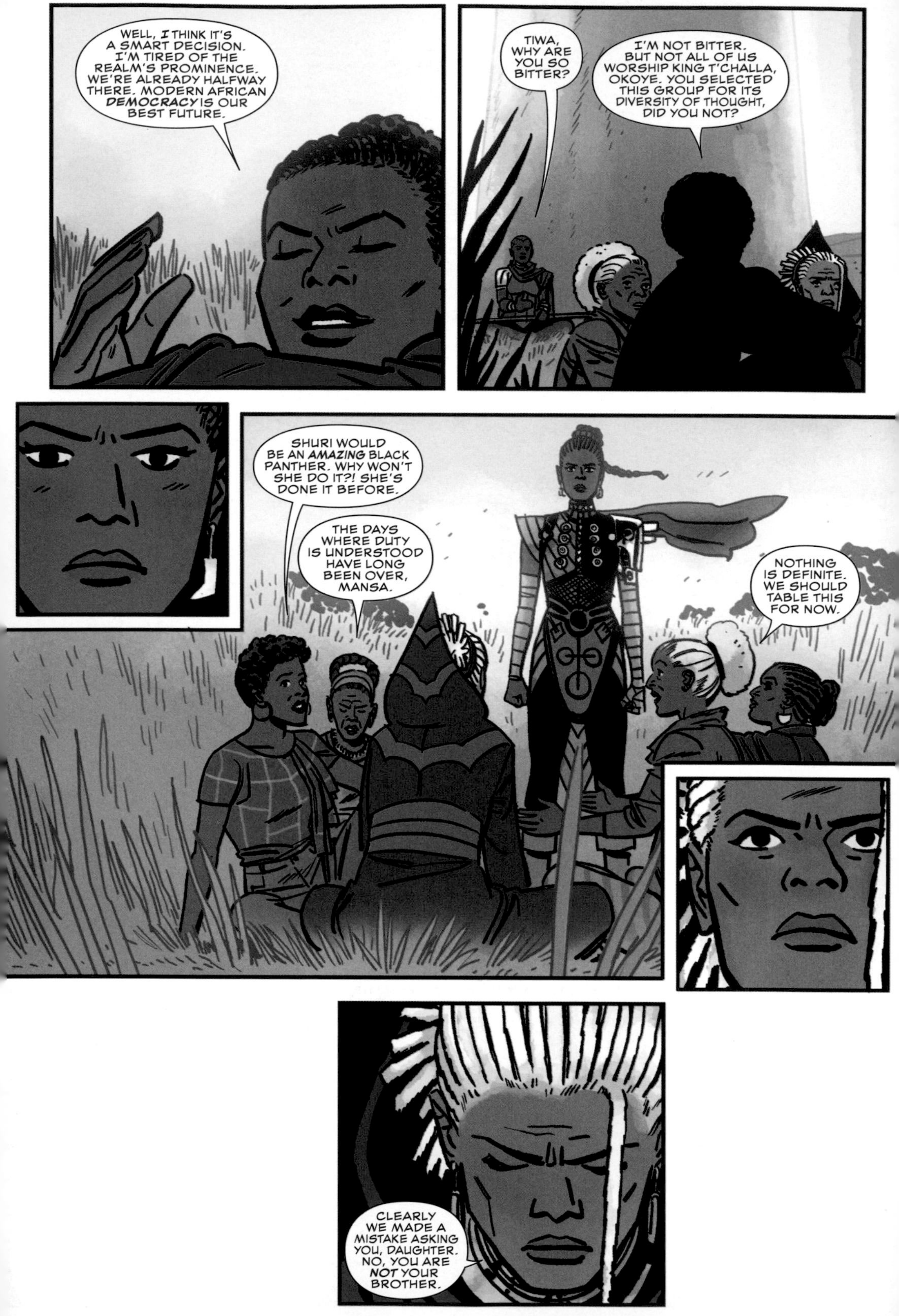
WELL, *I* THINK IT'S A SMART DECISION. I'M TIRED OF THE REALM'S PROMINENCE. WE'RE ALREADY HALFWAY THERE. MODERN AFRICAN *DEMOCRACY* IS OUR BEST FUTURE.
TIWA, WHY ARE YOU SO BITTER?
I'M NOT BITTER. BUT NOT ALL OF US WORSHIP KING T'CHALLA, OKOYE. YOU SELECTED THIS GROUP FOR ITS DIVERSITY OF THOUGHT, DID YOU NOT?
SHURI WOULD BE AN *AMAZING* BLACK PANTHER. WHY WON'T SHE DO IT?! SHE'S DONE IT BEFORE.
THE DAYS WHERE DUTY IS UNDERSTOOD HAVE LONG BEEN OVER, MANSA.
NOTHING IS DEFINITE. WE SHOULD TABLE THIS FOR NOW.
CLEARLY WE MADE A MISTAKE ASKING YOU, DAUGHTER. NO, YOU ARE *NOT* YOUR BROTHER.

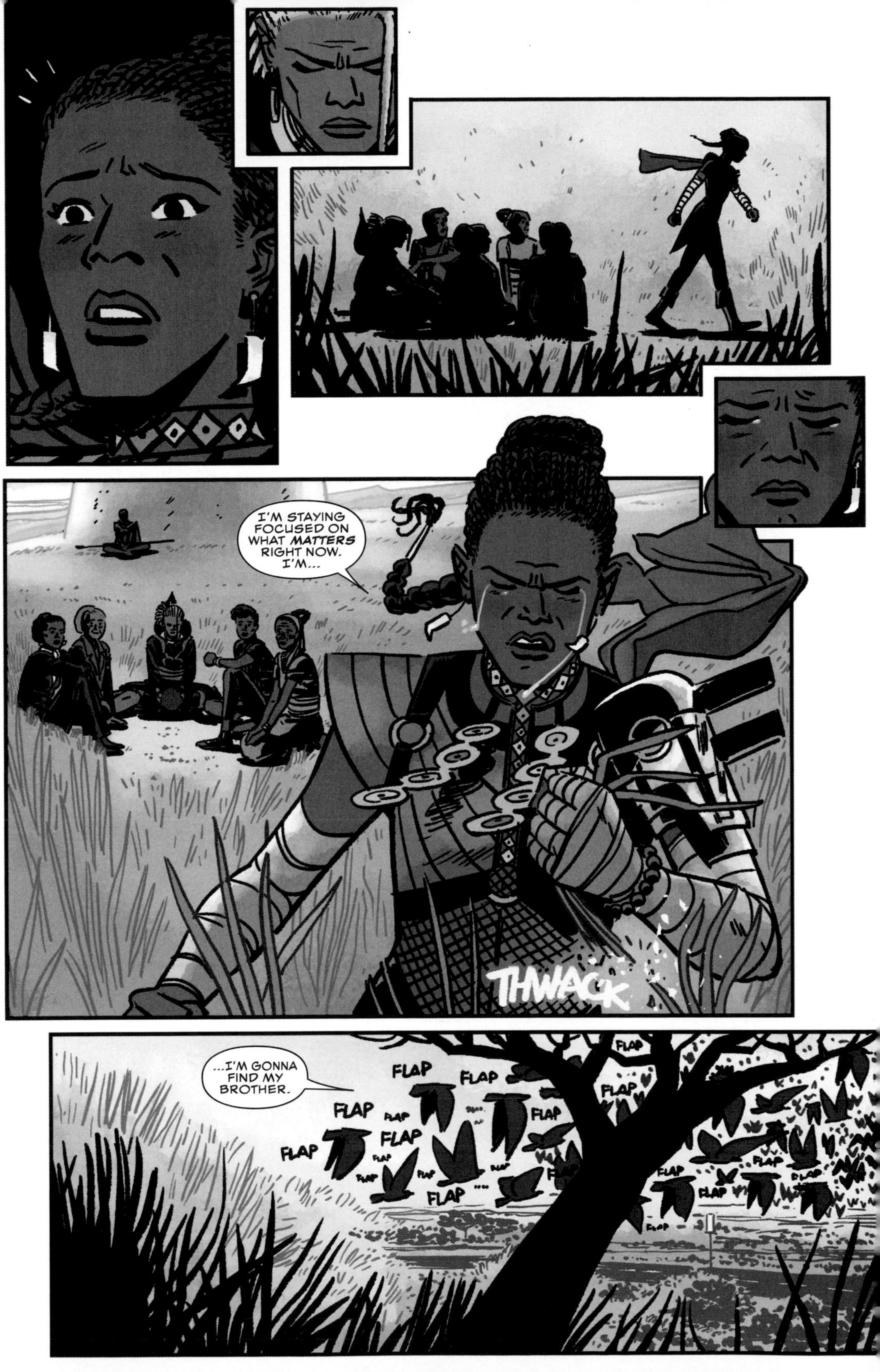
I'M STAYING FOCUSED ON WHAT MATTERS RIGHT NOW. I'M...
THWACK
...I'M GONNA FIND MY BROTHER.
FLAP
FLAP
FLAP
FLAP
FLAP
FLAP
FLAP
FLAP
FLAP

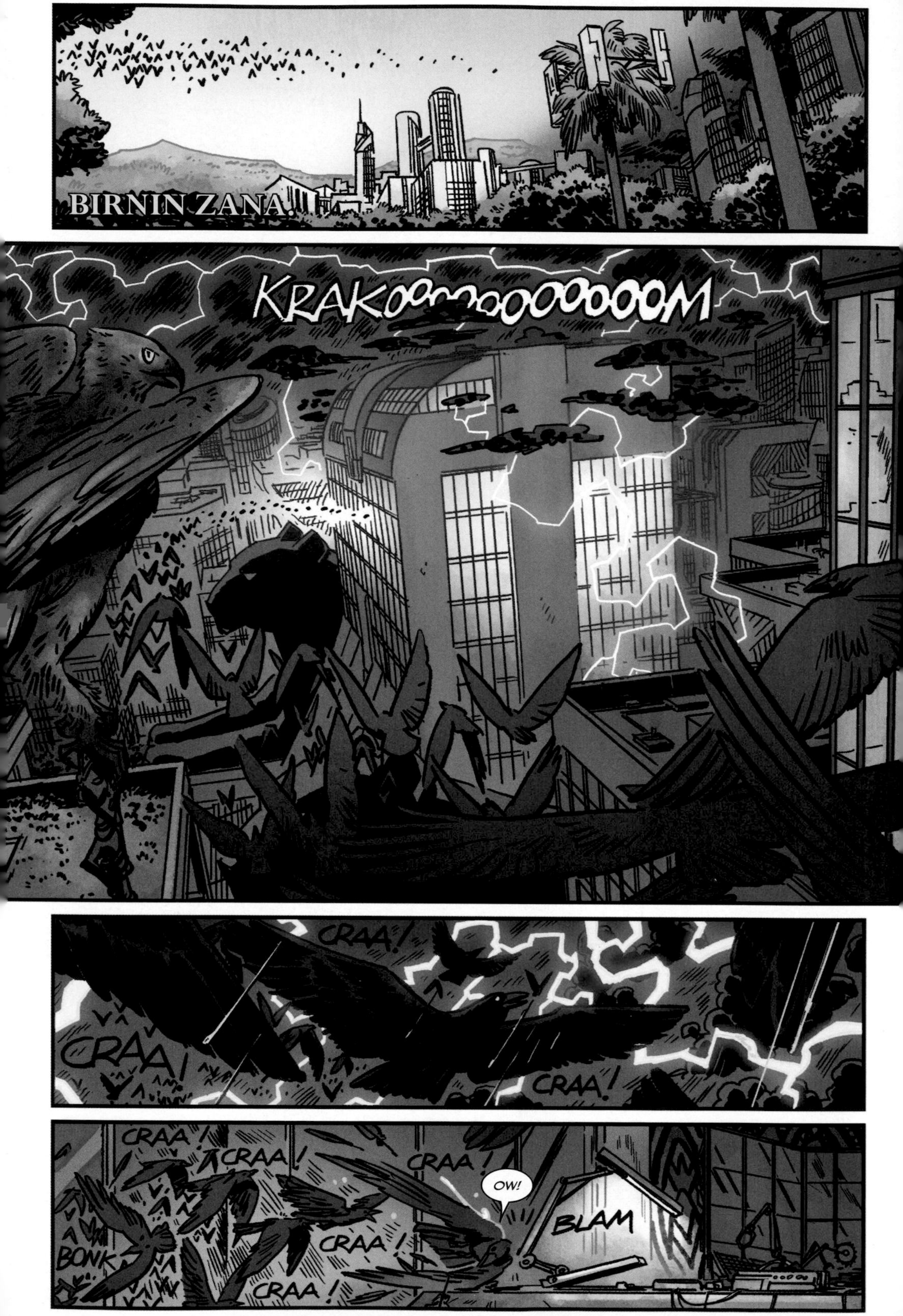

BIRNIN ZANA.
KRAKOOOOOOOOOOOM
CRAA!
CRAA!
CRAA!
CRAA!
CRAA!
CRAA!
OW!
BLAM
CRAA!
BONK
CRAA!

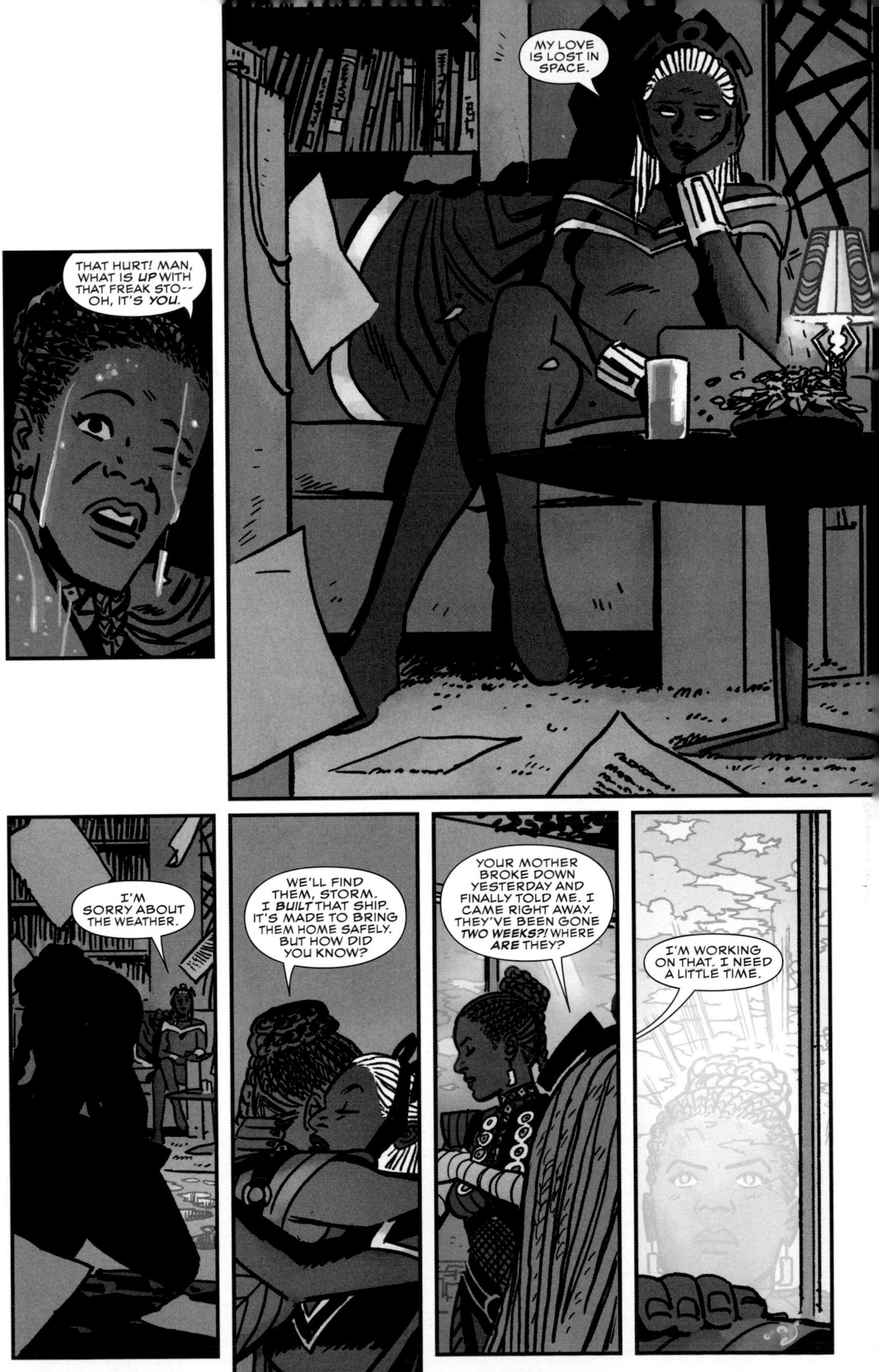
THAT HURT! MAN, WHAT IS UP WITH THAT FREAK STO-- OH, IT'S YOU.
MY LOVE IS LOST IN SPACE.
I'M SORRY ABOUT THE WEATHER.
WE'LL FIND THEM, STORM. I BUILT THAT SHIP. IT'S MADE TO BRING THEM HOME SAFELY. BUT HOW DID YOU KNOW?
YOUR MOTHER BROKE DOWN YESTERDAY AND FINALLY TOLD ME. I CAME RIGHT AWAY. THEY'VE BEEN GONE TWO WEEKS?! WHERE ARE THEY?
I'M WORKING ON THAT. I NEED A LITTLE TIME.

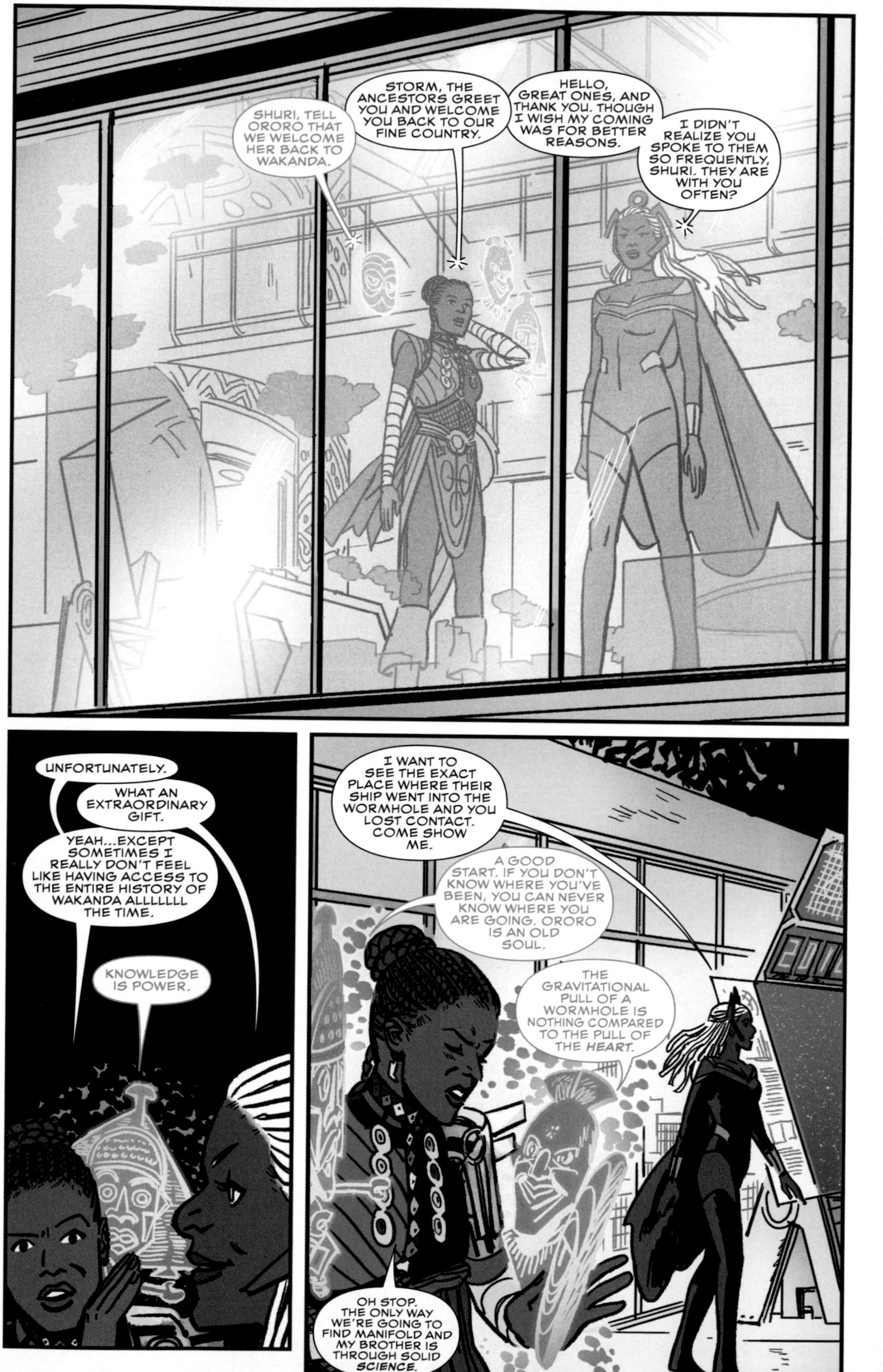
SHURI, TELL ORORO THAT WE WELCOME HER BACK TO WAKANDA.
STORM, THE ANCESTORS GREET YOU AND WELCOME YOU BACK TO OUR FINE COUNTRY.
HELLO, GREAT ONES, AND THANK YOU. THOUGH I WISH MY COMING WAS FOR BETTER REASONS.
I DIDN'T REALIZE YOU SPOKE TO THEM SO FREQUENTLY, SHURI. THEY ARE WITH YOU OFTEN?
UNFORTUNATELY.
WHAT AN EXTRAORDINARY GIFT.
YEAH...EXCEPT SOMETIMES I REALLY DON'T FEEL LIKE HAVING ACCESS TO THE ENTIRE HISTORY OF WAKANDA ALLLLLLL THE TIME.
KNOWLEDGE IS POWER.
I WANT TO SEE THE EXACT PLACE WHERE THEIR SHIP WENT INTO THE WORMHOLE AND YOU LOST CONTACT. COME SHOW ME.
A GOOD START. IF YOU DON'T KNOW WHERE YOU'VE BEEN, YOU CAN NEVER KNOW WHERE YOU ARE GOING. ORORO IS AN OLD SOUL.
THE GRAVITATIONAL PULL OF A WORMHOLE IS NOTHING COMPARED TO THE PULL OF THE *HEART*.
OH STOP. THE ONLY WAY WE'RE GOING TO FIND MANIFOLD AND MY BROTHER IS THROUGH SOLID *SCIENCE*.

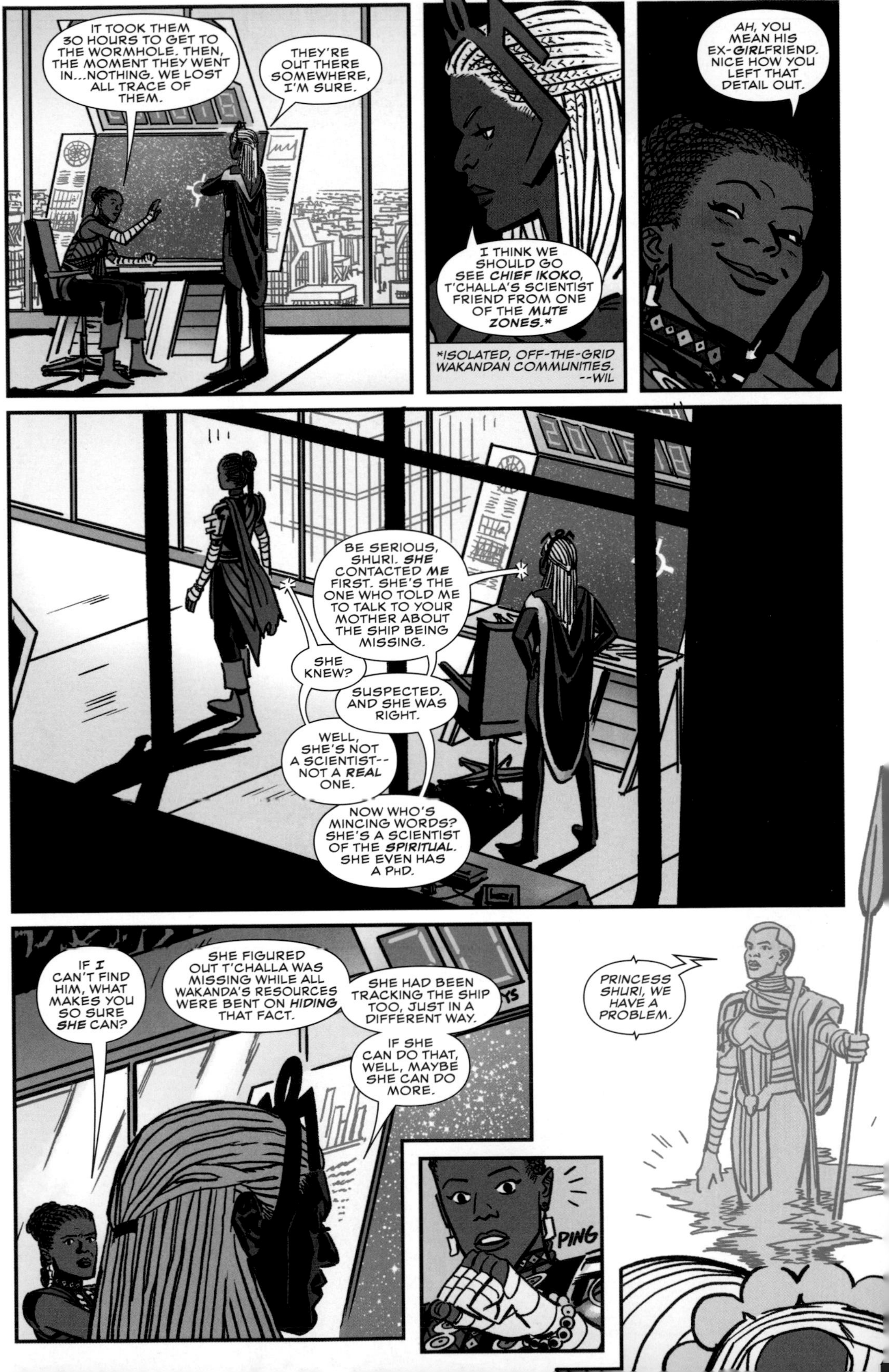
IT TOOK THEM 30 HOURS TO GET TO THE WORMHOLE. THEN, THE MOMENT THEY WENT IN...NOTHING. WE LOST ALL TRACE OF THEM.
THEY'RE OUT THERE SOMEWHERE, I'M SURE.
I THINK WE SHOULD GO SEE CHIEF IKOKO, T'CHALLA'S SCIENTIST FRIEND FROM ONE OF THE MUTE ZONES.*
*ISOLATED, OFF-THE-GRID WAKANDAN COMMUNITIES. --WIL
AH, YOU MEAN HIS EX-GIRLFRIEND. NICE HOW YOU LEFT THAT DETAIL OUT.
BE SERIOUS, SHURI. SHE CONTACTED ME FIRST. SHE'S THE ONE WHO TOLD ME TO TALK TO YOUR MOTHER ABOUT THE SHIP BEING MISSING.
SHE KNEW?
SUSPECTED. AND SHE WAS RIGHT.
WELL, SHE'S NOT A SCIENTIST-- NOT A REAL ONE.
NOW WHO'S MINCING WORDS? SHE'S A SCIENTIST OF THE SPIRITUAL. SHE EVEN HAS A PHD.
IF I CAN'T FIND HIM, WHAT MAKES YOU SO SURE SHE CAN?
SHE FIGURED OUT T'CHALLA WAS MISSING WHILE ALL WAKANDA'S RESOURCES WERE BENT ON HIDING THAT FACT.
SHE HAD BEEN TRACKING THE SHIP TOO, JUST IN A DIFFERENT WAY.
IF SHE CAN DO THAT, WELL, MAYBE SHE CAN DO MORE.
PING
PRINCESS SHURI, WE HAVE A PROBLEM.

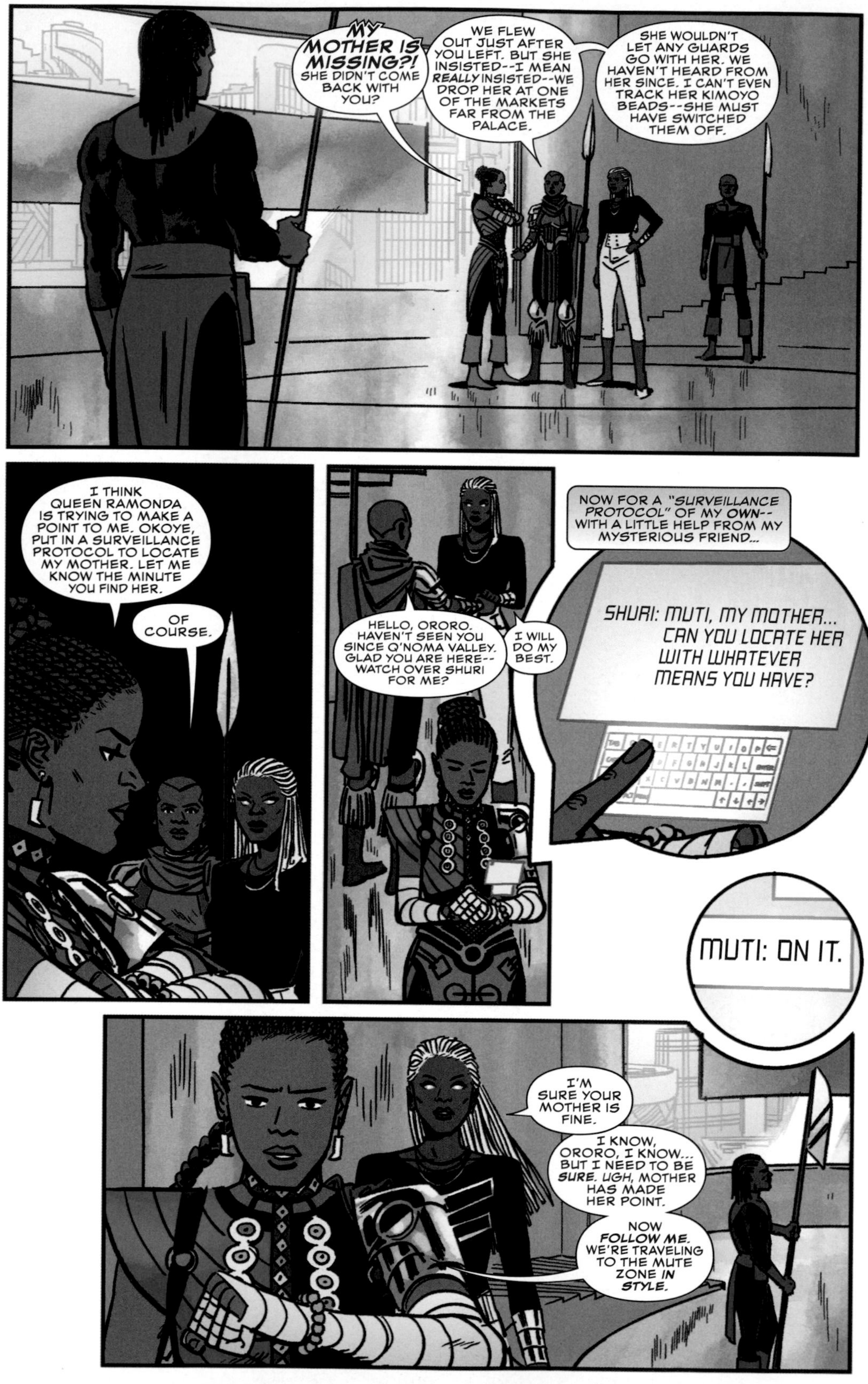

MY MOTHER IS MISSING?! SHE DIDN'T COME BACK WITH YOU?
WE FLEW OUT JUST AFTER YOU LEFT. BUT SHE INSISTED--I MEAN REALLY INSISTED--WE DROP HER AT ONE OF THE MARKETS FAR FROM THE PALACE.
SHE WOULDN'T LET ANY GUARDS GO WITH HER. WE HAVEN'T HEARD FROM HER SINCE. I CAN'T EVEN TRACK HER KIMOYO BEADS--SHE MUST HAVE SWITCHED THEM OFF.
I THINK QUEEN RAMONDA IS TRYING TO MAKE A POINT TO ME. OKOYE, PUT IN A SURVEILLANCE PROTOCOL TO LOCATE MY MOTHER. LET ME KNOW THE MINUTE YOU FIND HER.
OF COURSE.
HELLO, ORORO. HAVEN'T SEEN YOU SINCE Q'NOMA VALLEY. GLAD YOU ARE HERE--WATCH OVER SHURI FOR ME?
I WILL DO MY BEST.
NOW FOR A "SURVEILLANCE PROTOCOL" OF MY OWN--WITH A LITTLE HELP FROM MY MYSTERIOUS FRIEND...
SHURI: MUTI, MY MOTHER... CAN YOU LOCATE HER WITH WHATEVER MEANS YOU HAVE?
MUTI: ON IT.
I'M SURE YOUR MOTHER IS FINE.
I KNOW, ORORO, I KNOW... BUT I NEED TO BE SURE. UGH, MOTHER HAS MADE HER POINT.
NOW FOLLOW ME. WE'RE TRAVELING TO THE MUTE ZONE IN STYLE.

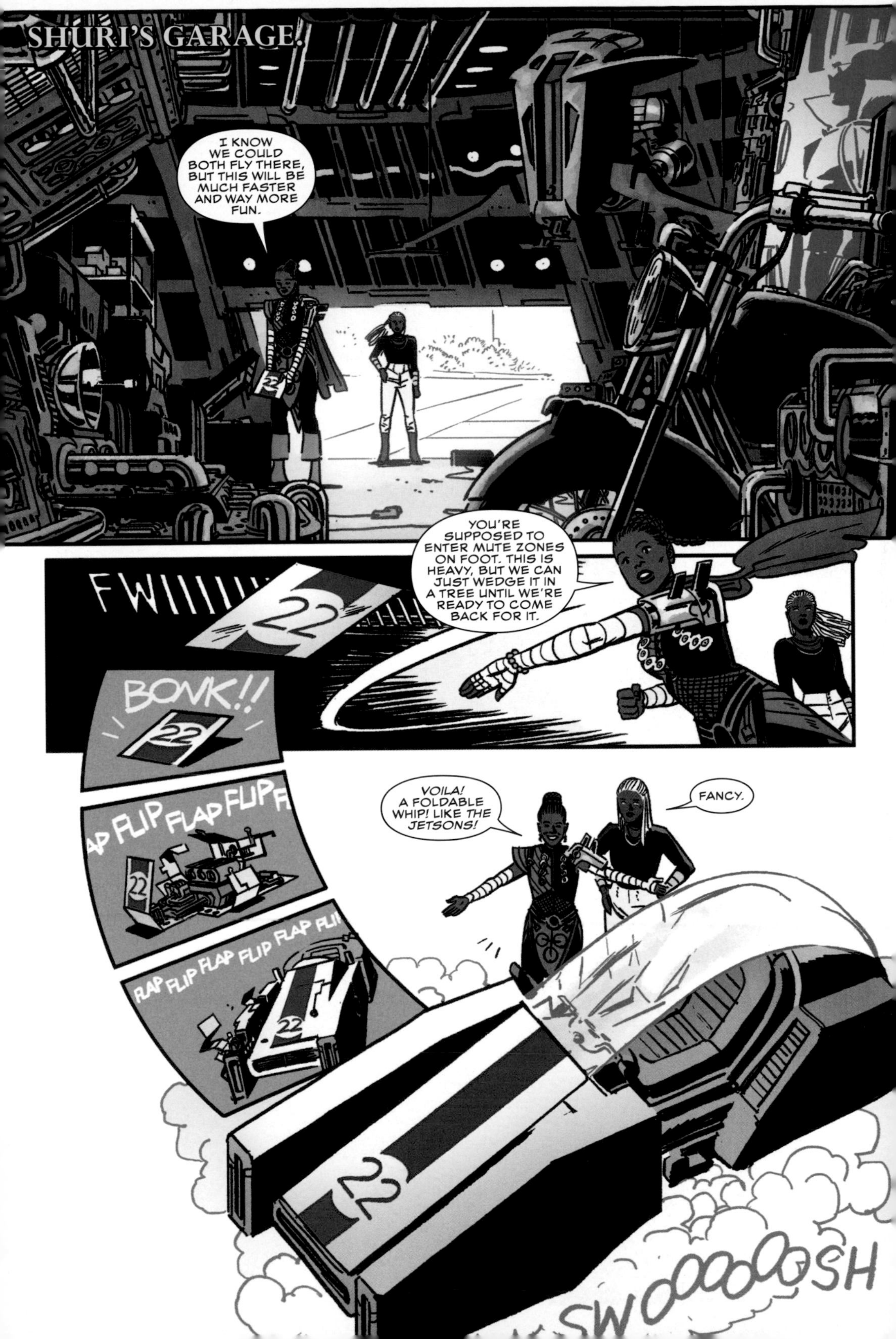
SHURI'S GARAGE.
I KNOW WE COULD BOTH FLY THERE, BUT THIS WILL BE MUCH FASTER AND WAY MORE FUN.
FWIIIIII
YOU'RE SUPPOSED TO ENTER MUTE ZONES ON FOOT. THIS IS HEAVY, BUT WE CAN JUST WEDGE IT IN A TREE UNTIL WE'RE READY TO COME BACK FOR IT.
BONK!!
FLIP FLAP FLIP
FLAP FLIP FLAP FLIP FLAP
VOILA! A FOLDABLE WHIP! LIKE THE JETSONS!
FANCY.
SWOOOOOOOSH

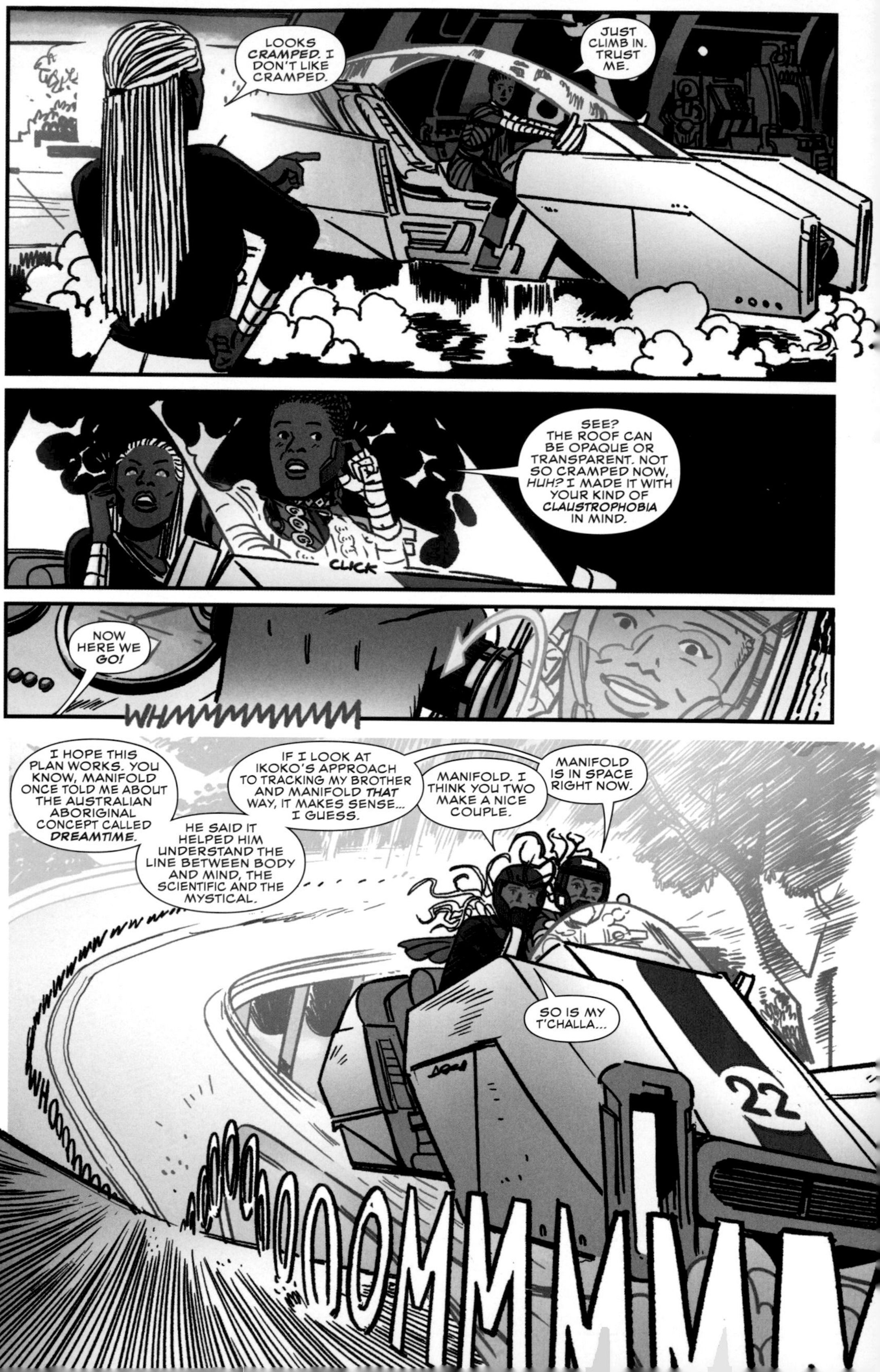
LOOKS CRAMPED. I DON'T LIKE CRAMPED.
JUST CLIMB IN. TRUST ME.
SEE? THE ROOF CAN BE OPAQUE OR TRANSPARENT. NOT SO CRAMPED NOW, HUH? I MADE IT WITH YOUR KIND OF CLAUSTROPHOBIA IN MIND.
CLICK
NOW HERE WE GO!
WHMMMMMMMM
I HOPE THIS PLAN WORKS. YOU KNOW, MANIFOLD ONCE TOLD ME ABOUT THE AUSTRALIAN ABORIGINAL CONCEPT CALLED DREAMTIME.
HE SAID IT HELPED HIM UNDERSTAND THE LINE BETWEEN BODY AND MIND, THE SCIENTIFIC AND THE MYSTICAL.
IF I LOOK AT IKOKO'S APPROACH TO TRACKING MY BROTHER AND MANIFOLD THAT WAY, IT MAKES SENSE... I GUESS.
MANIFOLD. I THINK YOU TWO MAKE A NICE COUPLE.
MANIFOLD IS IN SPACE RIGHT NOW.
SO IS MY T'CHALLA...
WHOOOOOOOMMMMM

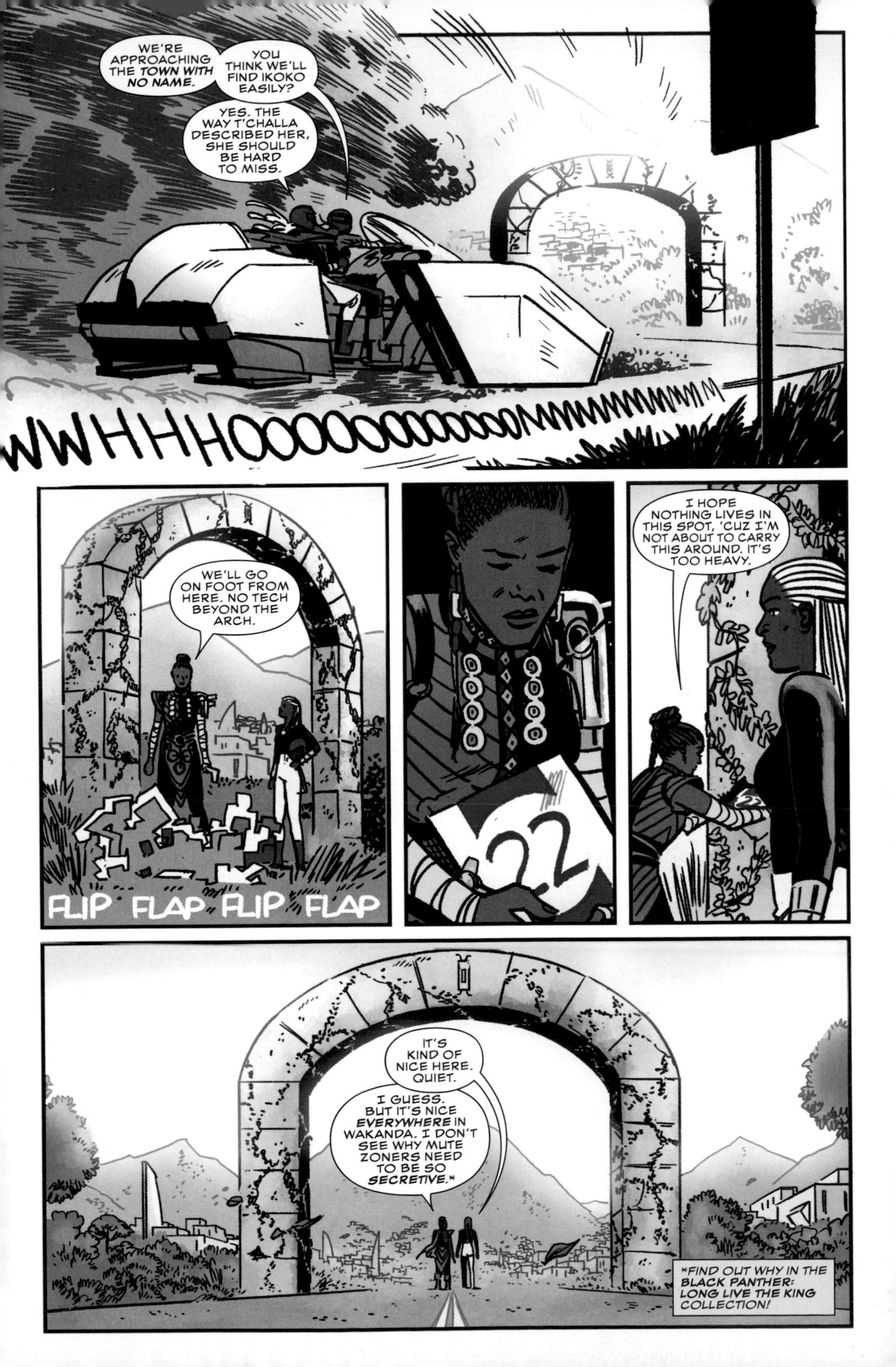
WE'RE APPROACHING THE *TOWN WITH NO NAME*.
YOU THINK WE'LL FIND IKOKO EASILY?
YES. THE WAY T'CHALLA DESCRIBED HER, SHE SHOULD BE HARD TO MISS.
WWHHHOOOOOOOOOOOOMMMMMMMMM
WE'LL GO ON FOOT FROM HERE. NO TECH BEYOND THE ARCH.
FLIP FLAP FLIP FLAP
22
I HOPE NOTHING LIVES IN THIS SPOT, 'CUZ I'M NOT ABOUT TO CARRY THIS AROUND. IT'S TOO HEAVY.
IT'S KIND OF NICE HERE. QUIET.
I GUESS. BUT IT'S NICE *EVERYWHERE* IN WAKANDA. I DON'T SEE WHY MUTE ZONERS NEED TO BE SO *SECRETIVE*.*
*FIND OUT WHY IN THE BLACK PANTHER: LONG LIVE THE KING COLLECTION!

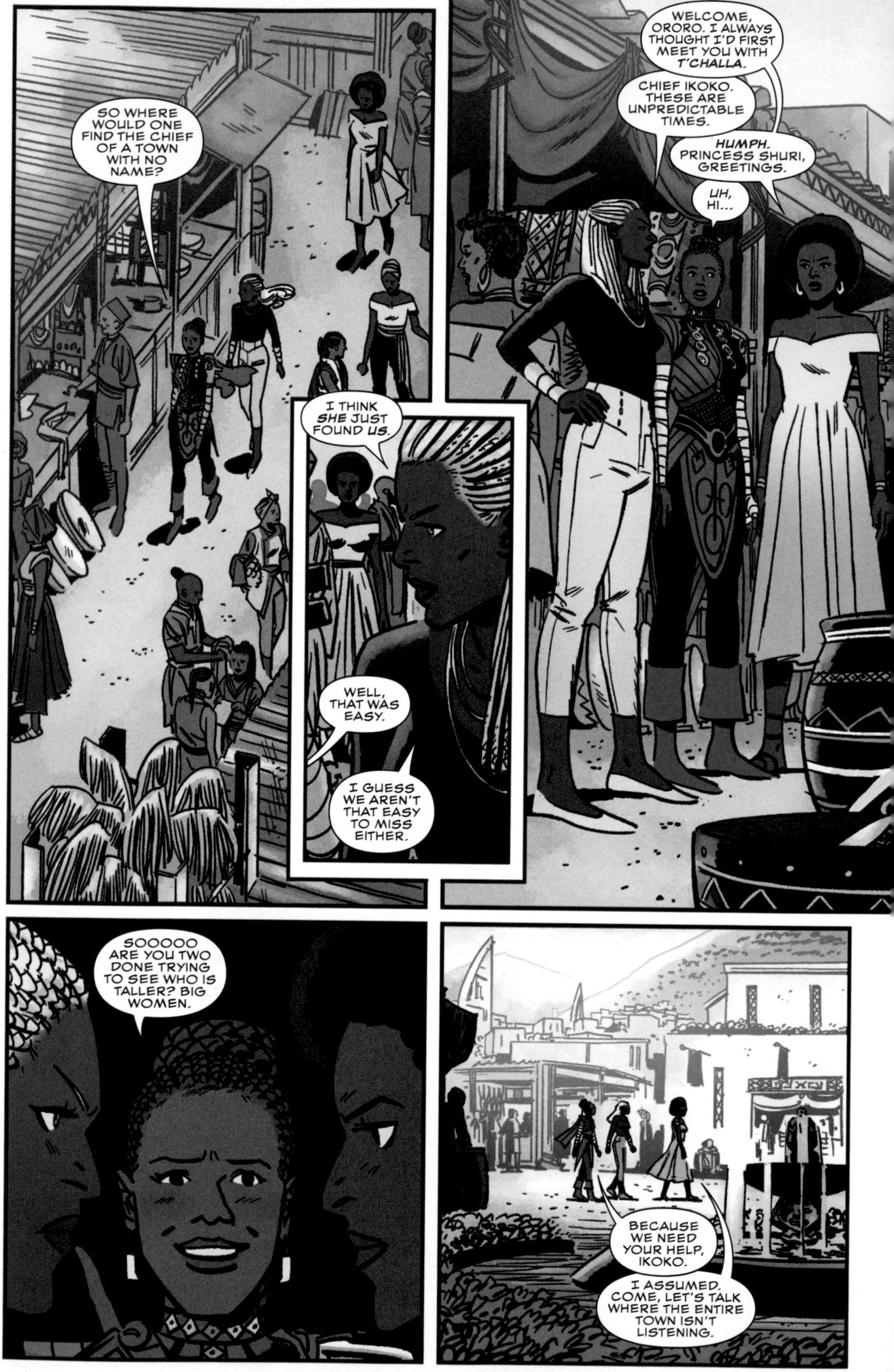
SO WHERE WOULD ONE FIND THE CHIEF OF A TOWN WITH NO NAME?
I THINK SHE JUST FOUND US.
WELL, THAT WAS EASY.
I GUESS WE AREN'T THAT EASY TO MISS EITHER.
WELCOME, ORORO. I ALWAYS THOUGHT I'D FIRST MEET YOU WITH T'CHALLA.
CHIEF IKOKO. THESE ARE UNPREDICTABLE TIMES.
HUMPH. PRINCESS SHURI, GREETINGS.
UH, HI...
SOOOOO ARE YOU TWO DONE TRYING TO SEE WHO IS TALLER? BIG WOMEN.
BECAUSE WE NEED YOUR HELP, IKOKO.
I ASSUMED. COME, LET'S TALK WHERE THE ENTIRE TOWN ISN'T LISTENING.

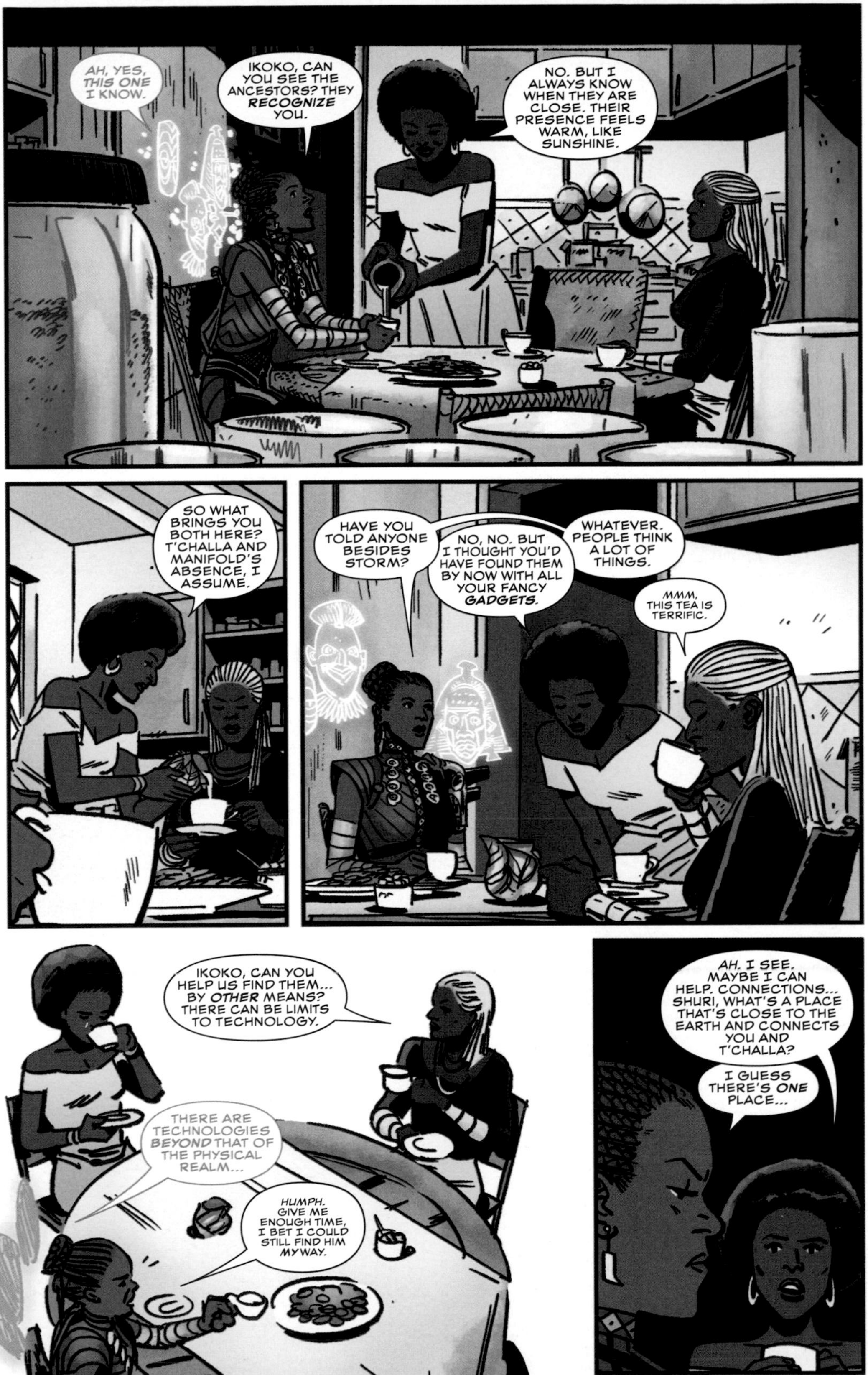
AH, YES, THIS ONE I KNOW.
IKOKO, CAN YOU SEE THE ANCESTORS? THEY RECOGNIZE YOU.
NO. BUT I ALWAYS KNOW WHEN THEY ARE CLOSE. THEIR PRESENCE FEELS WARM, LIKE SUNSHINE.
SO WHAT BRINGS YOU BOTH HERE? T'CHALLA AND MANIFOLD'S ABSENCE, I ASSUME.
HAVE YOU TOLD ANYONE BESIDES STORM?
NO, NO. BUT I THOUGHT YOU'D HAVE FOUND THEM BY NOW WITH ALL YOUR FANCY GADGETS.
WHATEVER. PEOPLE THINK A LOT OF THINGS.
MMM, THIS TEA IS TERRIFIC.
IKOKO, CAN YOU HELP US FIND THEM... BY OTHER MEANS? THERE CAN BE LIMITS TO TECHNOLOGY.
THERE ARE TECHNOLOGIES BEYOND THAT OF THE PHYSICAL REALM...
HUMPH. GIVE ME ENOUGH TIME, I BET I COULD STILL FIND HIM MY WAY.
AH. I SEE. MAYBE I CAN HELP. CONNECTIONS... SHURI, WHAT'S A PLACE THAT'S CLOSE TO THE EARTH AND CONNECTS YOU AND T'CHALLA?
I GUESS THERE'S ONE PLACE...

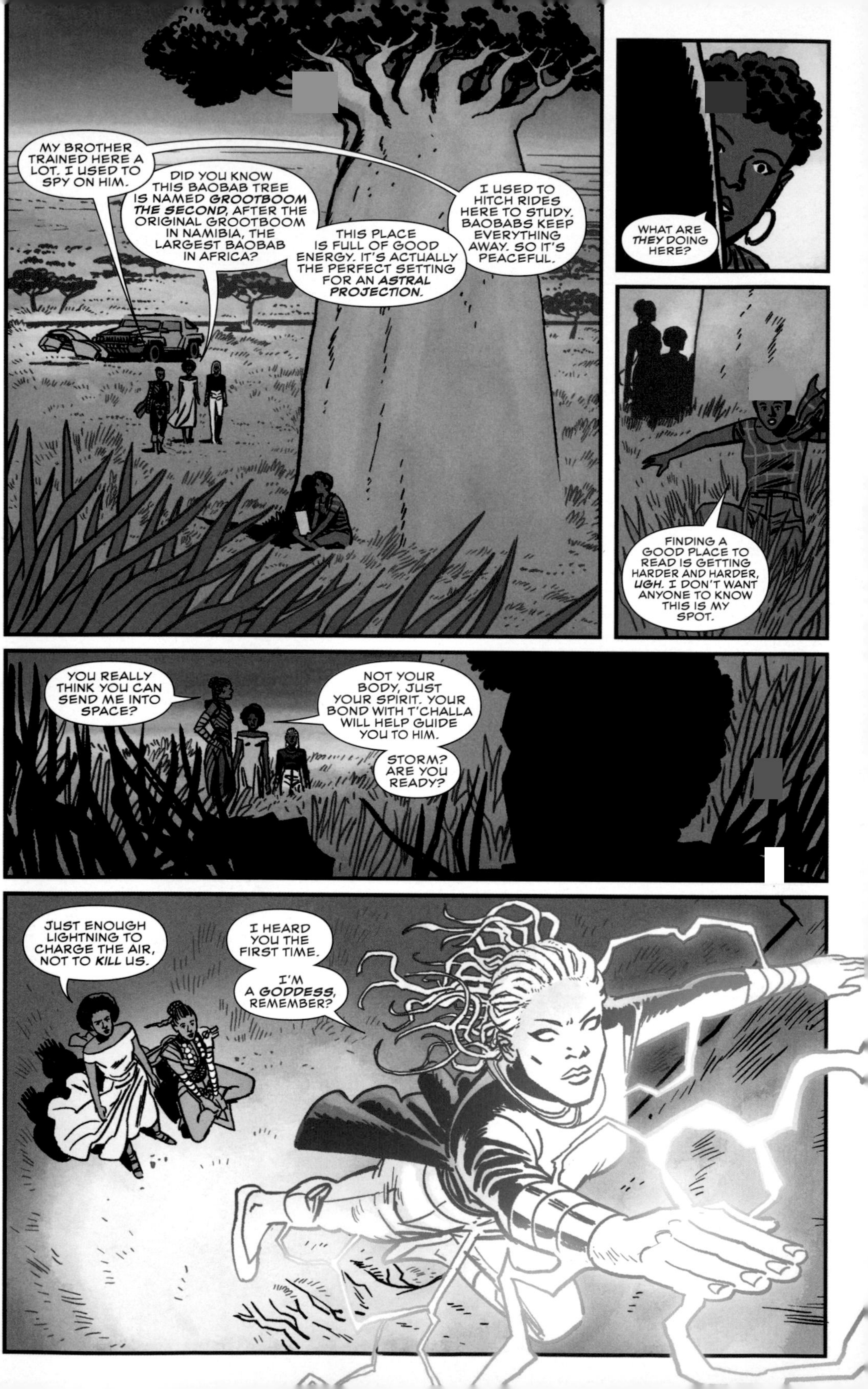

MY BROTHER TRAINED HERE A LOT. I USED TO SPY ON HIM.
DID YOU KNOW THIS BAOBAB TREE IS NAMED GROOTBOOM THE SECOND, AFTER THE ORIGINAL GROOTBOOM IN NAMIBIA, THE LARGEST BAOBAB IN AFRICA?
THIS PLACE IS FULL OF GOOD ENERGY. IT'S ACTUALLY THE PERFECT SETTING FOR AN ASTRAL PROJECTION.
I USED TO HITCH RIDES HERE TO STUDY. BAOBABS KEEP EVERYTHING AWAY. SO IT'S PEACEFUL.
WHAT ARE THEY DOING HERE?
FINDING A GOOD PLACE TO READ IS GETTING HARDER AND HARDER, UGH. I DON'T WANT ANYONE TO KNOW THIS IS MY SPOT.
YOU REALLY THINK YOU CAN SEND ME INTO SPACE?
NOT YOUR BODY, JUST YOUR SPIRIT. YOUR BOND WITH T'CHALLA WILL HELP GUIDE YOU TO HIM.
STORM? ARE YOU READY?
JUST ENOUGH LIGHTNING TO CHARGE THE AIR, NOT TO KILL US.
I HEARD YOU THE FIRST TIME.
I'M A GODDESS, REMEMBER?

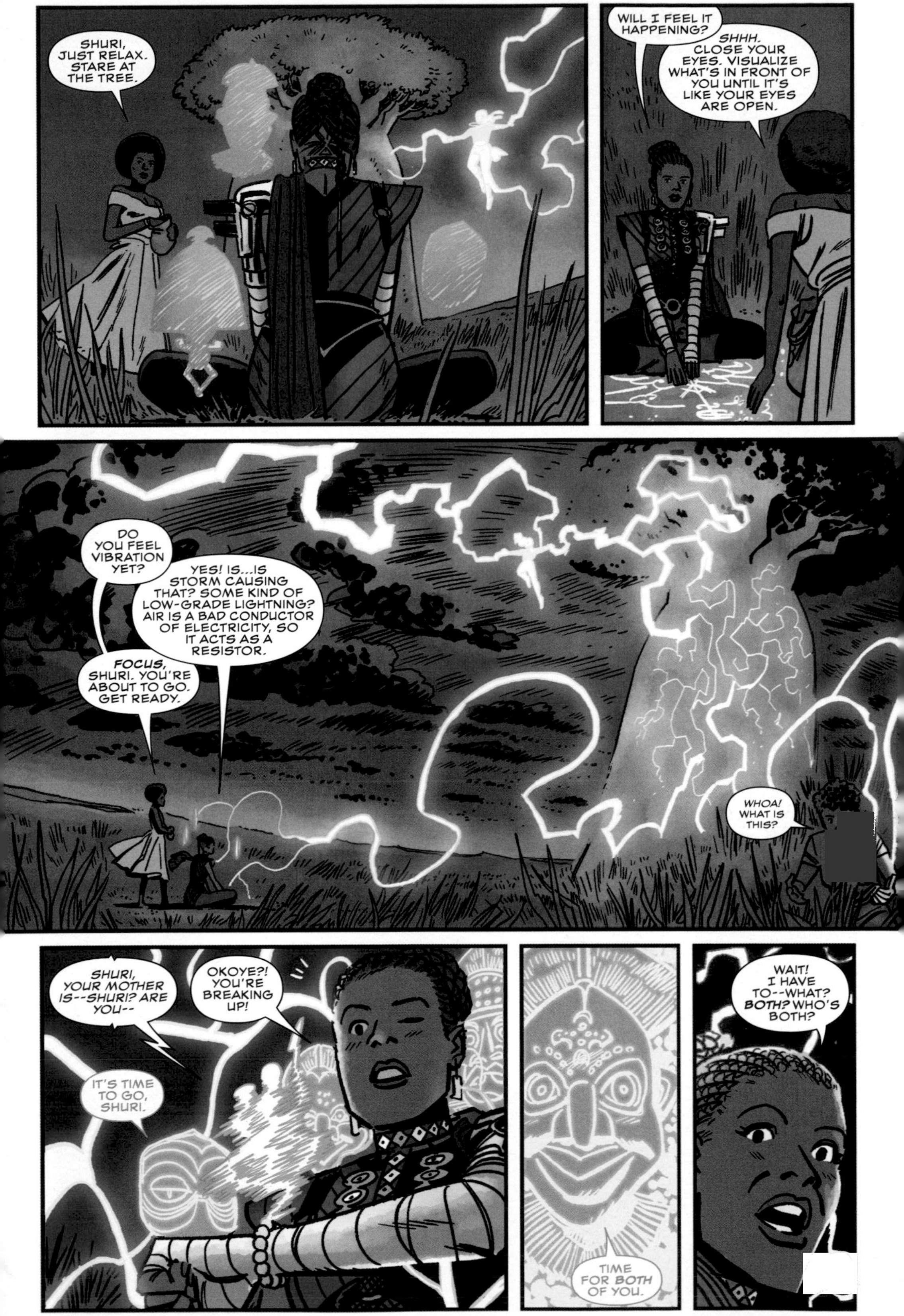
SHURI, JUST RELAX. STARE AT THE TREE.
WILL I FEEL IT HAPPENING?
SHHH. CLOSE YOUR EYES. VISUALIZE WHAT'S IN FRONT OF YOU UNTIL IT'S LIKE YOUR EYES ARE OPEN.
DO YOU FEEL VIBRATION YET?
YES! IS...IS STORM CAUSING THAT? SOME KIND OF LOW-GRADE LIGHTNING? AIR IS A BAD CONDUCTOR OF ELECTRICITY, SO IT ACTS AS A RESISTOR.
FOCUS, SHURI. YOU'RE ABOUT TO GO. GET READY.
WHOA! WHAT IS THIS?
SHURI, YOUR MOTHER IS--SHURI? ARE YOU--
OKOYE?! YOU'RE BREAKING UP!
IT'S TIME TO GO, SHURI.
TIME FOR BOTH OF YOU.
WAIT! I HAVE TO--WHAT? BOTH? WHO'S BOTH?

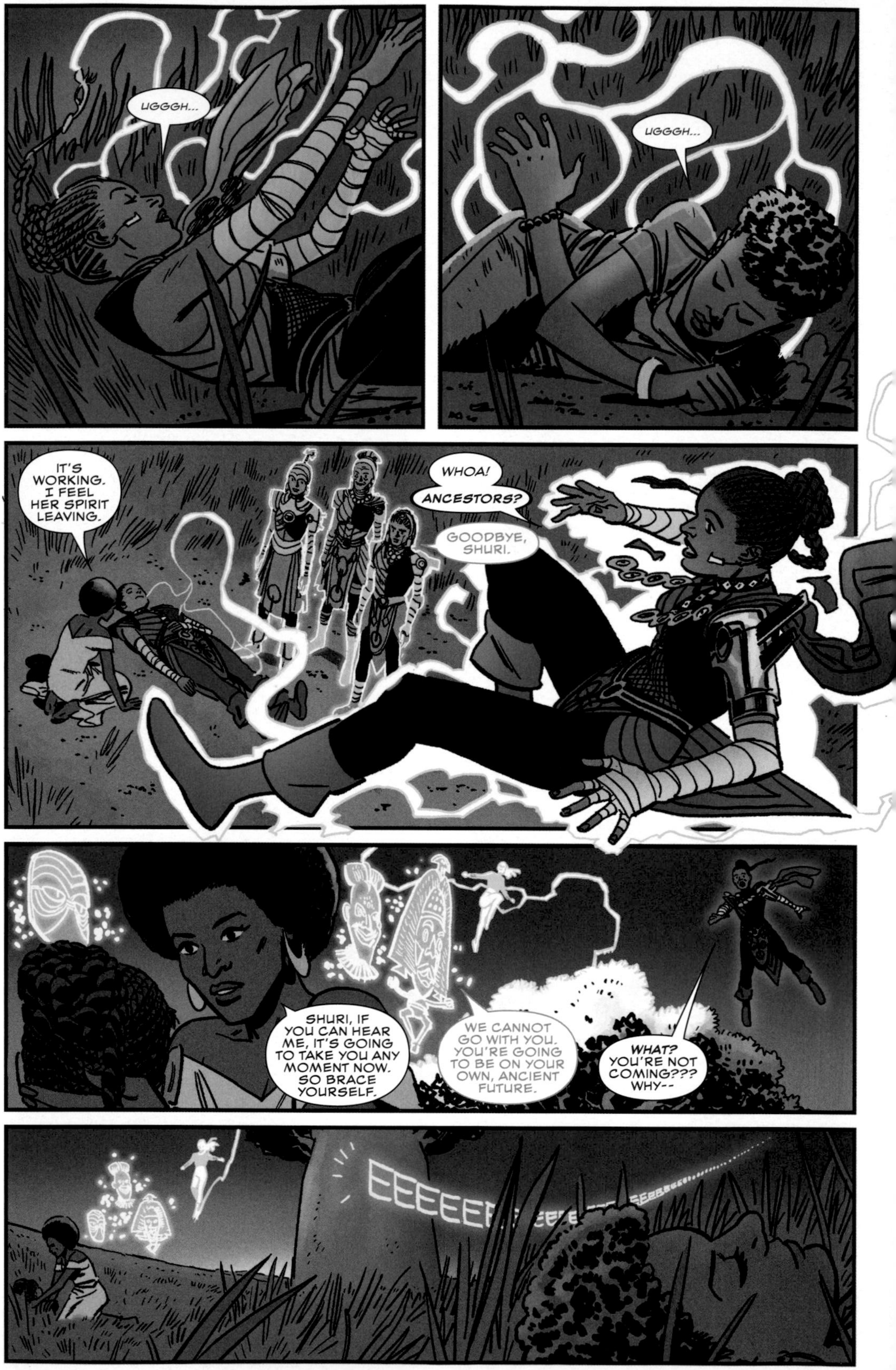
UGGGH...
UGGGH...
IT'S WORKING. I FEEL HER SPIRIT LEAVING.
WHOA!
ANCESTORS?
GOODBYE, SHURI.
SHURI, IF YOU CAN HEAR ME, IT'S GOING TO TAKE YOU ANY MOMENT NOW. SO BRACE YOURSELF.
WE CANNOT GO WITH YOU. YOU'RE GOING TO BE ON YOUR OWN, ANCIENT FUTURE.
WHAT? YOU'RE NOT COMING??? WHY--
EEEEEEEEEEEEEEE

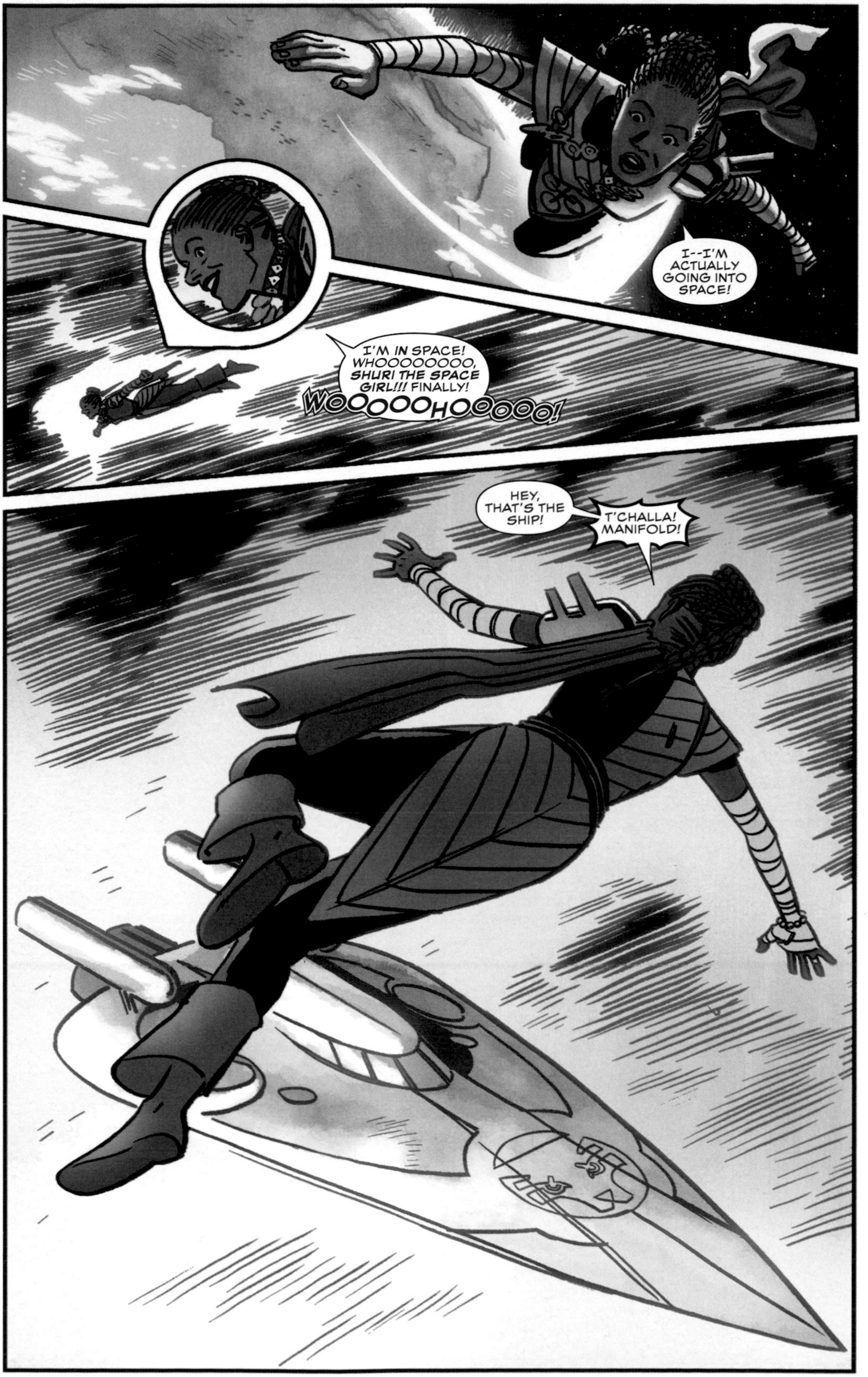
I--I'M ACTUALLY GOING INTO SPACE!
I'M IN SPACE! WHOOOOOOOOO, SHURI THE SPACE GIRL!!! FINALLY!
WOOOOOHOOOOO!
HEY, THAT'S THE SHIP!
T'CHALLA! MANIFOLD!

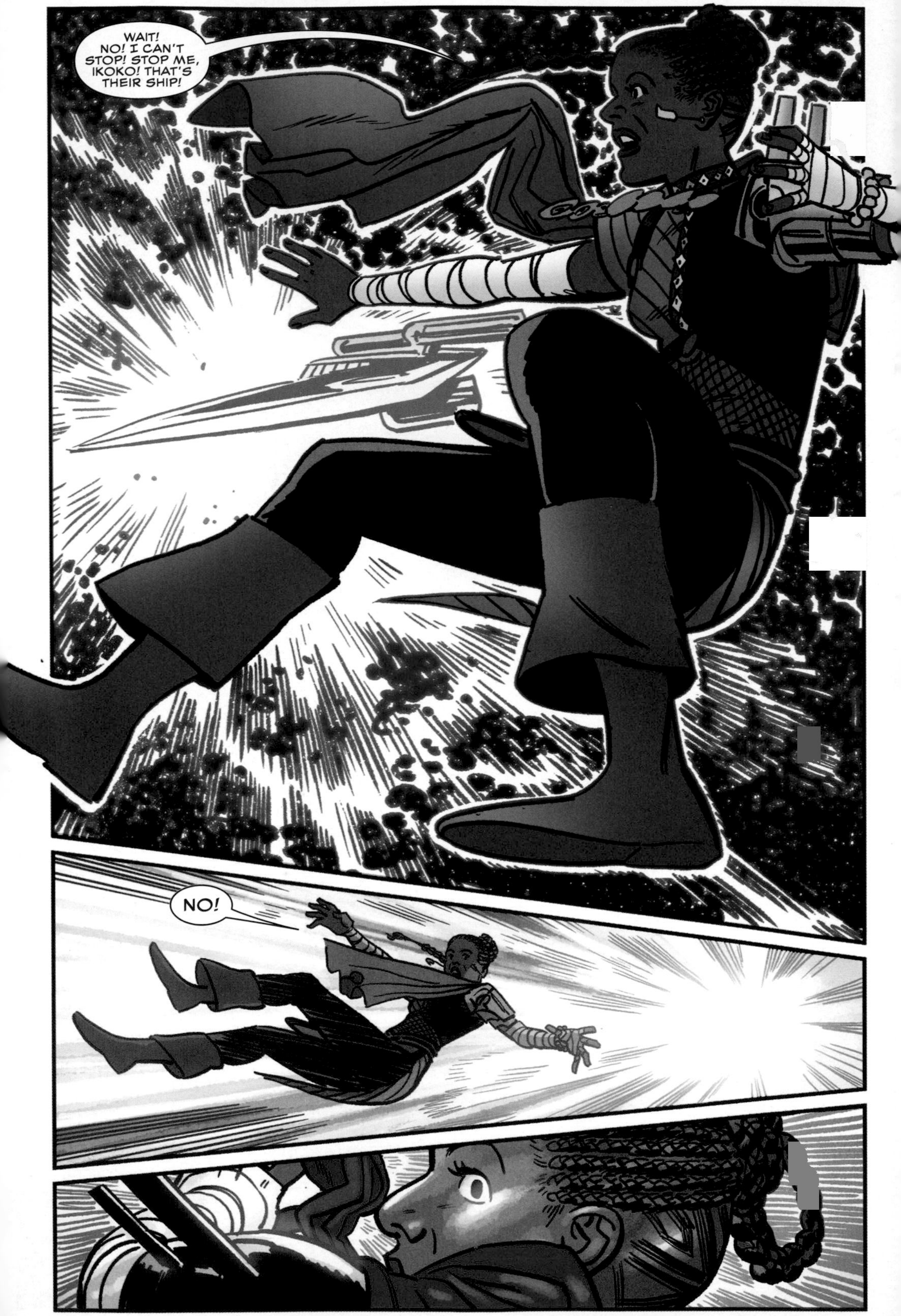
WAIT! NO! I CAN'T STOP! STOP ME, IKOKO! THAT'S THEIR SHIP!
NO!

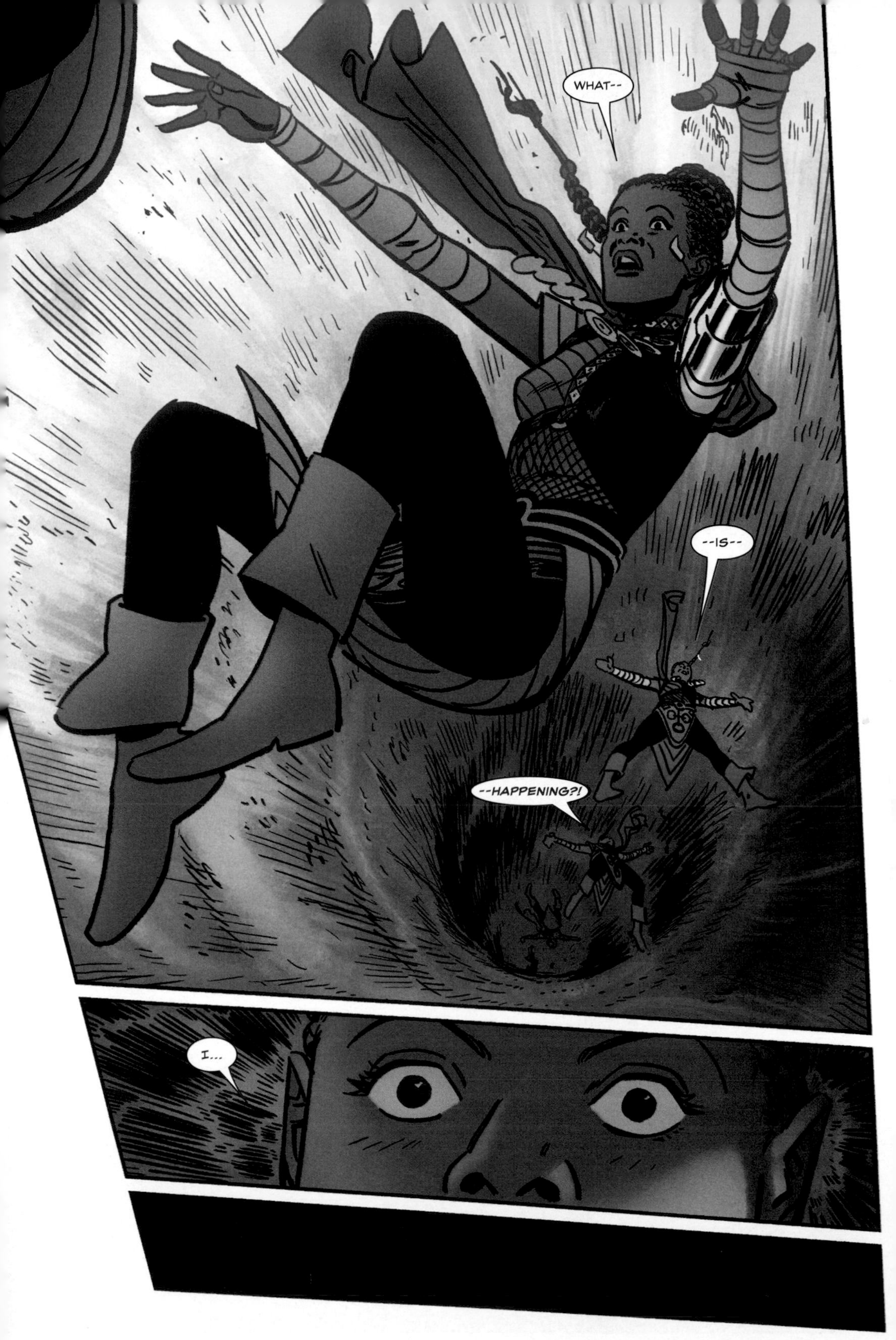
WHAT--
--IS--
--HAPPENING?!
I...

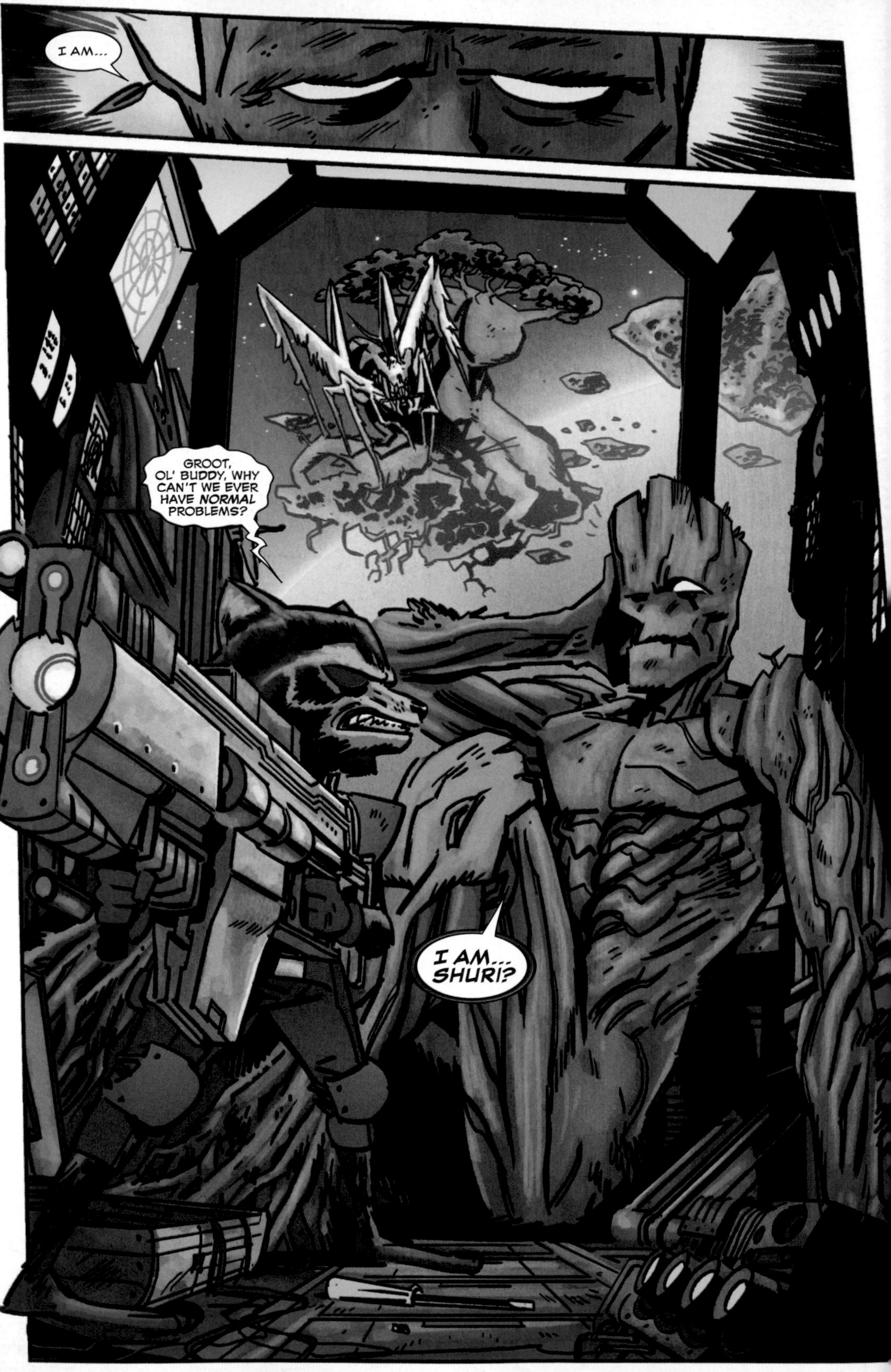
I AM...
GROOT, OL' BUDDY, WHY CAN'T WE EVER HAVE NORMAL PROBLEMS?
I AM... SHURI?

3

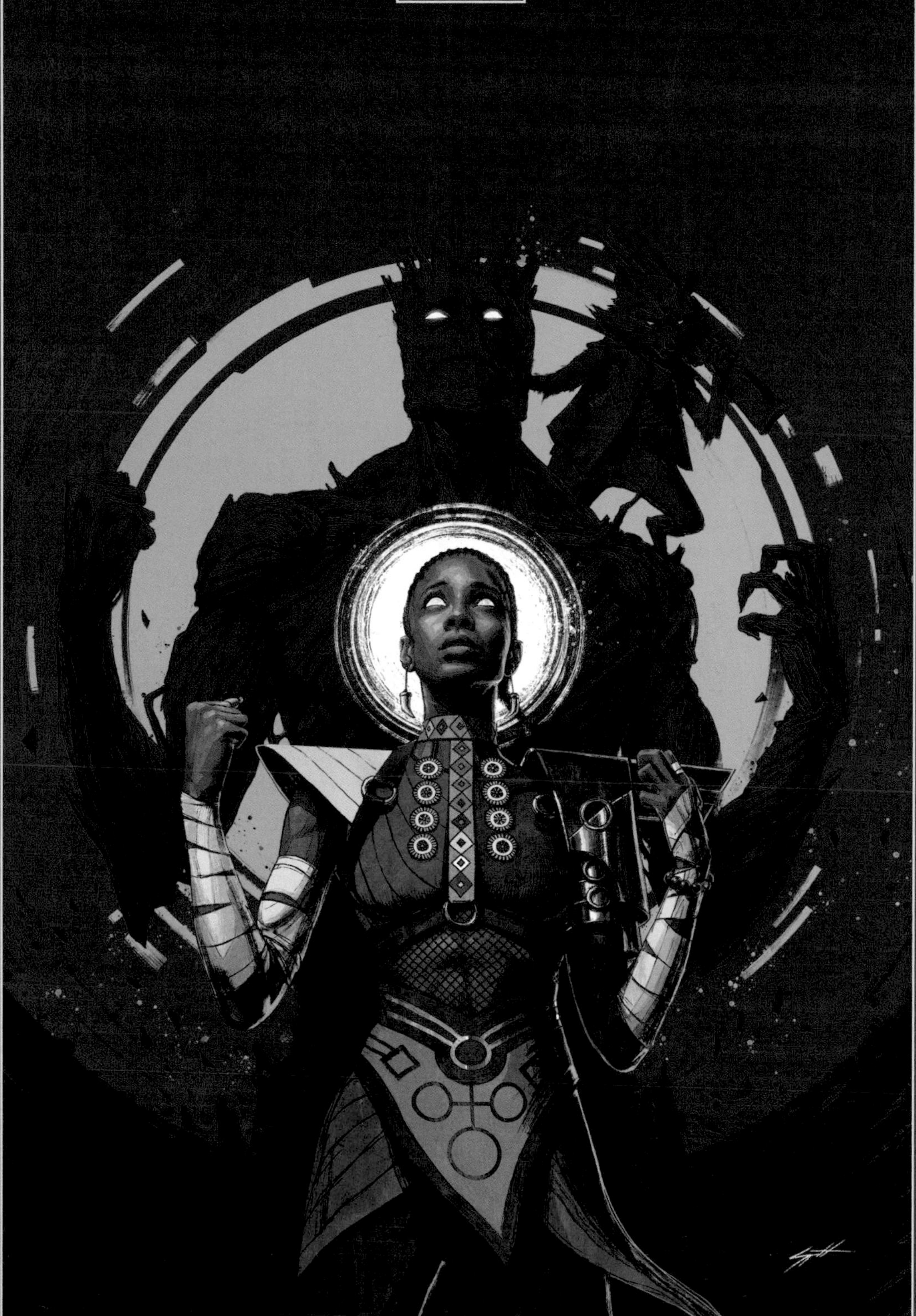

"GROOT BOOM"

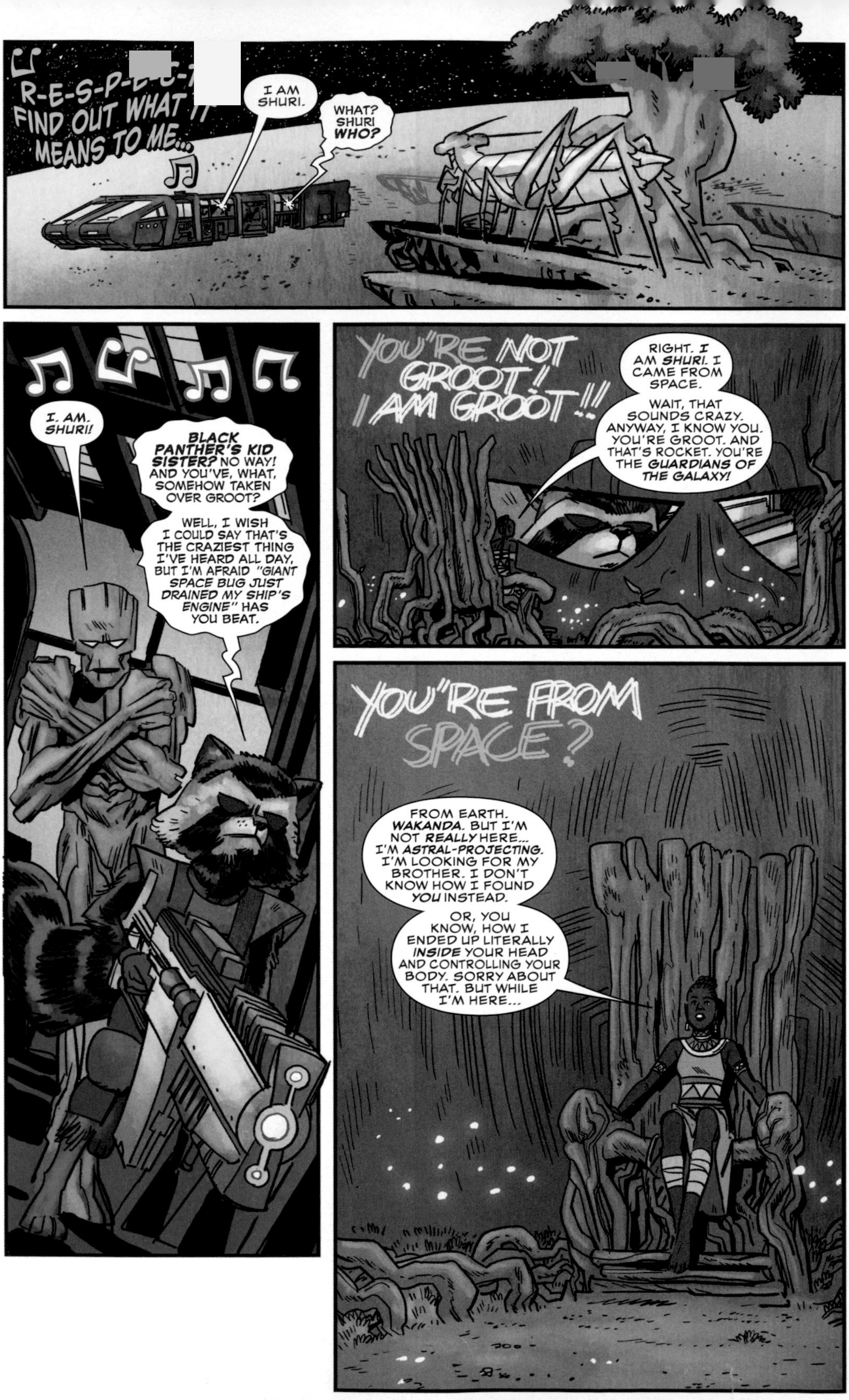

R-E-S-P-E-C-T FIND OUT WHAT IT MEANS TO ME...
I AM SHURI.
WHAT? SHURI WHO?
I. AM. SHURI!
BLACK PANTHER'S KID SISTER? NO WAY! AND YOU'VE, WHAT, SOMEHOW TAKEN OVER GROOT?
WELL, I WISH I COULD SAY THAT'S THE CRAZIEST THING I'VE HEARD ALL DAY, BUT I'M AFRAID "GIANT SPACE BUG JUST DRAINED MY SHIP'S ENGINE" HAS YOU BEAT.
YOU'RE NOT GROOT! I AM GROOT!!
RIGHT. I AM SHURI. I CAME FROM SPACE.
WAIT, THAT SOUNDS CRAZY. ANYWAY, I KNOW YOU. YOU'RE GROOT. AND THAT'S ROCKET. YOU'RE THE GUARDIANS OF THE GALAXY!
YOU'RE FROM SPACE?
FROM EARTH. WAKANDA. BUT I'M NOT REALLY HERE... I'M ASTRAL-PROJECTING. I'M LOOKING FOR MY BROTHER. I DON'T KNOW HOW I FOUND YOU INSTEAD.
OR, YOU KNOW, HOW I ENDED UP LITERALLY INSIDE YOUR HEAD AND CONTROLLING YOUR BODY. SORRY ABOUT THAT. BUT WHILE I'M HERE...

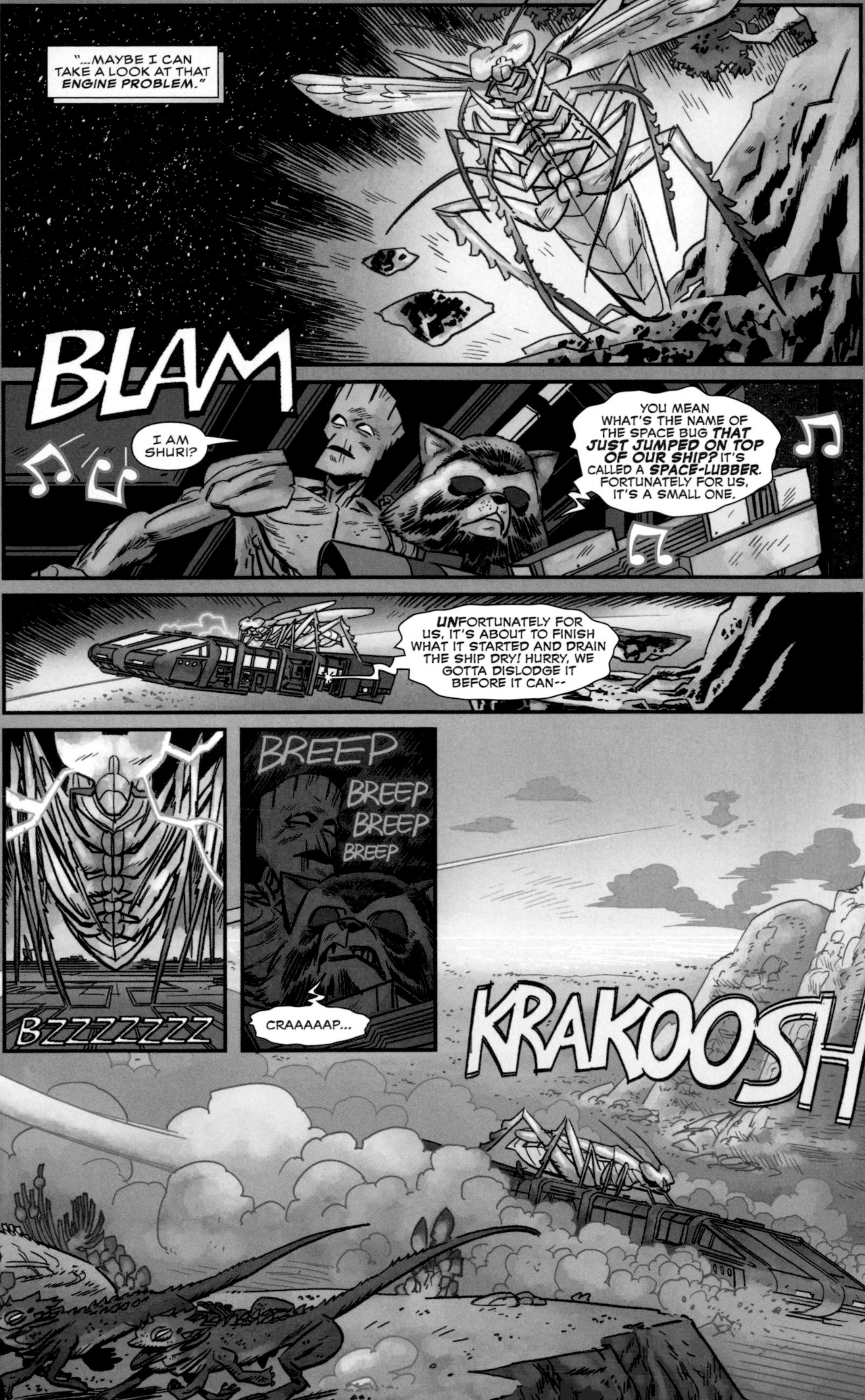

"...MAYBE I CAN TAKE A LOOK AT THAT ENGINE PROBLEM."
BLAM
I AM SHURI?
YOU MEAN WHAT'S THE NAME OF THE SPACE BUG THAT JUST JUMPED ON TOP OF OUR SHIP? IT'S CALLED A SPACE-LUBBER. FORTUNATELY FOR US, IT'S A SMALL ONE.
UNFORTUNATELY FOR US, IT'S ABOUT TO FINISH WHAT IT STARTED AND DRAIN THE SHIP DRY! HURRY, WE GOTTA DISLODGE IT BEFORE IT CAN--
BZZZZZZZ
BREEP
BREEP
BREEP
BREEP
CRAAAAAP...
KRAKOOSH

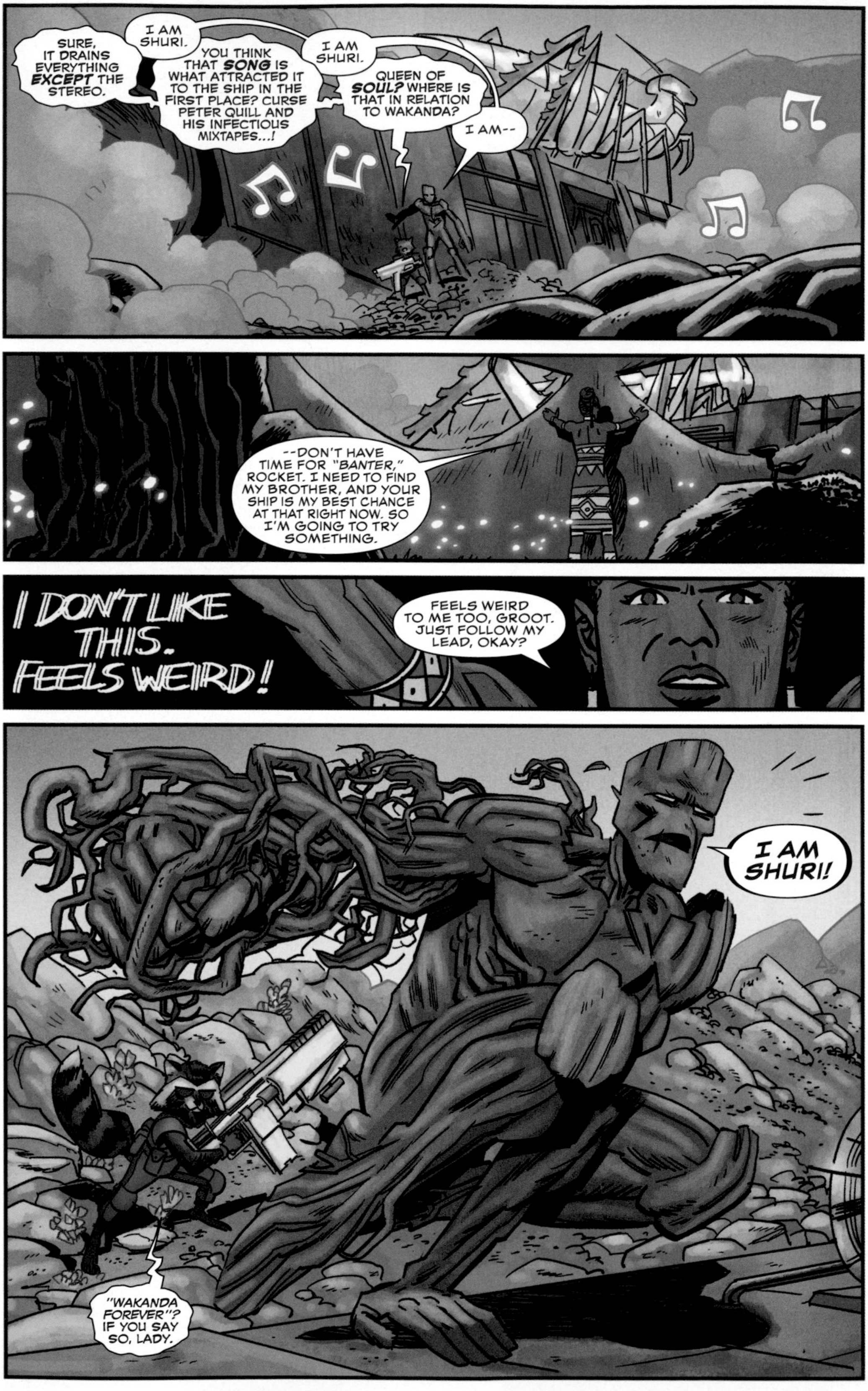
SURE, IT DRAINS EVERYTHING EXCEPT THE STEREO.
I AM SHURI.
YOU THINK THAT SONG IS WHAT ATTRACTED IT TO THE SHIP IN THE FIRST PLACE? CURSE PETER QUILL AND HIS INFECTIOUS MIXTAPES...!
I AM SHURI.
QUEEN OF SOUL? WHERE IS THAT IN RELATION TO WAKANDA?
I AM--
--DON'T HAVE TIME FOR "BANTER," ROCKET. I NEED TO FIND MY BROTHER, AND YOUR SHIP IS MY BEST CHANCE AT THAT RIGHT NOW. SO I'M GOING TO TRY SOMETHING.
I DON'T LIKE THIS.. FEELS WEIRD!
FEELS WEIRD TO ME TOO, GROOT. JUST FOLLOW MY LEAD, OKAY?
I AM SHURI!
"WAKANDA FOREVER"? IF YOU SAY SO, LADY.

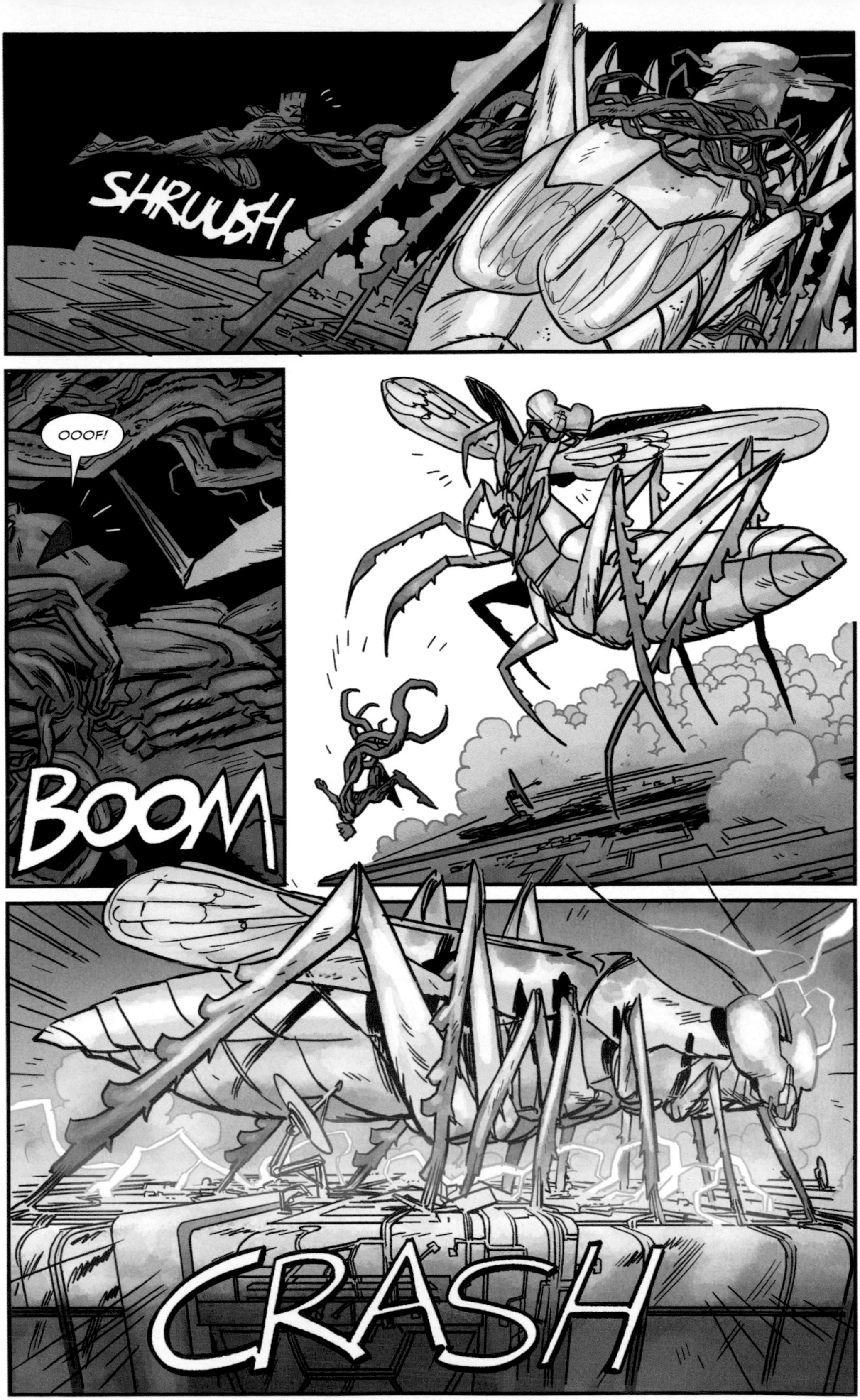
SHRUUSH
OOOF!
BOOM
CRASH

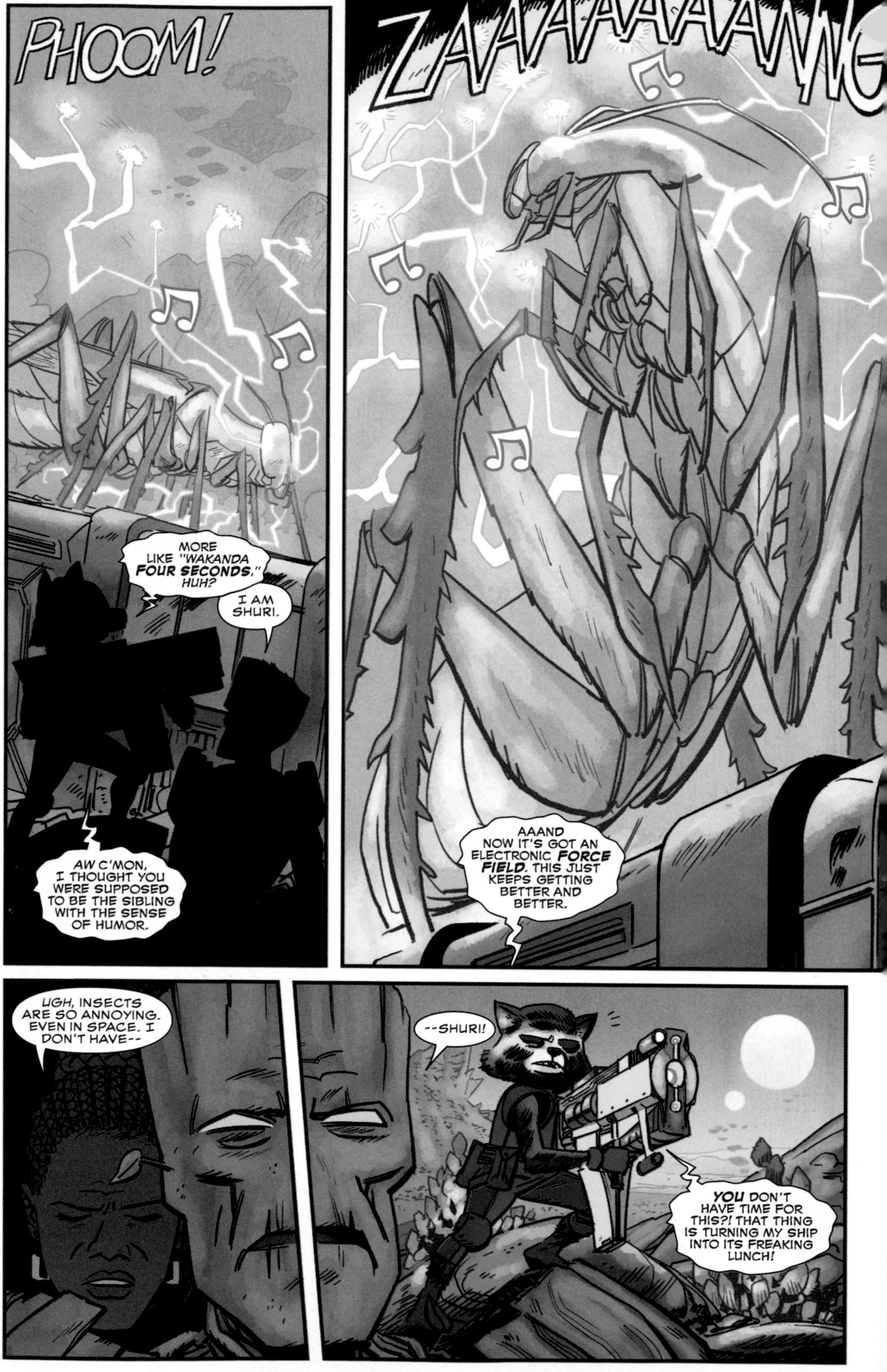
PHOOM!
MORE LIKE "WAKANDA FOUR SECONDS," HUH?
I AM SHURI.
AW C'MON, I THOUGHT YOU WERE SUPPOSED TO BE THE SIBLING WITH THE SENSE OF HUMOR.
ZAAAAAAAANNG
AAAND NOW IT'S GOT AN ELECTRONIC FORCE FIELD. THIS JUST KEEPS GETTING BETTER AND BETTER.
UGH, INSECTS ARE SO ANNOYING. EVEN IN SPACE. I DON'T HAVE--
--SHURI!
YOU DON'T HAVE TIME FOR THIS?! THAT THING IS TURNING MY SHIP INTO ITS FREAKING LUNCH!

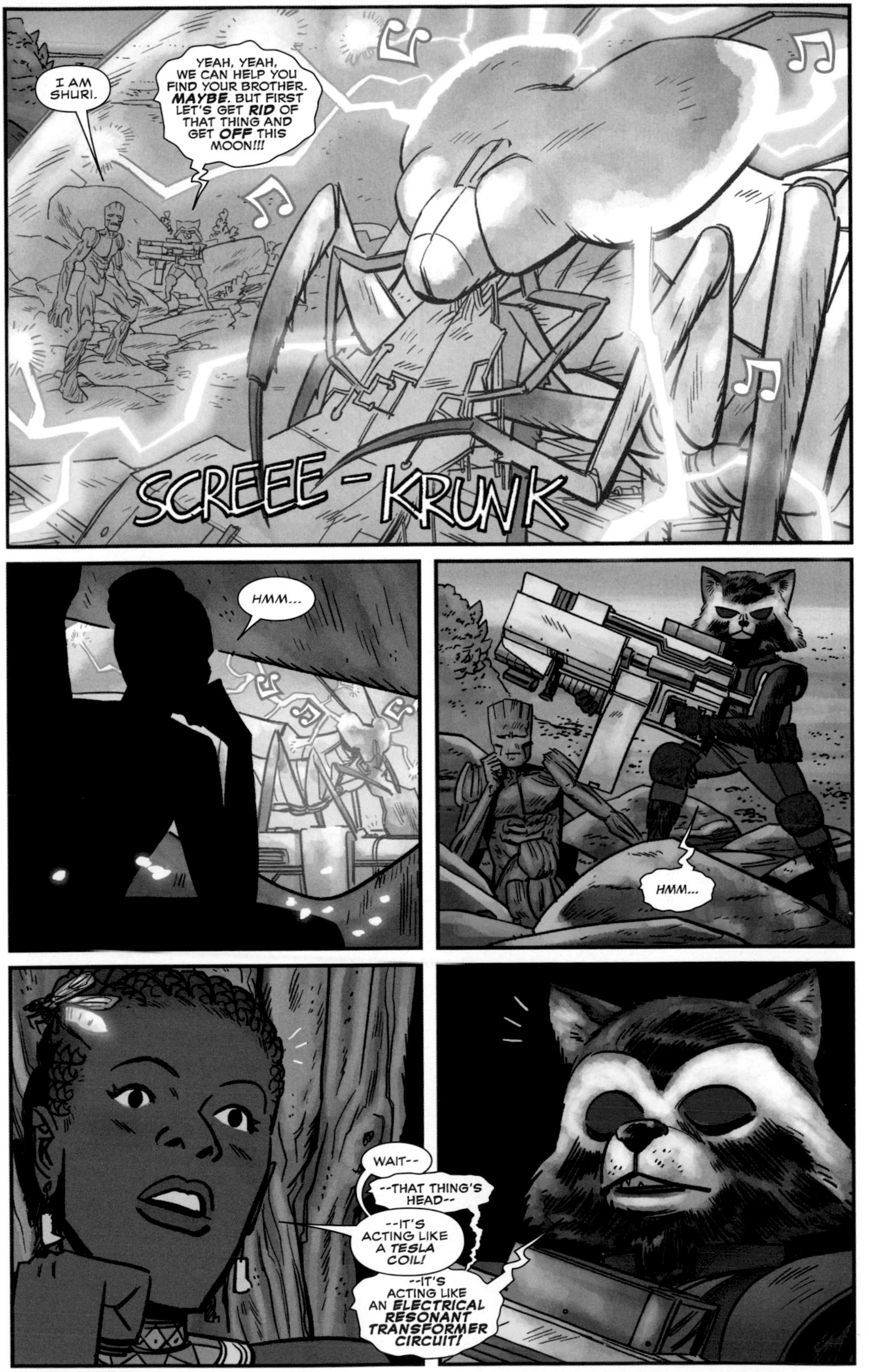
I AM SHURI.
YEAH, YEAH, WE CAN HELP YOU FIND YOUR BROTHER. **MAYBE.** BUT FIRST LET'S GET **RID** OF THAT THING AND GET **OFF** THIS MOON!!!
SCREEE-KRUNK
HMM...
HMM...
WAIT--
--THAT THING'S HEAD--
--IT'S ACTING LIKE A *TESLA* COIL!
--IT'S ACTING LIKE AN ***ELECTRICAL RESONANT TRANSFORMER CIRCUIT!***

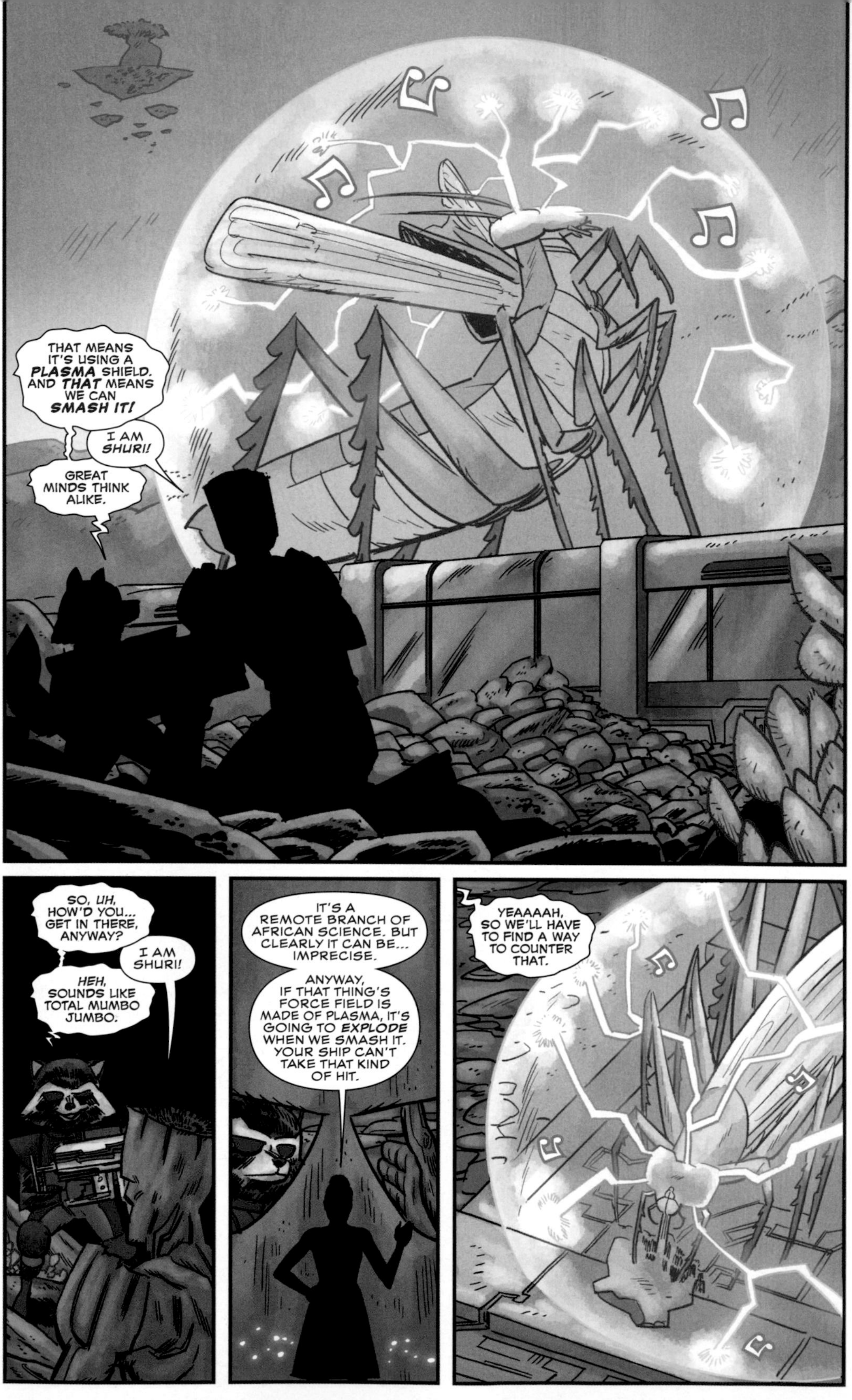
THAT MEANS IT'S USING A *PLASMA* SHIELD. AND *THAT* MEANS WE CAN *SMASH IT!*
I AM *SHURI!*
GREAT MINDS THINK ALIKE.
SO, *UH*, HOW'D YOU... GET IN THERE, ANYWAY?
I AM SHURI!
HEH, SOUNDS LIKE TOTAL MUMBO JUMBO.
IT'S A REMOTE BRANCH OF AFRICAN SCIENCE. BUT CLEARLY IT CAN BE... IMPRECISE.
ANYWAY, IF THAT THING'S FORCE FIELD IS MADE OF PLASMA, IT'S GOING TO *EXPLODE* WHEN WE SMASH IT. YOUR SHIP CAN'T TAKE THAT KIND OF HIT.
YEAAAAH, SO WE'LL HAVE TO FIND A WAY TO COUNTER THAT.

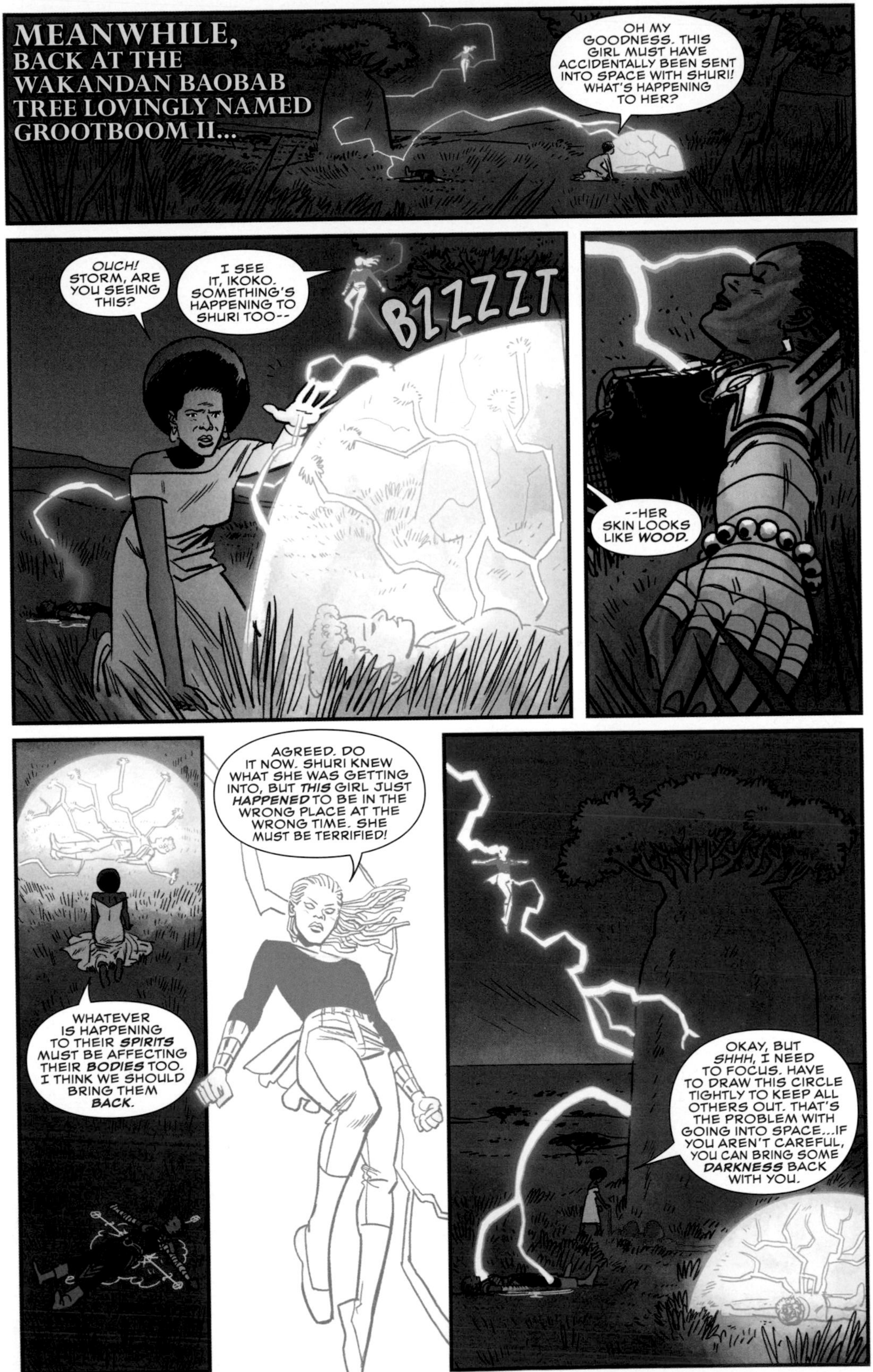
MEANWHILE, BACK AT THE WAKANDAN BAOBAB TREE LOVINGLY NAMED GROOTBOOM II...
OH MY GOODNESS. THIS GIRL MUST HAVE ACCIDENTALLY BEEN SENT INTO SPACE WITH SHURI! WHAT'S HAPPENING TO HER?
OUCH! STORM, ARE YOU SEEING THIS?
I SEE IT, IKOKO. SOMETHING'S HAPPENING TO SHURI TOO--
BZZZZT
--HER SKIN LOOKS LIKE WOOD.
AGREED. DO IT NOW. SHURI KNEW WHAT SHE WAS GETTING INTO, BUT THIS GIRL JUST HAPPENED TO BE IN THE WRONG PLACE AT THE WRONG TIME. SHE MUST BE TERRIFIED!
WHATEVER IS HAPPENING TO THEIR SPIRITS MUST BE AFFECTING THEIR BODIES TOO. I THINK WE SHOULD BRING THEM BACK.
OKAY, BUT SHHH, I NEED TO FOCUS. HAVE TO DRAW THIS CIRCLE TIGHTLY TO KEEP ALL OTHERS OUT. THAT'S THE PROBLEM WITH GOING INTO SPACE...IF YOU AREN'T CAREFUL, YOU CAN BRING SOME DARKNESS BACK WITH YOU.

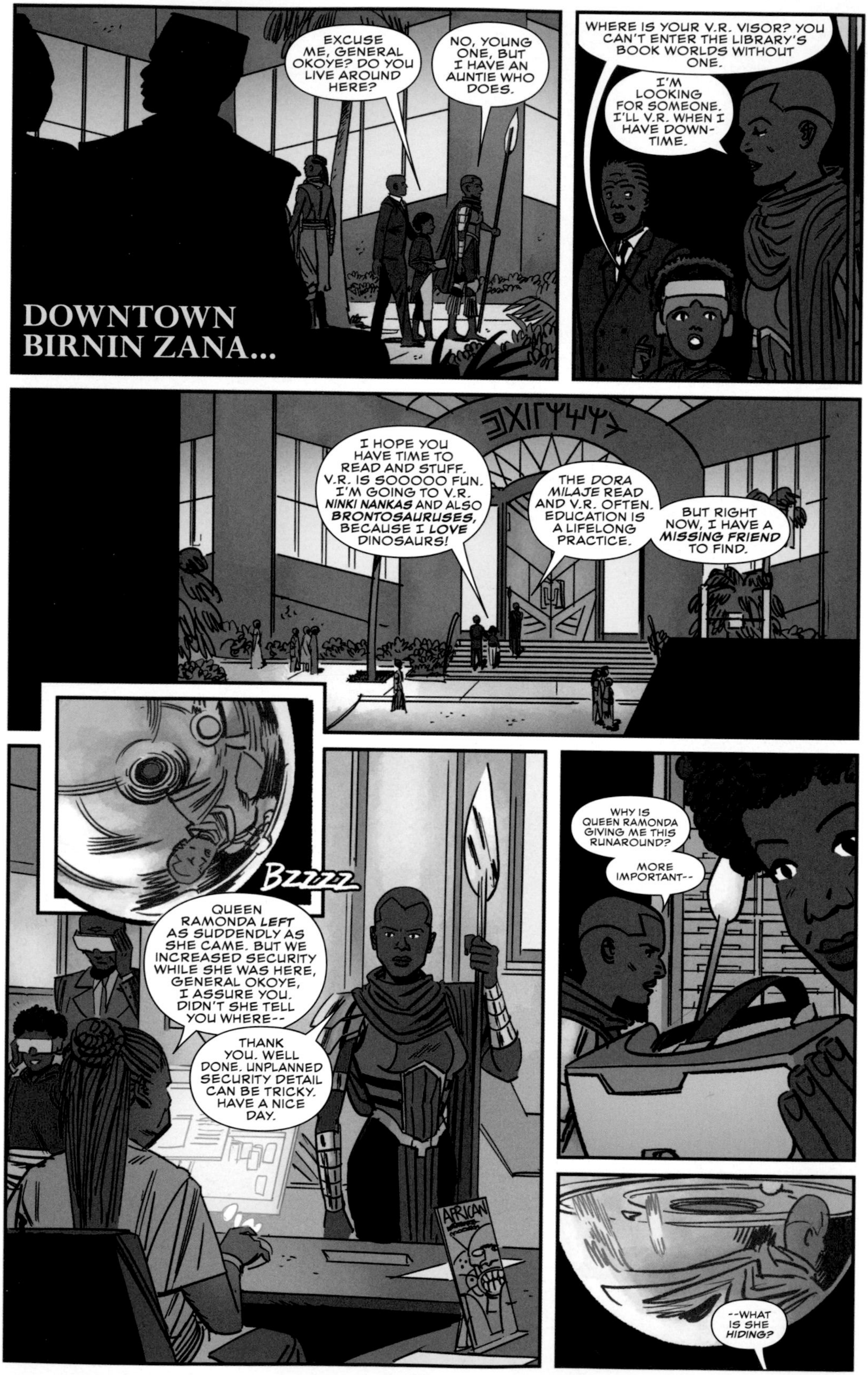
EXCUSE ME, GENERAL OKOYE? DO YOU LIVE AROUND HERE?
NO, YOUNG ONE, BUT I HAVE AN AUNTIE WHO DOES.
DOWNTOWN BIRNIN ZANA...
WHERE IS YOUR V.R. VISOR? YOU CAN'T ENTER THE LIBRARY'S BOOK WORLDS WITHOUT ONE.
I'M LOOKING FOR SOMEONE. I'LL V.R. WHEN I HAVE DOWN-TIME.
I HOPE YOU HAVE TIME TO READ AND STUFF. V.R. IS SOOOOO FUN. I'M GOING TO V.R. NINKI NANKAS AND ALSO BRONTOSAURUSES, BECAUSE I LOVE DINOSAURS!
THE DORA MILAJE READ AND V.R. OFTEN. EDUCATION IS A LIFELONG PRACTICE.
BUT RIGHT NOW, I HAVE A MISSING FRIEND TO FIND.
BZZZZZ
QUEEN RAMONDA LEFT AS SUDDENLY AS SHE CAME. BUT WE INCREASED SECURITY WHILE SHE WAS HERE, GENERAL OKOYE, I ASSURE YOU. DIDN'T SHE TELL YOU WHERE--
THANK YOU. WELL DONE. UNPLANNED SECURITY DETAIL CAN BE TRICKY. HAVE A NICE DAY.
AFRICAN
WHY IS QUEEN RAMONDA GIVING ME THIS RUNAROUND?
MORE IMPORTANT--
--WHAT IS SHE HIDING?

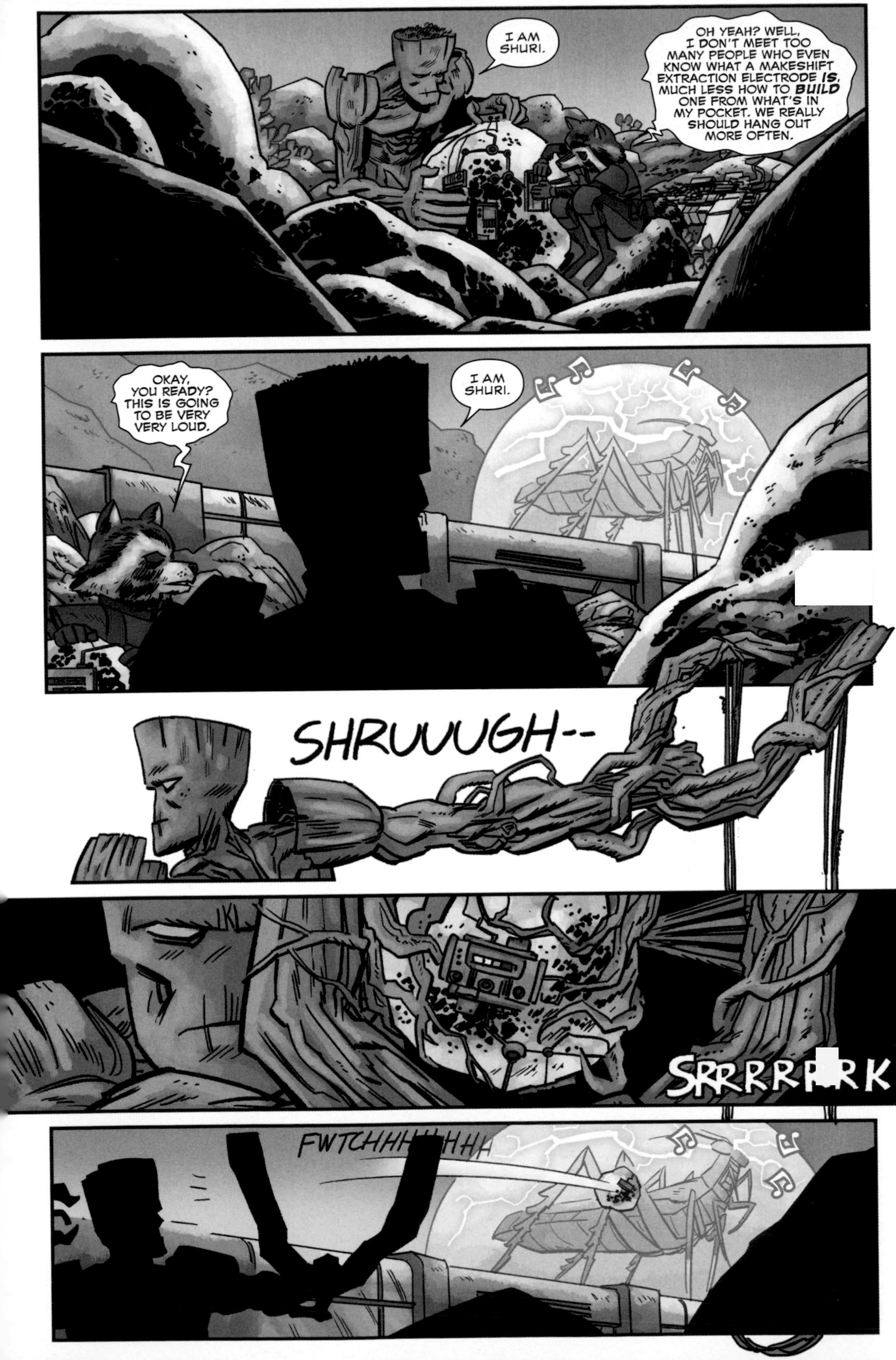
I AM SHURI.
OH YEAH? WELL, I DON'T MEET TOO MANY PEOPLE WHO EVEN KNOW WHAT A MAKESHIFT EXTRACTION ELECTRODE **IS**, MUCH LESS HOW TO **BUILD** ONE FROM WHAT'S IN MY POCKET. WE REALLY SHOULD HANG OUT MORE OFTEN.
OKAY, YOU READY? THIS IS GOING TO BE VERY VERY LOUD.
I AM SHURI.
SHRUUUGH--
SRRRRRRK
FWTCHHHHHH

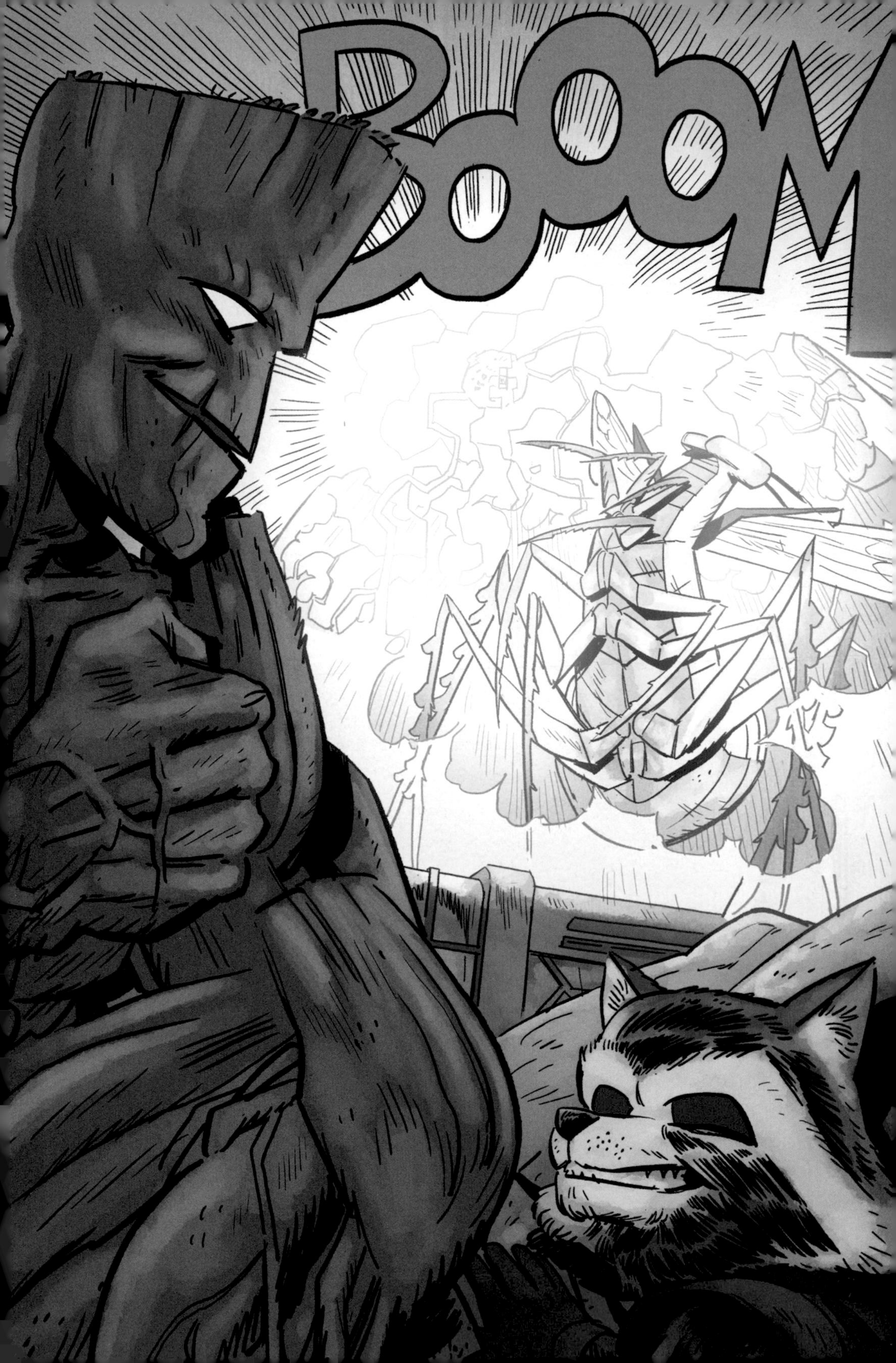
BOOOM

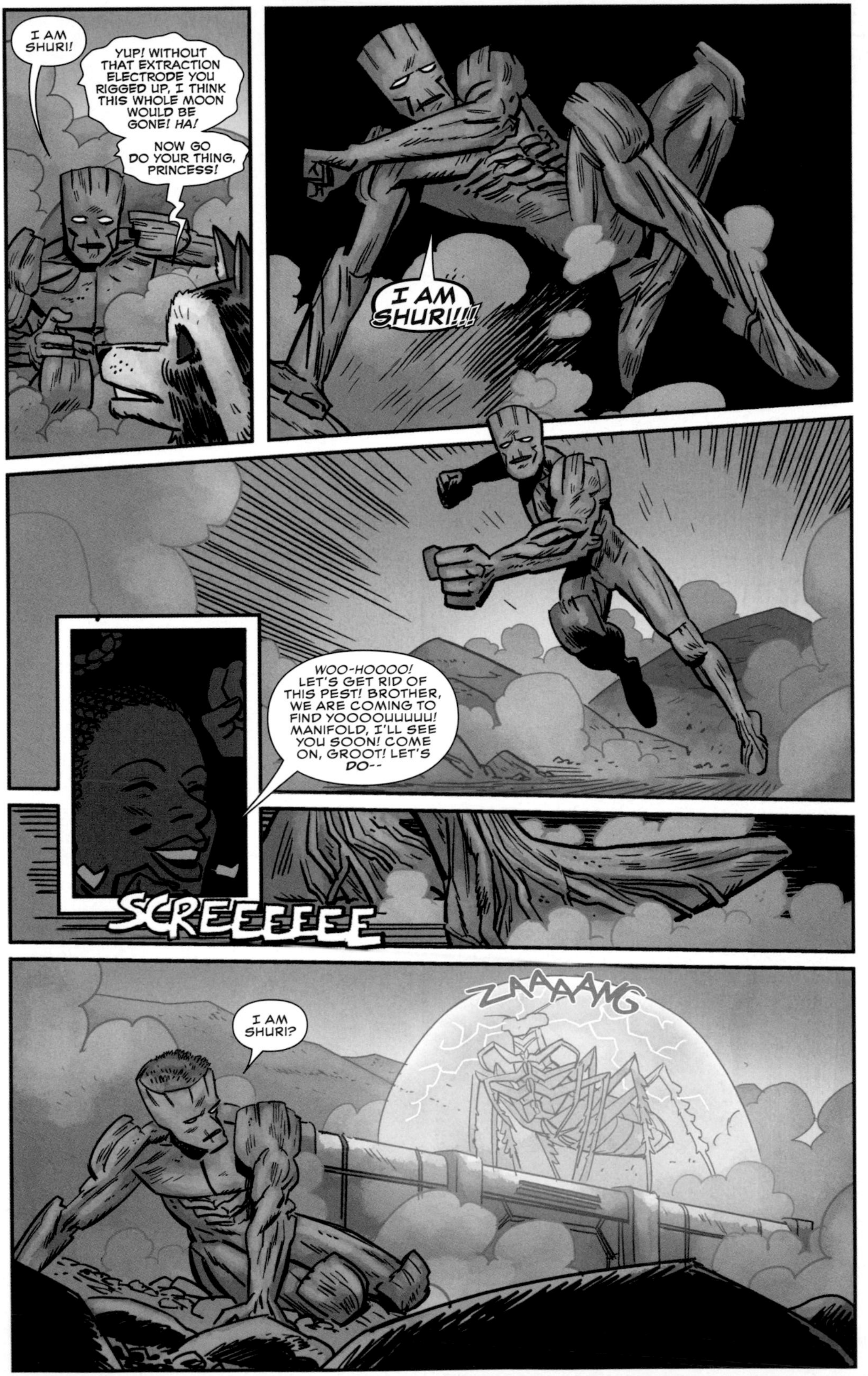
I AM SHURI!
YUP! WITHOUT THAT EXTRACTION ELECTRODE YOU RIGGED UP, I THINK THIS WHOLE MOON WOULD BE GONE! HA!
NOW GO DO YOUR THING, PRINCESS!
I AM SHURI!!!
WOO-HOOOO! LET'S GET RID OF THIS PEST! BROTHER, WE ARE COMING TO FIND YOOOOUUUUU! MANIFOLD, I'LL SEE YOU SOON! COME ON, GROOT! LET'S DO--
SCREEEEEEE
ZAAAAANG
I AM SHURI?

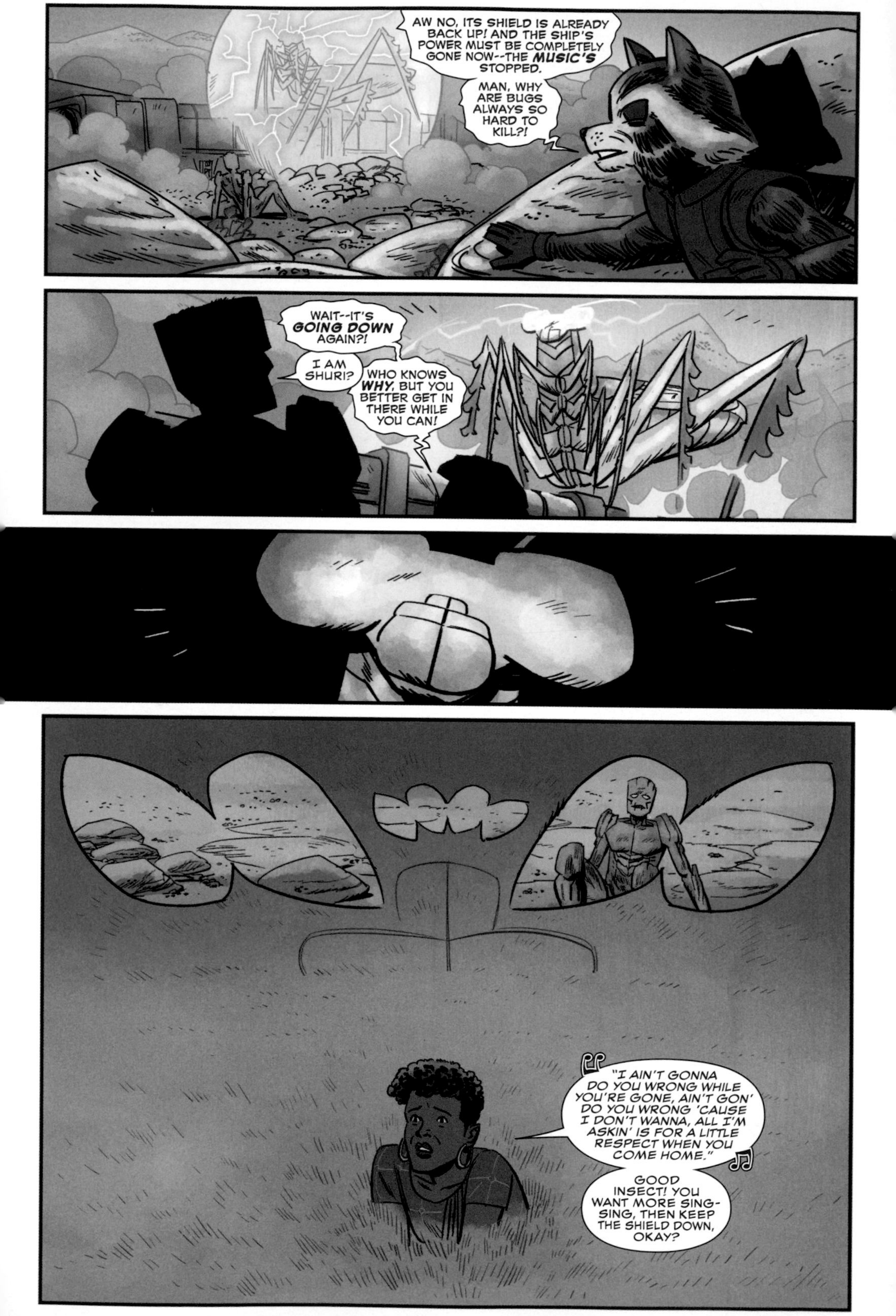
AW NO, ITS SHIELD IS ALREADY BACK UP! AND THE SHIP'S POWER MUST BE COMPLETELY GONE NOW--THE MUSIC'S STOPPED.
MAN, WHY ARE BUGS ALWAYS SO HARD TO KILL?!
WAIT--IT'S GOING DOWN AGAIN?!
I AM SHURI?
WHO KNOWS WHY, BUT YOU BETTER GET IN THERE WHILE YOU CAN!
"I AIN'T GONNA DO YOU WRONG WHILE YOU'RE GONE, AIN'T GON' DO YOU WRONG 'CAUSE I DON'T WANNA, ALL I'M ASKIN' IS FOR A LITTLE RESPECT WHEN YOU COME HOME."
GOOD INSECT! YOU WANT MORE SING-SING, THEN KEEP THE SHIELD DOWN, OKAY?

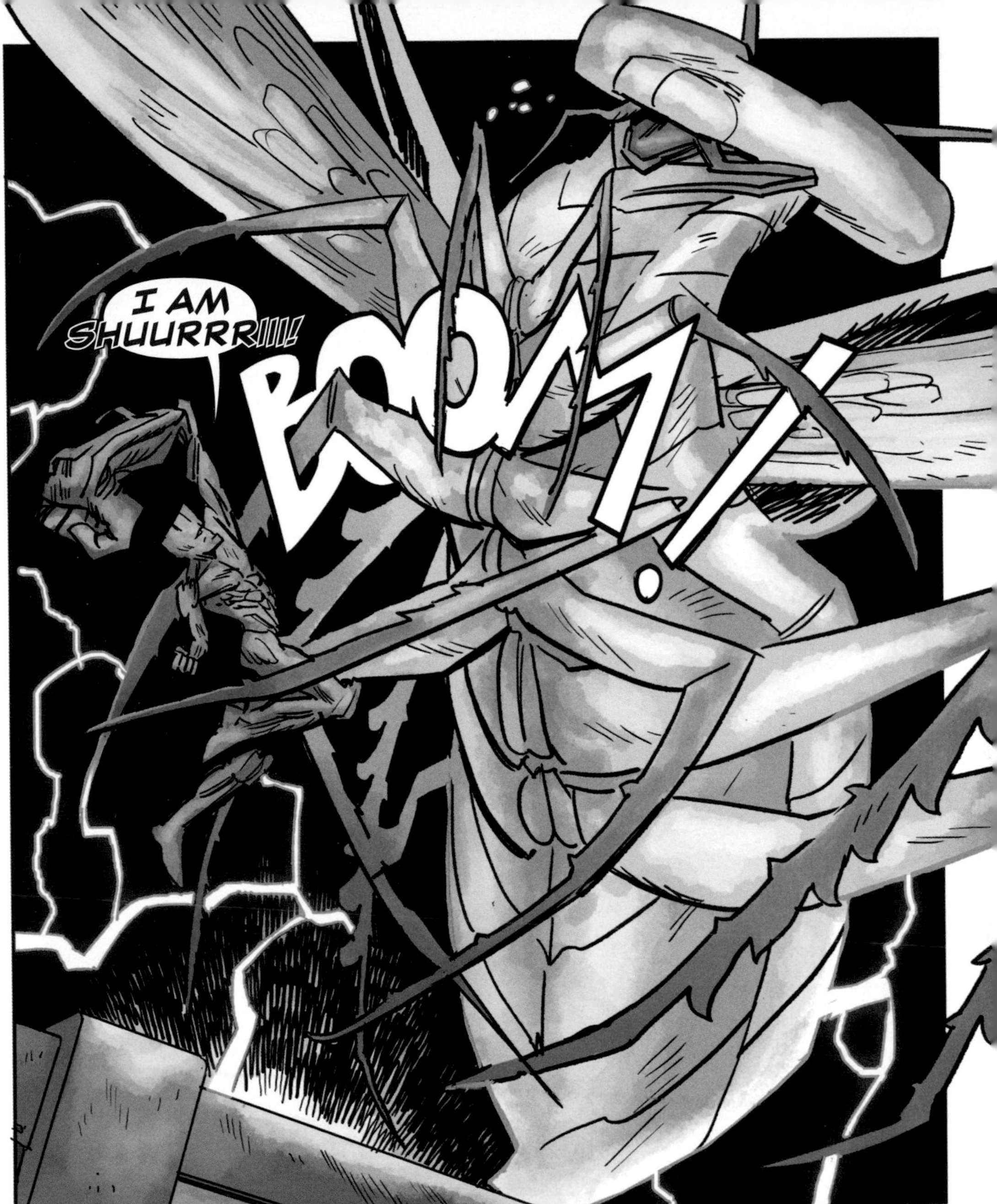
I AM SHUURRRIII!
BOOM!

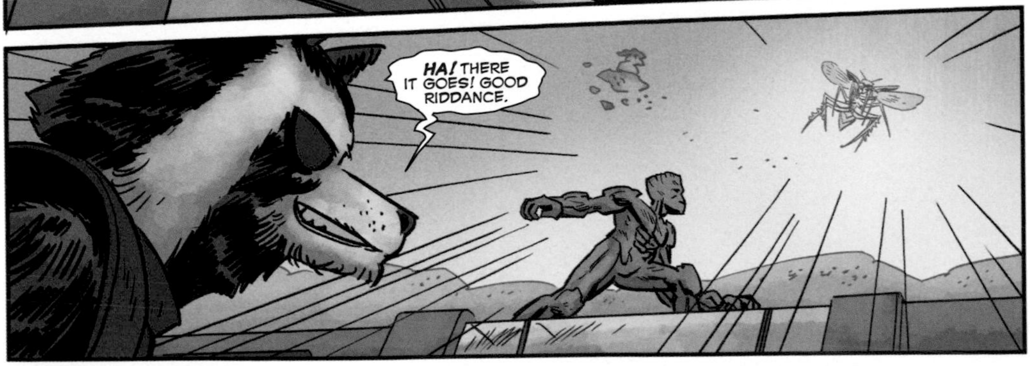
HA! THERE IT GOES! GOOD RIDDANCE.

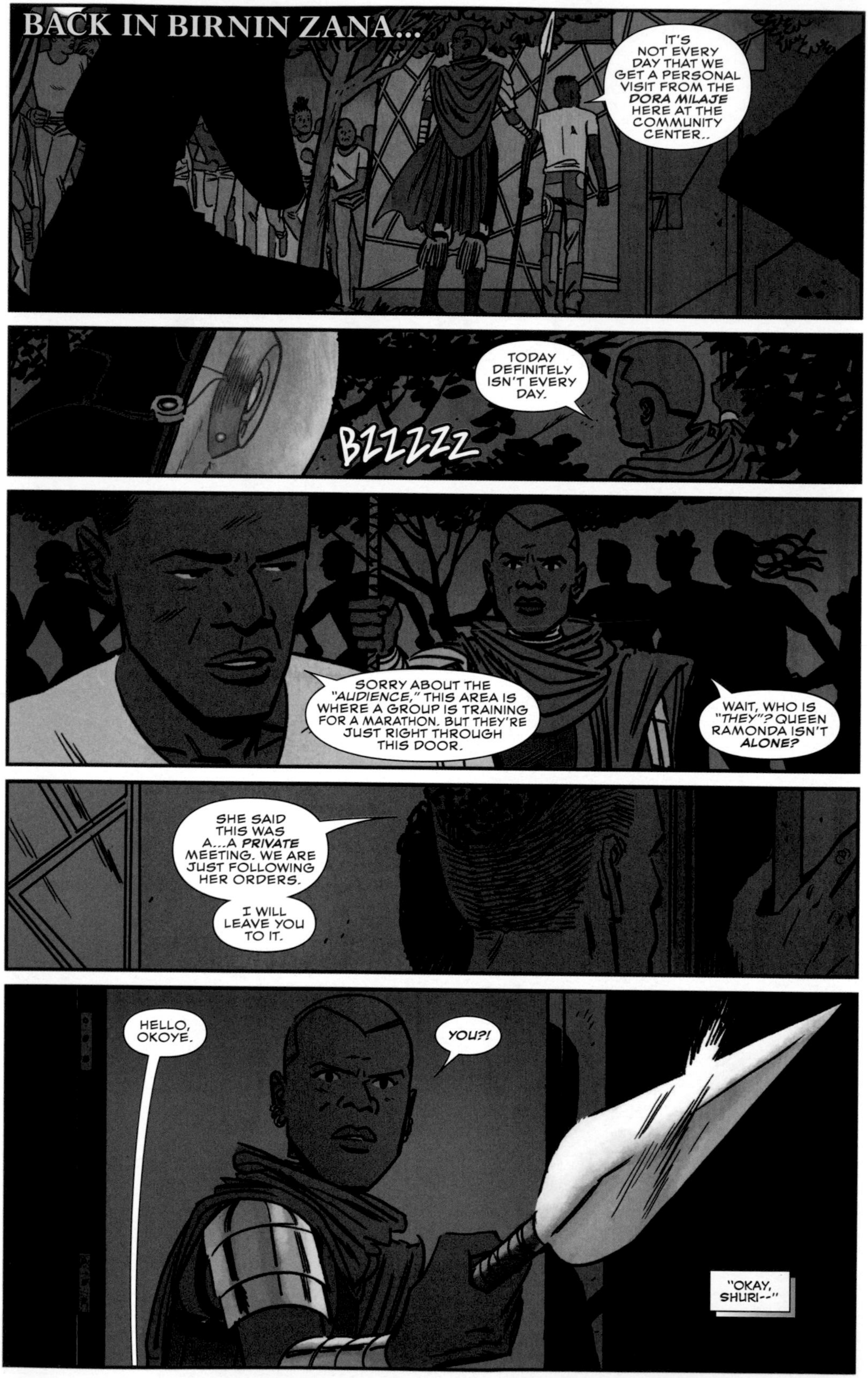
BACK IN BIRNIN ZANA...
IT'S NOT EVERY DAY THAT WE GET A PERSONAL VISIT FROM THE DORA MILAJE HERE AT THE COMMUNITY CENTER..
TODAY DEFINITELY ISN'T EVERY DAY.
BZZZZZ
SORRY ABOUT THE "AUDIENCE," THIS AREA IS WHERE A GROUP IS TRAINING FOR A MARATHON. BUT THEY'RE JUST RIGHT THROUGH THIS DOOR.
WAIT, WHO IS "THEY"? QUEEN RAMONDA ISN'T ALONE?
SHE SAID THIS WAS A...A PRIVATE MEETING. WE ARE JUST FOLLOWING HER ORDERS.
I WILL LEAVE YOU TO IT.
HELLO, OKOYE.
YOU?!
"OKAY, SHURI--"

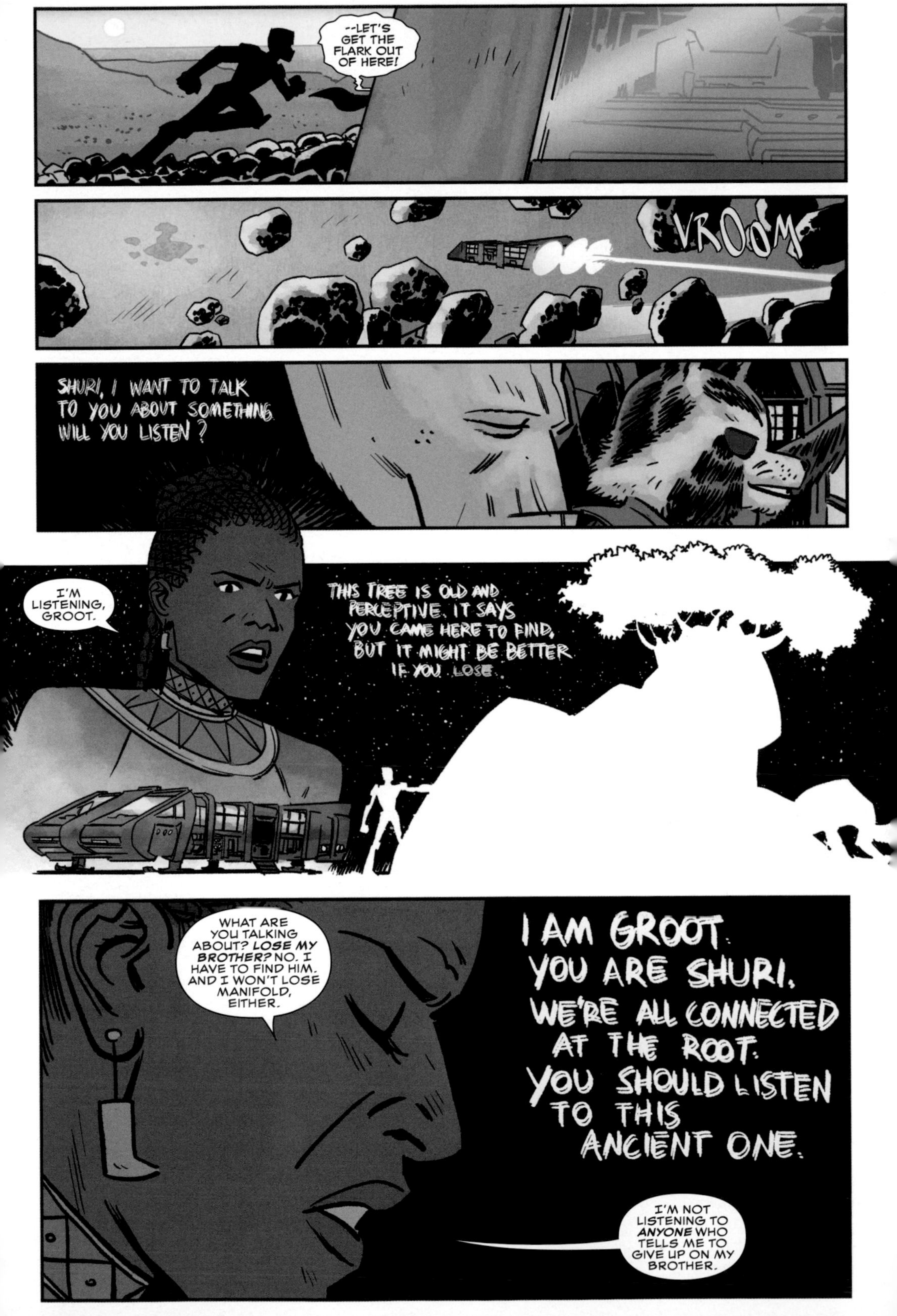

--LET'S GET THE FLARK OUT OF HERE!
VROOM
SHURI, I WANT TO TALK TO YOU ABOUT SOMETHING. WILL YOU LISTEN?
I'M LISTENING, GROOT.
THIS TREE IS OLD AND PERCEPTIVE. IT SAYS YOU CAME HERE TO FIND. BUT IT MIGHT BE BETTER IF YOU... LOSE.
WHAT ARE YOU TALKING ABOUT? LOSE MY BROTHER? NO. I HAVE TO FIND HIM. AND I WON'T LOSE MANIFOLD, EITHER.
I AM GROOT. YOU ARE SHURI. WE'RE ALL CONNECTED AT THE ROOT. YOU SHOULD LISTEN TO THIS ANCIENT ONE.
I'M NOT LISTENING TO ANYONE WHO TELLS ME TO GIVE UP ON MY BROTHER.

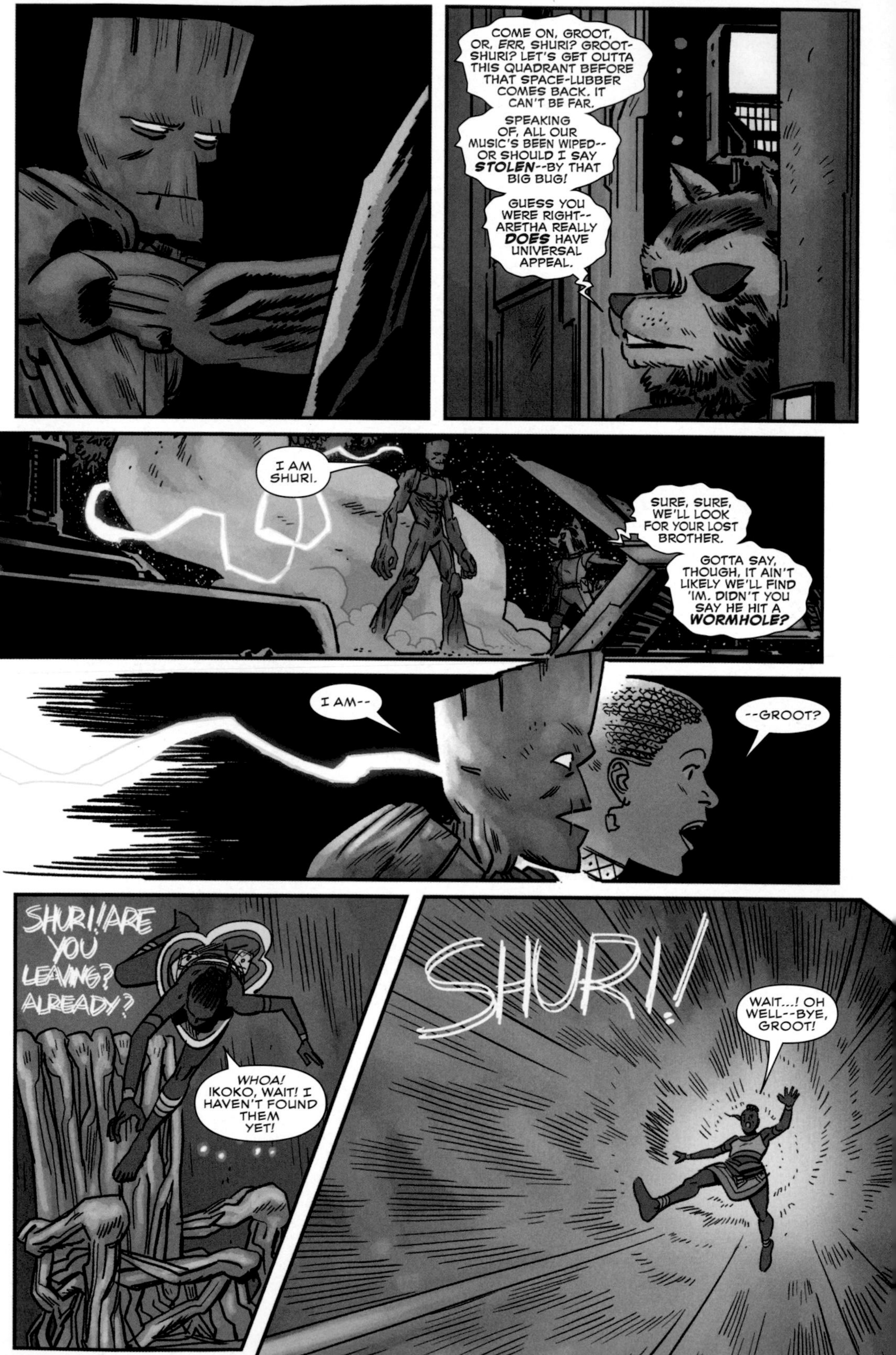
COME ON, GROOT, OR, ERR, SHURI? GROOT-SHURI? LET'S GET OUTTA THIS QUADRANT BEFORE THAT SPACE-LUBBER COMES BACK. IT CAN'T BE FAR.
SPEAKING OF, ALL OUR MUSIC'S BEEN WIPED--OR SHOULD I SAY STOLEN--BY THAT BIG BUG!
GUESS YOU WERE RIGHT--ARETHA REALLY DOES HAVE UNIVERSAL APPEAL.
I AM SHURI.
SURE, SURE, WE'LL LOOK FOR YOUR LOST BROTHER.
GOTTA SAY, THOUGH, IT AIN'T LIKELY WE'LL FIND 'IM. DIDN'T YOU SAY HE HIT A WORMHOLE?
I AM--
--GROOT?
SHURI! ARE YOU LEAVING? ALREADY?
WHOA! IKOKO, WAIT! I HAVEN'T FOUND THEM YET!
SHURI!
WAIT...! OH WELL--BYE, GROOT!

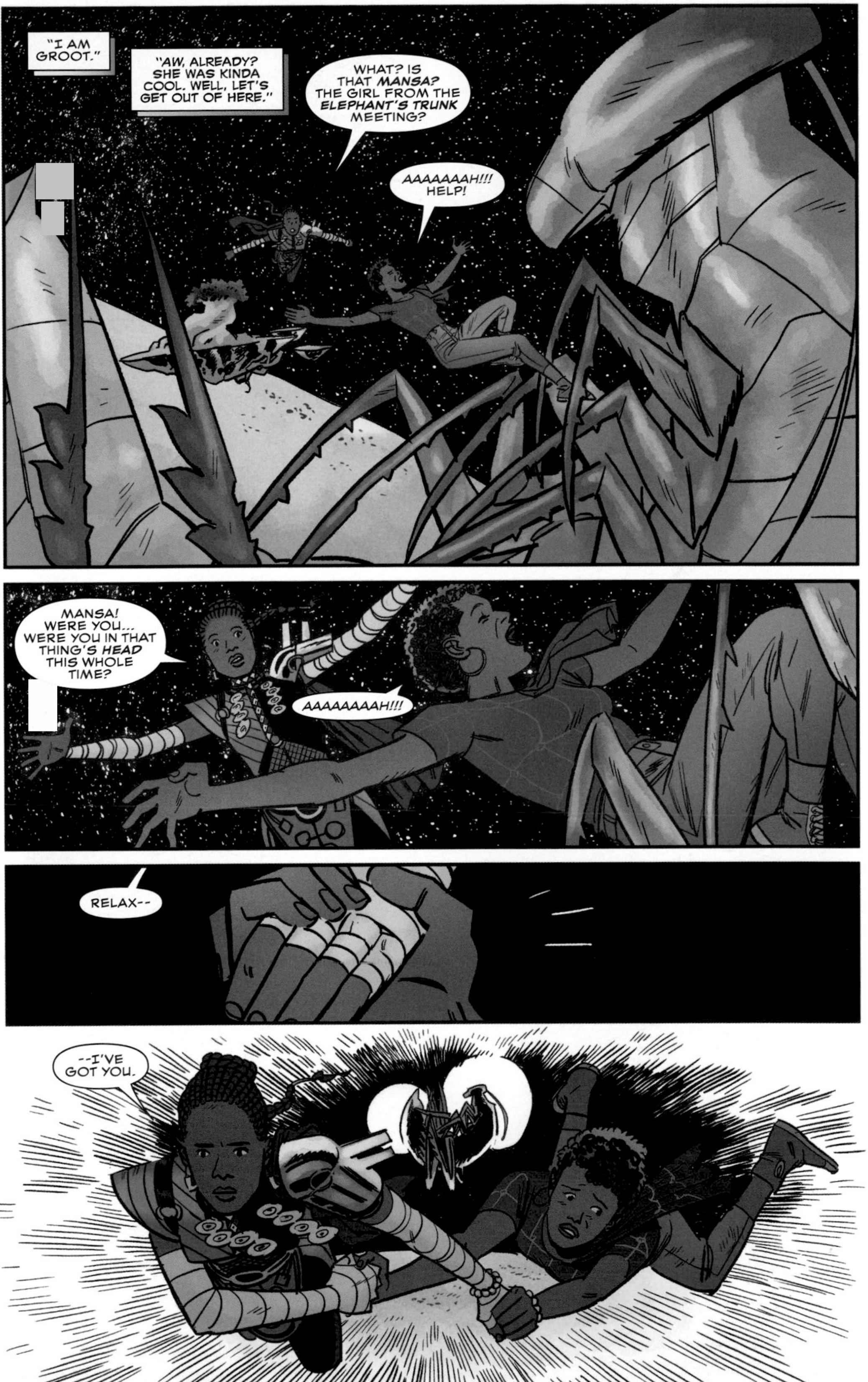
"I AM GROOT."
"AW, ALREADY? SHE WAS KINDA COOL. WELL, LET'S GET OUT OF HERE."
WHAT? IS THAT MANSA? THE GIRL FROM THE ELEPHANT'S TRUNK MEETING?
AAAAAAAH!!! HELP!
MANSA! WERE YOU... WERE YOU IN THAT THING'S HEAD THIS WHOLE TIME?
AAAAAAAAH!!!
RELAX--
--I'VE GOT YOU.

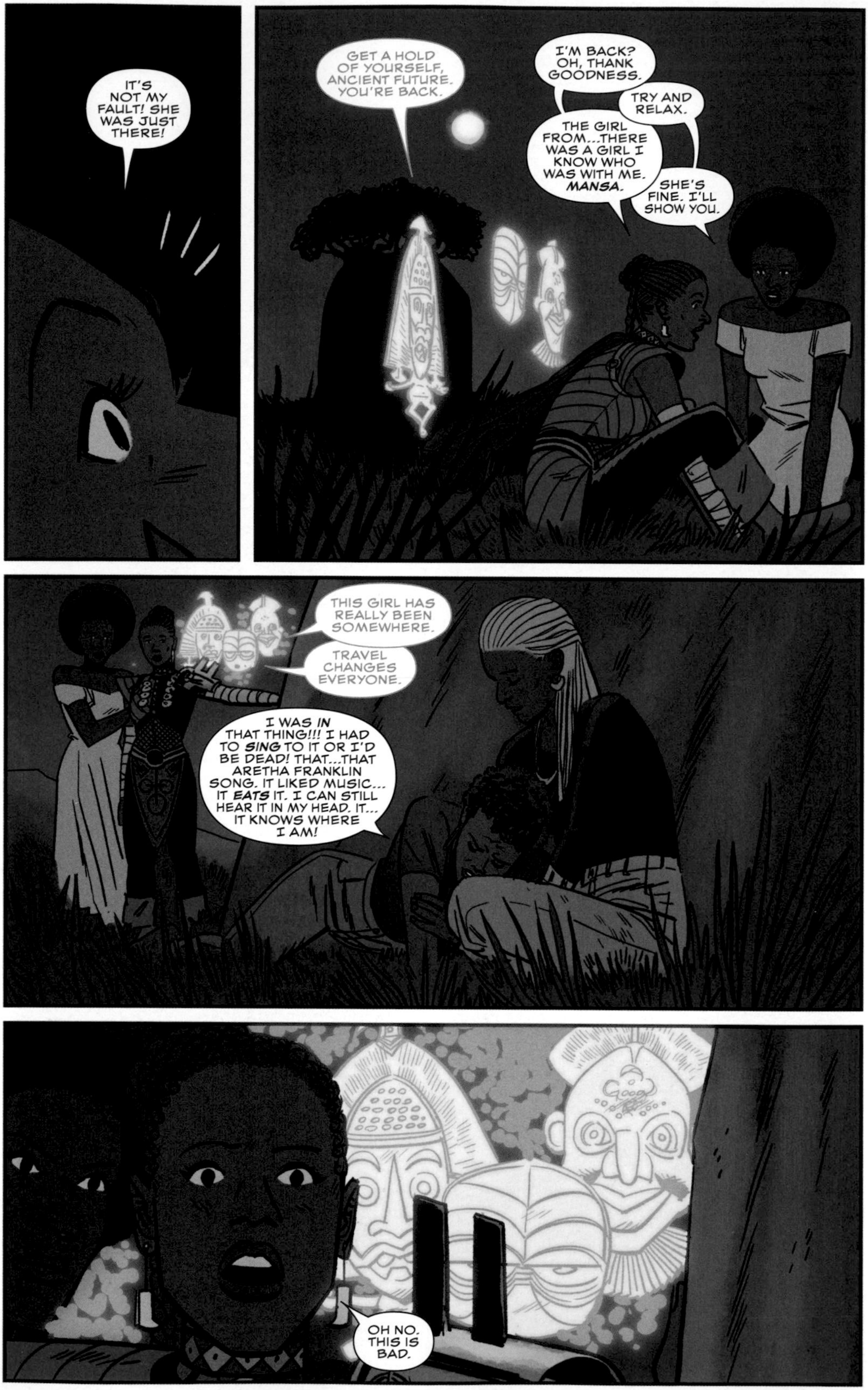
IT'S NOT MY FAULT! SHE WAS JUST THERE!
GET A HOLD OF YOURSELF, ANCIENT FUTURE. YOU'RE BACK.
I'M BACK? OH, THANK GOODNESS.
TRY AND RELAX.
THE GIRL FROM...THERE WAS A GIRL I KNOW WHO WAS WITH ME. MANSA.
SHE'S FINE. I'LL SHOW YOU.
THIS GIRL HAS REALLY BEEN SOMEWHERE.
TRAVEL CHANGES EVERYONE.
I WAS IN THAT THING!!! I HAD TO SING TO IT OR I'D BE DEAD! THAT...THAT ARETHA FRANKLIN SONG. IT LIKED MUSIC... IT EATS IT. I CAN STILL HEAR IT IN MY HEAD. IT... IT KNOWS WHERE I AM!
OH NO. THIS IS BAD.

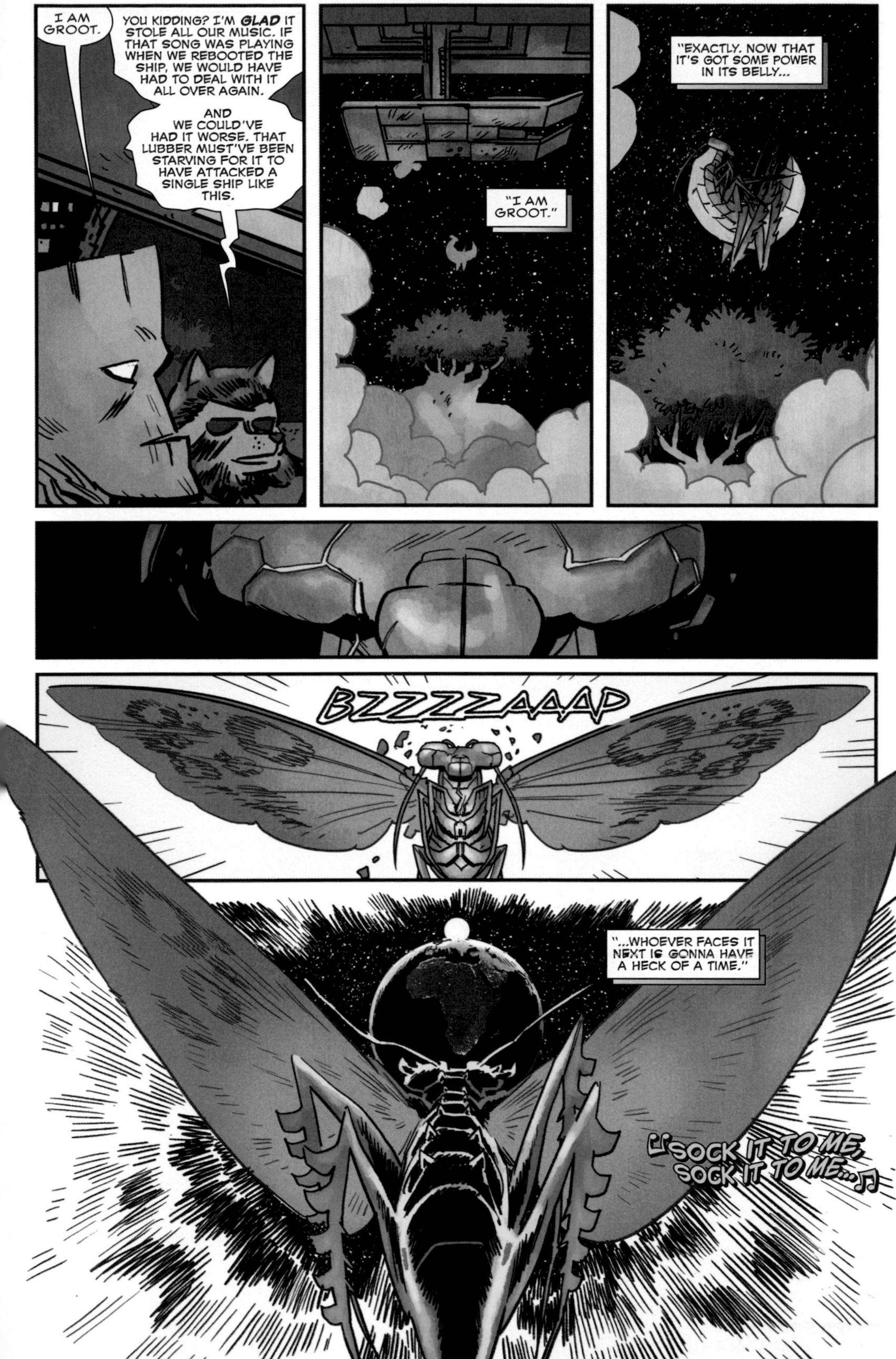
I AM GROOT.
YOU KIDDING? I'M GLAD IT STOLE ALL OUR MUSIC. IF THAT SONG WAS PLAYING WHEN WE REBOOTED THE SHIP, WE WOULD HAVE HAD TO DEAL WITH IT ALL OVER AGAIN.
AND WE COULD'VE HAD IT WORSE. THAT LUBBER MUST'VE BEEN STARVING FOR IT TO HAVE ATTACKED A SINGLE SHIP LIKE THIS.
"I AM GROOT."
"EXACTLY. NOW THAT IT'S GOT SOME POWER IN ITS BELLY...
BZZZZZAAAP
"...WHOEVER FACES IT NEXT IS GONNA HAVE A HECK OF A TIME."
♫SOCK IT TO ME, SOCK IT TO ME...♫

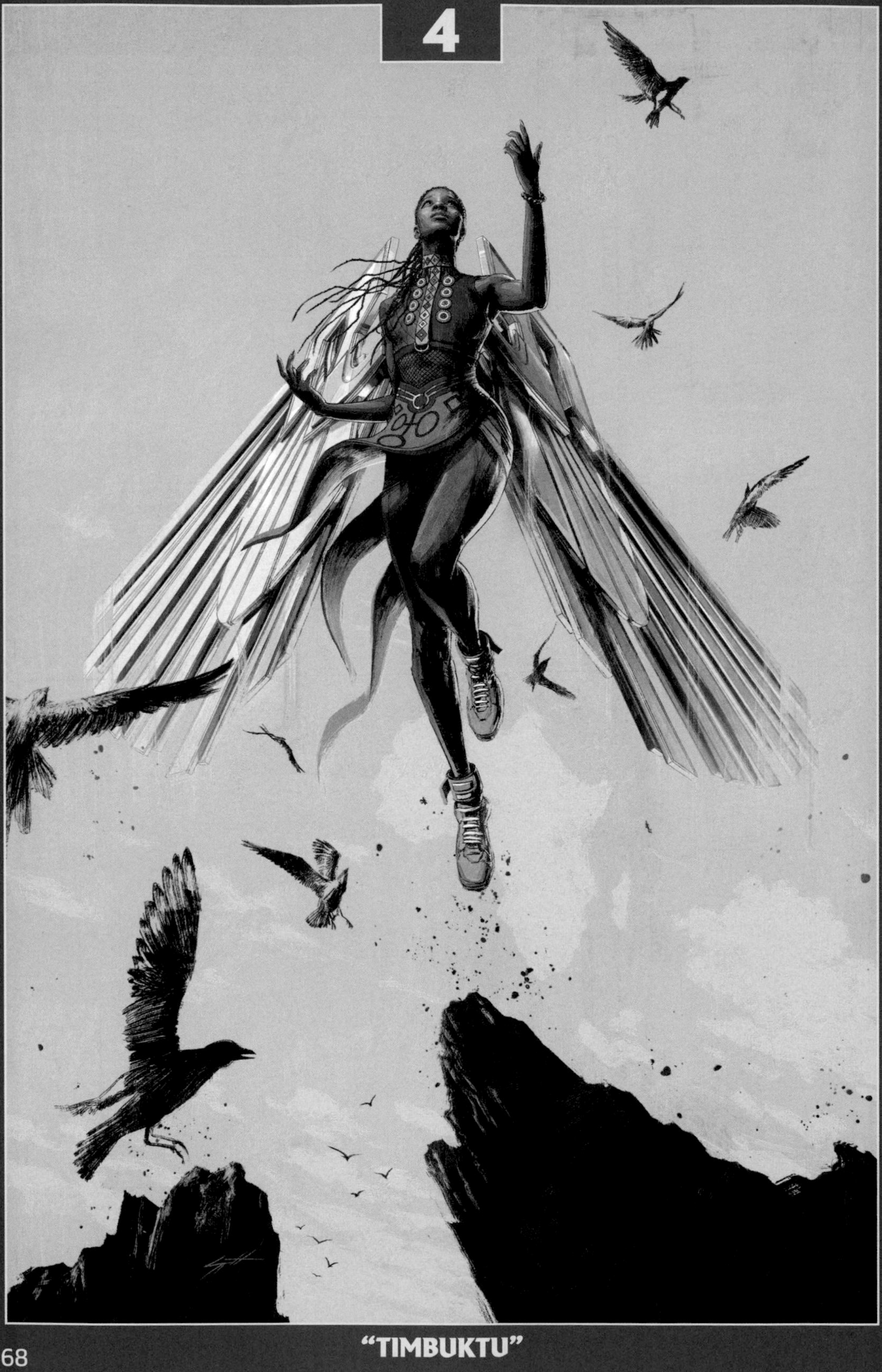
4

"TIMBUKTU"

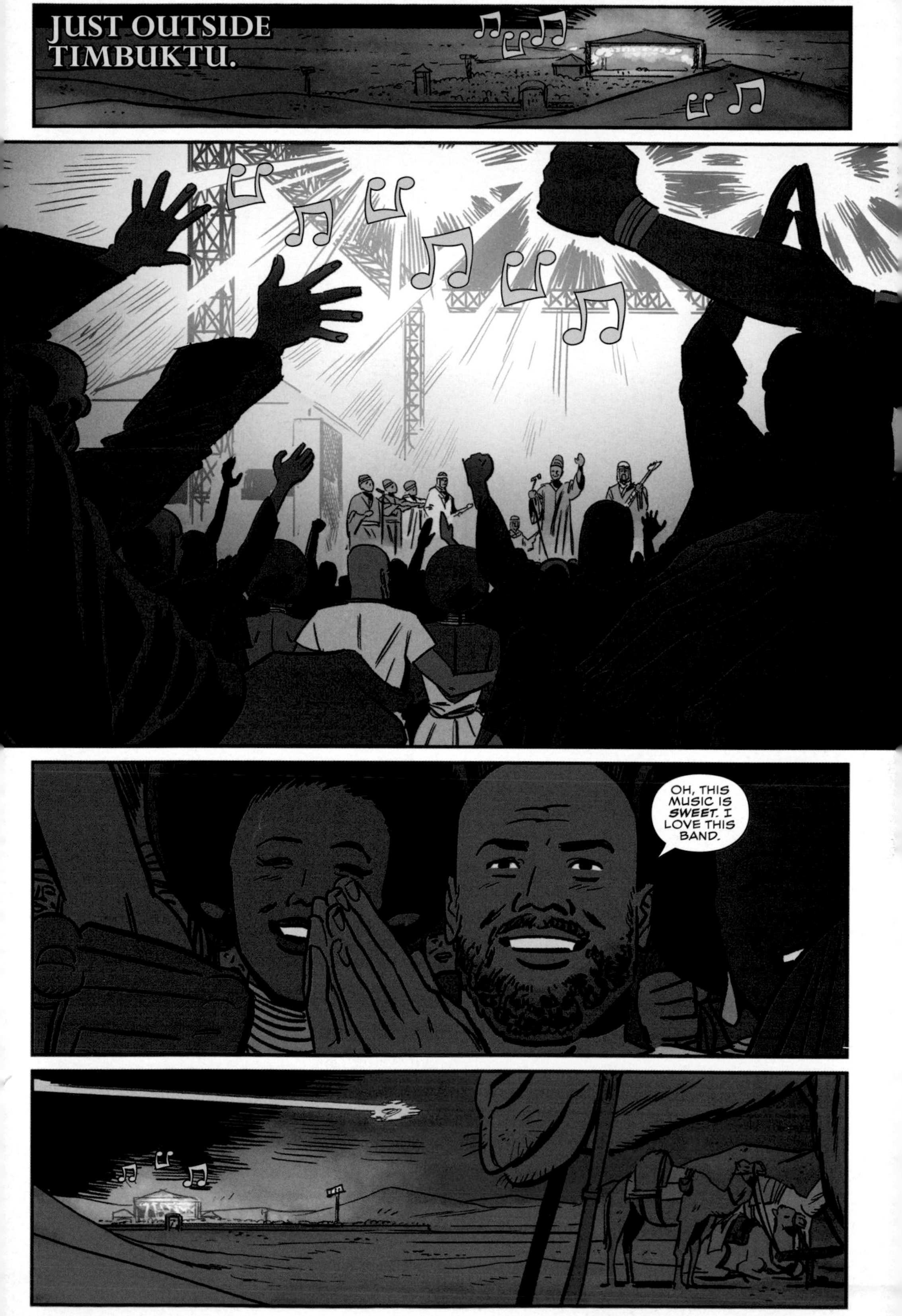
JUST OUTSIDE TIMBUKTU.
OH, THIS MUSIC IS SWEET. I LOVE THIS BAND.

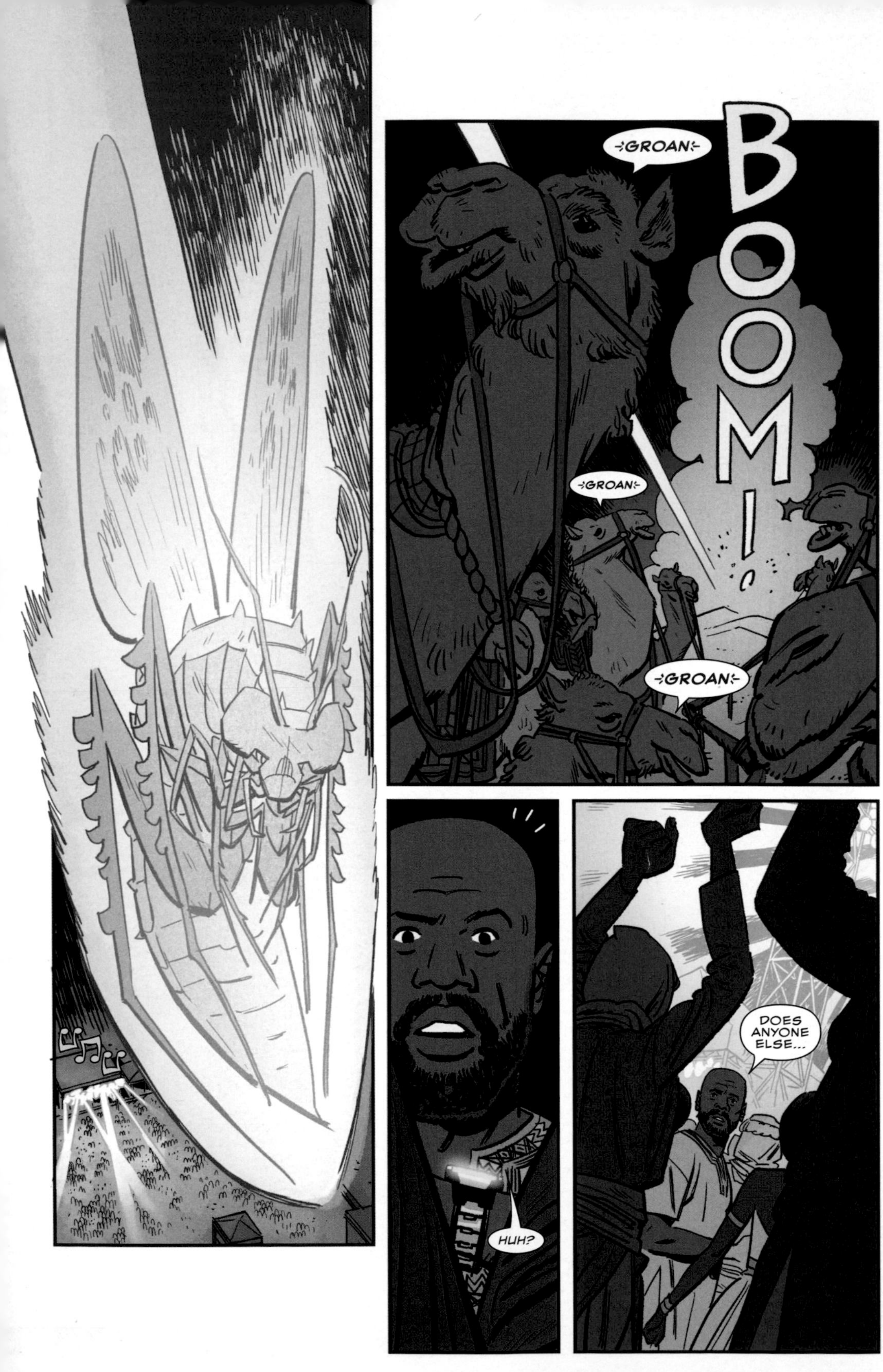
GROAN
BOOM!
GROAN
GROAN
HUH?
DOES ANYONE ELSE...

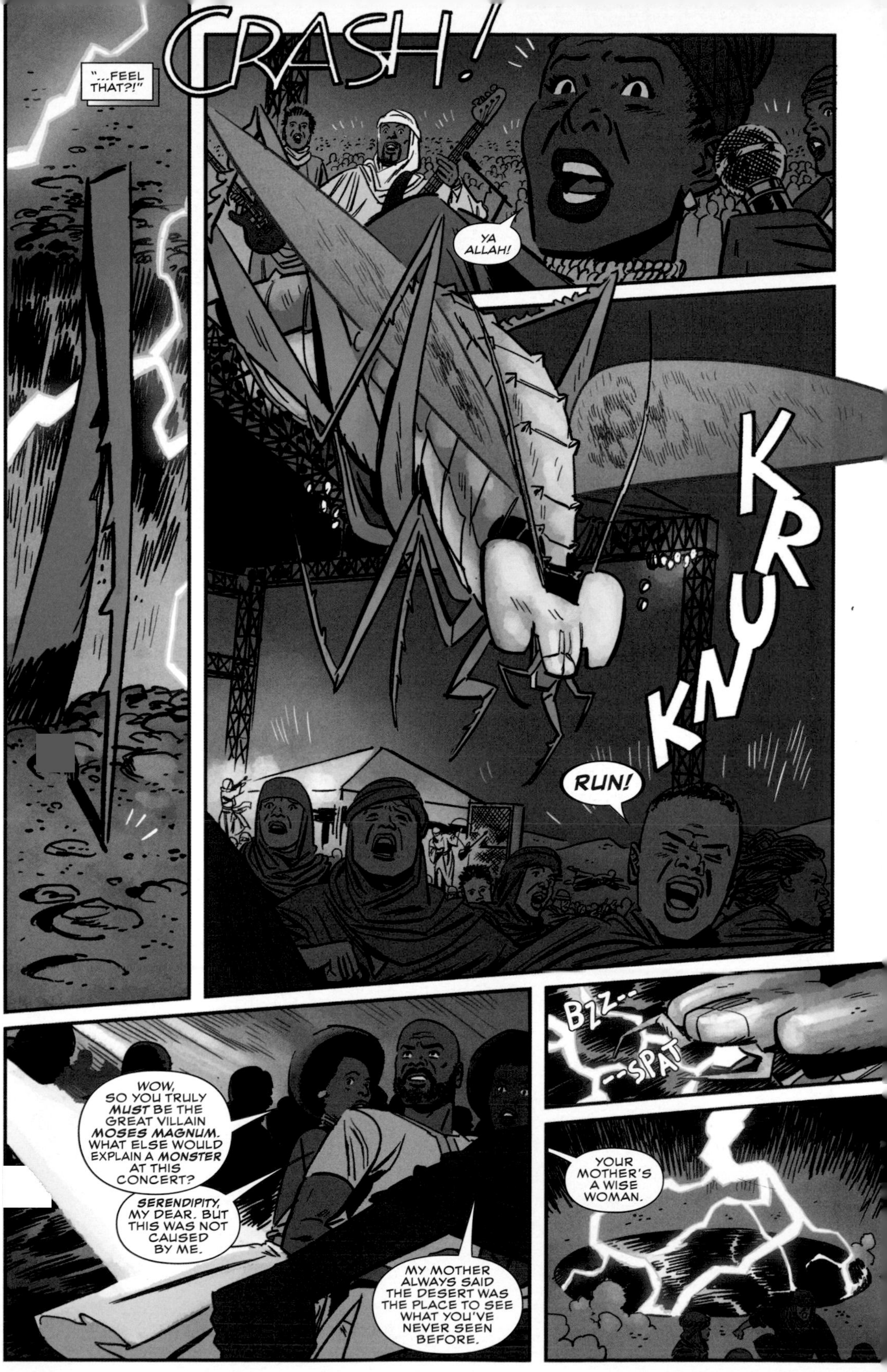
"...FEEL THAT?!"
CRASH!
YA ALLAH!
KRUNK
RUN!
WOW, SO YOU TRULY MUST BE THE GREAT VILLAIN MOSES MAGNUM. WHAT ELSE WOULD EXPLAIN A MONSTER AT THIS CONCERT?
SERENDIPITY, MY DEAR. BUT THIS WAS NOT CAUSED BY ME.
MY MOTHER ALWAYS SAID THE DESERT WAS THE PLACE TO SEE WHAT YOU'VE NEVER SEEN BEFORE.
BZZ--
--SPAT
YOUR MOTHER'S A WISE WOMAN.

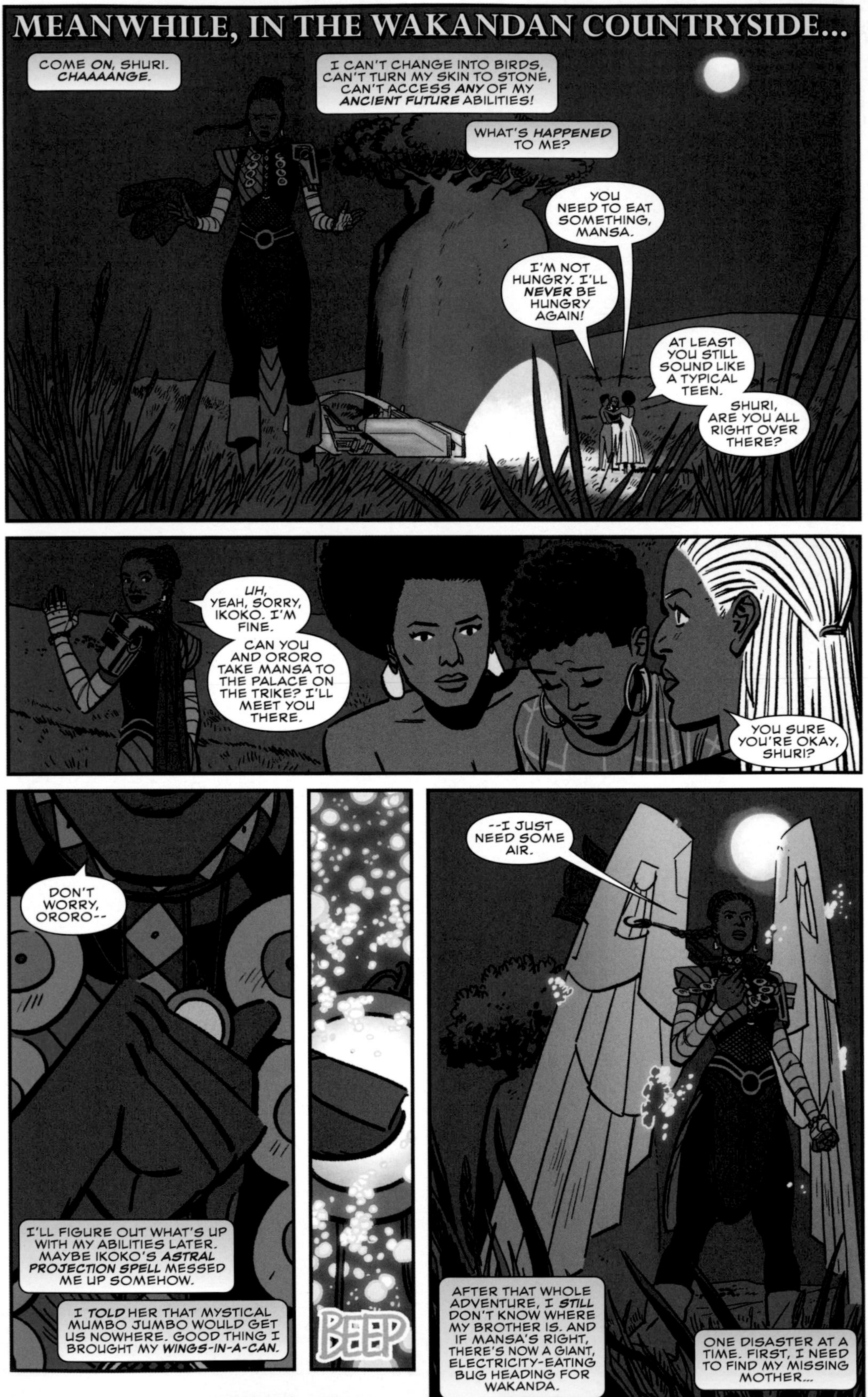
MEANWHILE, IN THE WAKANDAN COUNTRYSIDE...
COME ON, SHURI. CHAAAAANGE.
I CAN'T CHANGE INTO BIRDS, CAN'T TURN MY SKIN TO STONE, CAN'T ACCESS ANY OF MY ANCIENT FUTURE ABILITIES!
WHAT'S HAPPENED TO ME?
YOU NEED TO EAT SOMETHING, MANSA.
I'M NOT HUNGRY. I'LL NEVER BE HUNGRY AGAIN!
AT LEAST YOU STILL SOUND LIKE A TYPICAL TEEN.
SHURI, ARE YOU ALL RIGHT OVER THERE?
UH, YEAH, SORRY, IKOKO. I'M FINE.
CAN YOU AND ORORO TAKE MANSA TO THE PALACE ON THE TRIKE? I'LL MEET YOU THERE.
YOU SURE YOU'RE OKAY, SHURI?
DON'T WORRY, ORORO--
I'LL FIGURE OUT WHAT'S UP WITH MY ABILITIES LATER. MAYBE IKOKO'S ASTRAL PROJECTION SPELL MESSED ME UP SOMEHOW.
I TOLD HER THAT MYSTICAL MUMBO JUMBO WOULD GET US NOWHERE. GOOD THING I BROUGHT MY WINGS-IN-A-CAN.
BEEP
--I JUST NEED SOME AIR.
AFTER THAT WHOLE ADVENTURE, I STILL DON'T KNOW WHERE MY BROTHER IS. AND IF MANSA'S RIGHT, THERE'S NOW A GIANT, ELECTRICITY-EATING BUG HEADING FOR WAKANDA.
ONE DISASTER AT A TIME. FIRST, I NEED TO FIND MY MISSING MOTHER...

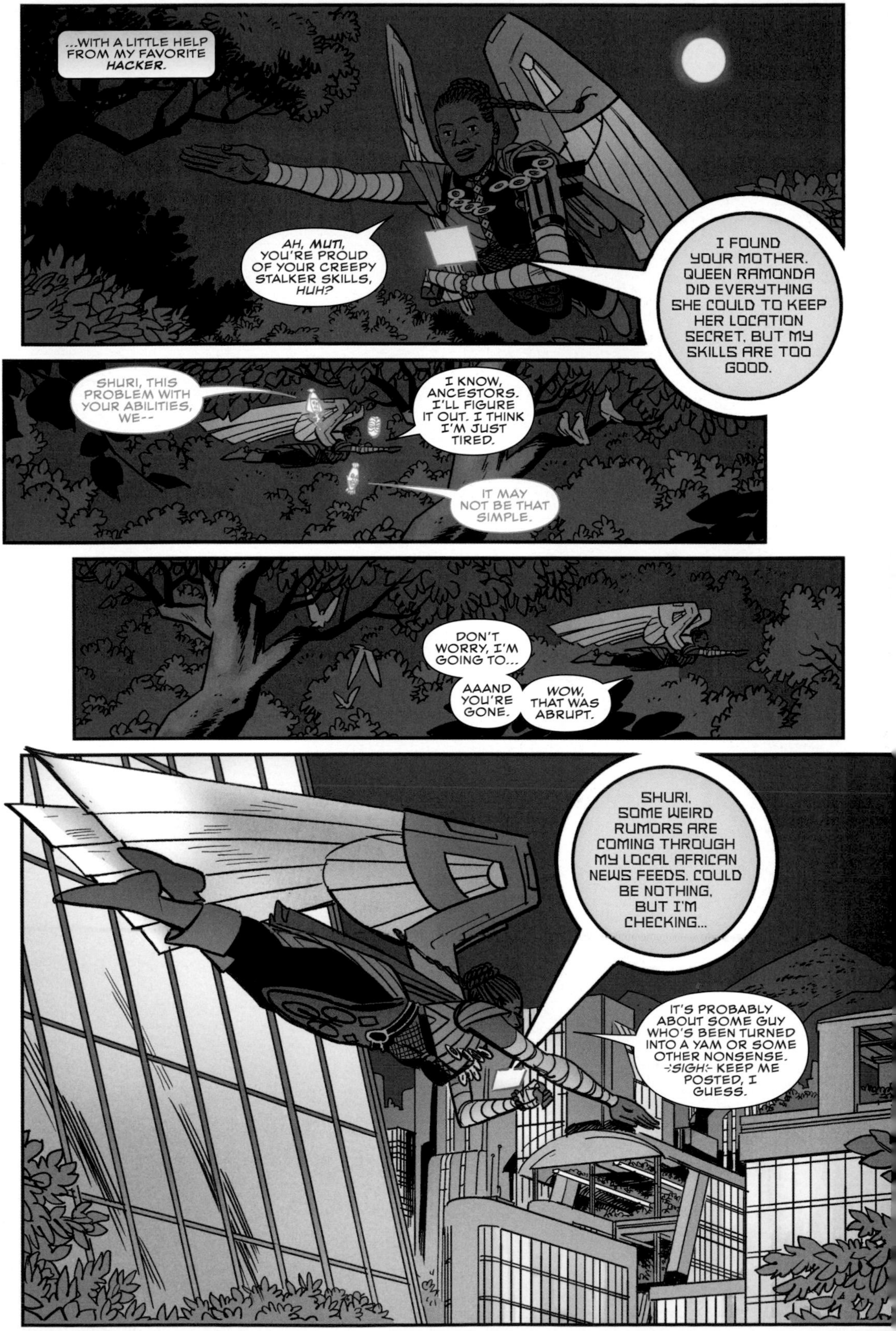
...WITH A LITTLE HELP FROM MY FAVORITE HACKER.
I FOUND YOUR MOTHER. QUEEN RAMONDA DID EVERYTHING SHE COULD TO KEEP HER LOCATION SECRET, BUT MY SKILLS ARE TOO GOOD.
AH, MUTI, YOU'RE PROUD OF YOUR CREEPY STALKER SKILLS, HUH?
SHURI, THIS PROBLEM WITH YOUR ABILITIES, WE--
I KNOW, ANCESTORS. I'LL FIGURE IT OUT. I THINK I'M JUST TIRED.
IT MAY NOT BE THAT SIMPLE.
DON'T WORRY, I'M GOING TO...
AAAND YOU'RE GONE.
WOW, THAT WAS ABRUPT.
SHURI, SOME WEIRD RUMORS ARE COMING THROUGH MY LOCAL AFRICAN NEWS FEEDS. COULD BE NOTHING, BUT I'M CHECKING...
IT'S PROBABLY ABOUT SOME GUY WHO'S BEEN TURNED INTO A YAM OR SOME OTHER NONSENSE. -SIGH- KEEP ME POSTED, I GUESS.

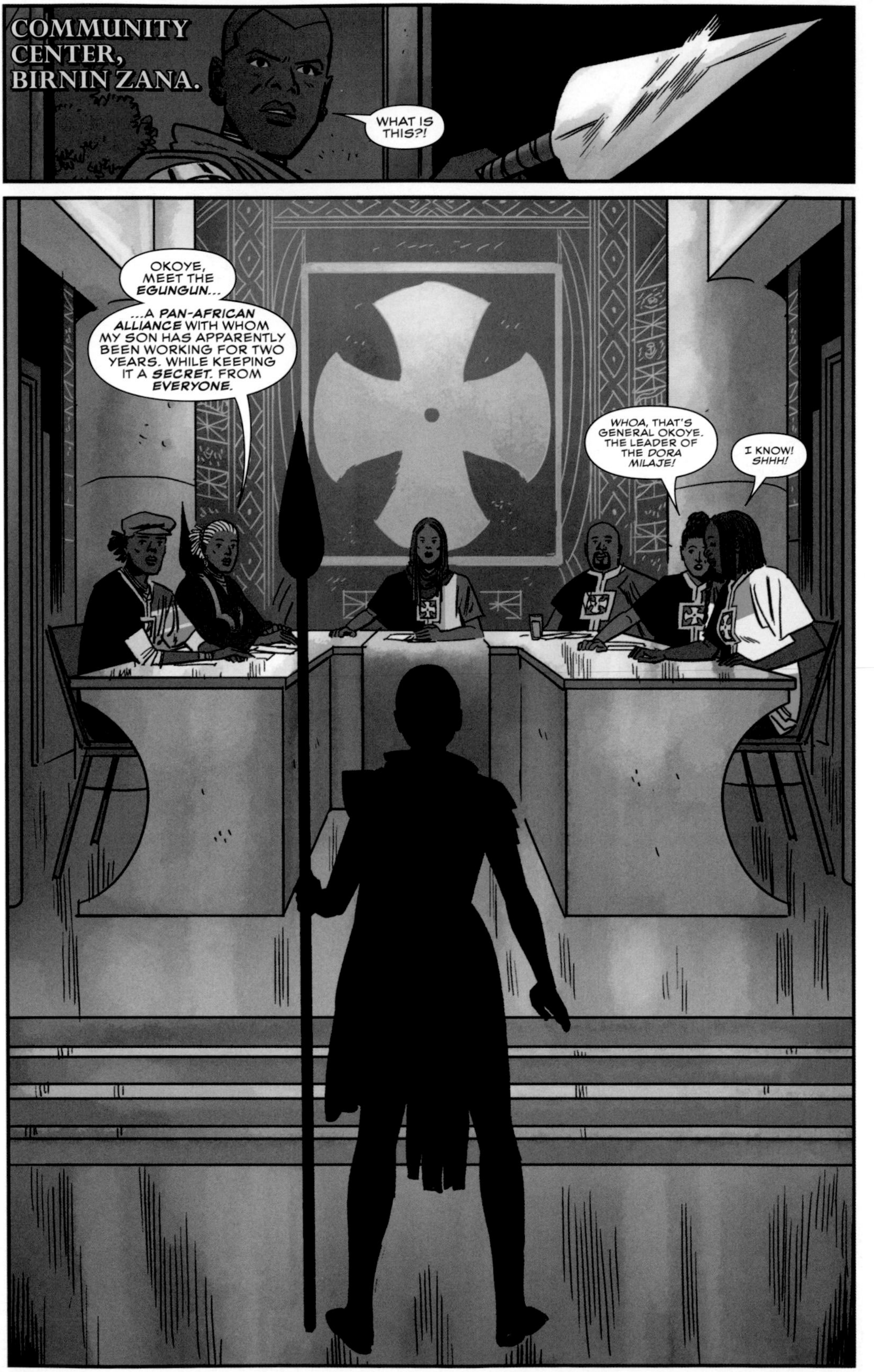
COMMUNITY CENTER, BIRNIN ZANA.
WHAT IS THIS?!
OKOYE, MEET THE EGUNGUN...
...A PAN-AFRICAN ALLIANCE WITH WHOM MY SON HAS APPARENTLY BEEN WORKING FOR TWO YEARS. WHILE KEEPING IT A SECRET. FROM EVERYONE.
WHOA, THAT'S GENERAL OKOYE. THE LEADER OF THE DORA MILAJE!
I KNOW! SHHH!

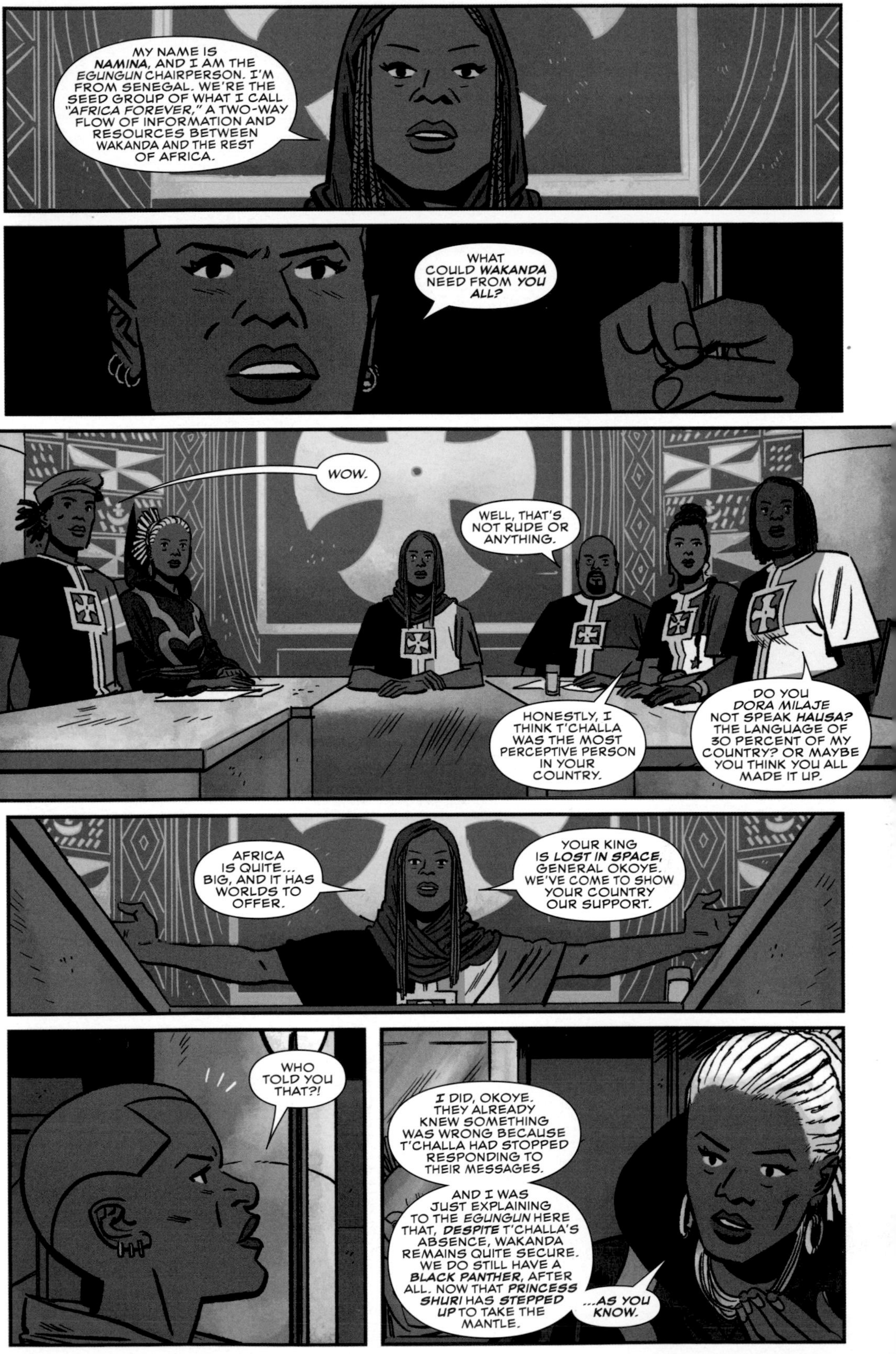

MY NAME IS NAMINA, AND I AM THE EGUNGUN CHAIRPERSON. I'M FROM SENEGAL. WE'RE THE SEED GROUP OF WHAT I CALL "AFRICA FOREVER," A TWO-WAY FLOW OF INFORMATION AND RESOURCES BETWEEN WAKANDA AND THE REST OF AFRICA.
WHAT COULD WAKANDA NEED FROM YOU ALL?
WOW.
WELL, THAT'S NOT RUDE OR ANYTHING.
HONESTLY, I THINK T'CHALLA WAS THE MOST PERCEPTIVE PERSON IN YOUR COUNTRY.
DO YOU DORA MILAJE NOT SPEAK HAUSA? THE LANGUAGE OF 30 PERCENT OF MY COUNTRY? OR MAYBE YOU THINK YOU ALL MADE IT UP.
AFRICA IS QUITE... BIG, AND IT HAS WORLDS TO OFFER.
YOUR KING IS LOST IN SPACE, GENERAL OKOYE. WE'VE COME TO SHOW YOUR COUNTRY OUR SUPPORT.
WHO TOLD YOU THAT?!
I DID, OKOYE. THEY ALREADY KNEW SOMETHING WAS WRONG BECAUSE T'CHALLA HAD STOPPED RESPONDING TO THEIR MESSAGES.
AND I WAS JUST EXPLAINING TO THE EGUNGUN HERE THAT, DESPITE T'CHALLA'S ABSENCE, WAKANDA REMAINS QUITE SECURE. WE DO STILL HAVE A BLACK PANTHER, AFTER ALL. NOW THAT PRINCESS SHURI HAS STEPPED UP TO TAKE THE MANTLE.
...AS YOU KNOW.

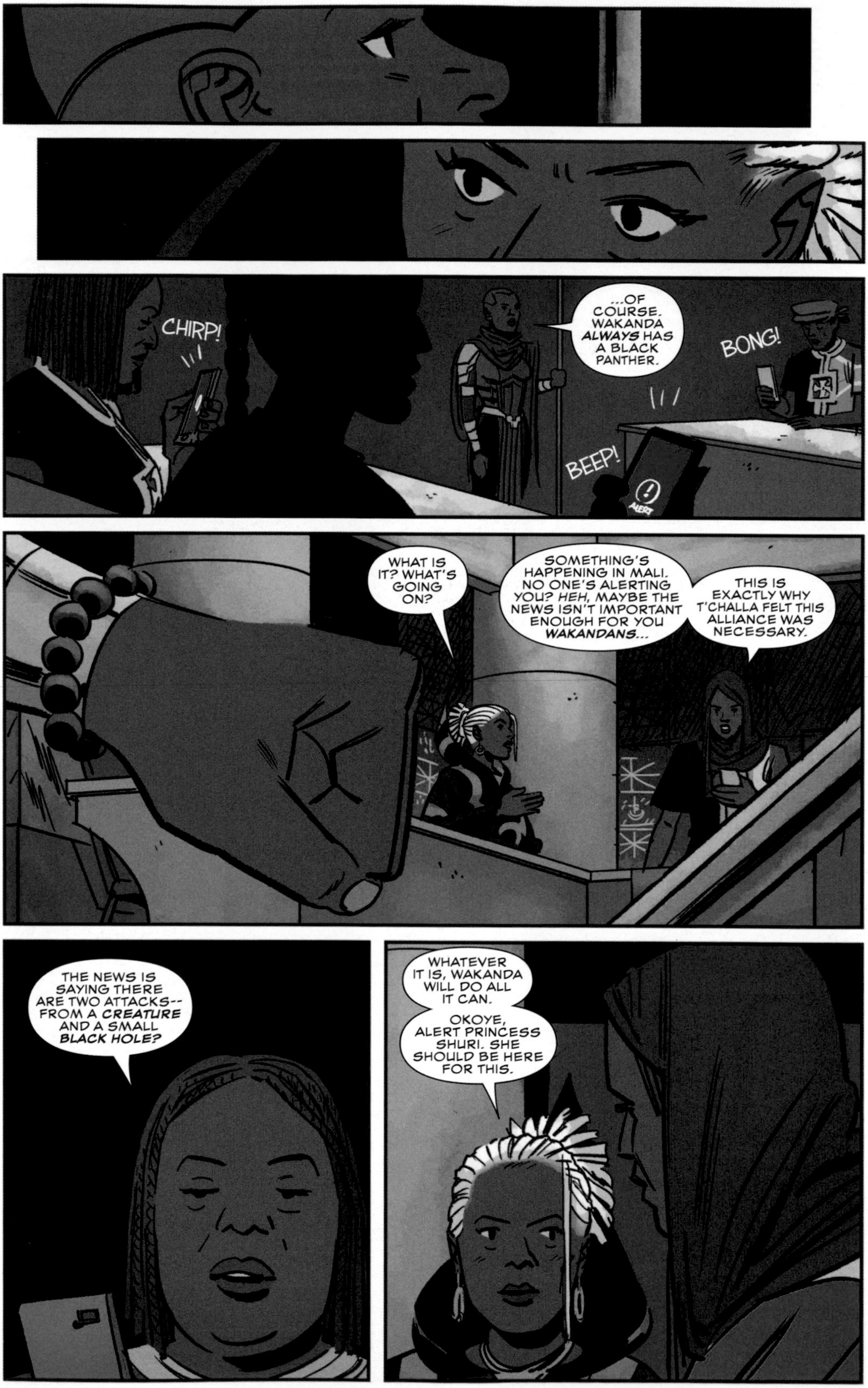
CHIRP!
...OF COURSE. WAKANDA ALWAYS HAS A BLACK PANTHER.
BONG!
BEEP!
WHAT IS IT? WHAT'S GOING ON?
SOMETHING'S HAPPENING IN MALI. NO ONE'S ALERTING YOU? HEH, MAYBE THE NEWS ISN'T IMPORTANT ENOUGH FOR YOU WAKANDANS...
THIS IS EXACTLY WHY T'CHALLA FELT THIS ALLIANCE WAS NECESSARY.
THE NEWS IS SAYING THERE ARE TWO ATTACKS--FROM A CREATURE AND A SMALL BLACK HOLE?
WHATEVER IT IS, WAKANDA WILL DO ALL IT CAN.
OKOYE, ALERT PRINCESS SHURI. SHE SHOULD BE HERE FOR THIS.

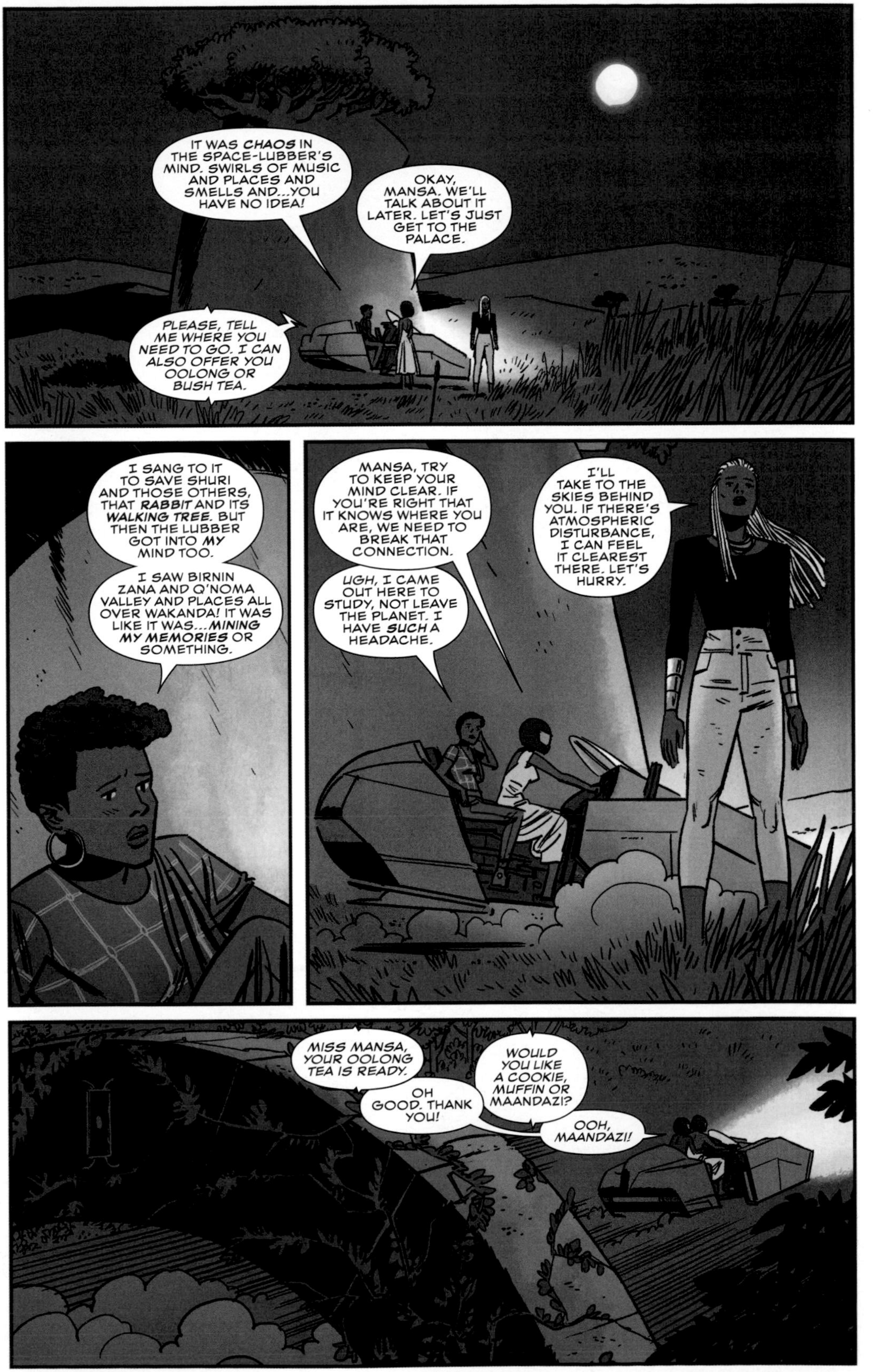
IT WAS *CHAOS* IN THE SPACE-LUBBER'S MIND. SWIRLS OF MUSIC AND PLACES AND SMELLS AND...YOU HAVE NO IDEA!
OKAY, MANSA. WE'LL TALK ABOUT IT LATER. LET'S JUST GET TO THE PALACE.
PLEASE, TELL ME WHERE YOU NEED TO GO. I CAN ALSO OFFER YOU OOLONG OR BUSH TEA.
I SANG TO IT TO SAVE SHURI AND THOSE OTHERS, THAT *RABBIT* AND ITS *WALKING TREE*. BUT THEN THE LUBBER GOT INTO *MY* MIND TOO.
I SAW BIRNIN ZANA AND Q'NOMA VALLEY AND PLACES ALL OVER WAKANDA! IT WAS LIKE IT WAS...*MINING MY MEMORIES* OR SOMETHING.
MANSA, TRY TO KEEP YOUR MIND CLEAR. IF YOU'RE RIGHT THAT IT KNOWS WHERE YOU ARE, WE NEED TO BREAK THAT CONNECTION.
UGH, I CAME OUT HERE TO STUDY, NOT LEAVE THE PLANET. I HAVE *SUCH* A HEADACHE.
I'LL TAKE TO THE SKIES BEHIND YOU. IF THERE'S ATMOSPHERIC DISTURBANCE, I CAN FEEL IT CLEAREST THERE. LET'S HURRY.
MISS MANSA, YOUR OOLONG TEA IS READY.
OH GOOD. THANK YOU!
WOULD YOU LIKE A COOKIE, MUFFIN OR MAANDAZI?
OOH, MAANDAZI!

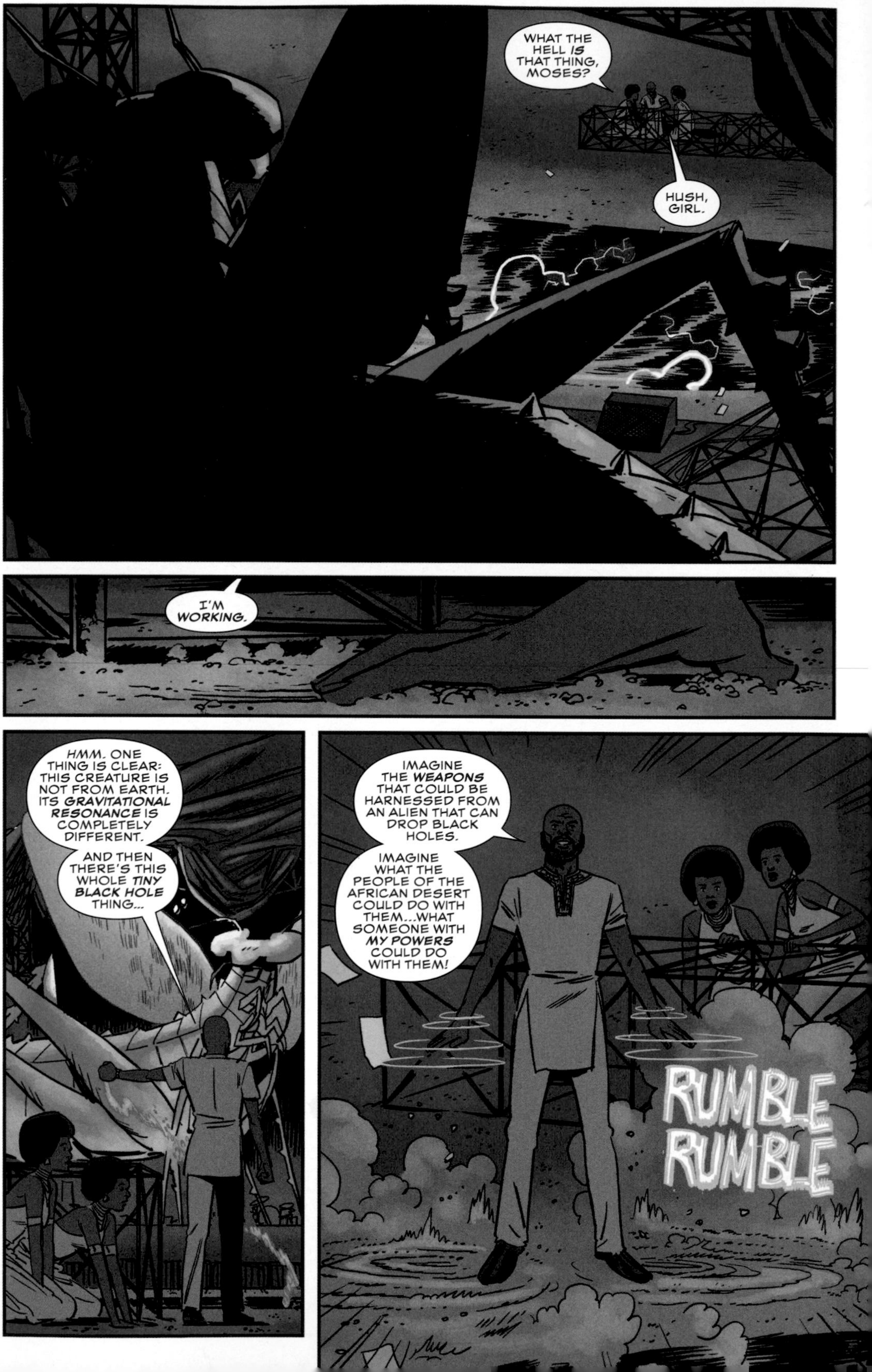
WHAT THE HELL *IS* THAT THING, MOSES?
HUSH, GIRL.
I'M *WORKING.*
HMM. ONE THING IS CLEAR: THIS CREATURE IS NOT FROM EARTH. ITS **GRAVITATIONAL RESONANCE** IS COMPLETELY DIFFERENT.
AND THEN THERE'S THIS WHOLE *TINY BLACK HOLE* THING...
IMAGINE THE **WEAPONS** THAT COULD BE HARNESSED FROM AN ALIEN THAT CAN DROP BLACK HOLES.
IMAGINE WHAT THE PEOPLE OF THE AFRICAN DESERT COULD DO WITH THEM...WHAT SOMEONE WITH **MY POWERS** COULD DO WITH THEM!
RUMBLE RUMBLE

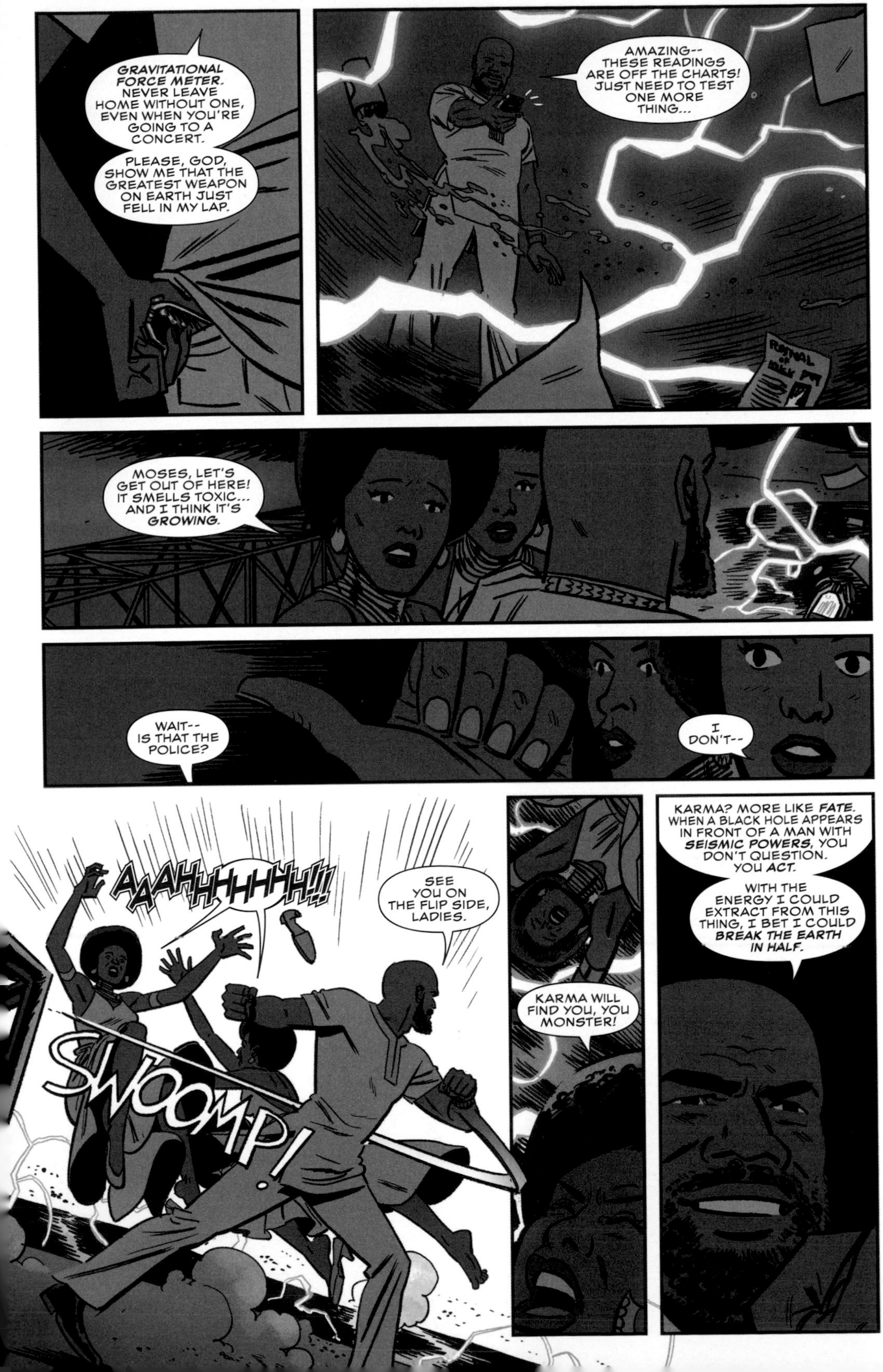

GRAVITATIONAL FORCE METER. NEVER LEAVE HOME WITHOUT ONE, EVEN WHEN YOU'RE GOING TO A CONCERT.
PLEASE, GOD, SHOW ME THAT THE GREATEST WEAPON ON EARTH JUST FELL IN MY LAP.
AMAZING-- THESE READINGS ARE OFF THE CHARTS! JUST NEED TO TEST ONE MORE THING...
MOSES, LET'S GET OUT OF HERE! IT SMELLS TOXIC... AND I THINK IT'S GROWING.
WAIT-- IS THAT THE POLICE?
I DON'T--
AAAHHHHHH!!!
SEE YOU ON THE FLIP SIDE, LADIES.
SWOOMP!
KARMA WILL FIND YOU, YOU MONSTER!
KARMA? MORE LIKE FATE. WHEN A BLACK HOLE APPEARS IN FRONT OF A MAN WITH SEISMIC POWERS, YOU DON'T QUESTION. YOU ACT.
WITH THE ENERGY I COULD EXTRACT FROM THIS THING, I BET I COULD BREAK THE EARTH IN HALF.

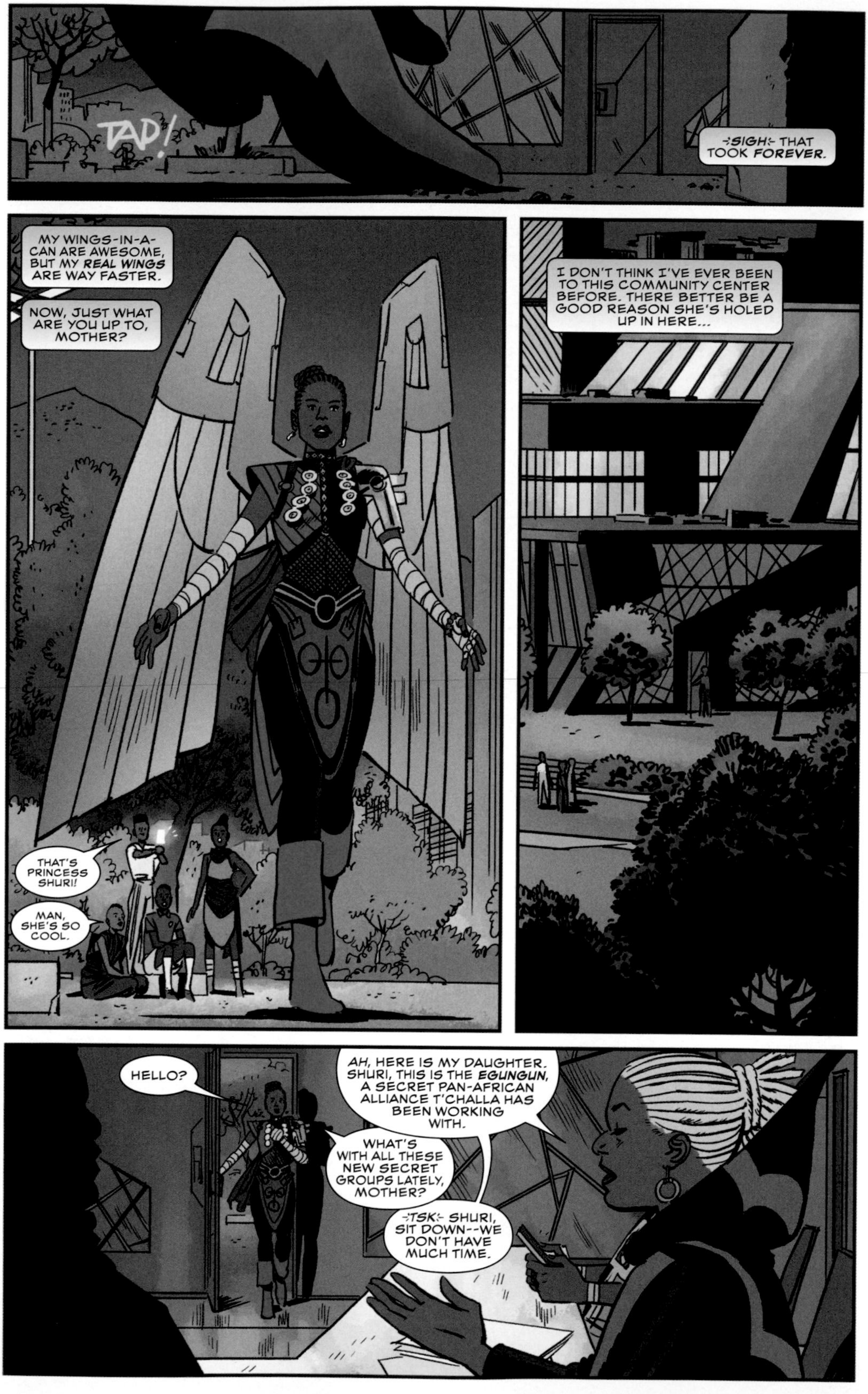
TAP!
-SIGH- THAT TOOK FOREVER.
MY WINGS-IN-A-CAN ARE AWESOME, BUT MY REAL WINGS ARE WAY FASTER.
NOW, JUST WHAT ARE YOU UP TO, MOTHER?
THAT'S PRINCESS SHURI!
MAN, SHE'S SO COOL.
I DON'T THINK I'VE EVER BEEN TO THIS COMMUNITY CENTER BEFORE. THERE BETTER BE A GOOD REASON SHE'S HOLED UP IN HERE...
HELLO?
AH, HERE IS MY DAUGHTER. SHURI, THIS IS THE EGUNGUN, A SECRET PAN-AFRICAN ALLIANCE T'CHALLA HAS BEEN WORKING WITH.
WHAT'S WITH ALL THESE NEW SECRET GROUPS LATELY, MOTHER?
-TSK- SHURI, SIT DOWN--WE DON'T HAVE MUCH TIME.

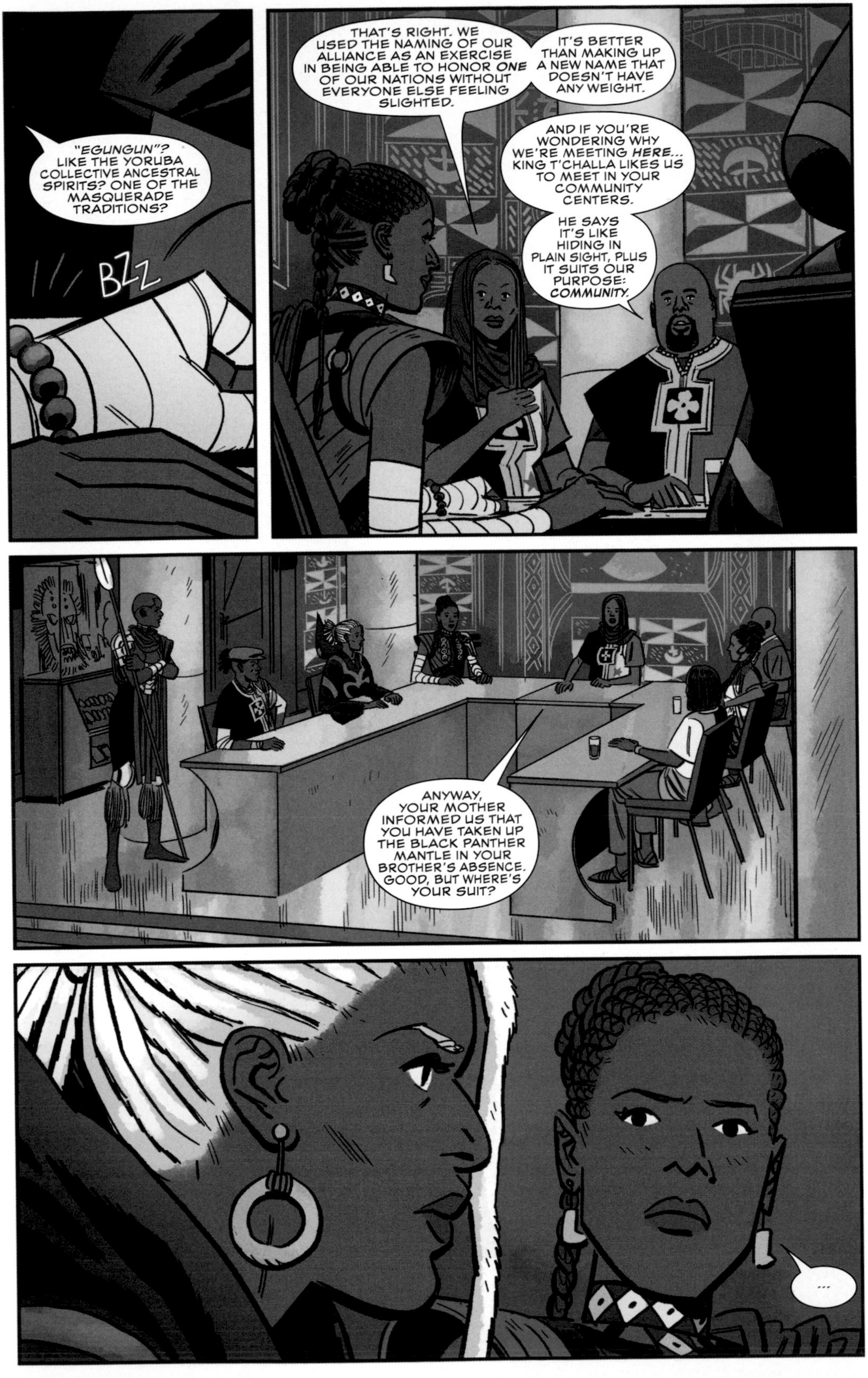
"EGUNGUN"? LIKE THE YORUBA COLLECTIVE ANCESTRAL SPIRITS? ONE OF THE MASQUERADE TRADITIONS?
BZZ
THAT'S RIGHT. WE USED THE NAMING OF OUR ALLIANCE AS AN EXERCISE IN BEING ABLE TO HONOR ONE OF OUR NATIONS WITHOUT EVERYONE ELSE FEELING SLIGHTED.
IT'S BETTER THAN MAKING UP A NEW NAME THAT DOESN'T HAVE ANY WEIGHT.
AND IF YOU'RE WONDERING WHY WE'RE MEETING HERE... KING T'CHALLA LIKES US TO MEET IN YOUR COMMUNITY CENTERS.
HE SAYS IT'S LIKE HIDING IN PLAIN SIGHT, PLUS IT SUITS OUR PURPOSE: COMMUNITY.
ANYWAY, YOUR MOTHER INFORMED US THAT YOU HAVE TAKEN UP THE BLACK PANTHER MANTLE IN YOUR BROTHER'S ABSENCE. GOOD, BUT WHERE'S YOUR SUIT?
...

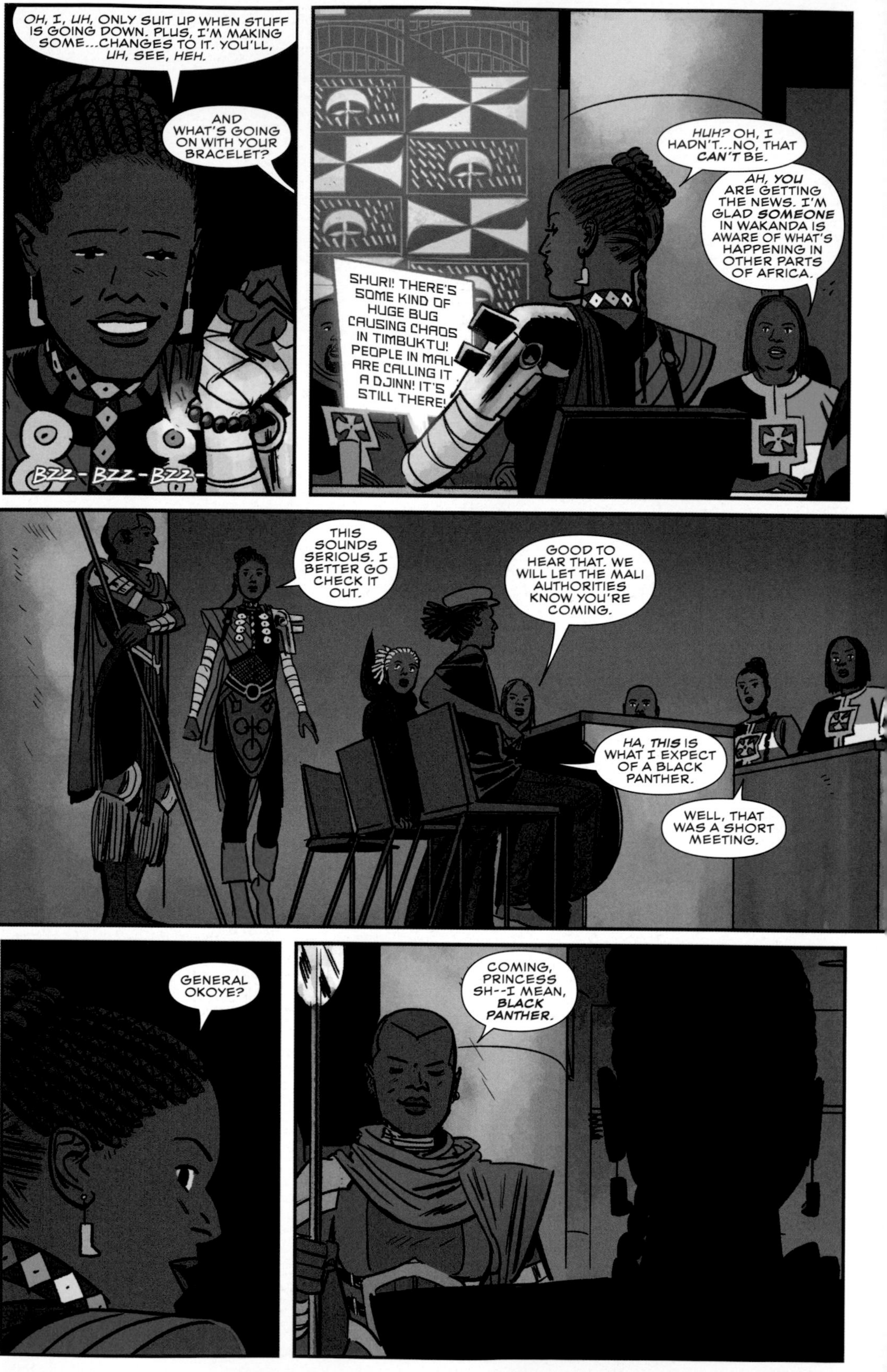
OH, I, UH, ONLY SUIT UP WHEN STUFF IS GOING DOWN. PLUS, I'M MAKING SOME...CHANGES TO IT. YOU'LL, UH, SEE, HEH.
AND WHAT'S GOING ON WITH YOUR BRACELET?
BZZ-BZZ-BZZ-
SHURI! THERE'S SOME KIND OF HUGE BUG CAUSING CHAOS IN TIMBUKTU! PEOPLE IN MALI ARE CALLING IT A DJINN! IT'S STILL THERE!
HUH? OH, I HADN'T...NO, THAT CAN'T BE.
AH, YOU ARE GETTING THE NEWS. I'M GLAD SOMEONE IN WAKANDA IS AWARE OF WHAT'S HAPPENING IN OTHER PARTS OF AFRICA.
THIS SOUNDS SERIOUS. I BETTER GO CHECK IT OUT.
GOOD TO HEAR THAT. WE WILL LET THE MALI AUTHORITIES KNOW YOU'RE COMING.
HA, THIS IS WHAT I EXPECT OF A BLACK PANTHER.
WELL, THAT WAS A SHORT MEETING.
GENERAL OKOYE?
COMING, PRINCESS SH--I MEAN, BLACK PANTHER.

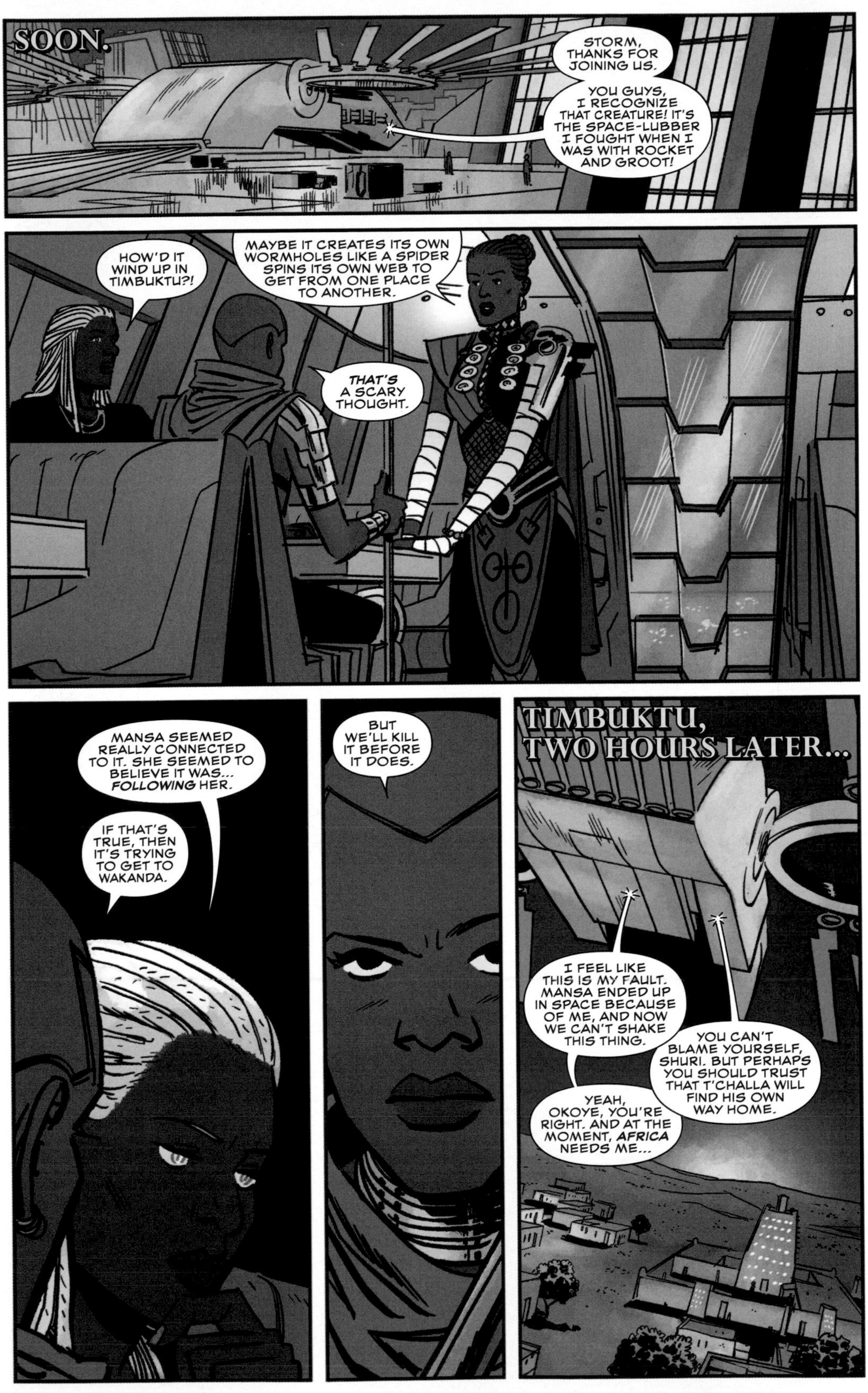
SOON.
STORM, THANKS FOR JOINING US.
YOU GUYS, I RECOGNIZE THAT CREATURE! IT'S THE SPACE-LUBBER I FOUGHT WHEN I WAS WITH ROCKET AND GROOT!
HOW'D IT WIND UP IN TIMBUKTU?!
MAYBE IT CREATES ITS OWN WORMHOLES LIKE A SPIDER SPINS ITS OWN WEB TO GET FROM ONE PLACE TO ANOTHER.
THAT'S A SCARY THOUGHT.
MANSA SEEMED REALLY CONNECTED TO IT. SHE SEEMED TO BELIEVE IT WAS... FOLLOWING HER.
IF THAT'S TRUE, THEN IT'S TRYING TO GET TO WAKANDA.
BUT WE'LL KILL IT BEFORE IT DOES.
TIMBUKTU, TWO HOURS LATER...
I FEEL LIKE THIS IS MY FAULT. MANSA ENDED UP IN SPACE BECAUSE OF ME, AND NOW WE CAN'T SHAKE THIS THING.
YOU CAN'T BLAME YOURSELF, SHURI. BUT PERHAPS YOU SHOULD TRUST THAT T'CHALLA WILL FIND HIS OWN WAY HOME.
YEAH, OKOYE, YOU'RE RIGHT. AND AT THE MOMENT, AFRICA NEEDS ME...

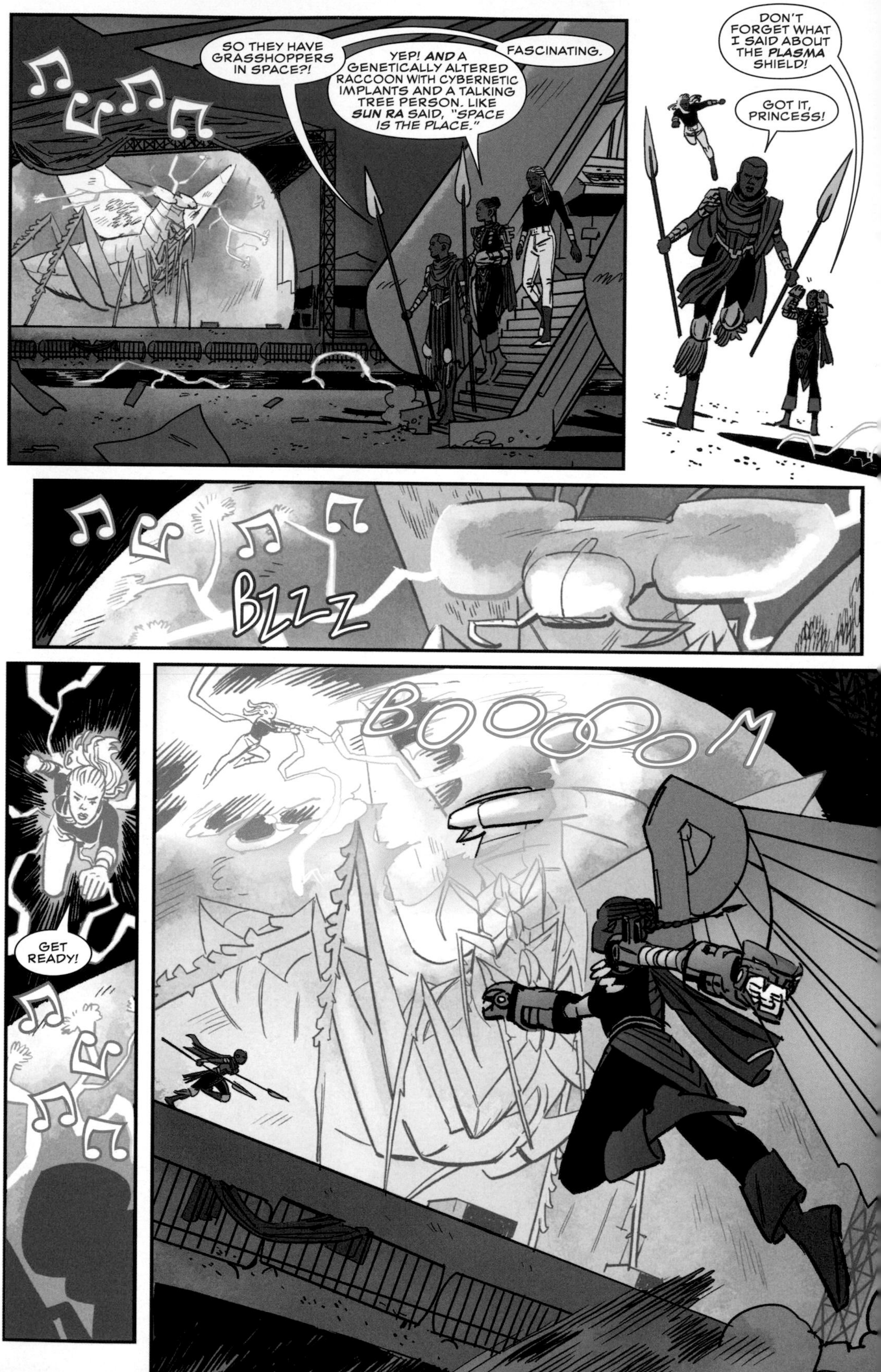
SO THEY HAVE GRASSHOPPERS IN SPACE?!
FASCINATING.
YEP! AND A GENETICALLY ALTERED RACCOON WITH CYBERNETIC IMPLANTS AND A TALKING TREE PERSON. LIKE SUN RA SAID, "SPACE IS THE PLACE."
DON'T FORGET WHAT I SAID ABOUT THE PLASMA SHIELD!
GOT IT, PRINCESS!
BZZZ
GET READY!
BOOOOOM

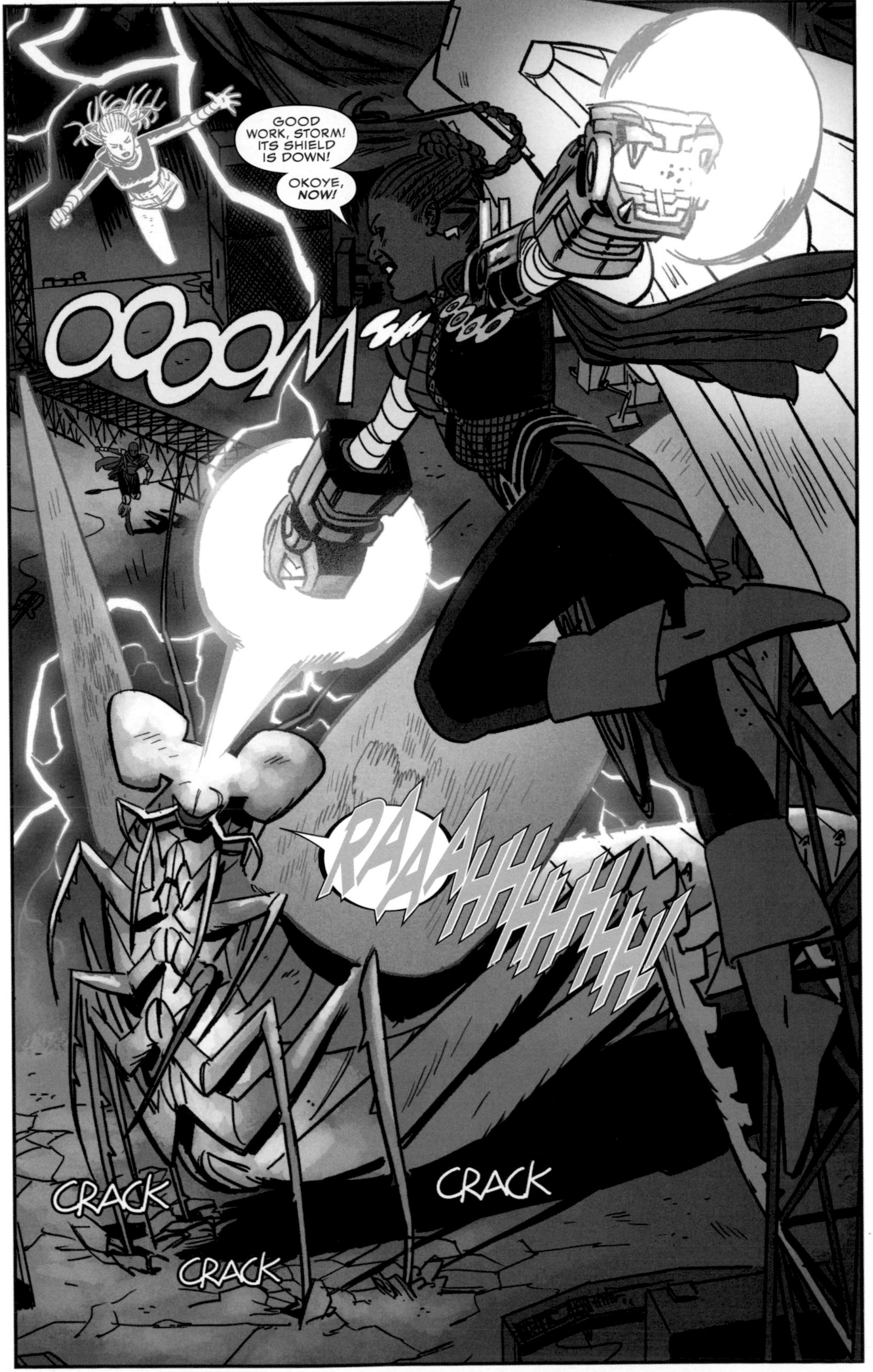
GOOD WORK, STORM! ITS SHIELD IS DOWN!
OKOYE, NOW!
OOOOM
RAAAHHHHHH!
CRACK
CRACK
CRACK

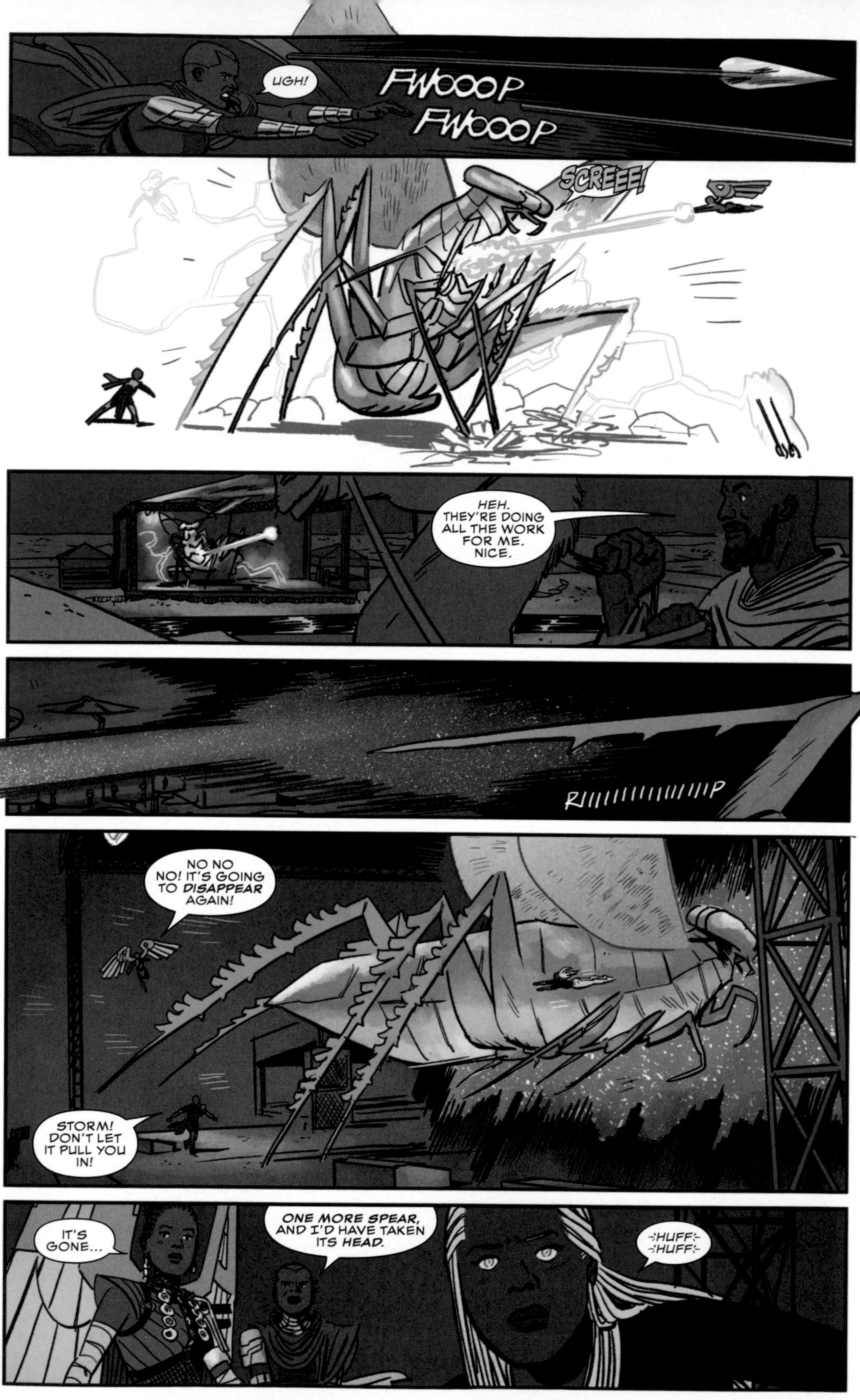
UGH!
FWOOOP
FWOOOP
SCREEE!
HEH. THEY'RE DOING ALL THE WORK FOR ME. NICE.
RIIIIIIIIIIIIIIIP
NO NO NO! IT'S GOING TO DISAPPEAR AGAIN!
STORM! DON'T LET IT PULL YOU IN!
IT'S GONE...
ONE MORE SPEAR, AND I'D HAVE TAKEN ITS HEAD.
HUFF
HUFF

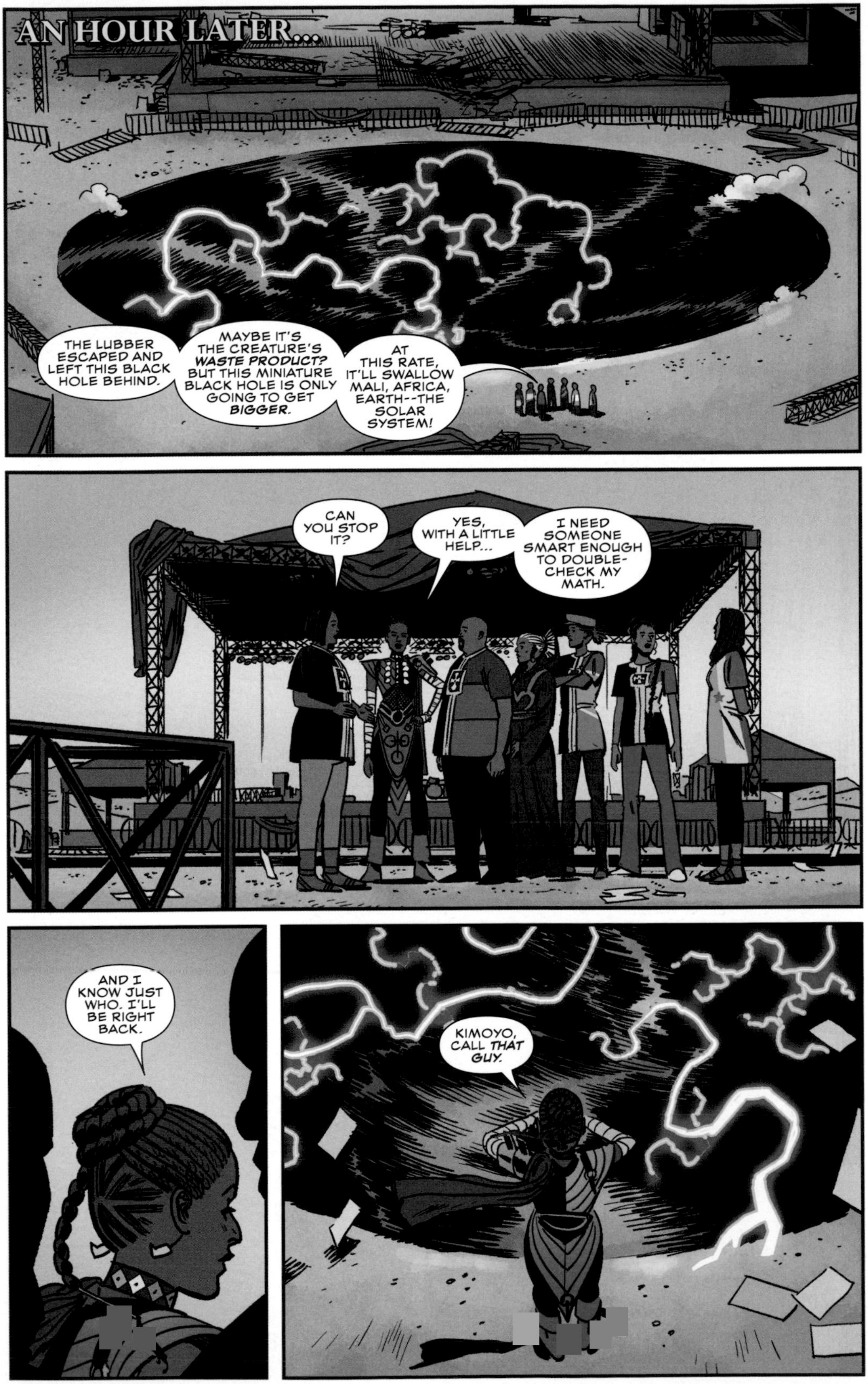
AN HOUR LATER...
THE LUBBER ESCAPED AND LEFT THIS BLACK HOLE BEHIND.
MAYBE IT'S THE CREATURE'S WASTE PRODUCT? BUT THIS MINIATURE BLACK HOLE IS ONLY GOING TO GET BIGGER.
AT THIS RATE, IT'LL SWALLOW MALI, AFRICA, EARTH--THE SOLAR SYSTEM!
CAN YOU STOP IT?
YES, WITH A LITTLE HELP...
I NEED SOMEONE SMART ENOUGH TO DOUBLE-CHECK MY MATH.
AND I KNOW JUST WHO. I'LL BE RIGHT BACK.
KIMOYO, CALL THAT GUY.

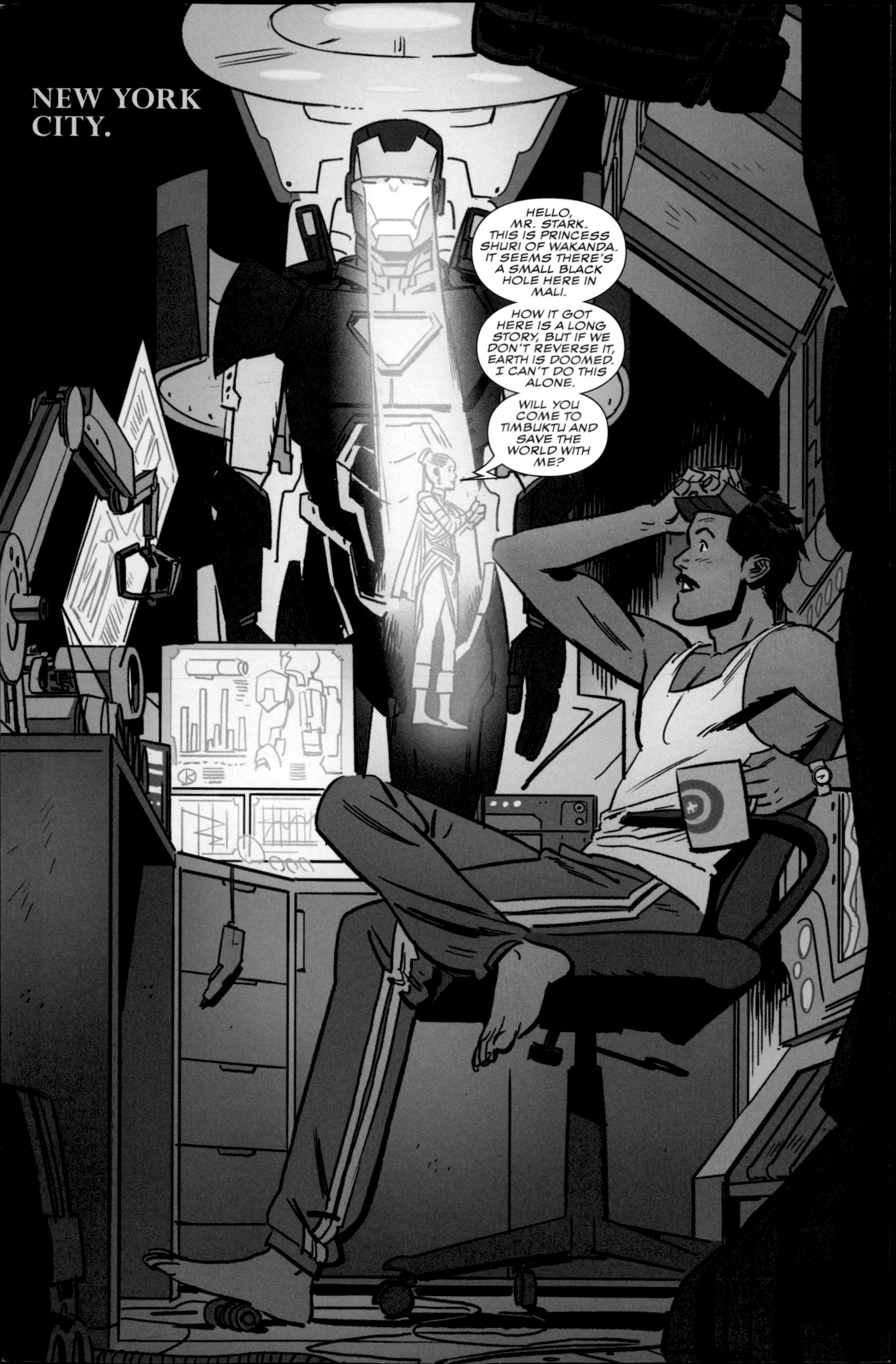
NEW YORK CITY.
HELLO, MR. STARK. THIS IS PRINCESS SHURI OF WAKANDA. IT SEEMS THERE'S A SMALL BLACK HOLE HERE IN MALI.
HOW IT GOT HERE IS A LONG STORY, BUT IF WE DON'T REVERSE IT, EARTH IS DOOMED. I CAN'T DO THIS ALONE.
WILL YOU COME TO TIMBUKTU AND SAVE THE WORLD WITH ME?

5

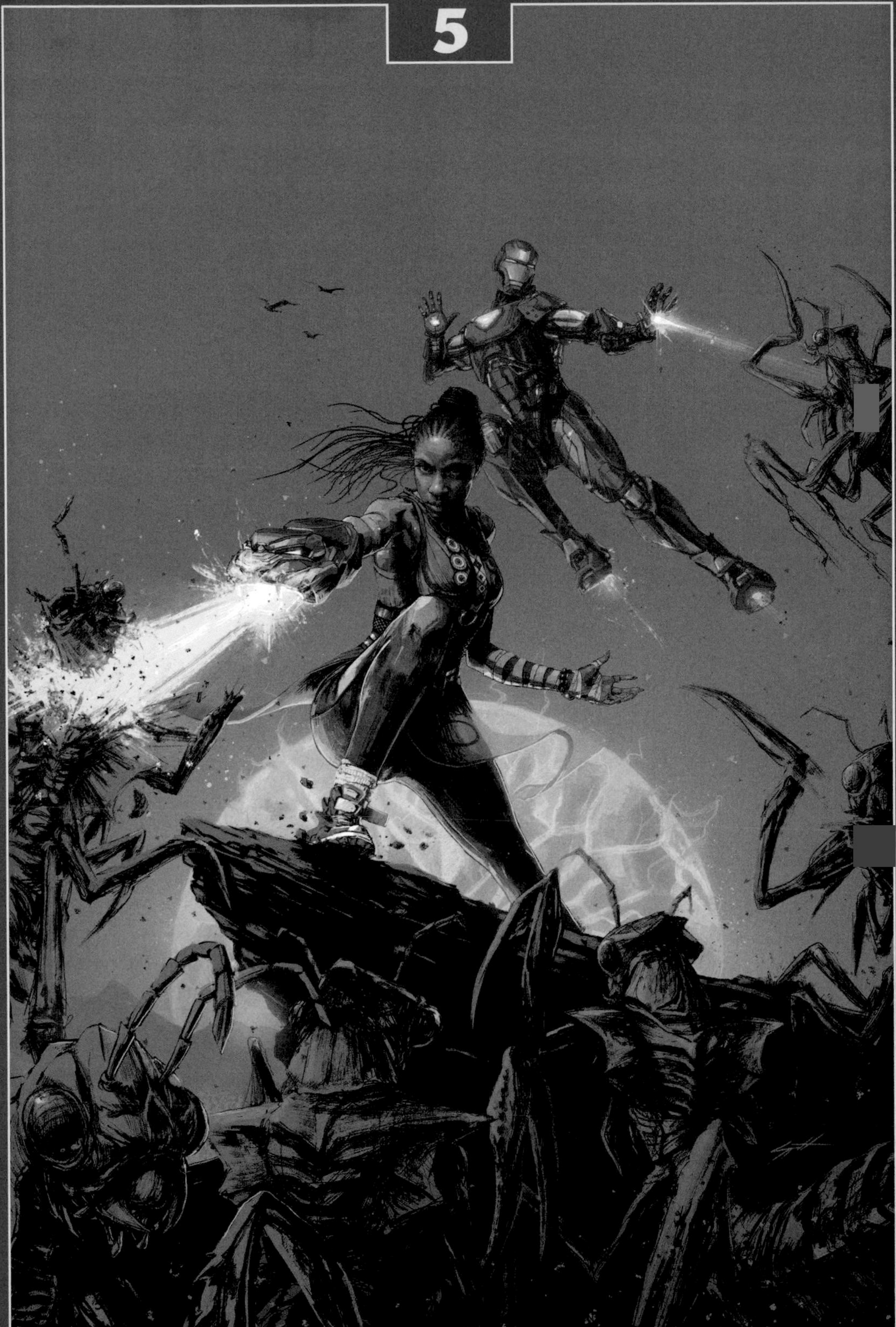

“THE END OF THE EARTH”

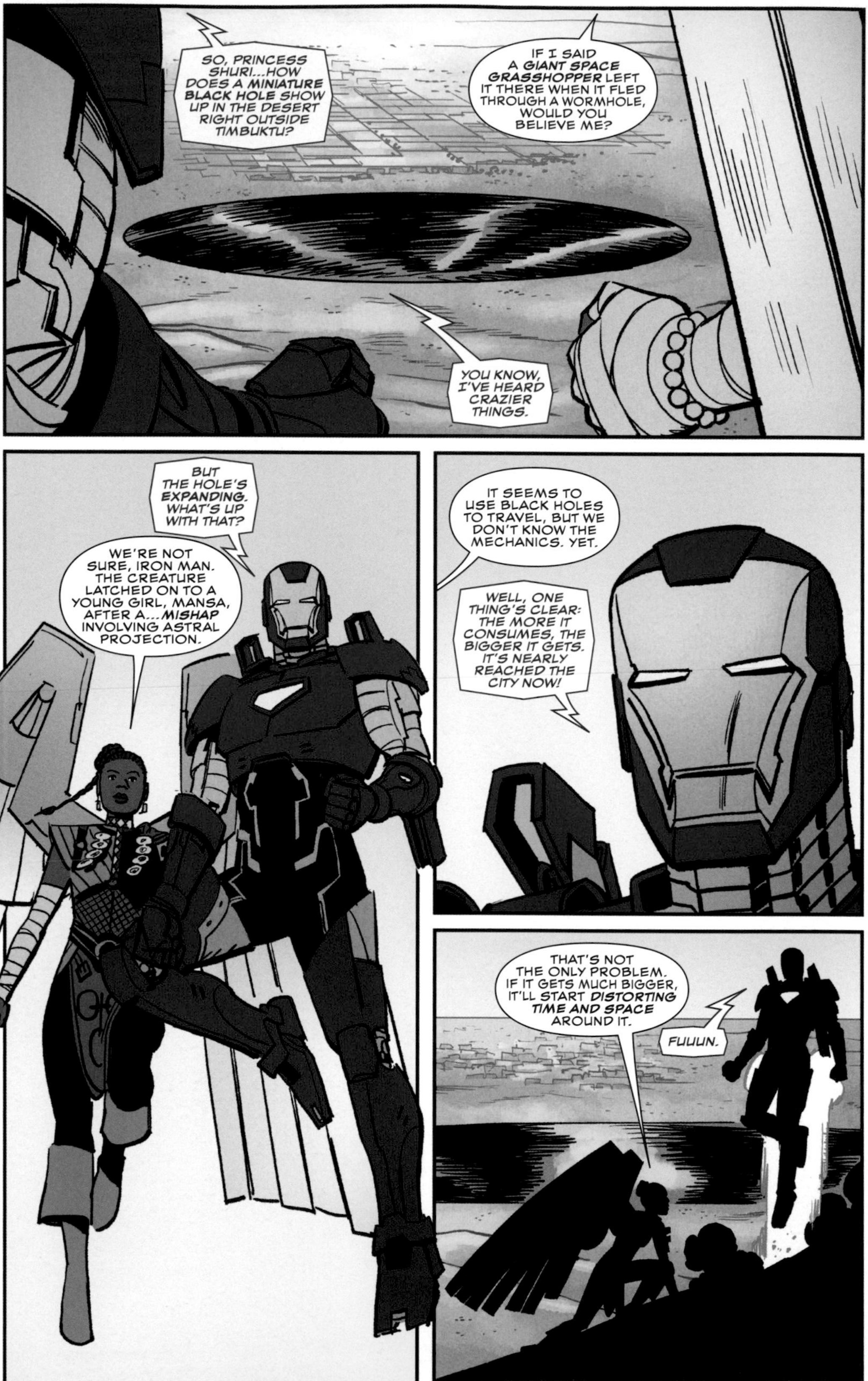
SO, PRINCESS SHURI...HOW DOES A MINIATURE BLACK HOLE SHOW UP IN THE DESERT RIGHT OUTSIDE TIMBUKTU?
IF I SAID A GIANT SPACE GRASSHOPPER LEFT IT THERE WHEN IT FLED THROUGH A WORMHOLE, WOULD YOU BELIEVE ME?
YOU KNOW, I'VE HEARD CRAZIER THINGS.
BUT THE HOLE'S EXPANDING. WHAT'S UP WITH THAT?
WE'RE NOT SURE, IRON MAN. THE CREATURE LATCHED ON TO A YOUNG GIRL, MANSA, AFTER A...MISHAP INVOLVING ASTRAL PROJECTION.
IT SEEMS TO USE BLACK HOLES TO TRAVEL, BUT WE DON'T KNOW THE MECHANICS. YET.
WELL, ONE THING'S CLEAR: THE MORE IT CONSUMES, THE BIGGER IT GETS. IT'S NEARLY REACHED THE CITY NOW!
THAT'S NOT THE ONLY PROBLEM. IF IT GETS MUCH BIGGER, IT'LL START DISTORTING TIME AND SPACE AROUND IT.
FUUUN.

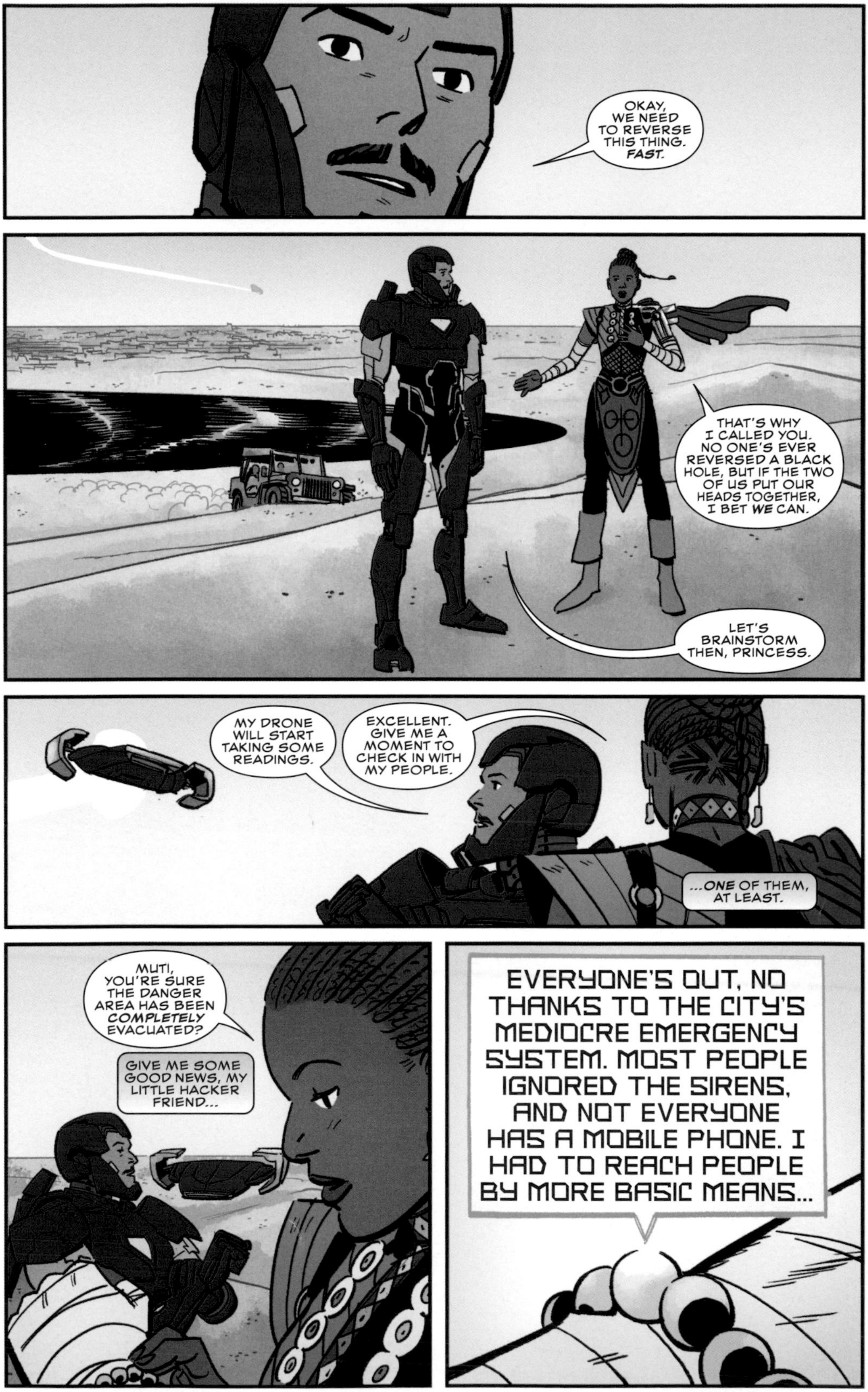
OKAY, WE NEED TO REVERSE THIS THING. FAST.
THAT'S WHY I CALLED YOU. NO ONE'S EVER REVERSED A BLACK HOLE, BUT IF THE TWO OF US PUT OUR HEADS TOGETHER, I BET WE CAN.
LET'S BRAINSTORM THEN, PRINCESS.
MY DRONE WILL START TAKING SOME READINGS.
EXCELLENT. GIVE ME A MOMENT TO CHECK IN WITH MY PEOPLE.
...ONE OF THEM, AT LEAST.
MUTI, YOU'RE SURE THE DANGER AREA HAS BEEN COMPLETELY EVACUATED?
GIVE ME SOME GOOD NEWS, MY LITTLE HACKER FRIEND...
EVERYONE'S OUT, NO THANKS TO THE CITY'S MEDIOCRE EMERGENCY SYSTEM. MOST PEOPLE IGNORED THE SIRENS, AND NOT EVERYONE HAS A MOBILE PHONE. I HAD TO REACH PEOPLE BY MORE BASIC MEANS...

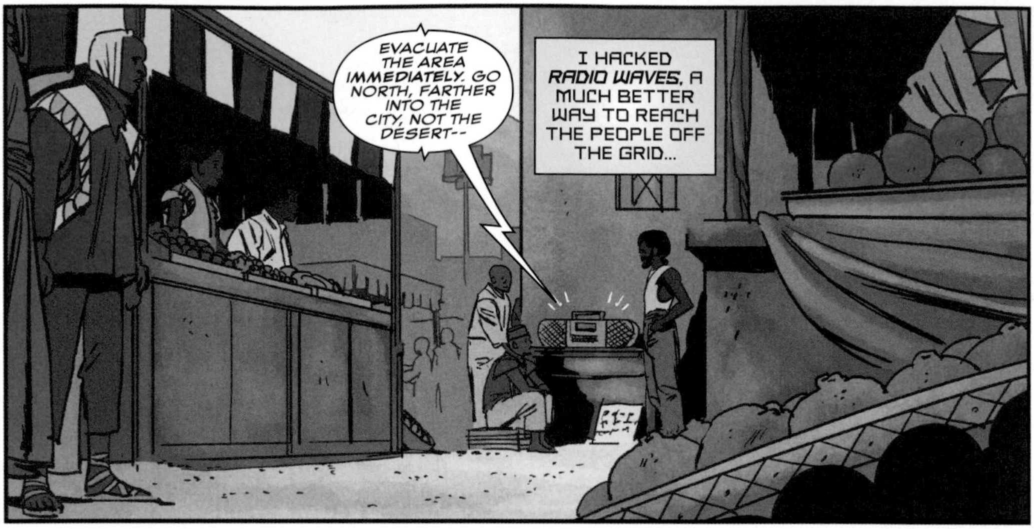
EVACUATE THE AREA IMMEDIATELY. GO NORTH, FARTHER INTO THE CITY, NOT THE DESERT--
I HACKED RADIO WAVES, A MUCH BETTER WAY TO REACH THE PEOPLE OFF THE GRID...

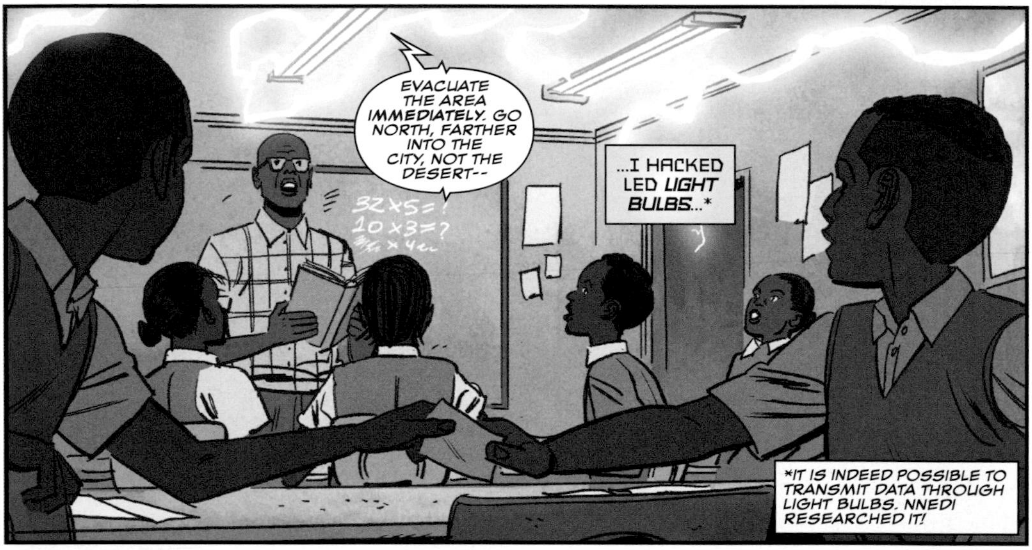
EVACUATE THE AREA IMMEDIATELY. GO NORTH, FARTHER INTO THE CITY, NOT THE DESERT--
...I HACKED LED LIGHT BULBS...*
32×5=!
10×3=?
*IT IS INDEED POSSIBLE TO TRANSMIT DATA THROUGH LIGHT BULBS. NNEDI RESEARCHED IT!

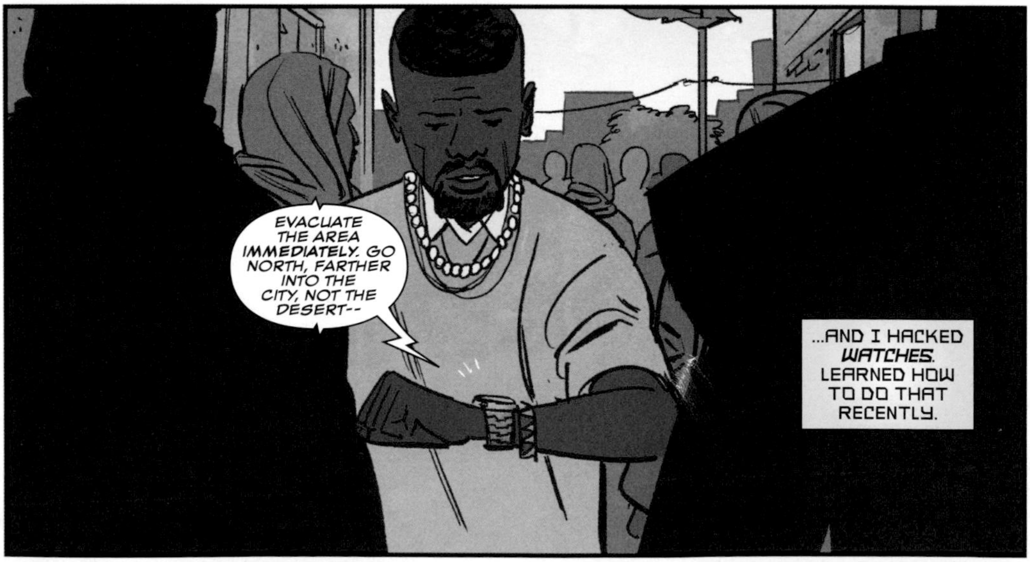
EVACUATE THE AREA IMMEDIATELY. GO NORTH, FARTHER INTO THE CITY, NOT THE DESERT--
...AND I HACKED WATCHES. LEARNED HOW TO DO THAT RECENTLY.

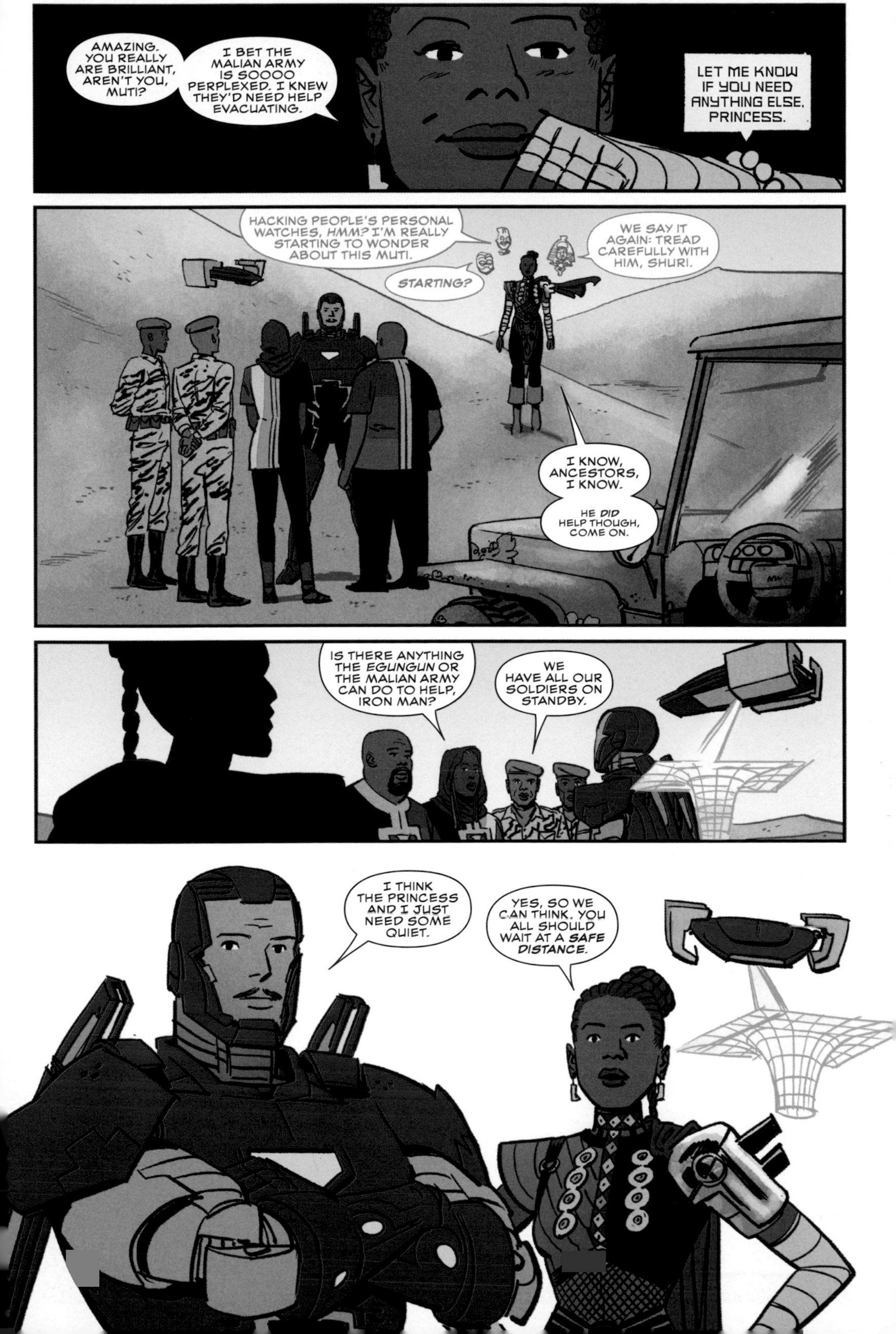
AMAZING. YOU REALLY ARE BRILLIANT, AREN'T YOU, MUTI?
I BET THE MALIAN ARMY IS SOOOO PERPLEXED. I KNEW THEY'D NEED HELP EVACUATING.
LET ME KNOW IF YOU NEED ANYTHING ELSE, PRINCESS.
HACKING PEOPLE'S PERSONAL WATCHES, HMM? I'M REALLY STARTING TO WONDER ABOUT THIS MUTI.
STARTING?
WE SAY IT AGAIN: TREAD CAREFULLY WITH HIM, SHURI.
I KNOW, ANCESTORS, I KNOW.
HE DID HELP THOUGH, COME ON.
IS THERE ANYTHING THE EGUNGUN OR THE MALIAN ARMY CAN DO TO HELP, IRON MAN?
WE HAVE ALL OUR SOLDIERS ON STANDBY.
I THINK THE PRINCESS AND I JUST NEED SOME QUIET.
YES, SO WE CAN THINK. YOU ALL SHOULD WAIT AT A SAFE DISTANCE.

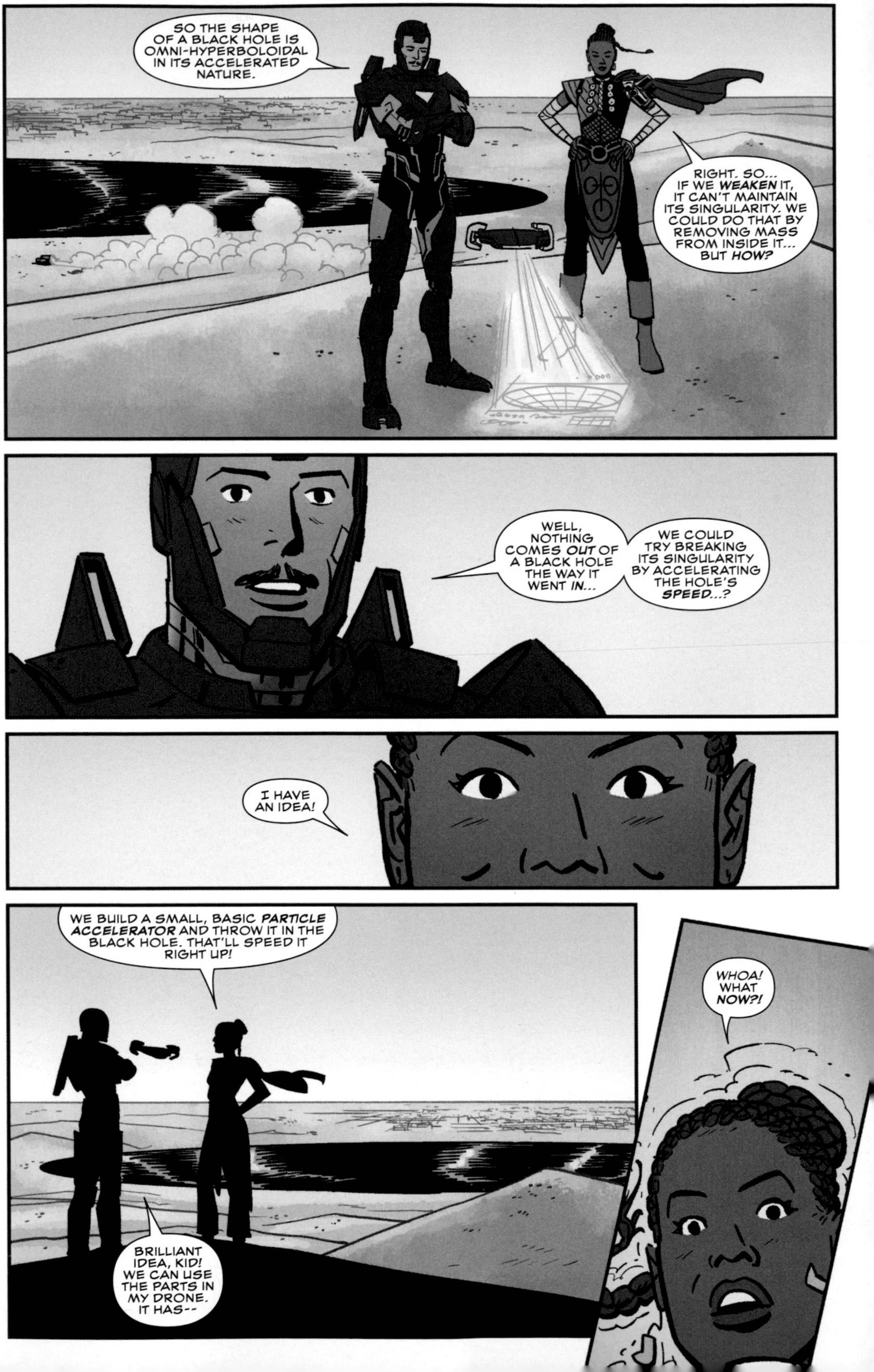
SO THE SHAPE OF A BLACK HOLE IS OMNI-HYPERBOLOIDAL IN ITS ACCELERATED NATURE.
RIGHT. SO... IF WE *WEAKEN* IT, IT CAN'T MAINTAIN ITS SINGULARITY. WE COULD DO THAT BY REMOVING MASS FROM INSIDE IT... BUT *HOW?*
WELL, NOTHING COMES *OUT* OF A BLACK HOLE THE WAY IT WENT *IN*...
WE COULD TRY BREAKING ITS SINGULARITY BY ACCELERATING THE HOLE'S *SPEED*...?
I HAVE AN IDEA!
WE BUILD A SMALL, BASIC *PARTICLE ACCELERATOR* AND THROW IT IN THE BLACK HOLE. THAT'LL SPEED IT RIGHT UP!
BRILLIANT IDEA, KID! WE CAN USE THE PARTS IN MY DRONE. IT HAS--
WHOA! WHAT NOW?!

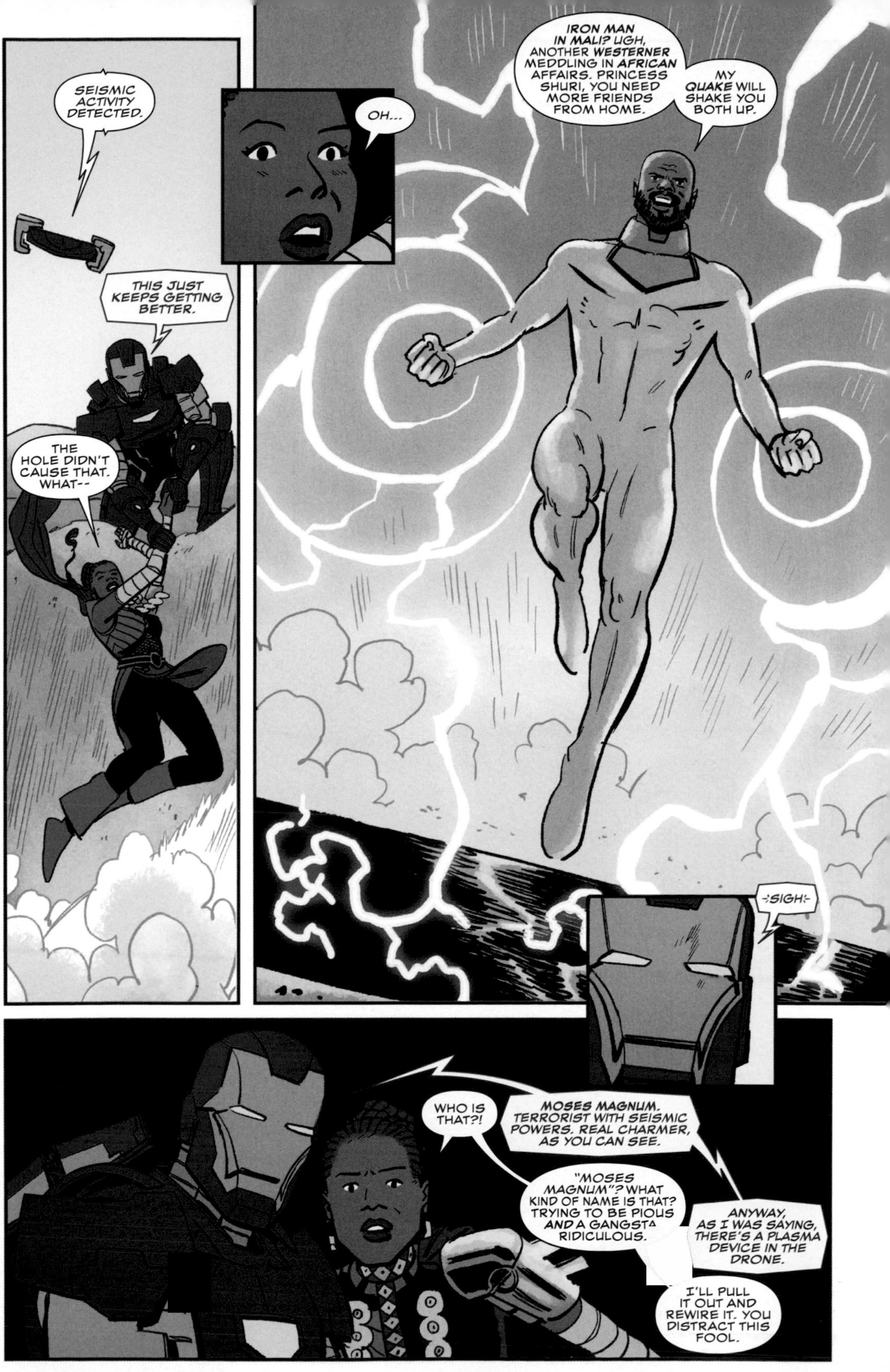
SEISMIC ACTIVITY DETECTED.
THIS JUST KEEPS GETTING BETTER.
THE HOLE DIDN'T CAUSE THAT. WHAT--
OH...
IRON MAN IN MALI? UGH, ANOTHER WESTERNER MEDDLING IN AFRICAN AFFAIRS. PRINCESS SHURI, YOU NEED MORE FRIENDS FROM HOME.
MY QUAKE WILL SHAKE YOU BOTH UP.
-SIGH-
WHO IS THAT?!
MOSES MAGNUM. TERRORIST WITH SEISMIC POWERS. REAL CHARMER, AS YOU CAN SEE.
"MOSES MAGNUM"? WHAT KIND OF NAME IS THAT? TRYING TO BE PIOUS AND A GANGSTA RIDICULOUS.
ANYWAY, AS I WAS SAYING, THERE'S A PLASMA DEVICE IN THE DRONE.
I'LL PULL IT OUT AND REWIRE IT. YOU DISTRACT THIS FOOL.

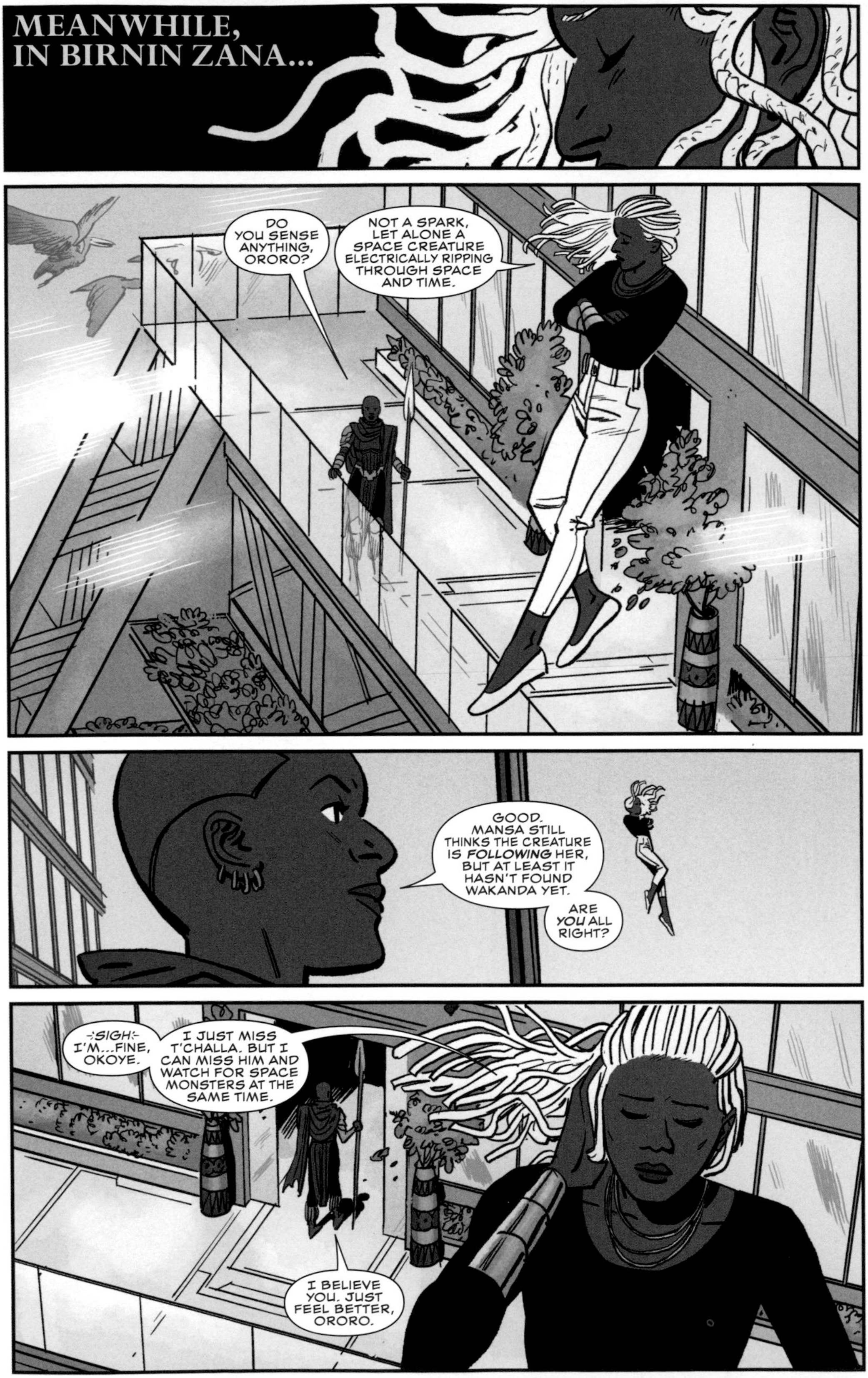

MEANWHILE, IN BIRNIN ZANA...
DO YOU SENSE ANYTHING, ORORO?
NOT A SPARK, LET ALONE A SPACE CREATURE ELECTRICALLY RIPPING THROUGH SPACE AND TIME.
GOOD. MANSA STILL THINKS THE CREATURE IS FOLLOWING HER, BUT AT LEAST IT HASN'T FOUND WAKANDA YET.
ARE YOU ALL RIGHT?
-SIGH- I'M...FINE, OKOYE.
I JUST MISS T'CHALLA. BUT I CAN MISS HIM AND WATCH FOR SPACE MONSTERS AT THE SAME TIME.
I BELIEVE YOU. JUST FEEL BETTER, ORORO.

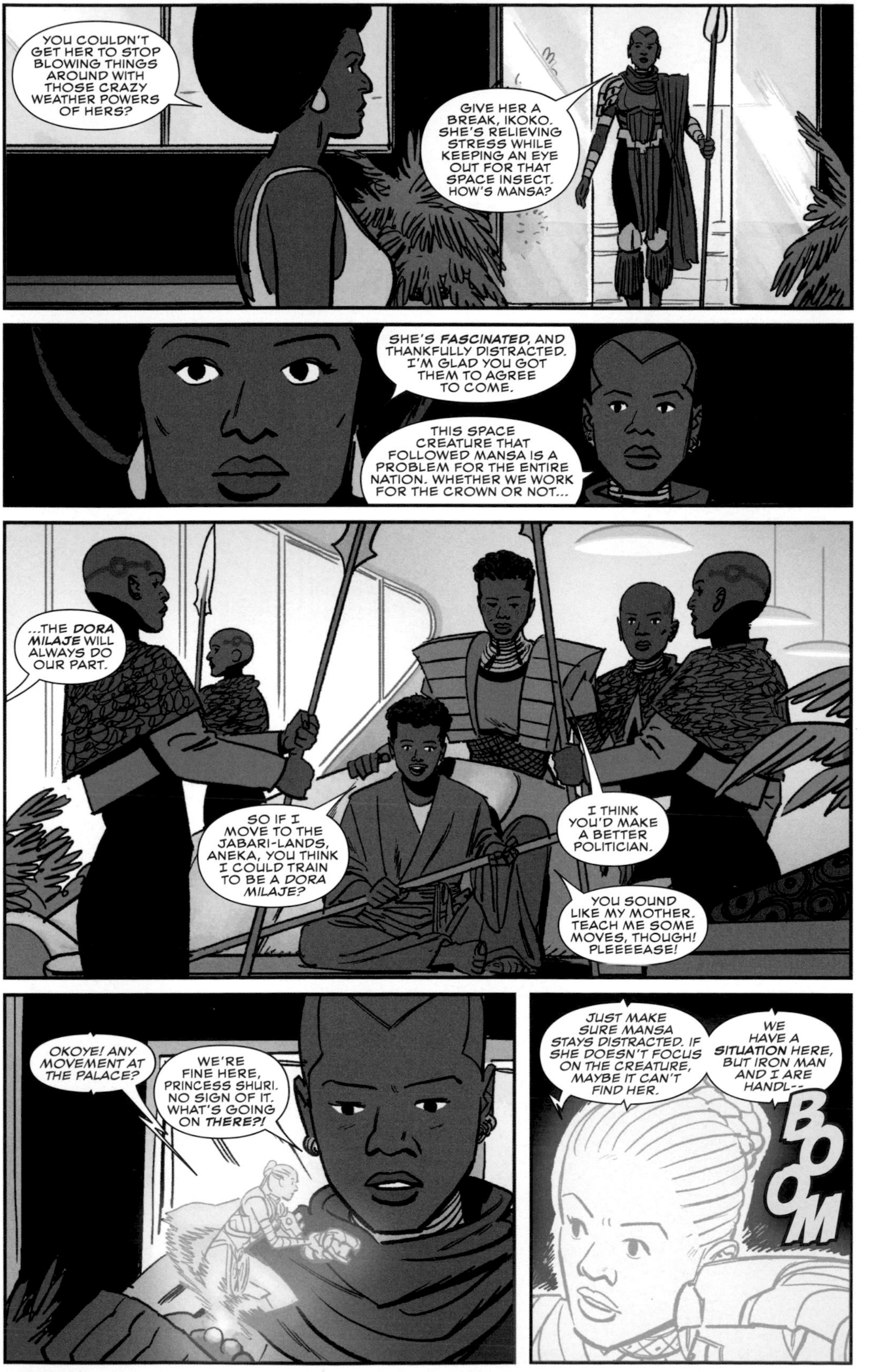
YOU COULDN'T GET HER TO STOP BLOWING THINGS AROUND WITH THOSE CRAZY WEATHER POWERS OF HERS?
GIVE HER A BREAK, IKOKO. SHE'S RELIEVING STRESS WHILE KEEPING AN EYE OUT FOR THAT SPACE INSECT. HOW'S MANSA?
SHE'S FASCINATED, AND THANKFULLY DISTRACTED. I'M GLAD YOU GOT THEM TO AGREE TO COME.
THIS SPACE CREATURE THAT FOLLOWED MANSA IS A PROBLEM FOR THE ENTIRE NATION. WHETHER WE WORK FOR THE CROWN OR NOT...
...THE DORA MILAJE WILL ALWAYS DO OUR PART.
SO IF I MOVE TO THE JABARI-LANDS, ANEKA, YOU THINK I COULD TRAIN TO BE A DORA MILAJE?
I THINK YOU'D MAKE A BETTER POLITICIAN.
YOU SOUND LIKE MY MOTHER. TEACH ME SOME MOVES, THOUGH! PLEEEEASE!
OKOYE! ANY MOVEMENT AT THE PALACE?
WE'RE FINE HERE, PRINCESS SHURI. NO SIGN OF IT. WHAT'S GOING ON THERE?!
JUST MAKE SURE MANSA STAYS DISTRACTED. IF SHE DOESN'T FOCUS ON THE CREATURE, MAYBE IT CAN'T FIND HER.
WE HAVE A SITUATION HERE, BUT IRON MAN AND I ARE HANDL--
BOOM

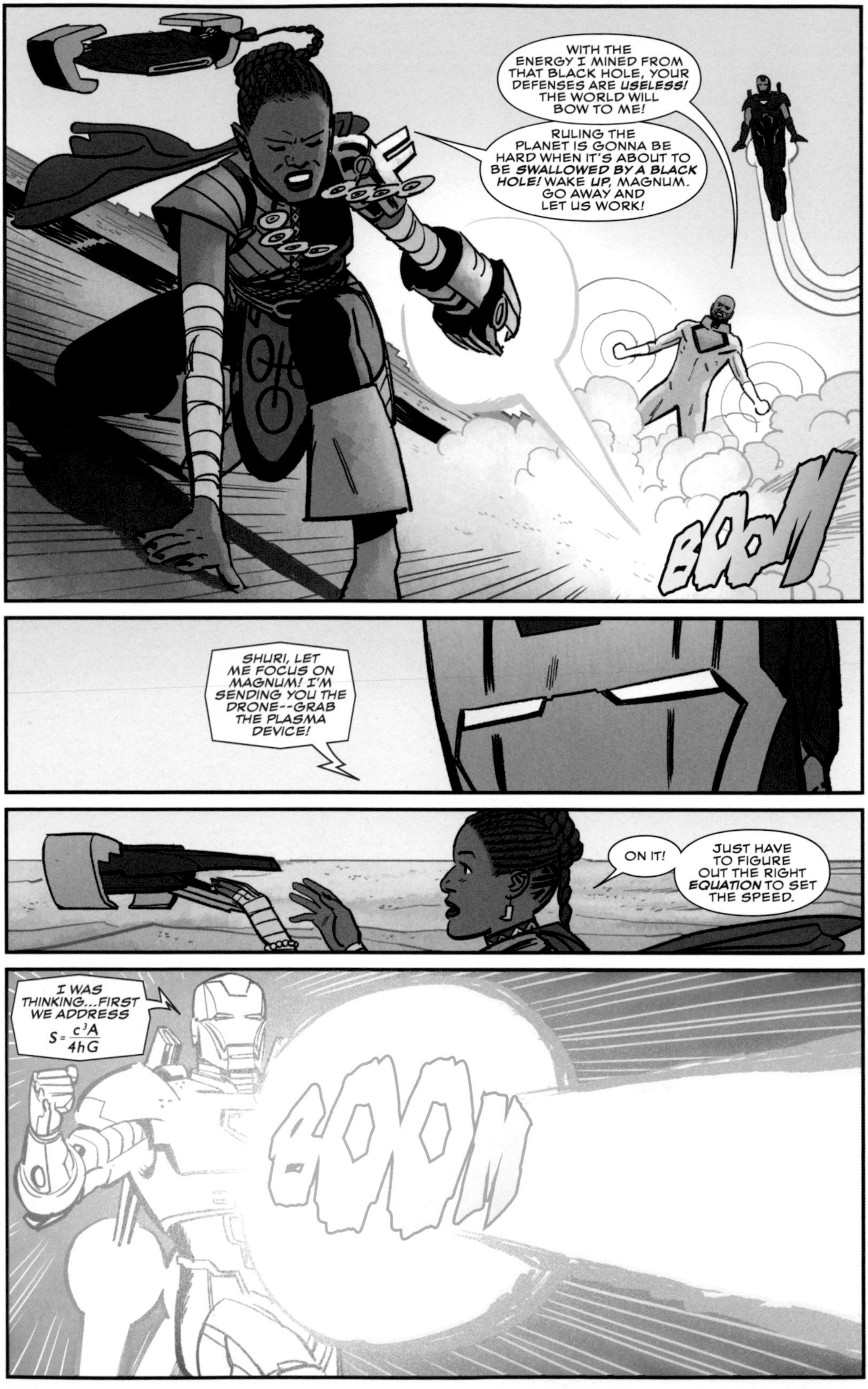
WITH THE ENERGY I MINED FROM THAT BLACK HOLE, YOUR DEFENSES ARE *USELESS!* THE WORLD WILL BOW TO ME!
RULING THE PLANET IS GONNA BE HARD WHEN IT'S ABOUT TO BE ***SWALLOWED BY A BLACK HOLE!*** WAKE *UP*, MAGNUM. GO AWAY AND LET US WORK!
BOOM
SHURI, LET ME FOCUS ON MAGNUM! I'M SENDING YOU THE DRONE--GRAB THE PLASMA DEVICE!
ON IT!
JUST HAVE TO FIGURE OUT THE RIGHT ***EQUATION*** TO SET THE SPEED.
I WAS THINKING...FIRST WE ADDRESS $S = \frac{c^3A}{4hG}$
BOOM

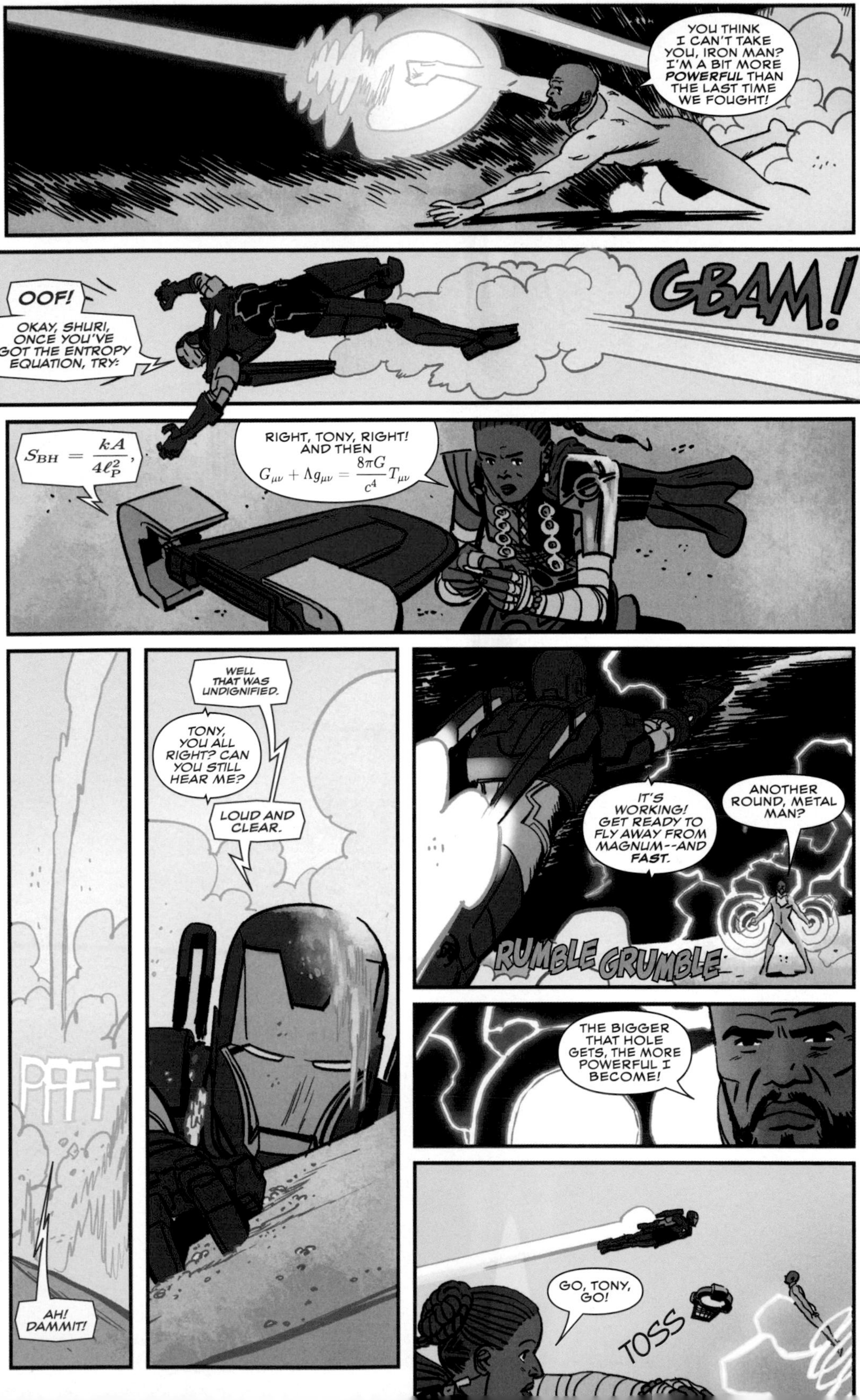
YOU THINK I CAN'T TAKE YOU, IRON MAN? I'M A BIT MORE POWERFUL THAN THE LAST TIME WE FOUGHT!
OOF!
OKAY, SHURI, ONCE YOU'VE GOT THE ENTROPY EQUATION, TRY:
GBAM!
$S_{BH} = \frac{kA}{4\ell_P^2}$,
RIGHT, TONY, RIGHT! AND THEN $G_{\mu\nu} + \Lambda g_{\mu\nu} = \frac{8\pi G}{c^4} T_{\mu\nu}$
PFFF
AH! DAMMIT!
WELL THAT WAS UNDIGNIFIED.
TONY, YOU ALL RIGHT? CAN YOU STILL HEAR ME?
LOUD AND CLEAR.
IT'S WORKING! GET READY TO FLY AWAY FROM MAGNUM--AND FAST.
ANOTHER ROUND, METAL MAN?
RUMBLE GRUMBLE
THE BIGGER THAT HOLE GETS, THE MORE POWERFUL I BECOME!
GO, TONY, GO!
TOSS

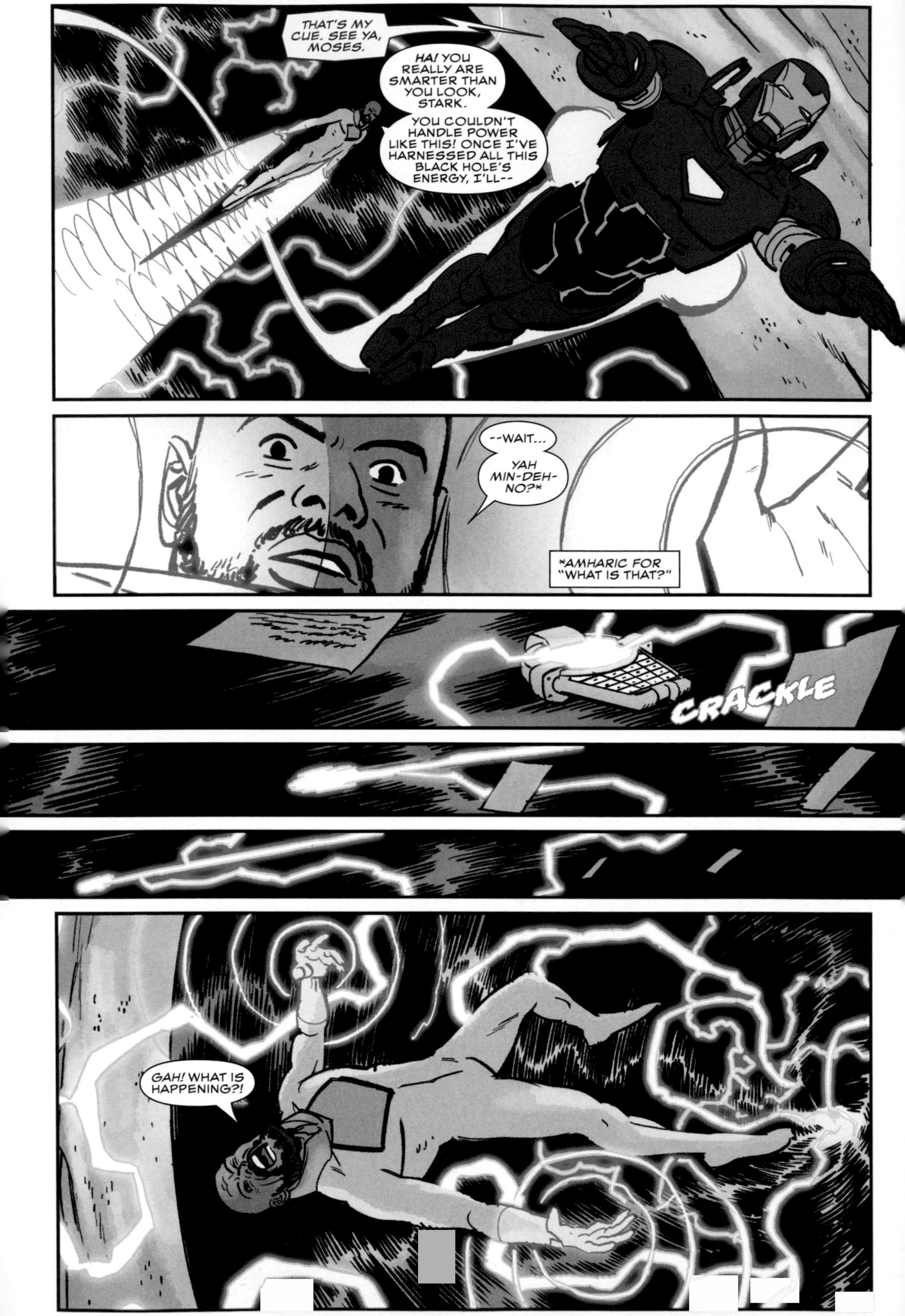
THAT'S MY CUE. SEE YA, MOSES.
HA! YOU REALLY ARE SMARTER THAN YOU LOOK, STARK.
YOU COULDN'T HANDLE POWER LIKE THIS! ONCE I'VE HARNESSED ALL THIS BLACK HOLE'S ENERGY, I'LL--
--WAIT...
YAH MIN-DEH-NO?*
*AMHARIC FOR "WHAT IS THAT?"
CRACKLE
GAH! WHAT IS HAPPENING?!

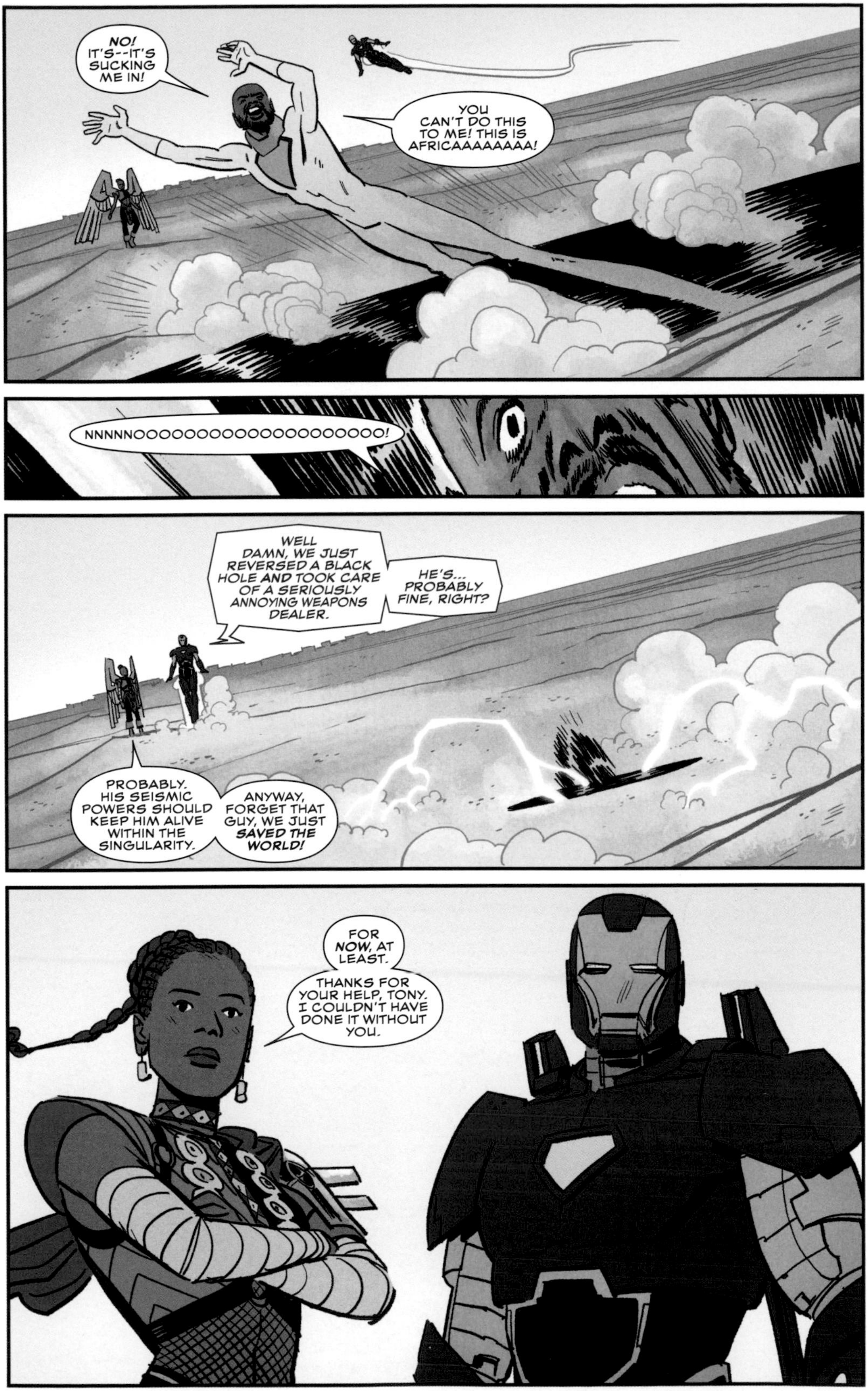
NO! IT'S--IT'S SUCKING ME IN!
YOU CAN'T DO THIS TO ME! THIS IS AFRICAAAAAAAA!
NNNNNOOOOOOOOOOOOOOOOOOOOOO!
WELL DAMN, WE JUST REVERSED A BLACK HOLE AND TOOK CARE OF A SERIOUSLY ANNOYING WEAPONS DEALER.
HE'S... PROBABLY FINE, RIGHT?
PROBABLY. HIS SEISMIC POWERS SHOULD KEEP HIM ALIVE WITHIN THE SINGULARITY.
ANYWAY, FORGET THAT GUY, WE JUST SAVED THE WORLD!
FOR NOW, AT LEAST.
THANKS FOR YOUR HELP, TONY. I COULDN'T HAVE DONE IT WITHOUT YOU.

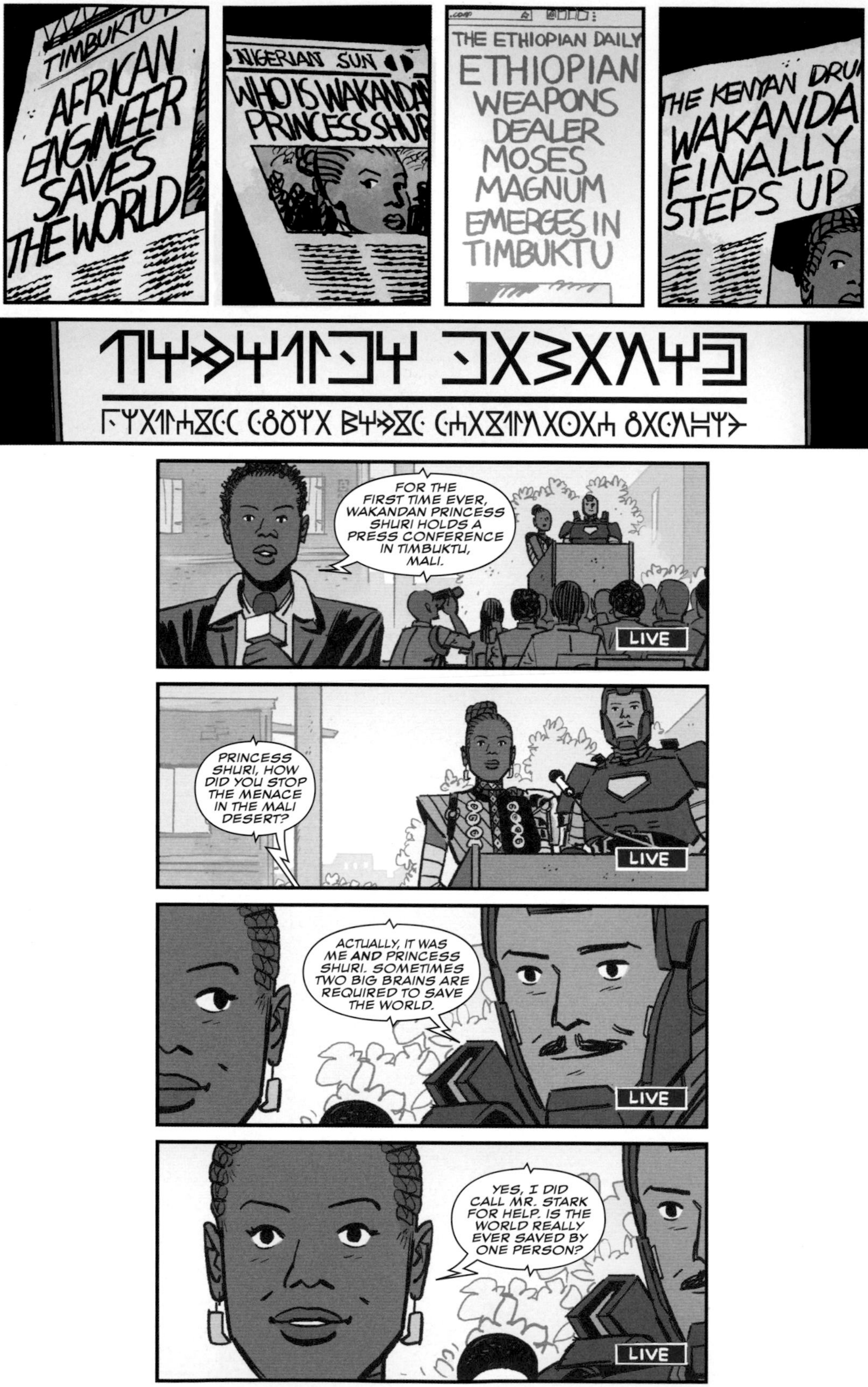
TIMBUKTU
AFRICAN ENGINEER SAVES THE WORLD
NIGERIAN SUN
WHO IS WAKANDA'S PRINCESS SHURI
THE ETHIOPIAN DAILY
ETHIOPIAN WEAPONS DEALER MOSES MAGNUM EMERGES IN TIMBUKTU
THE KENYAN DRU
WAKANDA FINALLY STEPS UP
FOR THE FIRST TIME EVER, WAKANDAN PRINCESS SHURI HOLDS A PRESS CONFERENCE IN TIMBUKTU, MALI.
LIVE
PRINCESS SHURI, HOW DID YOU STOP THE MENACE IN THE MALI DESERT?
LIVE
ACTUALLY, IT WAS ME AND PRINCESS SHURI. SOMETIMES TWO BIG BRAINS ARE REQUIRED TO SAVE THE WORLD.
LIVE
YES, I DID CALL MR. STARK FOR HELP. IS THE WORLD REALLY EVER SAVED BY ONE PERSON?
LIVE

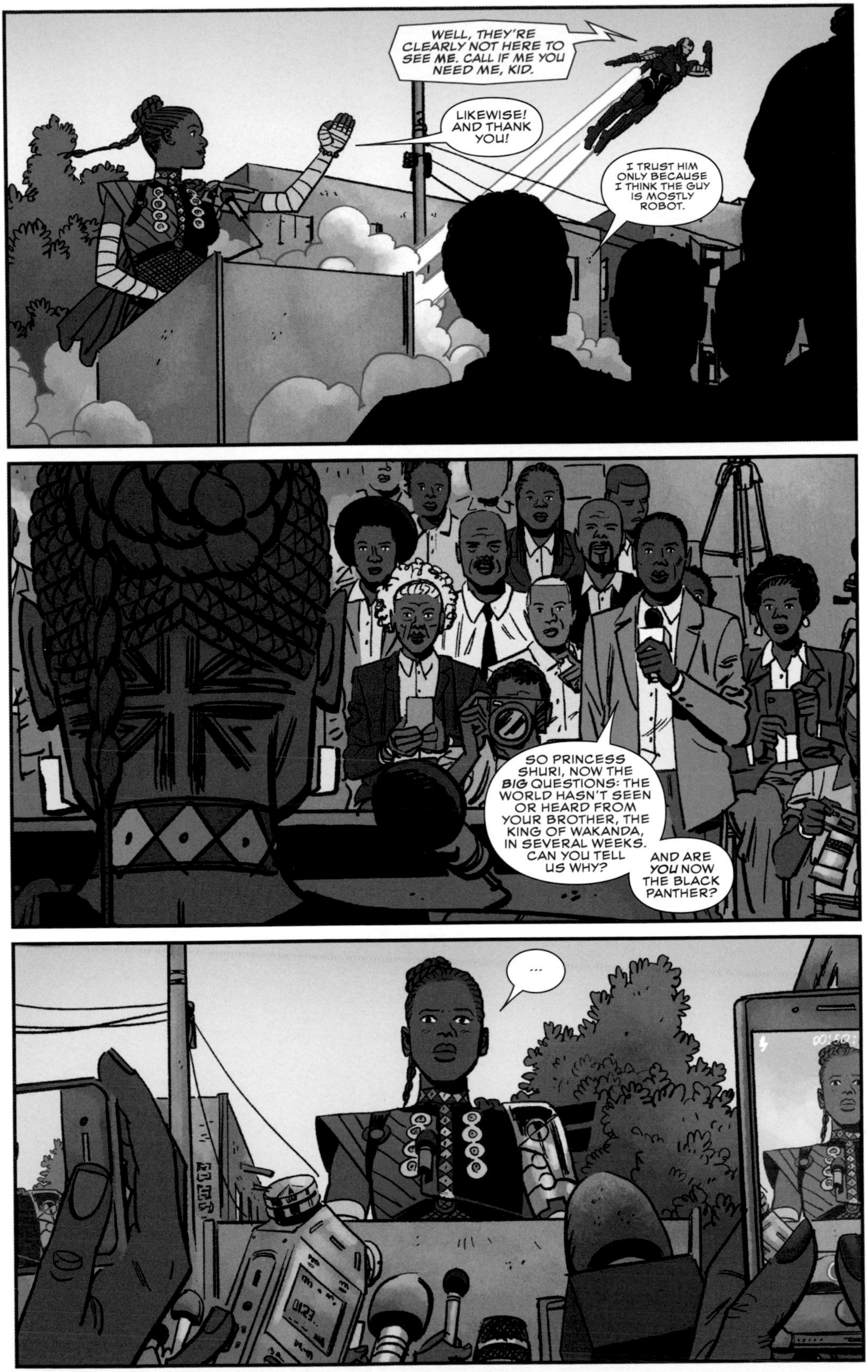
WELL, THEY'RE CLEARLY NOT HERE TO SEE ME. CALL IF ME YOU NEED ME, KID.
LIKEWISE! AND THANK YOU!
I TRUST HIM ONLY BECAUSE I THINK THE GUY IS MOSTLY ROBOT.
SO PRINCESS SHURI, NOW THE BIG QUESTIONS: THE WORLD HASN'T SEEN OR HEARD FROM YOUR BROTHER, THE KING OF WAKANDA, IN SEVERAL WEEKS. CAN YOU TELL US WHY?
AND ARE YOU NOW THE BLACK PANTHER?
...

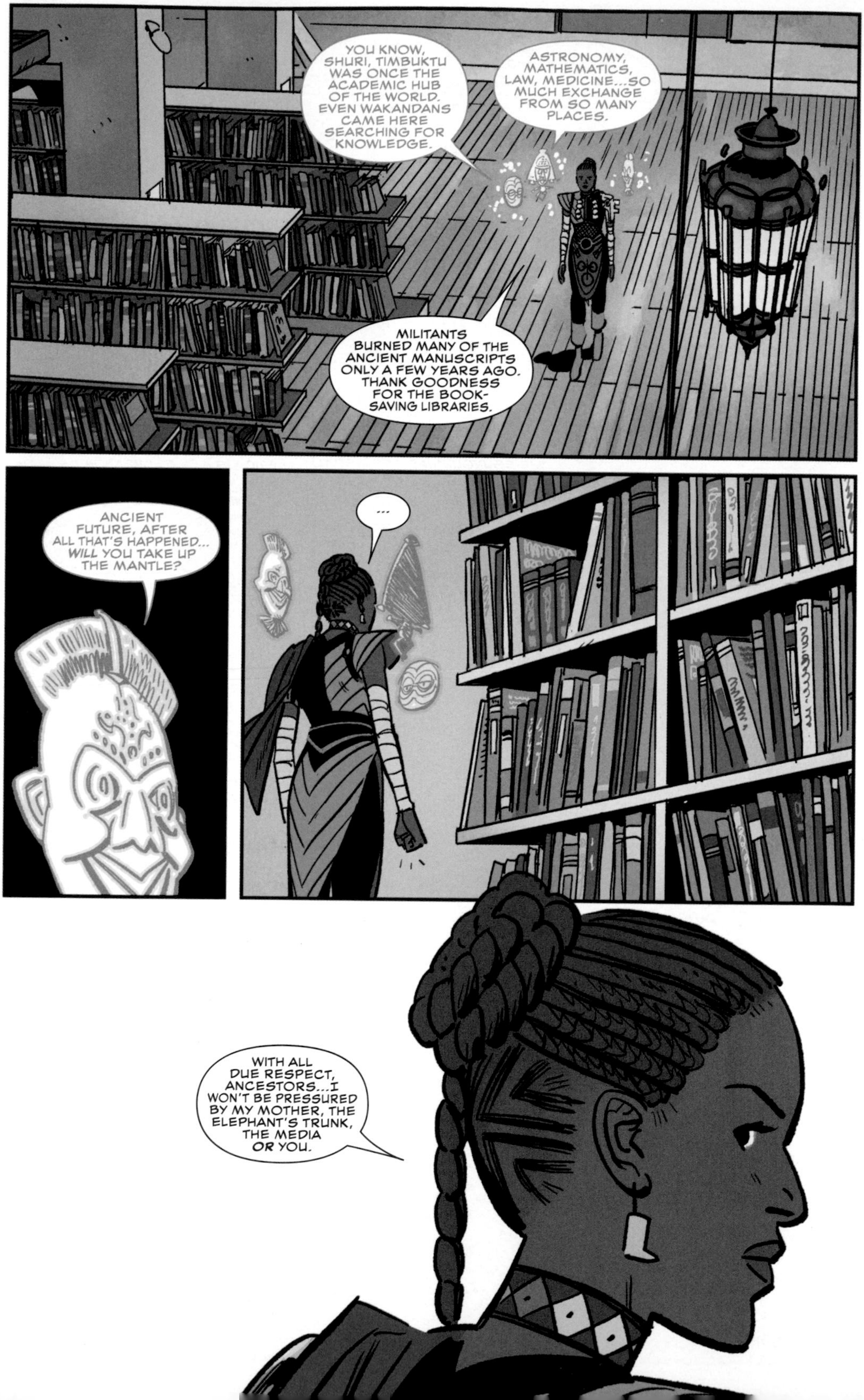
YOU KNOW, SHURI, TIMBUKTU WAS ONCE THE ACADEMIC HUB OF THE WORLD. EVEN WAKANDANS CAME HERE SEARCHING FOR KNOWLEDGE.
ASTRONOMY, MATHEMATICS, LAW, MEDICINE...SO MUCH EXCHANGE FROM SO MANY PLACES.
MILITANTS BURNED MANY OF THE ANCIENT MANUSCRIPTS ONLY A FEW YEARS AGO. THANK GOODNESS FOR THE BOOK-SAVING LIBRARIES.
ANCIENT FUTURE, AFTER ALL THAT'S HAPPENED... WILL YOU TAKE UP THE MANTLE?
...
WITH ALL DUE RESPECT, ANCESTORS...I WON'T BE PRESSURED BY MY MOTHER, THE ELEPHANT'S TRUNK, THE MEDIA OR YOU.

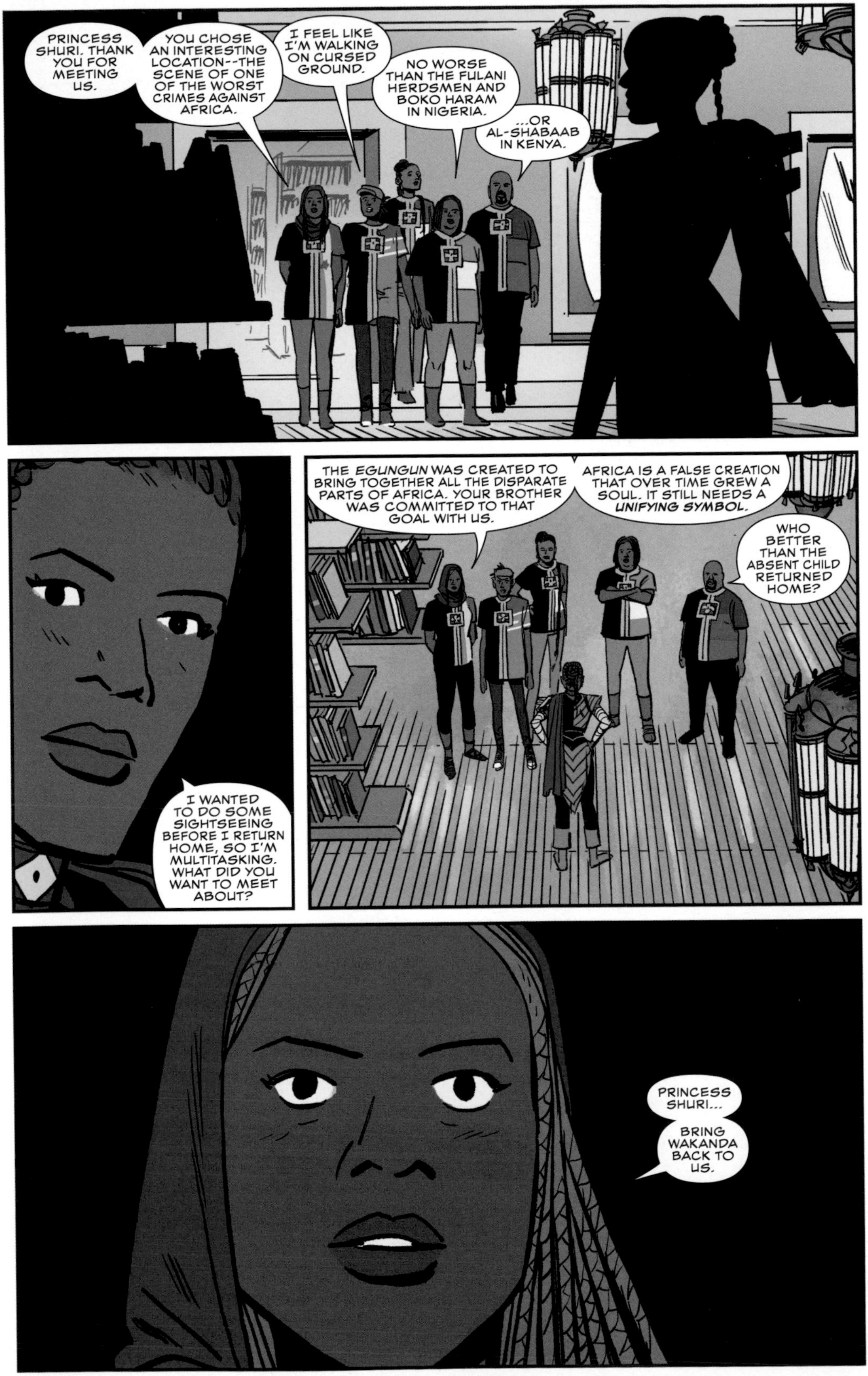
PRINCESS SHURI. THANK YOU FOR MEETING US.
YOU CHOSE AN INTERESTING LOCATION--THE SCENE OF ONE OF THE WORST CRIMES AGAINST AFRICA.
I FEEL LIKE I'M WALKING ON CURSED GROUND.
NO WORSE THAN THE FULANI HERDSMEN AND BOKO HARAM IN NIGERIA.
...OR AL-SHABAAB IN KENYA.
I WANTED TO DO SOME SIGHTSEEING BEFORE I RETURN HOME, SO I'M MULTITASKING. WHAT DID YOU WANT TO MEET ABOUT?
THE *EGUNGUN* WAS CREATED TO BRING TOGETHER ALL THE DISPARATE PARTS OF AFRICA. YOUR BROTHER WAS COMMITTED TO THAT GOAL WITH US.
AFRICA IS A FALSE CREATION THAT OVER TIME GREW A SOUL. IT STILL NEEDS A ***UNIFYING SYMBOL.***
WHO BETTER THAN THE ABSENT CHILD RETURNED HOME?
PRINCESS SHURI...
BRING WAKANDA BACK TO US.

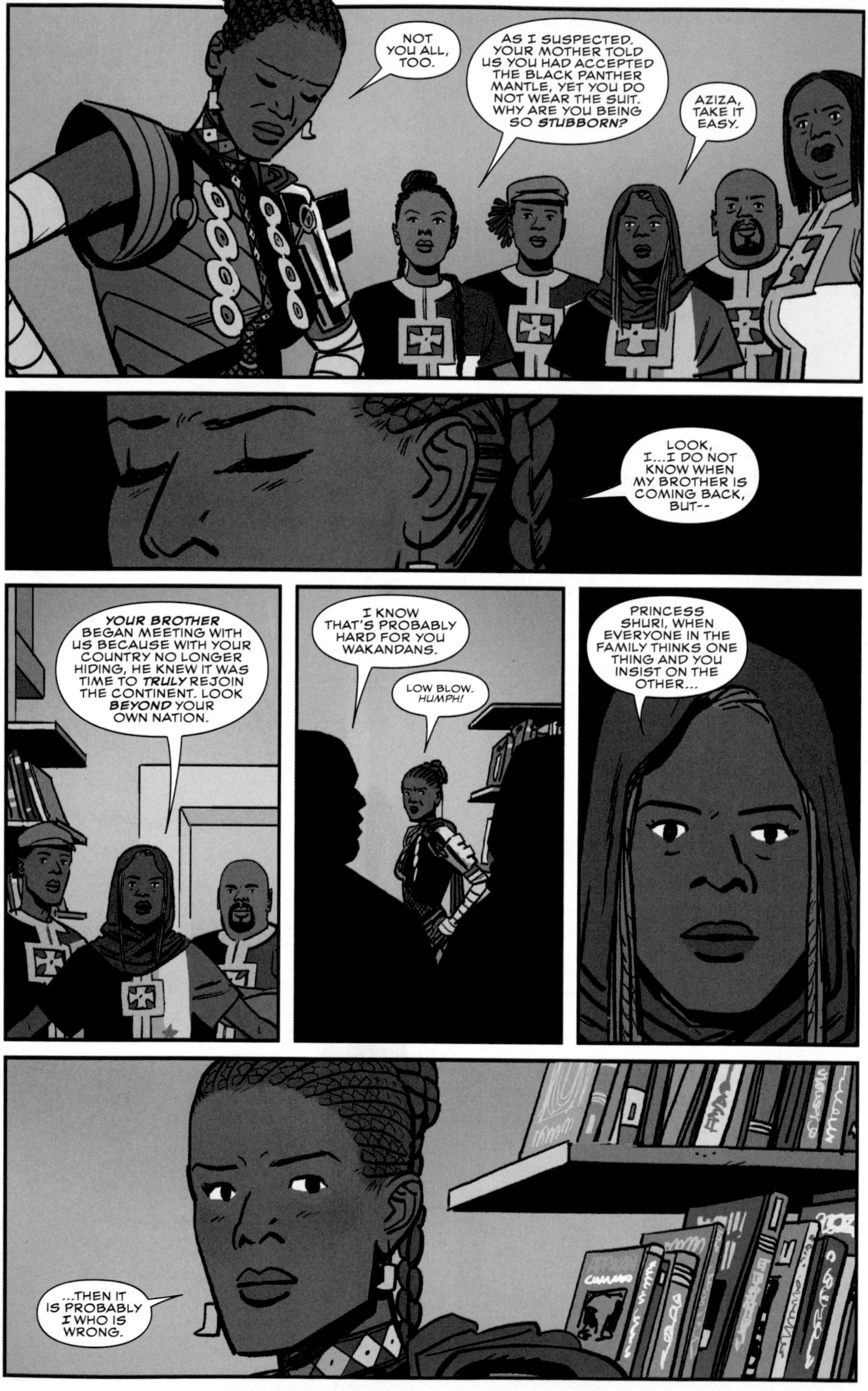
NOT YOU ALL, TOO.
AS I SUSPECTED. YOUR MOTHER TOLD US YOU HAD ACCEPTED THE BLACK PANTHER MANTLE, YET YOU DO NOT WEAR THE SUIT. WHY ARE YOU BEING SO *STUBBORN?*
AZIZA, TAKE IT EASY.
LOOK, I...I DO NOT KNOW WHEN MY BROTHER IS COMING BACK, BUT--
YOUR BROTHER BEGAN MEETING WITH US BECAUSE WITH YOUR COUNTRY NO LONGER HIDING, HE KNEW IT WAS TIME TO *TRULY* REJOIN THE CONTINENT. LOOK *BEYOND* YOUR OWN NATION.
I KNOW THAT'S PROBABLY HARD FOR YOU WAKANDANS.
LOW BLOW. *HUMPH!*
PRINCESS SHURI, WHEN EVERYONE IN THE FAMILY THINKS ONE THING AND YOU INSIST ON THE OTHER...
...THEN IT IS PROBABLY *I* WHO IS WRONG.

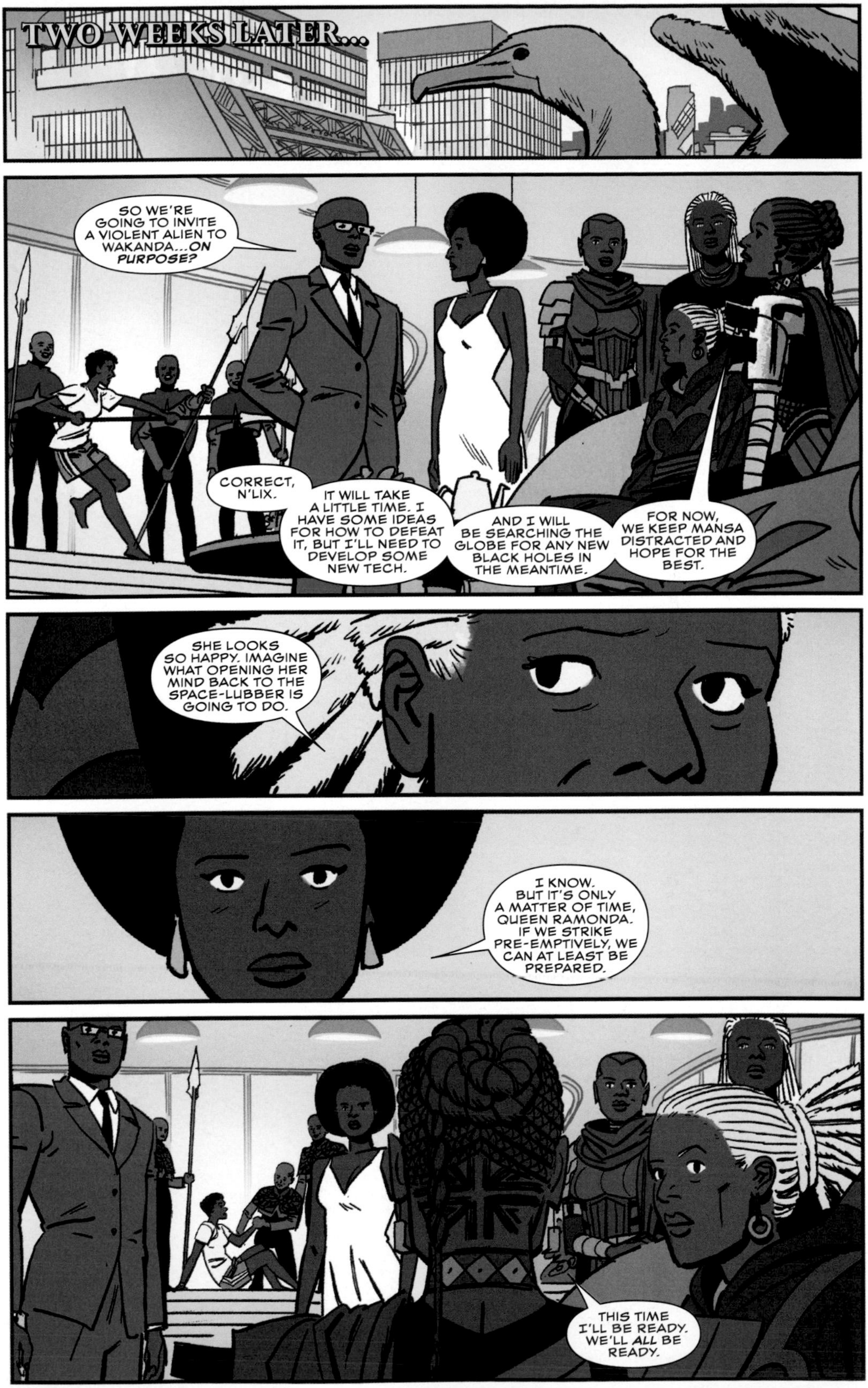
TWO WEEKS LATER...
SO WE'RE GOING TO INVITE A VIOLENT ALIEN TO WAKANDA...*ON PURPOSE?*
CORRECT, N'LIX.
IT WILL TAKE A LITTLE TIME. I HAVE SOME IDEAS FOR HOW TO DEFEAT IT, BUT I'LL NEED TO DEVELOP SOME NEW TECH.
AND I WILL BE SEARCHING THE GLOBE FOR ANY NEW BLACK HOLES IN THE MEANTIME.
FOR NOW, WE KEEP MANSA DISTRACTED AND HOPE FOR THE BEST.
SHE LOOKS SO HAPPY. IMAGINE WHAT OPENING HER MIND BACK TO THE SPACE-LUBBER IS GOING TO DO.
I KNOW. BUT IT'S ONLY A MATTER OF TIME, QUEEN RAMONDA. IF WE STRIKE PRE-EMPTIVELY, WE CAN AT LEAST BE PREPARED.
THIS TIME I'LL BE READY. WE'LL *ALL* BE READY.

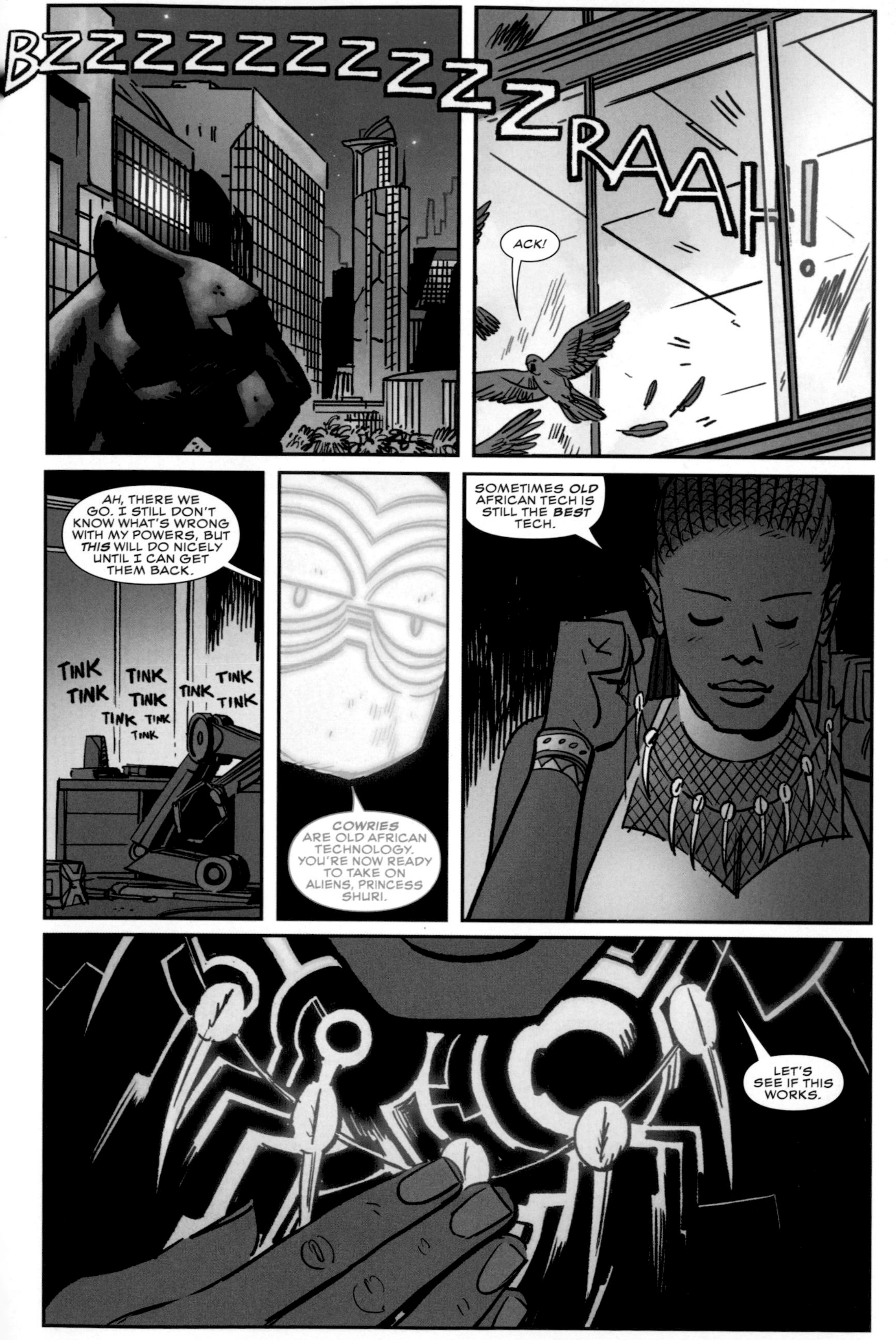
BZZZZZZZZZZZRAAH!
ACK!
AH, THERE WE GO. I STILL DON'T KNOW WHAT'S WRONG WITH MY POWERS, BUT THIS WILL DO NICELY UNTIL I CAN GET THEM BACK.
TINK TINK TINK TINK TINK TINK TINK TINK TINK TINK TINK
COWRIES ARE OLD AFRICAN TECHNOLOGY. YOU'RE NOW READY TO TAKE ON ALIENS, PRINCESS SHURI.
SOMETIMES OLD AFRICAN TECH IS STILL THE BEST TECH.
LET'S SEE IF THIS WORKS.

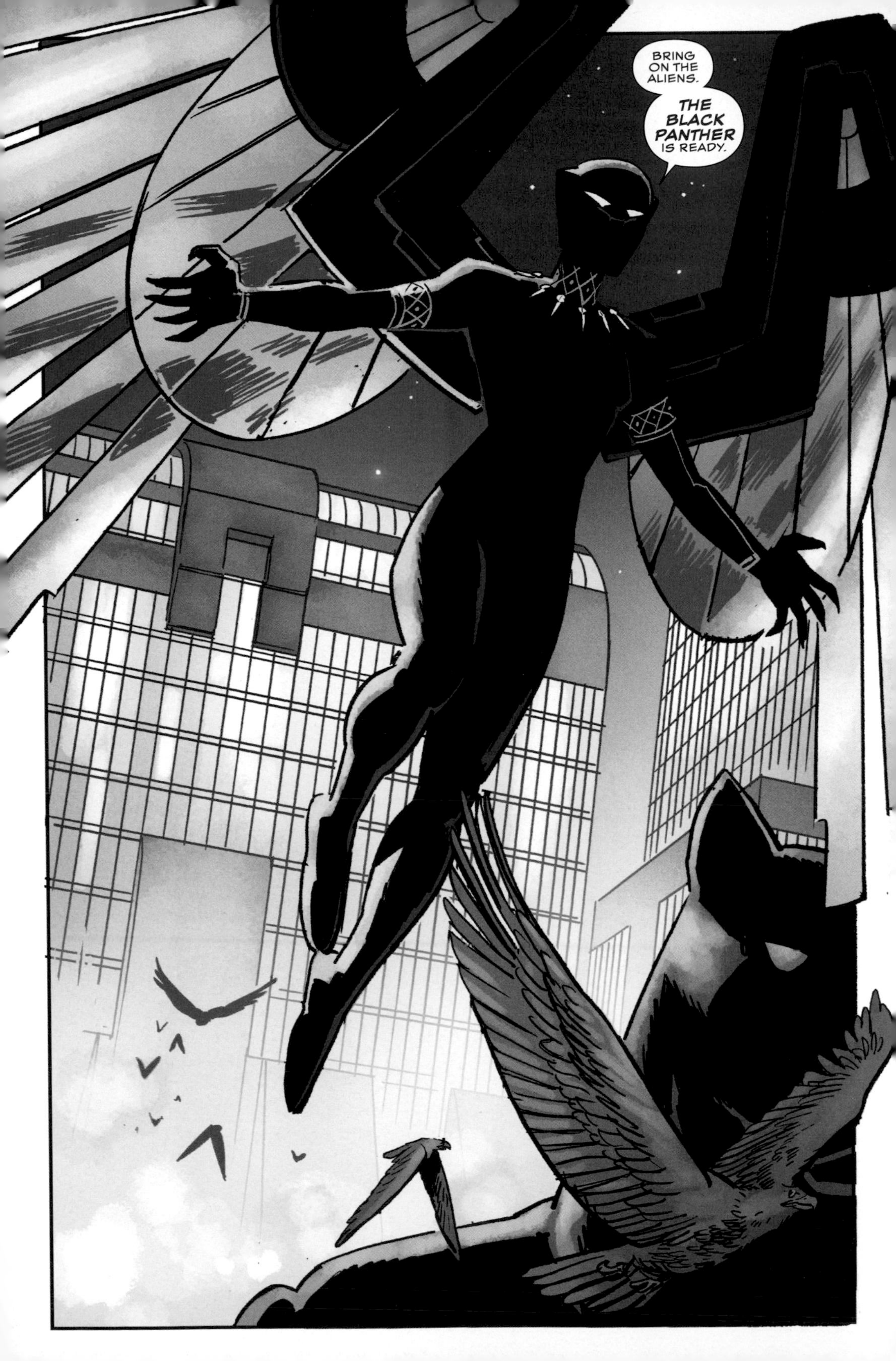
BRING ON THE ALIENS.
THE BLACK PANTHER IS READY.

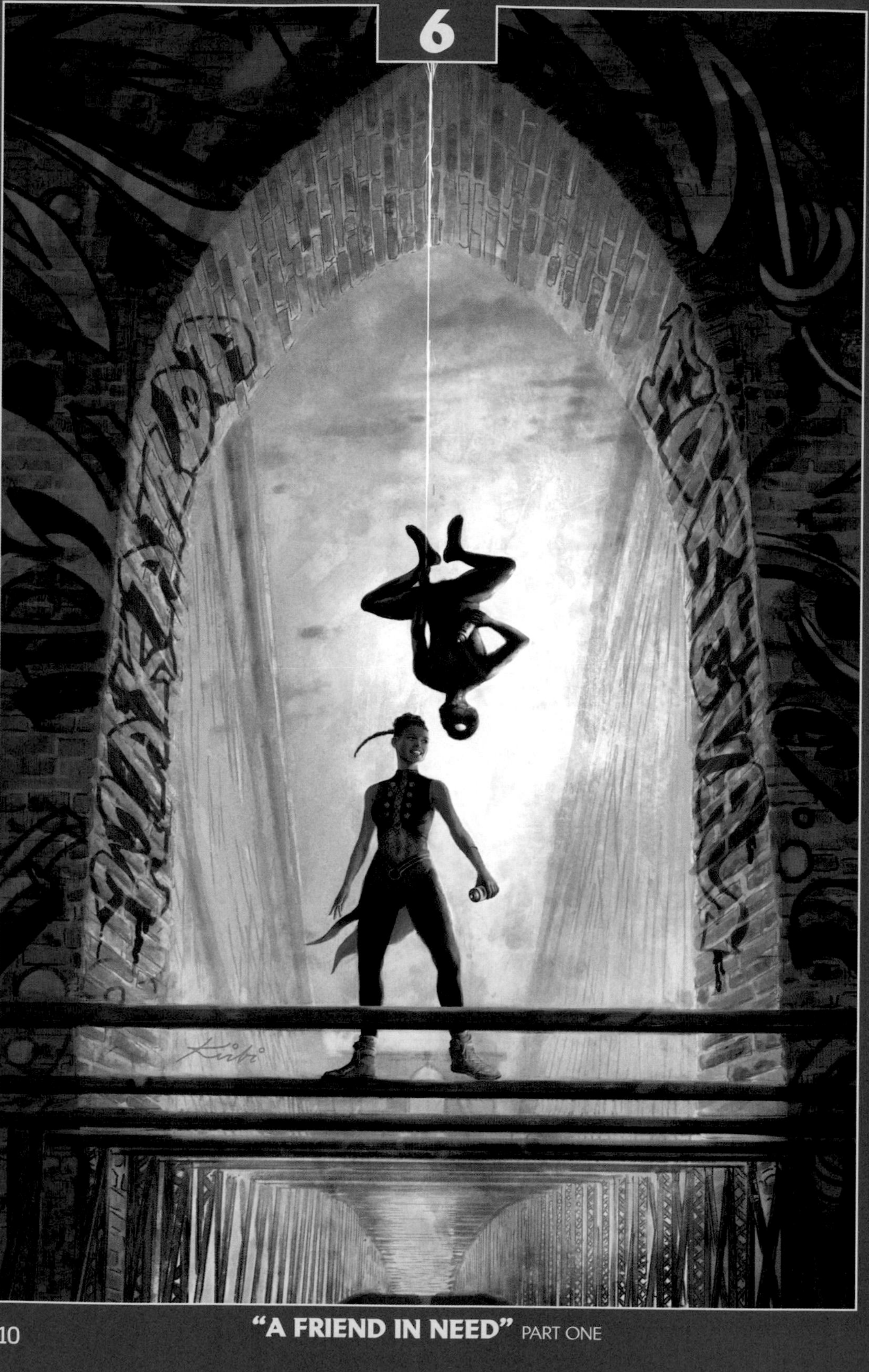
6

"A FRIEND IN NEED" PART ONE

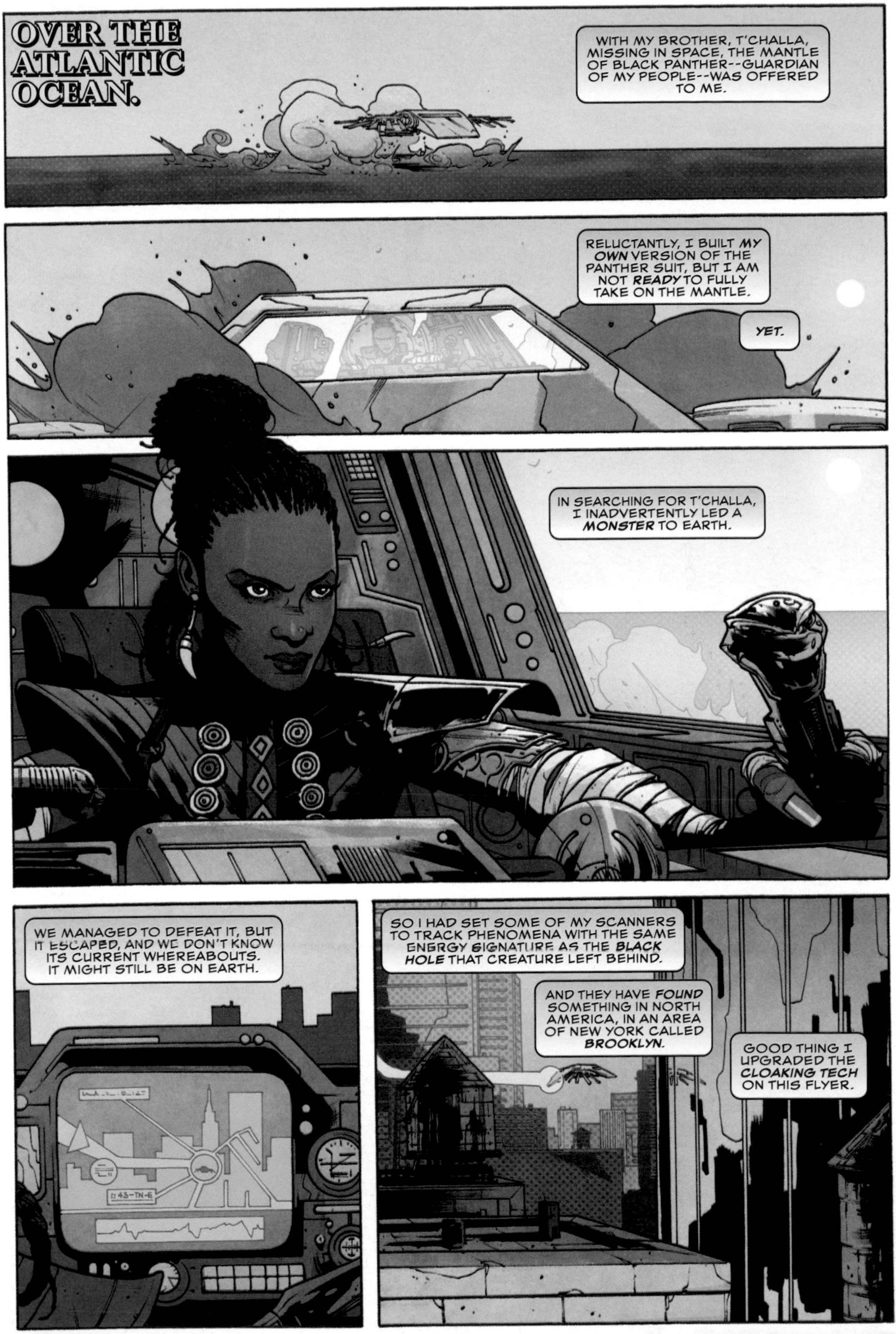
OVER THE ATLANTIC OCEAN.
WITH MY BROTHER, T'CHALLA, MISSING IN SPACE, THE MANTLE OF BLACK PANTHER--GUARDIAN OF MY PEOPLE--WAS OFFERED TO ME.
RELUCTANTLY, I BUILT MY OWN VERSION OF THE PANTHER SUIT, BUT I AM NOT READY TO FULLY TAKE ON THE MANTLE.
YET.
IN SEARCHING FOR T'CHALLA, I INADVERTENTLY LED A MONSTER TO EARTH.
WE MANAGED TO DEFEAT IT, BUT IT ESCAPED, AND WE DON'T KNOW ITS CURRENT WHEREABOUTS. IT MIGHT STILL BE ON EARTH.
SO I HAD SET SOME OF MY SCANNERS TO TRACK PHENOMENA WITH THE SAME ENERGY SIGNATURE AS THE BLACK HOLE THAT CREATURE LEFT BEHIND.
AND THEY HAVE FOUND SOMETHING IN NORTH AMERICA, IN AN AREA OF NEW YORK CALLED BROOKLYN.
GOOD THING I UPGRADED THE CLOAKING TECH ON THIS FLYER.

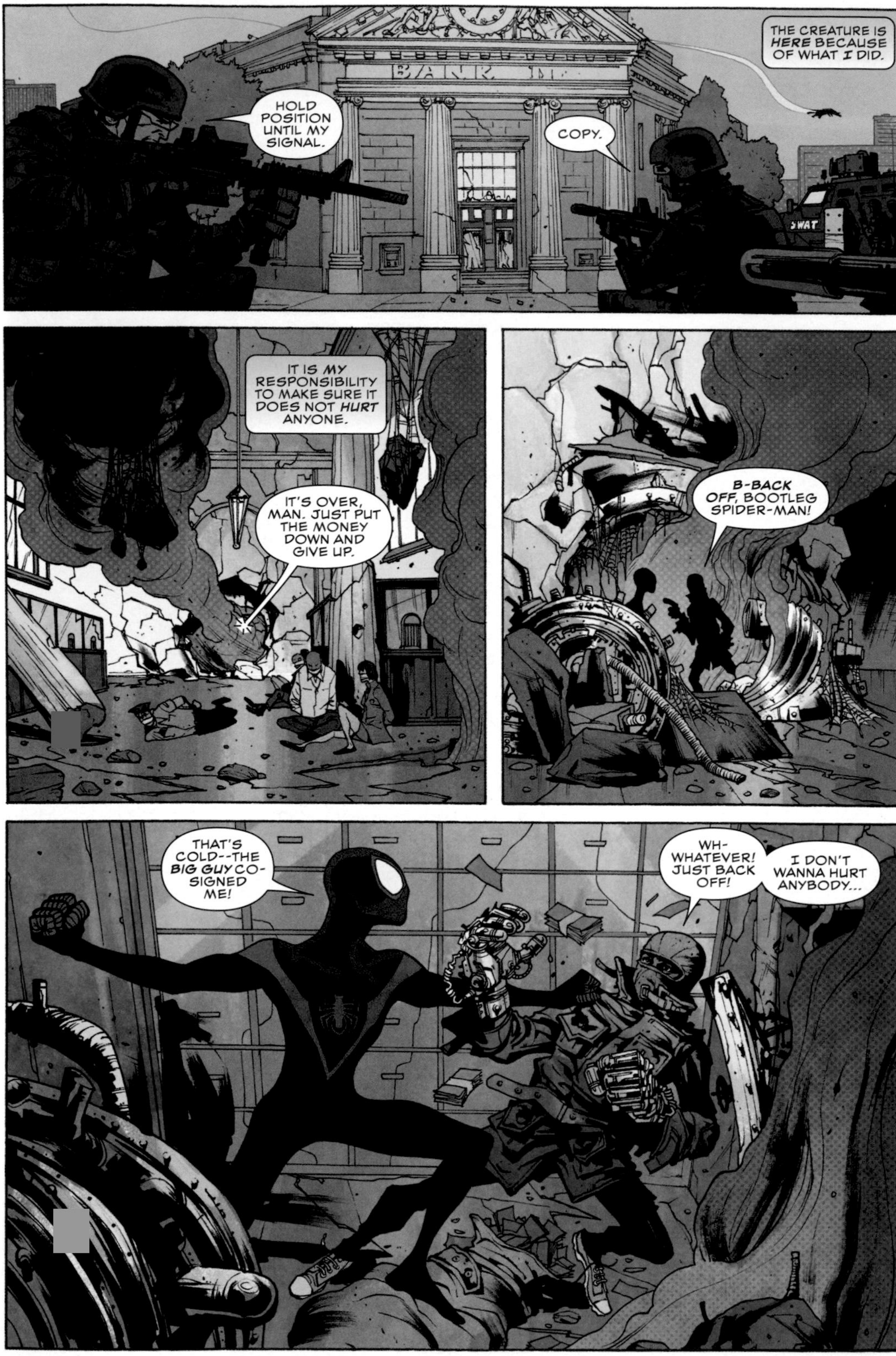
THE CREATURE IS HERE BECAUSE OF WHAT I DID.
HOLD POSITION UNTIL MY SIGNAL.
COPY.
SWAT
IT IS MY RESPONSIBILITY TO MAKE SURE IT DOES NOT HURT ANYONE.
IT'S OVER, MAN. JUST PUT THE MONEY DOWN AND GIVE UP.
B-BACK OFF, BOOTLEG SPIDER-MAN!
THAT'S COLD--THE BIG GUY CO-SIGNED ME!
WH-WHATEVER! JUST BACK OFF!
I DON'T WANNA HURT ANYBODY...

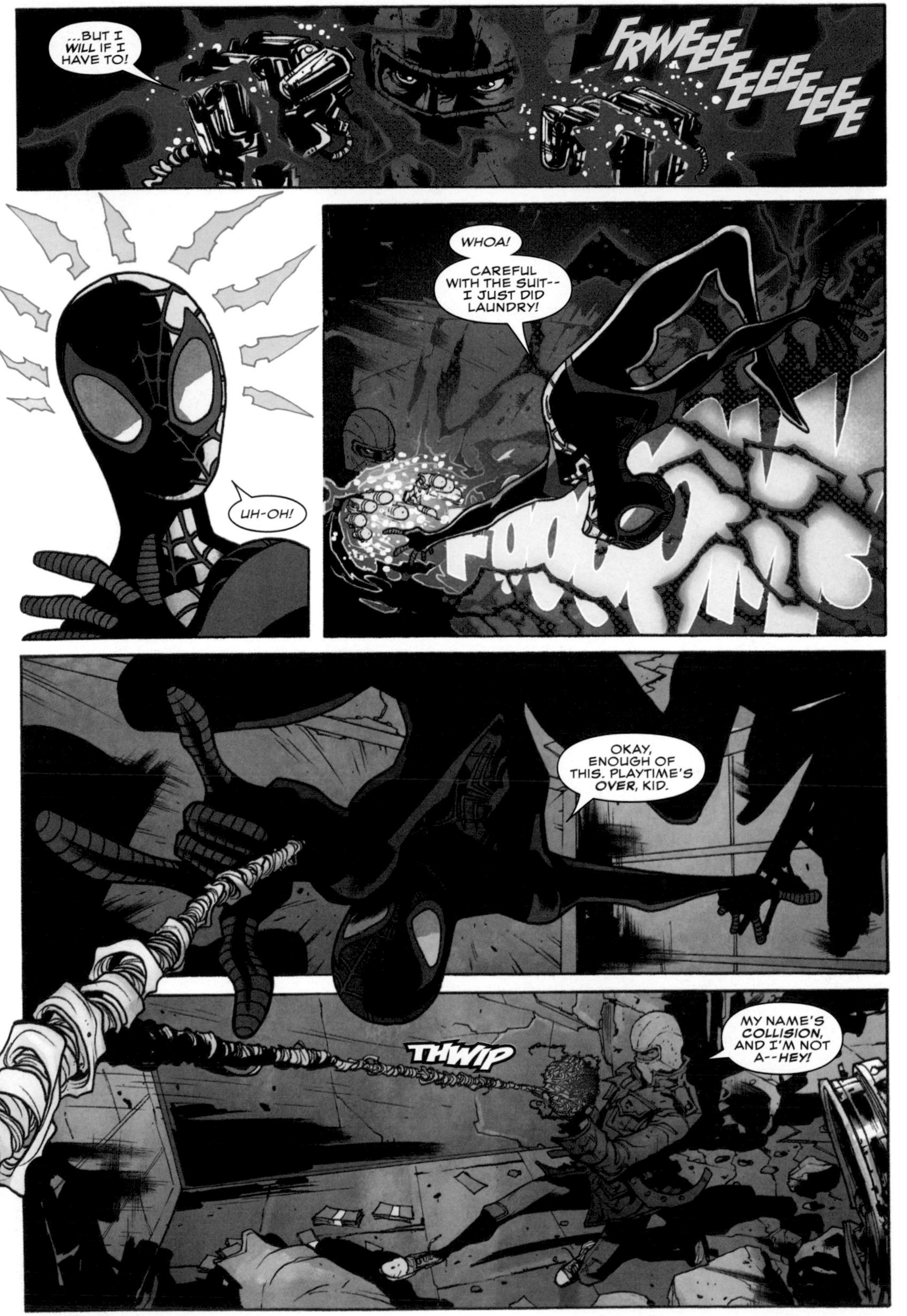
...BUT I WILL IF I HAVE TO!
FRWEEEEEEEEEEEE
UH-OH!
WHOA!
CAREFUL WITH THE SUIT-- I JUST DID LAUNDRY!
OKAY, ENOUGH OF THIS. PLAYTIME'S OVER, KID.
THWIP
MY NAME'S COLLISION, AND I'M NOT A--HEY!

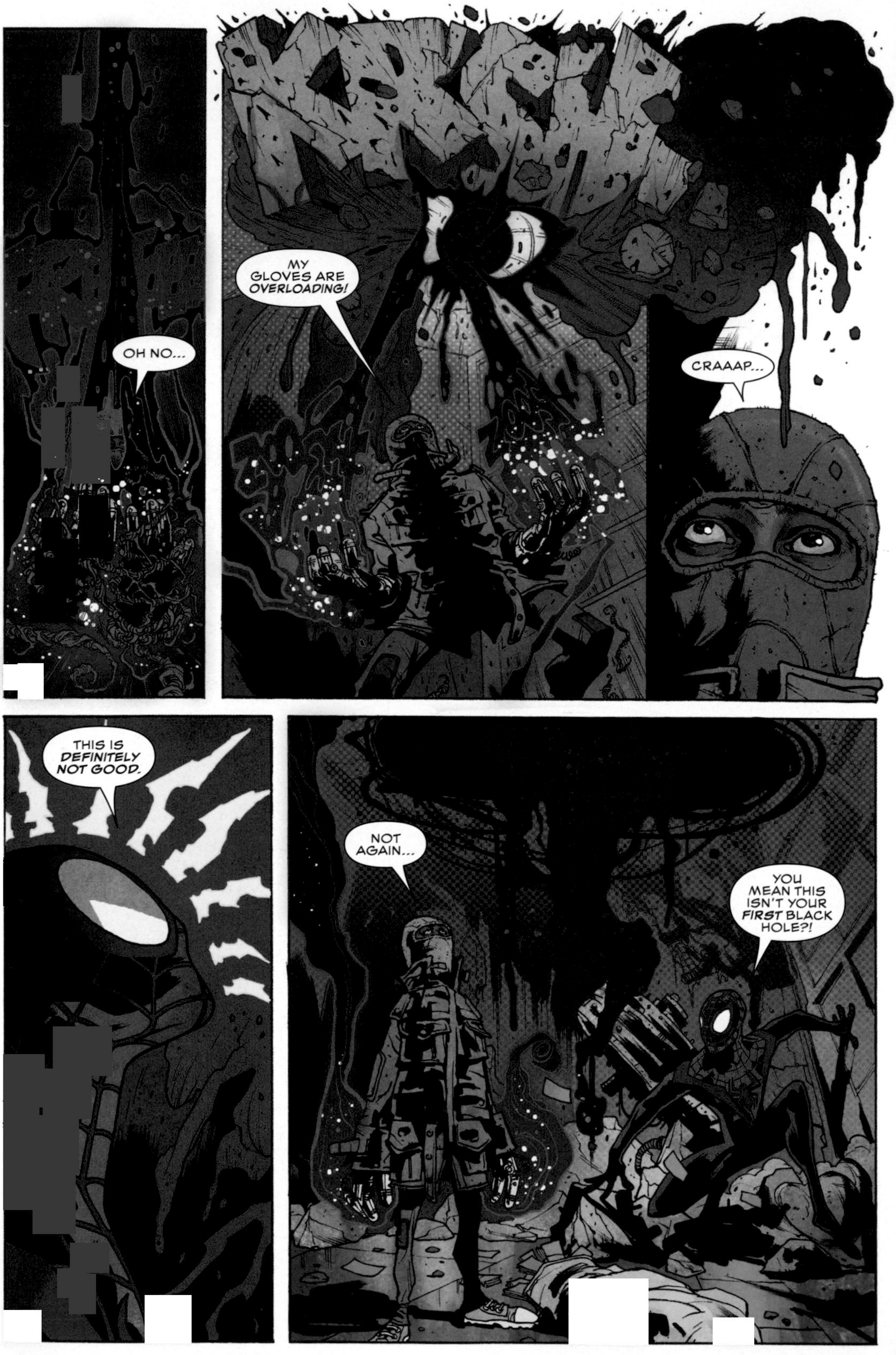
OH NO...
MY GLOVES ARE OVERLOADING!
CRAAAP...
THIS IS DEFINITELY NOT GOOD.
NOT AGAIN...
YOU MEAN THIS ISN'T YOUR FIRST BLACK HOLE?!

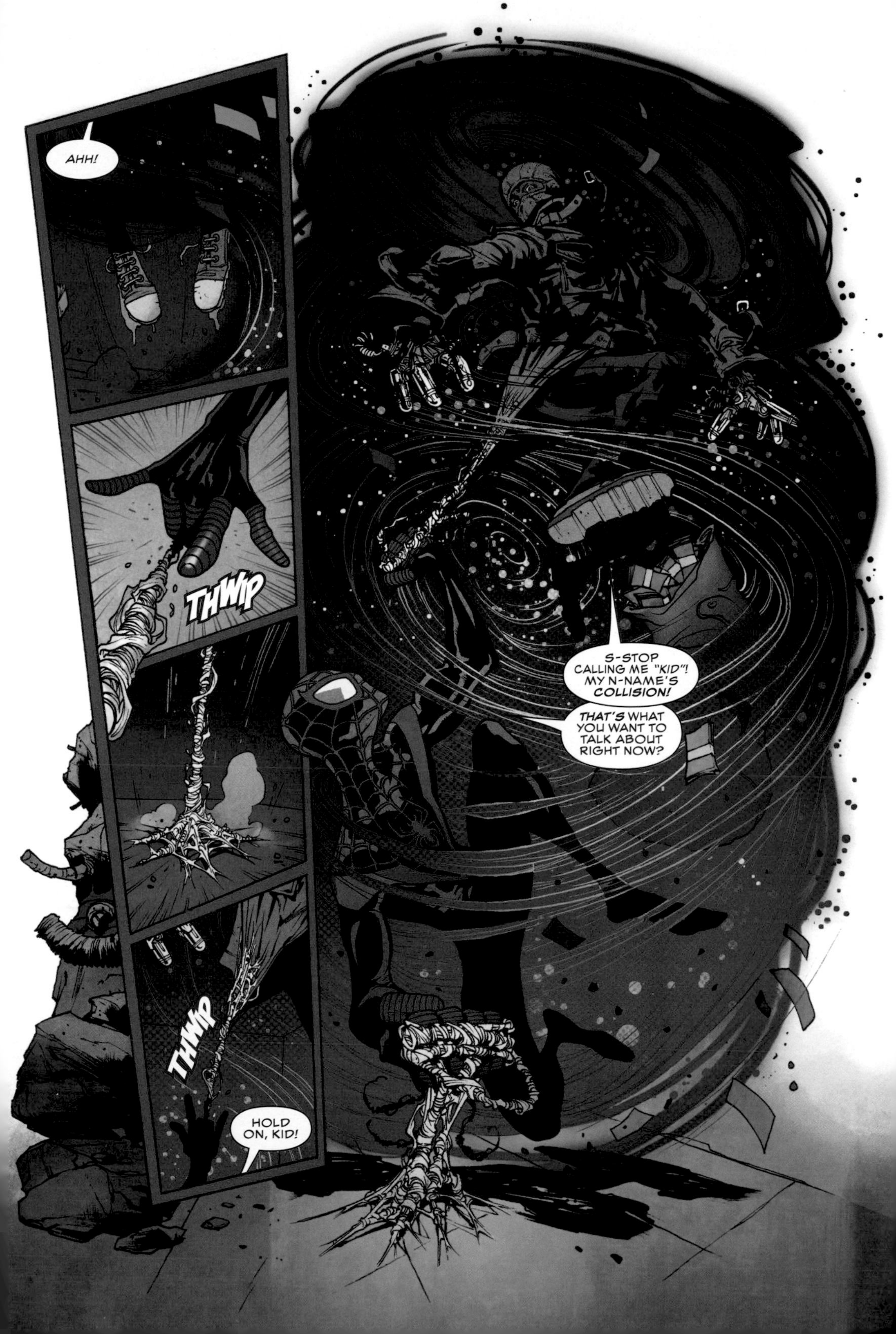
AHH!
THWIP
THWIP
HOLD ON, KID!
S-STOP CALLING ME "KID"! MY N-NAME'S COLLISION!
THAT'S WHAT YOU WANT TO TALK ABOUT RIGHT NOW?

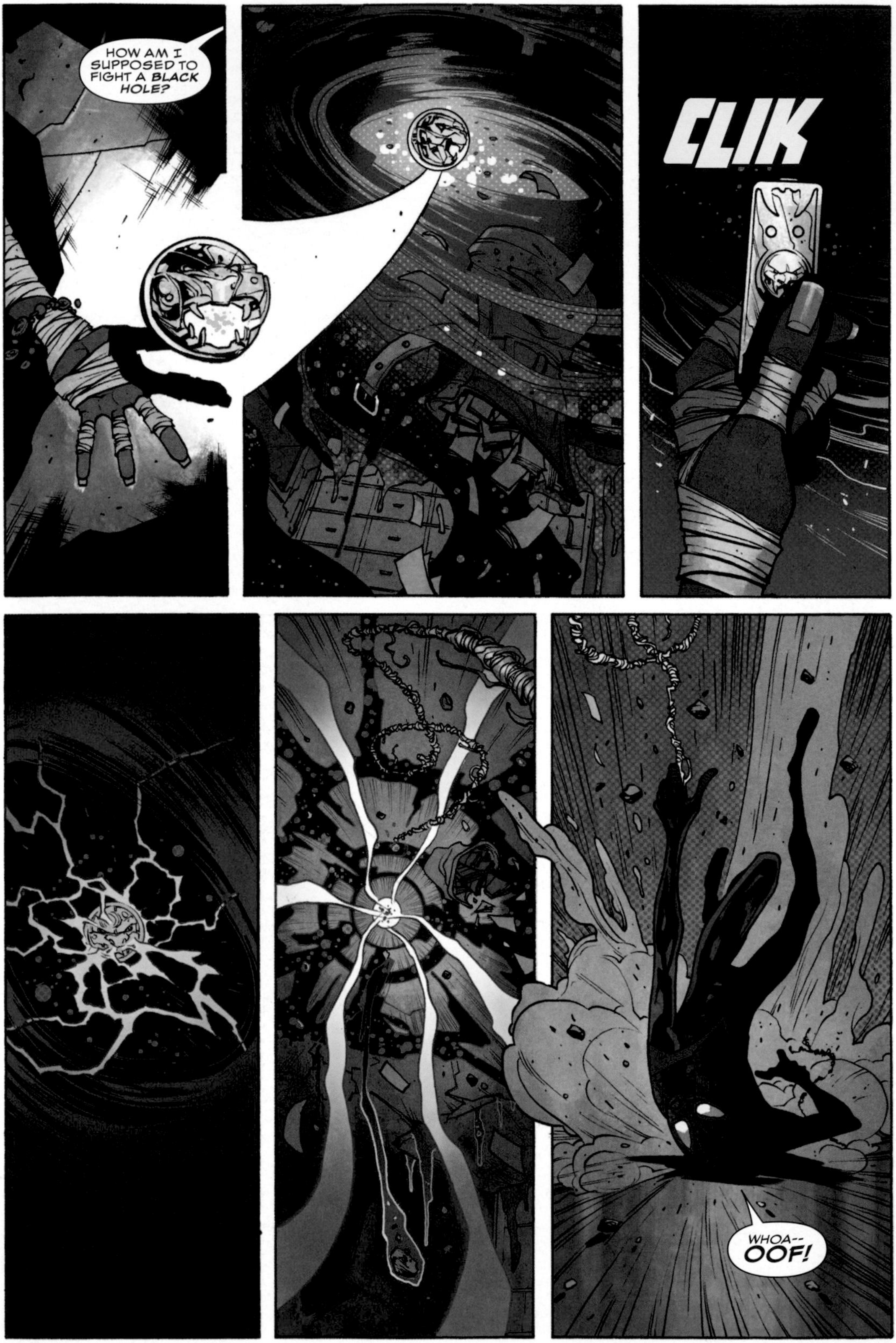
HOW AM I SUPPOSED TO FIGHT A BLACK HOLE?
CLIK
WHOA-- OOF!

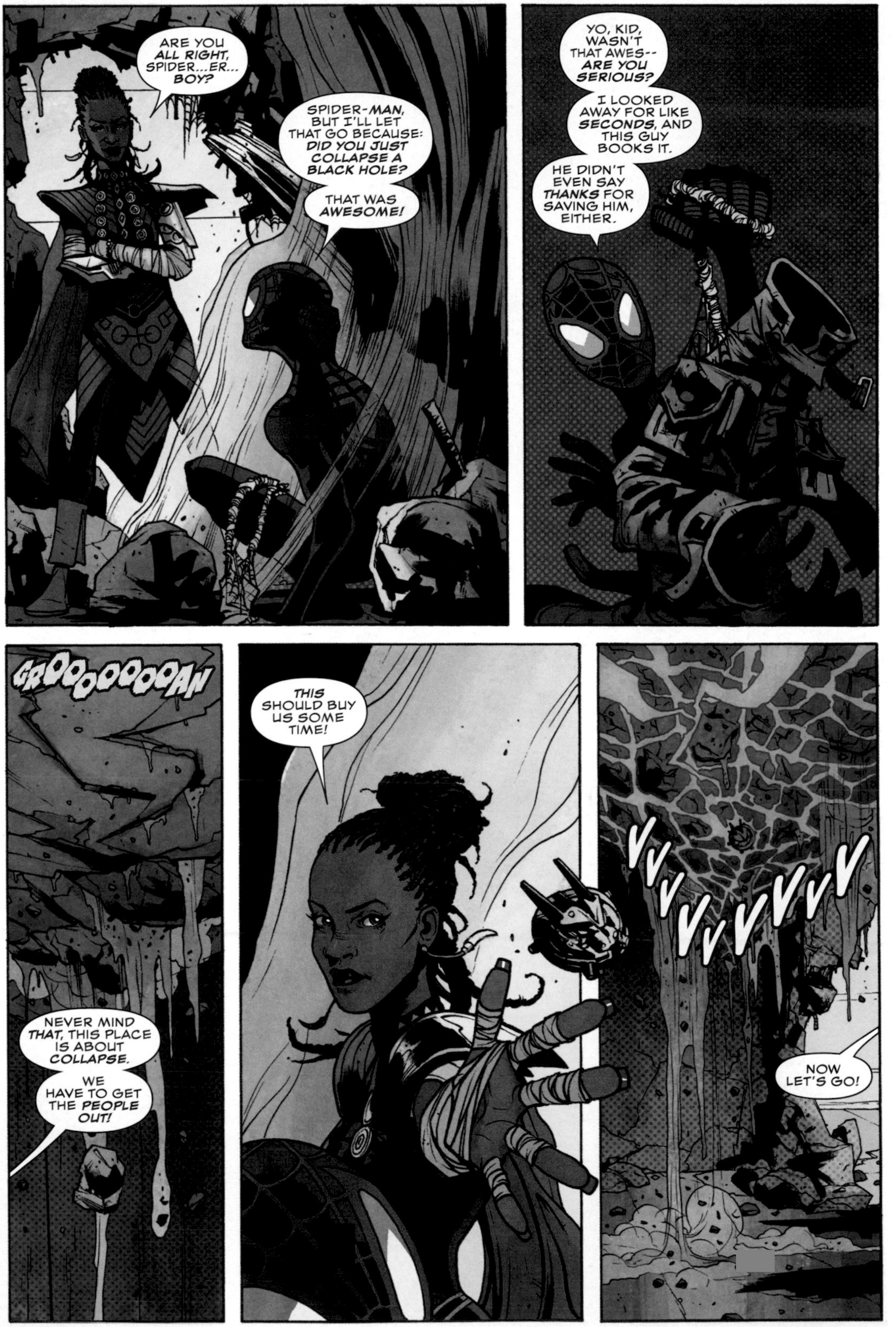
ARE YOU ALL RIGHT, SPIDER...ER... BOY?
SPIDER-MAN, BUT I'LL LET THAT GO BECAUSE: DID YOU JUST COLLAPSE A BLACK HOLE?
THAT WAS AWESOME!
YO, KID, WASN'T THAT AWES-- ARE YOU SERIOUS?
I LOOKED AWAY FOR LIKE SECONDS, AND THIS GUY BOOKS IT.
HE DIDN'T EVEN SAY THANKS FOR SAVING HIM, EITHER.
GROOOOOOOOAN
NEVER MIND THAT, THIS PLACE IS ABOUT COLLAPSE.
WE HAVE TO GET THE PEOPLE OUT!
THIS SHOULD BUY US SOME TIME!
VVVVVVVVVVVV
NOW LET'S GO!

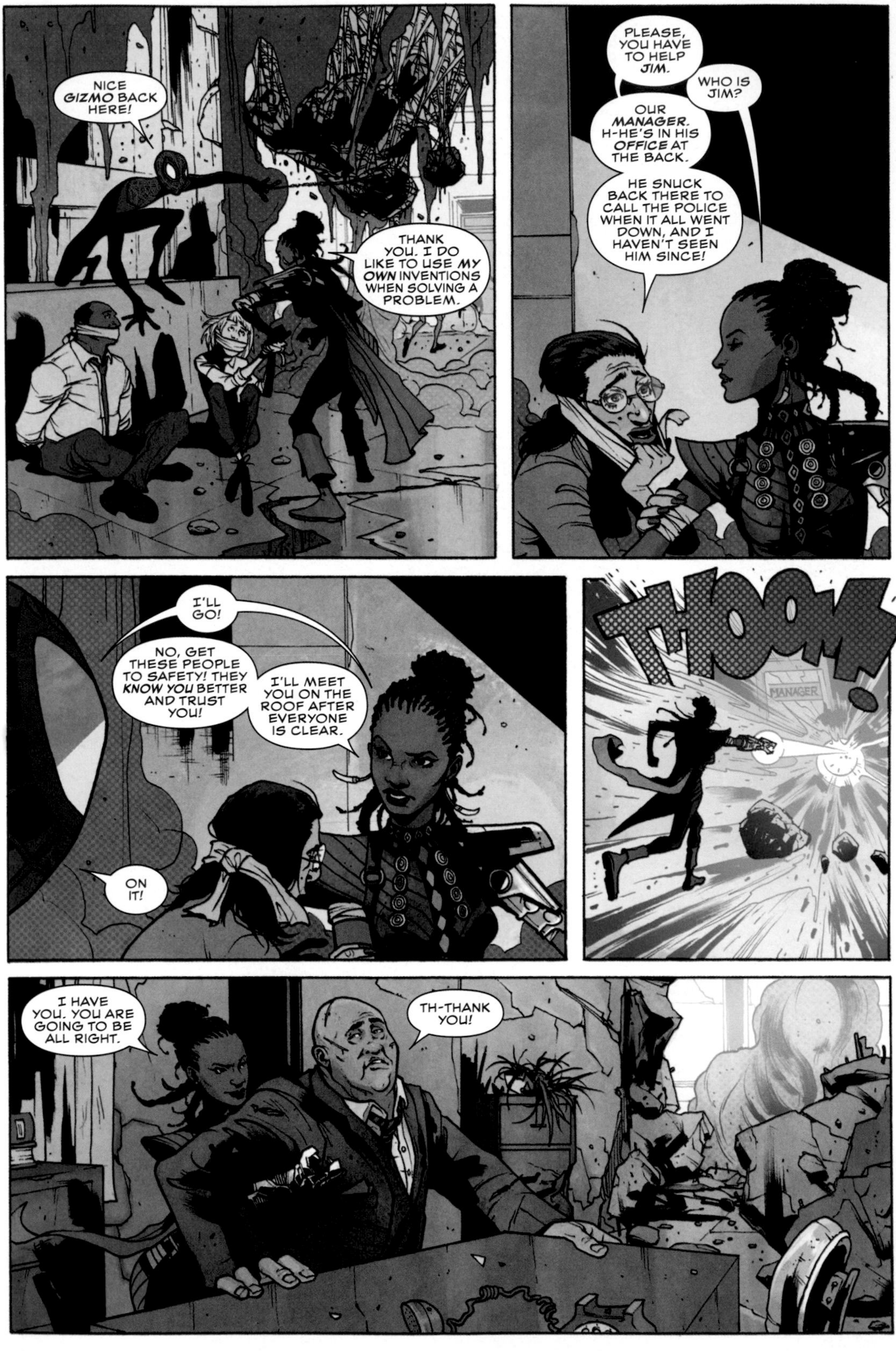
NICE GIZMO BACK HERE!
THANK YOU. I DO LIKE TO USE MY OWN INVENTIONS WHEN SOLVING A PROBLEM.
PLEASE, YOU HAVE TO HELP JIM.
WHO IS JIM?
OUR MANAGER. H-HE'S IN HIS OFFICE AT THE BACK.
HE SNUCK BACK THERE TO CALL THE POLICE WHEN IT ALL WENT DOWN, AND I HAVEN'T SEEN HIM SINCE!
I'LL GO!
NO, GET THESE PEOPLE TO SAFETY! THEY KNOW YOU BETTER AND TRUST YOU!
I'LL MEET YOU ON THE ROOF AFTER EVERYONE IS CLEAR.
ON IT!
THOOM!
MANAGER
I HAVE YOU. YOU ARE GOING TO BE ALL RIGHT.
TH-THANK YOU!

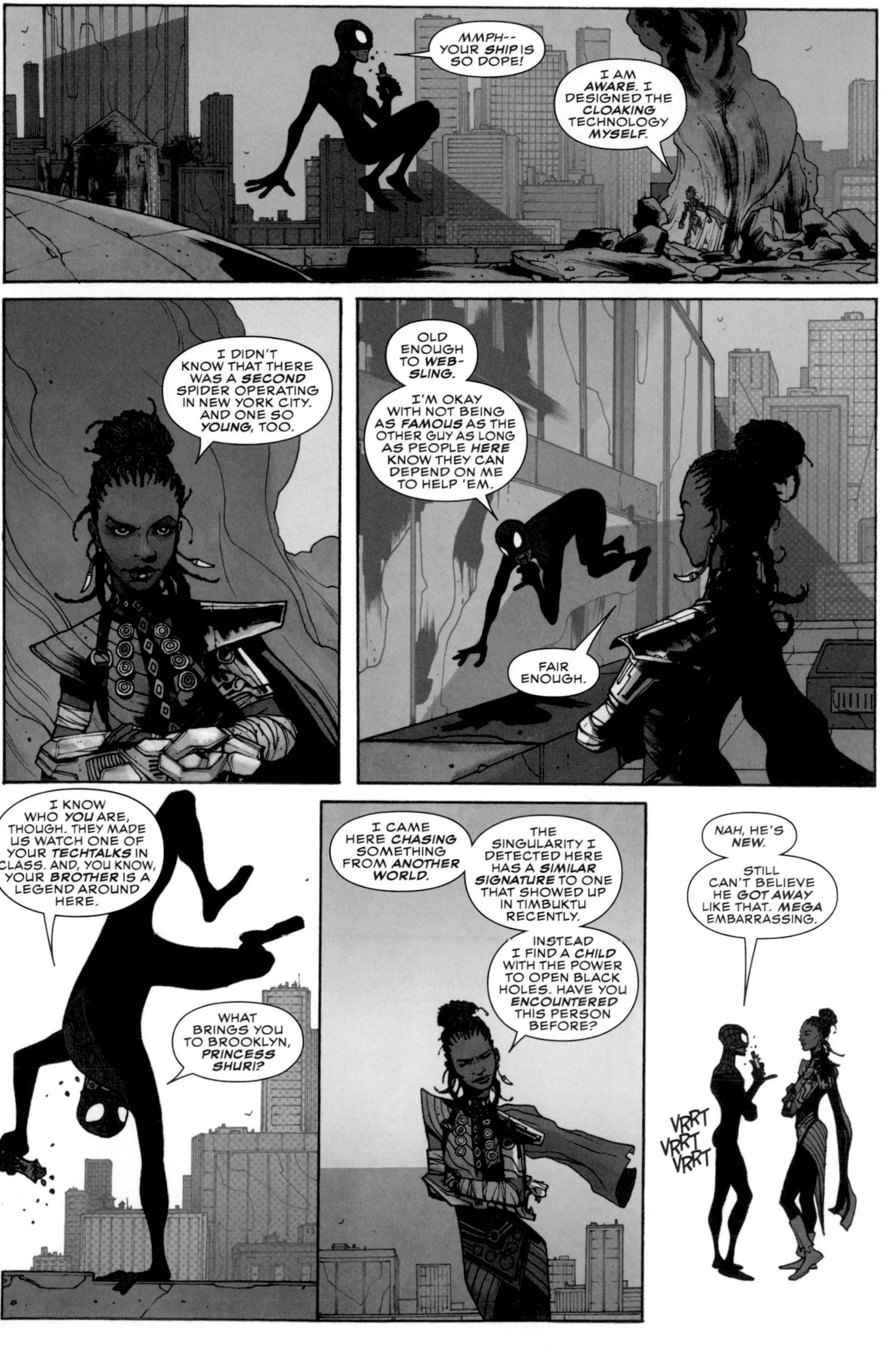
MMPH-- YOUR SHIP IS SO DOPE!
I AM AWARE. I DESIGNED THE CLOAKING TECHNOLOGY MYSELF.
I DIDN'T KNOW THAT THERE WAS A SECOND SPIDER OPERATING IN NEW YORK CITY. AND ONE SO YOUNG, TOO.
OLD ENOUGH TO WEB-SLING.
I'M OKAY WITH NOT BEING AS FAMOUS AS THE OTHER GUY AS LONG AS PEOPLE HERE KNOW THEY CAN DEPEND ON ME TO HELP 'EM.
FAIR ENOUGH.
I KNOW WHO YOU ARE, THOUGH. THEY MADE US WATCH ONE OF YOUR TECHTALKS IN CLASS. AND, YOU KNOW, YOUR BROTHER IS A LEGEND AROUND HERE.
WHAT BRINGS YOU TO BROOKLYN, PRINCESS SHURI?
I CAME HERE CHASING SOMETHING FROM ANOTHER WORLD.
THE SINGULARITY I DETECTED HERE HAS A SIMILAR SIGNATURE TO ONE THAT SHOWED UP IN TIMBUKTU RECENTLY.
INSTEAD I FIND A CHILD WITH THE POWER TO OPEN BLACK HOLES. HAVE YOU ENCOUNTERED THIS PERSON BEFORE?
NAH, HE'S NEW.
STILL CAN'T BELIEVE HE GOT AWAY LIKE THAT. MEGA EMBARRASSING.
VRRT VRRT VRRT

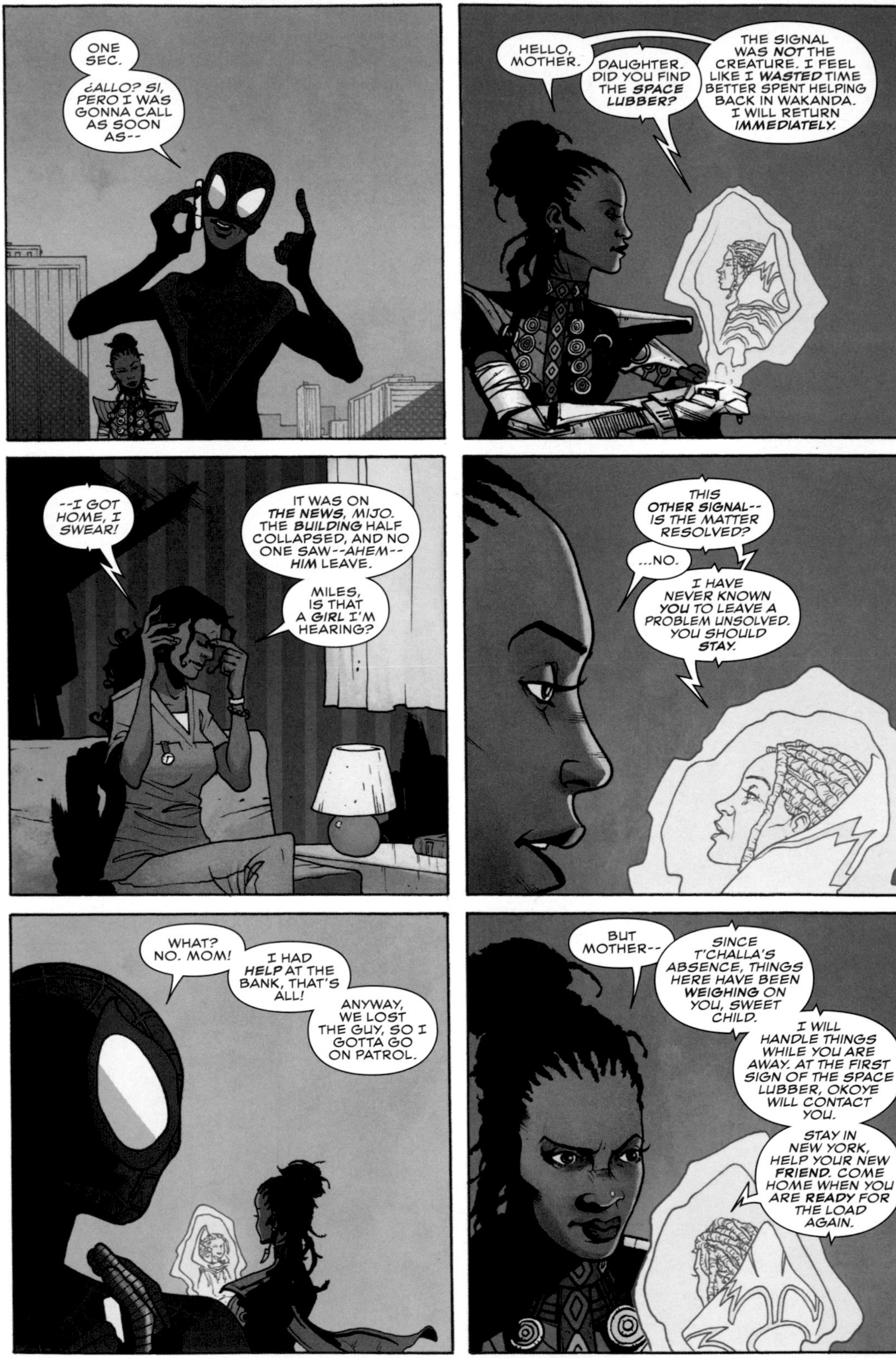
ONE SEC.
¿ALLO? SI, PERO I WAS GONNA CALL AS SOON AS--
HELLO, MOTHER.
DAUGHTER. DID YOU FIND THE SPACE LUBBER?
THE SIGNAL WAS NOT THE CREATURE. I FEEL LIKE I WASTED TIME BETTER SPENT HELPING BACK IN WAKANDA. I WILL RETURN IMMEDIATELY.
--I GOT HOME, I SWEAR!
IT WAS ON THE NEWS, MIJO. THE BUILDING HALF COLLAPSED, AND NO ONE SAW--AHEM--HIM LEAVE.
MILES, IS THAT A GIRL I'M HEARING?
THIS OTHER SIGNAL-- IS THE MATTER RESOLVED?
...NO.
I HAVE NEVER KNOWN YOU TO LEAVE A PROBLEM UNSOLVED. YOU SHOULD STAY.
WHAT? NO. MOM!
I HAD HELP AT THE BANK, THAT'S ALL!
ANYWAY, WE LOST THE GUY, SO I GOTTA GO ON PATROL.
BUT MOTHER--
SINCE T'CHALLA'S ABSENCE, THINGS HERE HAVE BEEN WEIGHING ON YOU, SWEET CHILD.
I WILL HANDLE THINGS WHILE YOU ARE AWAY. AT THE FIRST SIGN OF THE SPACE LUBBER, OKOYE WILL CONTACT YOU.
STAY IN NEW YORK, HELP YOUR NEW FRIEND. COME HOME WHEN YOU ARE READY FOR THE LOAD AGAIN.

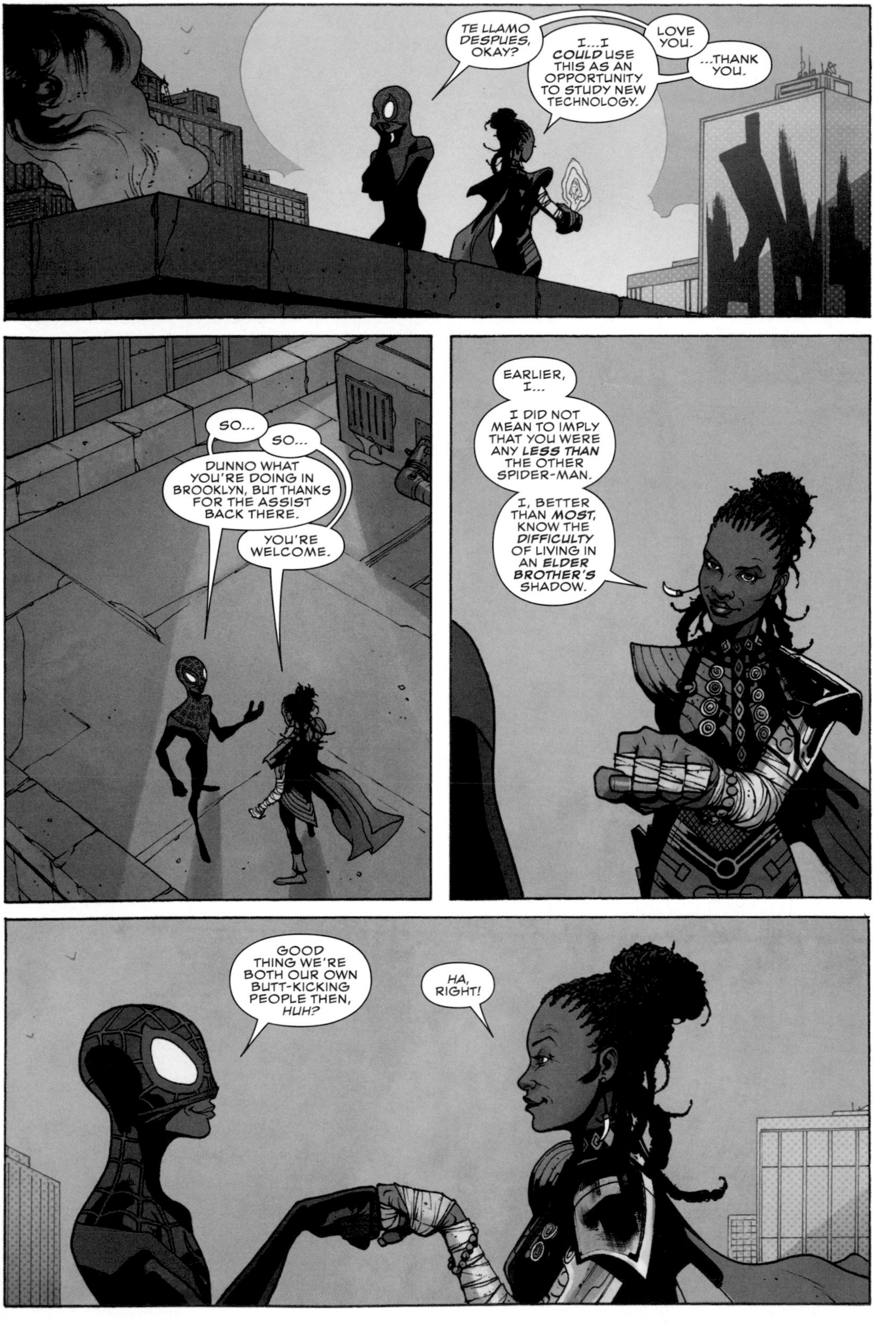

TE LLAMO DESPUES, OKAY?
LOVE YOU.
I...I COULD USE THIS AS AN OPPORTUNITY TO STUDY NEW TECHNOLOGY.
...THANK YOU.
SO...
SO...
DUNNO WHAT YOU'RE DOING IN BROOKLYN, BUT THANKS FOR THE ASSIST BACK THERE.
YOU'RE WELCOME.
EARLIER, I...
I DID NOT MEAN TO IMPLY THAT YOU WERE ANY LESS THAN THE OTHER SPIDER-MAN.
I, BETTER THAN MOST, KNOW THE DIFFICULTY OF LIVING IN AN ELDER BROTHER'S SHADOW.
GOOD THING WE'RE BOTH OUR OWN BUTT-KICKING PEOPLE THEN, HUH?
HA, RIGHT!

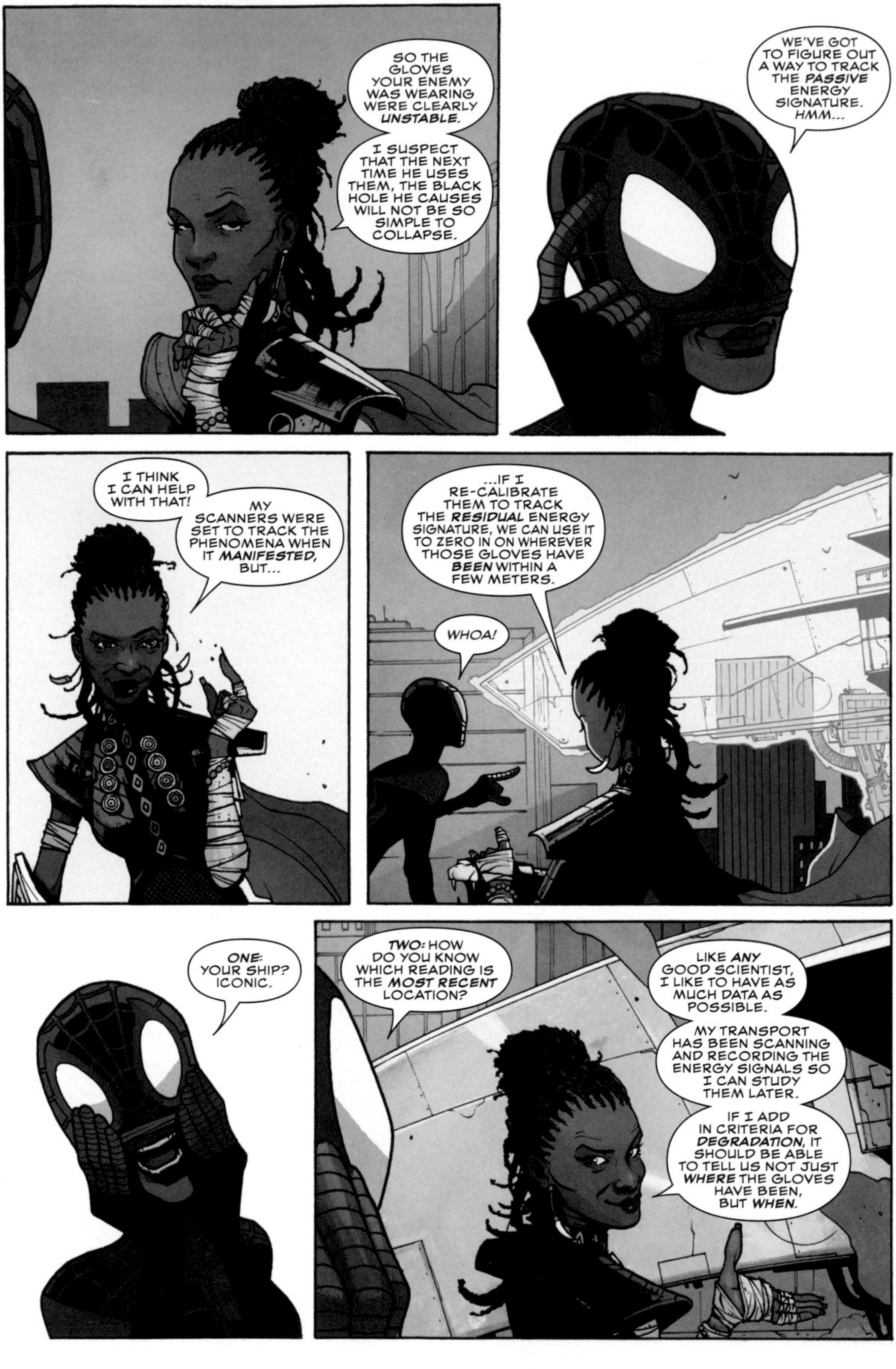
SO THE GLOVES YOUR ENEMY WAS WEARING WERE CLEARLY UNSTABLE.
I SUSPECT THAT THE NEXT TIME HE USES THEM, THE BLACK HOLE HE CAUSES WILL NOT BE SO SIMPLE TO COLLAPSE.
WE'VE GOT TO FIGURE OUT A WAY TO TRACK THE PASSIVE ENERGY SIGNATURE. HMM...
I THINK I CAN HELP WITH THAT!
MY SCANNERS WERE SET TO TRACK THE PHENOMENA WHEN IT MANIFESTED, BUT...
...IF I RE-CALIBRATE THEM TO TRACK THE RESIDUAL ENERGY SIGNATURE, WE CAN USE IT TO ZERO IN ON WHEREVER THOSE GLOVES HAVE BEEN WITHIN A FEW METERS.
WHOA!
ONE: YOUR SHIP? ICONIC.
TWO: HOW DO YOU KNOW WHICH READING IS THE MOST RECENT LOCATION?
LIKE ANY GOOD SCIENTIST, I LIKE TO HAVE AS MUCH DATA AS POSSIBLE.
MY TRANSPORT HAS BEEN SCANNING AND RECORDING THE ENERGY SIGNALS SO I CAN STUDY THEM LATER.
IF I ADD IN CRITERIA FOR DEGRADATION, IT SHOULD BE ABLE TO TELL US NOT JUST WHERE THE GLOVES HAVE BEEN, BUT WHEN.

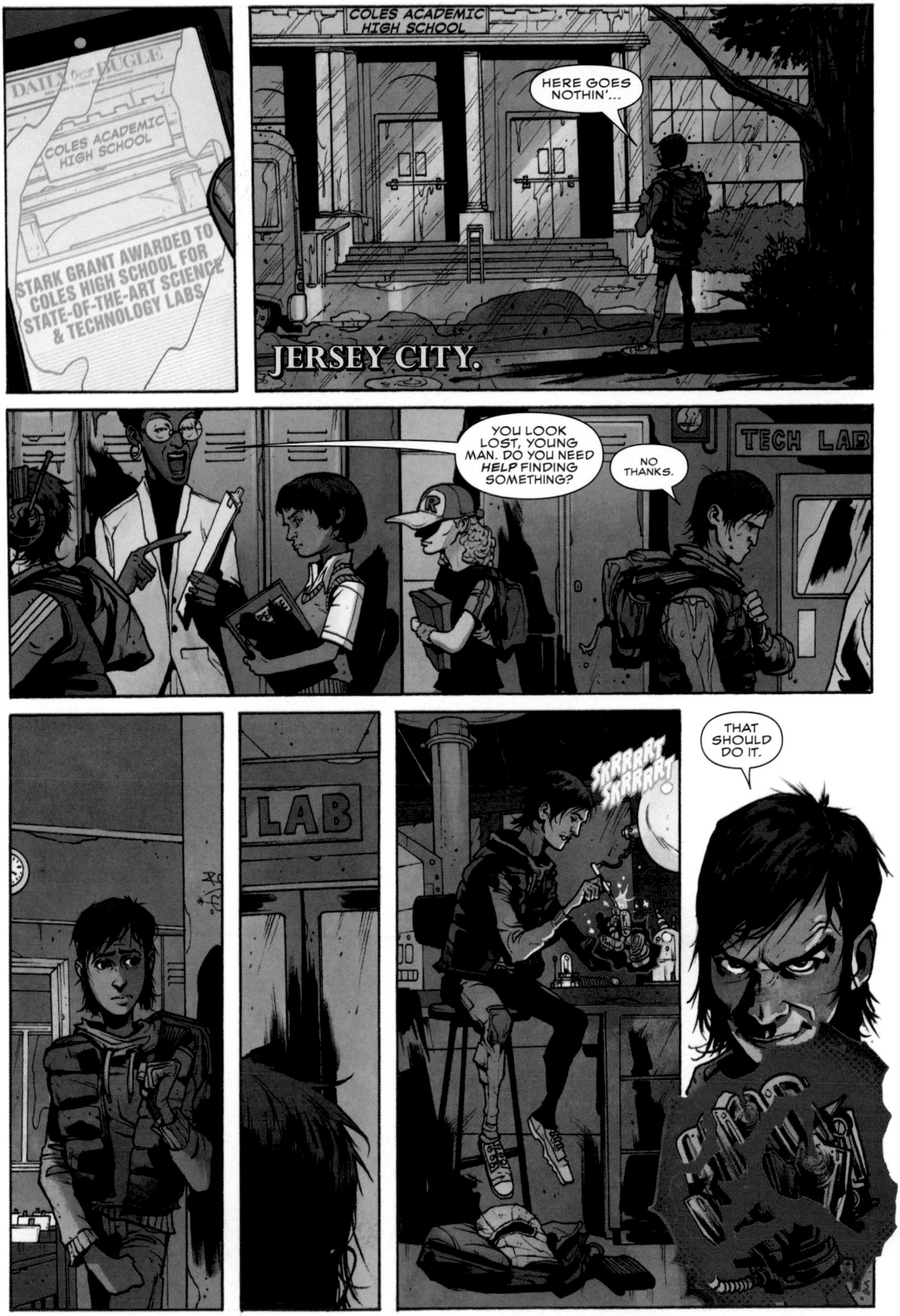
DAILY BUGLE
COLES ACADEMIC HIGH SCHOOL
STARK GRANT AWARDED TO COLES HIGH SCHOOL FOR STATE-OF-THE-ART SCIENCE & TECHNOLOGY LABS
COLES ACADEMIC HIGH SCHOOL
HERE GOES NOTHIN'...
JERSEY CITY.
YOU LOOK LOST, YOUNG MAN. DO YOU NEED *HELP* FINDING SOMETHING?
NO THANKS.
TECH LAB
LAB
SKRRRRT SKRRRRT
THAT SHOULD DO IT.

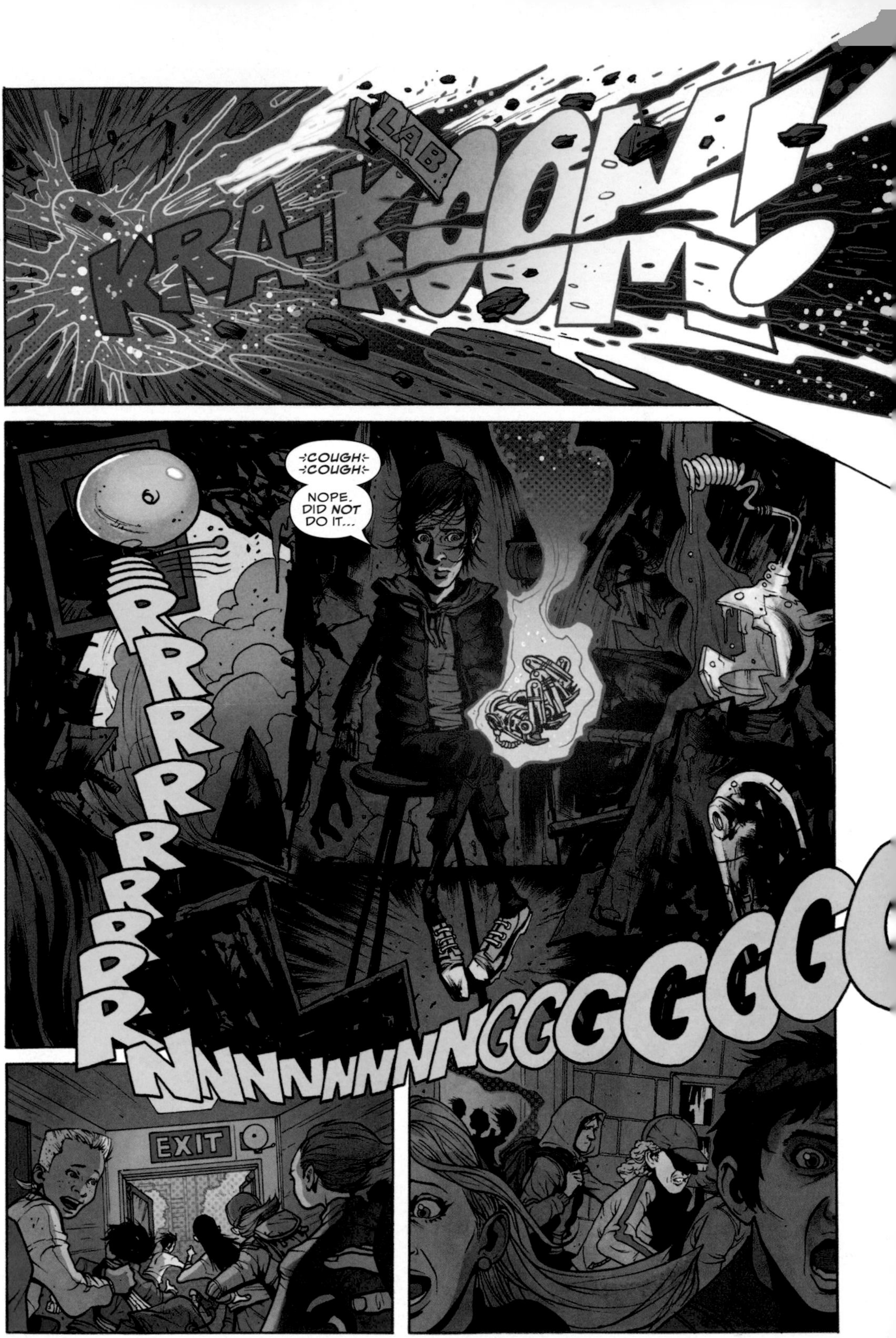

LAB
KRA-KOOOM!
COUGH
COUGH
NOPE. DID NOT DO IT...
RRRRRRRRRNNNNNNNNGGGGGG
EXIT

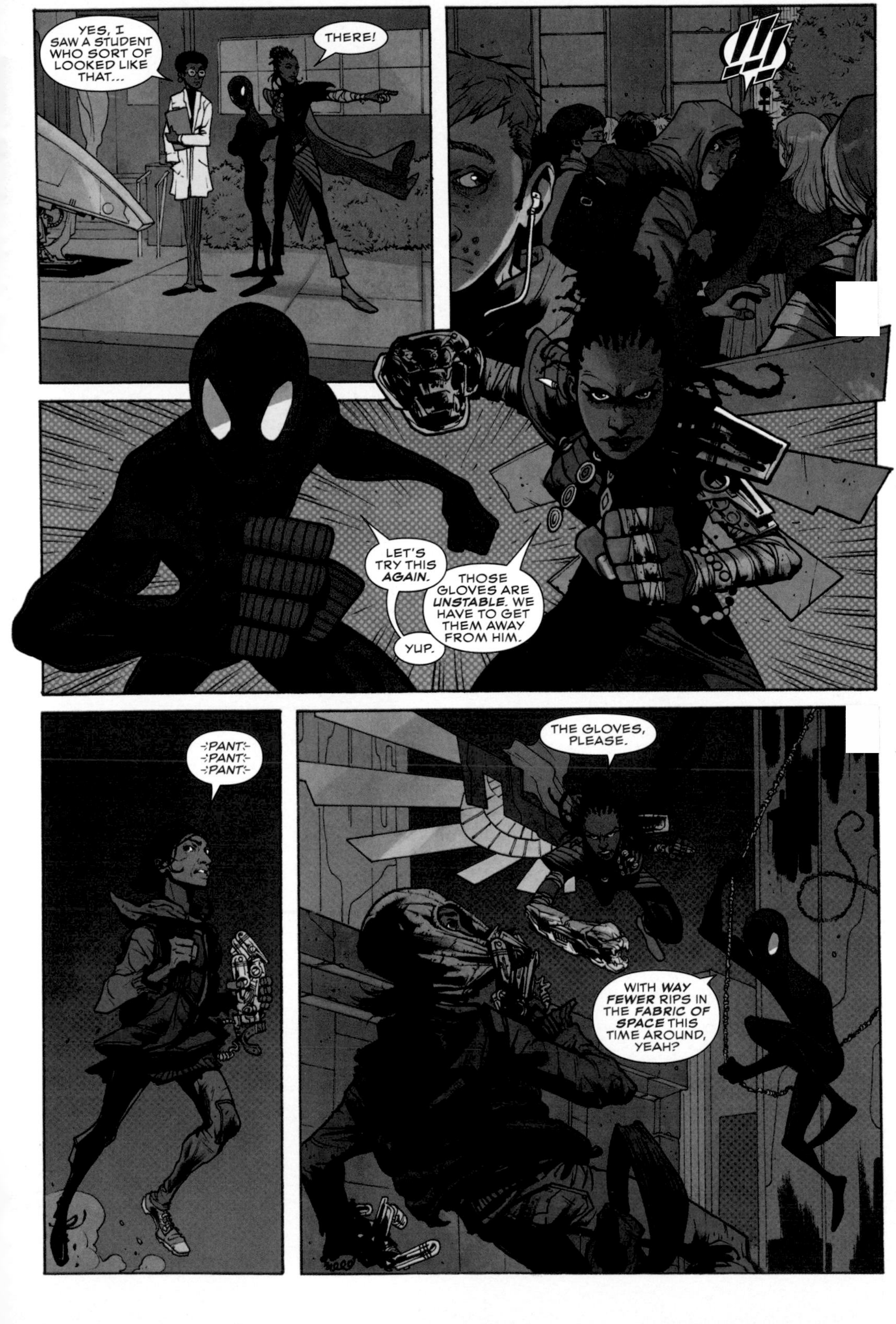
YES, I SAW A STUDENT WHO SORT OF LOOKED LIKE THAT...
THERE!
LET'S TRY THIS AGAIN.
THOSE GLOVES ARE UNSTABLE. WE HAVE TO GET THEM AWAY FROM HIM.
YUP.
PANT PANT PANT
THE GLOVES, PLEASE.
WITH WAY FEWER RIPS IN THE FABRIC OF SPACE THIS TIME AROUND, YEAH?

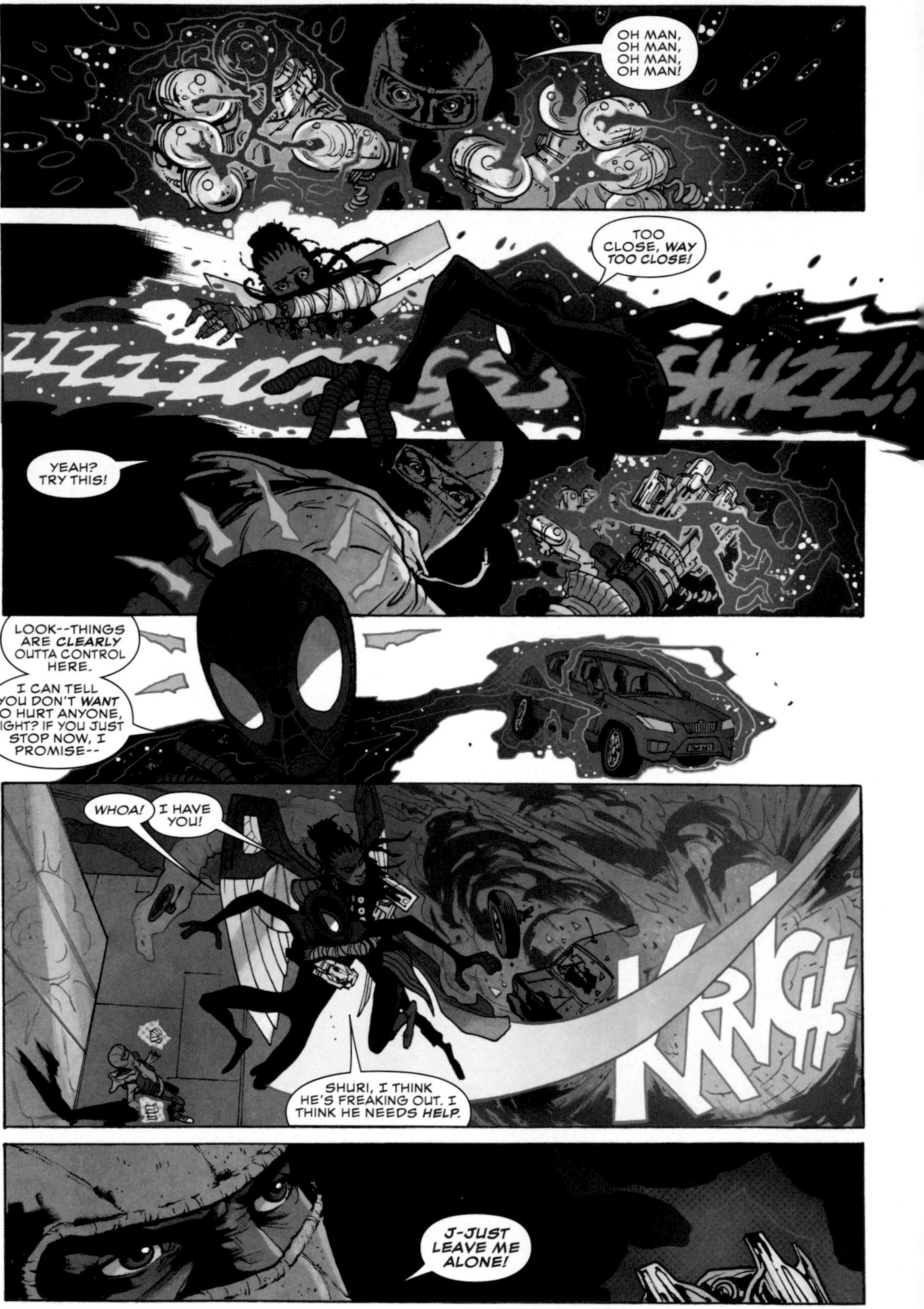
OH MAN, OH MAN, OH MAN, OH MAN!
TOO CLOSE, WAY TOO CLOSE!
ZZZZZOOMSSSSHHZZ!!
YEAH? TRY THIS!
LOOK--THINGS ARE CLEARLY OUTTA CONTROL HERE.
I CAN TELL YOU DON'T WANT TO HURT ANYONE, RIGHT? IF YOU JUST STOP NOW, I PROMISE--
WHOA!
I HAVE YOU!
KRRUNCH
SHURI, I THINK HE'S FREAKING OUT. I THINK HE NEEDS HELP.
J-JUST LEAVE ME ALONE!

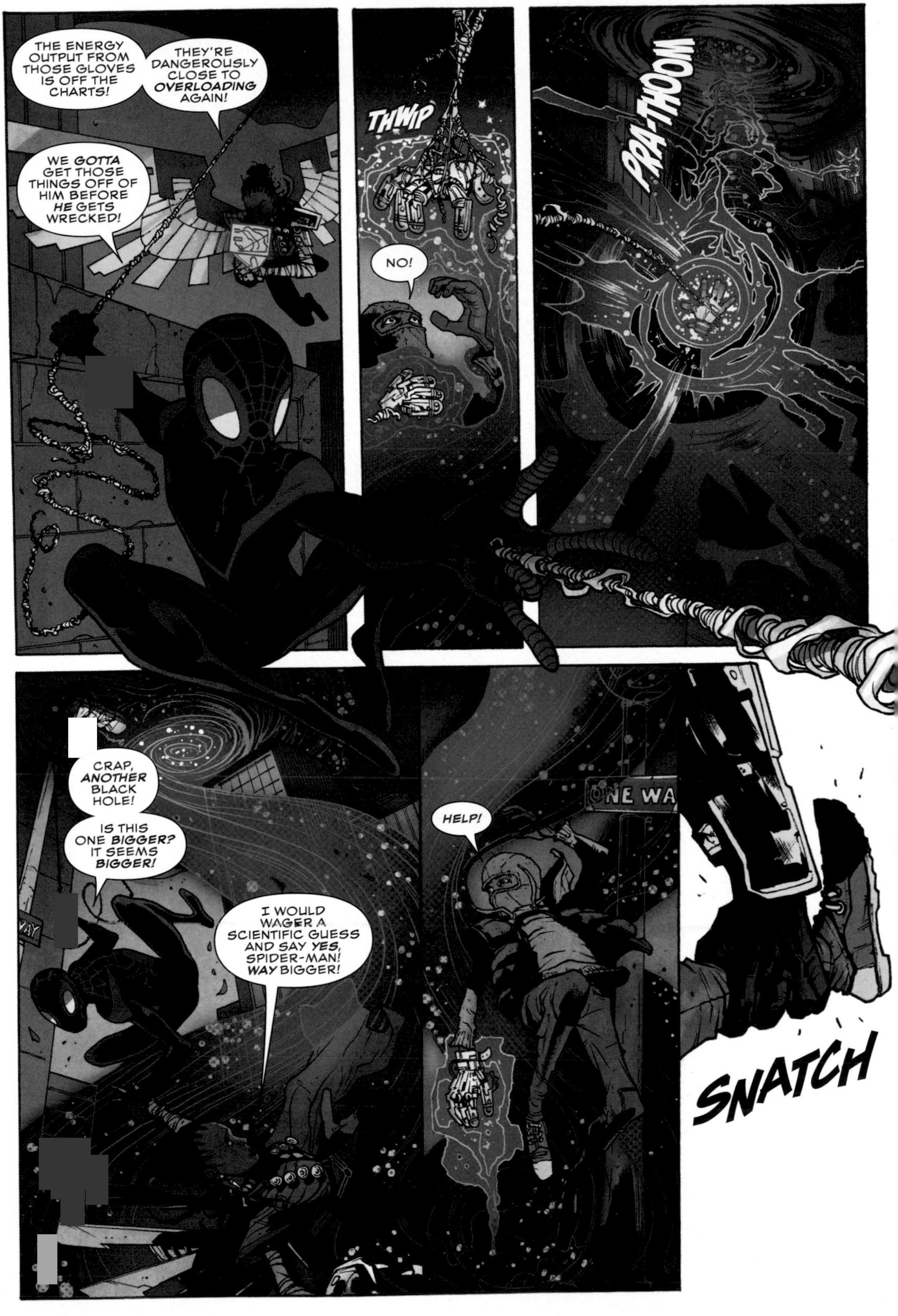
THE ENERGY OUTPUT FROM THOSE GLOVES IS OFF THE CHARTS!
THEY'RE DANGEROUSLY CLOSE TO OVERLOADING AGAIN!
WE GOTTA GET THOSE THINGS OFF OF HIM BEFORE HE GETS WRECKED!
THWIP
NO!
PRA-THOOM
CRAP, ANOTHER BLACK HOLE!
IS THIS ONE BIGGER? IT SEEMS BIGGER!
I WOULD WAGER A SCIENTIFIC GUESS AND SAY YES, SPIDER-MAN! WAY BIGGER!
ONE WA
HELP!
SNATCH

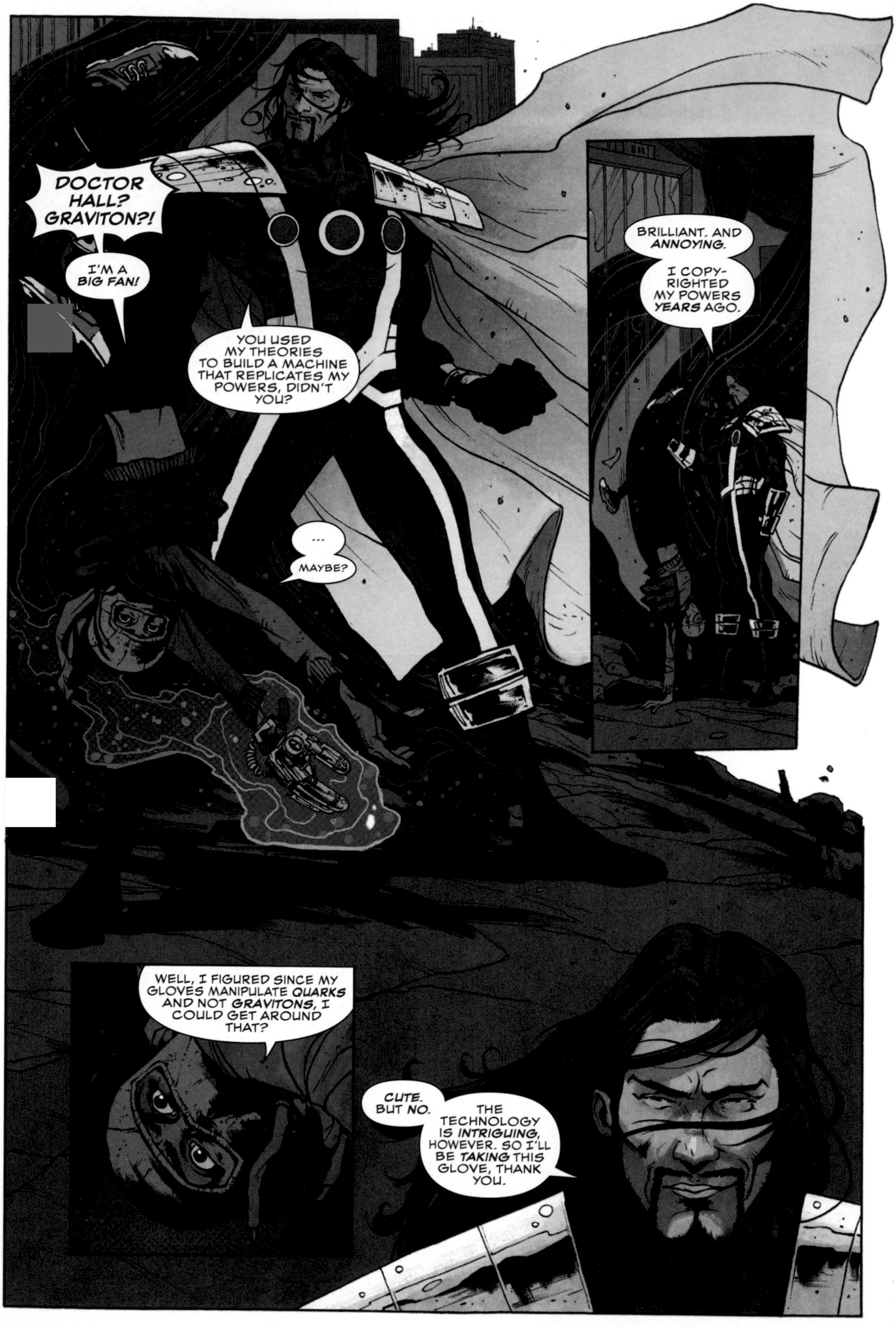
DOCTOR HALL? GRAVITON?!
I'M A BIG FAN!
YOU USED MY THEORIES TO BUILD A MACHINE THAT REPLICATES MY POWERS, DIDN'T YOU?
...
MAYBE?
BRILLIANT. AND ANNOYING.
I COPY-RIGHTED MY POWERS YEARS AGO.
WELL, I FIGURED SINCE MY GLOVES MANIPULATE QUARKS AND NOT GRAVITONS, I COULD GET AROUND THAT?
CUTE. BUT NO.
THE TECHNOLOGY IS INTRIGUING, HOWEVER. SO I'LL BE TAKING THIS GLOVE, THANK YOU.

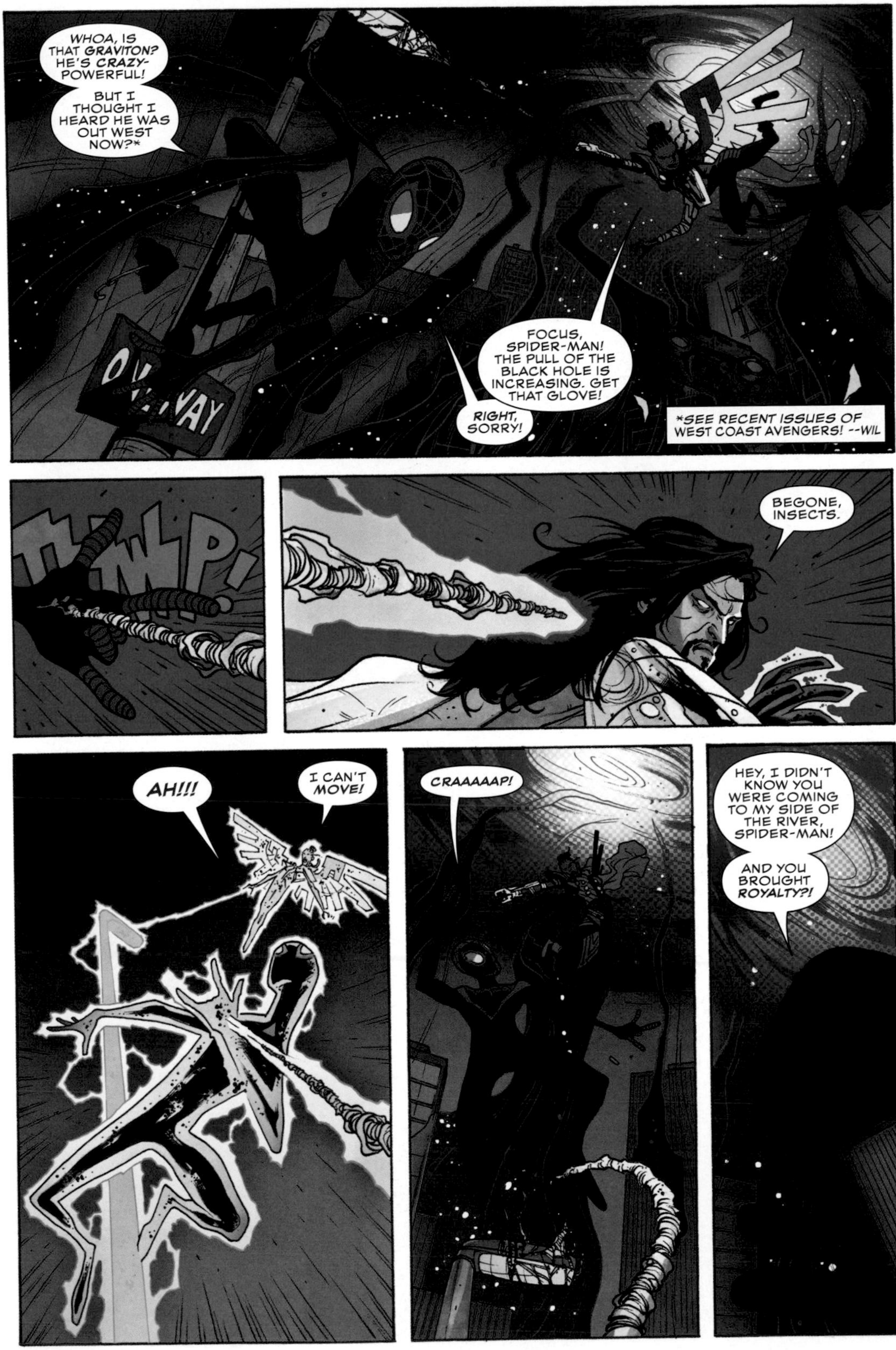
WHOA, IS THAT GRAVITON? HE'S CRAZY-POWERFUL!
BUT I THOUGHT I HEARD HE WAS OUT WEST NOW?*
FOCUS, SPIDER-MAN! THE PULL OF THE BLACK HOLE IS INCREASING. GET THAT GLOVE!
RIGHT, SORRY!
*SEE RECENT ISSUES OF WEST COAST AVENGERS! --WIL
THWIP!
BEGONE, INSECTS.
AH!!!
I CAN'T MOVE!
CRAAAAAP!
HEY, I DIDN'T KNOW YOU WERE COMING TO MY SIDE OF THE RIVER, SPIDER-MAN!
AND YOU BROUGHT ROYALTY?!

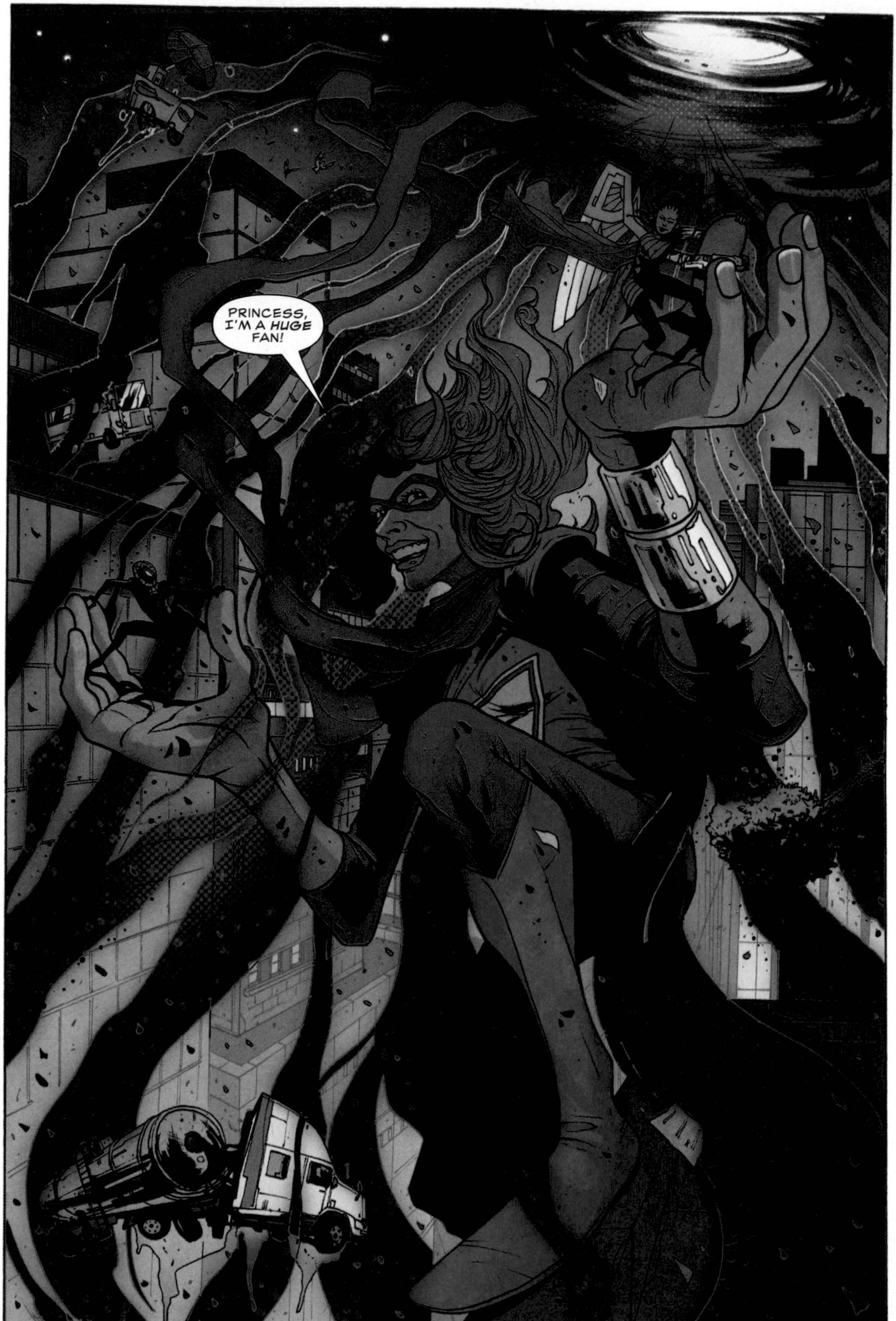
PRINCESS, I'M A *HUGE* FAN!

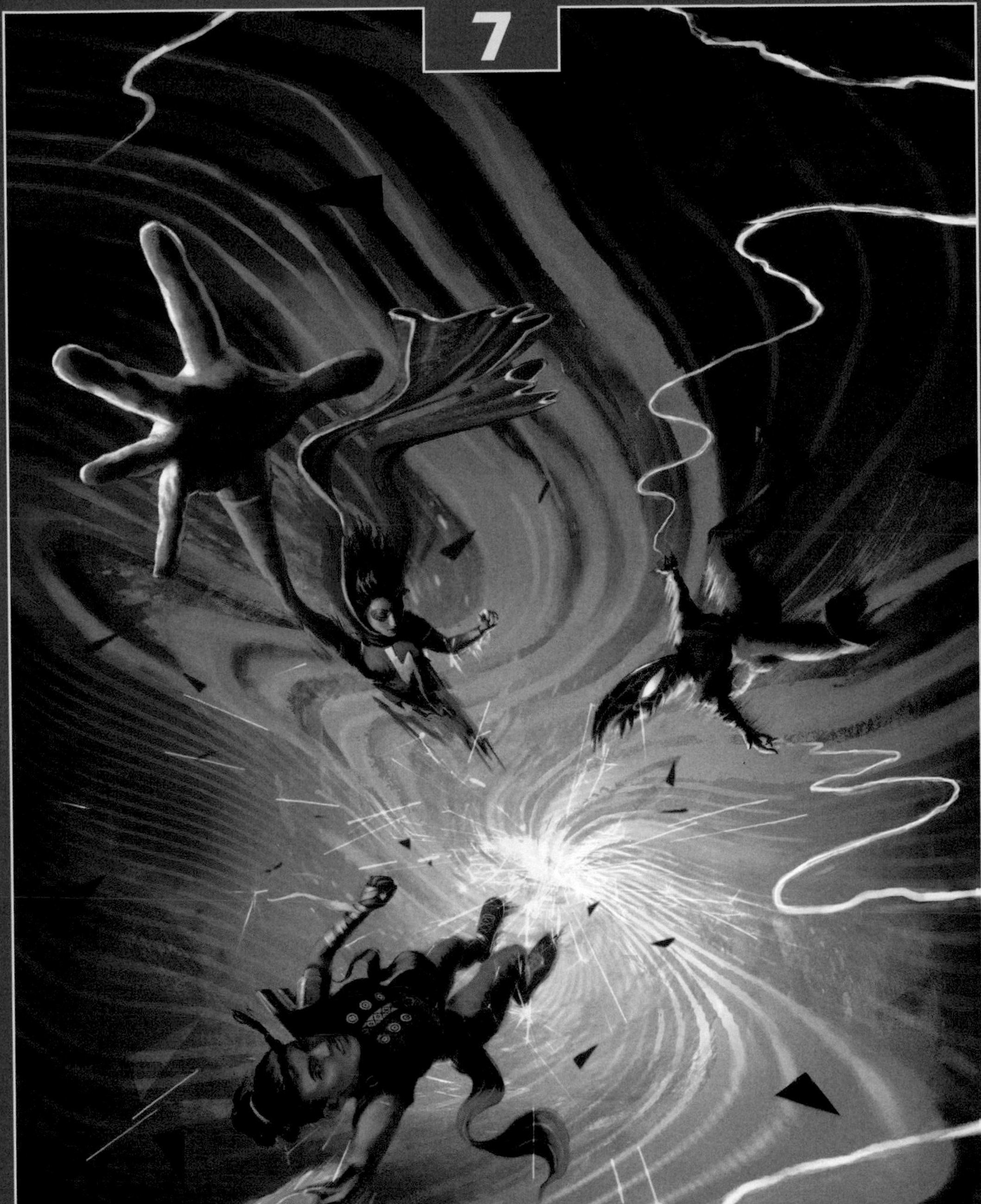
7

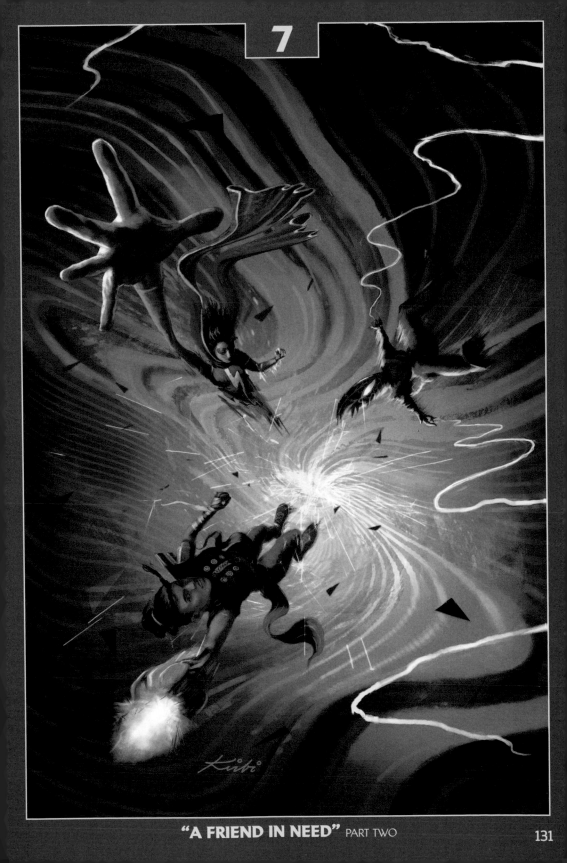

"A FRIEND IN NEED" PART TWO

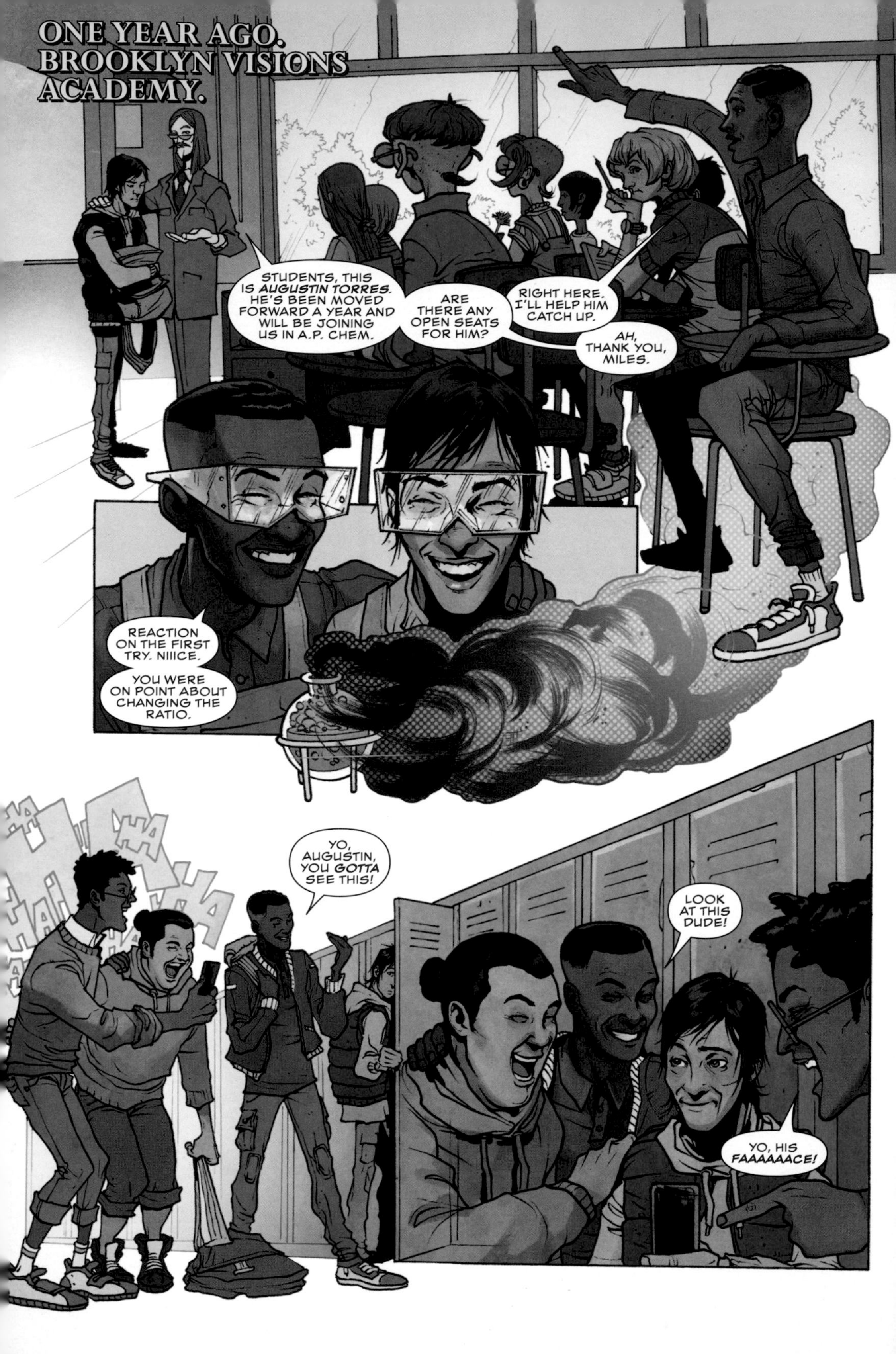
ONE YEAR AGO. BROOKLYN VISIONS ACADEMY.
STUDENTS, THIS IS AUGUSTIN TORRES. HE'S BEEN MOVED FORWARD A YEAR AND WILL BE JOINING US IN A.P. CHEM.
ARE THERE ANY OPEN SEATS FOR HIM?
RIGHT HERE. I'LL HELP HIM CATCH UP.
AH, THANK YOU, MILES.
REACTION ON THE FIRST TRY. NIIICE.
YOU WERE ON POINT ABOUT CHANGING THE RATIO.
YO, AUGUSTIN, YOU GOTTA SEE THIS!
LOOK AT THIS DUDE!
YO, HIS FAAAAAACE!

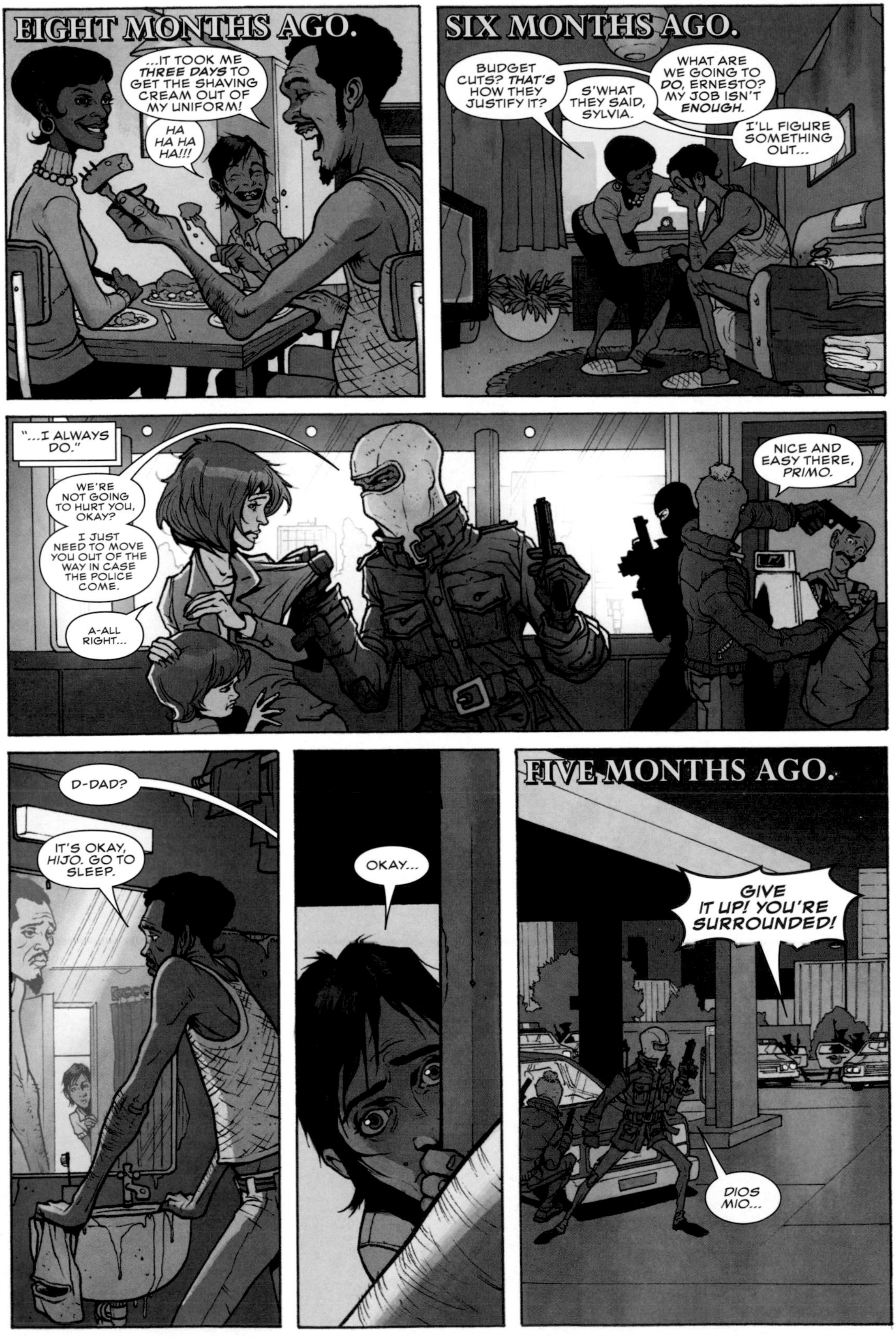
EIGHT MONTHS AGO.
...IT TOOK ME THREE DAYS TO GET THE SHAVING CREAM OUT OF MY UNIFORM!
HA HA HA HA!!!
SIX MONTHS AGO.
BUDGET CUTS? THAT'S HOW THEY JUSTIFY IT?
S'WHAT THEY SAID, SYLVIA.
WHAT ARE WE GOING TO DO, ERNESTO? MY JOB ISN'T ENOUGH.
I'LL FIGURE SOMETHING OUT...
"...I ALWAYS DO."
WE'RE NOT GOING TO HURT YOU, OKAY?
I JUST NEED TO MOVE YOU OUT OF THE WAY IN CASE THE POLICE COME.
A-ALL RIGHT...
NICE AND EASY THERE, PRIMO.
D-DAD?
IT'S OKAY, HIJO. GO TO SLEEP.
OKAY...
FIVE MONTHS AGO.
GIVE IT UP! YOU'RE SURROUNDED!
DIOS MIO...

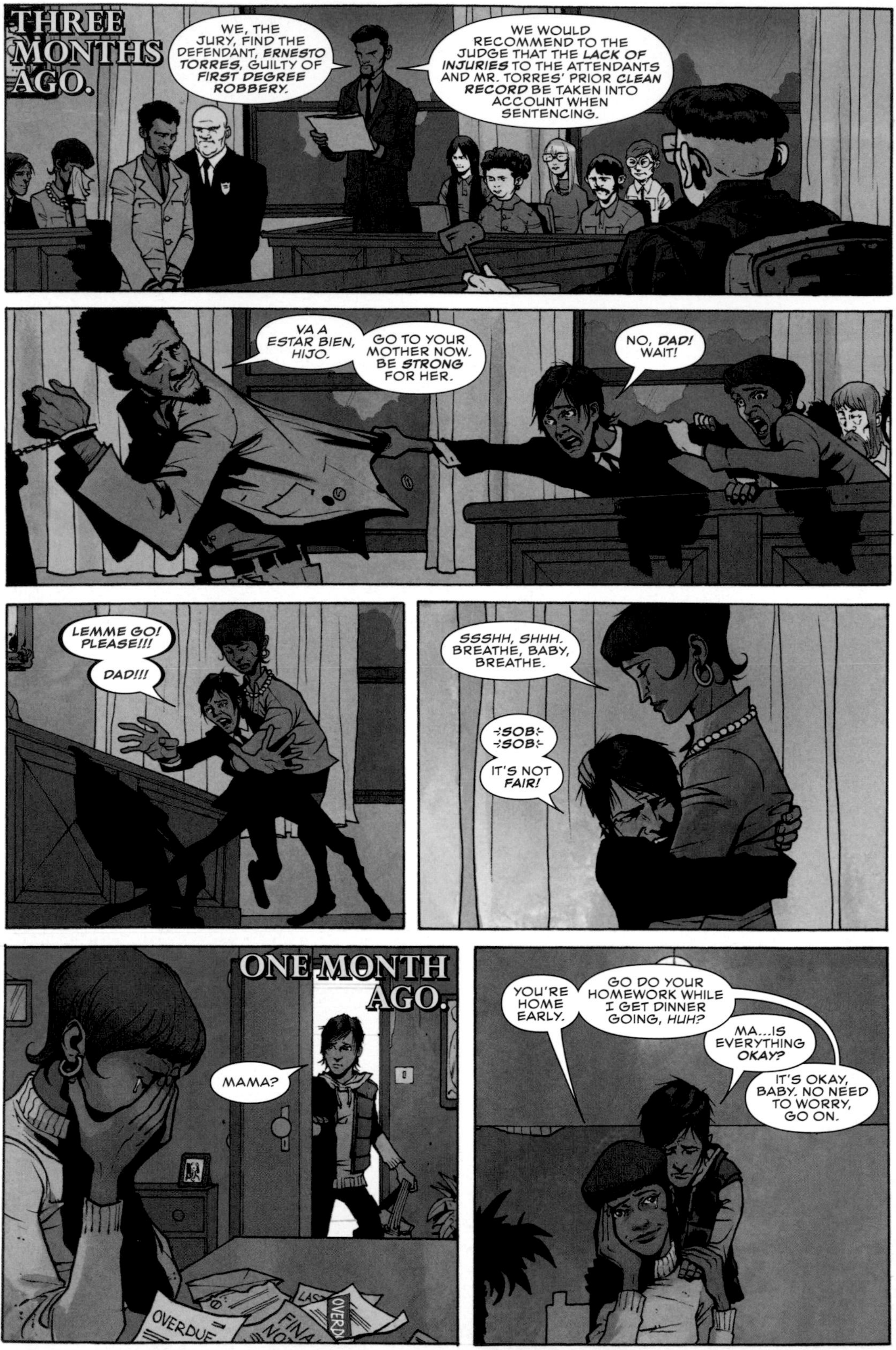
THREE MONTHS AGO.
WE, THE JURY, FIND THE DEFENDANT, ERNESTO TORRES, GUILTY OF FIRST DEGREE ROBBERY.
WE WOULD RECOMMEND TO THE JUDGE THAT THE LACK OF INJURIES TO THE ATTENDANTS AND MR. TORRES' PRIOR CLEAN RECORD BE TAKEN INTO ACCOUNT WHEN SENTENCING.
VA A ESTAR BIEN, HIJO.
GO TO YOUR MOTHER NOW. BE STRONG FOR HER.
NO, DAD! WAIT!
LEMME GO! PLEASE!!!
DAD!!!
SSSHH, SHHH. BREATHE, BABY, BREATHE.
SOB
SOB
IT'S NOT FAIR!
ONE MONTH AGO.
MAMA?
OVERDUE
LAST
YOU'RE HOME EARLY.
GO DO YOUR HOMEWORK WHILE I GET DINNER GOING, HUH?
MA...IS EVERYTHING OKAY?
IT'S OKAY, BABY. NO NEED TO WORRY, GO ON.

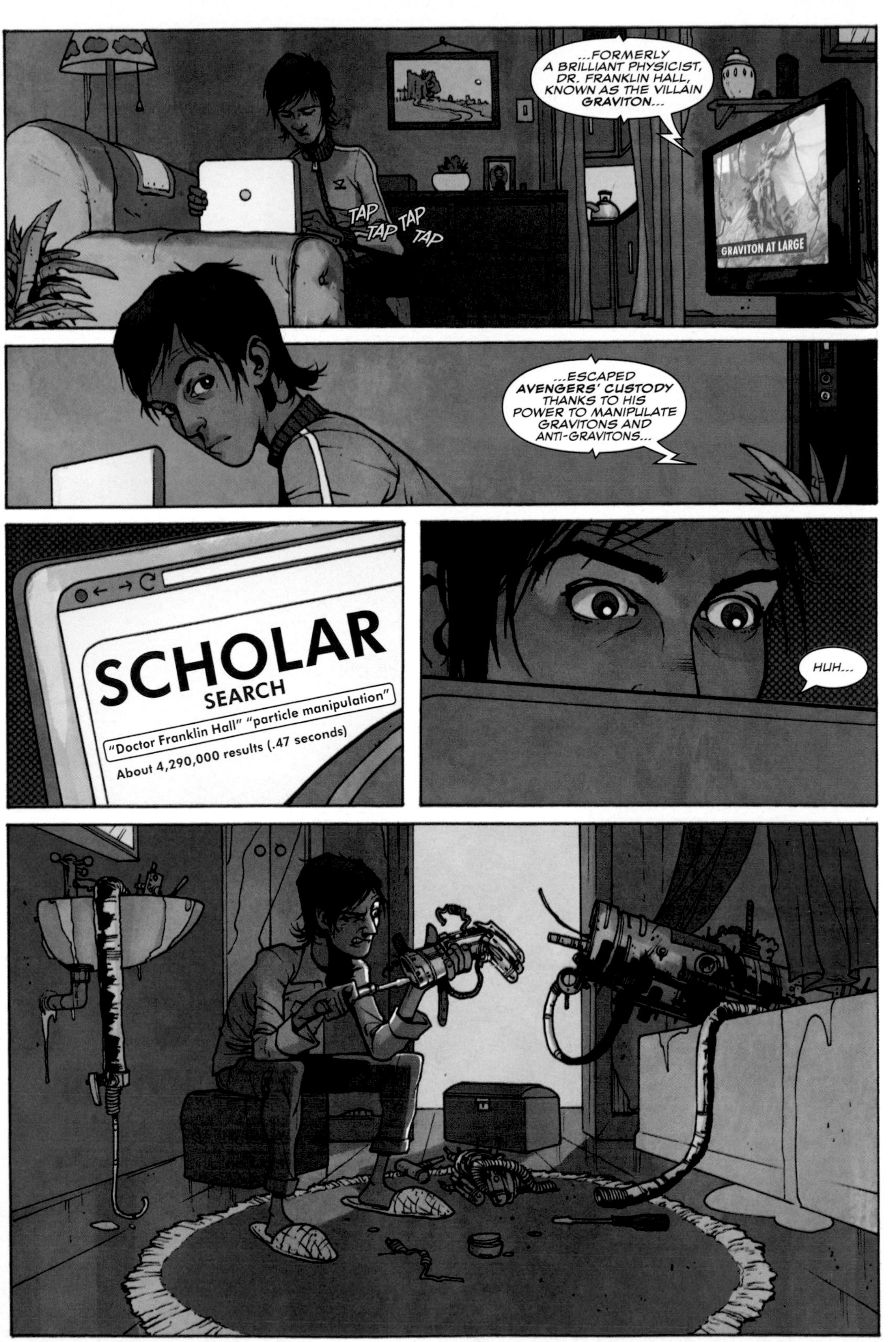
...FORMERLY A BRILLIANT PHYSICIST, DR. FRANKLIN HALL, KNOWN AS THE VILLAIN GRAVITON...
TAP TAP TAP TAP
GRAVITON AT LARGE
...ESCAPED AVENGERS' CUSTODY THANKS TO HIS POWER TO MANIPULATE GRAVITONS AND ANTI-GRAVITONS...
SCHOLAR
SEARCH
"Doctor Franklin Hall" "particle manipulation"
About 4,290,000 results (.47 seconds)
HUH...

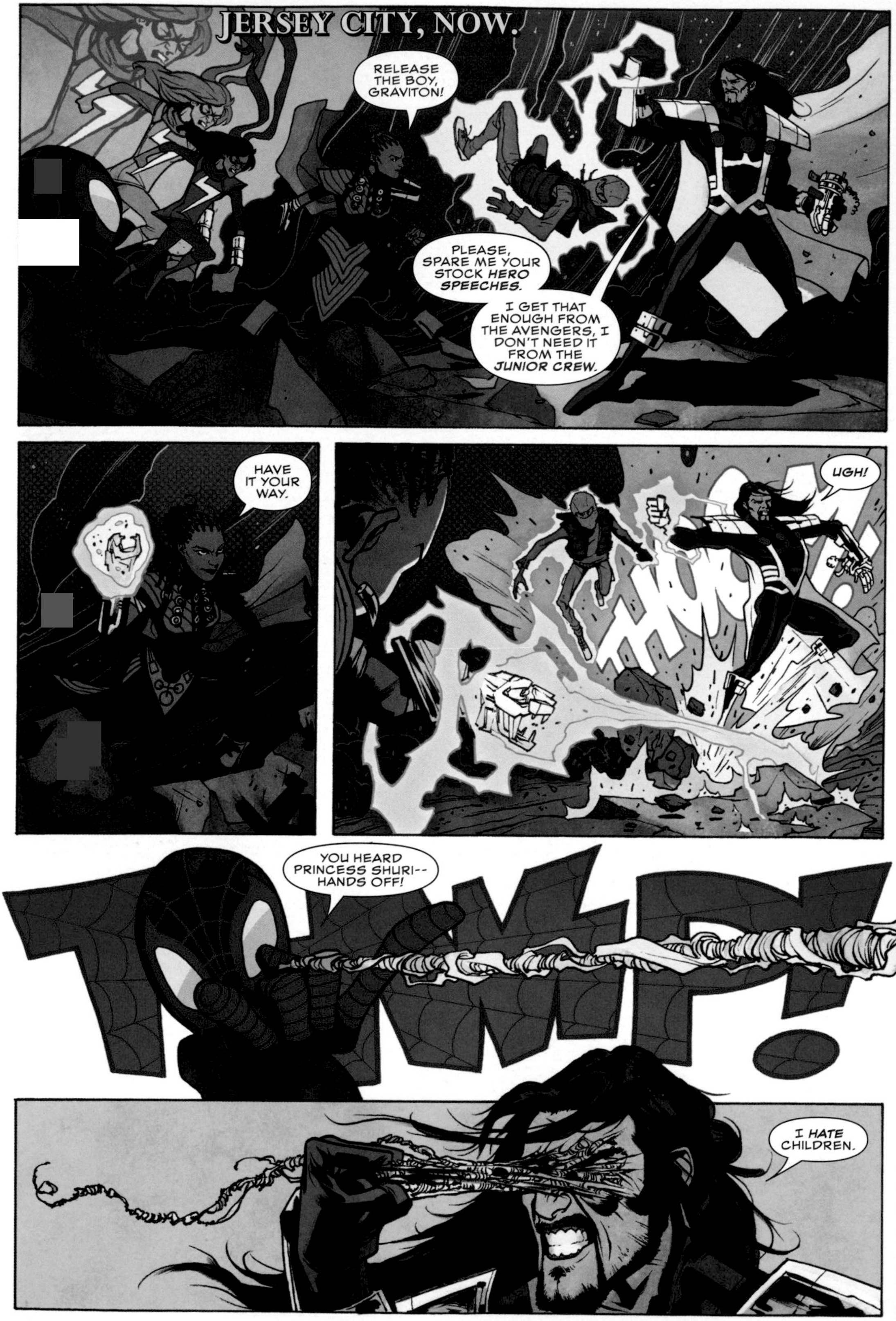
JERSEY CITY, NOW.
RELEASE THE BOY, GRAVITON!
PLEASE, SPARE ME YOUR STOCK HERO SPEECHES.
I GET THAT ENOUGH FROM THE AVENGERS, I DON'T NEED IT FROM THE JUNIOR CREW.
HAVE IT YOUR WAY.
UGH!
YOU HEARD PRINCESS SHURI-- HANDS OFF!
I HATE CHILDREN.

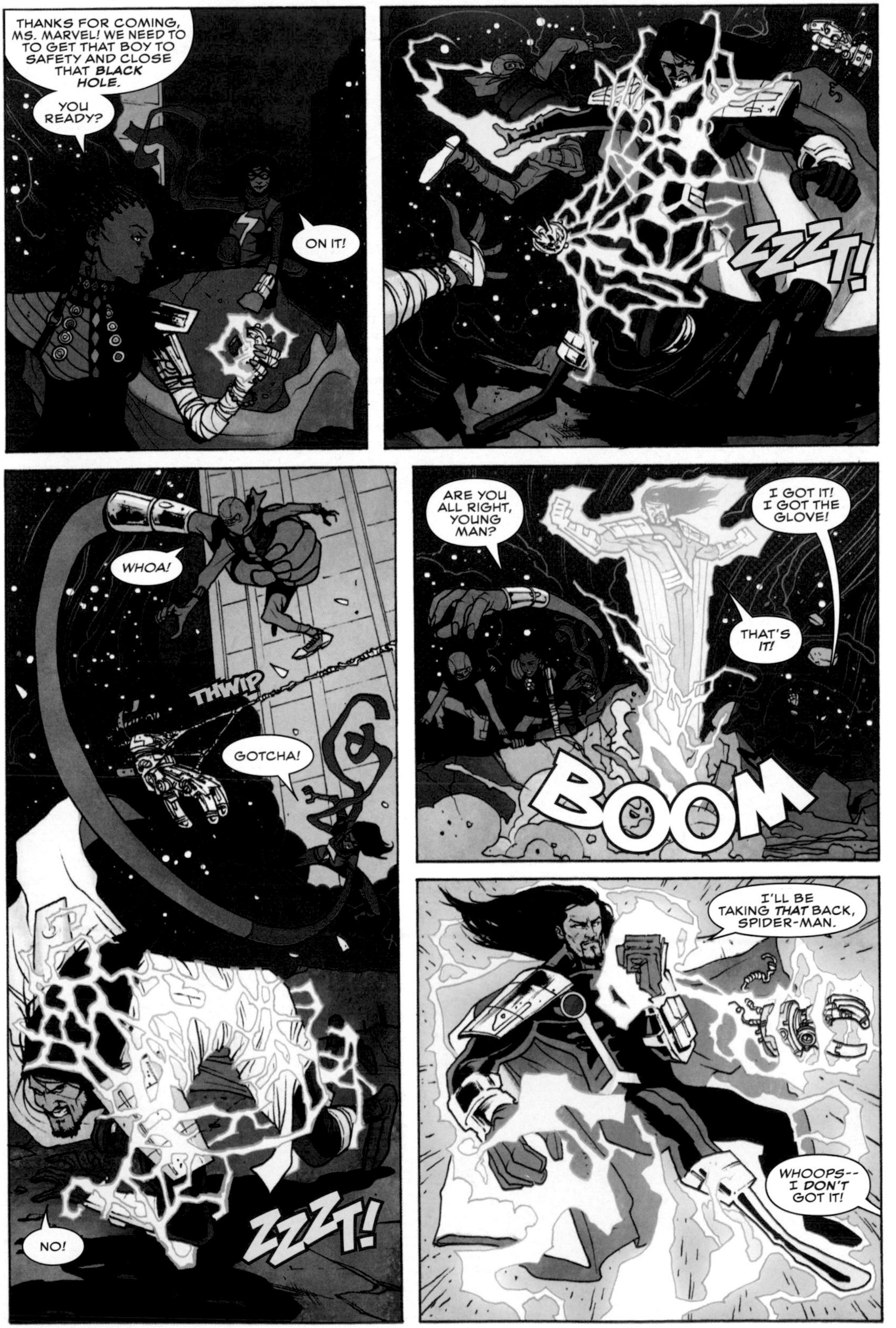

THANKS FOR COMING, MS. MARVEL! WE NEED TO TO GET THAT BOY TO SAFETY AND CLOSE THAT BLACK HOLE.
YOU READY?
ON IT!
ZZZT!
WHOA!
THWIP
GOTCHA!
NO!
ZZZT!
ARE YOU ALL RIGHT, YOUNG MAN?
I GOT IT! I GOT THE GLOVE!
THAT'S IT!
BOOM
I'LL BE TAKING THAT BACK, SPIDER-MAN.
WHOOPS-- I DON'T GOT IT!

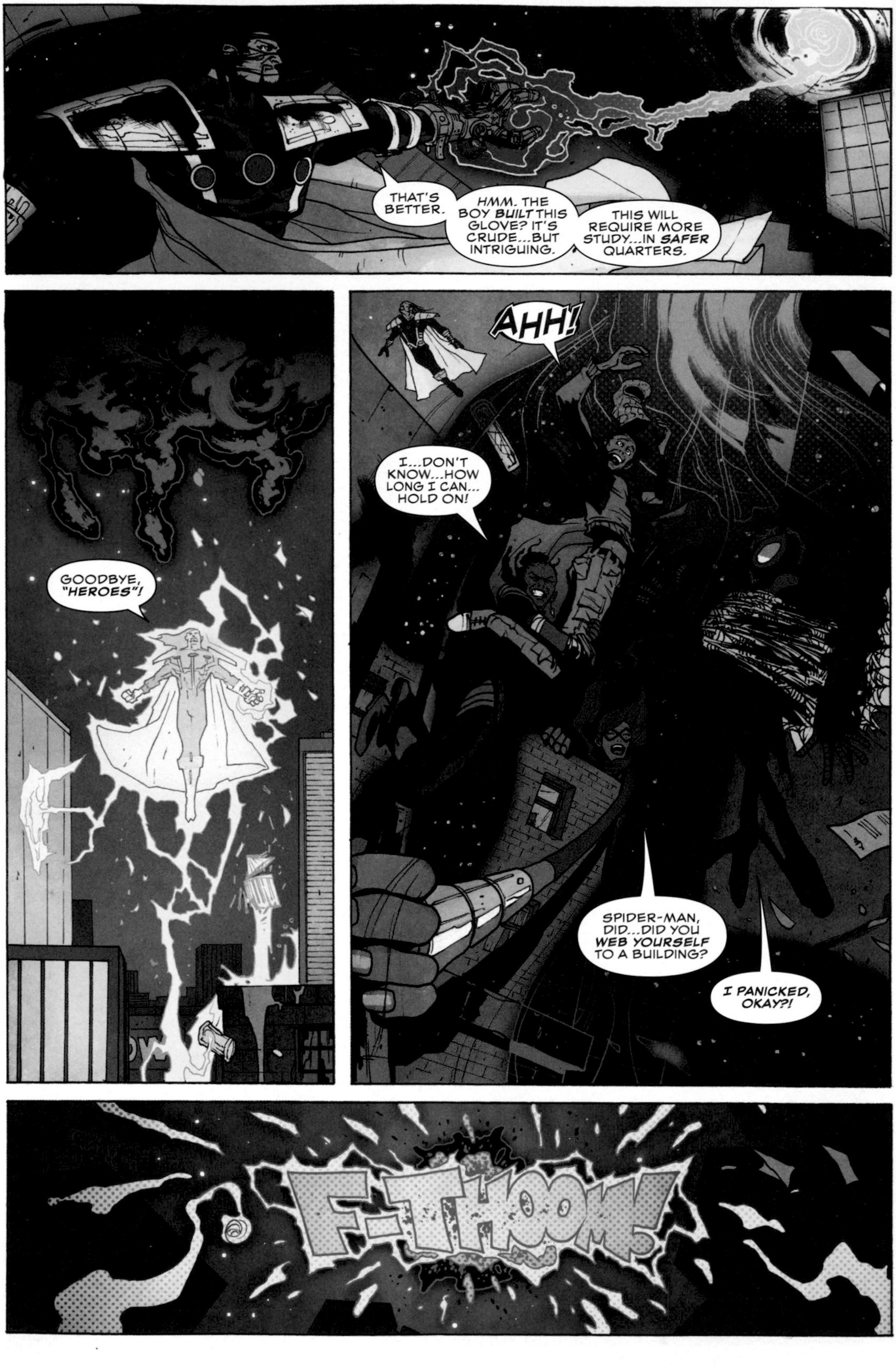
THAT'S BETTER.
HMM. THE BOY BUILT THIS GLOVE? IT'S CRUDE...BUT INTRIGUING.
THIS WILL REQUIRE MORE STUDY...IN SAFER QUARTERS.
GOODBYE, "HEROES"!
AHH!
I...DON'T KNOW...HOW LONG I CAN... HOLD ON!
SPIDER-MAN, DID...DID YOU WEB YOURSELF TO A BUILDING?
I PANICKED, OKAY?!
F-THOOM!

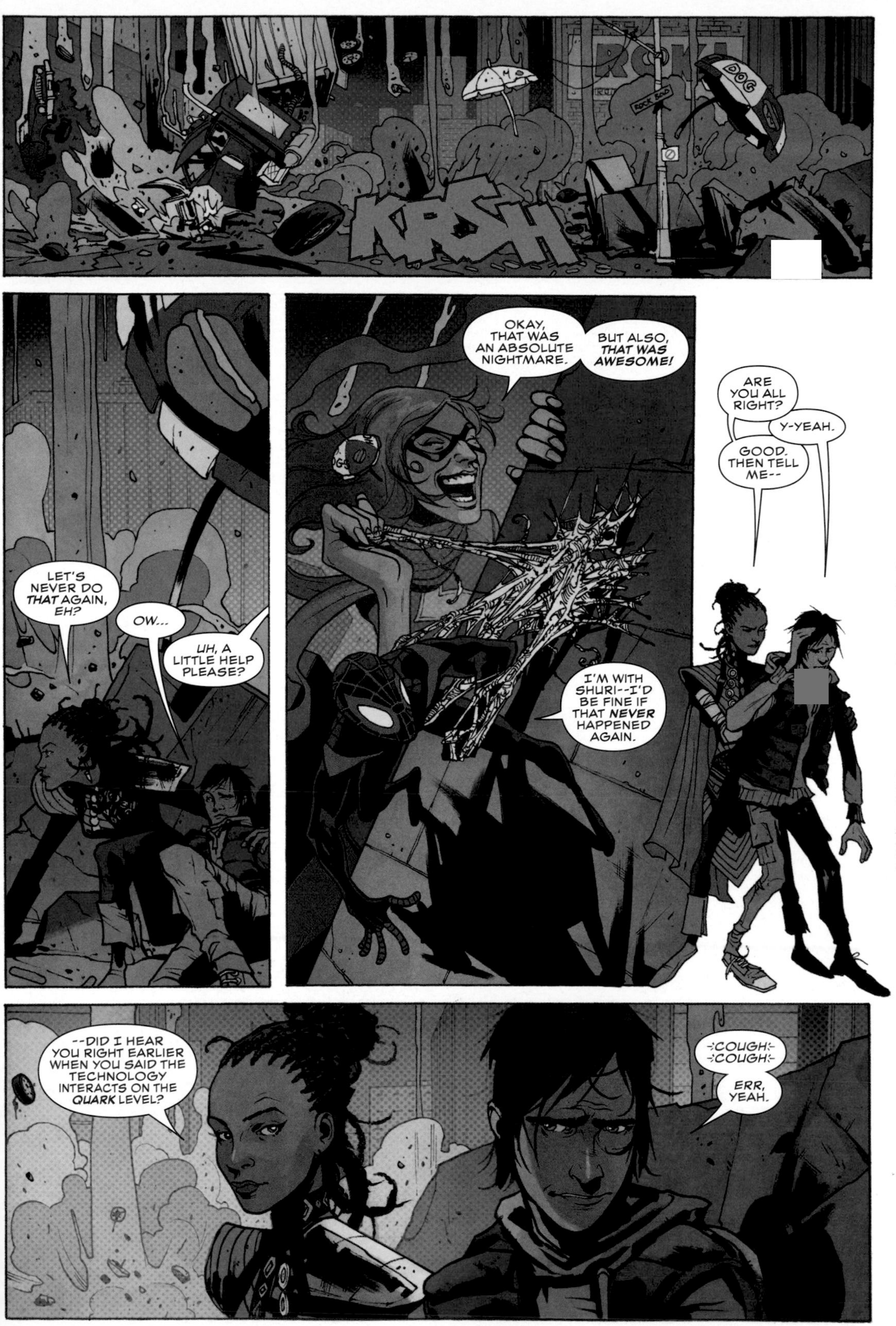
KRSH
ROCK
DOG
LET'S NEVER DO *THAT* AGAIN, EH?
OW...
UH, A LITTLE HELP PLEASE?
OKAY, THAT WAS AN ABSOLUTE NIGHTMARE.
BUT ALSO, ***THAT WAS AWESOME!***
I'M WITH SHURI--I'D BE FINE IF THAT ***NEVER*** HAPPENED AGAIN.
ARE YOU ALL RIGHT?
Y-YEAH.
GOOD. THEN TELL ME--
--DID I HEAR YOU RIGHT EARLIER WHEN YOU SAID THE TECHNOLOGY INTERACTS ON THE ***QUARK*** LEVEL?
COUGH
COUGH
ERR, YEAH.

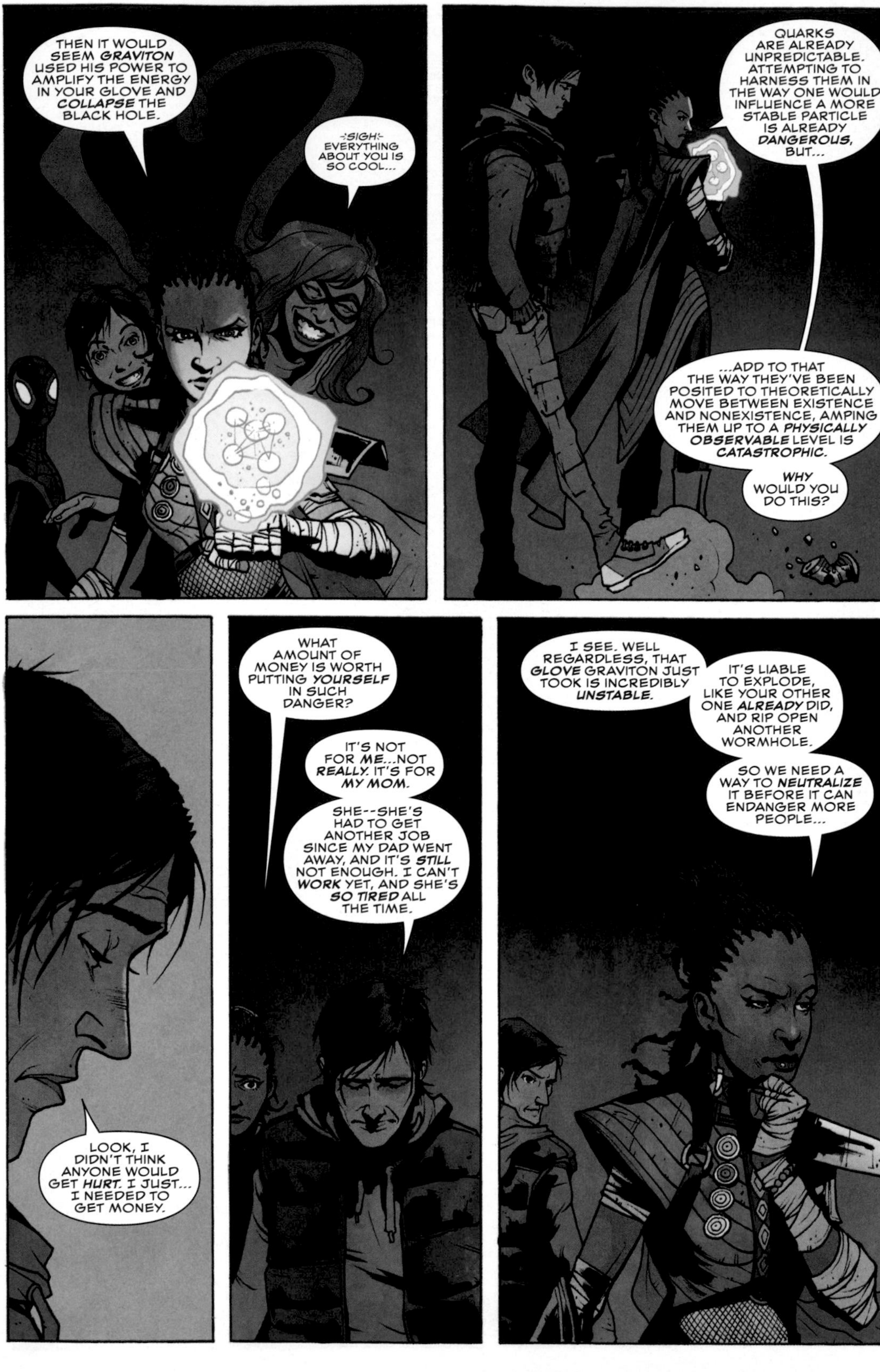
THEN IT WOULD SEEM GRAVITON USED HIS POWER TO AMPLIFY THE ENERGY IN YOUR GLOVE AND COLLAPSE THE BLACK HOLE.
-SIGH- EVERYTHING ABOUT YOU IS SO COOL...
QUARKS ARE ALREADY UNPREDICTABLE. ATTEMPTING TO HARNESS THEM IN THE WAY ONE WOULD INFLUENCE A MORE STABLE PARTICLE IS ALREADY DANGEROUS, BUT...
...ADD TO THAT THE WAY THEY'VE BEEN POSITED TO THEORETICALLY MOVE BETWEEN EXISTENCE AND NONEXISTENCE, AMPING THEM UP TO A PHYSICALLY OBSERVABLE LEVEL IS CATASTROPHIC.
WHY WOULD YOU DO THIS?
LOOK, I DIDN'T THINK ANYONE WOULD GET HURT. I JUST... I NEEDED TO GET MONEY.
WHAT AMOUNT OF MONEY IS WORTH PUTTING YOURSELF IN SUCH DANGER?
IT'S NOT FOR ME...NOT REALLY. IT'S FOR MY MOM.
SHE--SHE'S HAD TO GET ANOTHER JOB SINCE MY DAD WENT AWAY, AND IT'S STILL NOT ENOUGH. I CAN'T WORK YET, AND SHE'S SO TIRED ALL THE TIME.
I SEE. WELL REGARDLESS, THAT GLOVE GRAVITON JUST TOOK IS INCREDIBLY UNSTABLE.
IT'S LIABLE TO EXPLODE, LIKE YOUR OTHER ONE ALREADY DID, AND RIP OPEN ANOTHER WORMHOLE.
SO WE NEED A WAY TO NEUTRALIZE IT BEFORE IT CAN ENDANGER MORE PEOPLE...

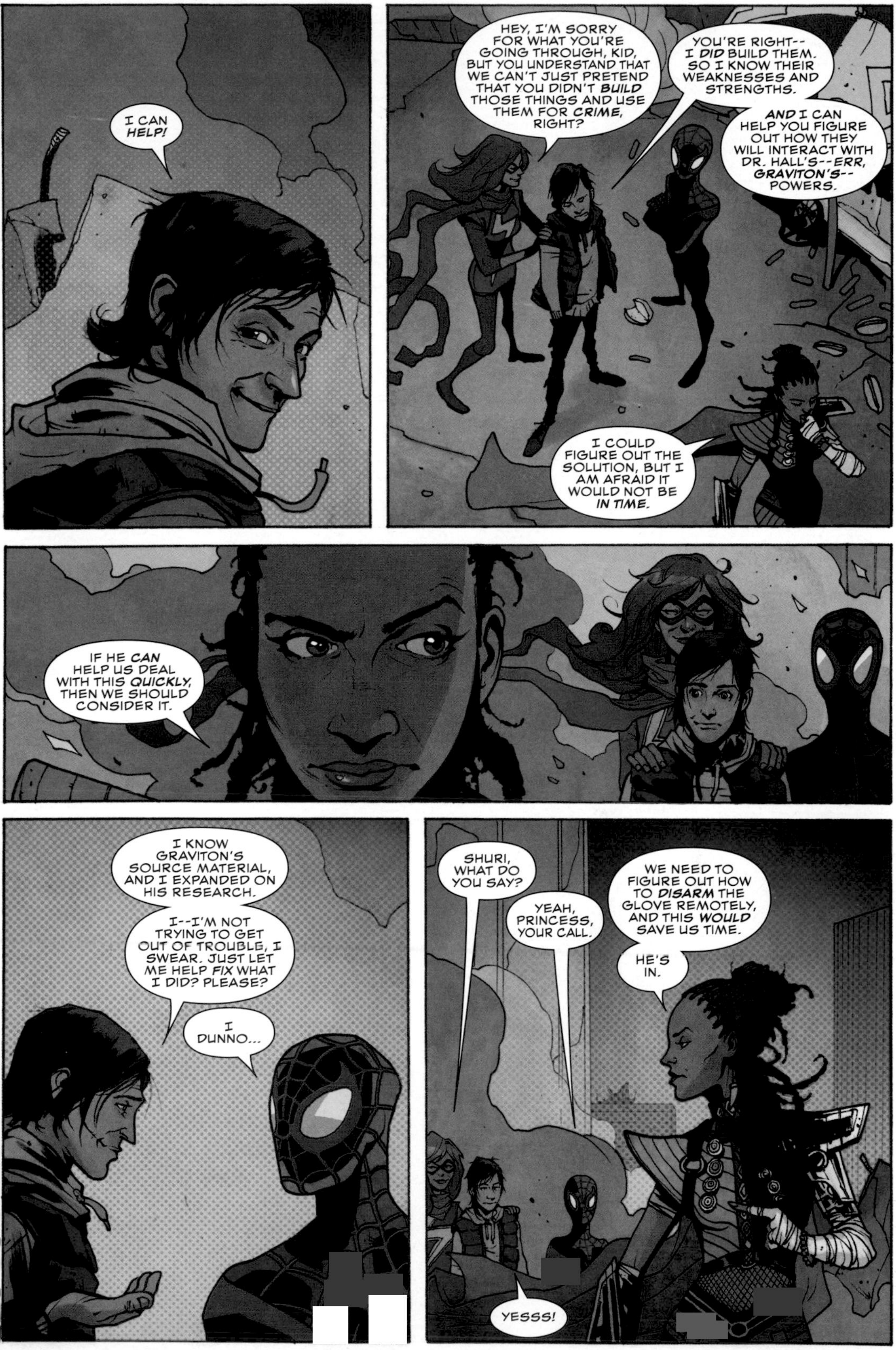
I CAN *HELP!*
HEY, I'M SORRY FOR WHAT YOU'RE GOING THROUGH, KID, BUT YOU UNDERSTAND THAT WE CAN'T JUST PRETEND THAT YOU DIDN'T *BUILD* THOSE THINGS AND USE THEM FOR *CRIME*, RIGHT?
YOU'RE RIGHT-- I *DID* BUILD THEM. SO I KNOW THEIR WEAKNESSES AND STRENGTHS.
AND I CAN HELP YOU FIGURE OUT HOW THEY WILL INTERACT WITH DR. HALL'S--*ERR, GRAVITON'S*-- POWERS.
I COULD FIGURE OUT THE SOLUTION, BUT I AM AFRAID IT WOULD NOT BE *IN TIME.*
IF HE *CAN* HELP US DEAL WITH THIS *QUICKLY*, THEN WE SHOULD CONSIDER IT.
I KNOW GRAVITON'S SOURCE MATERIAL, AND I EXPANDED ON HIS RESEARCH.
I--I'M NOT TRYING TO GET OUT OF TROUBLE, I SWEAR. JUST LET ME HELP *FIX* WHAT I DID? PLEASE?
I DUNNO...
SHURI, WHAT DO YOU SAY?
YEAH, PRINCESS, YOUR CALL.
WE NEED TO FIGURE OUT HOW TO *DISARM* THE GLOVE REMOTELY, AND THIS *WOULD* SAVE US TIME.
HE'S IN.
YESSS!

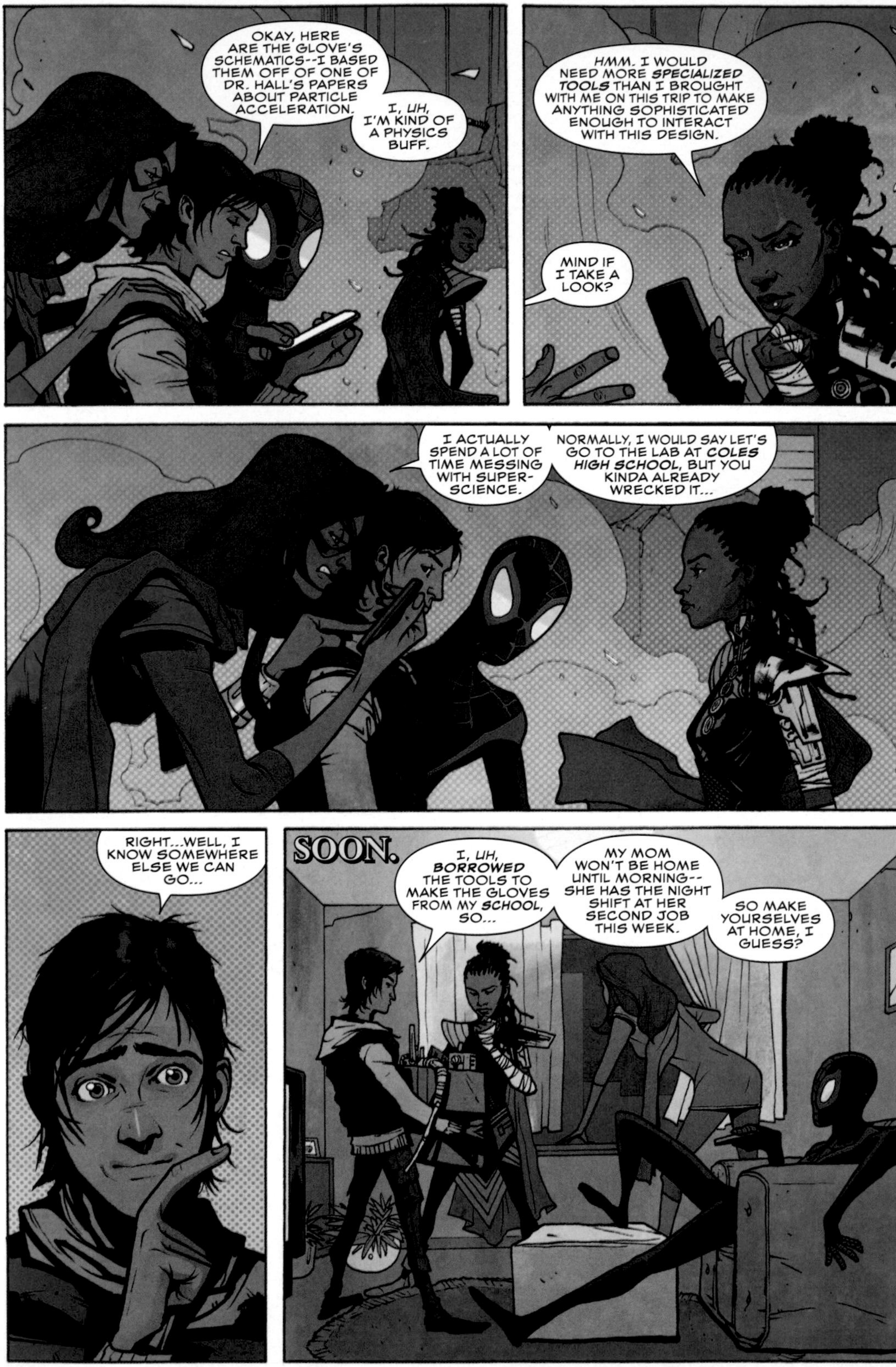
OKAY, HERE ARE THE GLOVE'S SCHEMATICS--I BASED THEM OFF OF ONE OF DR. HALL'S PAPERS ABOUT PARTICLE ACCELERATION.
I, *UH*, I'M KIND OF A PHYSICS BUFF.
HMM. I WOULD NEED MORE ***SPECIALIZED TOOLS*** THAN I BROUGHT WITH ME ON THIS TRIP TO MAKE ANYTHING SOPHISTICATED ENOUGH TO INTERACT WITH THIS DESIGN.
MIND IF I TAKE A LOOK?
I ACTUALLY SPEND A LOT OF TIME MESSING WITH SUPER-SCIENCE.
NORMALLY, I WOULD SAY LET'S GO TO THE LAB AT ***COLES HIGH SCHOOL***, BUT YOU KINDA ALREADY WRECKED IT...
RIGHT...WELL, I KNOW SOMEWHERE ELSE WE CAN GO...
SOON.
I, *UH*, ***BORROWED*** THE TOOLS TO MAKE THE GLOVES FROM MY ***SCHOOL***, SO...
MY MOM WON'T BE HOME UNTIL MORNING--SHE HAS THE NIGHT SHIFT AT HER SECOND JOB THIS WEEK.
SO MAKE YOURSELVES AT HOME, I GUESS?

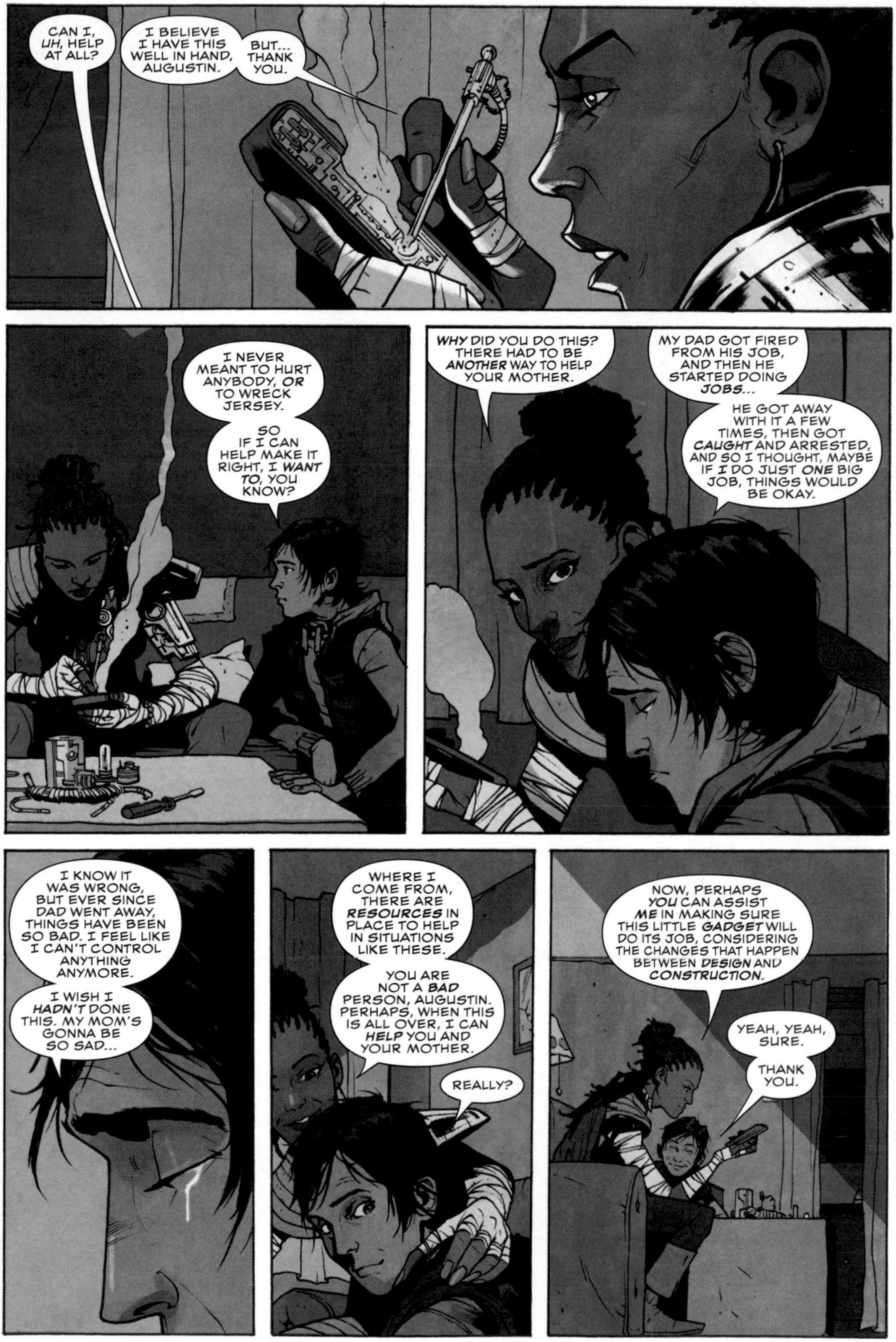
CAN I, UH, HELP AT ALL?
I BELIEVE I HAVE THIS WELL IN HAND, AUGUSTIN.
BUT... THANK YOU.
I NEVER MEANT TO HURT ANYBODY, OR TO WRECK JERSEY.
SO IF I CAN HELP MAKE IT RIGHT, I WANT TO, YOU KNOW?
WHY DID YOU DO THIS? THERE HAD TO BE ANOTHER WAY TO HELP YOUR MOTHER.
MY DAD GOT FIRED FROM HIS JOB, AND THEN HE STARTED DOING JOBS...
HE GOT AWAY WITH IT A FEW TIMES, THEN GOT CAUGHT AND ARRESTED, AND SO I THOUGHT, MAYBE IF I DO JUST ONE BIG JOB, THINGS WOULD BE OKAY.
I KNOW IT WAS WRONG, BUT EVER SINCE DAD WENT AWAY, THINGS HAVE BEEN SO BAD. I FEEL LIKE I CAN'T CONTROL ANYTHING ANYMORE.
I WISH I HADN'T DONE THIS. MY MOM'S GONNA BE SO SAD...
WHERE I COME FROM, THERE ARE RESOURCES IN PLACE TO HELP IN SITUATIONS LIKE THESE.
YOU ARE NOT A BAD PERSON, AUGUSTIN. PERHAPS, WHEN THIS IS ALL OVER, I CAN HELP YOU AND YOUR MOTHER.
REALLY?
NOW, PERHAPS YOU CAN ASSIST ME IN MAKING SURE THIS LITTLE GADGET WILL DO ITS JOB, CONSIDERING THE CHANGES THAT HAPPEN BETWEEN DESIGN AND CONSTRUCTION.
YEAH, YEAH, SURE.
THANK YOU.

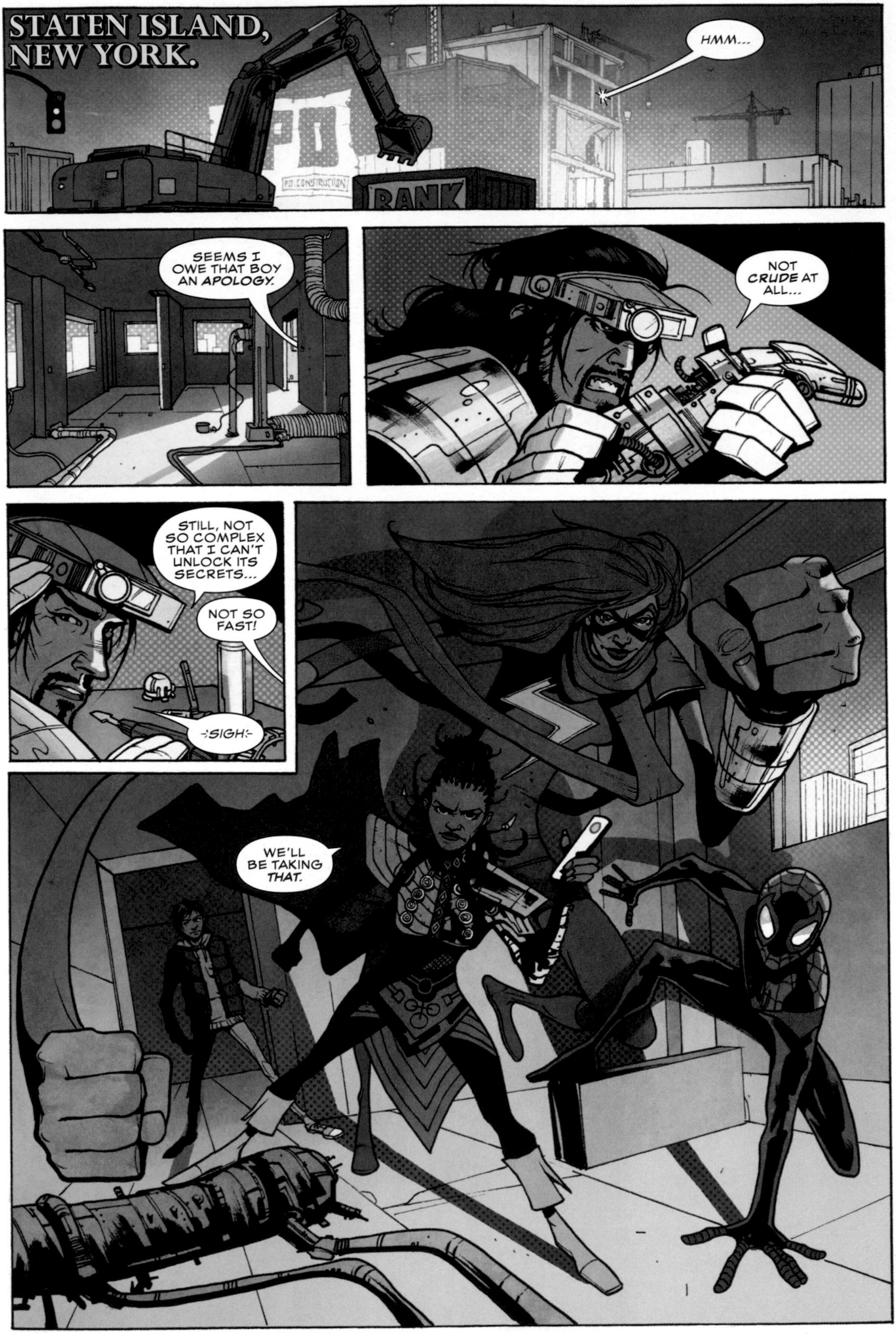
STATEN ISLAND, NEW YORK.
HMM...
PD CONSTRUCTION
BANK
SEEMS I OWE THAT BOY AN *APOLOGY*.
NOT *CRUDE* AT ALL...
STILL, NOT SO COMPLEX THAT I CAN'T UNLOCK ITS SECRETS...
NOT SO FAST!
-SIGH-
WE'LL BE TAKING *THAT*.

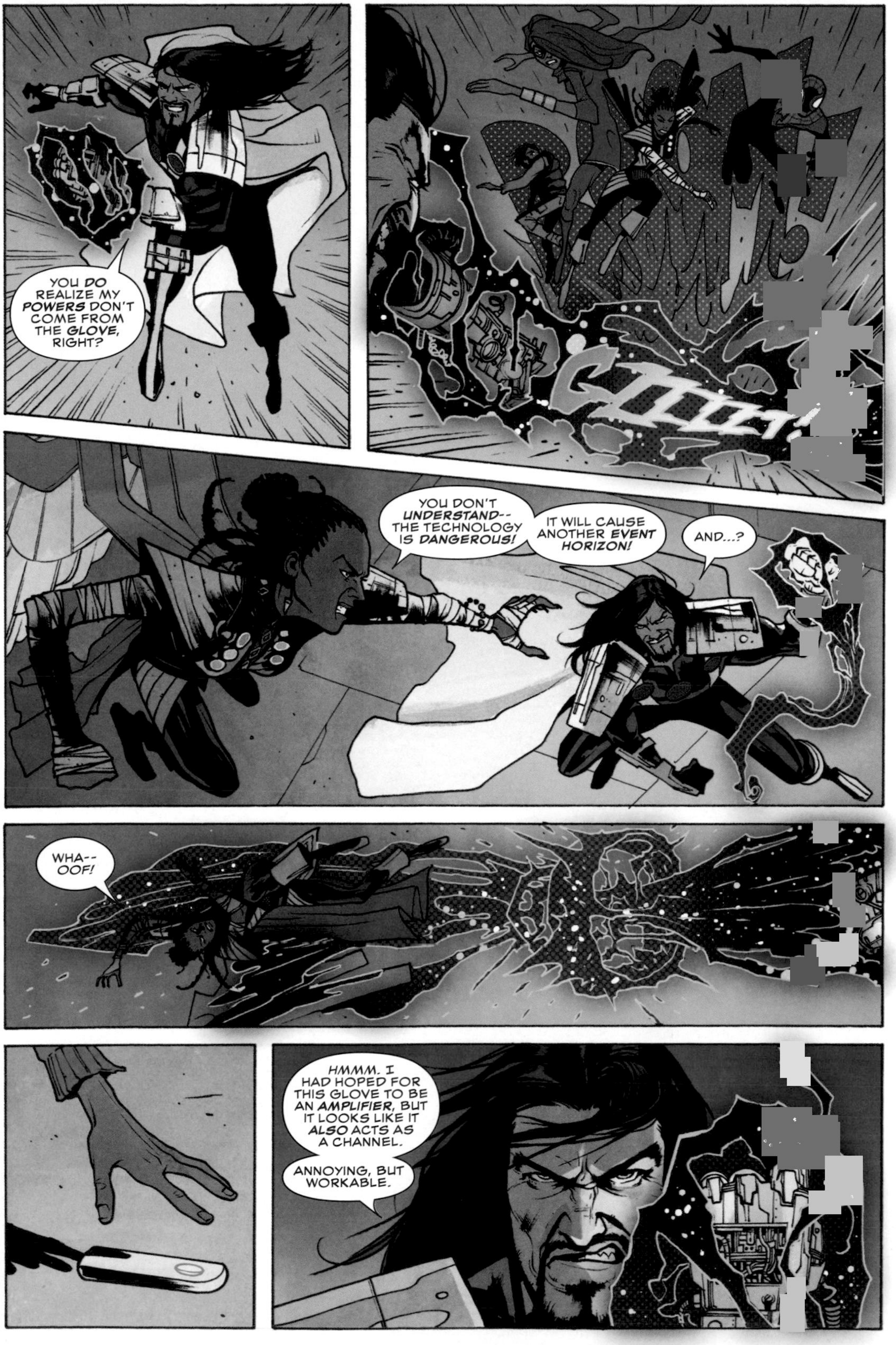
YOU DO REALIZE MY POWERS DON'T COME FROM THE GLOVE, RIGHT?
YOU DON'T UNDERSTAND-- THE TECHNOLOGY IS DANGEROUS!
IT WILL CAUSE ANOTHER EVENT HORIZON!
AND...?
WHA-- OOF!
HMMM. I HAD HOPED FOR THIS GLOVE TO BE AN AMPLIFIER, BUT IT LOOKS LIKE IT ALSO ACTS AS A CHANNEL.
ANNOYING, BUT WORKABLE.

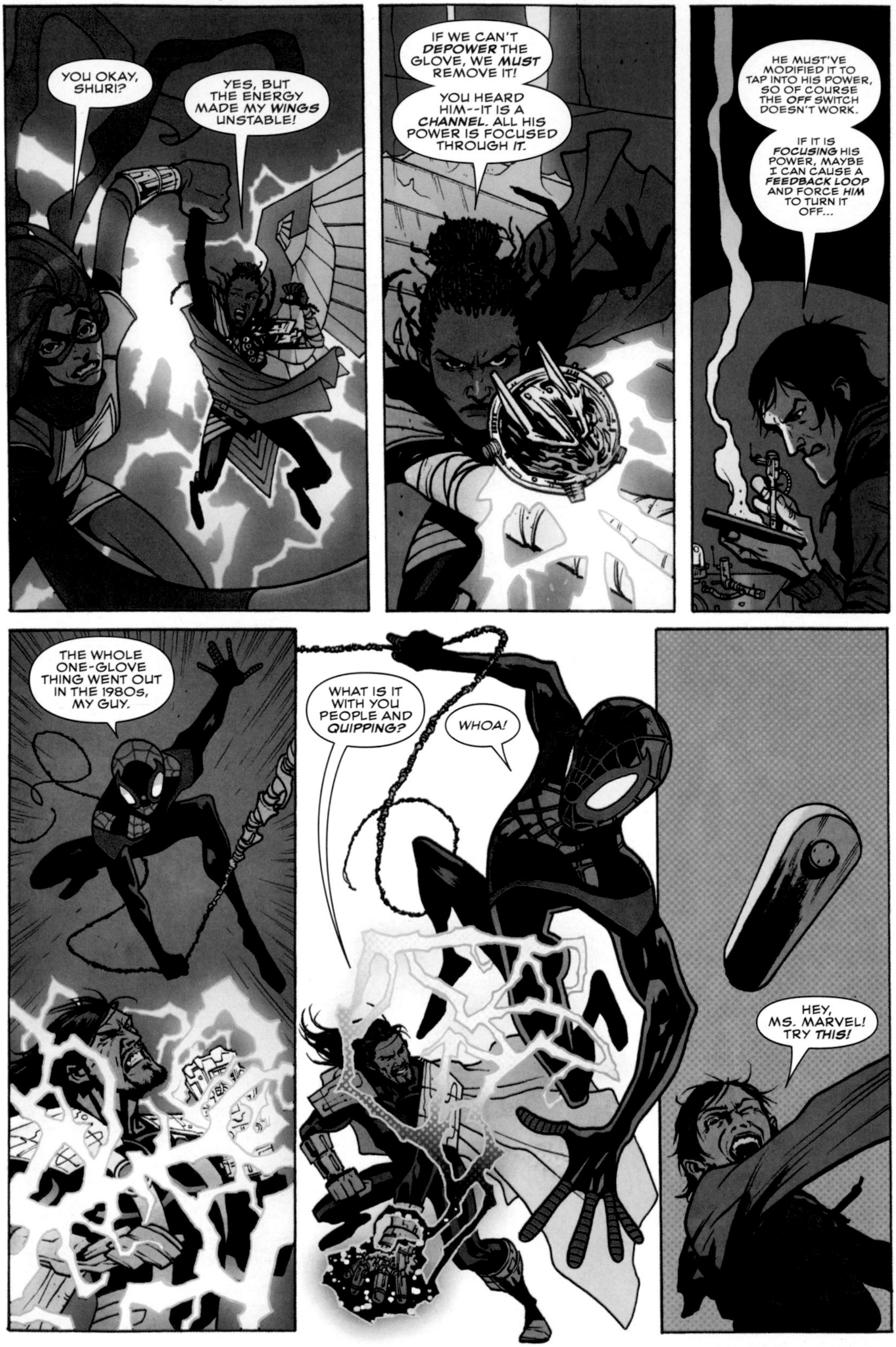
YOU OKAY, SHURI?
YES, BUT THE ENERGY MADE MY WINGS UNSTABLE!
IF WE CAN'T DEPOWER THE GLOVE, WE MUST REMOVE IT!
YOU HEARD HIM--IT IS A CHANNEL. ALL HIS POWER IS FOCUSED THROUGH IT.
HE MUST'VE MODIFIED IT TO TAP INTO HIS POWER, SO OF COURSE THE OFF SWITCH DOESN'T WORK.
IF IT IS FOCUSING HIS POWER, MAYBE I CAN CAUSE A FEEDBACK LOOP AND FORCE HIM TO TURN IT OFF...
THE WHOLE ONE-GLOVE THING WENT OUT IN THE 1980s, MY GUY.
WHAT IS IT WITH YOU PEOPLE AND QUIPPING?
WHOA!
HEY, MS. MARVEL! TRY THIS!

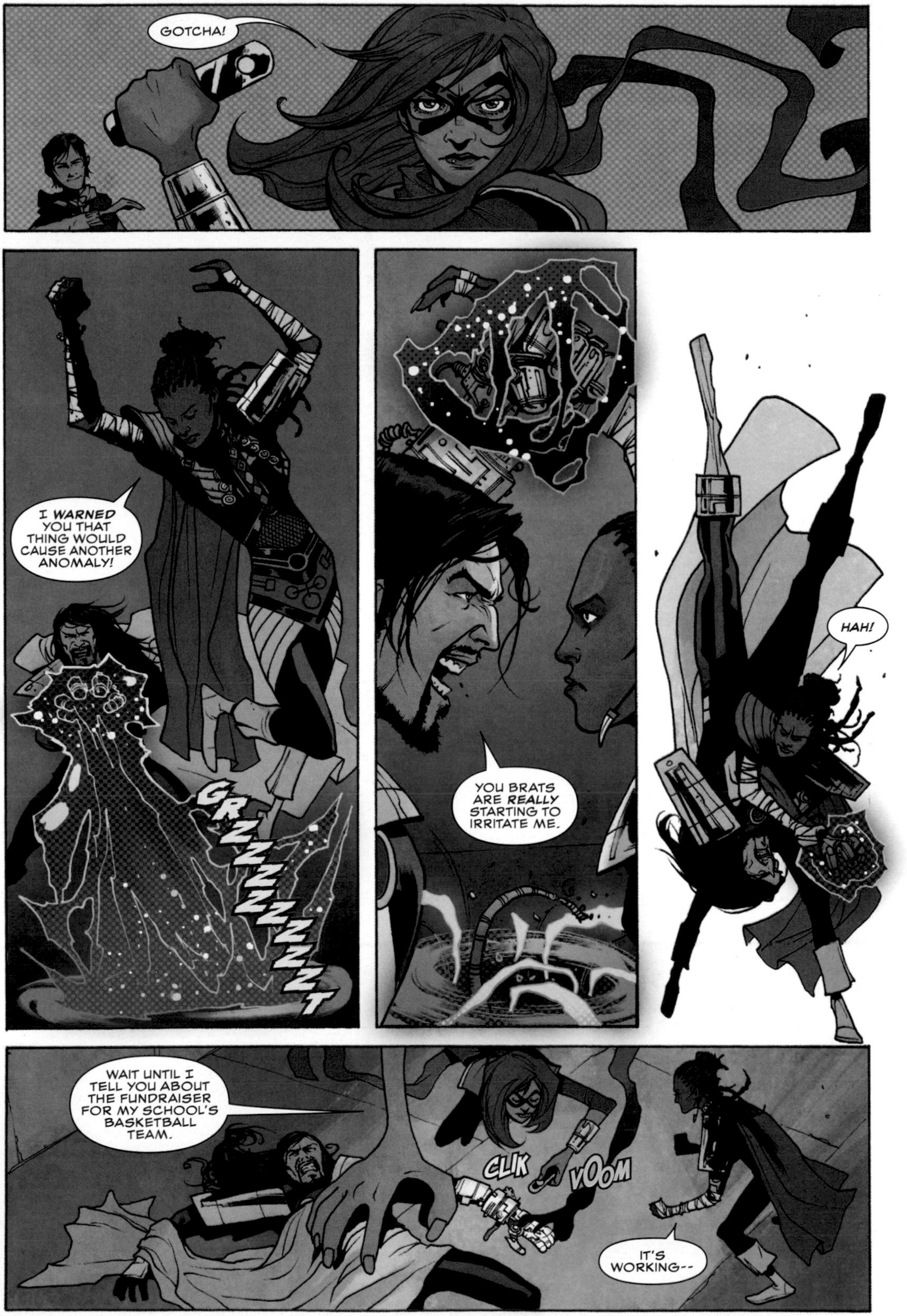
GOTCHA!
I WARNED YOU THAT THING WOULD CAUSE ANOTHER ANOMALY!
GRZZZZZZZT
YOU BRATS ARE REALLY STARTING TO IRRITATE ME.
HAH!
WAIT UNTIL I TELL YOU ABOUT THE FUNDRAISER FOR MY SCHOOL'S BASKETBALL TEAM.
CLIK
VOOM
IT'S WORKING--

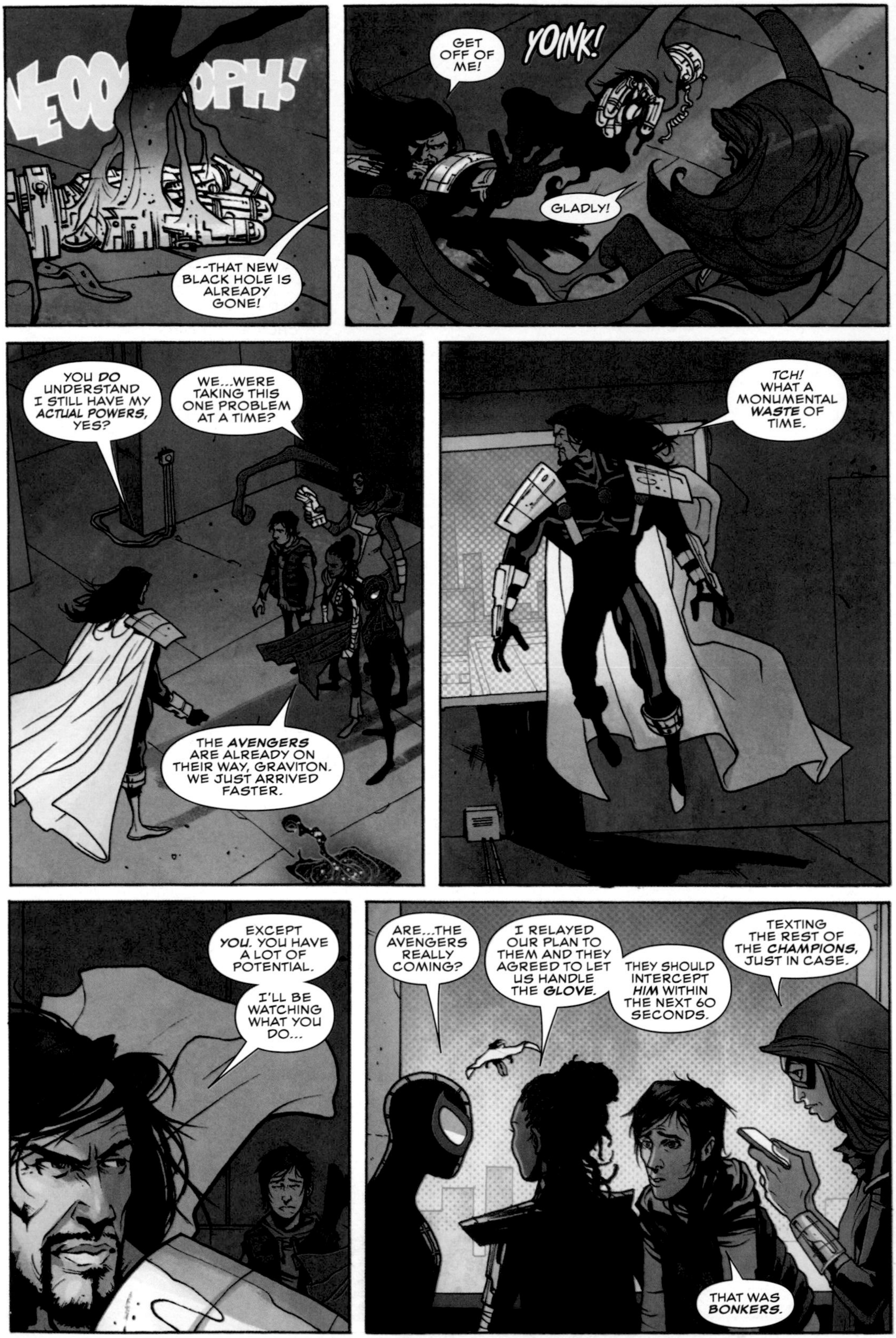

NEOOOOOPH!
--THAT NEW BLACK HOLE IS ALREADY GONE!
GET OFF OF ME!
YOINK!
GLADLY!
YOU DO UNDERSTAND I STILL HAVE MY ACTUAL POWERS, YES?
WE...WERE TAKING THIS ONE PROBLEM AT A TIME?
THE AVENGERS ARE ALREADY ON THEIR WAY, GRAVITON. WE JUST ARRIVED FASTER.
TCH! WHAT A MONUMENTAL WASTE OF TIME.
EXCEPT YOU. YOU HAVE A LOT OF POTENTIAL.
I'LL BE WATCHING WHAT YOU DO...
ARE...THE AVENGERS REALLY COMING?
I RELAYED OUR PLAN TO THEM AND THEY AGREED TO LET US HANDLE THE GLOVE.
THEY SHOULD INTERCEPT HIM WITHIN THE NEXT 60 SECONDS.
TEXTING THE REST OF THE CHAMPIONS, JUST IN CASE.
THAT WAS BONKERS.

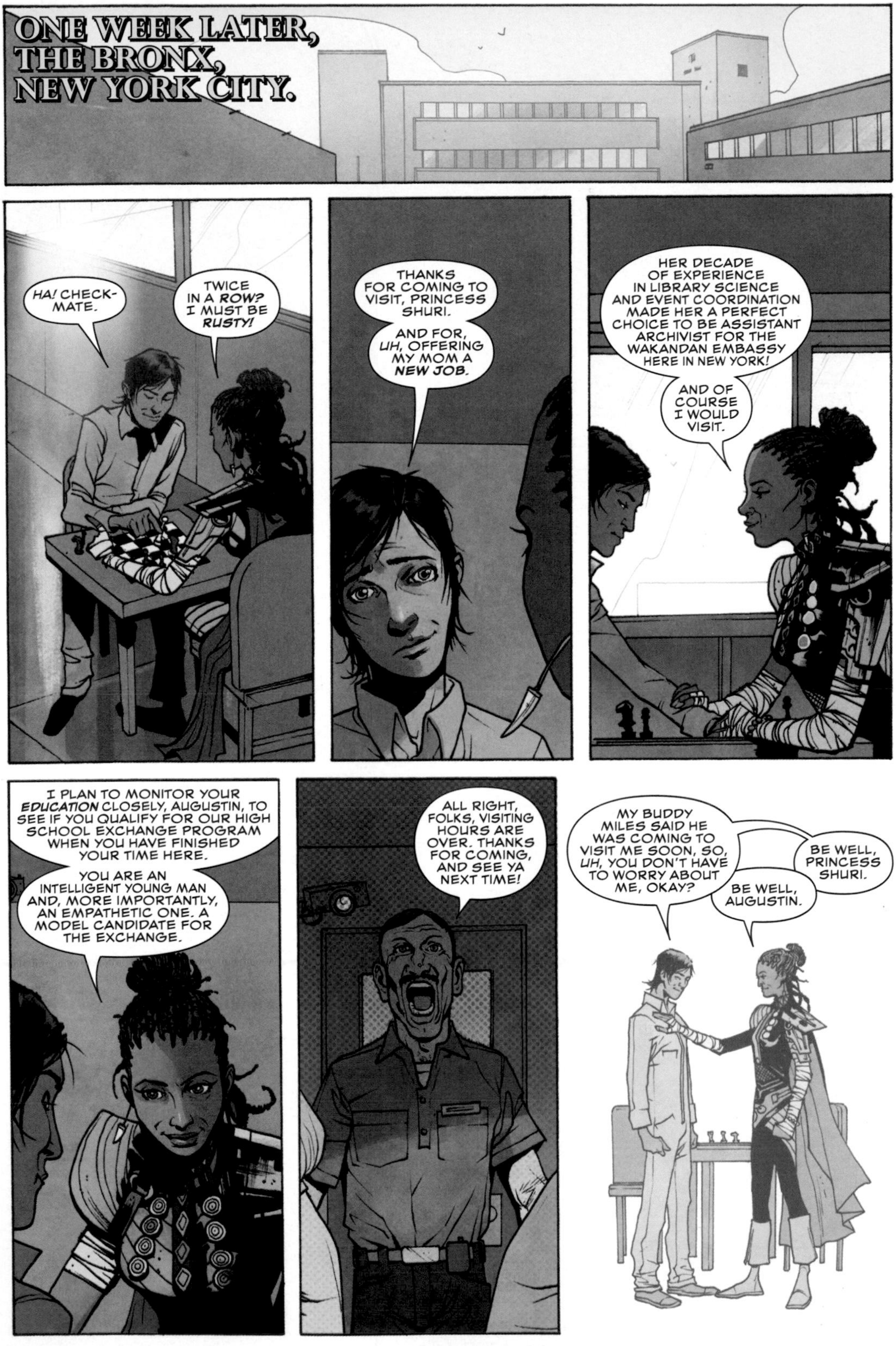
ONE WEEK LATER, THE BRONX, NEW YORK CITY.
HA! CHECK-MATE.
TWICE IN A ROW? I MUST BE RUSTY!
THANKS FOR COMING TO VISIT, PRINCESS SHURI.
AND FOR, UH, OFFERING MY MOM A NEW JOB.
HER DECADE OF EXPERIENCE IN LIBRARY SCIENCE AND EVENT COORDINATION MADE HER A PERFECT CHOICE TO BE ASSISTANT ARCHIVIST FOR THE WAKANDAN EMBASSY HERE IN NEW YORK!
AND OF COURSE I WOULD VISIT.
I PLAN TO MONITOR YOUR EDUCATION CLOSELY, AUGUSTIN, TO SEE IF YOU QUALIFY FOR OUR HIGH SCHOOL EXCHANGE PROGRAM WHEN YOU HAVE FINISHED YOUR TIME HERE.
YOU ARE AN INTELLIGENT YOUNG MAN AND, MORE IMPORTANTLY, AN EMPATHETIC ONE. A MODEL CANDIDATE FOR THE EXCHANGE.
ALL RIGHT, FOLKS, VISITING HOURS ARE OVER. THANKS FOR COMING, AND SEE YA NEXT TIME!
MY BUDDY MILES SAID HE WAS COMING TO VISIT ME SOON, SO, UH, YOU DON'T HAVE TO WORRY ABOUT ME, OKAY?
BE WELL, PRINCESS SHURI.
BE WELL, AUGUSTIN.

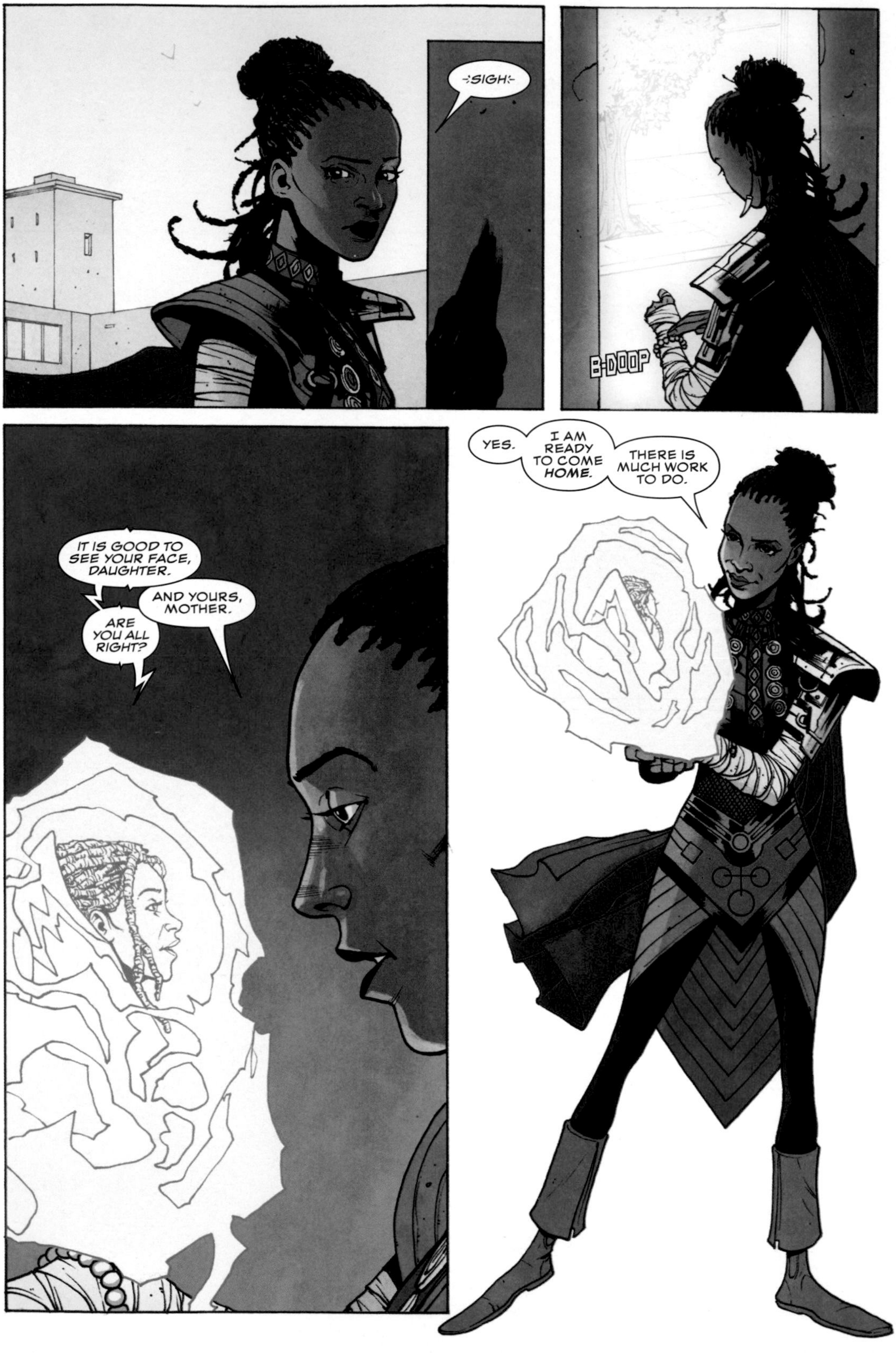
-SIGH-
B-DOOP
IT IS GOOD TO SEE YOUR FACE, DAUGHTER.
ARE YOU ALL RIGHT?
AND YOURS, MOTHER.
YES.
I AM READY TO COME *HOME*.
THERE IS MUCH WORK TO DO.

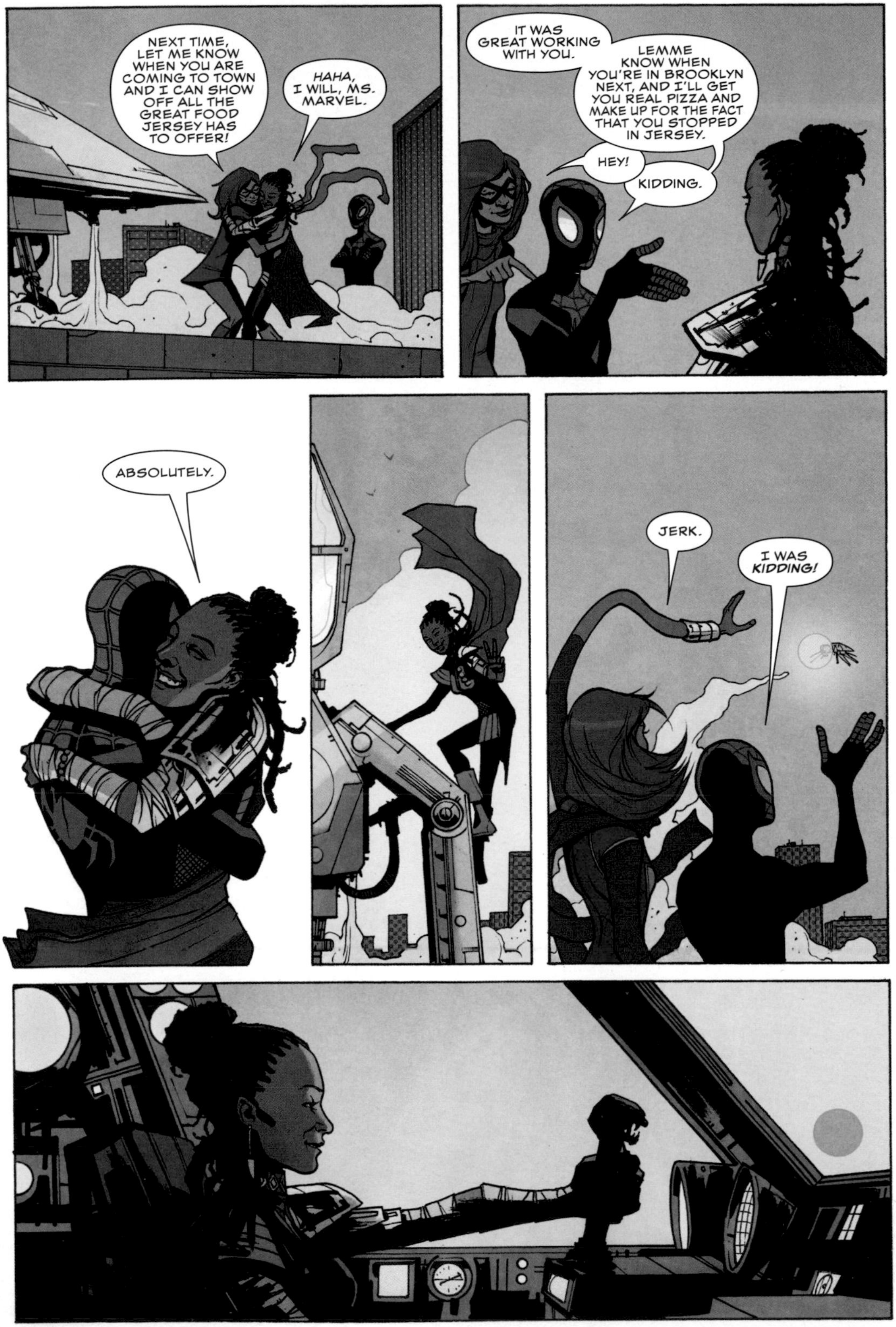
NEXT TIME, LET ME KNOW WHEN YOU ARE COMING TO TOWN AND I CAN SHOW OFF ALL THE GREAT FOOD JERSEY HAS TO OFFER!
HAHA, I WILL, MS. MARVEL.
IT WAS GREAT WORKING WITH YOU.
LEMME KNOW WHEN YOU'RE IN BROOKLYN NEXT, AND I'LL GET YOU REAL PIZZA AND MAKE UP FOR THE FACT THAT YOU STOPPED IN JERSEY.
HEY!
KIDDING.
ABSOLUTELY.
JERK.
I WAS KIDDING!

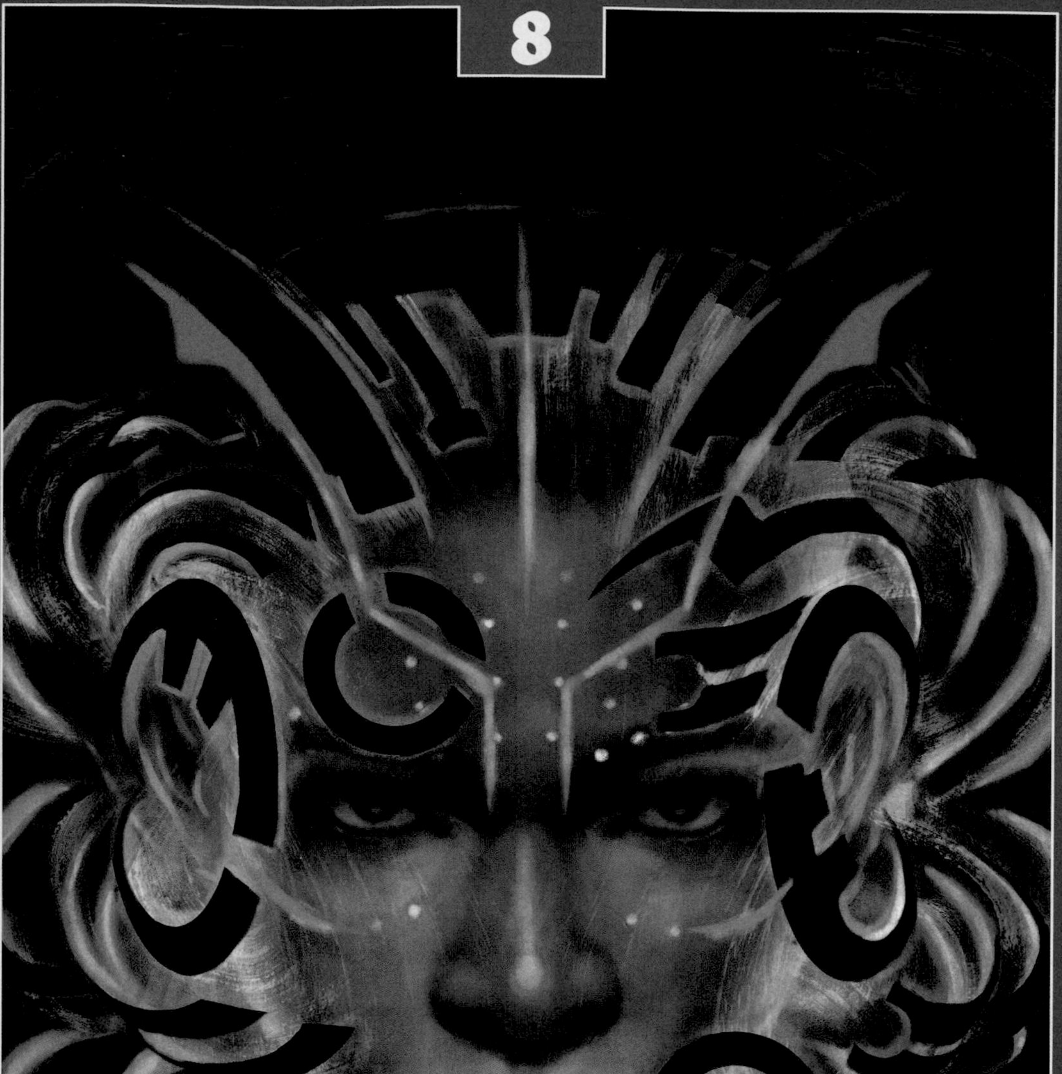
8

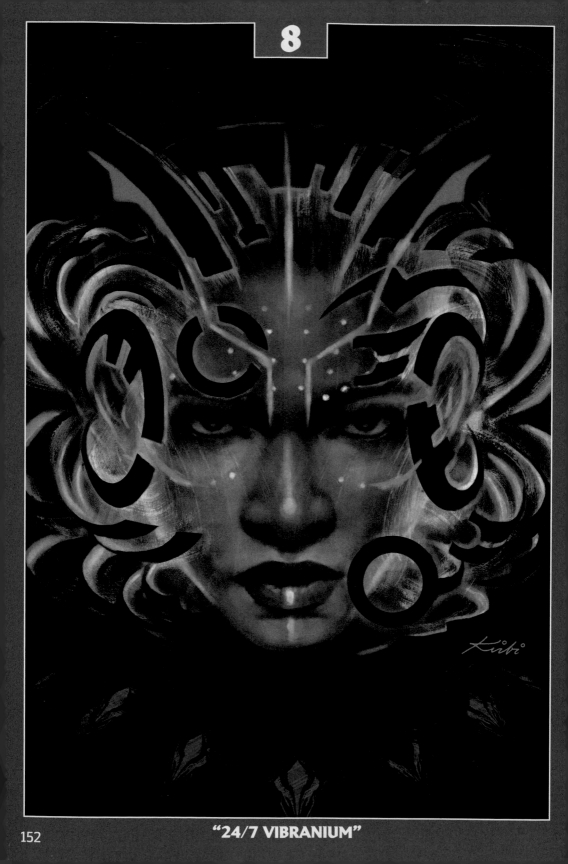

"24/7 VIBRANIUM"

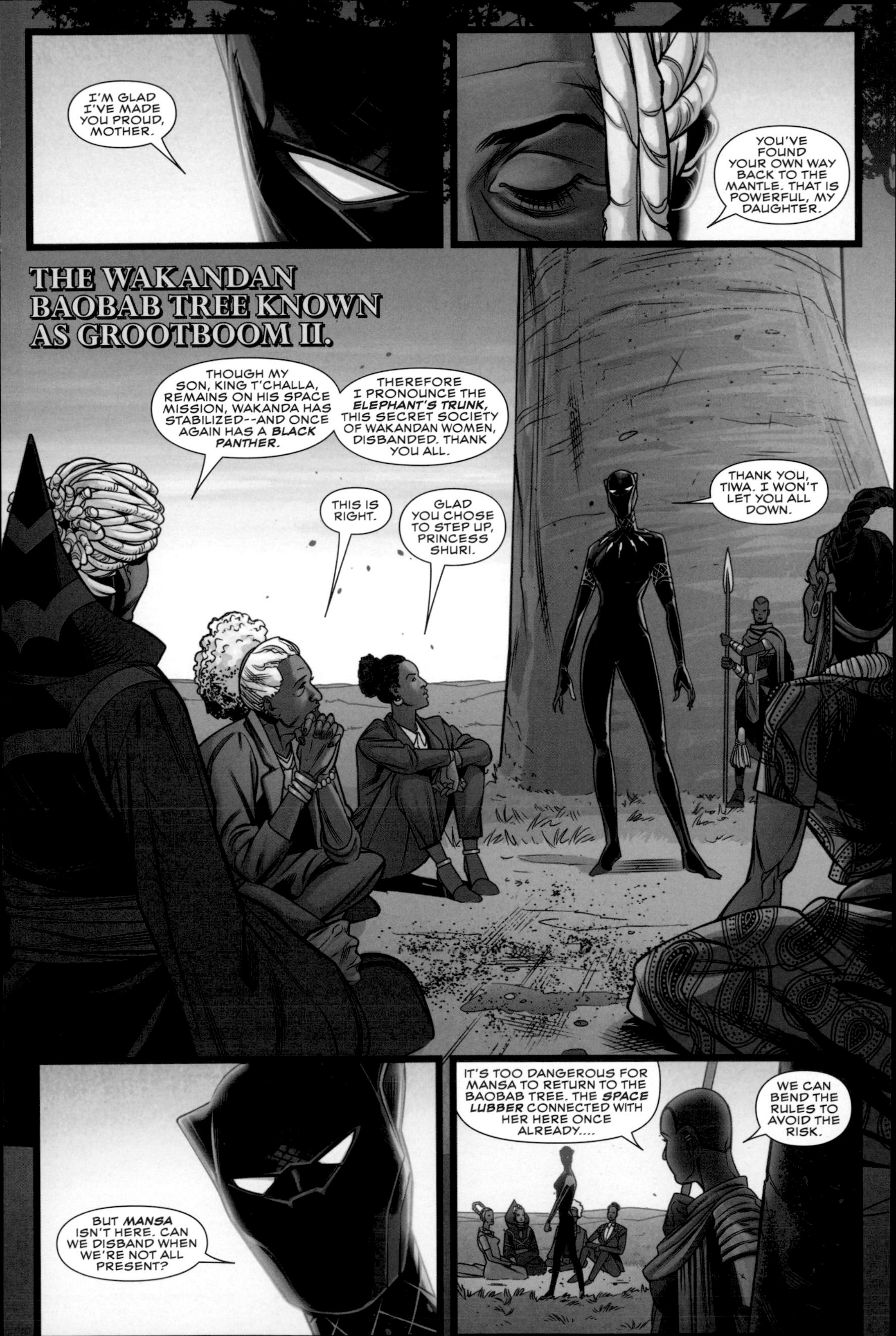
I'M GLAD I'VE MADE YOU PROUD, MOTHER.
YOU'VE FOUND YOUR OWN WAY BACK TO THE MANTLE. THAT IS POWERFUL, MY DAUGHTER.
THE WAKANDAN BAOBAB TREE KNOWN AS GROOTBOOM II.
THOUGH MY SON, KING T'CHALLA, REMAINS ON HIS SPACE MISSION, WAKANDA HAS STABILIZED--AND ONCE AGAIN HAS A BLACK PANTHER.
THEREFORE I PRONOUNCE THE ELEPHANT'S TRUNK, THIS SECRET SOCIETY OF WAKANDAN WOMEN, DISBANDED. THANK YOU ALL.
THIS IS RIGHT.
GLAD YOU CHOSE TO STEP UP, PRINCESS SHURI.
THANK YOU, TIWA. I WON'T LET YOU ALL DOWN.
BUT MANSA ISN'T HERE. CAN WE DISBAND WHEN WE'RE NOT ALL PRESENT?
IT'S TOO DANGEROUS FOR MANSA TO RETURN TO THE BAOBAB TREE. THE SPACE LUBBER CONNECTED WITH HER HERE ONCE ALREADY....
WE CAN BEND THE RULES TO AVOID THE RISK.

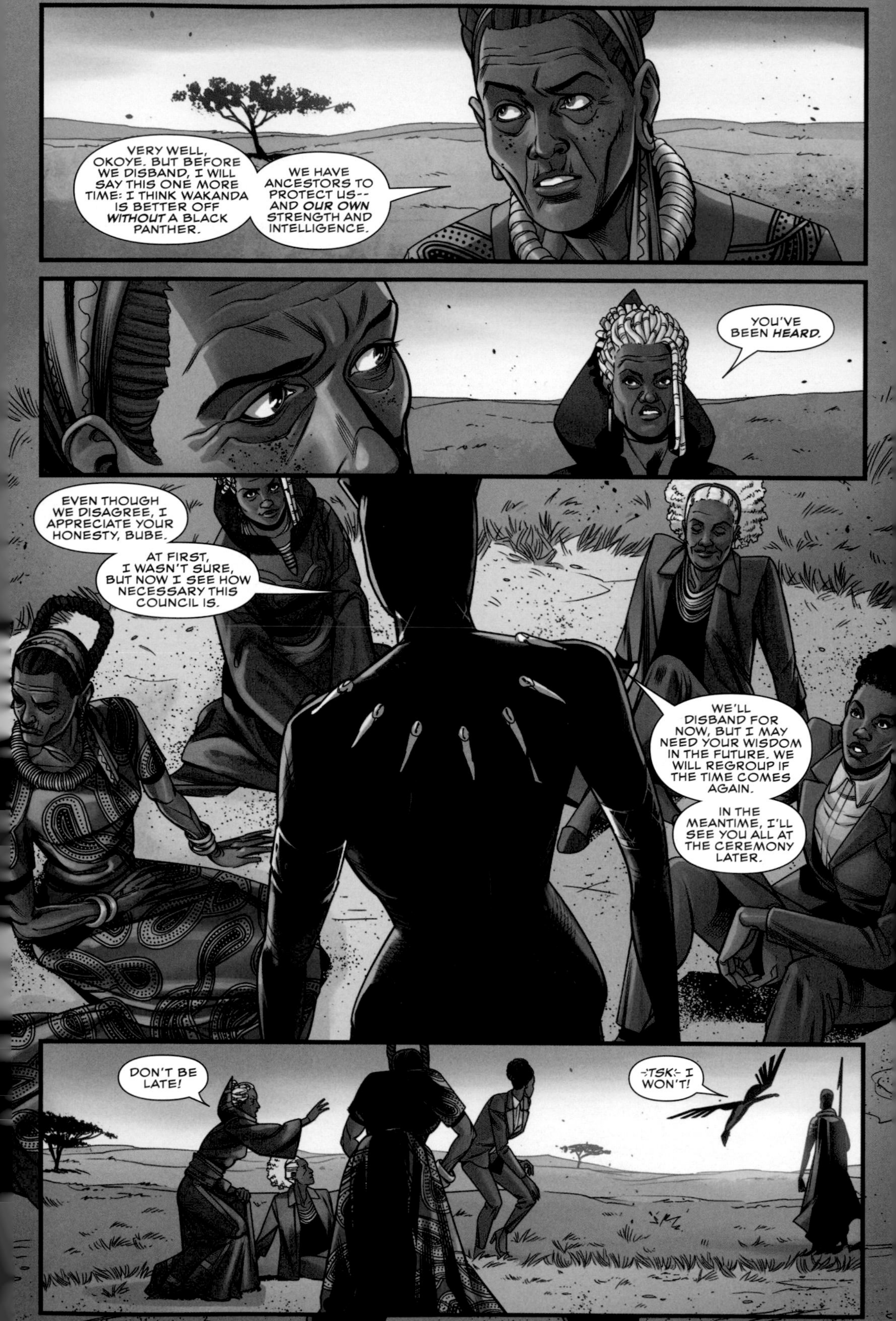
VERY WELL, OKOYE. BUT BEFORE WE DISBAND, I WILL SAY THIS ONE MORE TIME: I THINK WAKANDA IS BETTER OFF *WITHOUT* A BLACK PANTHER.
WE HAVE ANCESTORS TO PROTECT US-- AND *OUR OWN* STRENGTH AND INTELLIGENCE.
YOU'VE BEEN *HEARD.*
EVEN THOUGH WE DISAGREE, I APPRECIATE YOUR HONESTY, BUBE.
AT FIRST, I WASN'T SURE, BUT NOW I SEE HOW NECESSARY THIS COUNCIL IS.
WE'LL DISBAND FOR NOW, BUT I MAY NEED YOUR WISDOM IN THE FUTURE. WE WILL REGROUP IF THE TIME COMES AGAIN.
IN THE MEANTIME, I'LL SEE YOU ALL AT THE CEREMONY LATER.
DON'T BE LATE!
-TSK- I WON'T!

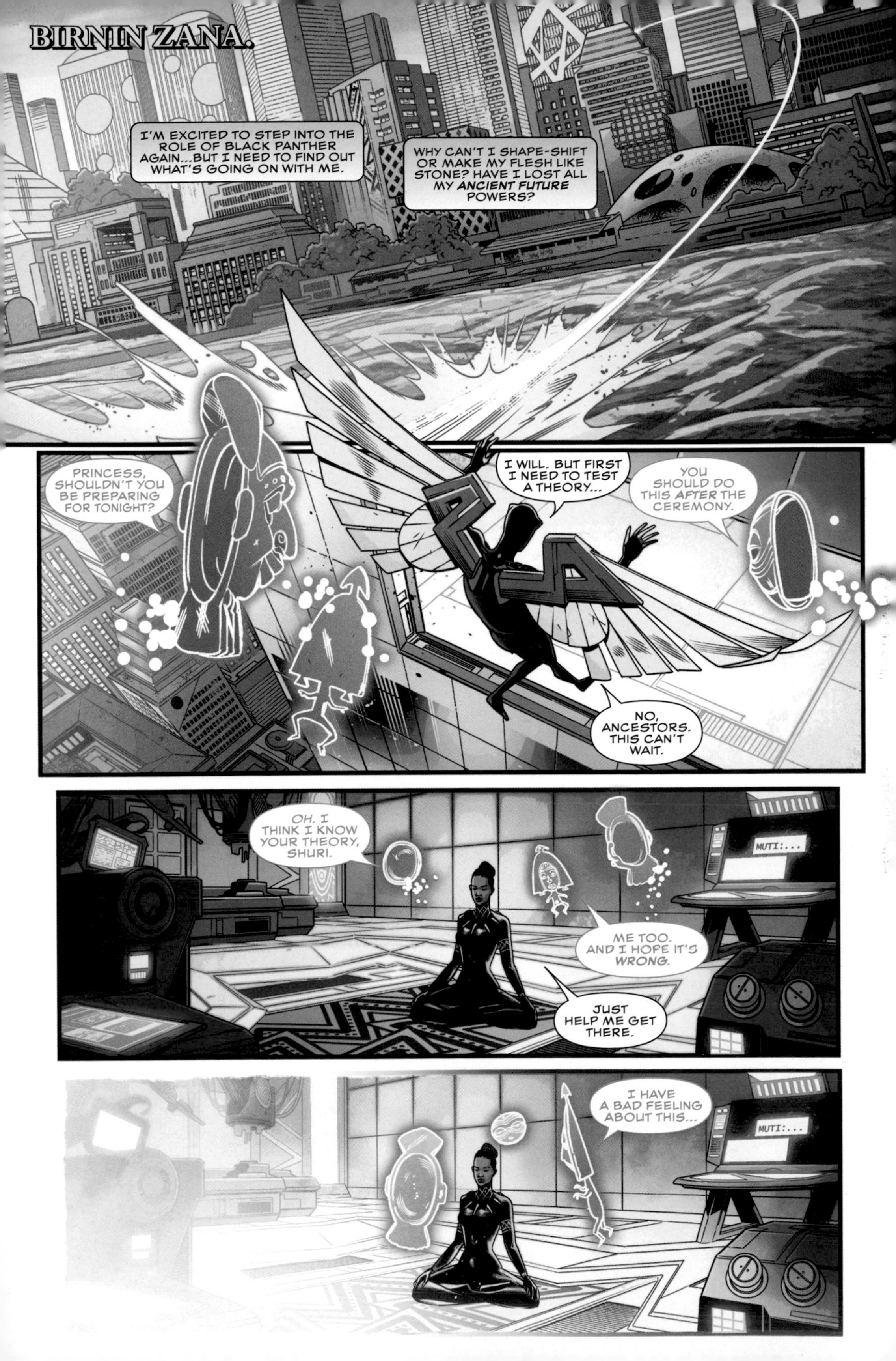
BIRNIN ZANA.
I'M EXCITED TO STEP INTO THE ROLE OF BLACK PANTHER AGAIN...BUT I NEED TO FIND OUT WHAT'S GOING ON WITH ME.
WHY CAN'T I SHAPE-SHIFT OR MAKE MY FLESH LIKE STONE? HAVE I LOST ALL MY ANCIENT FUTURE POWERS?
PRINCESS, SHOULDN'T YOU BE PREPARING FOR TONIGHT?
I WILL. BUT FIRST I NEED TO TEST A THEORY...
YOU SHOULD DO THIS AFTER THE CEREMONY.
NO, ANCESTORS. THIS CAN'T WAIT.
OH. I THINK I KNOW YOUR THEORY, SHURI.
MUTI:...
ME TOO. AND I HOPE IT'S WRONG.
JUST HELP ME GET THERE.
I HAVE A BAD FEELING ABOUT THIS...
MUTI:...

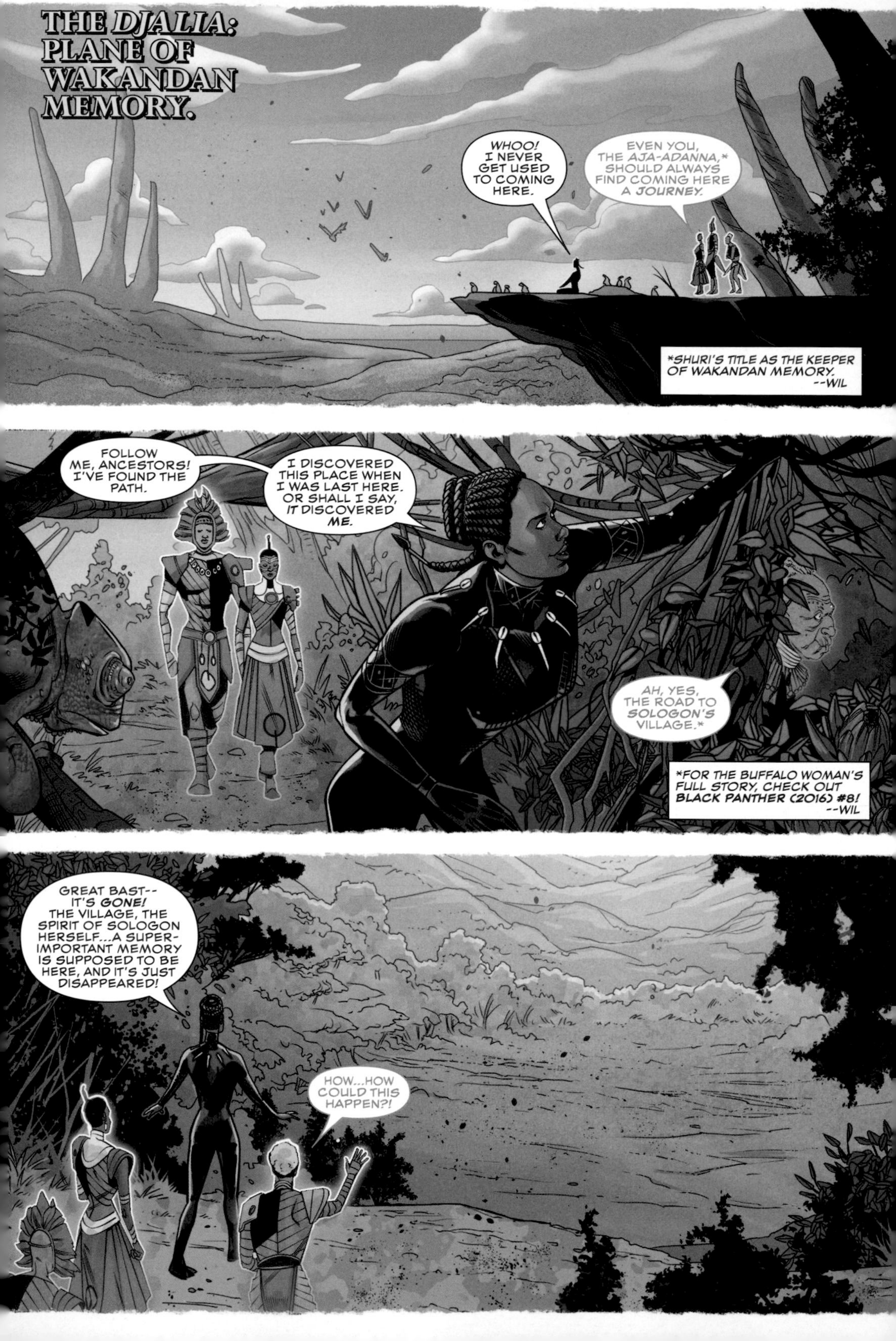
THE *DJALIA*: PLANE OF WAKANDAN MEMORY.
WHOO! I NEVER GET USED TO COMING HERE.
EVEN YOU, THE *AJA-ADANNA*,* SHOULD ALWAYS FIND COMING HERE A *JOURNEY*.
*SHURI'S TITLE AS THE KEEPER OF WAKANDAN MEMORY. --WIL
FOLLOW ME, ANCESTORS! I'VE FOUND THE PATH.
I DISCOVERED THIS PLACE WHEN I WAS LAST HERE. OR SHALL I SAY, *IT* DISCOVERED **ME**.
AH, YES, THE ROAD TO *SOLOGON'S* VILLAGE.*
*FOR THE BUFFALO WOMAN'S FULL STORY, CHECK OUT **BLACK PANTHER (2016) #8!** --WIL
GREAT BAST-- IT'S **GONE!** THE VILLAGE, THE SPIRIT OF SOLOGON HERSELF...A SUPER-IMPORTANT MEMORY IS SUPPOSED TO BE HERE, AND IT'S JUST DISAPPEARED!
HOW...HOW COULD THIS HAPPEN?!

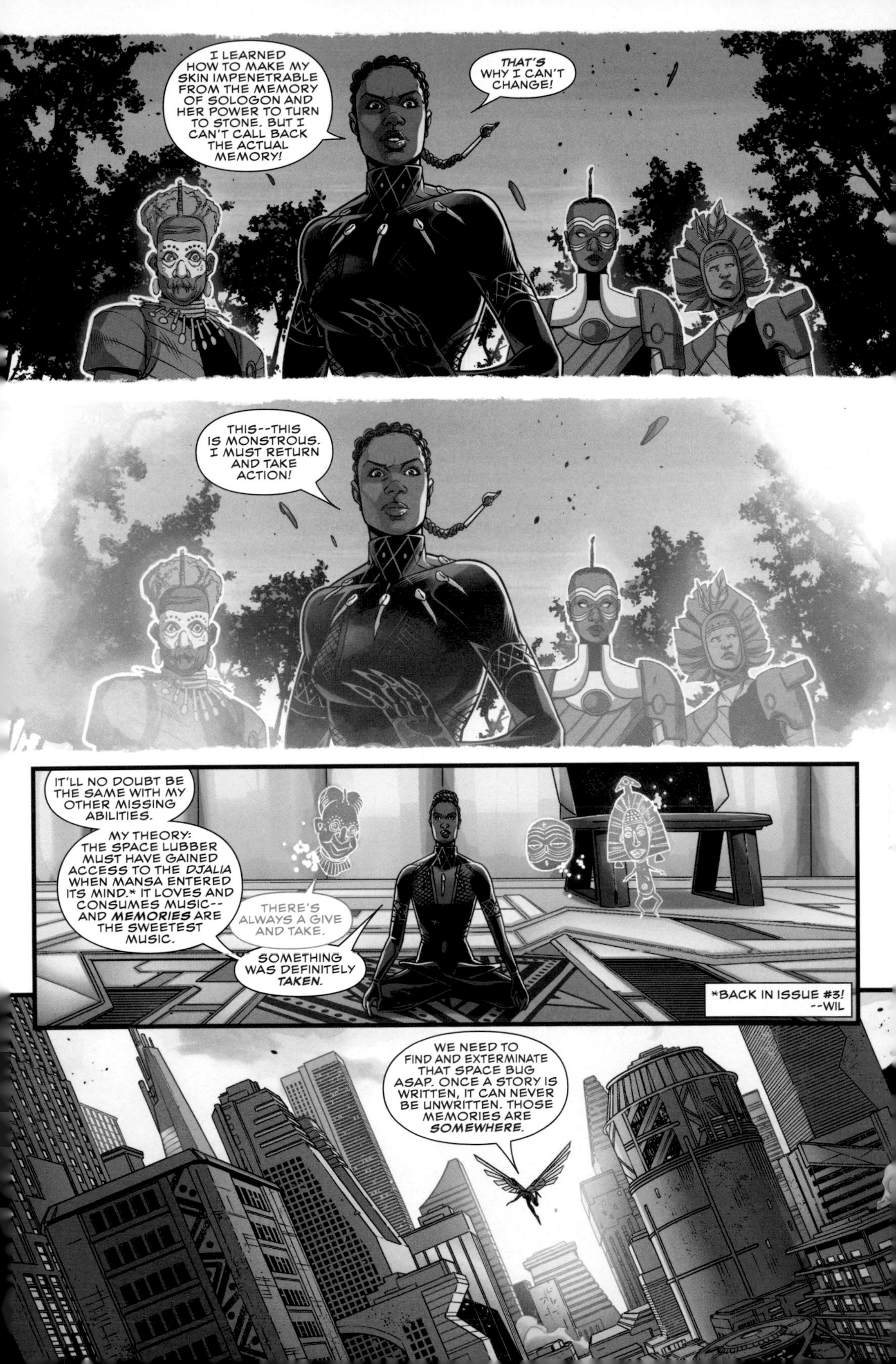

I LEARNED HOW TO MAKE MY SKIN IMPENETRABLE FROM THE MEMORY OF SOLOGON AND HER POWER TO TURN TO STONE. BUT I CAN'T CALL BACK THE ACTUAL MEMORY!
THAT'S WHY I CAN'T CHANGE!
THIS--THIS IS MONSTROUS. I MUST RETURN AND TAKE ACTION!
IT'LL NO DOUBT BE THE SAME WITH MY OTHER MISSING ABILITIES.
MY THEORY: THE SPACE LUBBER MUST HAVE GAINED ACCESS TO THE DJALIA WHEN MANSA ENTERED ITS MIND.* IT LOVES AND CONSUMES MUSIC-- AND MEMORIES ARE THE SWEETEST MUSIC.
THERE'S ALWAYS A GIVE AND TAKE.
SOMETHING WAS DEFINITELY TAKEN.
*BACK IN ISSUE #3! --WIL
WE NEED TO FIND AND EXTERMINATE THAT SPACE BUG ASAP. ONCE A STORY IS WRITTEN, IT CAN NEVER BE UNWRITTEN. THOSE MEMORIES ARE SOMEWHERE.

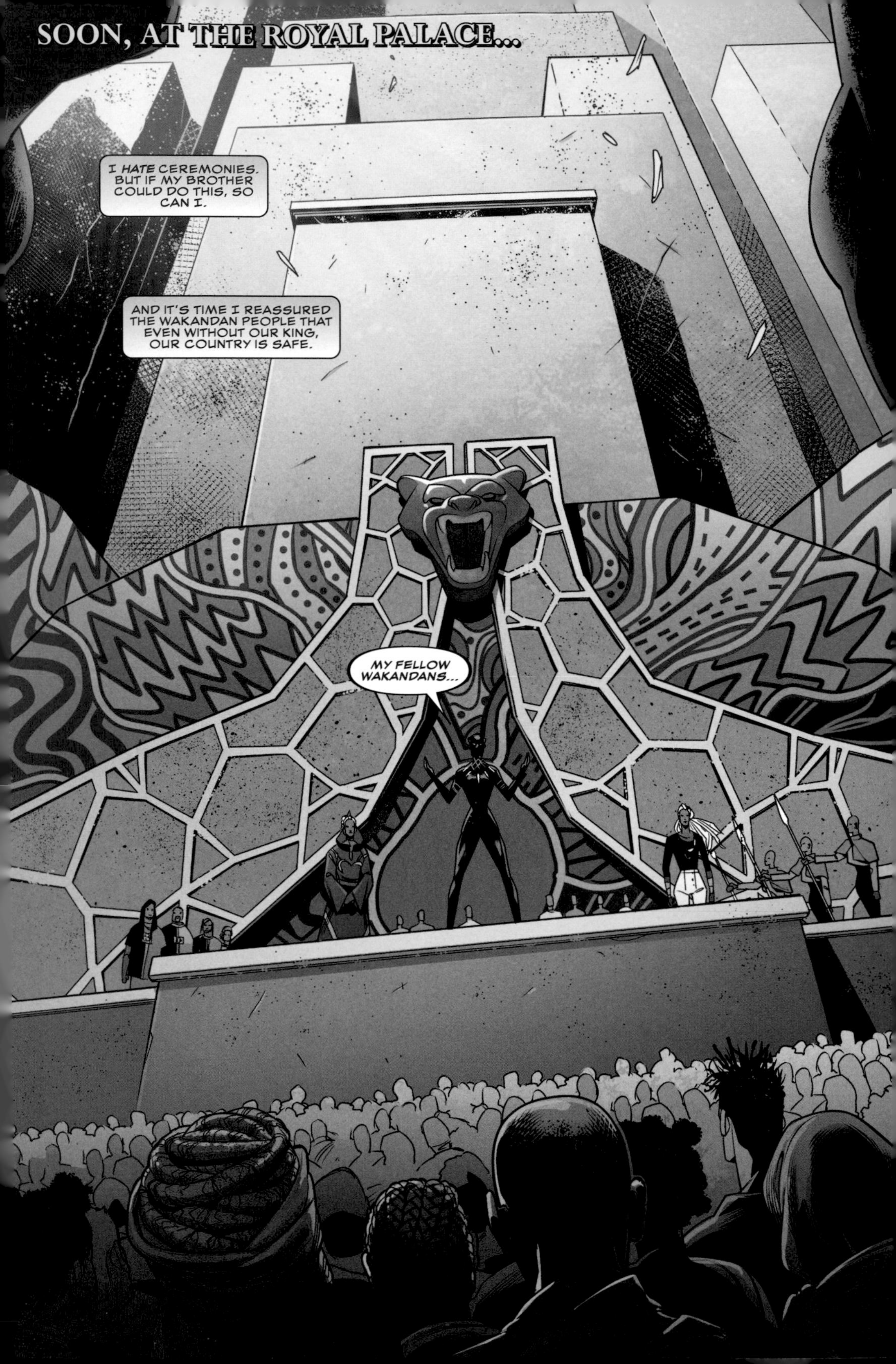
SOON, AT THE ROYAL PALACE...
I HATE CEREMONIES. BUT IF MY BROTHER COULD DO THIS, SO CAN I.
AND IT'S TIME I REASSURED THE WAKANDAN PEOPLE THAT EVEN WITHOUT OUR KING, OUR COUNTRY IS SAFE.
MY FELLOW WAKANDANS...

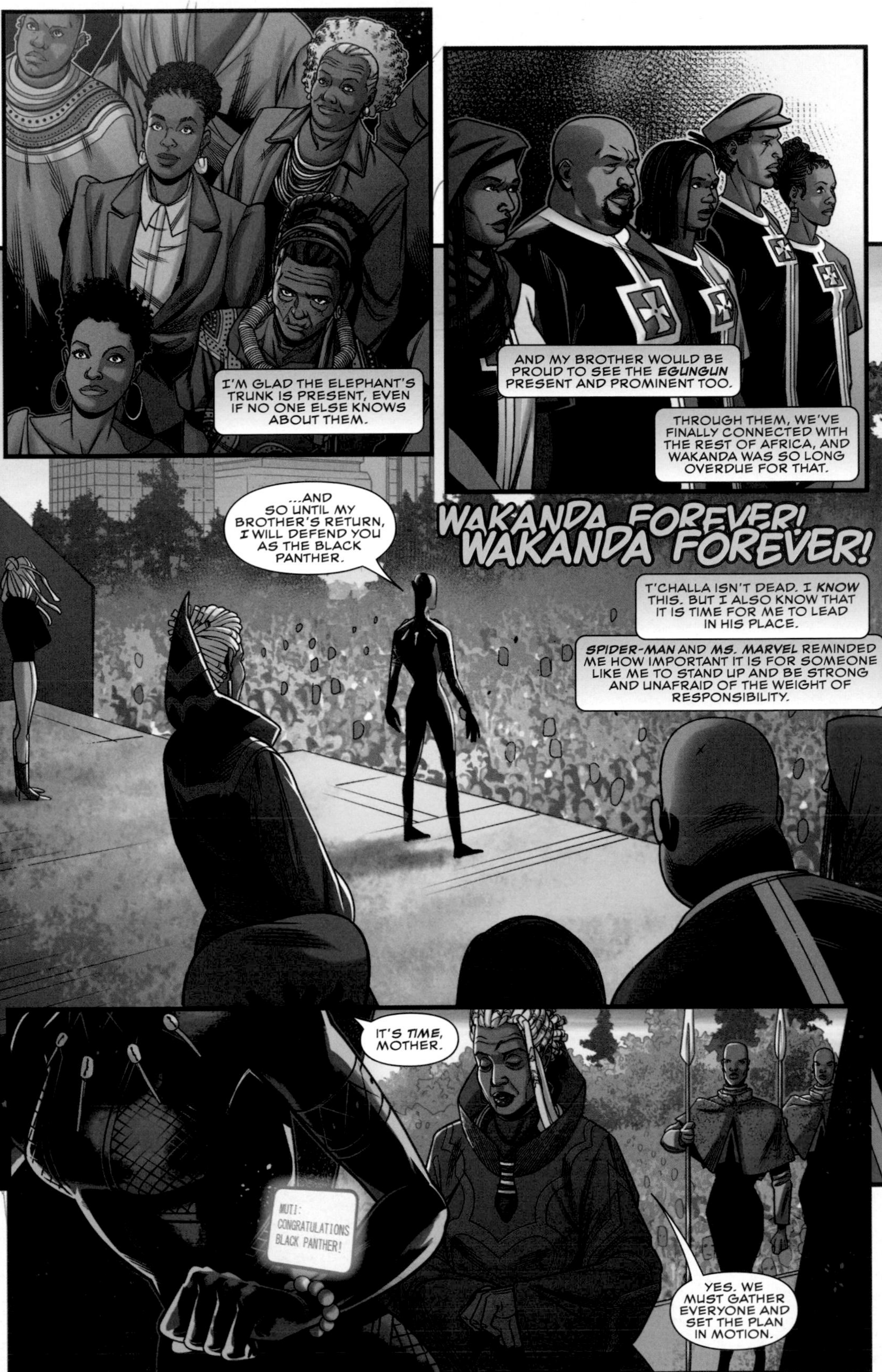
I'M GLAD THE ELEPHANT'S TRUNK IS PRESENT, EVEN IF NO ONE ELSE KNOWS ABOUT THEM.
AND MY BROTHER WOULD BE PROUD TO SEE THE *EGUNGUN* PRESENT AND PROMINENT TOO.
THROUGH THEM, WE'VE FINALLY CONNECTED WITH THE REST OF AFRICA, AND WAKANDA WAS SO LONG OVERDUE FOR THAT.
...AND SO UNTIL MY BROTHER'S RETURN, *I* WILL DEFEND YOU AS THE BLACK PANTHER.
WAKANDA FOREVER! WAKANDA FOREVER!
T'CHALLA ISN'T DEAD. I *KNOW* THIS. BUT I ALSO KNOW THAT IT IS TIME FOR ME TO LEAD IN HIS PLACE.
SPIDER-MAN AND *MS. MARVEL* REMINDED ME HOW IMPORTANT IT IS FOR SOMEONE LIKE ME TO STAND UP AND BE STRONG AND UNAFRAID OF THE WEIGHT OF RESPONSIBILITY.
IT'S *TIME*, MOTHER.
MUTI: CONGRATULATIONS BLACK PANTHER!
YES. WE MUST GATHER EVERYONE AND SET THE PLAN IN MOTION.

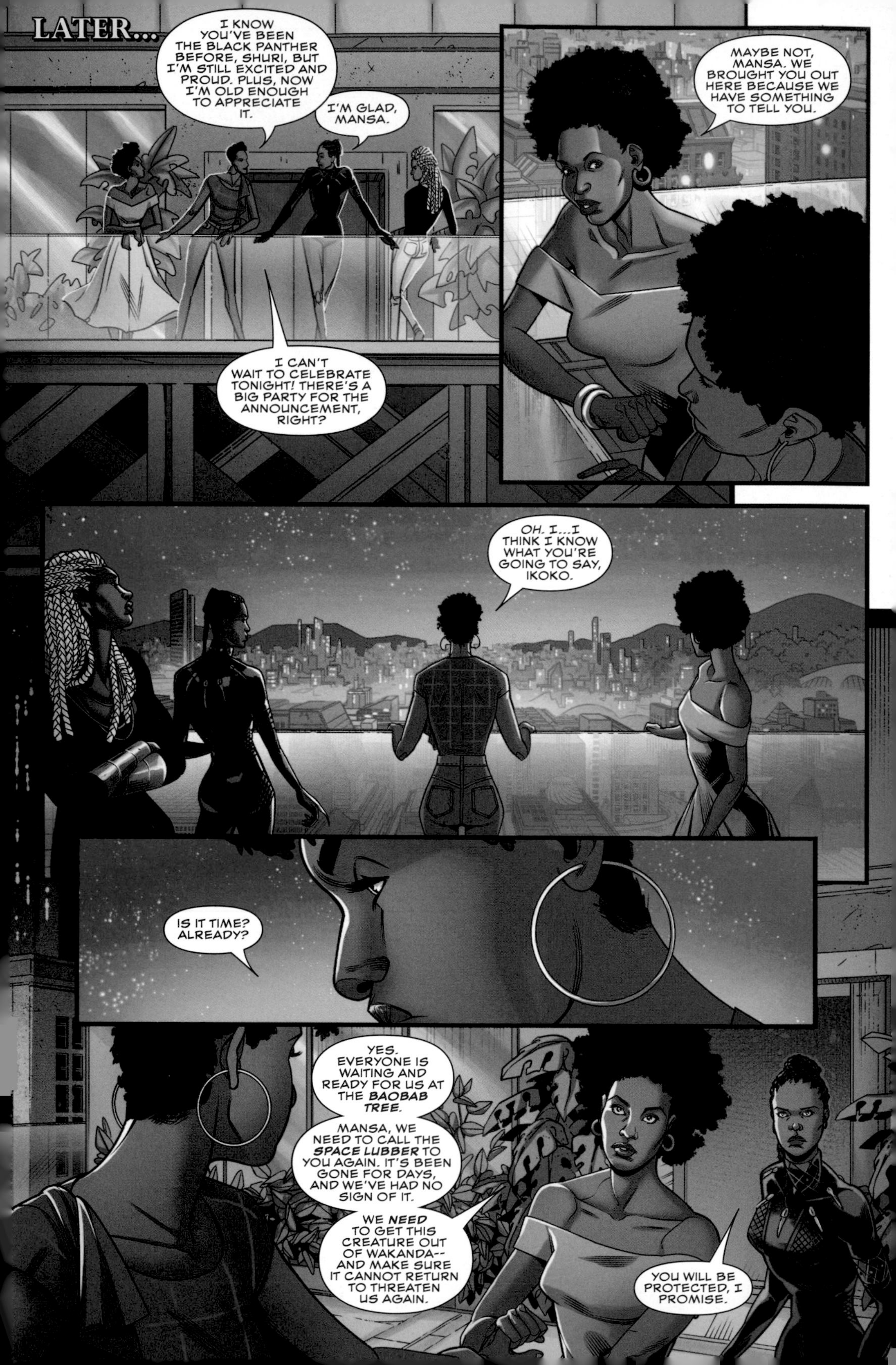
LATER...
I KNOW YOU'VE BEEN THE BLACK PANTHER BEFORE, SHURI, BUT I'M STILL EXCITED AND PROUD. PLUS, NOW I'M OLD ENOUGH TO APPRECIATE IT.
I'M GLAD, MANSA.
I CAN'T WAIT TO CELEBRATE TONIGHT! THERE'S A BIG PARTY FOR THE ANNOUNCEMENT, RIGHT?
MAYBE NOT, MANSA. WE BROUGHT YOU OUT HERE BECAUSE WE HAVE SOMETHING TO TELL YOU.
OH. I...I THINK I KNOW WHAT YOU'RE GOING TO SAY, IKOKO.
IS IT TIME? ALREADY?
YES. EVERYONE IS WAITING AND READY FOR US AT THE BAOBAB TREE.
MANSA, WE NEED TO CALL THE SPACE LUBBER TO YOU AGAIN. IT'S BEEN GONE FOR DAYS, AND WE'VE HAD NO SIGN OF IT.
WE NEED TO GET THIS CREATURE OUT OF WAKANDA--AND MAKE SURE IT CANNOT RETURN TO THREATEN US AGAIN.
YOU WILL BE PROTECTED, I PROMISE.

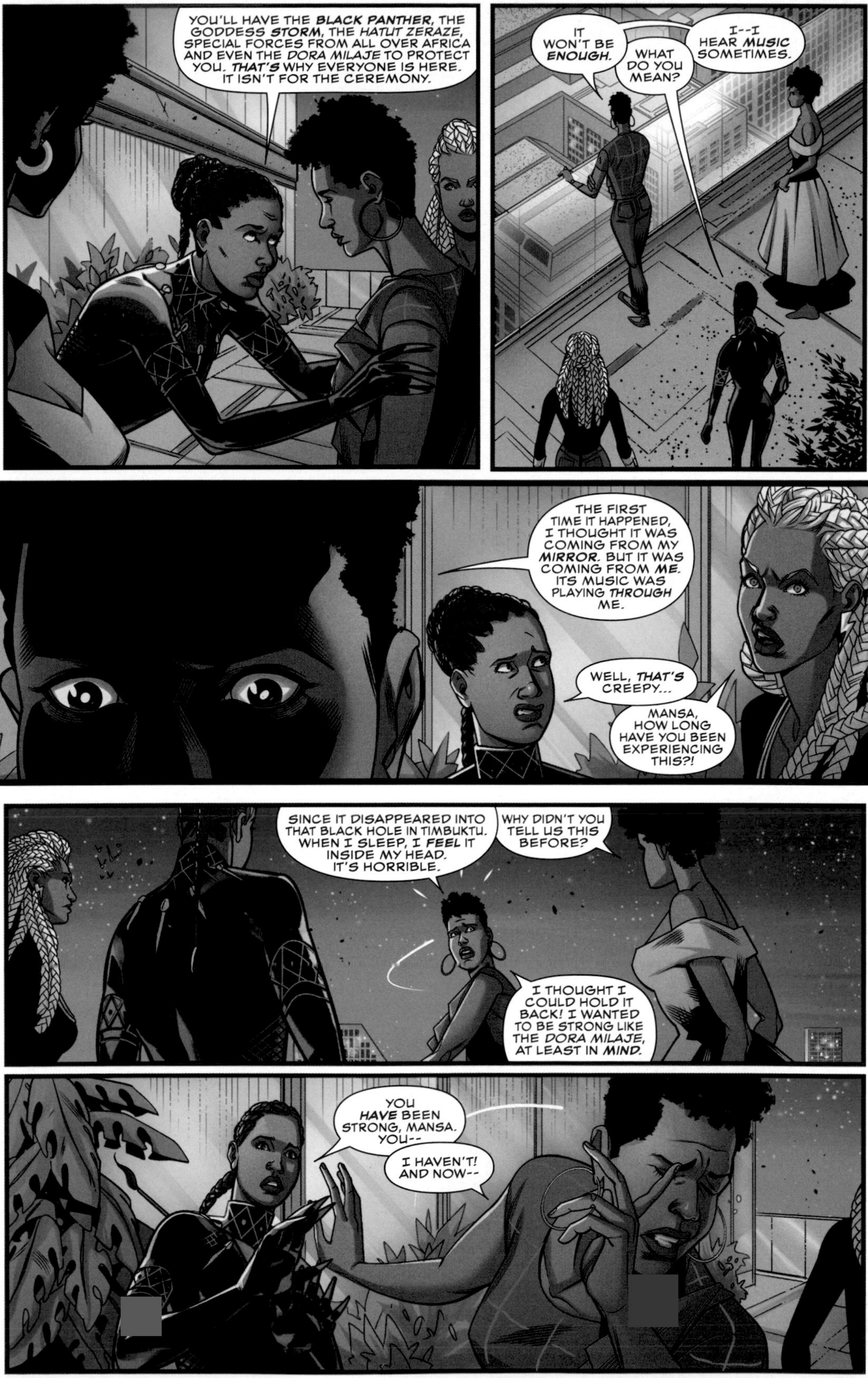
YOU'LL HAVE THE BLACK PANTHER, THE GODDESS STORM, THE HATUT ZERAZE, SPECIAL FORCES FROM ALL OVER AFRICA AND EVEN THE DORA MILAJE TO PROTECT YOU. THAT'S WHY EVERYONE IS HERE. IT ISN'T FOR THE CEREMONY.
IT WON'T BE ENOUGH.
WHAT DO YOU MEAN?
I--I HEAR MUSIC SOMETIMES.
THE FIRST TIME IT HAPPENED, I THOUGHT IT WAS COMING FROM MY MIRROR. BUT IT WAS COMING FROM ME. ITS MUSIC WAS PLAYING THROUGH ME.
WELL, THAT'S CREEPY...
MANSA, HOW LONG HAVE YOU BEEN EXPERIENCING THIS?!
SINCE IT DISAPPEARED INTO THAT BLACK HOLE IN TIMBUKTU. WHEN I SLEEP, I FEEL IT INSIDE MY HEAD. IT'S HORRIBLE.
WHY DIDN'T YOU TELL US THIS BEFORE?
I THOUGHT I COULD HOLD IT BACK! I WANTED TO BE STRONG LIKE THE DORA MILAJE, AT LEAST IN MIND.
YOU HAVE BEEN STRONG, MANSA. YOU--
I HAVEN'T! AND NOW--

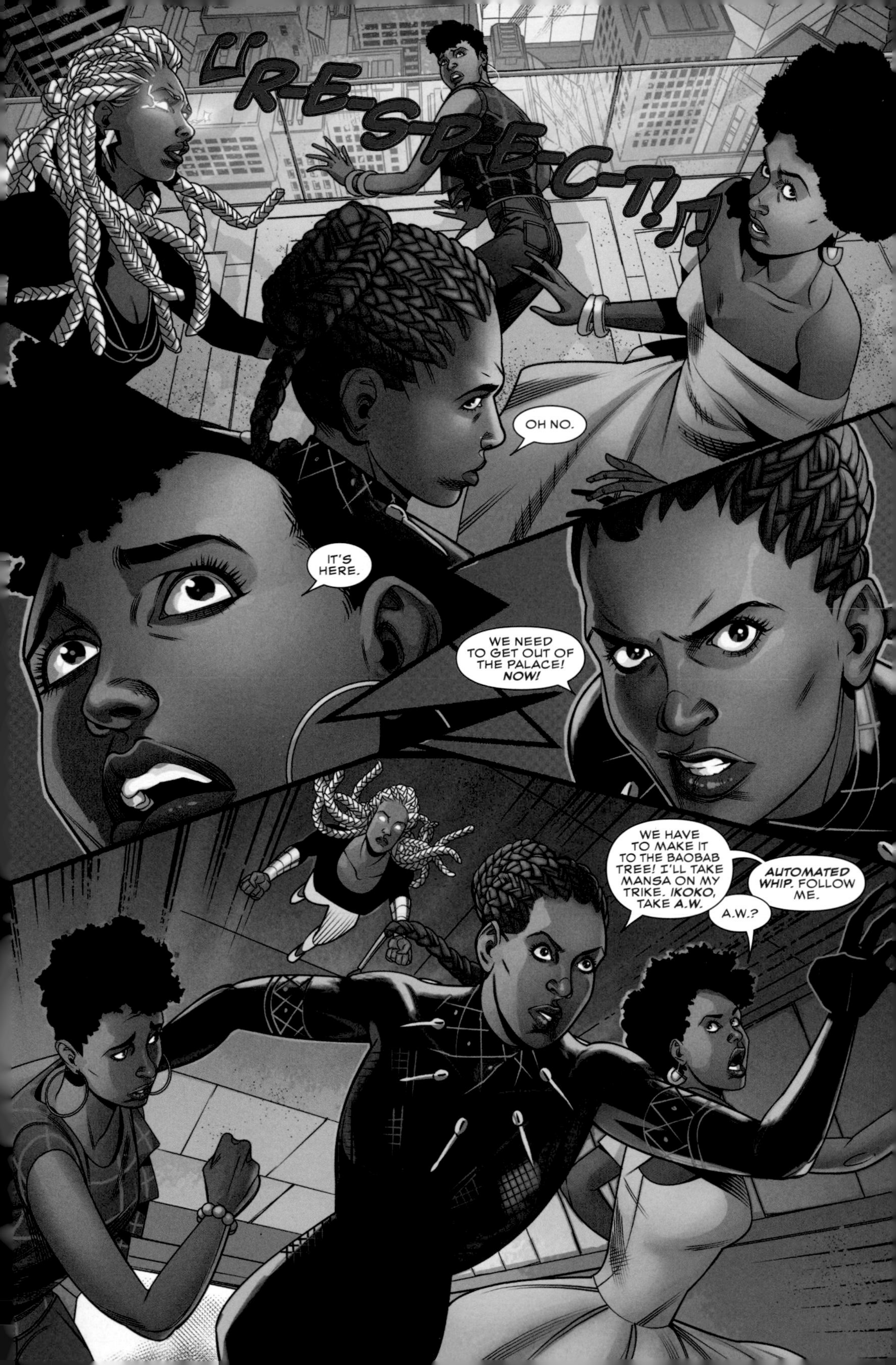

C-R-E-S-P-E-C-T!
OH NO.
IT'S HERE.
WE NEED TO GET OUT OF THE PALACE! NOW!
WE HAVE TO MAKE IT TO THE BAOBAB TREE! I'LL TAKE MANSA ON MY TRIKE. IKOKO, TAKE A.W.
A.W.?
AUTOMATED WHIP. FOLLOW ME.

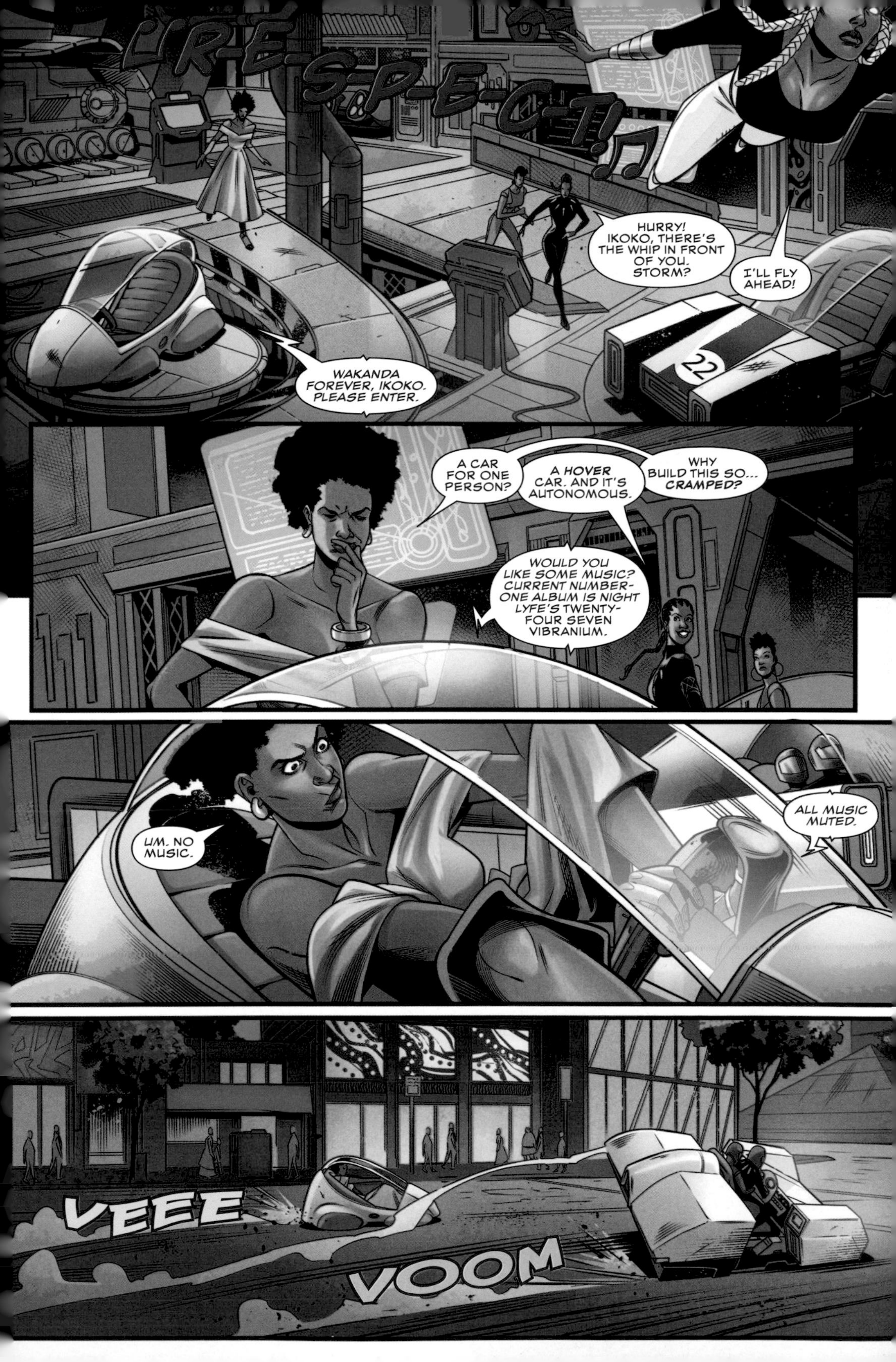
R-E-S-P-E-C-T!
HURRY! IKOKO, THERE'S THE WHIP IN FRONT OF YOU. STORM?
I'LL FLY AHEAD!
WAKANDA FOREVER, IKOKO. PLEASE ENTER.
22
A CAR FOR ONE PERSON?
A *HOVER* CAR. AND IT'S AUTONOMOUS.
WHY BUILD THIS SO... *CRAMPED?*
WOULD YOU LIKE SOME MUSIC? CURRENT NUMBER-ONE ALBUM IS NIGHT LYFE'S TWENTY-FOUR SEVEN VIBRANIUM.
UM. NO MUSIC.
ALL MUSIC MUTED.
VEEE
VOOM

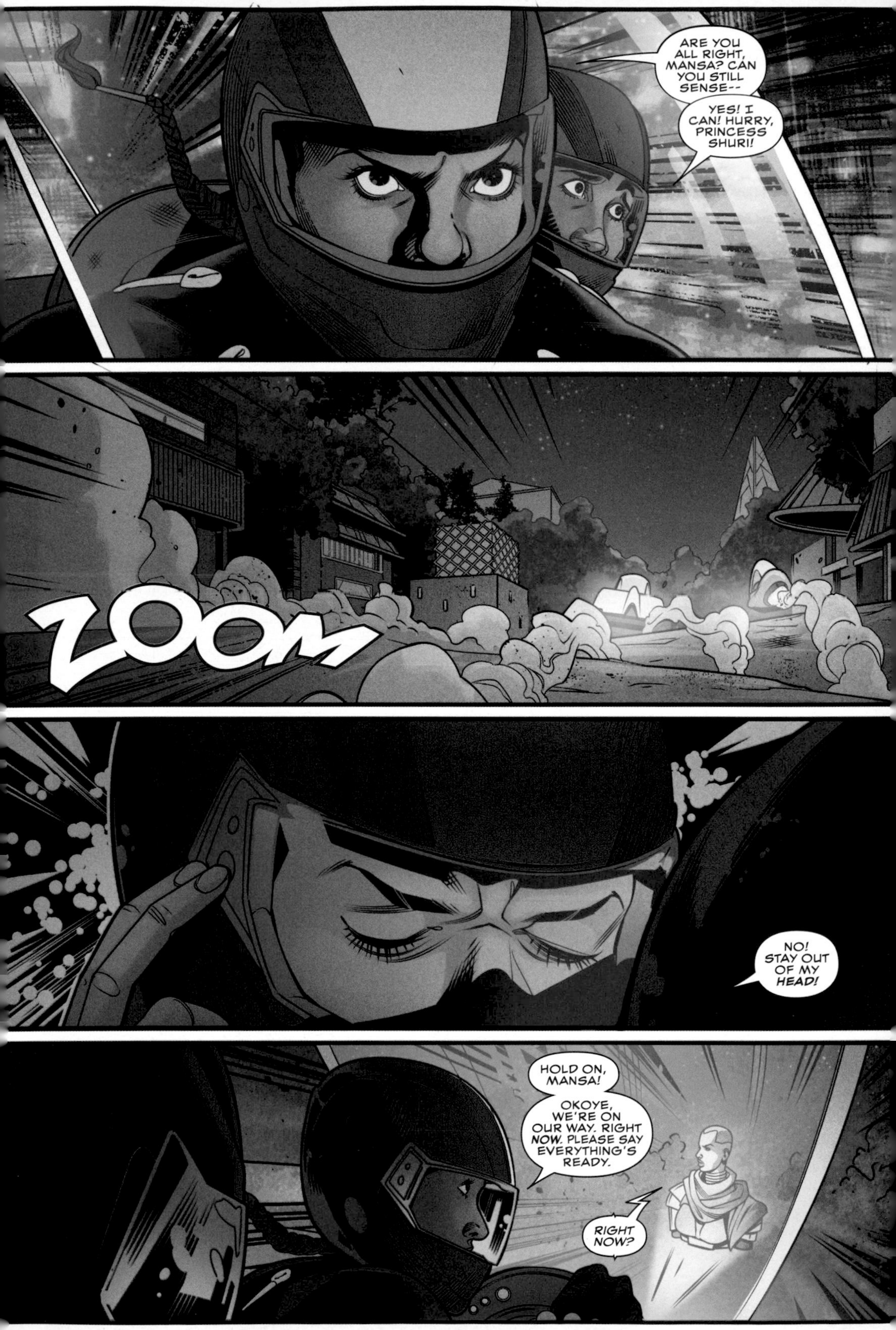
ARE YOU ALL RIGHT, MANSA? CAN YOU STILL SENSE--
YES! I CAN! HURRY, PRINCESS SHURI!
ZOOM
NO! STAY OUT OF MY HEAD!
HOLD ON, MANSA!
OKOYE, WE'RE ON OUR WAY. RIGHT NOW. PLEASE SAY EVERYTHING'S READY.
RIGHT NOW?

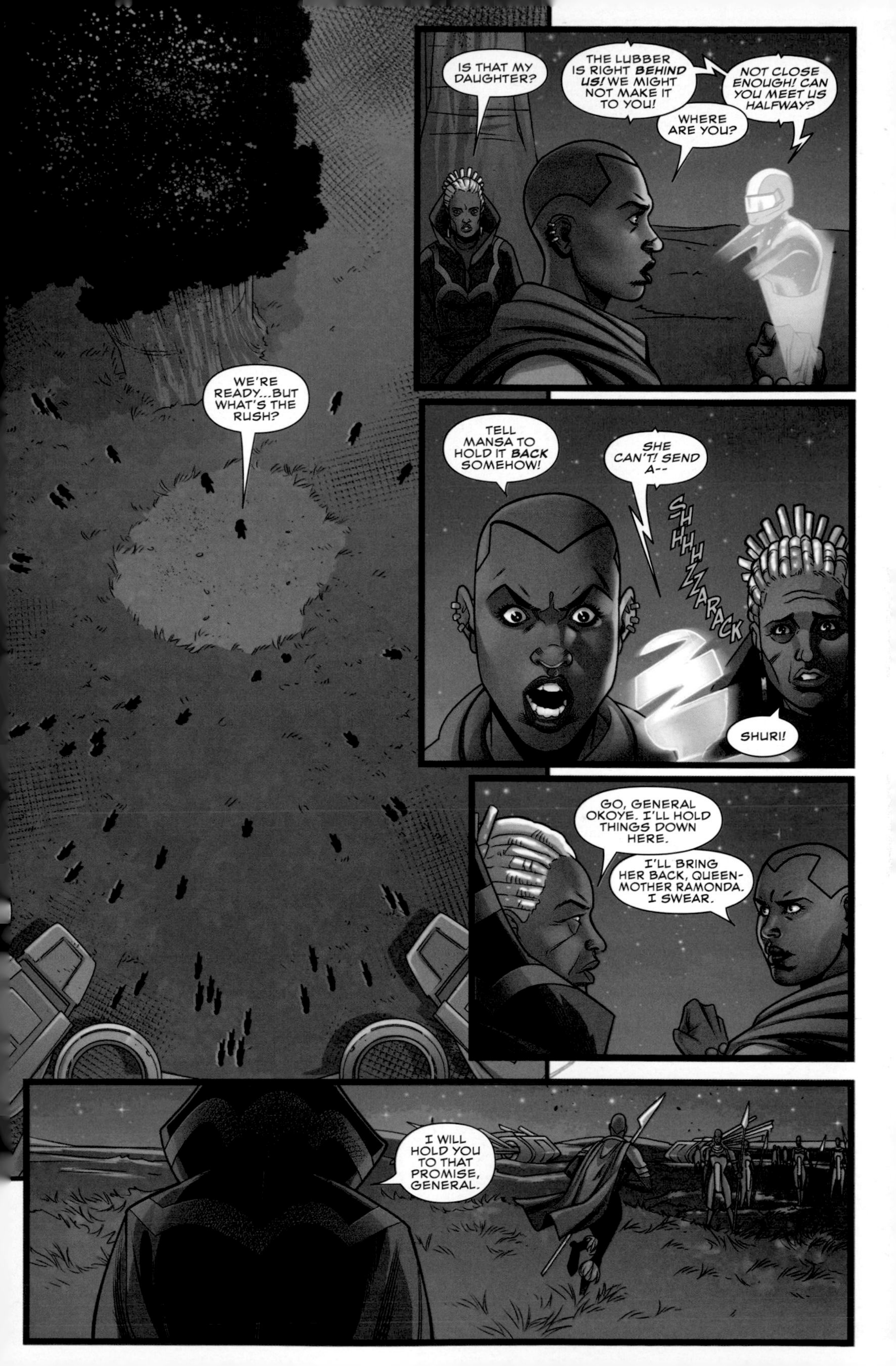
WE'RE READY...BUT WHAT'S THE RUSH?
IS THAT MY DAUGHTER?
THE LUBBER IS RIGHT BEHIND US! WE MIGHT NOT MAKE IT TO YOU!
NOT CLOSE ENOUGH! CAN YOU MEET US HALFWAY?
WHERE ARE YOU?
TELL MANSA TO HOLD IT BACK SOMEHOW!
SHE CAN'T! SEND A--
SHHHZZARACK
SHURI!
GO, GENERAL OKOYE. I'LL HOLD THINGS DOWN HERE.
I'LL BRING HER BACK, QUEEN-MOTHER RAMONDA. I SWEAR.
I WILL HOLD YOU TO THAT PROMISE, GENERAL.

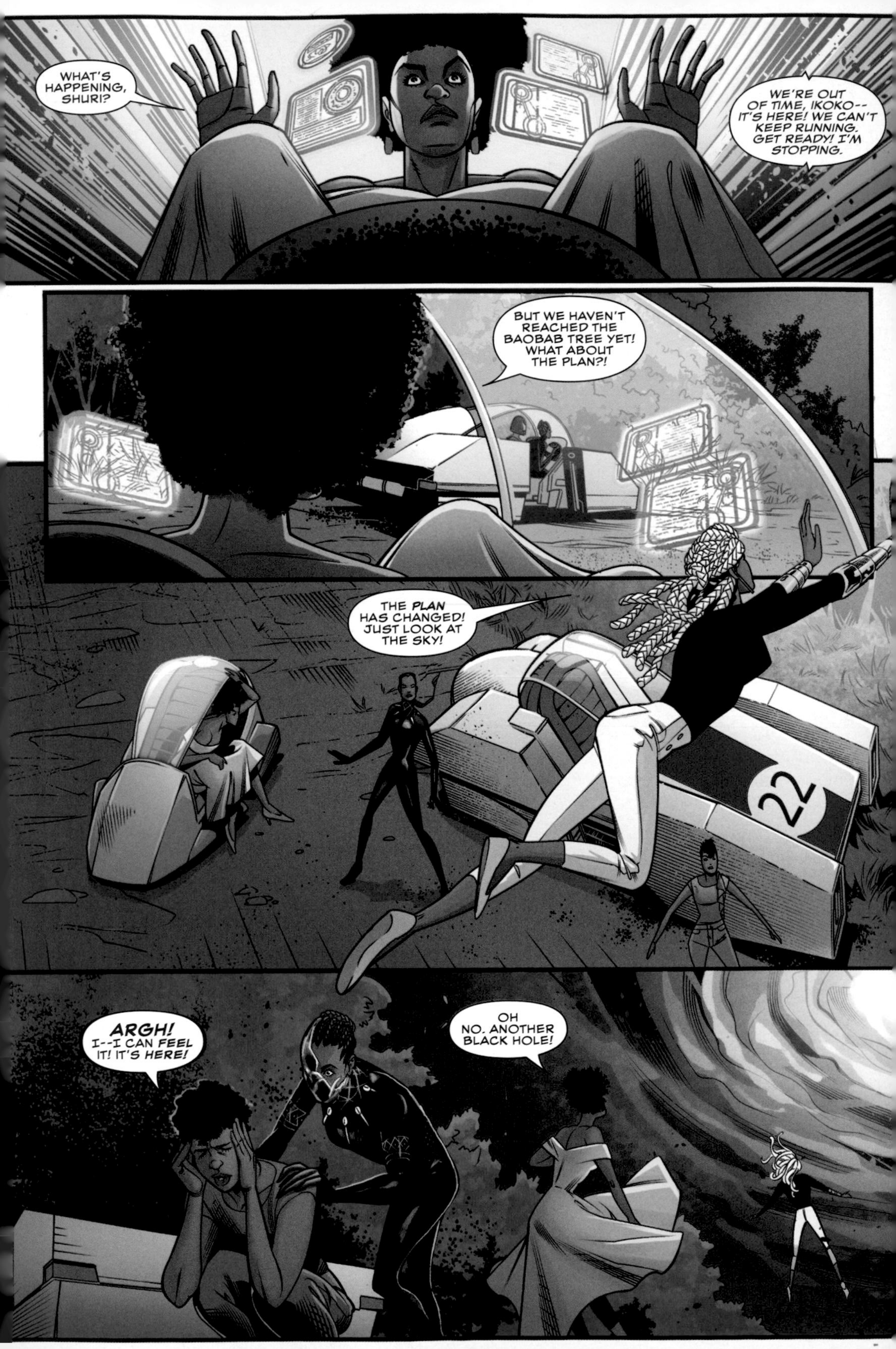
WHAT'S HAPPENING, SHURI?
WE'RE OUT OF TIME, IKOKO-- IT'S HERE! WE CAN'T KEEP RUNNING. GET READY! I'M STOPPING.
BUT WE HAVEN'T REACHED THE BAOBAB TREE YET! WHAT ABOUT THE PLAN?!
THE PLAN HAS CHANGED! JUST LOOK AT THE SKY!
22
ARGH! I--I CAN FEEL IT! IT'S HERE!
OH NO. ANOTHER BLACK HOLE!

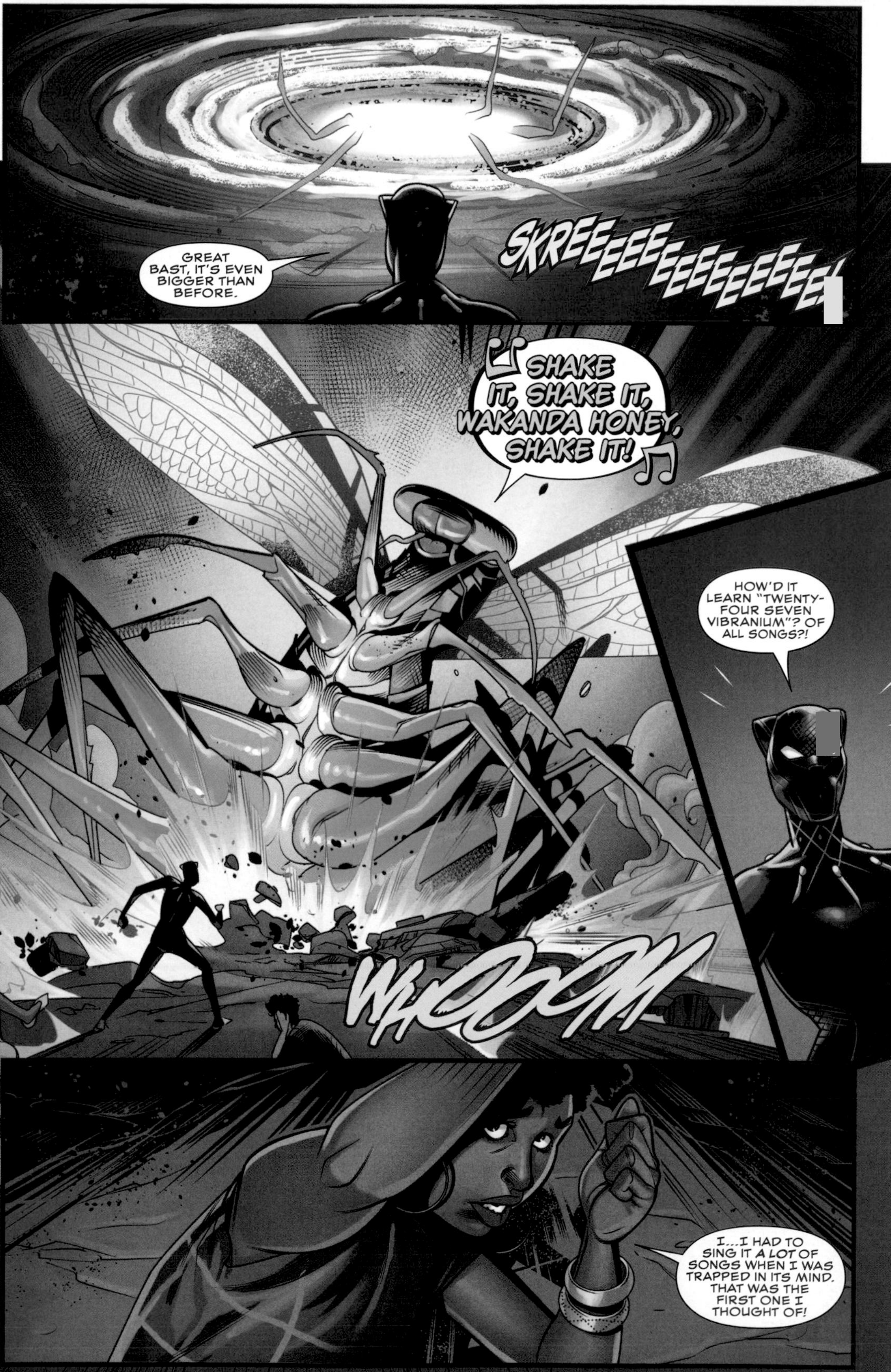

GREAT BAST, IT'S EVEN BIGGER THAN BEFORE.
SKREEEEEEEEEEEEEEE
SHAKE IT, SHAKE IT, WAKANDA HONEY, SHAKE IT!
HOW'D IT LEARN "TWENTY-FOUR SEVEN VIBRANIUM"? OF ALL SONGS?!
WHOOM
I...I HAD TO SING IT A LOT OF SONGS WHEN I WAS TRAPPED IN ITS MIND. THAT WAS THE FIRST ONE I THOUGHT OF!

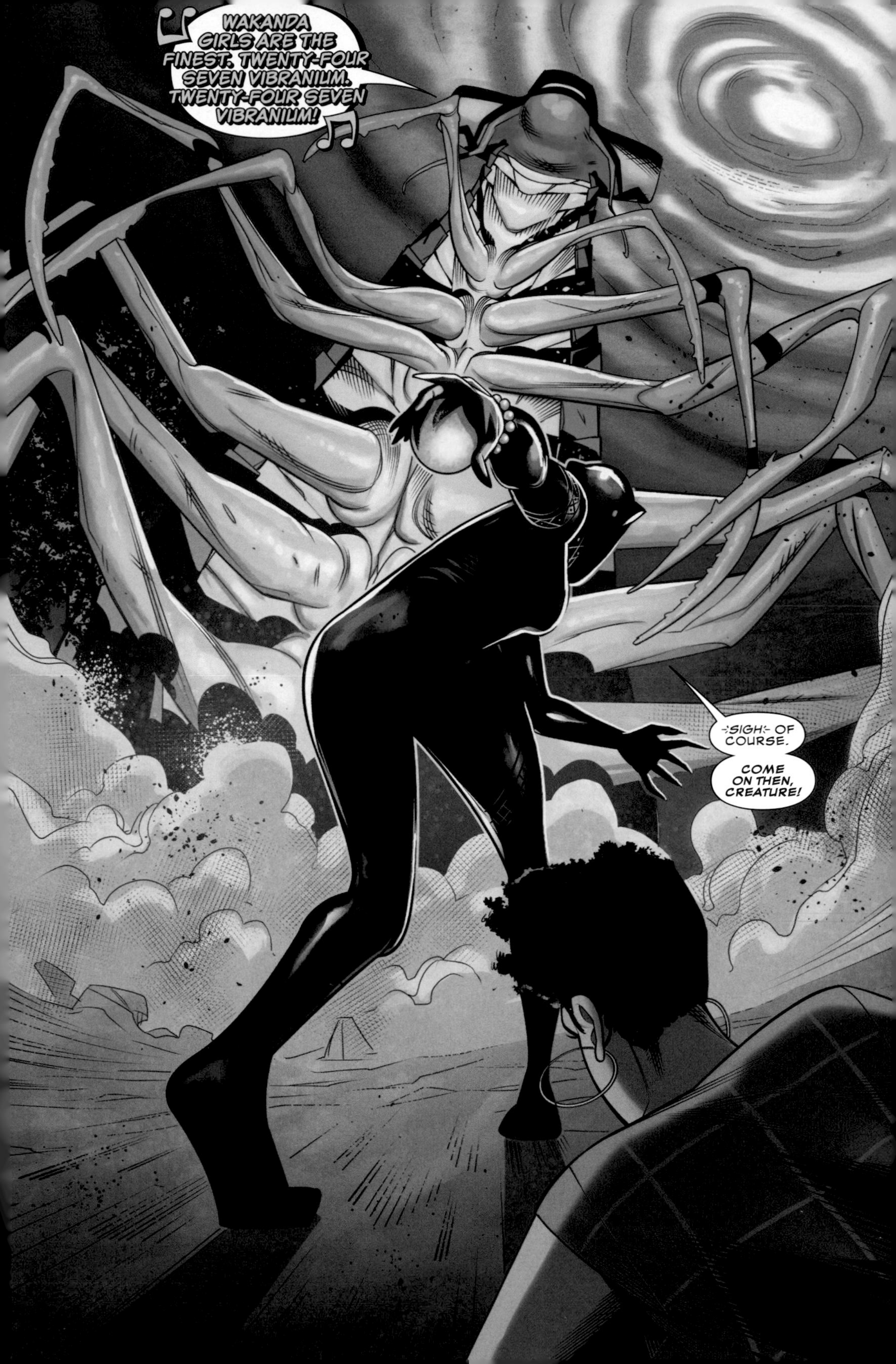
WAKANDA GIRLS ARE THE FINEST. TWENTY-FOUR SEVEN VIBRANIUM. TWENTY-FOUR SEVEN VIBRANIUM!
-SIGH- OF COURSE.
COME ON THEN, CREATURE!

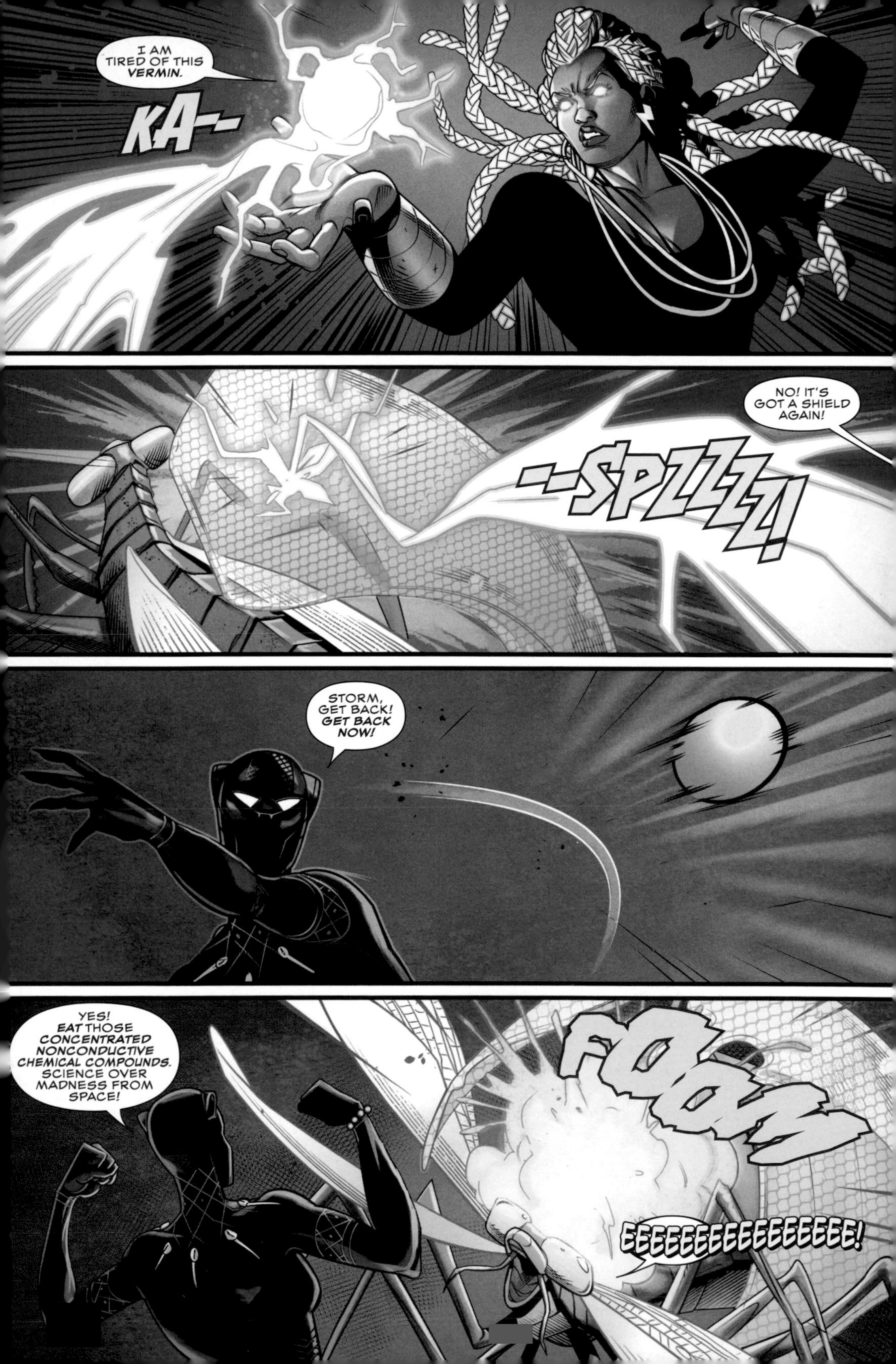
I AM TIRED OF THIS VERMIN.
KA--
NO! IT'S GOT A SHIELD AGAIN!
--SPZZZZ!
STORM, GET BACK! GET BACK NOW!
YES! EAT THOSE CONCENTRATED NONCONDUCTIVE CHEMICAL COMPOUNDS. SCIENCE OVER MADNESS FROM SPACE!
FOOM
EEEEEEEEEEEEEEEEE!

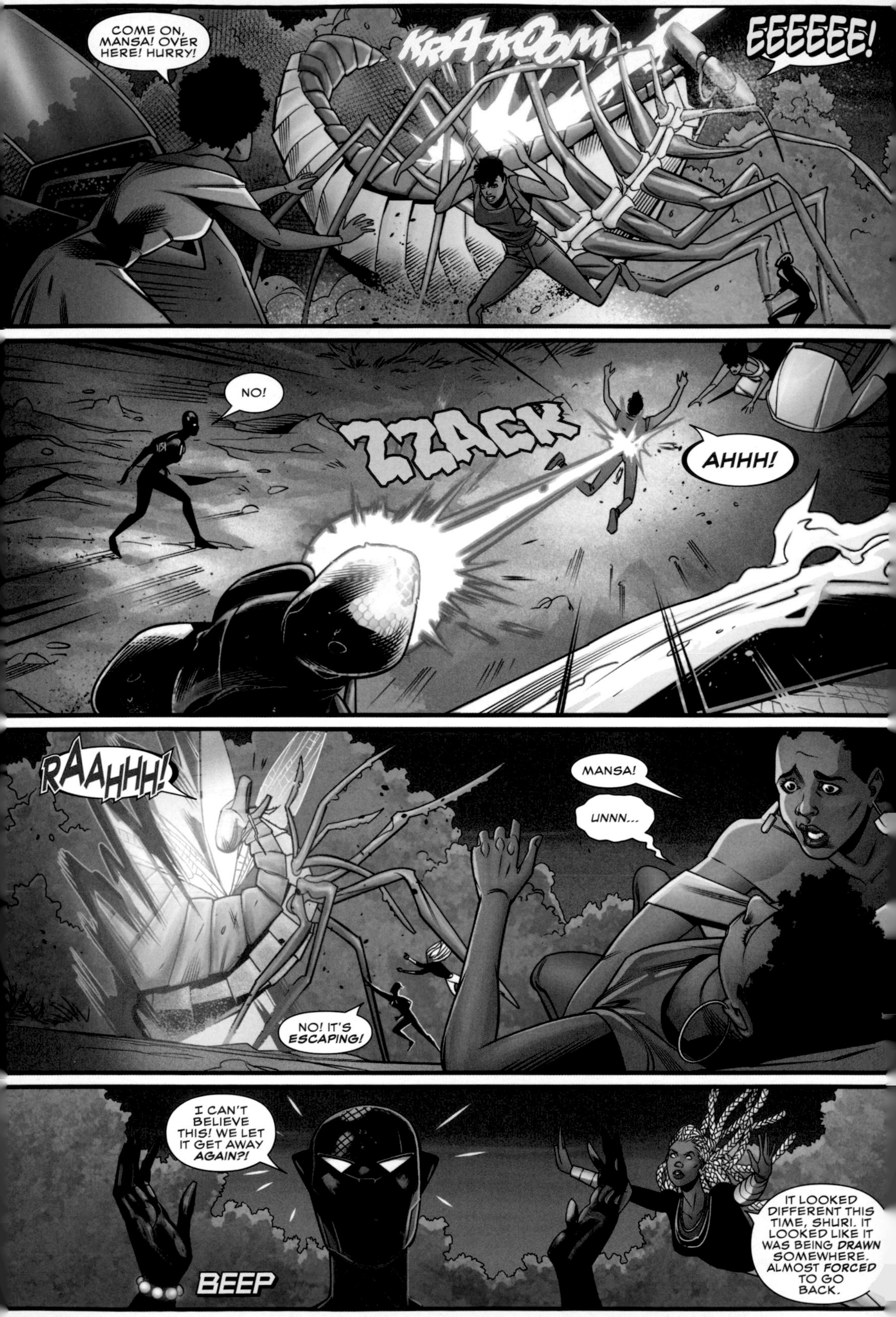
COME ON, MANSA! OVER HERE! HURRY!
KRA-KOOM
EEEEEEE!
NO!
ZZACK
AHHH!
RAAHHH!
MANSA!
UNNN...
NO! IT'S ESCAPING!
I CAN'T BELIEVE THIS! WE LET IT GET AWAY AGAIN?!
IT LOOKED DIFFERENT THIS TIME, SHURI. IT LOOKED LIKE IT WAS BEING DRAWN SOMEWHERE. ALMOST FORCED TO GO BACK.
BEEP

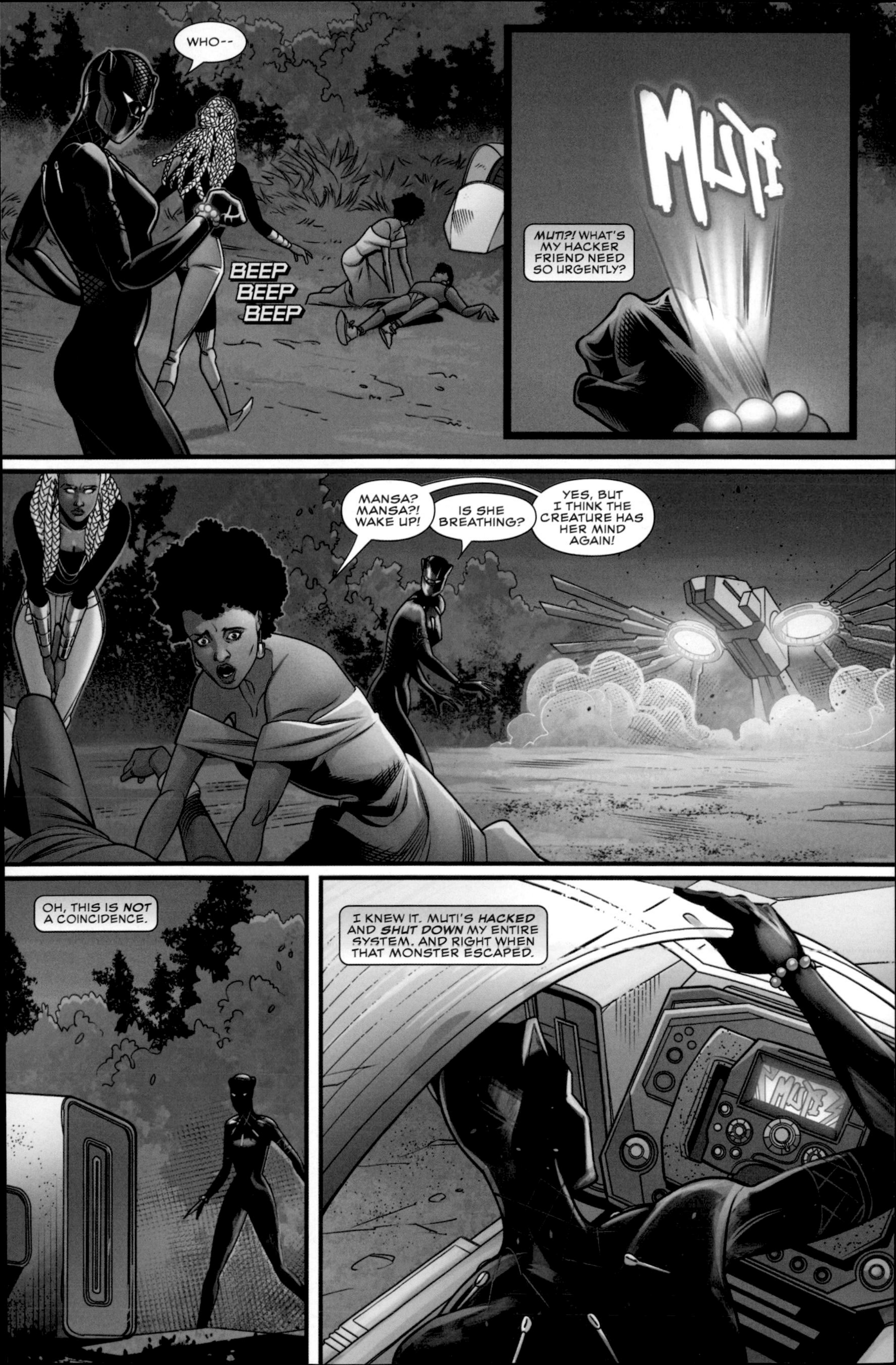
WHO--
BEEP
BEEP
BEEP
MUTI
MUTI?! WHAT'S MY HACKER FRIEND NEED SO URGENTLY?
MANSA? MANSA?! WAKE UP!
IS SHE BREATHING?
YES, BUT I THINK THE CREATURE HAS HER MIND AGAIN!
OH, THIS IS NOT A COINCIDENCE.
I KNEW IT. MUTI'S HACKED AND SHUT DOWN MY ENTIRE SYSTEM. AND RIGHT WHEN THAT MONSTER ESCAPED.

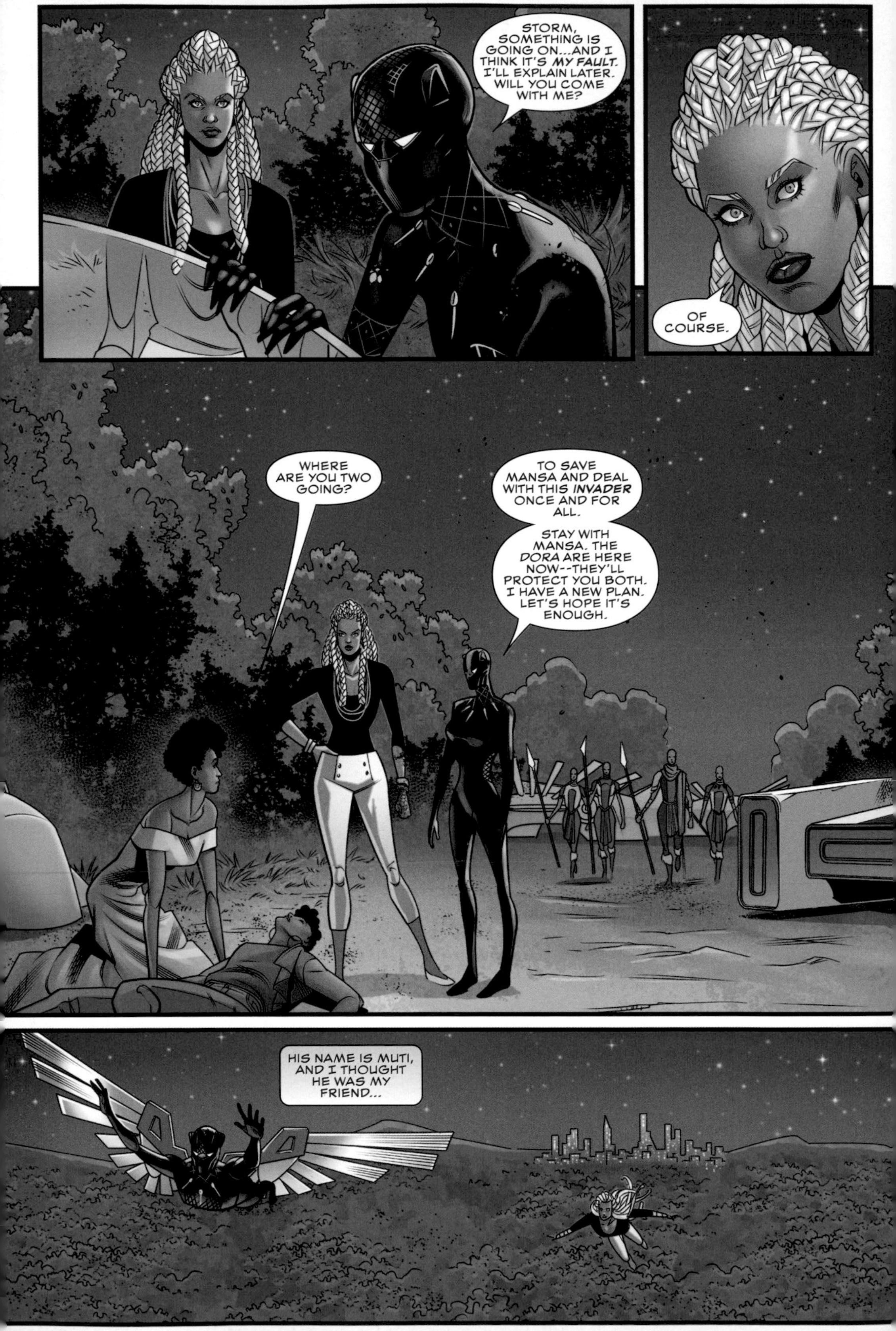

STORM, SOMETHING IS GOING ON...AND I THINK IT'S MY FAULT. I'LL EXPLAIN LATER. WILL YOU COME WITH ME?
OF COURSE.
WHERE ARE YOU TWO GOING?
TO SAVE MANSA AND DEAL WITH THIS INVADER ONCE AND FOR ALL.
STAY WITH MANSA. THE DORA ARE HERE NOW--THEY'LL PROTECT YOU BOTH. I HAVE A NEW PLAN. LET'S HOPE IT'S ENOUGH.
HIS NAME IS MUTI, AND I THOUGHT HE WAS MY FRIEND...

9

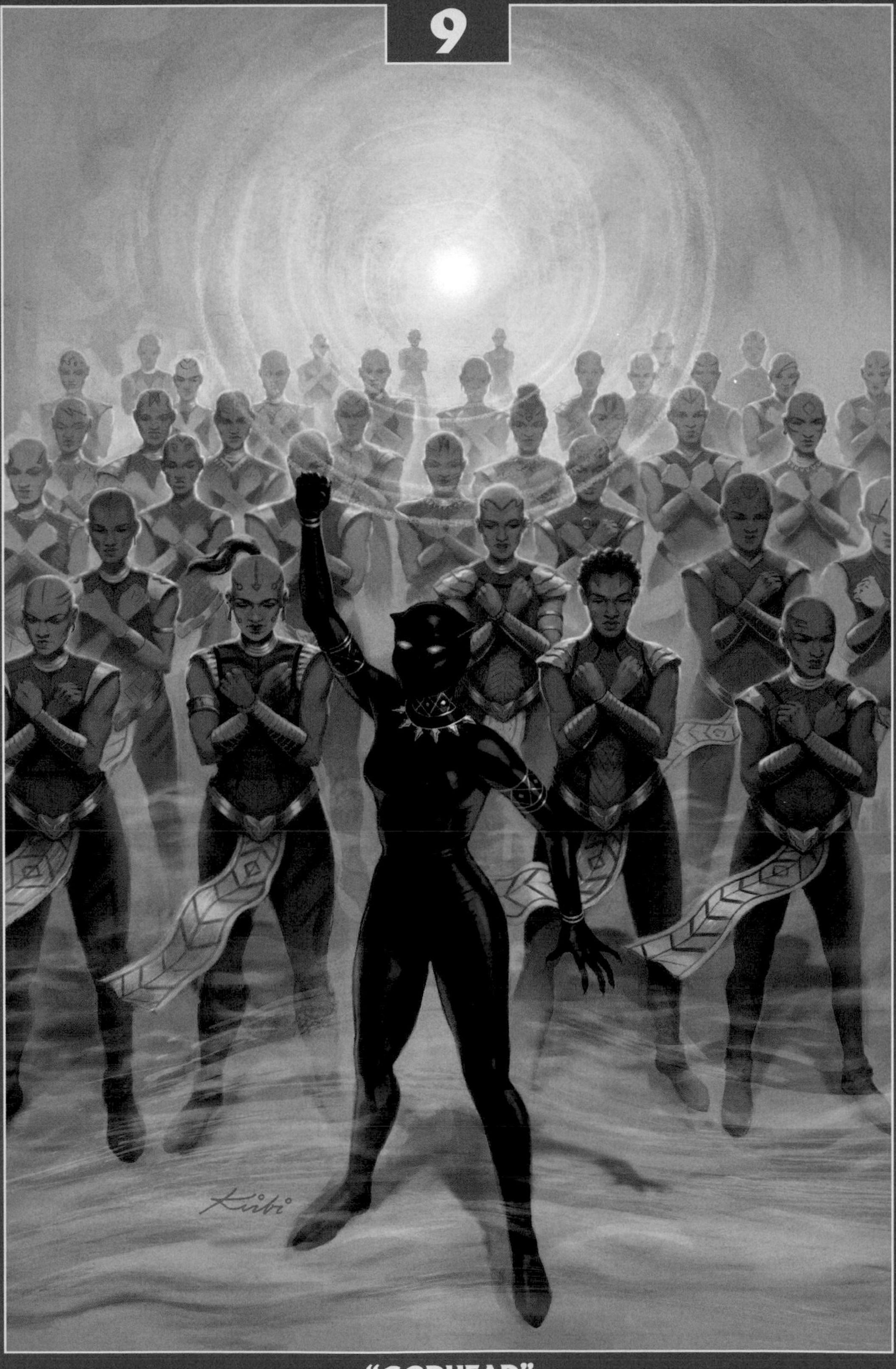

"GODHEAD"

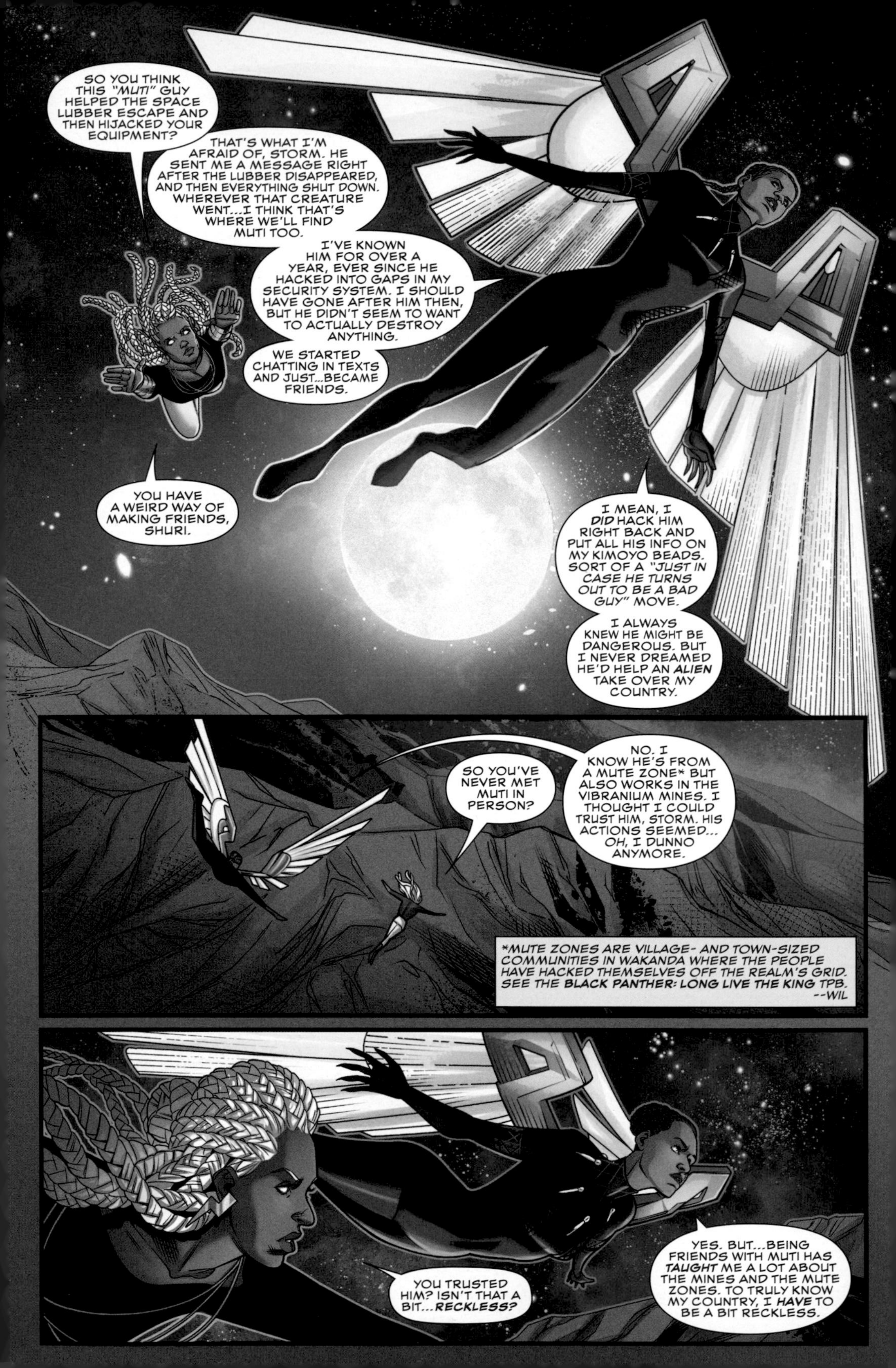
SO YOU THINK THIS "MUTI" GUY HELPED THE SPACE LUBBER ESCAPE AND THEN HIJACKED YOUR EQUIPMENT?
THAT'S WHAT I'M AFRAID OF, STORM. HE SENT ME A MESSAGE RIGHT AFTER THE LUBBER DISAPPEARED, AND THEN EVERYTHING SHUT DOWN. WHEREVER THAT CREATURE WENT...I THINK THAT'S WHERE WE'LL FIND MUTI TOO.
I'VE KNOWN HIM FOR OVER A YEAR, EVER SINCE HE HACKED INTO GAPS IN MY SECURITY SYSTEM. I SHOULD HAVE GONE AFTER HIM THEN, BUT HE DIDN'T SEEM TO WANT TO ACTUALLY DESTROY ANYTHING.
WE STARTED CHATTING IN TEXTS AND JUST...BECAME FRIENDS.
YOU HAVE A WEIRD WAY OF MAKING FRIENDS, SHURI.
I MEAN, I DID HACK HIM RIGHT BACK AND PUT ALL HIS INFO ON MY KIMOYO BEADS. SORT OF A "JUST IN CASE HE TURNS OUT TO BE A BAD GUY" MOVE.
I ALWAYS KNEW HE MIGHT BE DANGEROUS. BUT I NEVER DREAMED HE'D HELP AN ALIEN TAKE OVER MY COUNTRY.
SO YOU'VE NEVER MET MUTI IN PERSON?
NO. I KNOW HE'S FROM A MUTE ZONE* BUT ALSO WORKS IN THE VIBRANIUM MINES. I THOUGHT I COULD TRUST HIM, STORM. HIS ACTIONS SEEMED... OH, I DUNNO ANYMORE.
*MUTE ZONES ARE VILLAGE- AND TOWN-SIZED COMMUNITIES IN WAKANDA WHERE THE PEOPLE HAVE HACKED THEMSELVES OFF THE REALM'S GRID. SEE THE BLACK PANTHER: LONG LIVE THE KING TPB. --WIL
YOU TRUSTED HIM? ISN'T THAT A BIT...RECKLESS?
YES. BUT...BEING FRIENDS WITH MUTI HAS TAUGHT ME A LOT ABOUT THE MINES AND THE MUTE ZONES. TO TRULY KNOW MY COUNTRY, I HAVE TO BE A BIT RECKLESS.

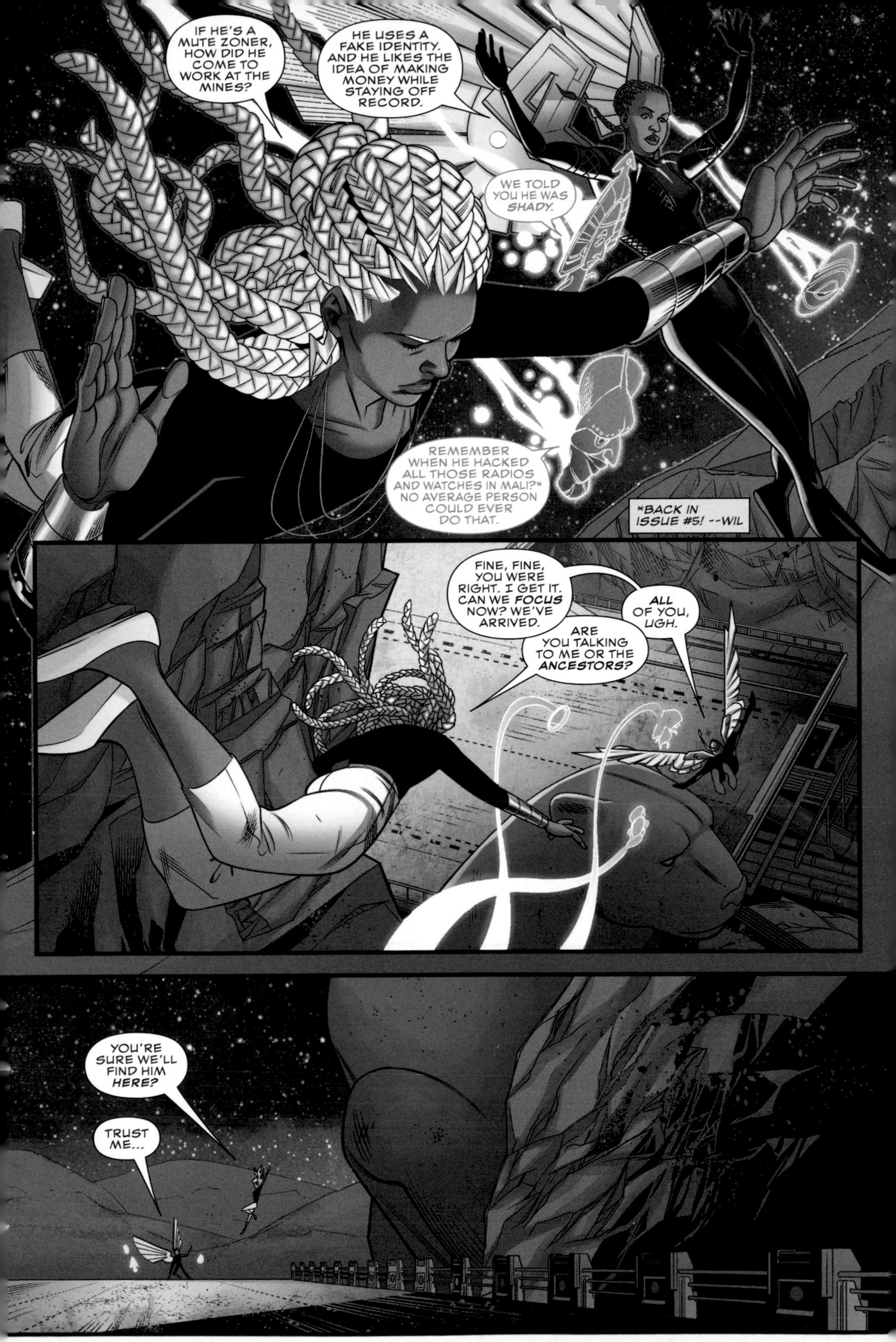
IF HE'S A MUTE ZONER, HOW DID HE COME TO WORK AT THE MINES?
HE USES A FAKE IDENTITY. AND HE LIKES THE IDEA OF MAKING MONEY WHILE STAYING OFF RECORD.
WE TOLD YOU HE WAS SHADY.
REMEMBER WHEN HE HACKED ALL THOSE RADIOS AND WATCHES IN MALI?* NO AVERAGE PERSON COULD EVER DO THAT.
*BACK IN ISSUE #5! --WIL
FINE, FINE, YOU WERE RIGHT. I GET IT. CAN WE FOCUS NOW? WE'VE ARRIVED.
ARE YOU TALKING TO ME OR THE ANCESTORS?
ALL OF YOU, UGH.
YOU'RE SURE WE'LL FIND HIM HERE?
TRUST ME...

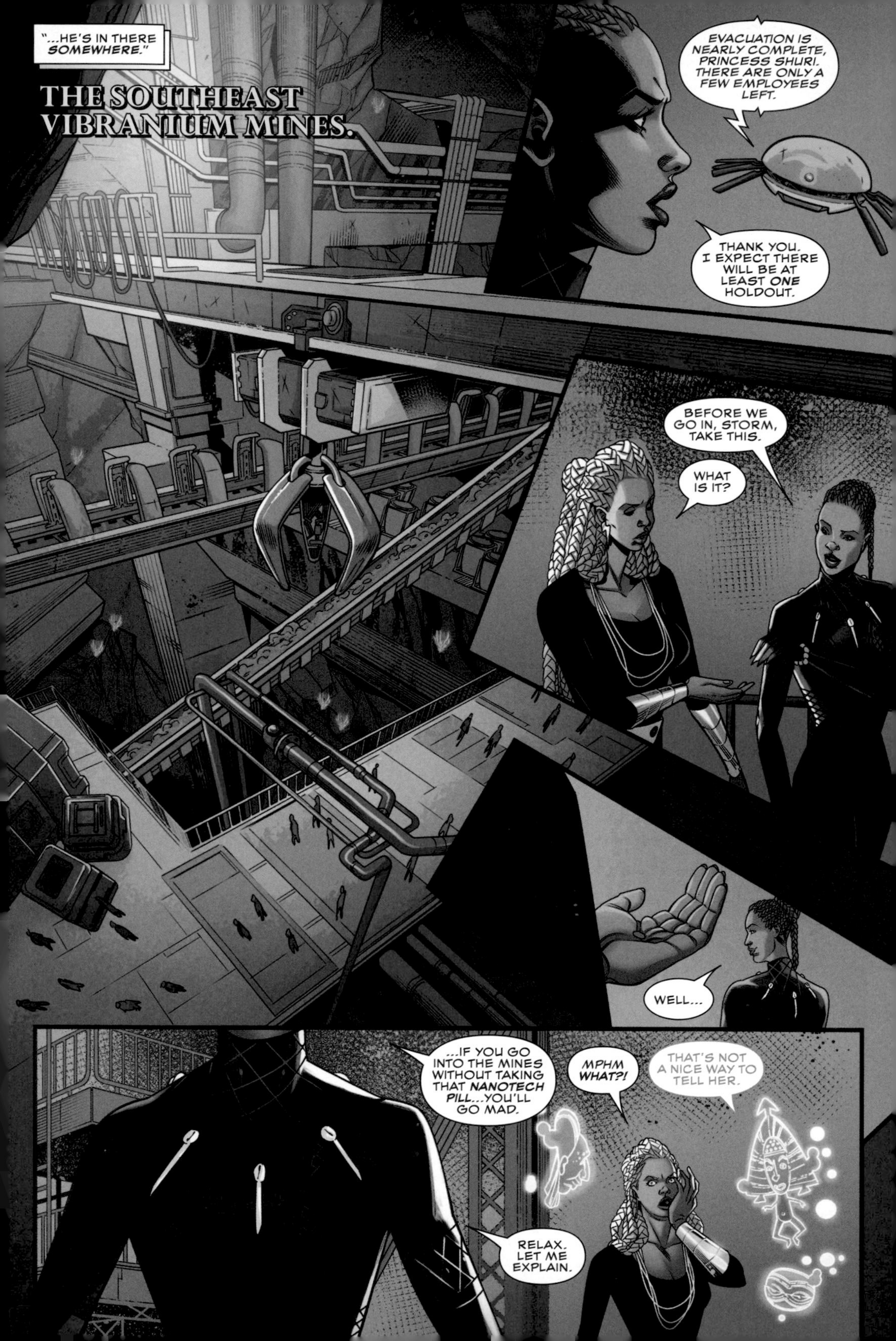
"...HE'S IN THERE SOMEWHERE."
THE SOUTHEAST VIBRANIUM MINES.
EVACUATION IS NEARLY COMPLETE, PRINCESS SHURI. THERE ARE ONLY A FEW EMPLOYEES LEFT.
THANK YOU. I EXPECT THERE WILL BE AT LEAST ONE HOLDOUT.
BEFORE WE GO IN, STORM, TAKE THIS.
WHAT IS IT?
WELL...
...IF YOU GO INTO THE MINES WITHOUT TAKING THAT NANOTECH PILL...YOU'LL GO MAD.
MPHM WHAT?!
THAT'S NOT A NICE WAY TO TELL HER.
RELAX. LET ME EXPLAIN.

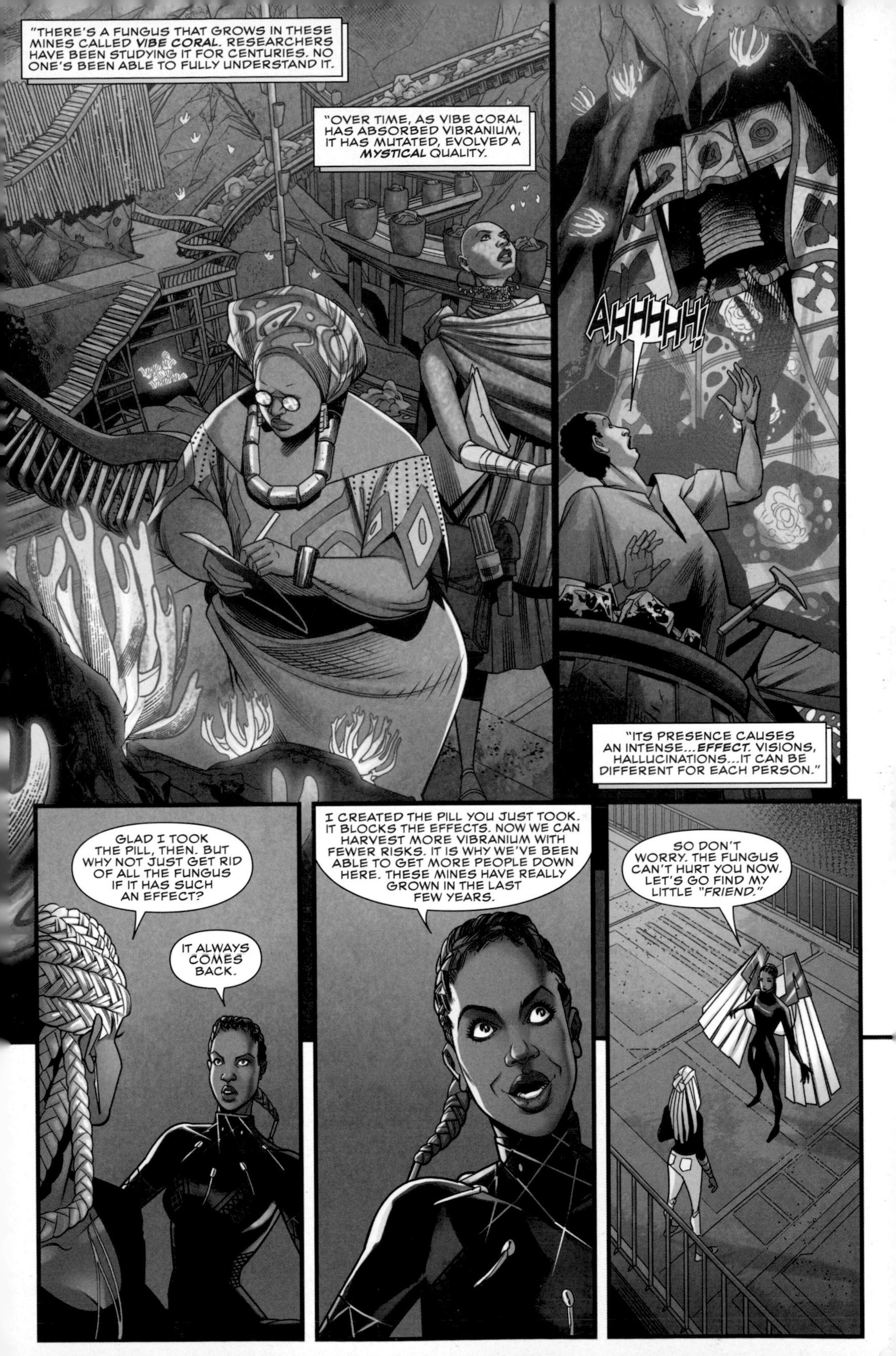
"THERE'S A FUNGUS THAT GROWS IN THESE MINES CALLED *VIBE CORAL*. RESEARCHERS HAVE BEEN STUDYING IT FOR CENTURIES. NO ONE'S BEEN ABLE TO FULLY UNDERSTAND IT.
"OVER TIME, AS VIBE CORAL HAS ABSORBED VIBRANIUM, IT HAS MUTATED, EVOLVED A *MYSTICAL* QUALITY.
AHHHH!
"ITS PRESENCE CAUSES AN INTENSE...*EFFECT*. VISIONS, HALLUCINATIONS...IT CAN BE DIFFERENT FOR EACH PERSON."
GLAD I TOOK THE PILL, THEN. BUT WHY NOT JUST GET RID OF ALL THE FUNGUS IF IT HAS SUCH AN EFFECT?
IT ALWAYS COMES BACK.
I CREATED THE PILL YOU JUST TOOK. IT BLOCKS THE EFFECTS. NOW WE CAN HARVEST MORE VIBRANIUM WITH FEWER RISKS. IT IS WHY WE'VE BEEN ABLE TO GET MORE PEOPLE DOWN HERE. THESE MINES HAVE REALLY GROWN IN THE LAST FEW YEARS.
SO DON'T WORRY. THE FUNGUS CAN'T HURT YOU NOW. LET'S GO FIND MY LITTLE "*FRIEND*."

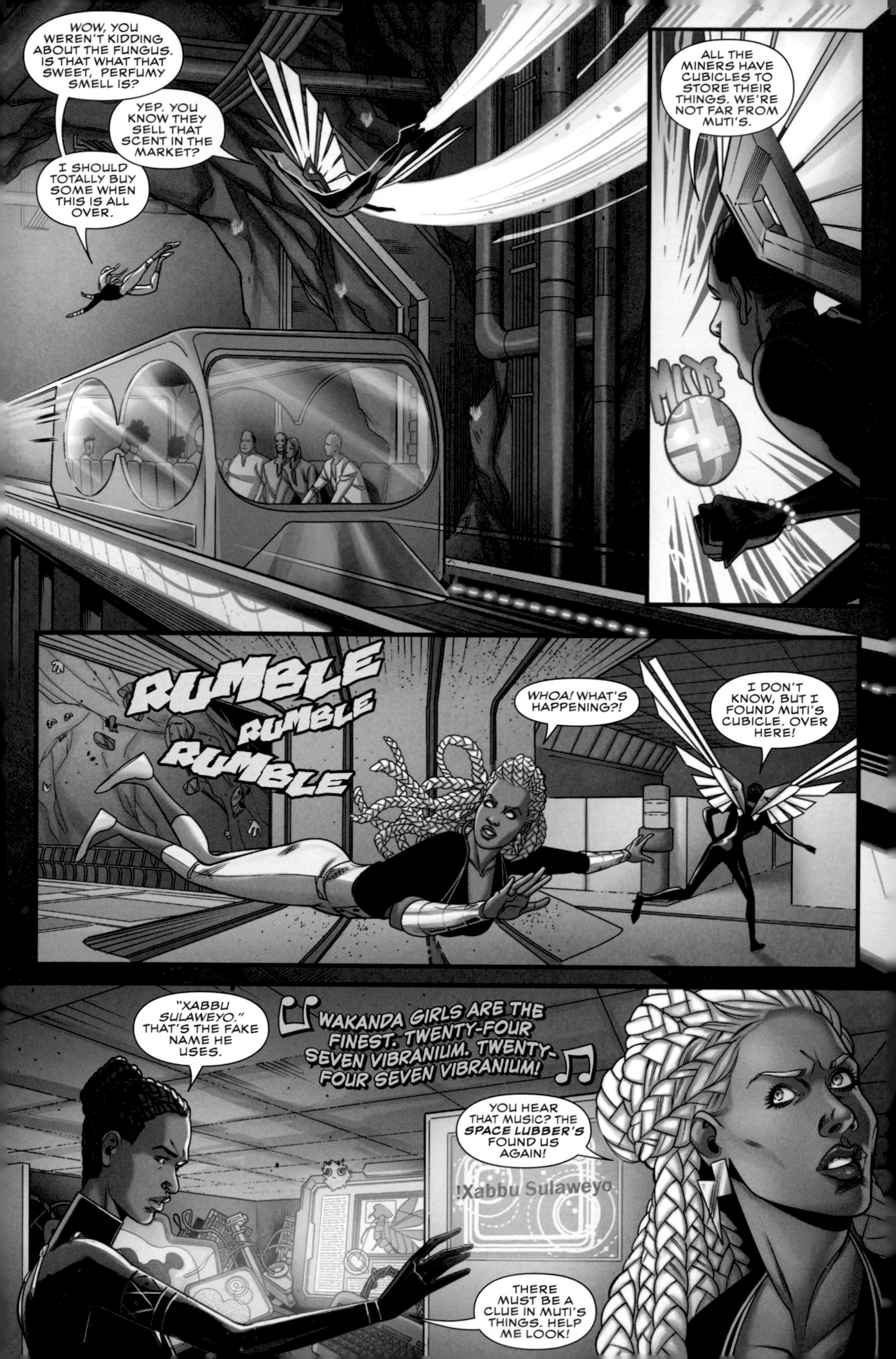
WOW, YOU WEREN'T KIDDING ABOUT THE FUNGUS. IS THAT WHAT THAT SWEET, PERFUMY SMELL IS?
YEP. YOU KNOW THEY SELL THAT SCENT IN THE MARKET?
I SHOULD TOTALLY BUY SOME WHEN THIS IS ALL OVER.
ALL THE MINERS HAVE CUBICLES TO STORE THEIR THINGS. WE'RE NOT FAR FROM MUTI'S.
RUMBLE RUMBLE RUMBLE
WHOA! WHAT'S HAPPENING?!
I DON'T KNOW, BUT I FOUND MUTI'S CUBICLE. OVER HERE!
"XABBU SULAWEYO." THAT'S THE FAKE NAME HE USES.
WAKANDA GIRLS ARE THE FINEST. TWENTY-FOUR SEVEN VIBRANIUM. TWENTY-FOUR SEVEN VIBRANIUM!
YOU HEAR THAT MUSIC? THE SPACE LUBBER'S FOUND US AGAIN!
!Xabbu Sulaweyo
THERE MUST BE A CLUE IN MUTI'S THINGS. HELP ME LOOK!

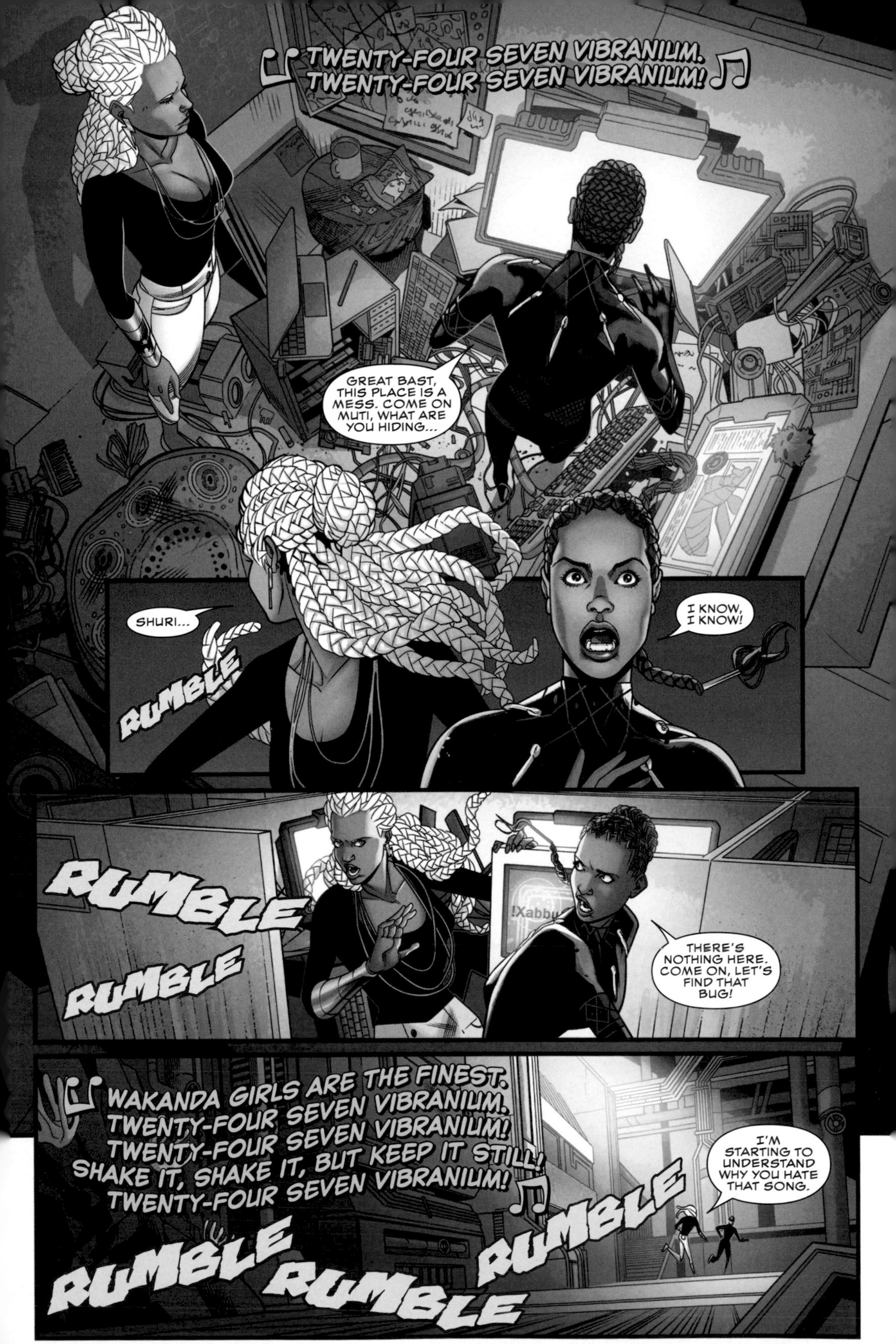
TWENTY-FOUR SEVEN VIBRANIUM. TWENTY-FOUR SEVEN VIBRANIUM!
GREAT BAST, THIS PLACE IS A MESS. COME ON MUTI, WHAT ARE YOU HIDING...
SHURI...
RUMBLE
I KNOW, I KNOW!
RUMBLE
RUMBLE
!Xabbu
THERE'S NOTHING HERE. COME ON, LET'S FIND THAT BUG!
WAKANDA GIRLS ARE THE FINEST. TWENTY-FOUR SEVEN VIBRANIUM. TWENTY-FOUR SEVEN VIBRANIUM! TWENTY-FOUR SEVEN VIBRANIUM! SHAKE IT, SHAKE IT, BUT KEEP IT STILL! TWENTY-FOUR SEVEN VIBRANIUM!
I'M STARTING TO UNDERSTAND WHY YOU HATE THAT SONG.
RUMBLE RUMBLE RUMBLE

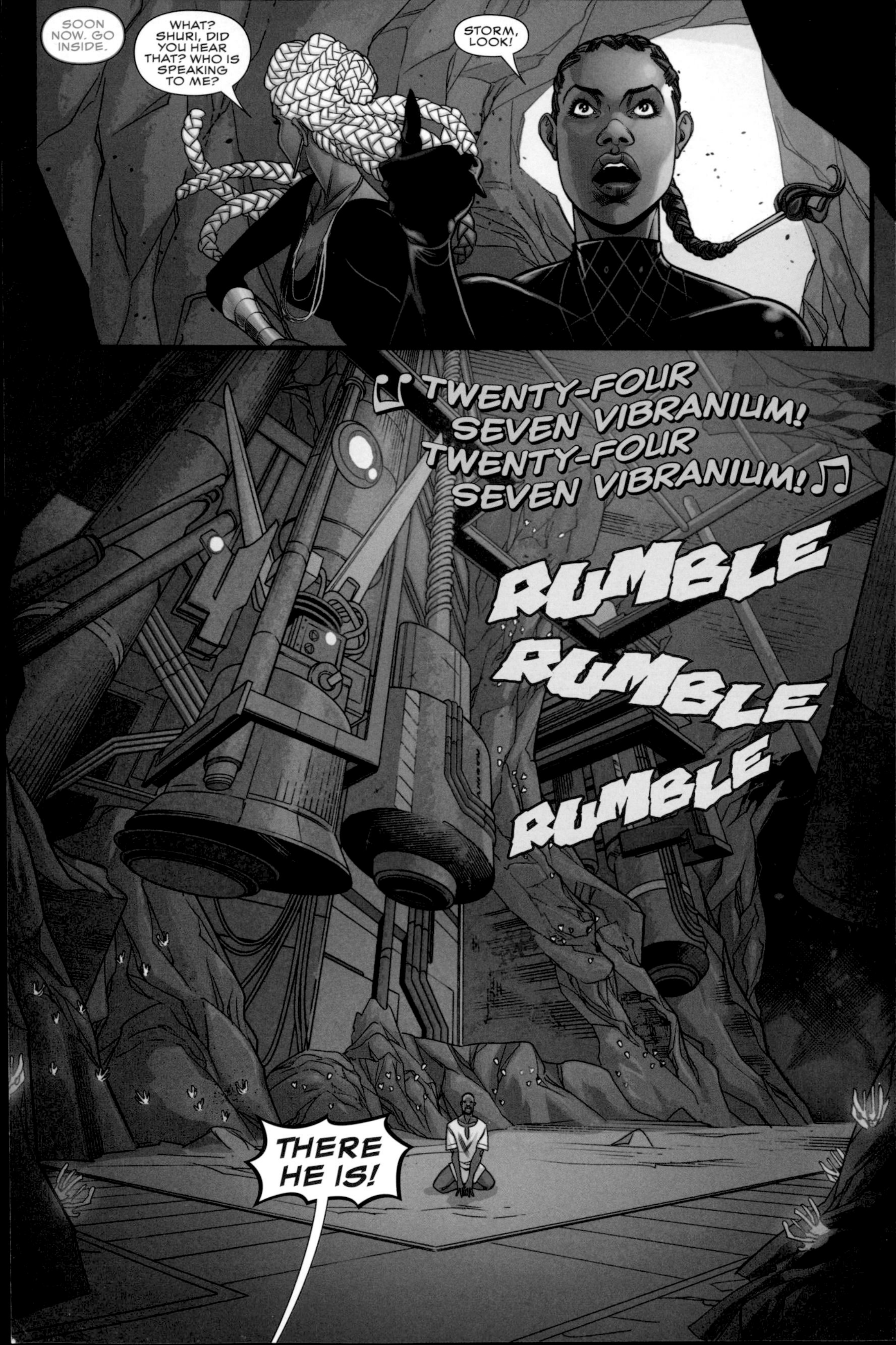
SOON NOW. GO INSIDE.
WHAT? SHURI, DID YOU HEAR THAT? WHO IS SPEAKING TO ME?
STORM, LOOK!
♫ TWENTY-FOUR SEVEN VIBRANIUM! TWENTY-FOUR SEVEN VIBRANIUM! ♫
RUMBLE RUMBLE RUMBLE
THERE HE IS!

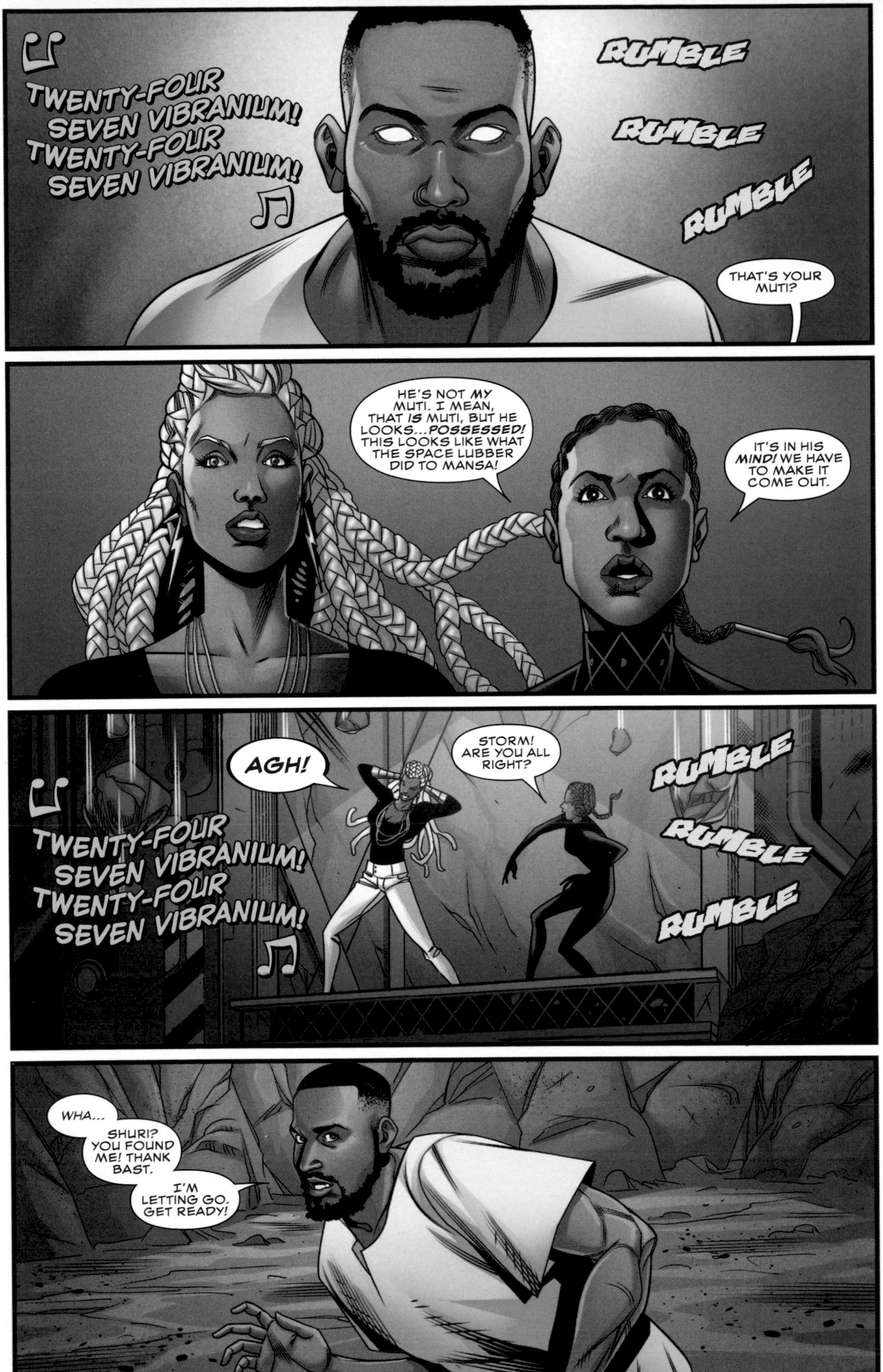
TWENTY-FOUR SEVEN VIBRANIUM! TWENTY-FOUR SEVEN VIBRANIUM!
RUMBLE
RUMBLE
RUMBLE
THAT'S YOUR MUTI?
HE'S NOT MY MUTI. I MEAN, THAT IS MUTI, BUT HE LOOKS...POSSESSED! THIS LOOKS LIKE WHAT THE SPACE LUBBER DID TO MANSA!
IT'S IN HIS MIND! WE HAVE TO MAKE IT COME OUT.
TWENTY-FOUR SEVEN VIBRANIUM! TWENTY-FOUR SEVEN VIBRANIUM!
AGH!
STORM! ARE YOU ALL RIGHT?
RUMBLE
RUMBLE
RUMBLE
WHA...
SHURI? YOU FOUND ME! THANK BAST.
I'M LETTING GO. GET READY!

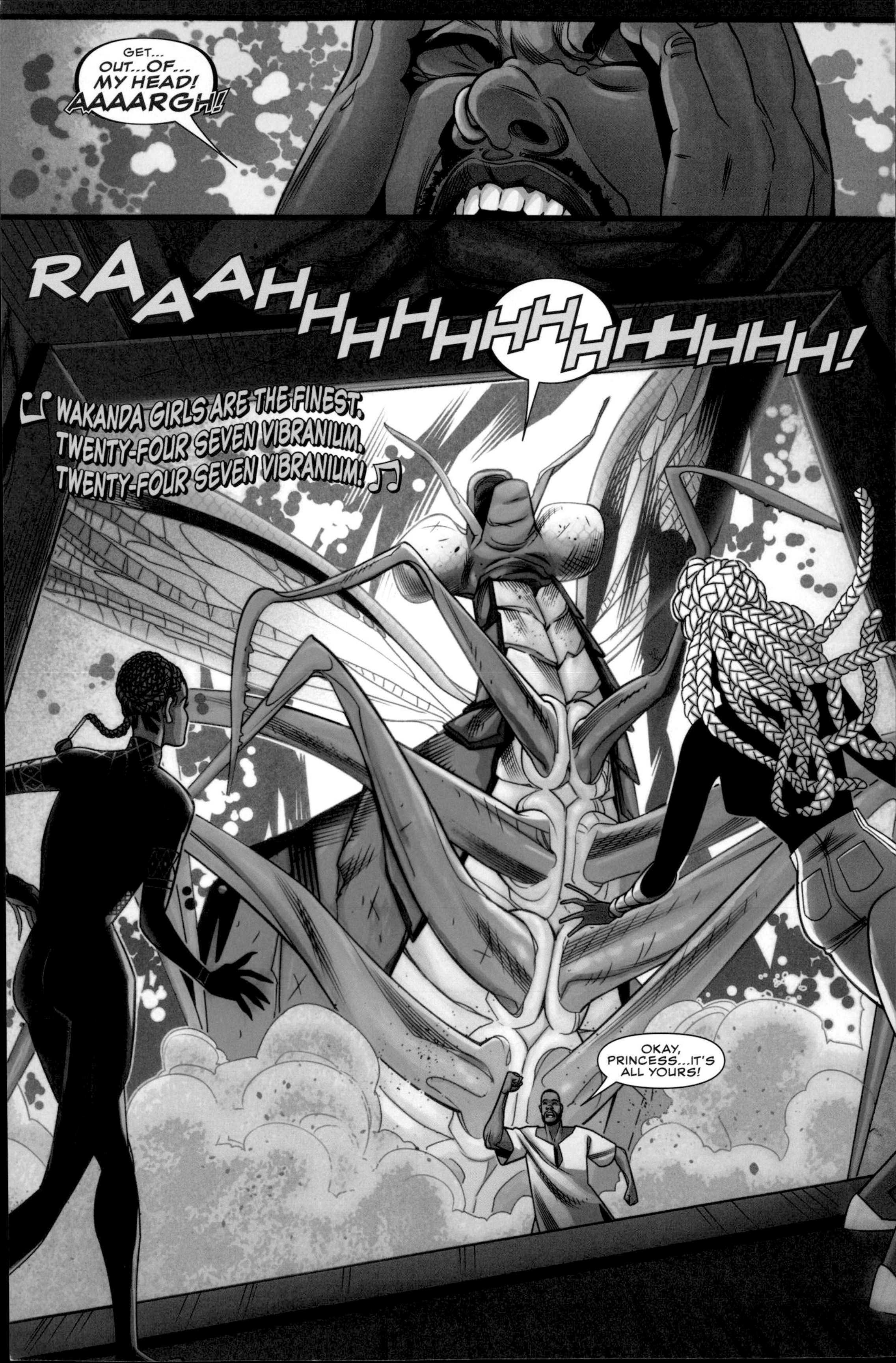
GET... OUT...OF... MY HEAD! AAAARGH!
RAAAHHHHHHHHHHHHH!
WAKANDA GIRLS ARE THE FINEST. TWENTY-FOUR SEVEN VIBRANIUM. TWENTY-FOUR SEVEN VIBRANIUM!
OKAY, PRINCESS...IT'S ALL YOURS!

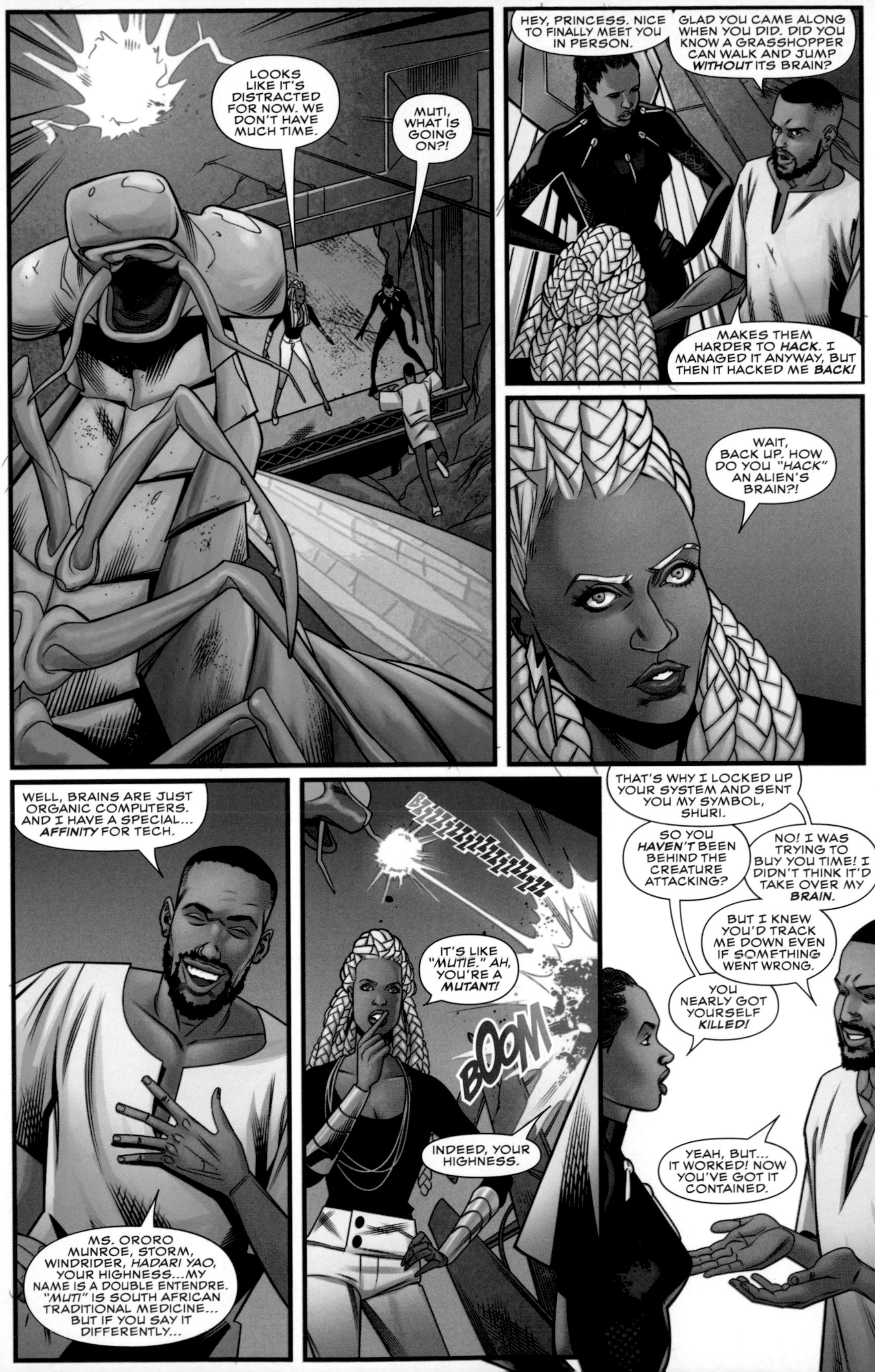

LOOKS LIKE IT'S DISTRACTED FOR NOW. WE DON'T HAVE MUCH TIME.
MUTI, WHAT IS GOING ON?!
HEY, PRINCESS. NICE TO FINALLY MEET YOU IN PERSON.
GLAD YOU CAME ALONG WHEN YOU DID. DID YOU KNOW A GRASSHOPPER CAN WALK AND JUMP *WITHOUT* ITS BRAIN?
MAKES THEM HARDER TO *HACK*. I MANAGED IT ANYWAY, BUT THEN IT HACKED ME *BACK!*
WAIT, BACK UP. HOW DO YOU *"HACK"* AN ALIEN'S BRAIN?!
WELL, BRAINS ARE JUST ORGANIC COMPUTERS. AND I HAVE A SPECIAL... *AFFINITY* FOR TECH.
MS. ORORO MUNROE, STORM, WINDRIDER, *HADARI YAO*, YOUR HIGHNESS...MY NAME IS A DOUBLE ENTENDRE. *"MUTI"* IS SOUTH AFRICAN TRADITIONAL MEDICINE... BUT IF YOU SAY IT DIFFERENTLY...
BZZZZZZZZZZZZZZZZZ
IT'S LIKE *"MUTIE."* AH, YOU'RE A *MUTANT!*
BOOM
INDEED, YOUR HIGHNESS.
THAT'S WHY I LOCKED UP YOUR SYSTEM AND SENT YOU MY SYMBOL, SHURI.
SO YOU *HAVEN'T* BEEN BEHIND THE CREATURE ATTACKING?
NO! I WAS TRYING TO BUY YOU TIME! I DIDN'T THINK IT'D TAKE OVER MY *BRAIN.*
BUT I KNEW YOU'D TRACK ME DOWN EVEN IF SOMETHING WENT WRONG.
YOU NEARLY GOT YOURSELF *KILLED!*
YEAH, BUT... IT WORKED! NOW YOU'VE GOT IT CONTAINED.

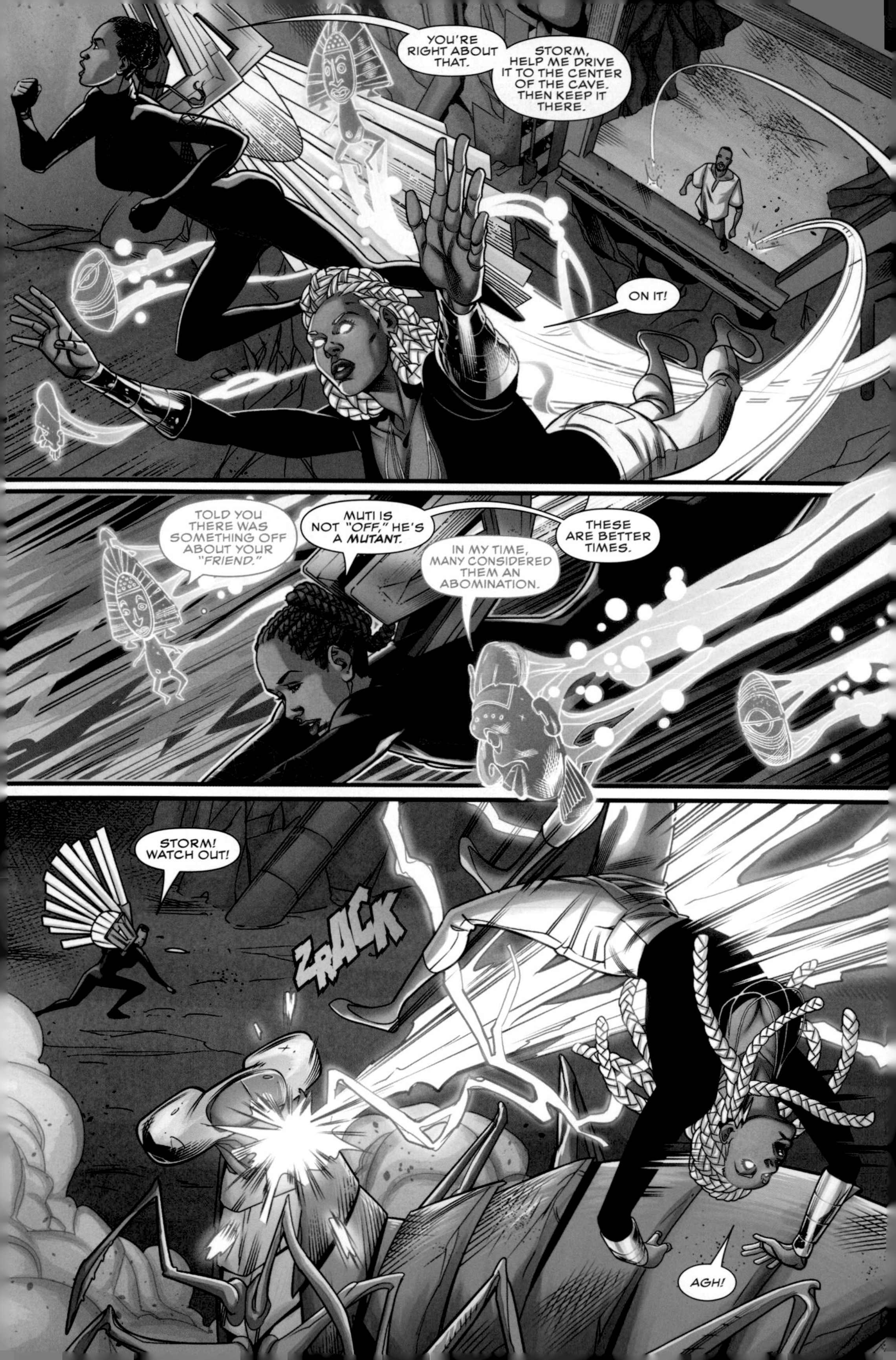
YOU'RE RIGHT ABOUT THAT.
STORM, HELP ME DRIVE IT TO THE CENTER OF THE CAVE. THEN KEEP IT THERE.
ON IT!
TOLD YOU THERE WAS SOMETHING OFF ABOUT YOUR "FRIEND."
MUTI IS NOT "OFF," HE'S A MUTANT.
IN MY TIME, MANY CONSIDERED THEM AN ABOMINATION.
THESE ARE BETTER TIMES.
STORM! WATCH OUT!
ZRACK
AGH!

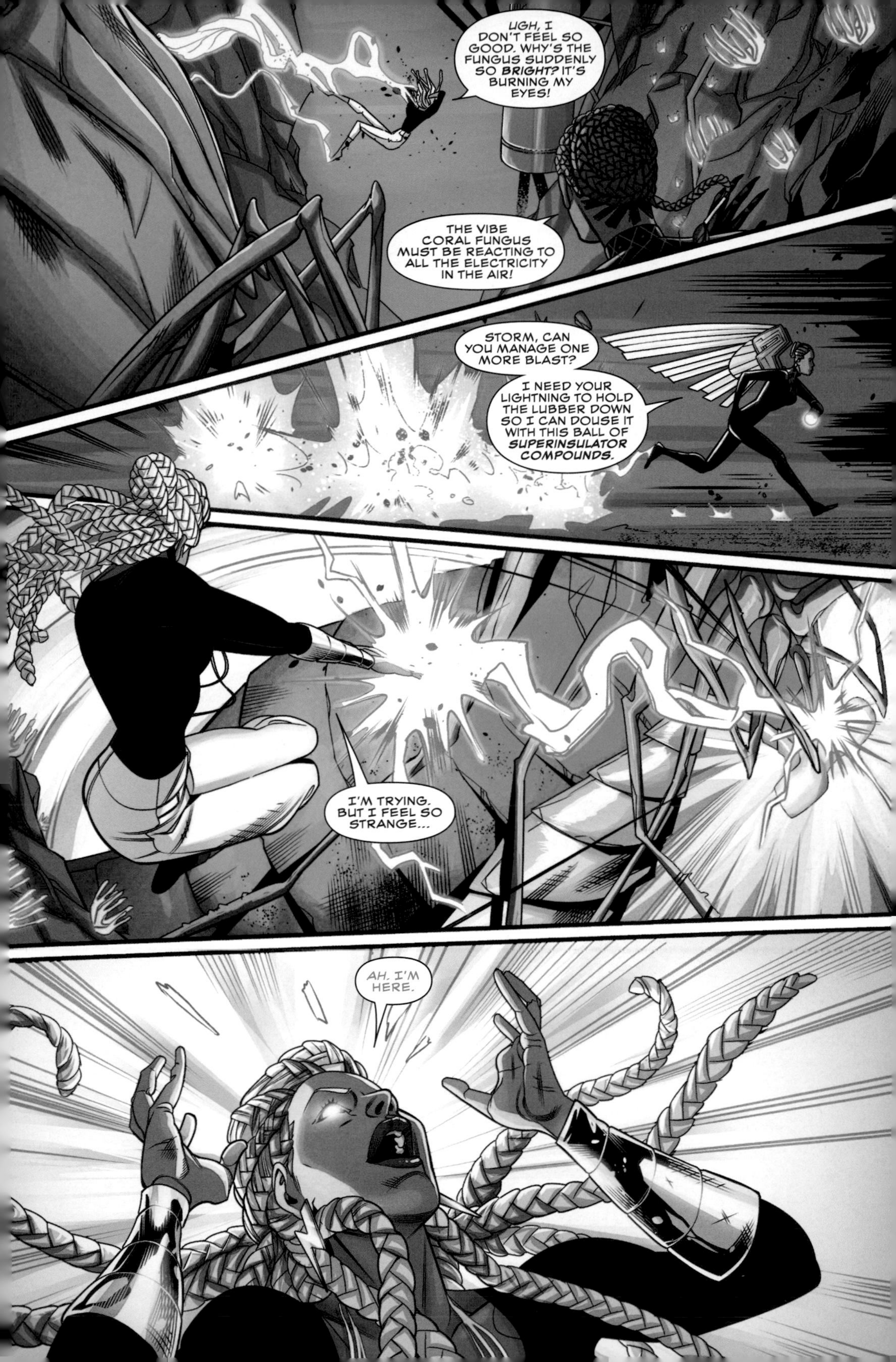
UGH, I DON'T FEEL SO GOOD. WHY'S THE FUNGUS SUDDENLY SO BRIGHT? IT'S BURNING MY EYES!
THE VIBE CORAL FUNGUS MUST BE REACTING TO ALL THE ELECTRICITY IN THE AIR!
STORM, CAN YOU MANAGE ONE MORE BLAST?
I NEED YOUR LIGHTNING TO HOLD THE LUBBER DOWN SO I CAN DOUSE IT WITH THIS BALL OF SUPERINSULATOR COMPOUNDS.
I'M TRYING. BUT I FEEL SO STRANGE...
AH. I'M HERE.

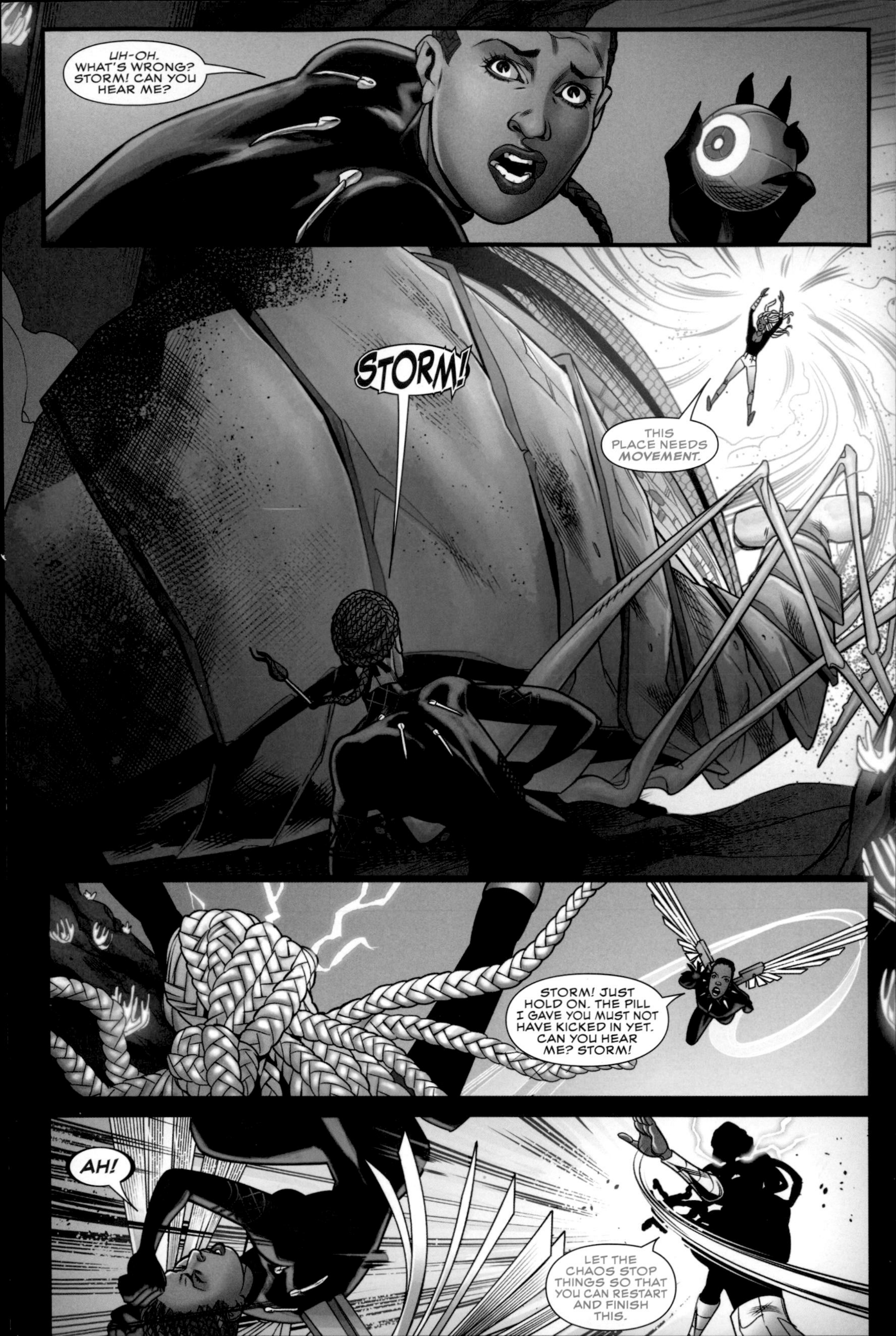
UH-OH. WHAT'S WRONG? STORM! CAN YOU HEAR ME?
STORM!
THIS PLACE NEEDS MOVEMENT.
STORM! JUST HOLD ON. THE PILL I GAVE YOU MUST NOT HAVE KICKED IN YET. CAN YOU HEAR ME? STORM!
AH!
LET THE CHAOS STOP THINGS SO THAT YOU CAN RESTART AND FINISH THIS.

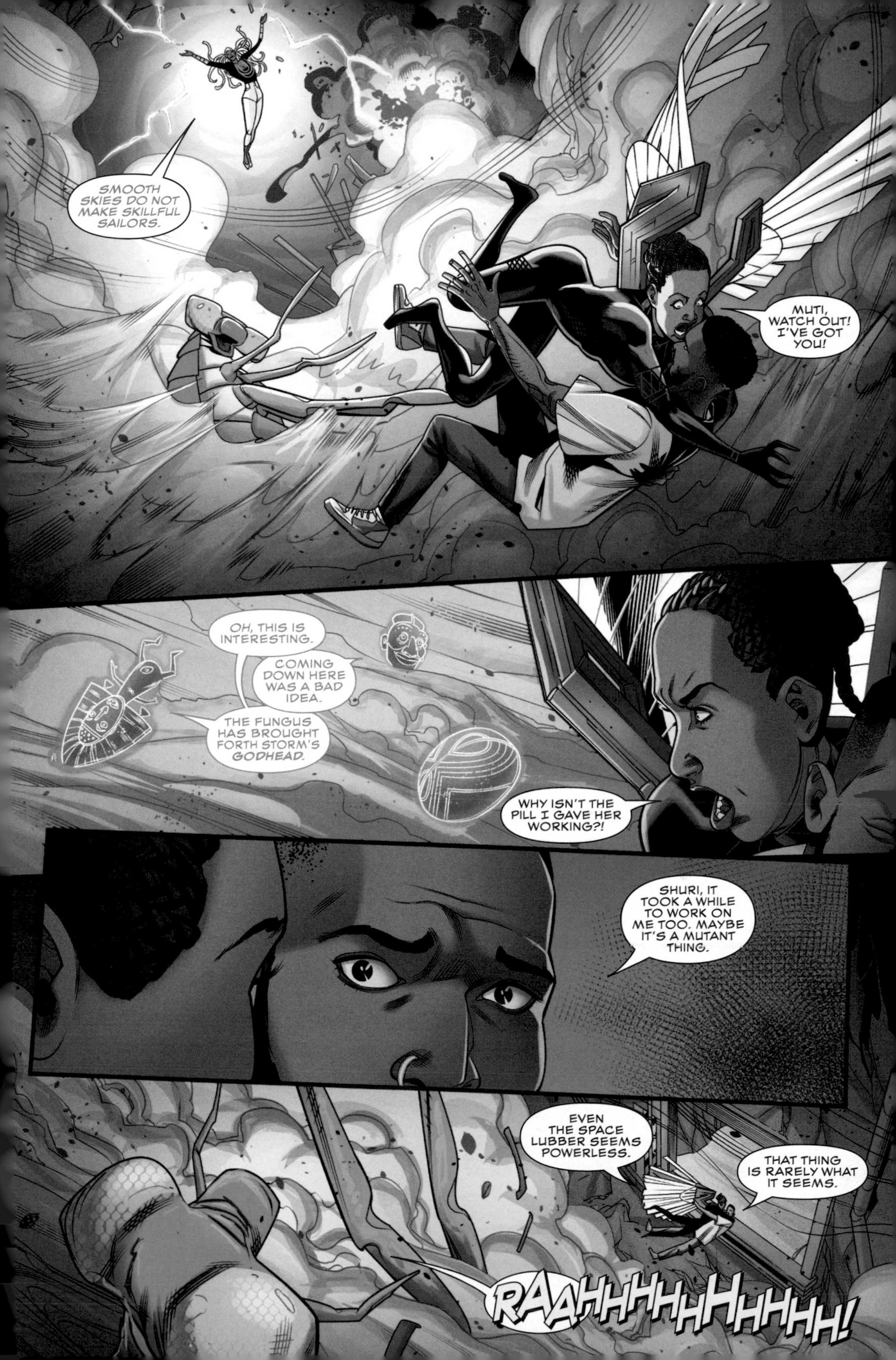
SMOOTH SKIES DO NOT MAKE SKILLFUL SAILORS.
MUTI, WATCH OUT! I'VE GOT YOU!
OH, THIS IS INTERESTING.
COMING DOWN HERE WAS A BAD IDEA.
THE FUNGUS HAS BROUGHT FORTH STORM'S GODHEAD.
WHY ISN'T THE PILL I GAVE HER WORKING?!
SHURI, IT TOOK A WHILE TO WORK ON ME TOO. MAYBE IT'S A MUTANT THING.
EVEN THE SPACE LUBBER SEEMS POWERLESS.
THAT THING IS RARELY WHAT IT SEEMS.
RAAHHHHHHHHHHH!

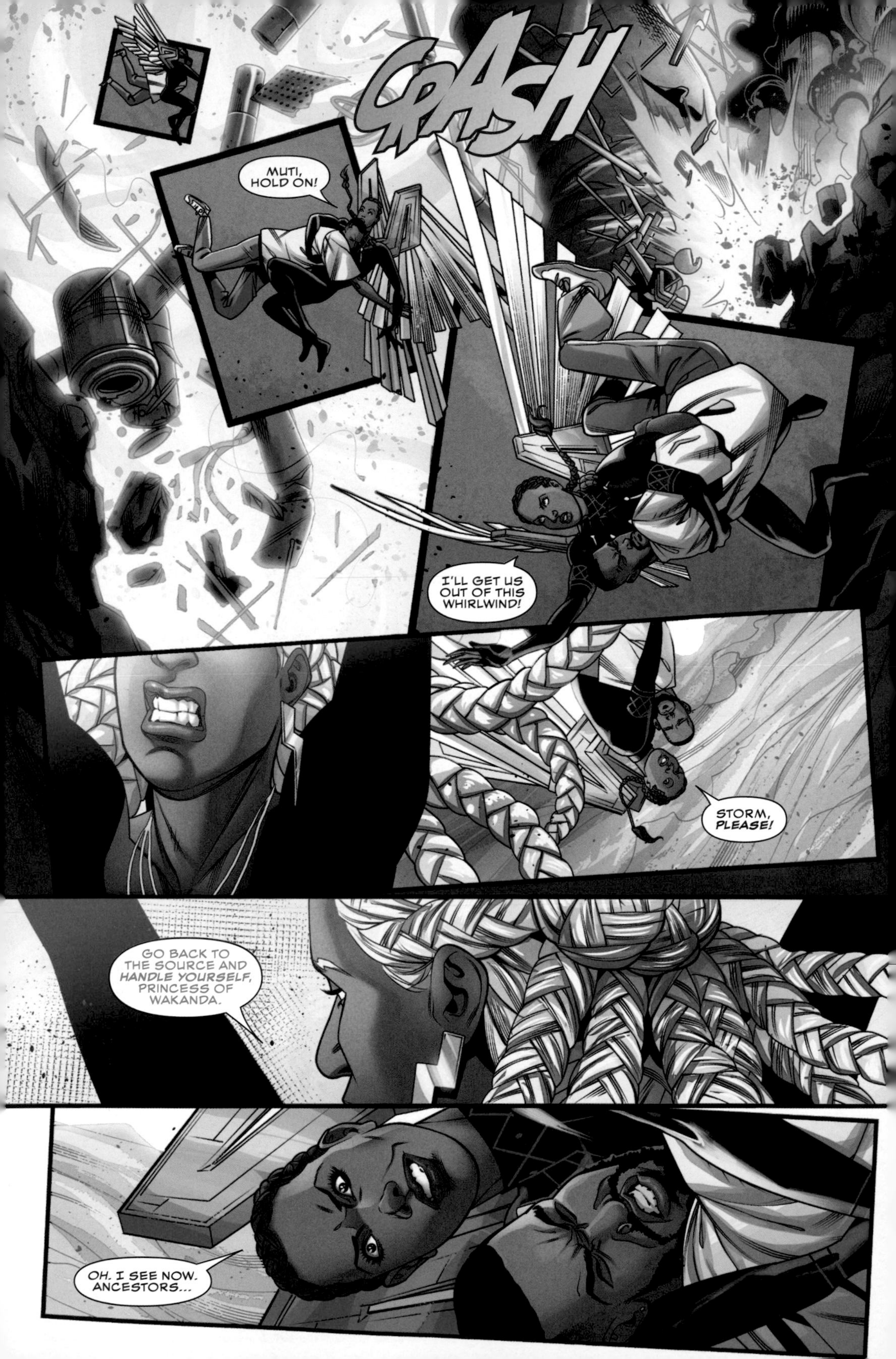
CRASH
MUTI, HOLD ON!
I'LL GET US OUT OF THIS WHIRLWIND!
STORM, *PLEASE!*
GO BACK TO THE SOURCE AND *HANDLE YOURSELF,* PRINCESS OF WAKANDA.
OH. I SEE NOW. ANCESTORS...

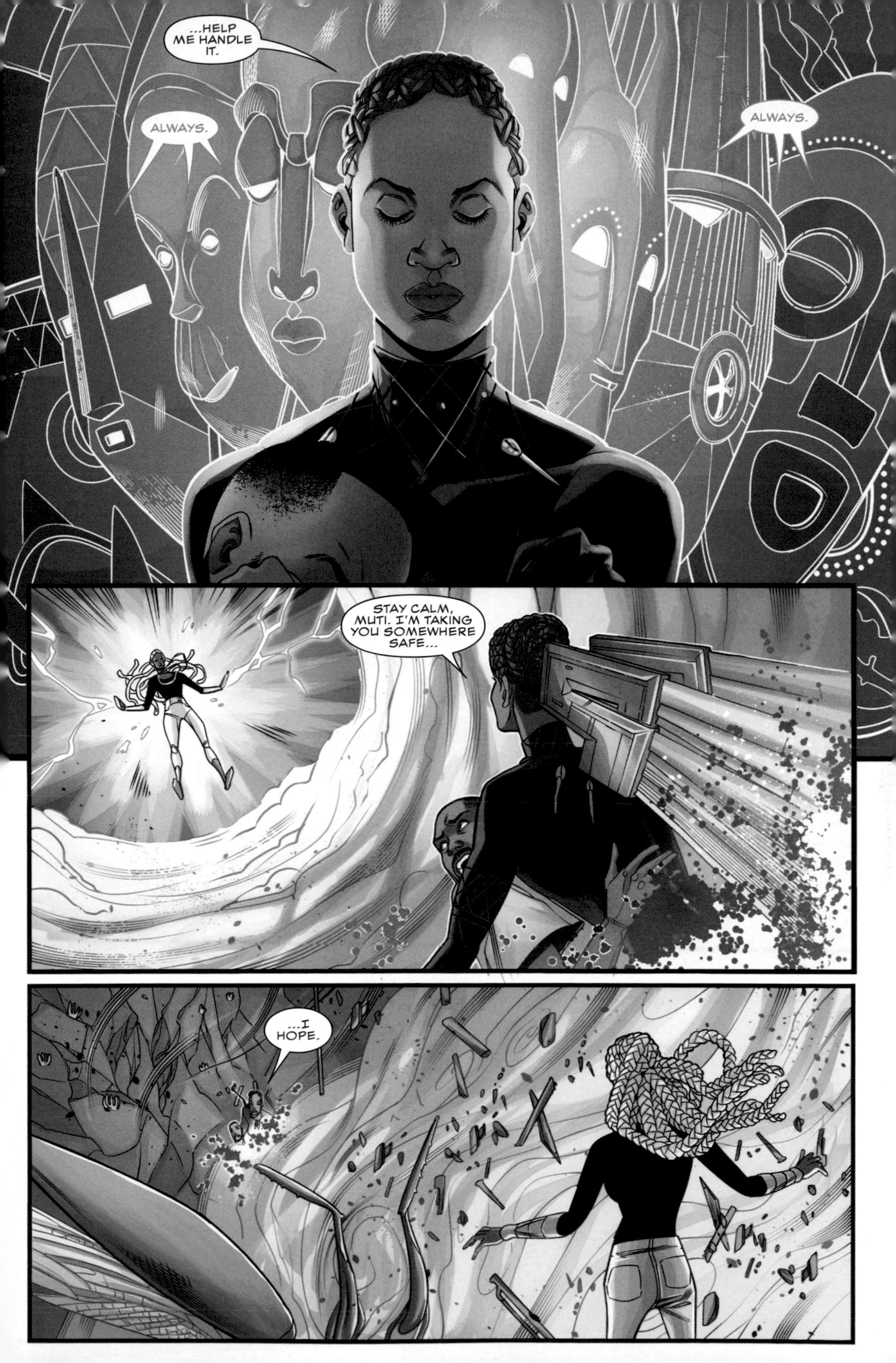
...HELP ME HANDLE IT.
ALWAYS.
ALWAYS.
STAY CALM, MUTI. I'M TAKING YOU SOMEWHERE SAFE...
...I HOPE.

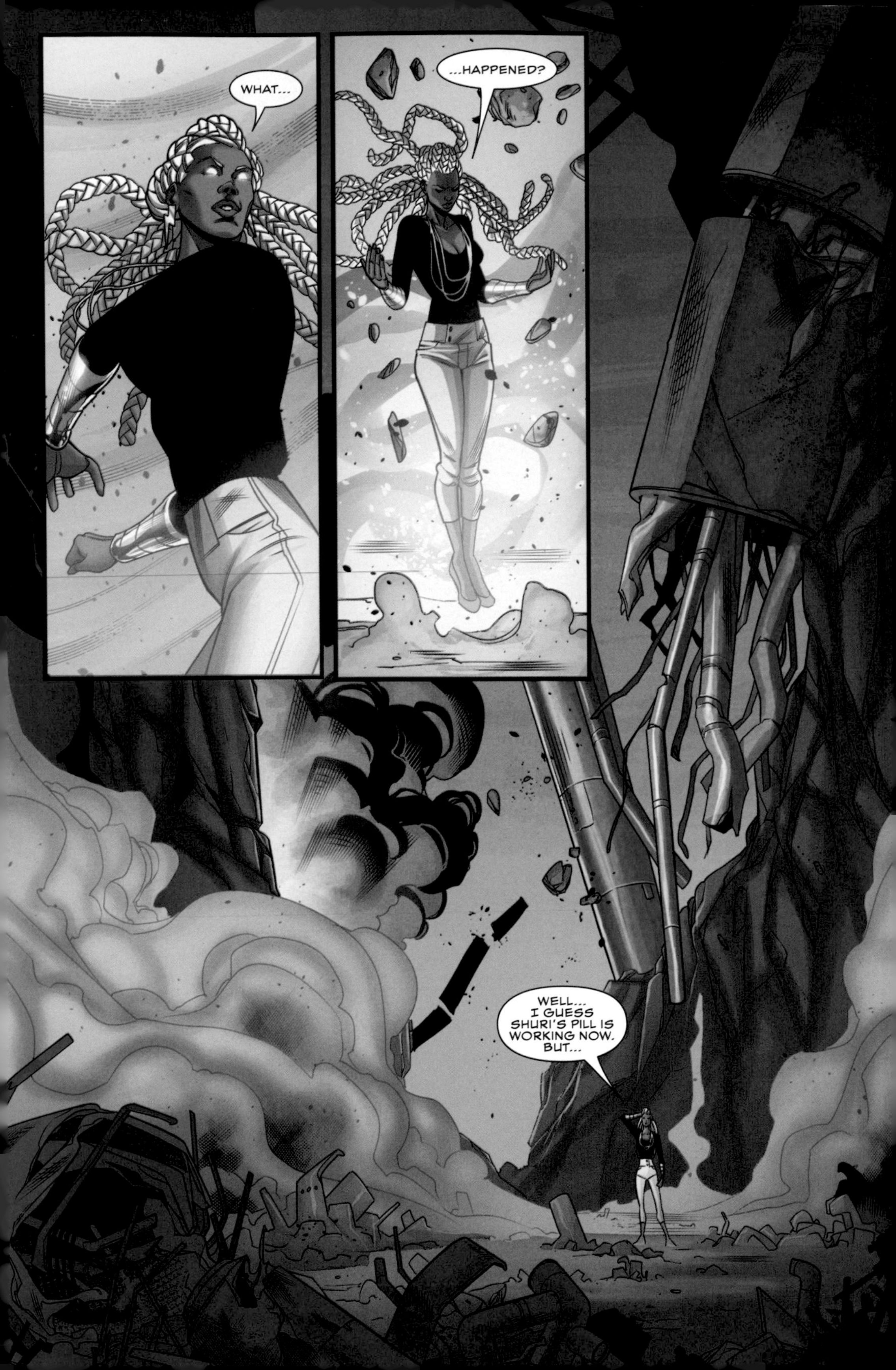
WHAT...
...HAPPENED?
WELL... I GUESS SHURI'S PILL IS WORKING NOW. BUT...

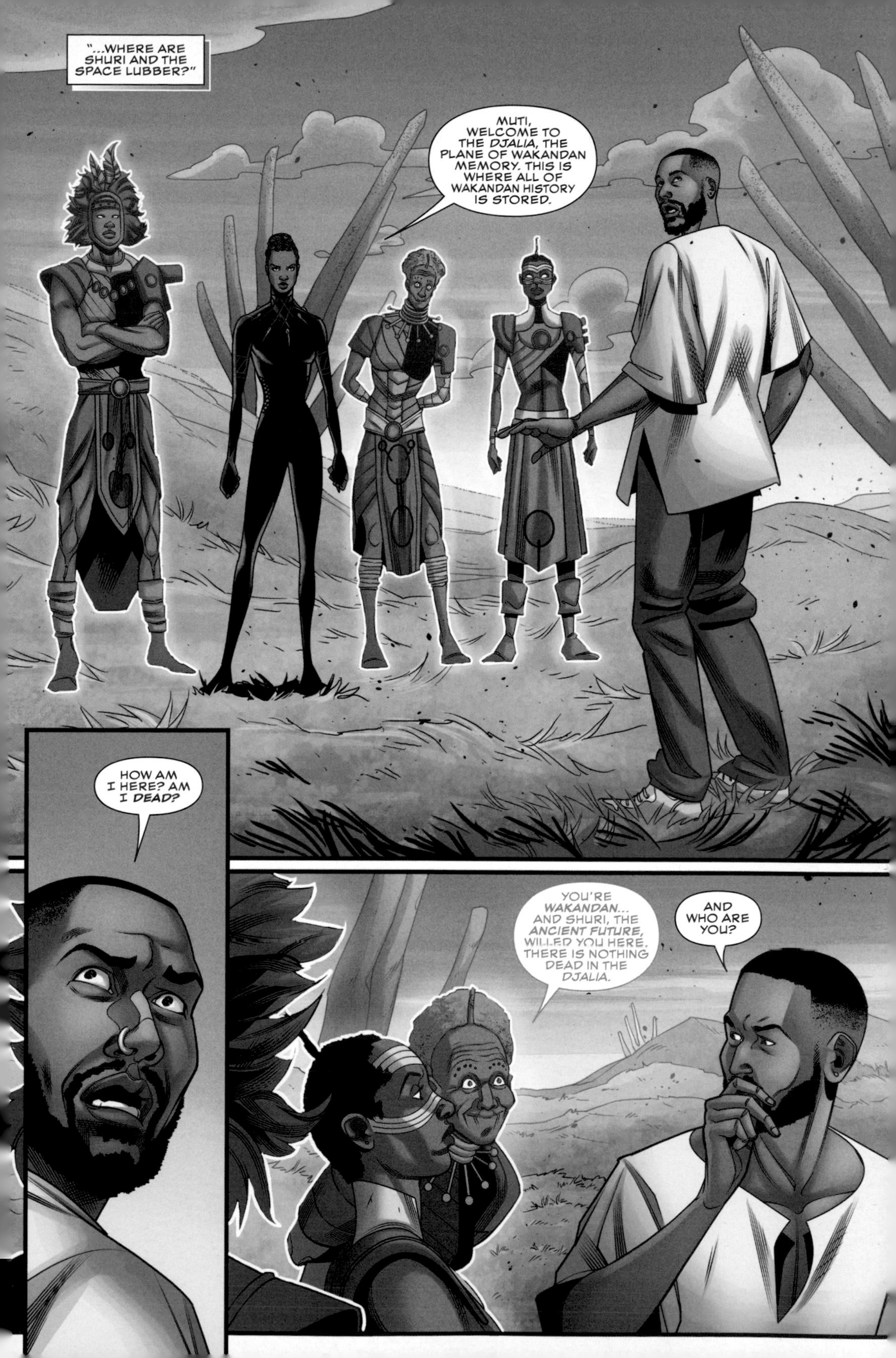
"...WHERE ARE SHURI AND THE SPACE LUBBER?"
MUTI, WELCOME TO THE *DJALIA*, THE PLANE OF WAKANDAN MEMORY. THIS IS WHERE ALL OF WAKANDAN HISTORY IS STORED.
HOW AM I HERE? AM I *DEAD?*
YOU'RE *WAKANDAN...* AND SHURI, THE *ANCIENT FUTURE*, WILLED YOU HERE. THERE IS NOTHING DEAD IN THE *DJALIA*.
AND WHO ARE YOU?

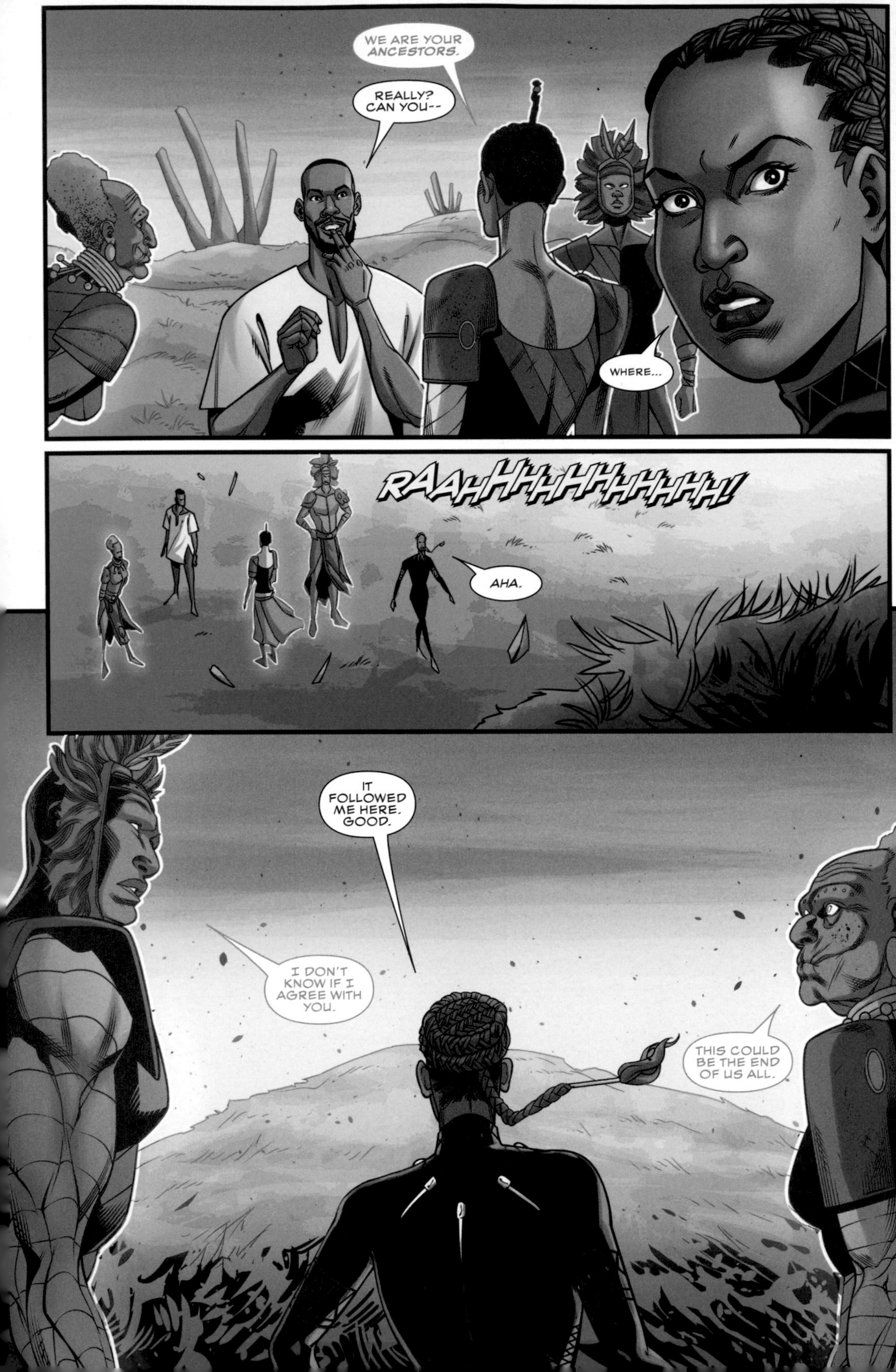
WE ARE YOUR ANCESTORS.
REALLY? CAN YOU--
WHERE...
RAAHHHHHHHHHHH!
AHA.
IT FOLLOWED ME HERE. GOOD.
I DON'T KNOW IF I AGREE WITH YOU.
THIS COULD BE THE END OF US ALL.

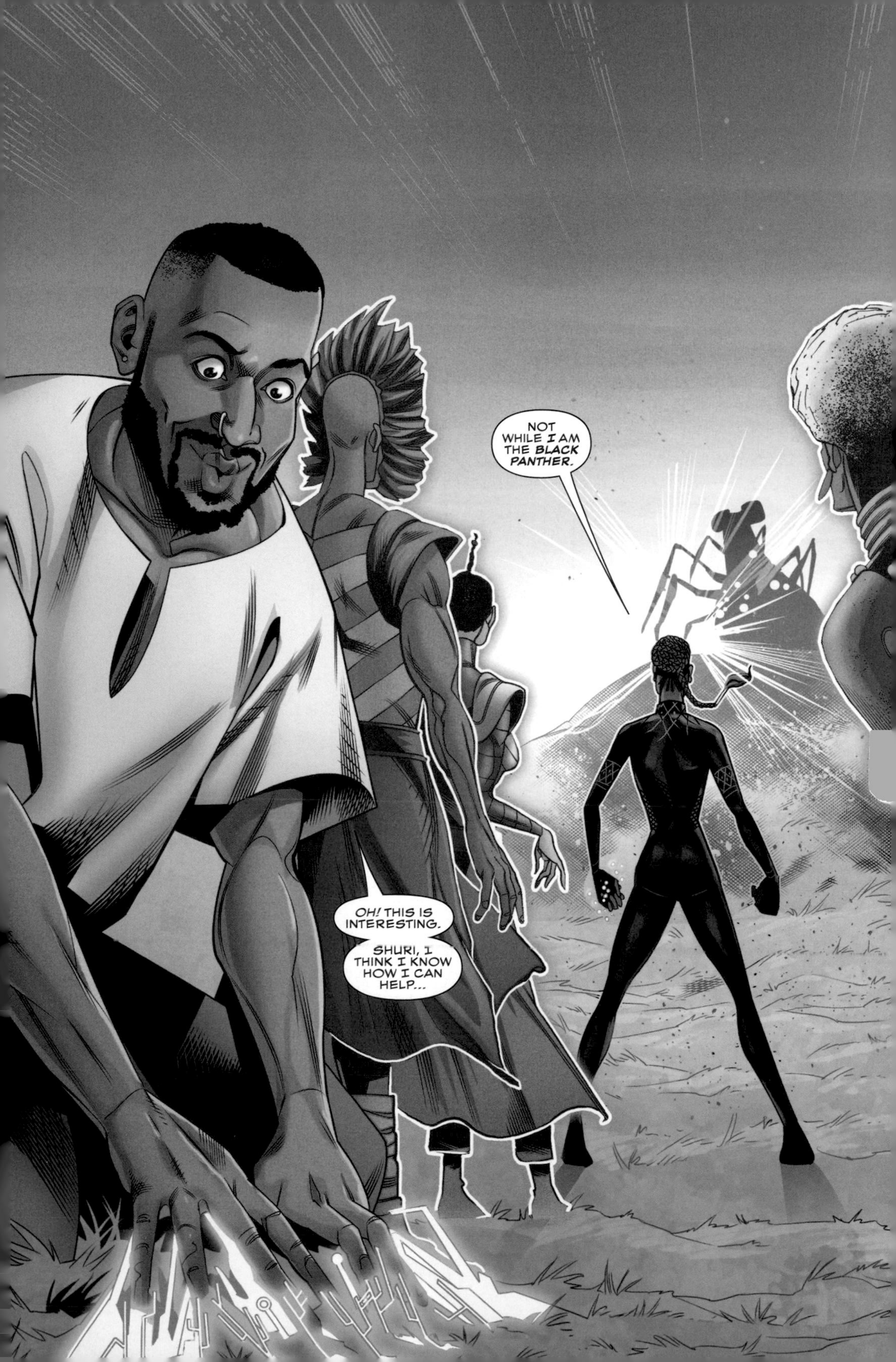
NOT WHILE I AM THE BLACK PANTHER.
OH! THIS IS INTERESTING.
SHURI, I THINK I KNOW HOW I CAN HELP...

10

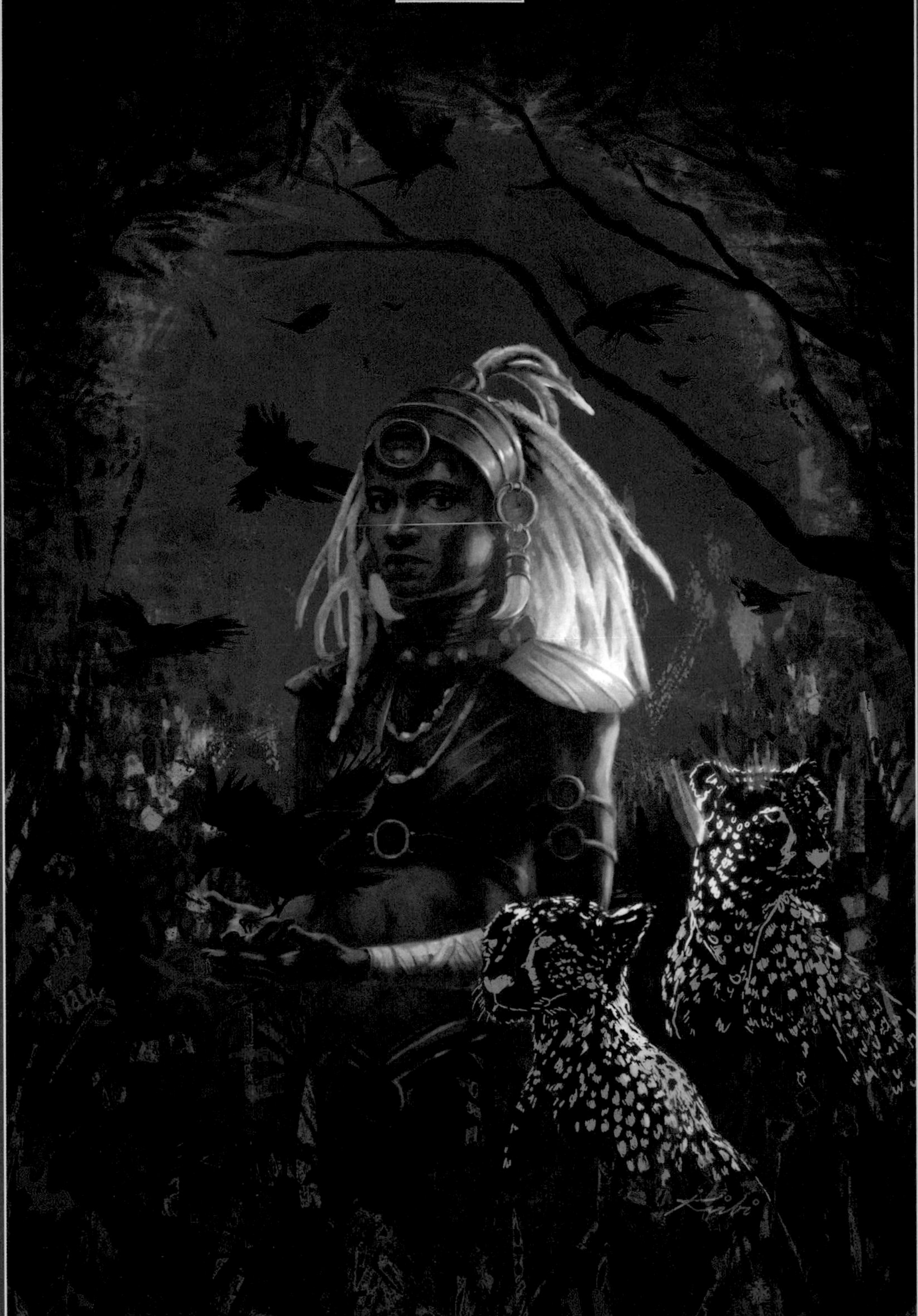

"LIVING MEMORY"

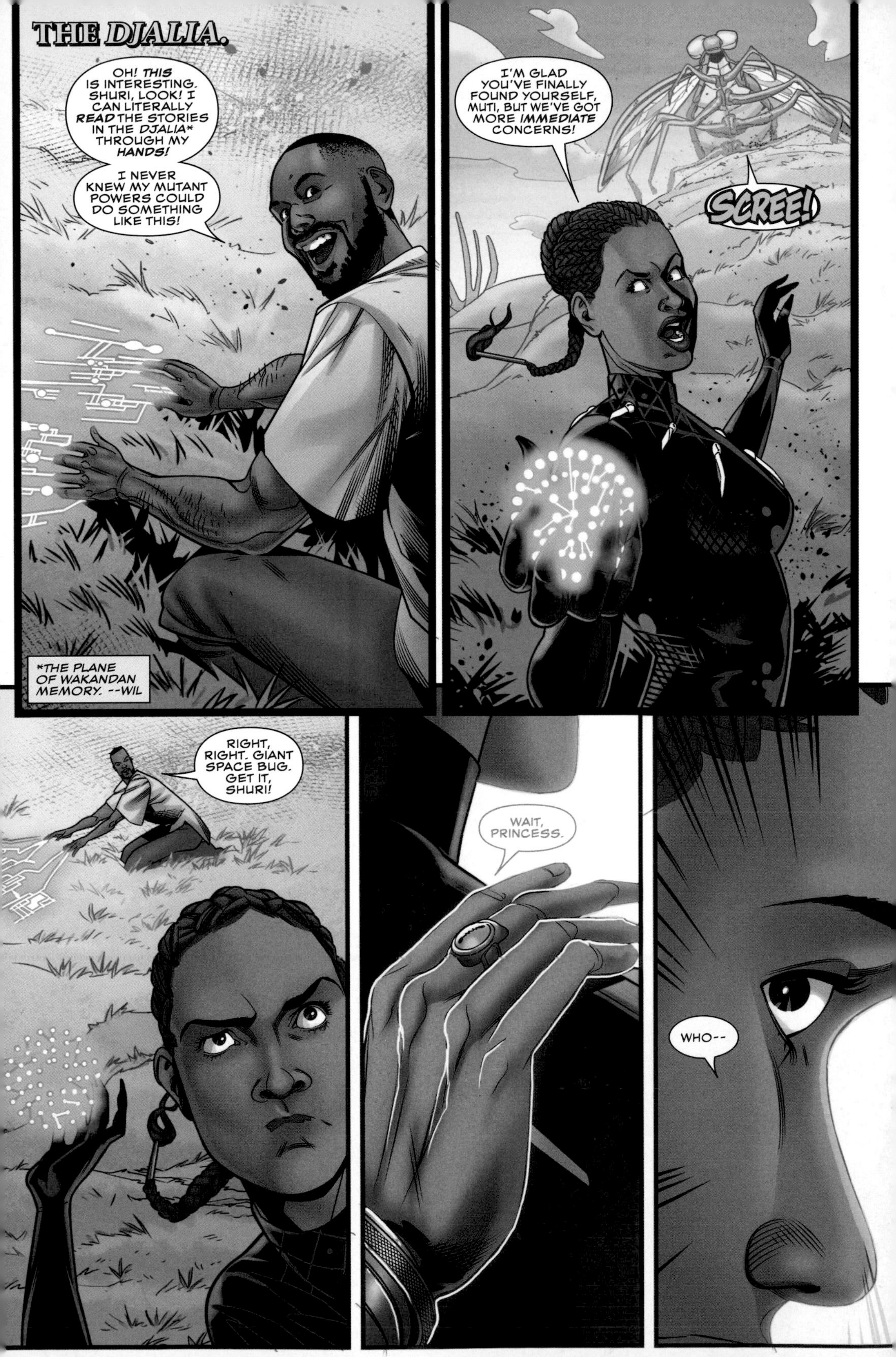
THE DJALIA.
OH! THIS IS INTERESTING. SHURI, LOOK! I CAN LITERALLY READ THE STORIES IN THE DJALIA* THROUGH MY HANDS!
I NEVER KNEW MY MUTANT POWERS COULD DO SOMETHING LIKE THIS!
*THE PLANE OF WAKANDAN MEMORY. --WIL
I'M GLAD YOU'VE FINALLY FOUND YOURSELF, MUTI, BUT WE'VE GOT MORE IMMEDIATE CONCERNS!
SCREE!
RIGHT, RIGHT. GIANT SPACE BUG. GET IT, SHURI!
WAIT, PRINCESS.
WHO--

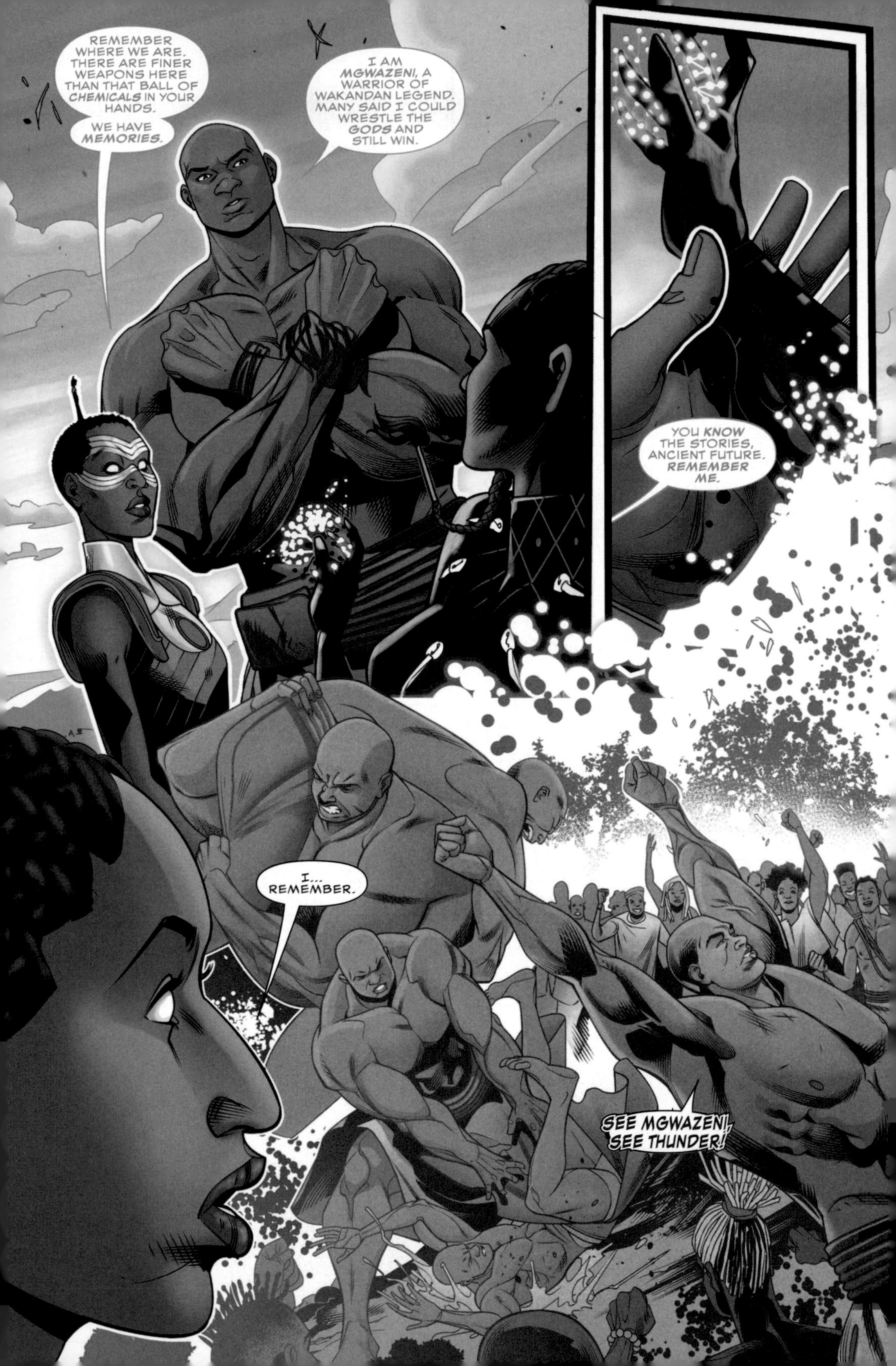
REMEMBER WHERE WE ARE. THERE ARE FINER WEAPONS HERE THAN THAT BALL OF CHEMICALS IN YOUR HANDS.
WE HAVE MEMORIES.
I AM MGWAZENI, A WARRIOR OF WAKANDAN LEGEND. MANY SAID I COULD WRESTLE THE GODS AND STILL WIN.
YOU KNOW THE STORIES, ANCIENT FUTURE. REMEMBER ME.
I... REMEMBER.
SEE MGWAZENI, SEE THUNDER!

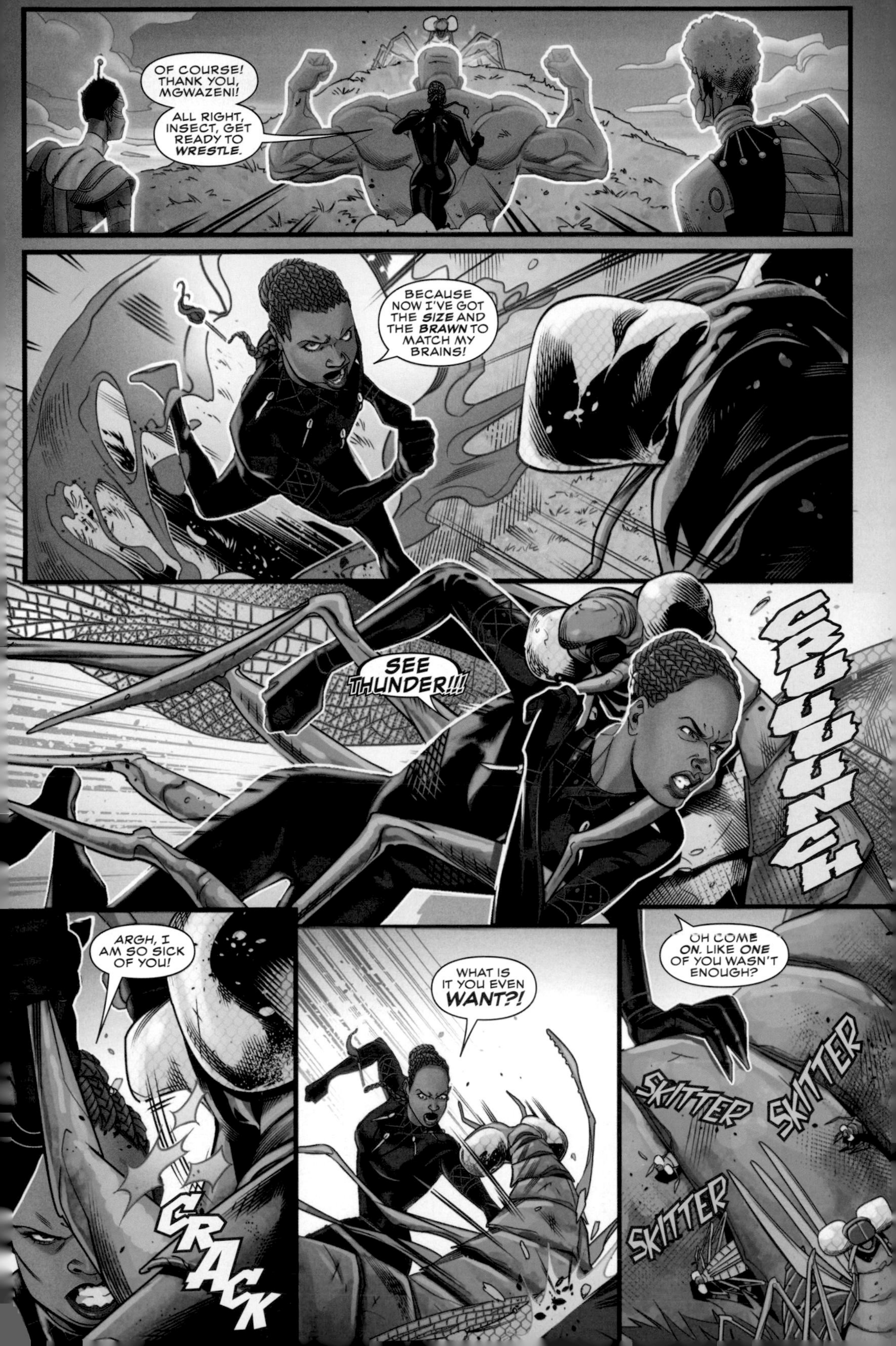
OF COURSE! THANK YOU, MGWAZENI!
ALL RIGHT, INSECT, GET READY TO *WRESTLE*.
BECAUSE NOW I'VE GOT THE *SIZE* AND THE *BRAWN* TO MATCH MY BRAINS!
SEE THUNDER!!!
CRUUNCH
ARGH, I AM SO SICK OF YOU!
CRACK
WHAT IS IT YOU EVEN *WANT?!*
OH COME *ON*. LIKE *ONE* OF YOU WASN'T ENOUGH?
SKITTER
SKITTER
SKITTER

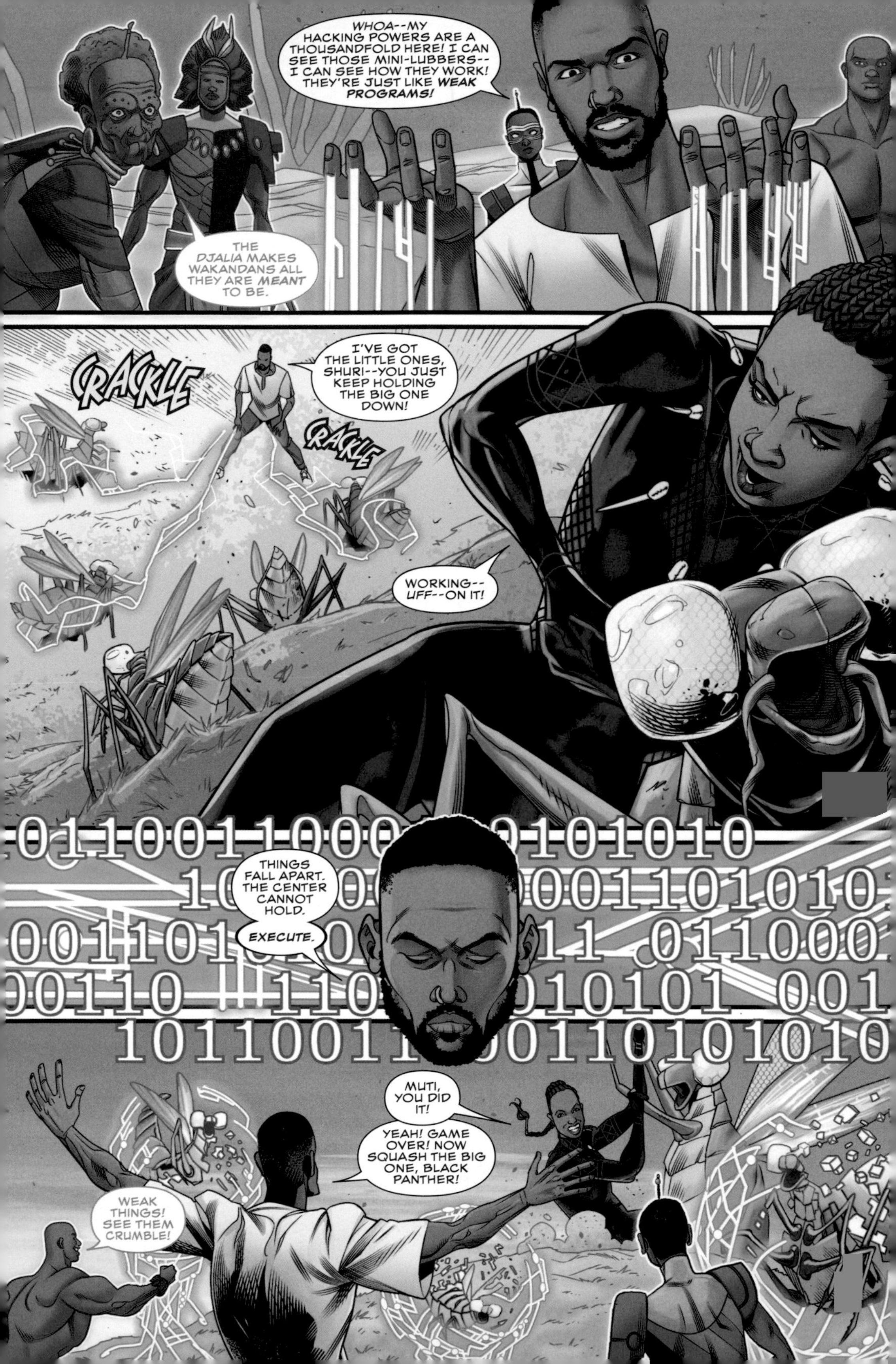

WHOA--MY HACKING POWERS ARE A THOUSANDFOLD HERE! I CAN SEE THOSE MINI-LUBBERS--I CAN SEE HOW THEY WORK! THEY'RE JUST LIKE WEAK PROGRAMS!
THE DJALIA MAKES WAKANDANS ALL THEY ARE MEANT TO BE.
CRACKLE
I'VE GOT THE LITTLE ONES, SHURI--YOU JUST KEEP HOLDING THE BIG ONE DOWN!
CRACKLE
WORKING--UFF--ON IT!
THINGS FALL APART. THE CENTER CANNOT HOLD.
EXECUTE.
MUTI, YOU DID IT!
YEAH! GAME OVER! NOW SQUASH THE BIG ONE, BLACK PANTHER!
WEAK THINGS! SEE THEM CRUMBLE!

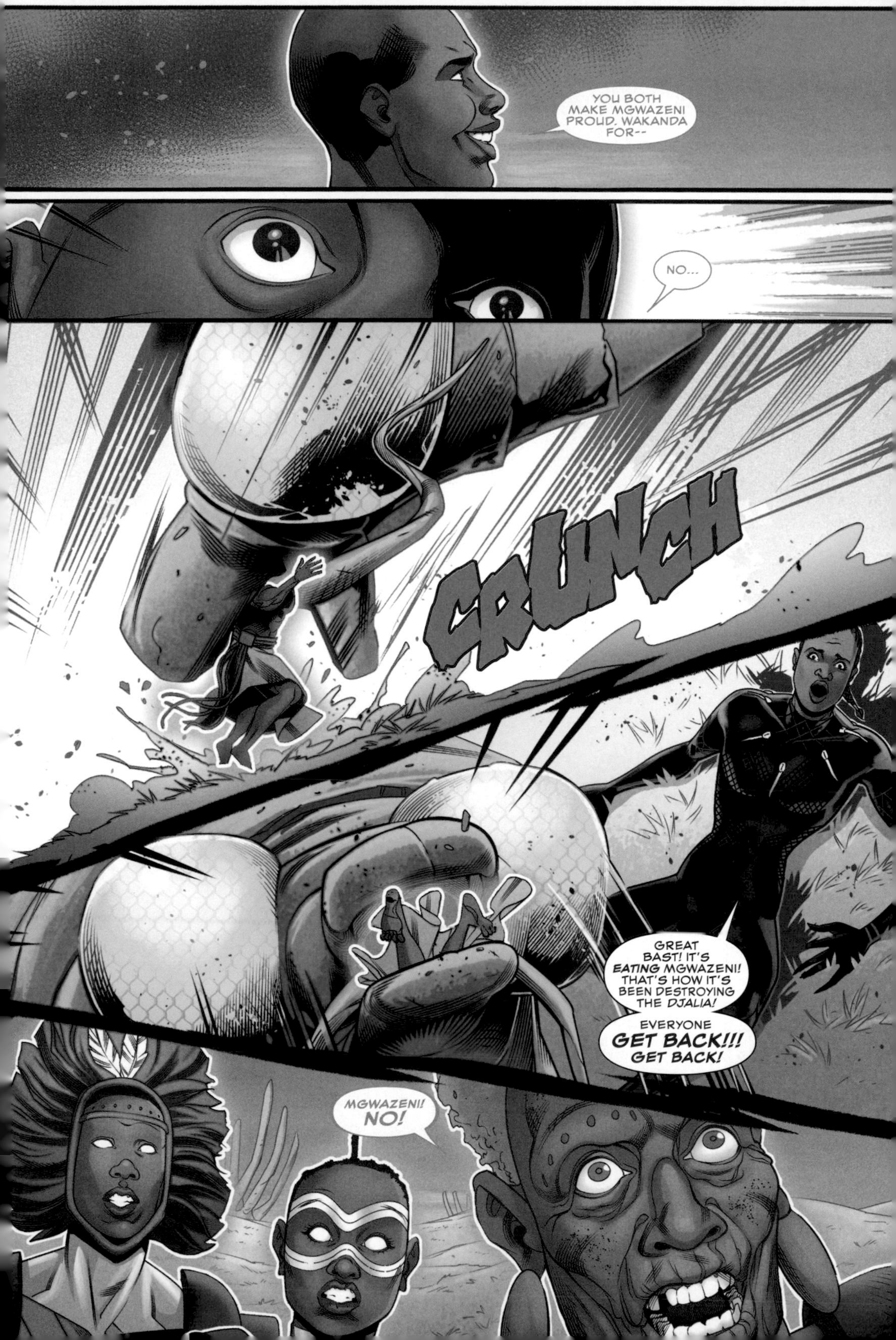
YOU BOTH MAKE MGWAZENI PROUD. WAKANDA FOR--
NO...
CRUNCH
GREAT BAST! IT'S *EATING* MGWAZENI! THAT'S HOW IT'S BEEN DESTROYING THE *DJALIA!*
EVERYONE **GET BACK!!!** GET BACK!
MGWAZENI! NO!

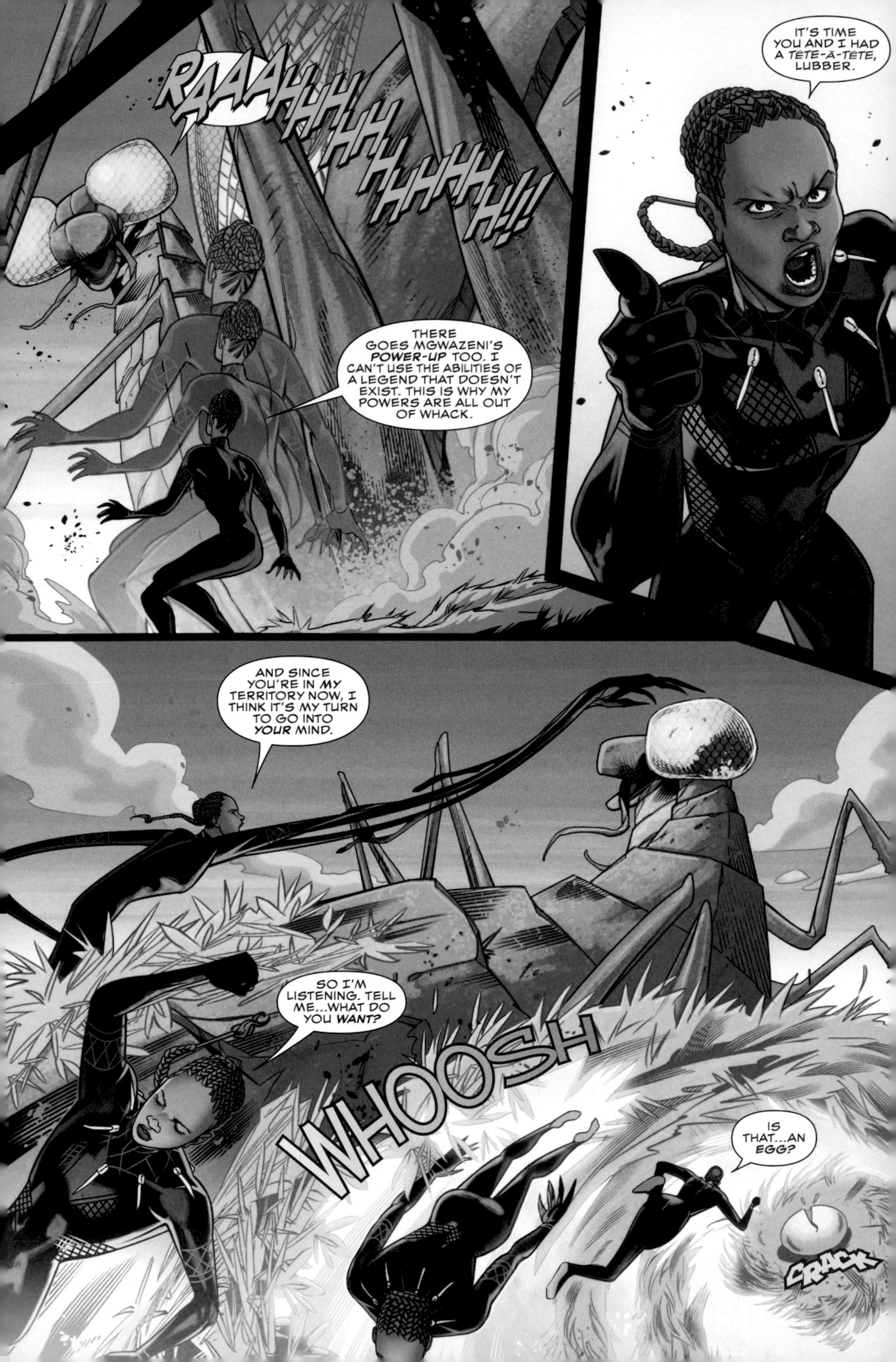
RAAAHHHHHHHHHH!!!
THERE GOES MGWAZENI'S POWER-UP TOO. I CAN'T USE THE ABILITIES OF A LEGEND THAT DOESN'T EXIST. THIS IS WHY MY POWERS ARE ALL OUT OF WHACK.
IT'S TIME YOU AND I HAD A TÊTE-À-TÊTE, LUBBER.
AND SINCE YOU'RE IN MY TERRITORY NOW, I THINK IT'S MY TURN TO GO INTO YOUR MIND.
SO I'M LISTENING. TELL ME...WHAT DO YOU WANT?
WHOOSH
IS THAT...AN EGG?
CRACK

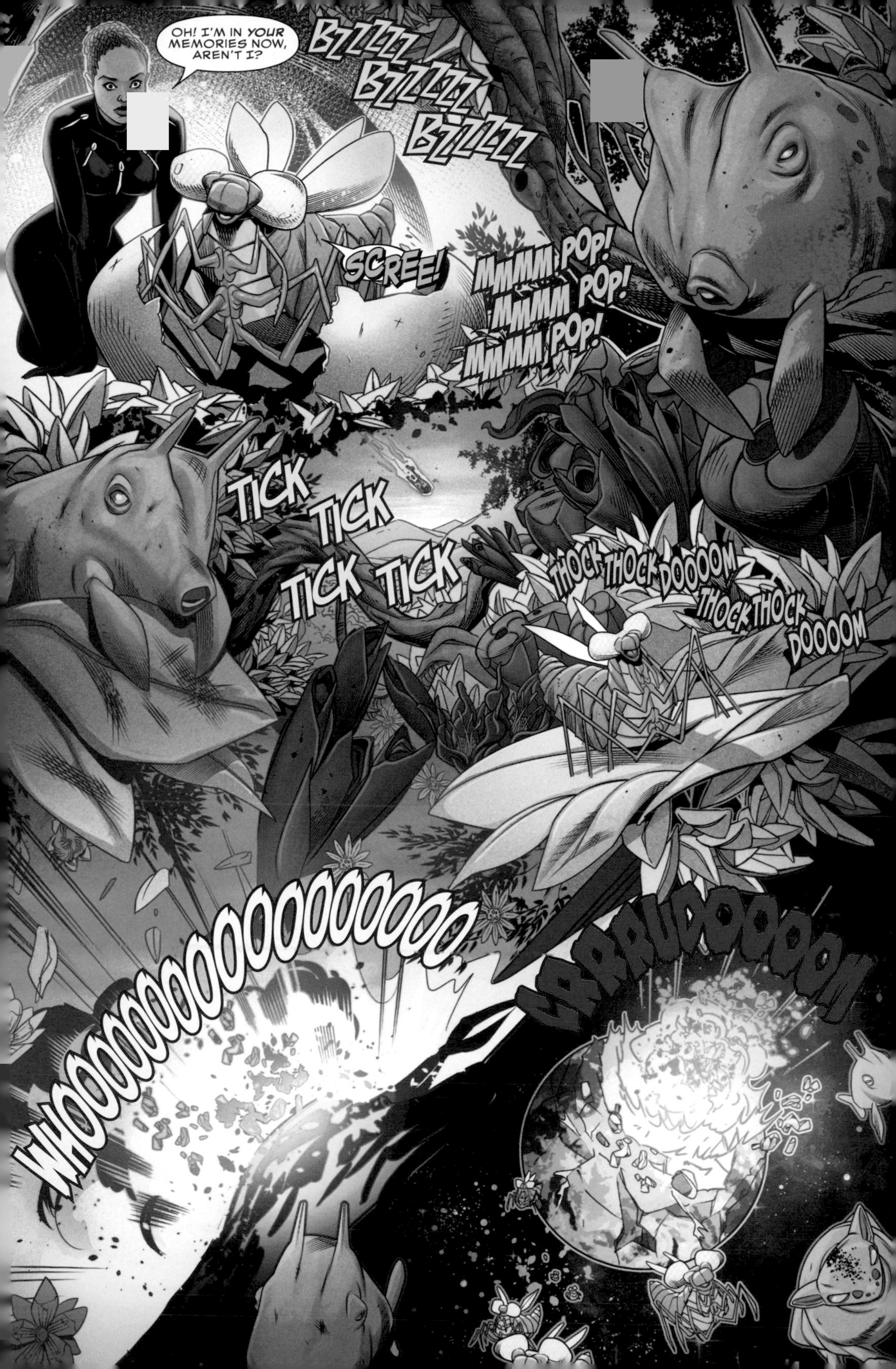
OH! I'M IN YOUR MEMORIES NOW, AREN'T I?
BZZZZZ BZZZZZ BZZZZZ
SCREE!
MMMM POP! MMMM POP! MMMM POP!
TICK TICK TICK TICK
THOCK THOCK DOOOOM THOCK THOCK DOOOOM
WHOOOOOOOOOOOOOOOOOO
GRRRUDOOOOOM

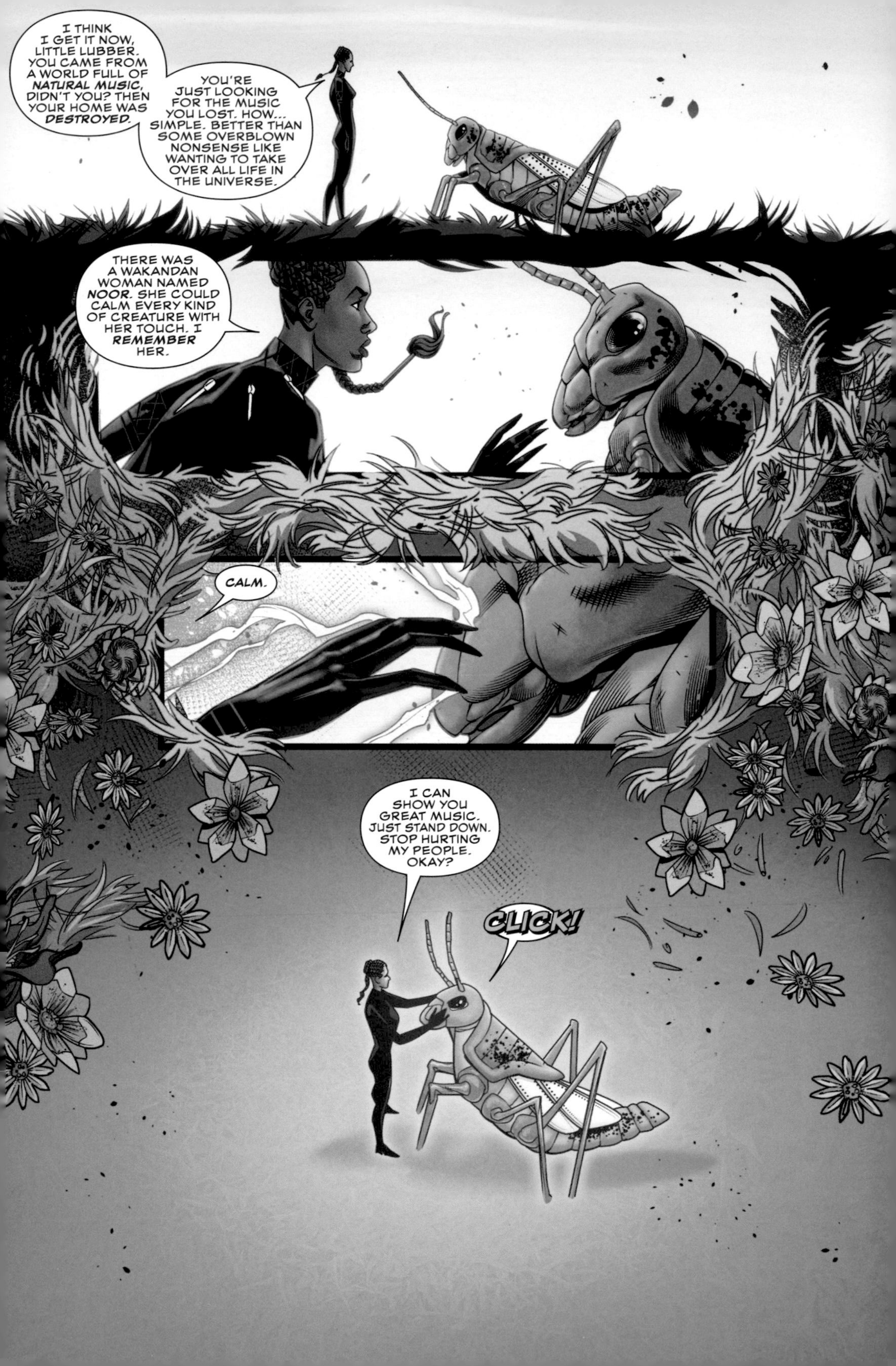

I THINK I GET IT NOW, LITTLE LUBBER. YOU CAME FROM A WORLD FULL OF NATURAL MUSIC, DIDN'T YOU? THEN YOUR HOME WAS DESTROYED.
YOU'RE JUST LOOKING FOR THE MUSIC YOU LOST. HOW... SIMPLE. BETTER THAN SOME OVERBLOWN NONSENSE LIKE WANTING TO TAKE OVER ALL LIFE IN THE UNIVERSE.
THERE WAS A WAKANDAN WOMAN NAMED NOOR. SHE COULD CALM EVERY KIND OF CREATURE WITH HER TOUCH. I REMEMBER HER.
CALM.
I CAN SHOW YOU GREAT MUSIC. JUST STAND DOWN. STOP HURTING MY PEOPLE. OKAY?
CLICK!

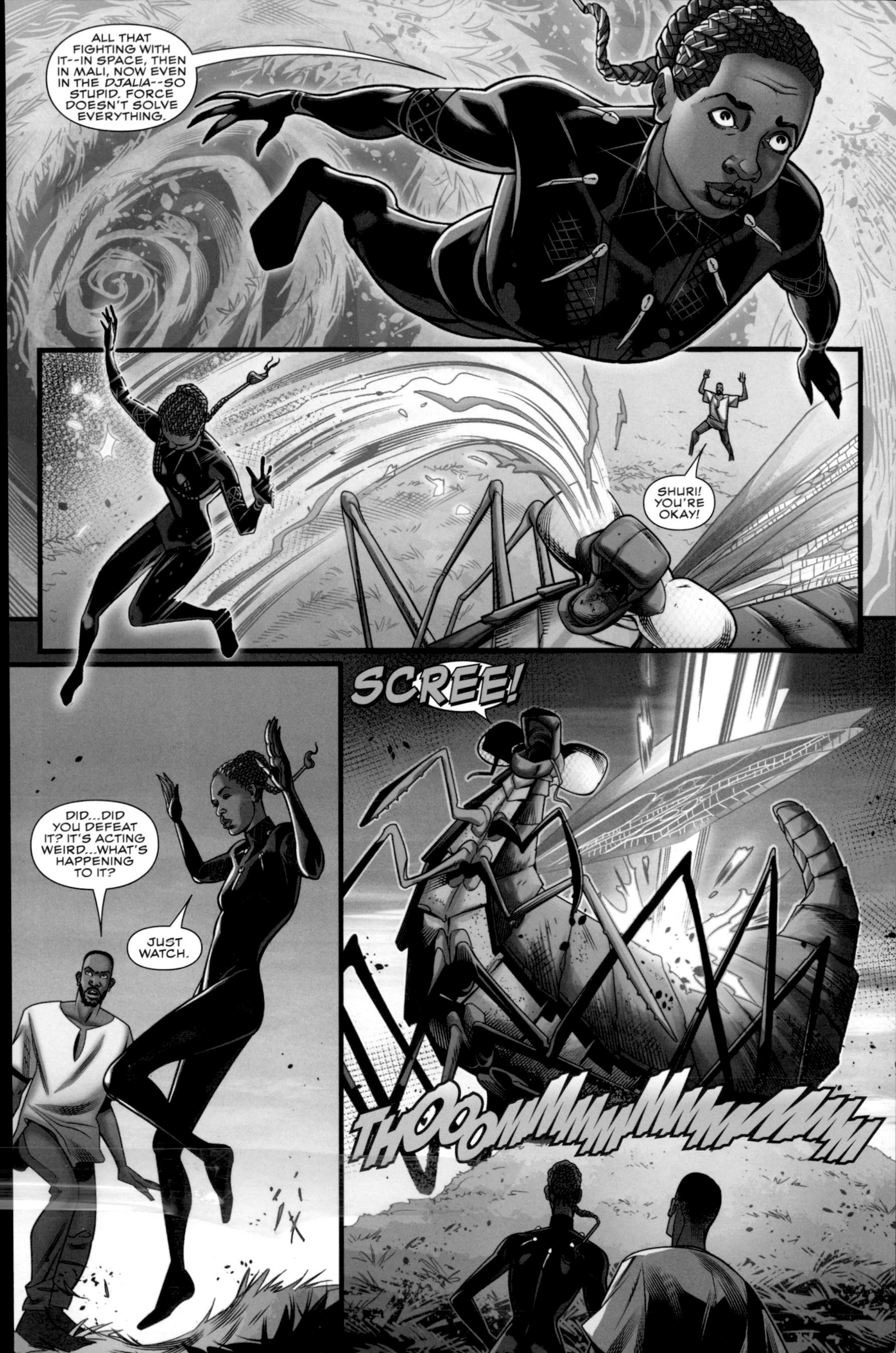
ALL THAT FIGHTING WITH IT--IN SPACE, THEN IN MALI, NOW EVEN IN THE *DJALIA*--SO STUPID. FORCE DOESN'T SOLVE EVERYTHING.
SHURI! YOU'RE OKAY!
SCREE!
DID...DID YOU DEFEAT IT? IT'S ACTING WEIRD...WHAT'S HAPPENING TO IT?
JUST WATCH.
THOOOMMMMMMMMMMMM

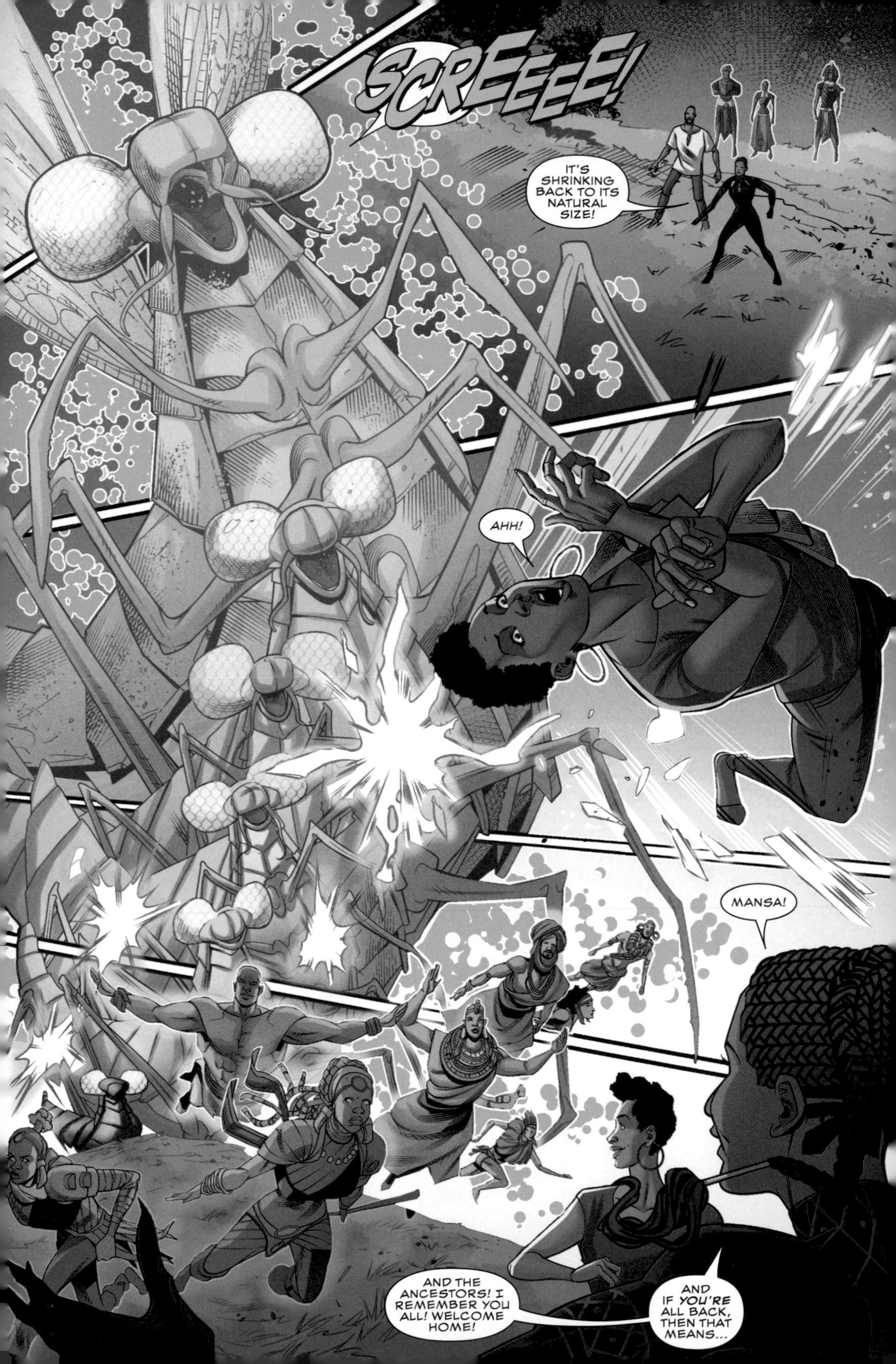
SCREEEEE!
IT'S SHRINKING BACK TO ITS NATURAL SIZE!
AHH!
MANSA!
AND THE ANCESTORS! I REMEMBER YOU ALL! WELCOME HOME!
AND IF YOU'RE ALL BACK, THEN THAT MEANS...

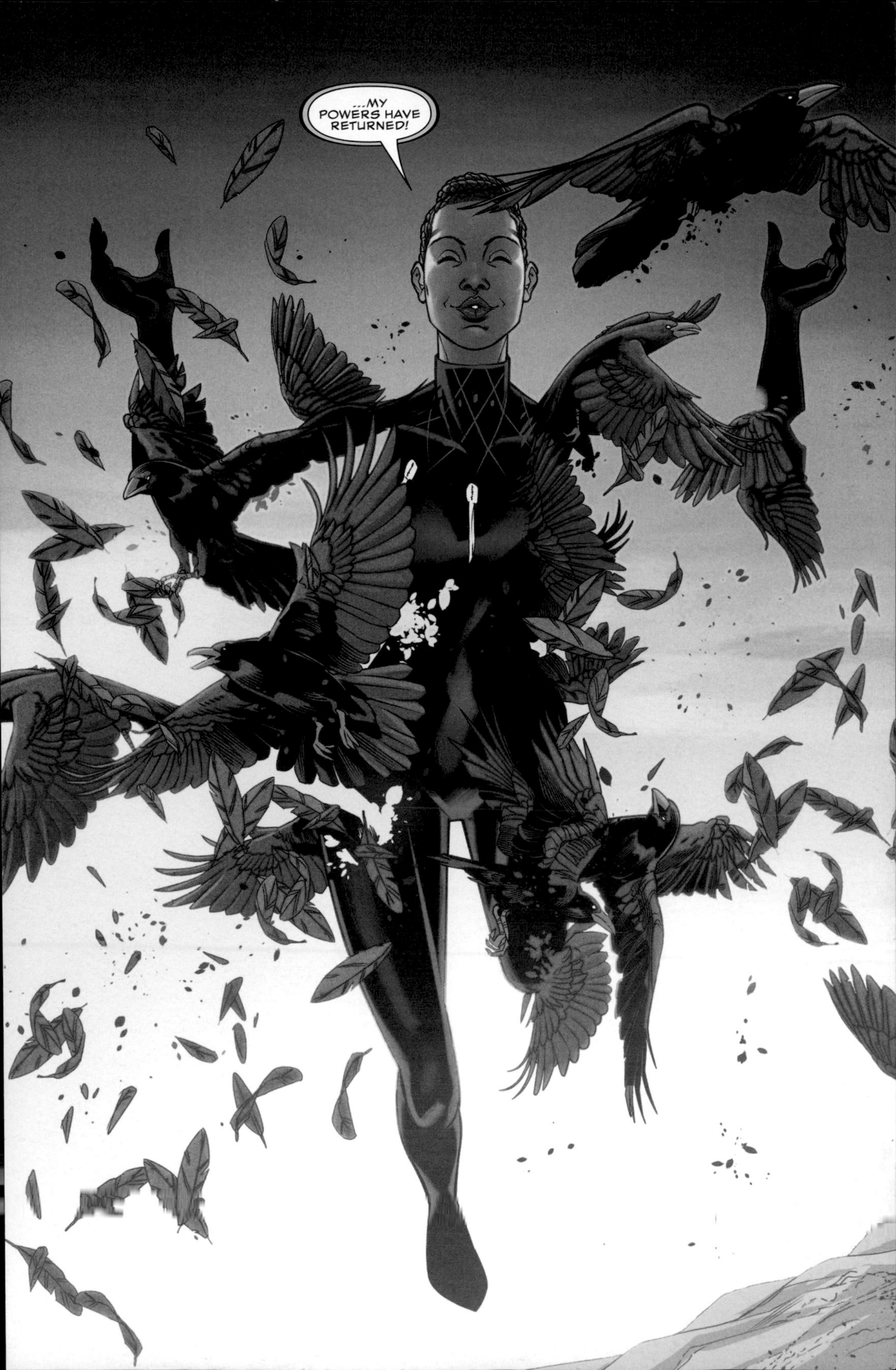
...MY POWERS HAVE RETURNED!

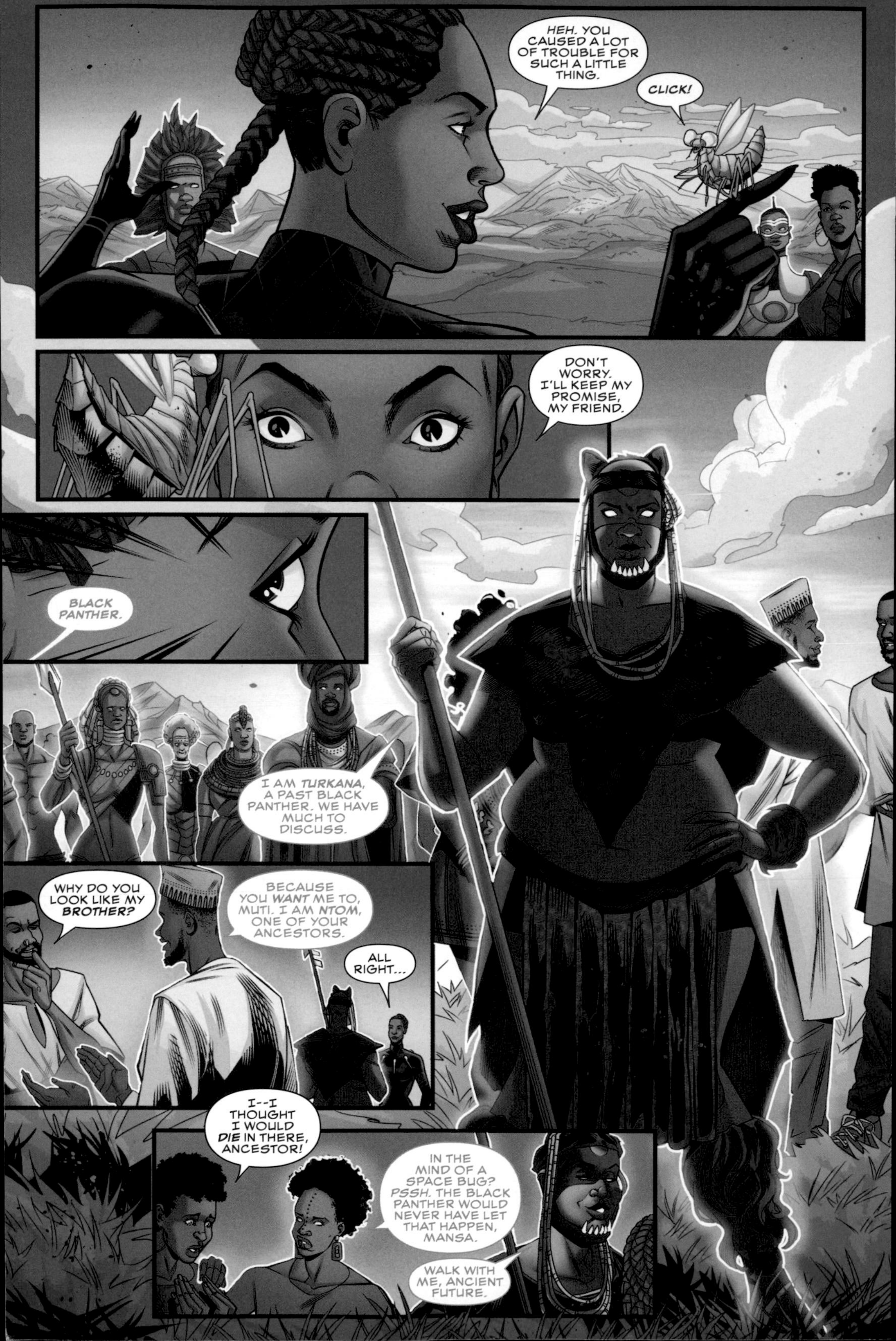
HEH. YOU CAUSED A LOT OF TROUBLE FOR SUCH A LITTLE THING.
CLICK!
DON'T WORRY. I'LL KEEP MY PROMISE, MY FRIEND.
BLACK PANTHER.
I AM TURKANA, A PAST BLACK PANTHER. WE HAVE MUCH TO DISCUSS.
WHY DO YOU LOOK LIKE MY BROTHER?
BECAUSE YOU WANT ME TO, MUTI. I AM NTOM, ONE OF YOUR ANCESTORS.
ALL RIGHT...
I--I THOUGHT I WOULD DIE IN THERE, ANCESTOR!
IN THE MIND OF A SPACE BUG? PSSH. THE BLACK PANTHER WOULD NEVER HAVE LET THAT HAPPEN, MANSA.
WALK WITH ME, ANCIENT FUTURE.

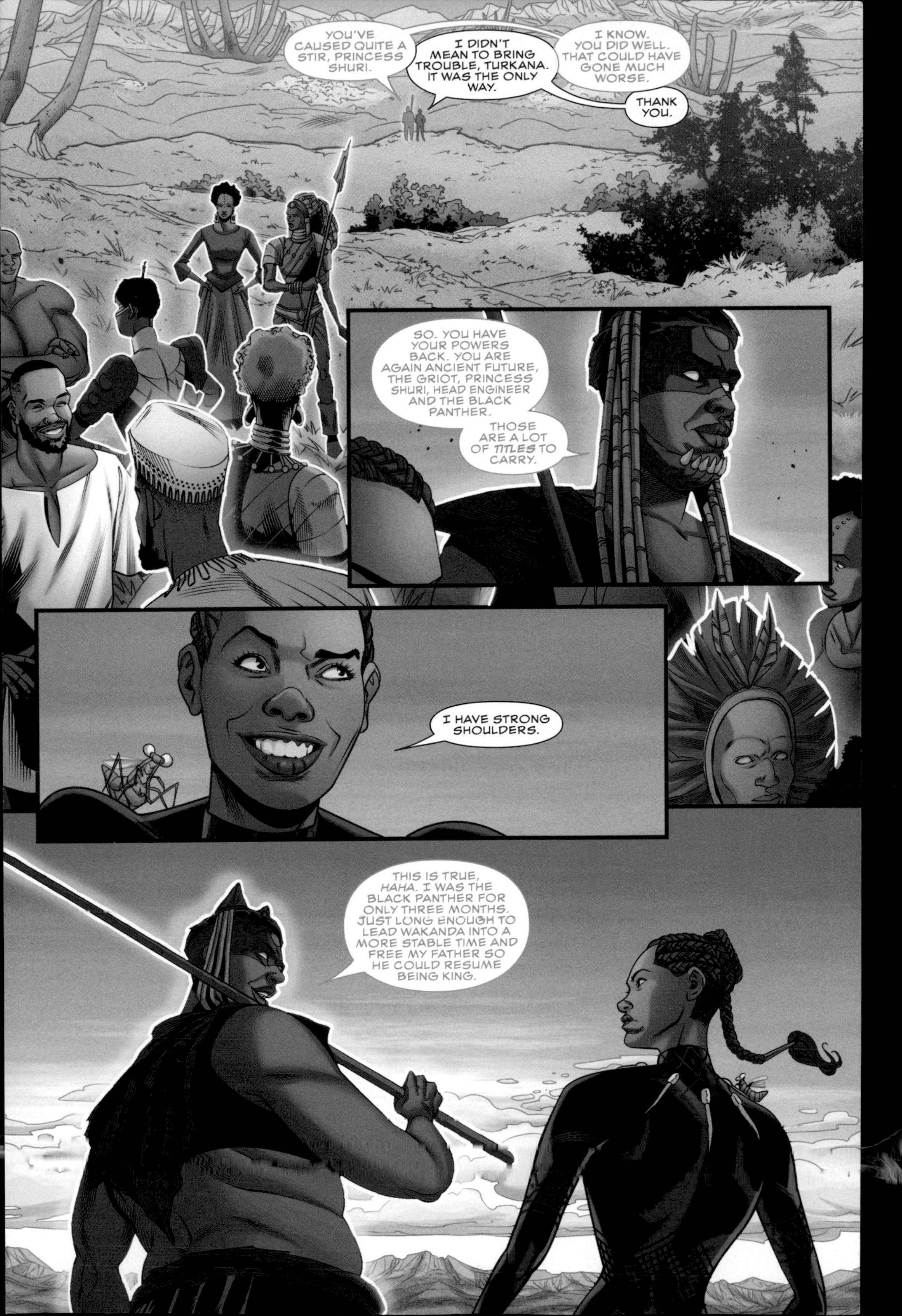

YOU'VE CAUSED QUITE A STIR, PRINCESS SHURI.
I DIDN'T MEAN TO BRING TROUBLE, TURKANA. IT WAS THE ONLY WAY.
I KNOW. YOU DID WELL. THAT COULD HAVE GONE MUCH WORSE.
THANK YOU.
SO. YOU HAVE YOUR POWERS BACK. YOU ARE AGAIN ANCIENT FUTURE, THE GRIOT, PRINCESS SHURI, HEAD ENGINEER AND THE BLACK PANTHER.
THOSE ARE A LOT OF *TITLES* TO CARRY.
I HAVE STRONG SHOULDERS.
THIS IS TRUE, *HAHA*. I WAS THE BLACK PANTHER FOR ONLY THREE MONTHS. JUST LONG ENOUGH TO LEAD WAKANDA INTO A MORE STABLE TIME AND FREE MY FATHER SO HE COULD RESUME BEING KING.

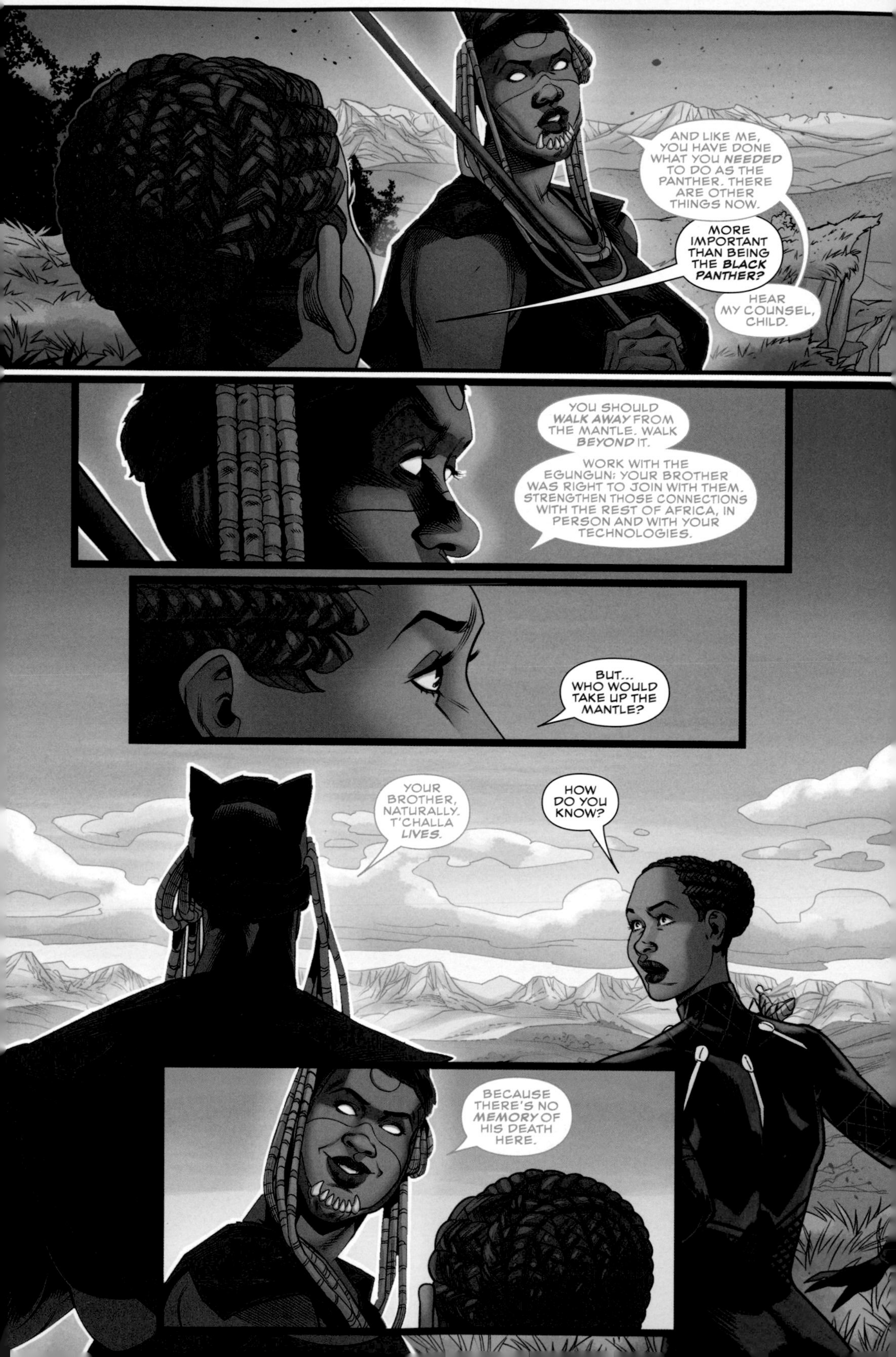
AND LIKE ME, YOU HAVE DONE WHAT YOU NEEDED TO DO AS THE PANTHER. THERE ARE OTHER THINGS NOW.
MORE IMPORTANT THAN BEING THE BLACK PANTHER?
HEAR MY COUNSEL, CHILD.
YOU SHOULD WALK AWAY FROM THE MANTLE. WALK BEYOND IT.
WORK WITH THE EGUNGUN; YOUR BROTHER WAS RIGHT TO JOIN WITH THEM. STRENGTHEN THOSE CONNECTIONS WITH THE REST OF AFRICA, IN PERSON AND WITH YOUR TECHNOLOGIES.
BUT... WHO WOULD TAKE UP THE MANTLE?
YOUR BROTHER, NATURALLY. T'CHALLA LIVES.
HOW DO YOU KNOW?
BECAUSE THERE'S NO MEMORY OF HIS DEATH HERE.

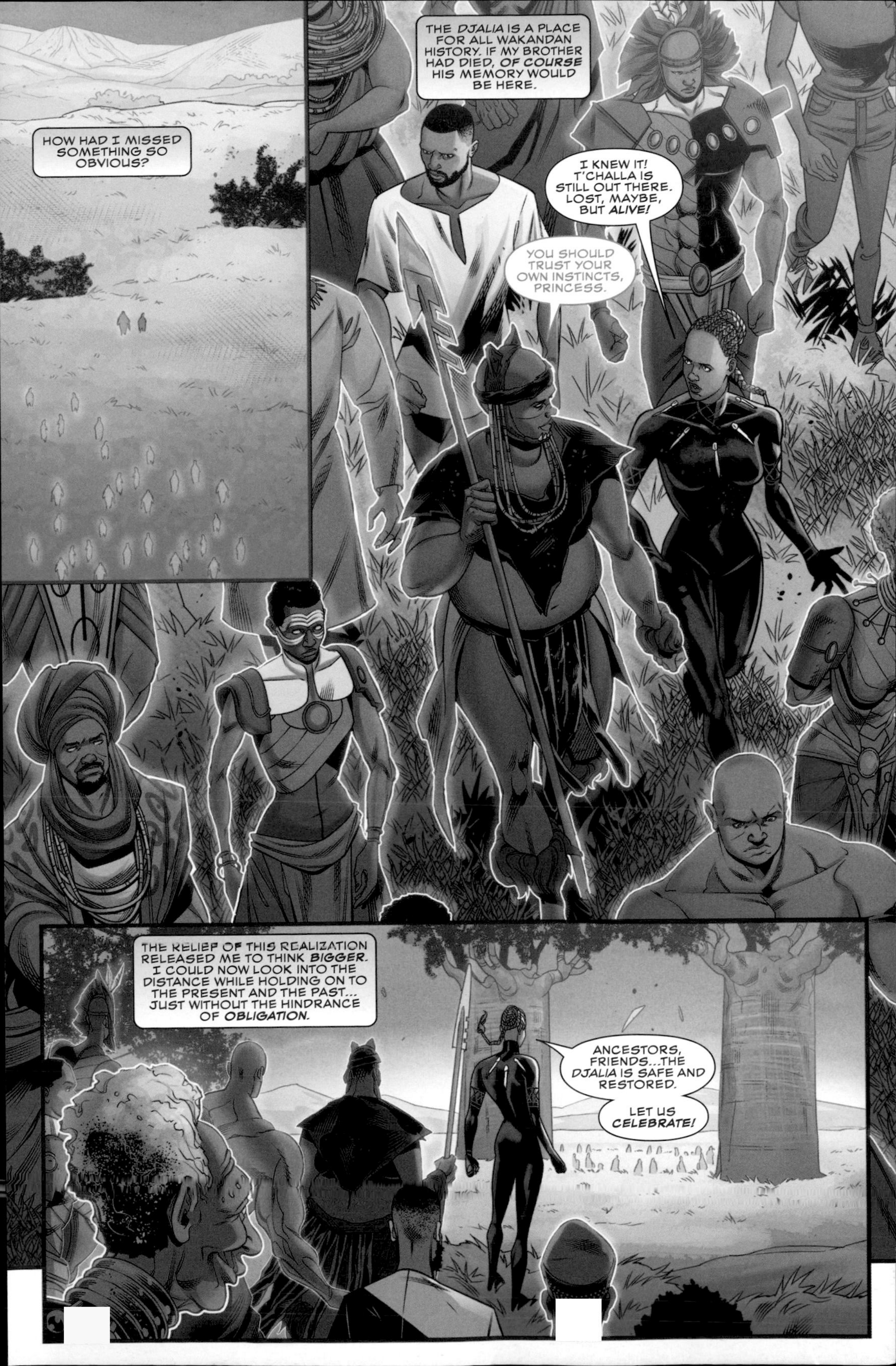

THE DJALIA IS A PLACE FOR ALL WAKANDAN HISTORY. IF MY BROTHER HAD DIED, OF COURSE HIS MEMORY WOULD BE HERE.
HOW HAD I MISSED SOMETHING SO OBVIOUS?
I KNEW IT! T'CHALLA IS STILL OUT THERE. LOST, MAYBE, BUT ALIVE!
YOU SHOULD TRUST YOUR OWN INSTINCTS, PRINCESS.
THE RELIEF OF THIS REALIZATION RELEASED ME TO THINK BIGGER. I COULD NOW LOOK INTO THE DISTANCE WHILE HOLDING ON TO THE PRESENT AND THE PAST... JUST WITHOUT THE HINDRANCE OF OBLIGATION.
ANCESTORS, FRIENDS...THE DJALIA IS SAFE AND RESTORED.
LET US CELEBRATE!

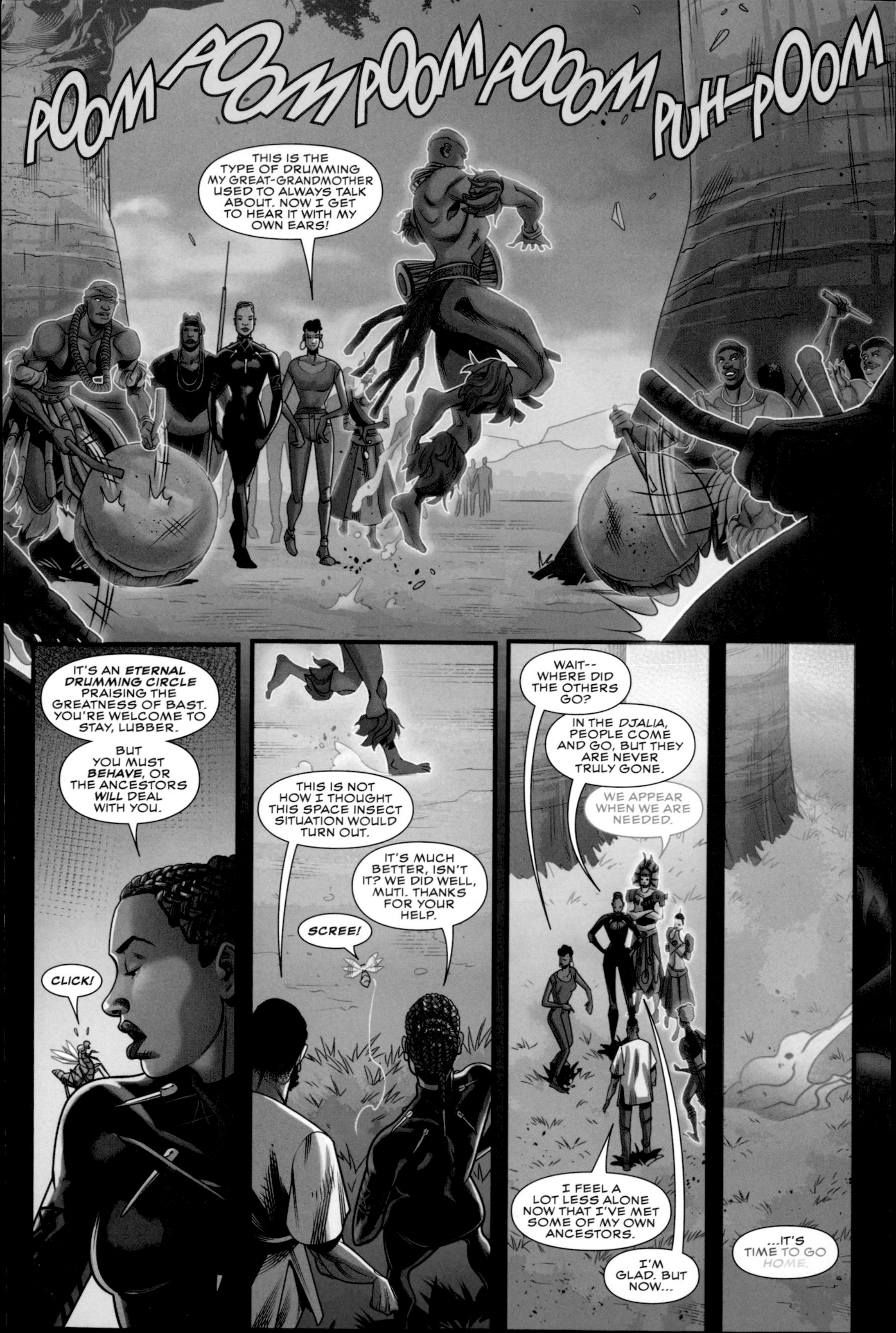
POOM POOM POOM POOOM PUH-POOM
THIS IS THE TYPE OF DRUMMING MY GREAT-GRANDMOTHER USED TO ALWAYS TALK ABOUT. NOW I GET TO HEAR IT WITH MY OWN EARS!
IT'S AN *ETERNAL DRUMMING CIRCLE* PRAISING THE GREATNESS OF BAST. YOU'RE WELCOME TO STAY, LUBBER.
BUT YOU MUST **BEHAVE**, OR THE ANCESTORS **WILL** DEAL WITH YOU.
CLICK!
THIS IS NOT HOW I THOUGHT THIS SPACE INSECT SITUATION WOULD TURN OUT.
IT'S MUCH BETTER, ISN'T IT? WE DID WELL, MUTI. THANKS FOR YOUR HELP.
SCREE!
WAIT-- WHERE DID THE OTHERS GO?
IN THE *DJALIA*, PEOPLE COME AND GO, BUT THEY ARE NEVER TRULY GONE.
WE APPEAR WHEN WE ARE NEEDED.
I FEEL A LOT LESS ALONE NOW THAT I'VE MET SOME OF MY OWN ANCESTORS.
I'M GLAD. BUT NOW...
...IT'S TIME TO GO *HOME*.

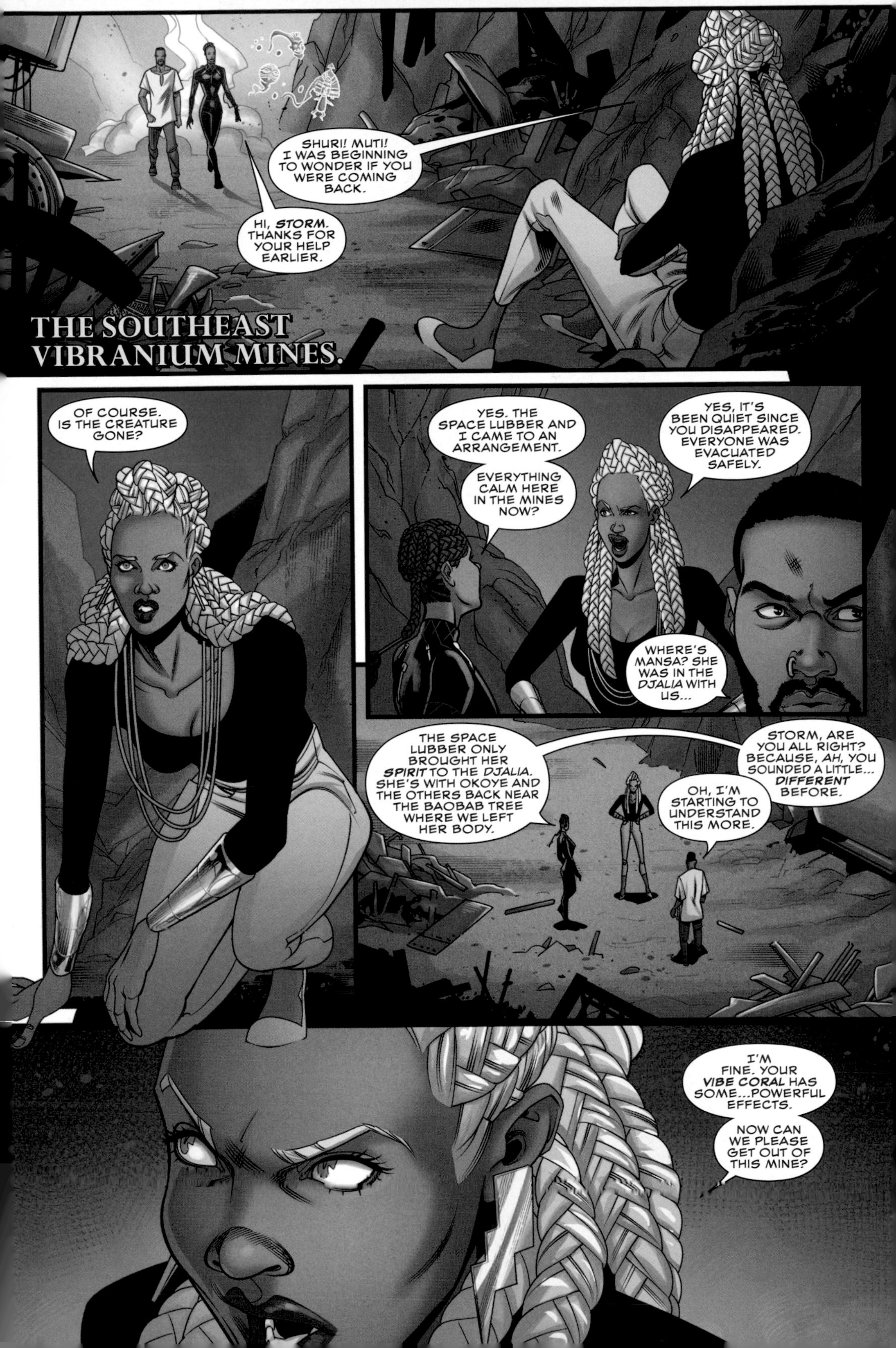
THE SOUTHEAST VIBRANIUM MINES.
SHURI! MUTI! I WAS BEGINNING TO WONDER IF YOU WERE COMING BACK.
HI, STORM. THANKS FOR YOUR HELP EARLIER.
OF COURSE. IS THE CREATURE GONE?
YES. THE SPACE LUBBER AND I CAME TO AN ARRANGEMENT.
EVERYTHING CALM HERE IN THE MINES NOW?
YES, IT'S BEEN QUIET SINCE YOU DISAPPEARED. EVERYONE WAS EVACUATED SAFELY.
WHERE'S MANSA? SHE WAS IN THE DJALIA WITH US...
THE SPACE LUBBER ONLY BROUGHT HER SPIRIT TO THE DJALIA. SHE'S WITH OKOYE AND THE OTHERS BACK NEAR THE BAOBAB TREE WHERE WE LEFT HER BODY.
STORM, ARE YOU ALL RIGHT? BECAUSE, AH, YOU SOUNDED A LITTLE... DIFFERENT BEFORE.
OH, I'M STARTING TO UNDERSTAND THIS MORE.
I'M FINE. YOUR VIBE CORAL HAS SOME...POWERFUL EFFECTS.
NOW CAN WE PLEASE GET OUT OF THIS MINE?

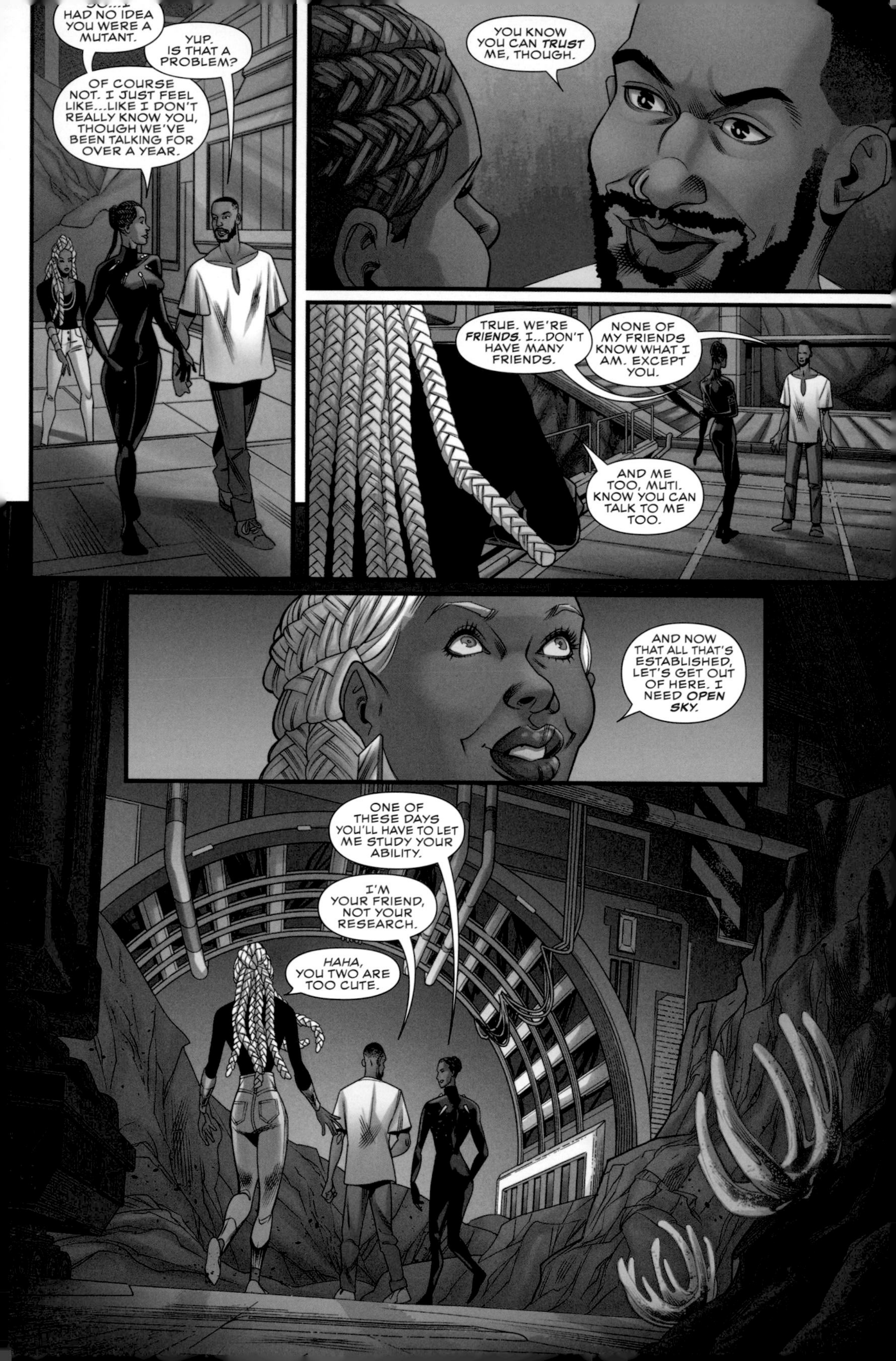
HAD NO IDEA YOU WERE A MUTANT.
YUP. IS THAT A PROBLEM?
OF COURSE NOT. I JUST FEEL LIKE...LIKE I DON'T REALLY KNOW YOU, THOUGH WE'VE BEEN TALKING FOR OVER A YEAR.
YOU KNOW YOU CAN TRUST ME, THOUGH.
TRUE. WE'RE FRIENDS. I...DON'T HAVE MANY FRIENDS.
NONE OF MY FRIENDS KNOW WHAT I AM. EXCEPT YOU.
AND ME TOO, MUTI. KNOW YOU CAN TALK TO ME TOO.
AND NOW THAT ALL THAT'S ESTABLISHED, LET'S GET OUT OF HERE. I NEED OPEN SKY.
ONE OF THESE DAYS YOU'LL HAVE TO LET ME STUDY YOUR ABILITY.
I'M YOUR FRIEND, NOT YOUR RESEARCH.
HAHA, YOU TWO ARE TOO CUTE.

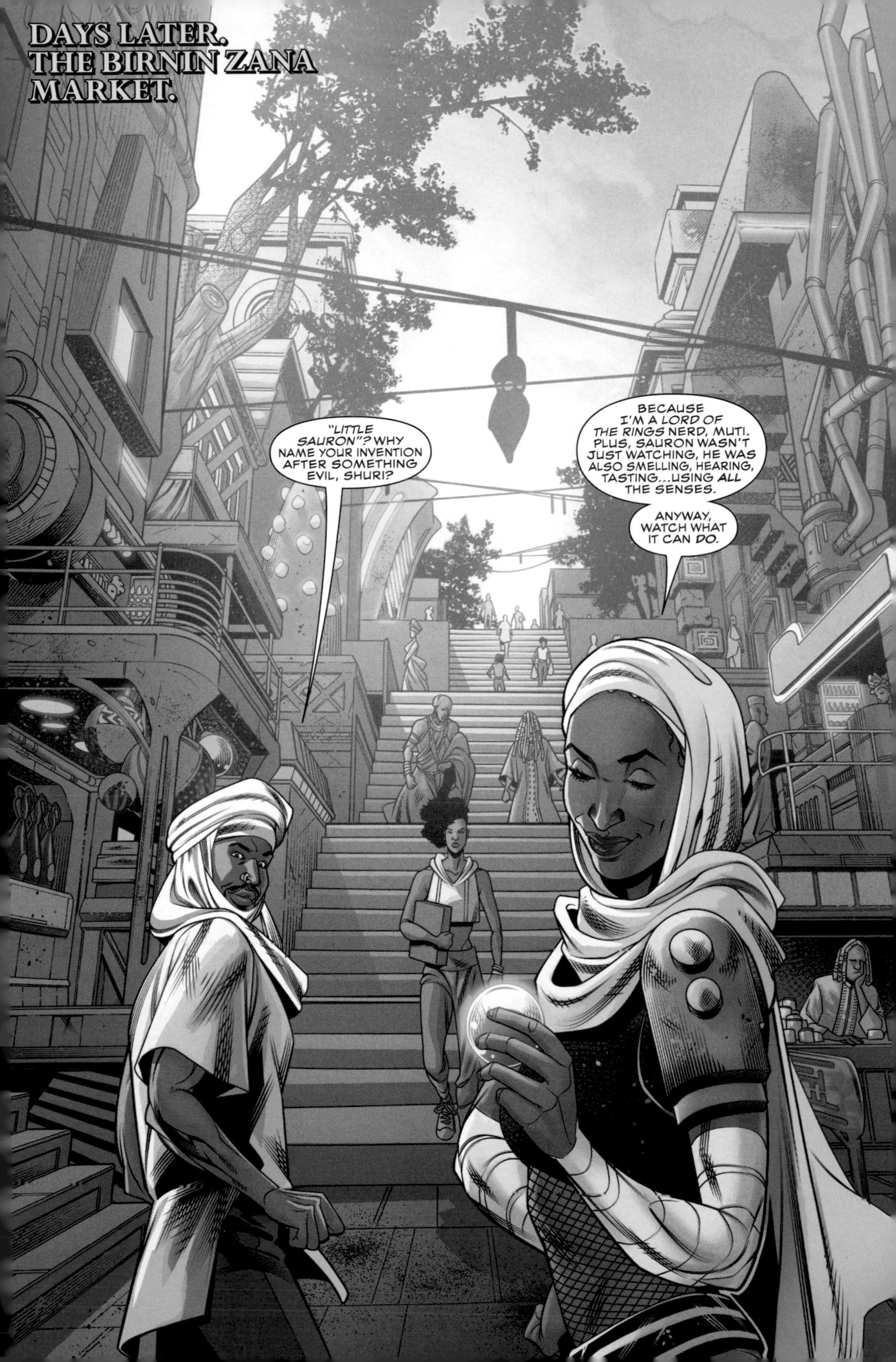
DAYS LATER. THE BIRNIN ZANA MARKET.
"LITTLE SAURON"? WHY NAME YOUR INVENTION AFTER SOMETHING EVIL, SHURI?
BECAUSE I'M A LORD OF THE RINGS NERD, MUTI. PLUS, SAURON WASN'T JUST WATCHING, HE WAS ALSO SMELLING, HEARING, TASTING...USING ALL THE SENSES.
ANYWAY, WATCH WHAT IT CAN DO.

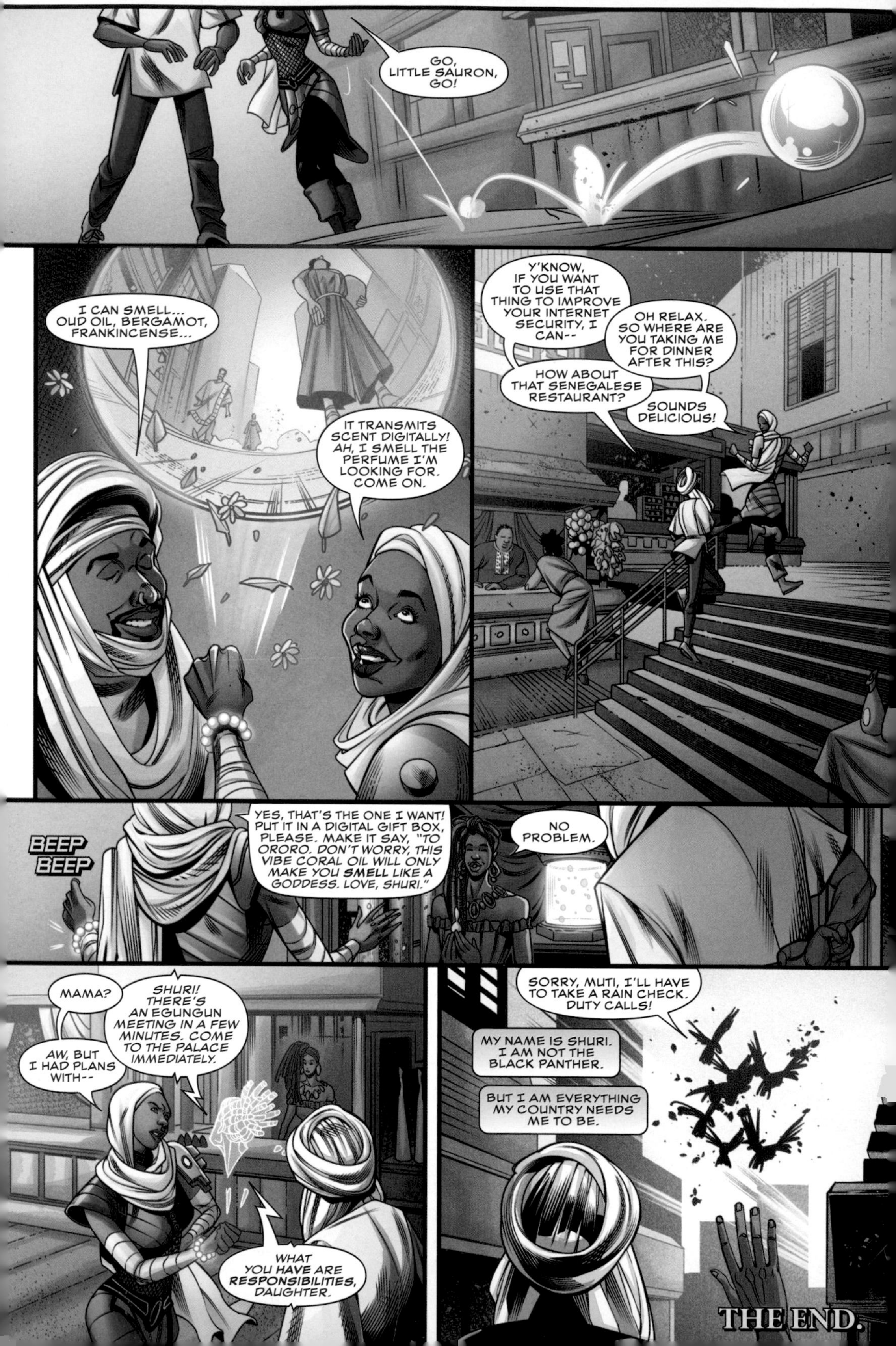
GO, LITTLE SAURON, GO!
I CAN SMELL... OUD OIL, BERGAMOT, FRANKINCENSE...
IT TRANSMITS SCENT DIGITALLY! AH, I SMELL THE PERFUME I'M LOOKING FOR. COME ON.
Y'KNOW, IF YOU WANT TO USE THAT THING TO IMPROVE YOUR INTERNET SECURITY, I CAN--
OH RELAX. SO WHERE ARE YOU TAKING ME FOR DINNER AFTER THIS?
HOW ABOUT THAT SENEGALESE RESTAURANT?
SOUNDS DELICIOUS!
BEEP BEEP
YES, THAT'S THE ONE I WANT! PUT IT IN A DIGITAL GIFT BOX, PLEASE. MAKE IT SAY, "TO ORORO. DON'T WORRY, THIS VIBE CORAL OIL WILL ONLY MAKE YOU SMELL LIKE A GODDESS. LOVE, SHURI."
NO PROBLEM.
MAMA?
SHURI! THERE'S AN EGUNGUN MEETING IN A FEW MINUTES. COME TO THE PALACE IMMEDIATELY.
AW, BUT I HAD PLANS WITH--
WHAT YOU HAVE ARE RESPONSIBILITIES, DAUGHTER.
SORRY, MUTI, I'LL HAVE TO TAKE A RAIN CHECK. DUTY CALLS!
MY NAME IS SHURI. I AM NOT THE BLACK PANTHER.
BUT I AM EVERYTHING MY COUNTRY NEEDS ME TO BE.
THE END.

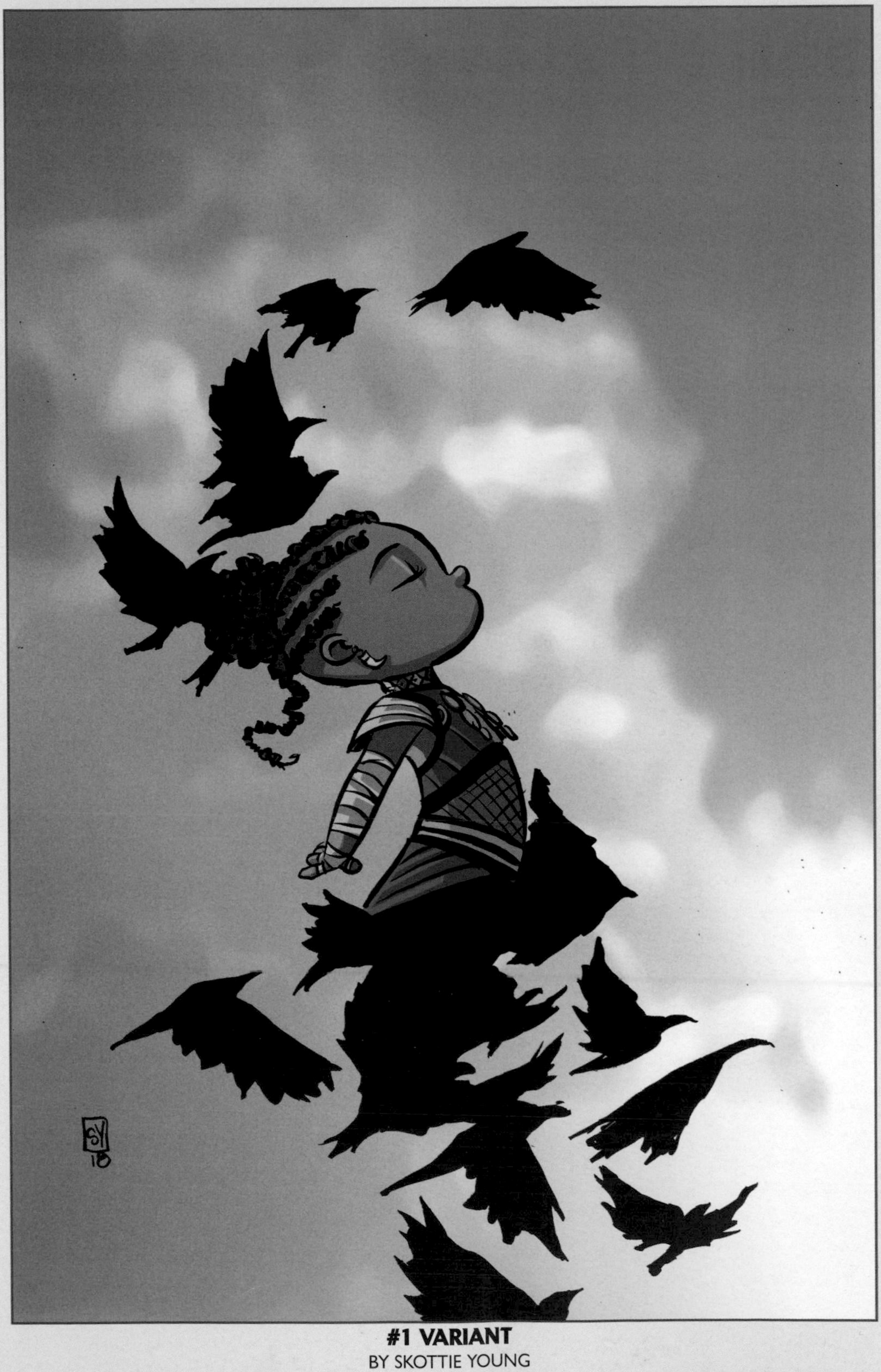
SY
18

#1 VARIANT

BY SKOTTIE YOUNG

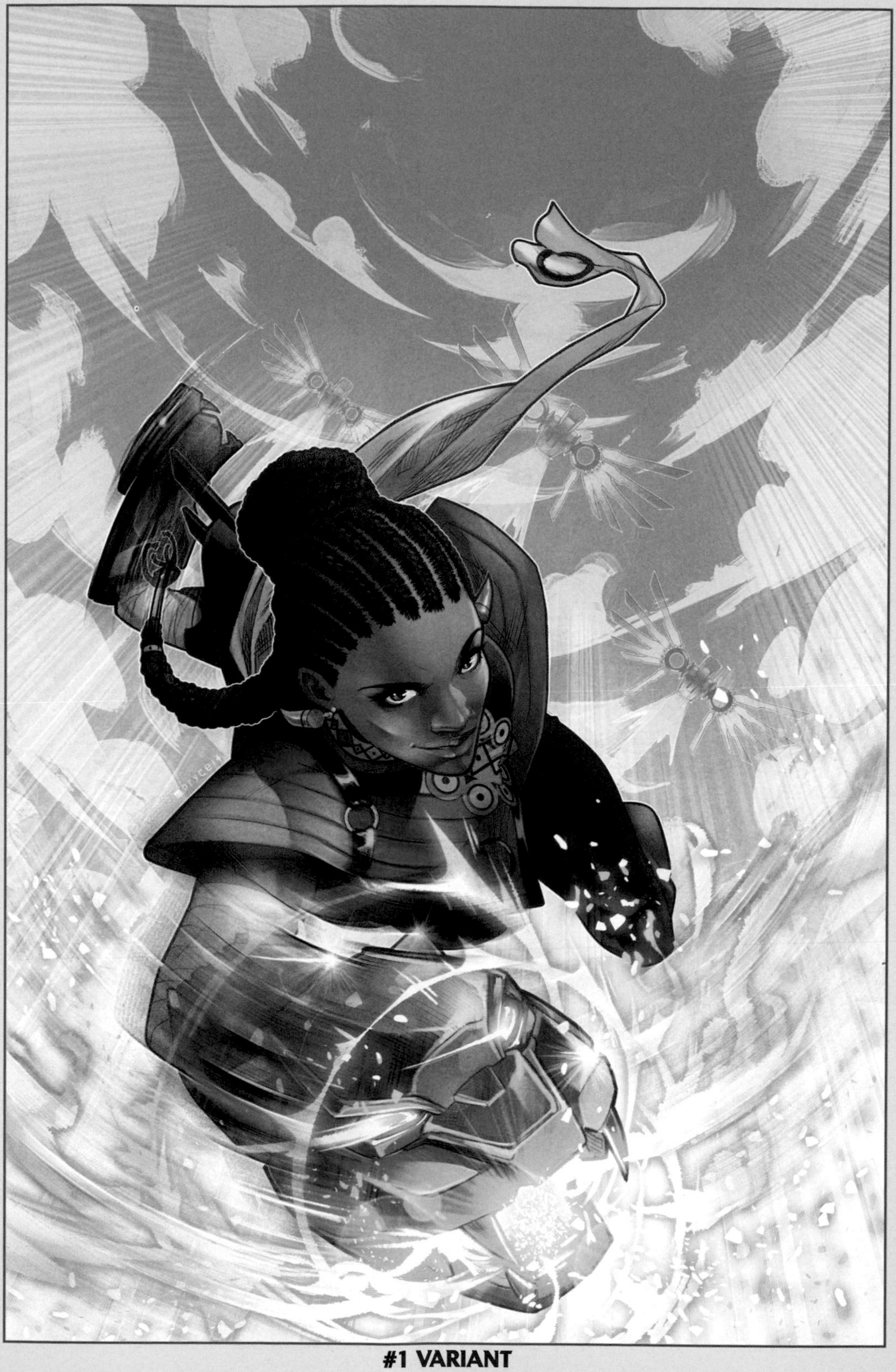

#1 VARIANT
BY JAMAL CAMPBELL

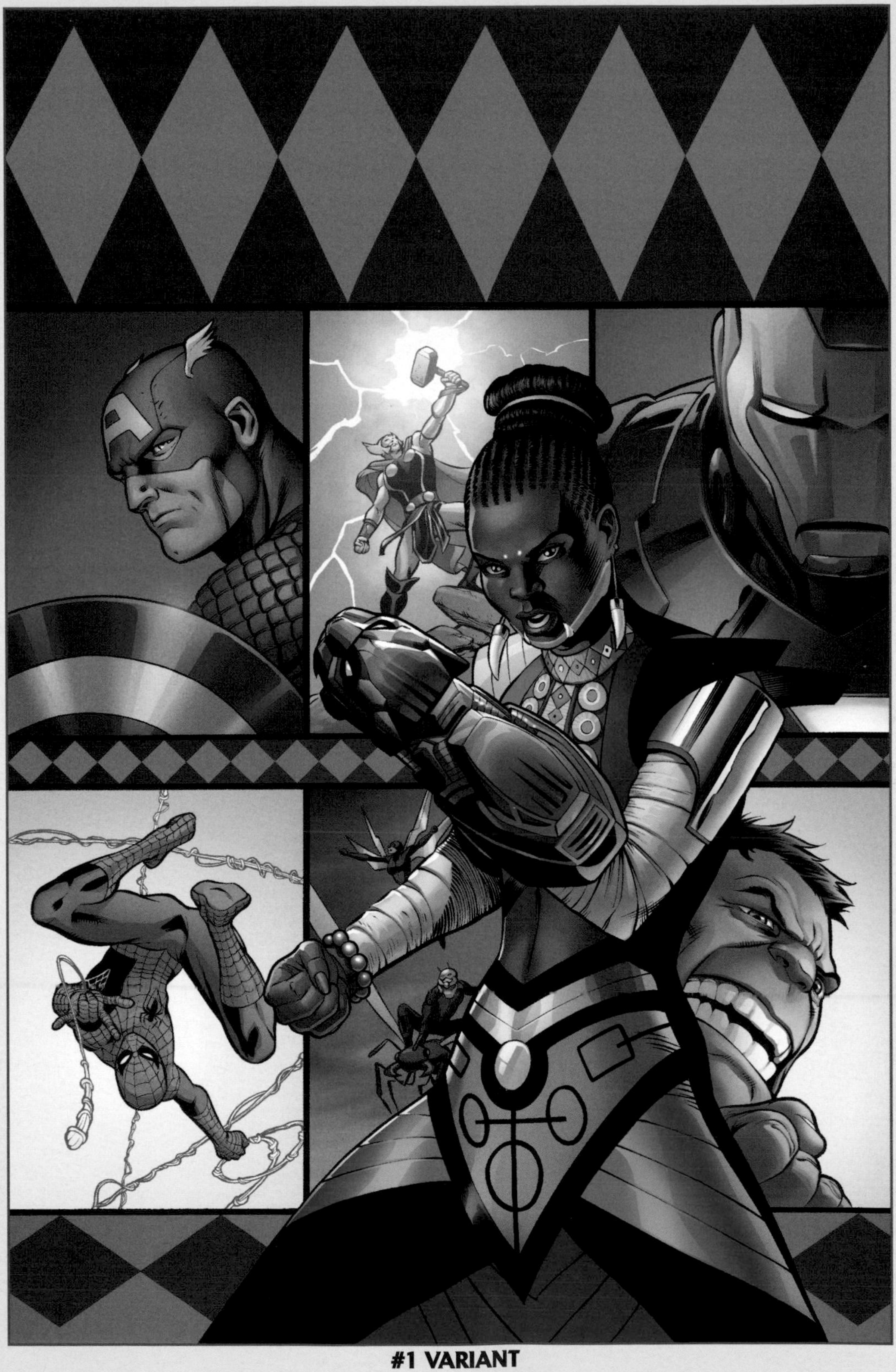

#1 VARIANT

BY CARLOS PACHECO, RAFAEL FONTERIZ & LAURA MARTIN

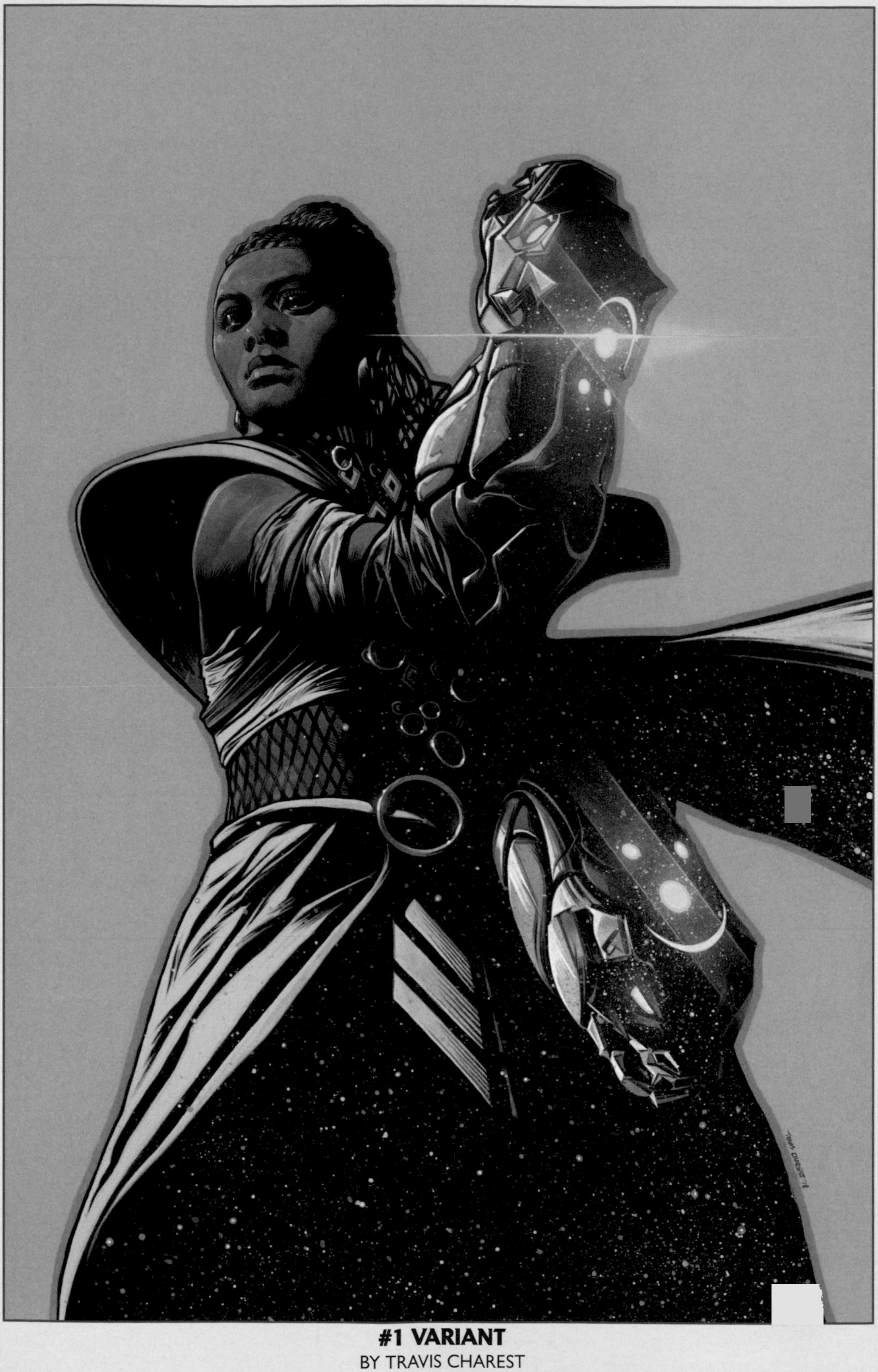

#1 VARIANT
BY TRAVIS CHAREST

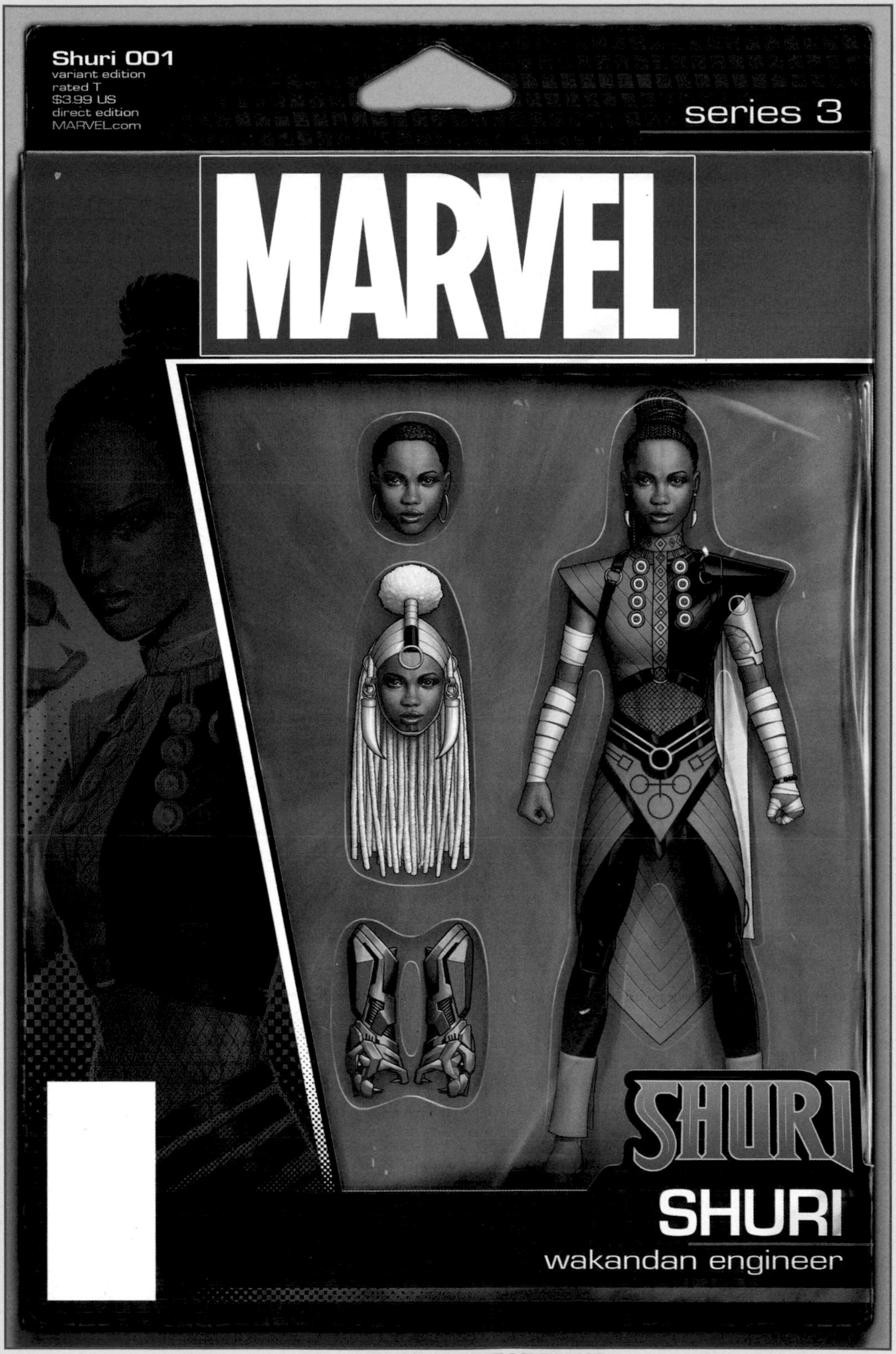
Shuri 001
variant edition
rated T
$3.99 US
direct edition
MARVEL.com
series 3
MARVEL
SHURI
SHURI
wakandan engineer

#1 ACTION FIGURE VARIANT
BY JOHN TYLER CHRISTOPHER

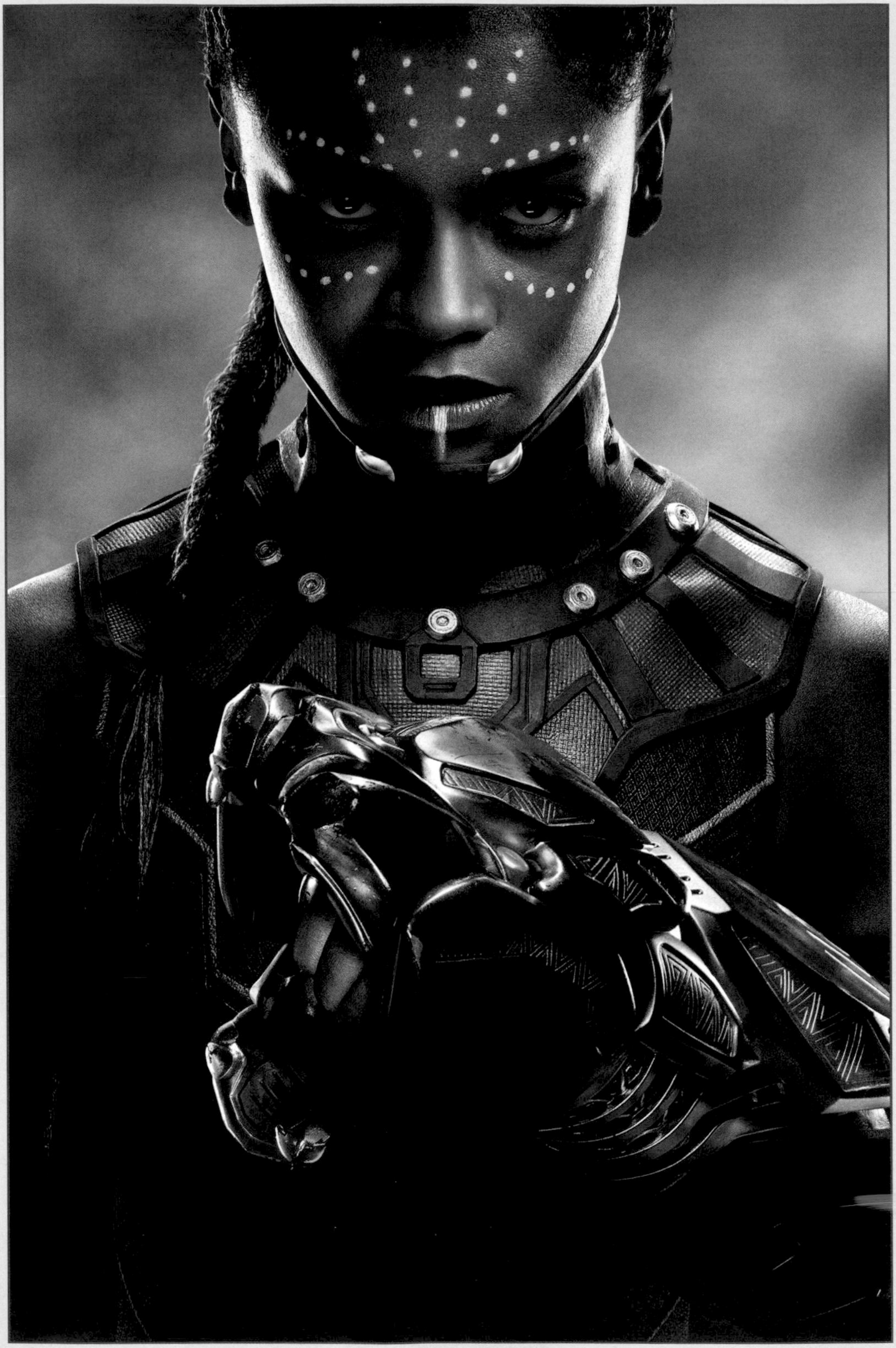

#2 MOVIE VARIANT

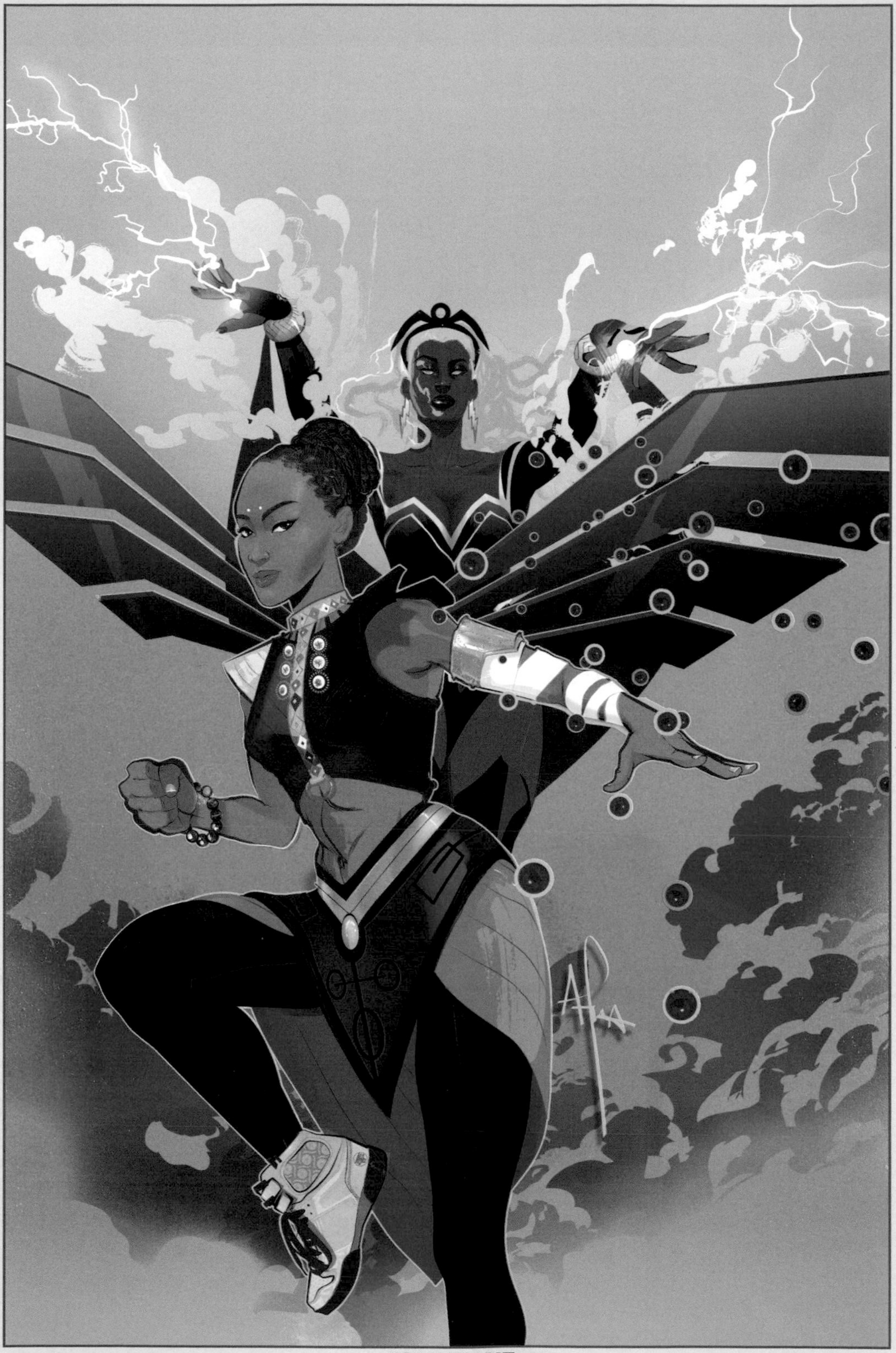

#2 VARIANT
BY AFUA RICHARDSON

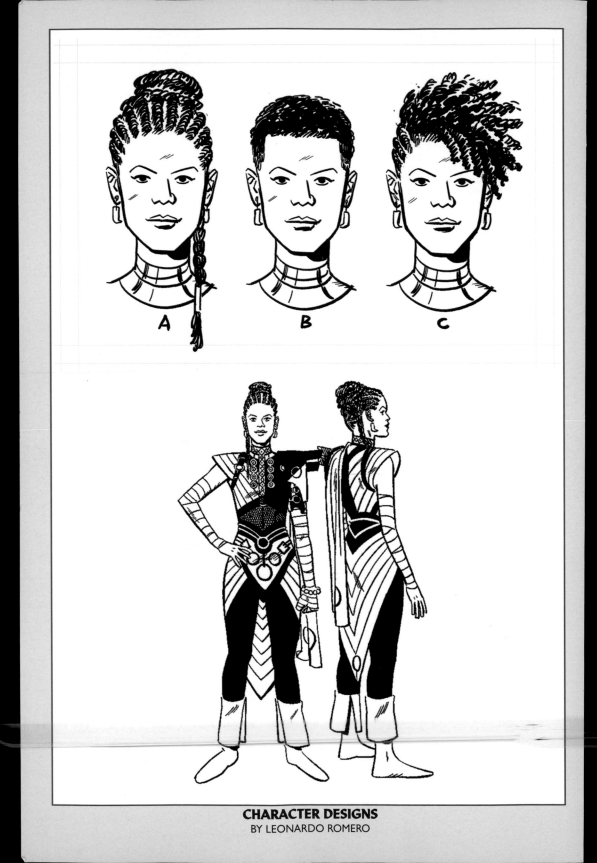

CHARACTER DESIGNS
BY LEONARDO ROMERO

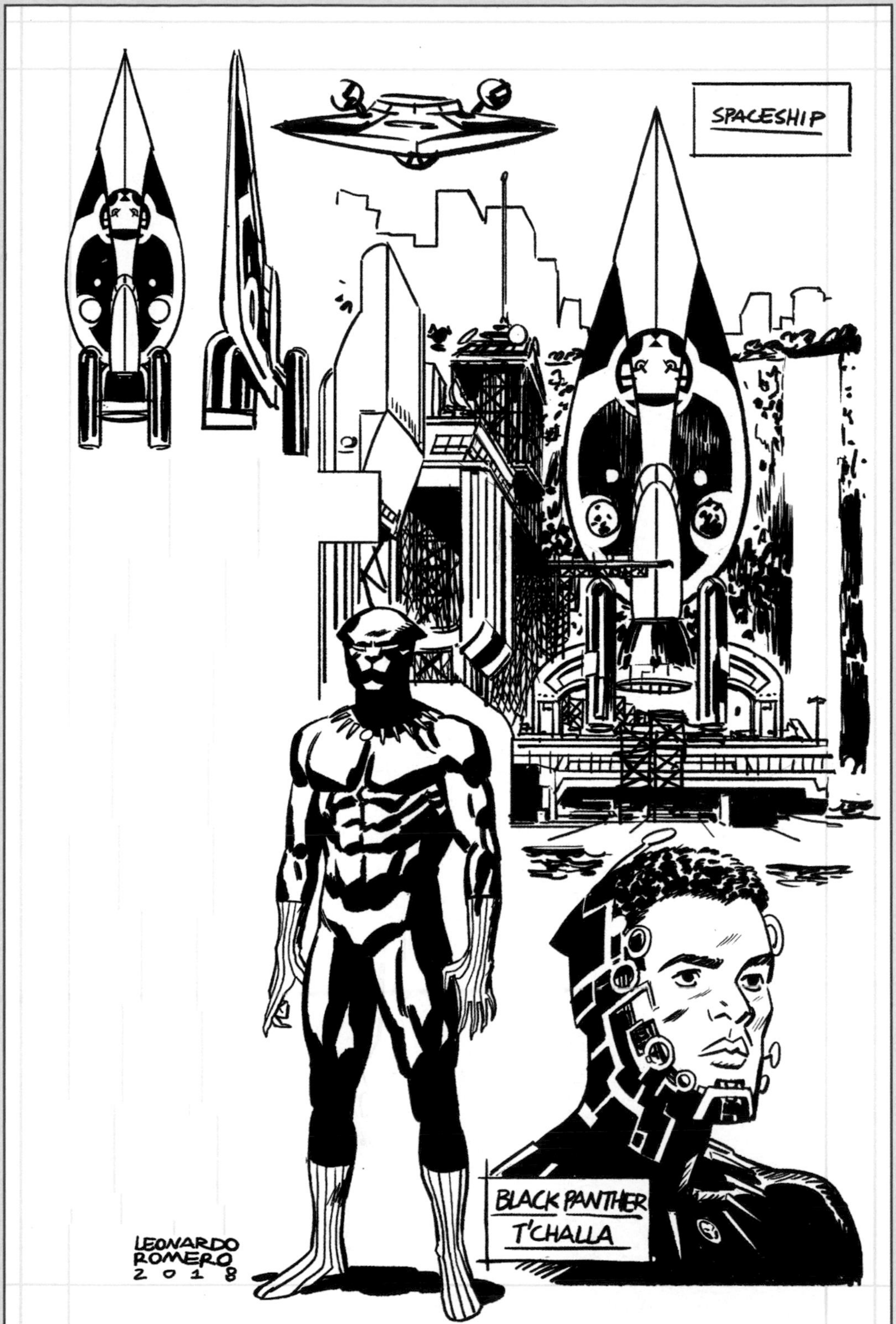
SPACESHIP
BLACK PANTHER
T'CHALLA
LEONARDO
ROMERO
2018

CHARACTER DESIGNS
BY LEONARDO ROMERO

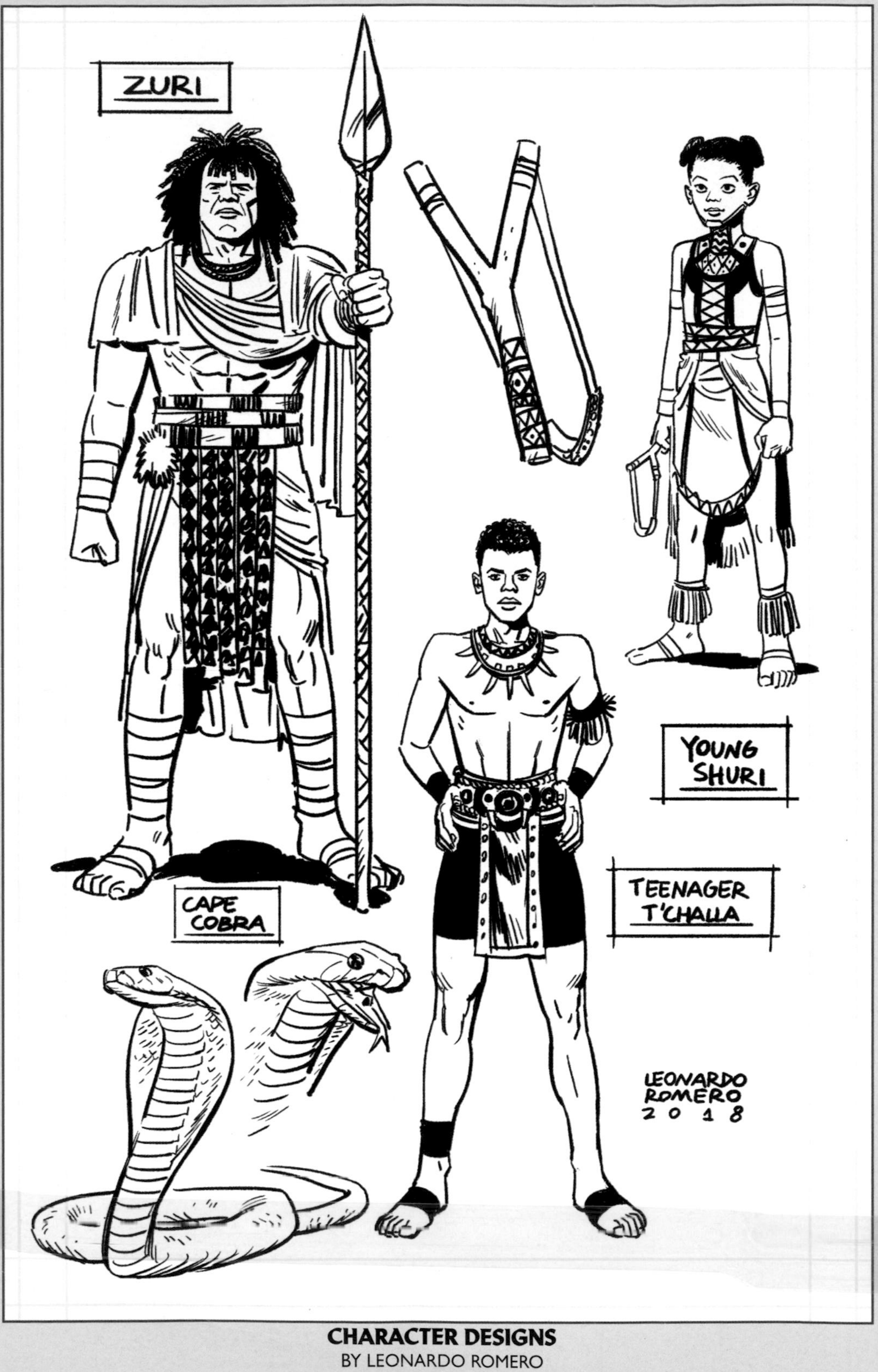

ZURI
YOUNG SHURI
TEENAGER T'CHALLA
CAPE COBRA
LEONARDO ROMERO 2018

CHARACTER DESIGNS
BY LEONARDO ROMERO